D1251582

THE LEGION OF
SHADOW

Also by Michael J. Ward from Gollancz:

The Legion of Shadow
The Heart of Fire

BOOK ONE

THE LEGION OF SHADOW

MICHAEL J. WARD

Copyright © Michael J. Ward 2012
All rights reserved

The right of Michael J. Ward to be identified as the author of this work
has been asserted by him in accordance with the
Copyright, Designs and Patents Act 1988.

First published in Great Britain in 2012
by Gollancz
An imprint of the Orion Publishing Group
Orion House, 5 Upper St Martin's Lane, London WC2H 9EA
An Hachette UK Company

This edition published in Great Britain in 2013 by Gollancz

1 3 5 7 9 10 8 6 4 2

A CIP catalogue record for this book is available
from the British Library

ISBN 978 0 575 11873 7

Typeset by Input Data Services Ltd, Bridgwater, Somerset

Printed and bound in Great Britain by
CPI Group (UK) Ltd, Croydon, CR0 4YY

The Orion Publishing Group's policy is to use papers that
are natural, renewable and recyclable products and made
from wood grown in sustainable forests. The logging and
manufacturing processes are expected to conform to the
environmental regulations of the country of origin.

www.destiny-quest.com
www.orionbooks.co.uk
www.gollancz.co.uk

For Mary
Who had the good fortune to let a
bona fide geek into her life.

This destiny would never have been realised, without the help of the following heroes:

Marcus Gipps: For giving me the phone call I've waited my whole life for – and taking a chance on a gamebook, of all things.

Paul Cheshire: For working stupid hours to produce the maps, logos and website art. And never complaining. Much.

Robbie Scourou: For doing 'all that coding malarkey' to turn my first-grade sketches into something resembling a website. Then teaching me how to actually use it . . .

Dominic Harman – For a stunning cover that paints 193,000 words.

And a big thank you to the friendly and talented team at Gollancz, who make all the magic happen. It's an honour to be a part of.

H E R O DQ S H E E T

NAME:

CLOAK

HEAD

GLOVES

MAIN HAND

CHEST

LEFT HAND

TALISMAN

FEET

MONEY POUCH

SPEED

BRAWN

MAGIC

ARMOUR

HEALTH

H E R O DQ S H E E T

PATH: **CAREER:**

NECKLACE

RING

RING

SPECIAL ABILITIES:

SPEED _____

_____

_____

COMBAT _____

_____

_____

PASSIVE _____

_____

_____

MODIFIER _____

_____

_____

BACKPACK:

NOTES:

H E R O DQ S H E E T

NAME:

CLOAK	HEAD	GLOVES

MAIN HAND	CHEST	LEFT HAND

TALISMAN	FEET	MONEY POUCH

SPEED	BRAWN	MAGIC	ARMOUR

HEALTH

H E R O DQ S H E E T

PATH: **CAREER:**

NECKLACE

RING

RING

SPECIAL ABILITIES:

SPEED _____

_____

_____

COMBAT _____

_____

_____

PASSIVE _____

_____

_____

MODIFIER _____

_____

_____

BACKPACK:

NOTES:

H E R O DQ S H E E T

NAME:

CLOAK

HEAD

GLOVES

MAIN HAND

CHEST

LEFT HAND

TALISMAN

FEET

MONEY POUCH

SPEED

BRAWN

MAGIC

ARMOUR

HEALTH

H E R O DO S H E E T

PATH: **CAREER:**

NECKLACE

RING

RING

SPECIAL ABILITIES:

SPEED _____

_____

_____

COMBAT _____

_____

_____

PASSIVE _____

_____

_____

MODIFIER _____

_____

_____

BACKPACK:

NOTES:

Welcome to DestinyQuest!

'It is through our choices that the seeds of destiny are sown.'
Carinold the Wise

Unlike ordinary storybooks, DestinyQuest puts *you* in charge of the action. As you guide your hero through this epic adventure, you will be choosing the danger that they face, the monsters that they fight and the treasures that they find. Every decision that you make will have an impact on the story and, ultimately, the fate of your hero.

Your choices, your hero
With hundreds of special items to discover in the game, you can completely customise your hero. You can choose their weapons, their armour, their special abilities – even the boots on their feet and the cloak on their back! No two heroes will ever be alike, which means your hero will always be unique to you. And even better, you can take your hero into battle against your friends' heroes too!

Limitless possibilities, endless adventure
You can play through DestinyQuest multiple times and never have the same adventure twice. With so many options and paths to choose from, the monsters that you encounter, the people that you meet and the loot that you find, will be different each time you play. There are numerous hidden secrets to discover, bonus items to collect and unique special abilities to unlock – in fact, every turn of the page could reveal something new for you and your hero.

Discover your destiny ...
The next few pages will take you through the rules of the game, outlining the hero creation process and the combat and quest system.

Don't worry, it won't take long – and then your first DestinyQuest adventure can begin!

The Hero Sheet

Let's start with one of the most important things in the game – your hero sheet. This is a visual record of your hero's abilities and equipment. You will be constantly updating this sheet throughout the game, as you train new abilities and find better armour and weapons for your hero. (Note: The hero sheet is also available as a free download from **www.destiny-quest.com**.)

Attributes

Every hero has five key attributes that determine their strengths and weaknesses. These are *speed, brawn, magic, armour* and *health*. The goal of DestinyQuest is to advance your hero from an inexperienced novice into a powerful champion – someone who can stand up to the biggest and baddest of foes and triumph!

To achieve this, you will need to complete the many quests throughout the lands of Valeron. These quests will reward you with new skills and equipment, such as weapons and armour. These will boost your hero's attributes and give you a better chance of survival when taking on tougher enemies.

The five attributes are:

* **Brawn**: As its name suggests, this score represents your hero's strength and muscle power. A hero with high *brawn* will be able to hit harder in combat, striking through their opponent's armour and dealing fatal blows.
  Brawn is the main attribute of the warrior.

* **Magic**: By mastering the arcane schools of fire, lightning, frost and shadow, a hero can command devastating spells and summon fiendish monsters. Heroes that choose this path should seek out the staffs, wands and arcane charms that will boost their *magic* score, granting them even deadlier powers to smite their foes.

Magic is the main attribute of the mage.

* **Speed**: The higher a hero's *speed* score, the more likely they are to score a hit against their opponent. A hero who puts points into *speed* can easily bring down stronger enemies thanks to their lightning-fast reflexes.
Speed is the main attribute of the rogue.

* **Armour**: Whenever a hero is hit in combat, by weapons or spells, they take damage. Wearing armour can help your hero to survive longer by absorbing some of this damage. Warriors will always have a high *armour* score, thanks to the heavy armour and shields that they can equip. Rogues and mages will typically have lower scores, relying instead on their powerful attacks to win the day.

* **Health**: This is your hero's most important attribute as it represents their life force. When *health* reaches zero, your hero is dead – so, it goes without saying that you should keep a very close eye on it! Armour and equipment can raise your hero's *health* score – and there are also potions and abilities to be discovered, to help your hero replenish their *health* during combat.

Starting attributes
Every hero begins their adventures with a zero score for *brawn*, *magic*, *speed* and *armour*. These attributes will be boosted throughout the course of your adventures. All starting heroes begin with **30 health**.

Equipment boxes
The hero sheet displays a number of important boxes. These boxes each represent a location on your hero where they can equip an item. Whenever your hero comes across a new item in the game, you will be told which box or boxes on the sheet you can place it in.

Backpack
Your hero also has a backpack that can hold five single items. On your travels you will come across many backpack items, including useful potions and quest items. Each backpack item you come across takes

up one space in your backpack – even if you have multiple versions of the same item (for example, health potions).

BACKPACK:				
Healing +4 health (1 use)	Healing +4 health (1 use)	Stone tablet	Forest dew full heal (2 uses)	Miracle grow +2 brawn (1 use)

Special abilities
The special abilities box, on the right of your sheet, is where you can record notes on your hero's special abilities. Every hero has two special abilities, which they learn when they train a career. Some items of equipment can also grant special abilities for your hero. All special abilities are explained in the glossary at the back of the book.

Paths and careers
Your hero starts their adventure as a simple traveller, with no remarkable skills or abilities. Once your hero has gained some experience however, three paths will become available to you – the paths of the warrior, the rogue and the mage. Your hero can only choose one of these paths, and once that decision is made, it can't be changed – so choose wisely. The chosen path will determine the careers and abilities that your hero can learn throughout their adventures.

Your hero's path and current career should always be recorded at the top of your hero sheet, and its special abilities should be recorded in the special abilities box on the right of your sheet. A hero can only be trained in *one career* at a time, but they can swap careers any time they wish, providing you have found the relevant trainer or reward item. When your hero trains for a new career, all abilities and bonuses from the old career are lost.

Gold
The main currency in Valeron is the gold crown. Your hero starts their adventure with 10 gold crowns. These can be used to purchase

potions and other special items whenever you visit a town, village or camp. More gold can be discovered by killing monsters and completing quests.

Quests and Monsters

The kingdom of Valeron is a dangerous place, full of ferocious monsters, wild beasts and deadly magical forces ... bad news for some people perhaps, but for a would-be adventurer it means plenty of paid work! By vanquishing foes and completing quests, your hero will grow stronger and more powerful, allowing you to take on tougher challenges and discover even greater rewards.

The maps
The story is divided into three chapters – known as 'Acts'. Each of the three Acts has a map, which shows you the locations of all the different quests that your hero can take part in. (The maps are available in the centre colour section of your book.) To select a quest you simply turn to the corresponding numbered entry in the book and read on from there, returning to the map when you have finished.

Choosing quests
Each map will provide you with a number of different quests. Some quests are harder than others. A simple colour-coded system ranks the quests in order of difficulty:

* **Green quests**: These are the easiest quests to complete. Heroes with even the most basic of equipment will still emerge victorious.

* **Orange quests**: Heroes will find these tasks a little more challenging, requiring them to defeat numerous enemies to succeed.

* **Blue quests**: Things get a lot tougher with blue quests. Monsters are more likely to have special abilities and higher attribute scores, meaning your hero will need to be fully prepared and equipped for the dangers they may face.

* **Red quests**: These quests should only be attempted once you have completed the majority of green, orange and blue quests. Your hero will need to use everything they've got to overcome these difficult challenges and triumph.

Quests can be done in any order you wish – although note that it is wiser to complete the easier quests (green and orange) before you attempt the harder ones (blue and red).

Legendary monsters

On each map you will also see some spider symbols. These represent special monsters that your hero can choose to fight if they so wish. Known as 'legendary monsters', these powerful foes will provide you with some of the toughest challenges in the game. Only the bravest of heroes, who are confident in their abilities and have good gear from their questing, should seek out and battle these mighty opponents.

Boss monsters

Each Act of the story has a final boss monster that must be defeated before you can advance the story to the next Act. These boss monsters are represented by the skull symbol on the map.

It goes without saying that these final bosses are no pushovers and should only be attempted once you have fully explored each map and completed most of the quests.

Towns, villages and camps

Every Act of the story has its own town, village or camp, which your hero can visit any time between quests. They are represented on the map by the building icon. Simply turn to the corresponding page entry whenever you wish to visit. These locations can provide your hero with items to purchase, additional quests, hints and tips and even some career trainers.

It is always a good idea to visit these areas first, whenever you start a new map. The inns and taverns can be a great source of rumour and information regarding the challenges ahead.

Upgrading equipment

The primary goal of DestinyQuest is to equip your hero with better weapons, armour and equipment. These will boost your hero's attributes such as *brawn* and *magic*, and help them to survive longer in battle.

At certain times in the story you will be offered a choice of rewards for your hero. Usually this will be the result of killing a monster or completing a quest, but there are also many other ways of gaining rewards – some easier to find than others.

When you are offered a choice of rewards, you will be told how many items you may pick from the selection. It is up to you to decide which reward/s will be best for your hero. These rewards, such as rings, pieces of armour, weapons and necklaces, will commonly give boosts to certain attributes. Select your rewards wisely to boost the attributes that are the most essential for your hero.

When you have chosen your reward, you write its name and details in the corresponding box on your hero sheet. Make sure to update any attributes that are affected by the new reward. Remember, it is your decision what rewards you take. You can always pass on items if they don't interest you.

Replacing equipment
Your hero can only carry one item in each box. When you choose a reward and your hero already has an item in the corresponding box, the new item *replaces* the old one – and the old item is *destroyed*. When you destroy the old item, all attribute bonuses and abilities that it provided are lost, to be replaced by those from the new item.

Combat

Valeron can be a wild and dangerous place. Most of the creatures you encounter will be hostile and it will be up to you (and your hero!) to battle and defeat these monsters, to emerge victorious.

When you enter into combat, you will be given your opponent's attributes. These are usually *speed*, *brawn* (or *magic*), *armour* and *health*.

Some may also have special abilities that you will need to take note of.

The combat sequence

Combat consists of a number of *combat rounds*. In each round of combat you roll dice to determine who hits who and who takes damage. (Note: A dice is considered to be a standard 6-sided dice.) Once damage has been applied, a new combat round starts. Combat continues until either your hero or their opponent is defeated.

In each combat round:

1. Roll *2 dice* for your hero and add their current *speed* score to the total. This is your hero's **attack speed**.

2. Roll *2 dice* for your opponent and add their *speed* score to the total. This is their **attack speed**.

3. The combatant with the highest attack speed wins the combat round. If both scores are the same, it is a stand off – the combat round ends (see step 7) and a new one begins.

4. The winner of the round rolls *1 die* and adds either their *brawn* score or their *magic* score to the total, whichever is highest. (Note: Monsters will only have one or the other, not both.) This will give you a **damage score**.

5. The loser of the round deducts their *armour* value from the damage score. Any remaining damage is then deducted from their *health*. (If the damage score was 8 and the loser had an *armour* of 2, they would take 6 *health* damage.)

6. If this damage takes your hero's or your opponent's *health* to zero, they are defeated. If both combatants have *health* remaining, then the combat continues.

7. At the end of each combat round, any damage from passive effects (such as *bleed* or *venom*) are applied to each combatant. If both opponents still have *health* remaining, then a new combat round begins. Return to step 1.

Example of combat

Sir Hugo has awoken a slumbering serpent and must now defend himself against its venomous attacks.

	Speed	Brawn	Magic	Armour	Health
Hugo	4	7	1	5	30

	Speed	Brawn	Magic	Armour	Health
Serpent	6	3	0	2	12

Special abilities

♥ Venom: Once you have taken health damage from the serpent, at the end of every combat round you must automatically lose 2 *health*.

Round one

1. Sir Hugo rolls 2 dice to determine his attack speed. He rolls a ⚄ and a ⚁ giving him a total of 6. He adds on his *speed* score of 4 to give him a final total of 10.

2. The serpent rolls 2 dice to determine its attack speed. The result is a ⚄ and a ⚅ making 11. The serpent's *speed* is 6, making its final total 17. The serpent has won the first round of combat.

3. A die is rolled for the serpent to determine its damage score. The result is a ⚅. Its *brawn* score is added onto this, to give a final total of 9.

4. Sir Hugo deducts his *armour* value from this total. This means he only takes 4 points of health damage (9−5=4). His *health* is reduced from 30 to 26.

5. Sir Hugo is also poisoned by the serpent's venom. He automatically takes another 2 points of health damage, reducing his *health* to 24.

Round two

1. As before, Sir Hugo and the Serpent roll 2 dice and add their *speed* to the result. Sir Hugo ends up with an attack speed of 15 and the serpent has an attack speed of 10. Sir Hugo wins.

2. Sir Hugo rolls a ⚁ for his damage score. He chooses to add on his *brawn* (which is higher than his *magic* score). His final total is 12.

3. The serpent has an *armour* value of 2, so takes 10 points of damage. The serpent is left with 2 *health*.

4. Because the serpent applied its venom special ability in the last round, Sir Hugo must now deduct another 2 points from his *health* – reducing it from 24 to 22.

Combat then moves to the next round, continuing until one combatant's *health* is reduced to zero.

Restoring health and attributes

Once you have defeated an enemy, your hero's *health* and any other attributes that have been affected by special attacks or abilities are **immediately restored** back to their normal values (unless otherwise stated in the text). In the above example, once Sir Hugo has defeated the serpent, he can return his *health* back to 30 and continue his adventures.

Using special abilities in combat

As your hero progresses through the story, they will discover many special abilities that they can use in combat. All abilities are explained in the glossary at the back of the book.

There are four types of special ability in DestinyQuest. These are: speed (sp), combat (co), modifier (mo) and passive (pa) abilities.

* **Speed (sp)**: These abilities can be used at the start of a combat round (before you roll for attack speed), and will usually influence how many dice you can roll or reduce the number of dice your opponent can roll for speed, You can only use one speed ability per combat round.

* **Combat (co)**: These abilities are used either before or after you (or your opponent) roll for damage. Usually these will increase the number of dice you can roll, or allow you to block or dodge

your opponent's attacks. You can only use one combat ability per combat round.

* **Modifier (mo)**: Modifier abilities allow you to boost your attribute scores or influence dice that you have already rolled. You can use as many different modifier abilities as you wish during a combat round.

* **Passive (pa)**: Passive abilities are typically applied at the end of a combat round, once you or your opponent has taken health damage. Abilities such as *venom* and *bleed* are passive abilities. These abilities happen automatically, based on their description.

Damage score and damage dice

Some special abilities will refer to a damage score and others will refer to rolling damage dice. A damage score is when your hero rolls one die and adds their *brawn* or *magic* to the total (as in the previous combat example). This is the most common means of applying damage to your opponent.

Some abilities allow you to roll damage dice instead. Damage dice are simply dice that are rolled for damage, but you do not add your *brawn* or *magic* score to the total. For example, the special ability *cleave* allows you to inflict 1 damage die to all your opponents, ignoring *armour*. You would simply roll 1 die and then deduct the result from each of your opponents' *health*. You do not add your *brawn* or *magic* to this total.

Using potions in combat

The outcome of many a combat can be decided by the clever use of potions. From restoring lost *health* to boosting your *speed*, never underestimate how useful these items can be in turning the tide of battle. However, you can only use one potion per combat round so choose wisely! Also note that every potion has a number of uses. Once these have been used up, they are gone forever.

Death is not the end

When your hero dies, their adventure isn't over. Simply make a note of the entry number where you died and then return to the quest map. Your *health* is immediately restored back to full, however any consumable items that you used in the combat (such as potions and elixirs) remain lost.

You can now do the following:

1. Return to the entry number where you died and try it again. (NOTE: You must fight monsters using their full *health* and original attributes.)

2. Explore a different location on the map, such as a town or another quest.

You can return to the entry number where you died any time you wish. If you are having difficulty with a particular combat, then try a different quest or purchase some helpful potions from a local vendor. Then you can return to the entry number where you died and try it again.

NOTE: In some quests, when your hero is defeated, there are special rules to follow. You will be given an entry number to turn to, where you can read on to see what happens to your hero.

Taking challenge tests

Occasionally, during your travels, you will be asked to take a challenge by testing one of your attributes (such as *speed* or *brawn*). Each challenge is given a number. For example:

Speed

Climb the cliff face   9

To take a challenge, simply roll 2 dice and add your hero's attribute score to the result. If the total is the same as or higher than the given number, then you have succeeded. For example, if Sir Hugo has a *speed* of 4 and rolls a ⚁ and a ⚂, then he would have a total of 9. This means he would have successfully completed the above challenge.

Take your adventures online!

Join the DestinyQuest community at **www.destiny-quest.com** for the latest information on DestinyQuest books, hints and tips, player forums and exclusive downloadable content (including printable hero sheets, hero vs. hero combat rules and extra bonus quests!).

It's time to begin

Before you start your adventure, don't forget to check that your hero sheet has been fully updated. It should display:

* Your hero's name
* A zero score in the *speed, brawn, magic,* and *armour* boxes
* A 30 in your hero's *health* box
* 10 gold crowns in your hero's money pouch.

Now, turn the page to begin your adventure ...

Prologue:
The knight's legacy

You are thrown from the dream, kicking and flailing. It is some seconds before you can catch your breath, images of black-scaled monsters and sharp fangs still swimming before your vision.

As your surroundings slowly come into focus, you find yourself lying on your back against the soggy ground, a steady patter of rain beating on the dead leaves and dirt. Above you, a full moon streams garish light through the treetops, picking out the charred, twisted remains that encircle you.

Bodies.

Corpses.

Frantically, you scramble to your feet, the cold rain making the ground slippery with mud. As you stand, an angry pain causes you to stagger, thumping against the inside of your head. Putting a hand to the back of your scalp, you feel for a wound or bruise. To your surprise, you find nothing.

All around you, the ground is scorched and smoking, forming a crater with you at its centre. Sprawled around its edge are over a dozen bodies – each one burnt beyond all recognition. You close your eyes, struggling to remember what happened ... how you came to be here.

You look down at your tattered clothing, rain soaked and smeared with mud. A splatter of blood covers one sleeve. Tentatively, you pull back the cloth, your eyes widening in surprise when you see the purple mark branded into the skin. The design is detailed and intricate, showing three diamond-bodied serpents intertwined in a dizzying pattern of spirals. Around them, a number of strange sigils glow with a soft purplish light.

You hear a groan coming from the trees ahead. Covering the strange mark, you stagger through the mud towards the sound. Instinctively, your hand goes to your belt, looking for a weapon. But there is none there. You are unarmed. Scanning the mud, you find a rusty-looking dagger next to one of the scorched bodies. You crouch down and pick it up, before heading into the dark trees.

A man is lying with his back against one of the trunks – no a boy, not much older than fifteen. He is clad in plate armour, his thick mud-spattered cloak bunched up around his shoulders. The shaft of an arrow protrudes from his lower chest, having pierced through the links between the metal plates.

The boy looks up as you approach, his face deathly white and dripping with rainwater. A trickle of blood seeps from the corner of his mouth.

'What ... what happened?' you ask, kneeling beside the wounded knight.

The boy fixes his watery eyes on your own. 'You don't remember?' he rasps hoarsely.

You say nothing, your attention shifting to the black-fletched arrow. 'Who did this? Who are those ... people?' You gesture back towards the clearing, where the scorched bodies lie in twisted repose.

'Brigands. Thieves,' gasps the boy, grimacing with pain. 'They attacked our camp.'

'Our camp?' you ask. You close your eyes, struggling to remember what happened – to find that part of yourself, that corner of your mind where some memory or trace of who you are might still remain. There is nothing – only a chill darkness, as cold and impenetrable as the night. When you open your eyes, they are misted with angry tears. 'I don't remember ... I don't remember anything.'

The boy gives a pained gasp as he struggles to raise one of his hands. With a trembling finger, he points to your head. 'You took a blow. Right before you killed those men.'

You draw back, inhaling sharply. 'I ... I did that ... back there?' Images of the charred, ruined bodies flash before your eyes. 'How?'

'Some magic,' whispers the boy. 'It came from the ... that mark on your arm.'

You flinch, clutching your arm protectively against your chest. The boy smirks at your reaction. 'You never mentioned it. I guess it was something you didn't want me to know about.'

'And this?' you ask, looking down at the black-fletched arrow.

'Assassin spitted me,' he grimaces. 'He was the only one to get away. Their leader ... I think.' Where the arrow shaft meets the skin, you can see green poison bubbling out of the wound.

The boy reads your fatal expression.

'I know, it's ... too late for me.'

Your shoulders sag. It is a grim thought – that this dying knight is the last remaining link to your past, to your previous life that is now forgotten. 'We know each other?' you ask hesitantly.

'We met yesterday,' rasps the boy. 'We were both travelling the same road ... to Tithebury Cross.'

You shake your head. The name means nothing to you.

'I'm an academy knight,' the boy wheezes. 'Just graduated, top of my class. I was going to apprentice ...' He stops as a wave of pain forces him to shudder. You put out your hand, gripping his shoulder and willing him to go on. 'I was going to apprentice with Avian Dale. The great Avian Dale ...' For a moment there is a flicker of life in his eyes, his pain forgotten as he stares wistfully up at the dark sky. 'It was my instructor's idea. He said I was the best in my year ... Avian doesn't accept just anyone. I was special ...' His face sours as he looks down at the arrow shaft. 'Now that life is over.'

Suddenly, from somewhere back in the forest, you hear a piercing shriek. You glance nervously over your shoulder.

'Harpies,' grimaces the boy. 'They hunt in packs. The scent ...' He lifts his hands, revealing palms soaked with his own blood. 'It will draw them here. You must go.'

'But I can't just leave you. I must find out ...'

'My pack. Fetch my pack.'

The boy tilts his head. Following his gaze, you see a brown back-pack lying at the base of one of the trees. You quickly retrieve it, surprised at its lightness as you lift it out of the mud. The boy gestures for you to open it. Inside, wedged between a bundle of clothes, is a rolled-up sheet of parchment.

'Take it,' whispers the boy. 'It's my letter from ... the academy.'

Unrolling the scroll, you see that it is covered in neat, flowing script. It is addressed to an Avian Dale, outlining the merits of a young academy knight. It ends in a green seal of wax, displaying the insignia of a winged dragon. 'I can't take this,' you protest, shaking your head.

The boy gives a wheezing cough, his body jerking painfully with the effort. 'It is ... no good to me. Take it. Start a new life. He'll never know.'

A screech draws your attention skywards. Black shapes are circling overhead, their spindly, feathered bodies silhouetted against the full moon. Harpies. Something inside you is urging you to flee ... the mark along your arm tingles as if sensing the same danger.

You roll up the scroll and stuff it into the pack. When you look over at the boy, you see that his head is now resting against his chest, his eyes closed. Death has finally taken him.

'I will find the assassin that did this. I promise.' You reach down and take the boy's sword. It is a well-balanced blade, the hilt and pommel studded with gems.

You have gained the following item (remember to add this item to your hero sheet, adding 1 to your *brawn* and *magic* scores):

The apprentice
(main hand: sword)
+1 brawn +1 magic

Another bird-like screech tears through the night. There are answering calls from all around you, worryingly close. Quickly, you shoulder the knight's pack and then start running.

You find comfort in purpose, keeping to a fast pace as you weave between the withered trees of the dark forest. After what feels like an age of battling through the cloying mud and driving rain, you spy a cave in the hollow of a hill. Having found shelter, you sit and await the dawn, shivering with more than just the cold.

* * *

The wooden signpost points southwards, where the marshy forest gives way to green rolling hills. 'Tithebury Cross. 3 miles.' You take a deep breath of the warm, morning air. 'A new life. A new start.' Peeling back your sleeve, you look down at the purple mark, glowing beneath your skin. Does this strange mark hold the key to your past?

And what of the future.

You scan the letter of introduction once again; a letter

recommending a talented knight to apprentice with one of the grand masters of the profession. 'Avian Dale.' It should have been the young boy – this was his future, his dream …

'It is … no good to me … take it. Start a new life. He'll never know …'

No one will ever know. Carefully, you roll up the letter and return it to your pack, before setting off down the long, dusty road towards Tithebury.

Turn to the first map to begin ACT 1 of your adventure (refer to the colour section at the centre of this book). Choose where you want to explore by turning to the entry number displayed next to the relevant shield. As a novice adventurer, you will want to start with the green quests first, as these are the easiest to complete. Return to the map when you want to choose a new quest or destination. Good luck!

1

The passageway ends in a square room filled with rubble and earth. Part of the left wall and ceiling has collapsed – pushed inwards by a series of enormous tree roots. Lodged between them is a small iron footlocker. Across the other side of the room is an archway, beyond which you can see a pale light falling on a stone tomb.

Will you:

Go through the archway?	154
Examine the footlocker?	93

2

There is a cheer from the assembled villagers as you re-emerge from the darkness of the well – cheers that quickly trail off one by one, as the onlookers notice the body you are carrying. Two of the men offer to take it from you, lifting it over the side of the well and laying it gently on the grass. You are then helped out of the swaying bucket, relieved to be back on solid ground again.

The white-robed priest walks over and kneels beside the body. With trembling hands he draws back the cloth and looks upon the face of his son.

'What … what happened?' asks one of the younger farmers, a tremor of fear in his voice.

'Burrower wurms,' says the priest solemnly. He rises to his feet, his expression grave. 'That acid is what they use to eat away the rock. Something must have disturbed them – or drawn them here.' He gives a heavy sigh, then reaches for the purse at his belt. 'I offer you my thanks, adventurer. You brought my son home to me.' He hands over the purse of money. (You have gained 10 gold crowns.) 'Now we have a better understanding of the dangers that we face.' He looks to each of the villagers in turn. 'Together we will exterminate this threat to our village and repair our well.'

The farmers look fearful but resolute. Your bravery has clearly served to bolster their spirits. You wish them luck in their task before returning to the village. (Return to the map to choose your next quest.)

3

'Excellent! We've not a moment to lose – come on!' The bird takes to the air, heading south towards a cluster of rocky hills. You do your best to keep up, jogging across the broken, uneven ground. Soon, you are clambering over jagged rocks and boulders to reach the top of a steep-sided mound.

At its summit, you find yourself surrounded by a circle of tall, weather-beaten stones. A discarded backpack lies in the middle of the circle, its contents spilling out onto the grass.

'Hurry! Hurry!' squawks the bird, alighting on one of the stones. 'I'm sure we don't have much time. You need to find out what happened!'

Will you:

Search through the backpack?	227
Examine the stones?	153

4
Quest: Rat extermination

You take the dusty track that leads out of Tithebury Cross and follow it up into the hills. Before too long you are passing endless fields of corn – the sun-bleached crop drooping listlessly over the cracked, dried earth. Further along the track you spot a man, sheltering beneath a tree from the heat of the midday sun. Noticing you, he beckons you over. As you approach, you see that the man is little more than a vagrant, his skin black with dirt and his clothes ragged and torn. Clearly he hasn't bathed for several days – possibly weeks – and the smell is almost overwhelming. You try and hide your revulsion as the man cracks open a smile.

'Good day, me good sir. A stranger in these parts I wager. Don't suppose I can be interesting you in a little work?' He scratches his cheek with a dirt-blackened finger. 'It's bloomin' rats,' he says. 'The blasted vermin have taken over me barn. They're everywhere!' He looks you over, his quick eyes darting back and forth between your weapons and your bulging backpack. 'Could do with someone like you to exterminate those critters. What do you say?'

Will you:

Ask why he can't do it himself?	12
Comment on his lack of hygiene?	27
State that you want a reward?	20
Agree to the quest and get started?	34

5

The girl claps her hands in delight. 'Oh he is so wonderful,' she gasps breathlessly. 'Not like the simple village boys. No, he's a travelling man, one of the gypsies. I don't think there's anywhere he hasn't been – the mountains to the east, the deserts of the south ... Gosh, he has such stories to tell, of adventure and lost treasures, and battles. It's so exciting!'

You nod your head, trying to look interested, but other more important things are starting to occupy your thoughts ... like the rapidly fading sunlight. You decide it is time that the girl was taken home to her father. Turn to 129.

6

The track you are following widens, becoming a dusty road that leads into the village of Tithebury Cross. It is a small settlement – its timber-framed buildings and cottages crowding in around a central, main square where four roads come together.

The lanes and paths are mostly deserted. You imagine that most sensible people are staying indoors, taking refuge from the sun's merciless heat. A couple of farmers pass you by, grumbling about the weather. Neither of them offers you a word of greeting.

Reaching the main square, you consider your options. Ahead of you is the local tavern, its painted sign showing a plump black bird pecking at a pie. To your left are the remnants of a small market, set up under a series of grey awnings. With few customers to view their wares, the traders look bored and listless. To your right, a narrow path leads past a row of houses and then rises steeply, climbing the side of a sun-scorched hill. At its summit you can see a stone well, with several villagers gathered around it, deep in conversation.

Will you:

Visit 'The Pie and Black Bird'?	11
Explore the market?	46
Visit the well (this starts a blue quest)?	72

7

You put the flame of your torch to the spider's web. The sparkling strands catch fire instantly, sizzling as the flames spread quickly across the interlaced pattern. With a chilling shriek of anger, the giant spider turns to face you, its immense black body seemingly untouched by the flames that rage around it. Turn to 60.

8

'Reward?' snaps one of the villagers, waving his pitchfork at you. 'A boy is in danger and you ask for a reward?' You hear several other angry mutterings from the crowd.

'Easy now,' says the elderly man, putting himself between you and the agitated villagers. 'I didn't see anyone else here wilfully volunteering to go down the well.' He looks at each of the men in turn – who all look away, embarrassed and ashamed. 'I have some coin I can give you,' he says, turning back to you. He opens his purse and produces 10 gold crowns, which he places in the palm of your hand. 'Half now and half when the task is done.'

Pocketing the coins, you agree to get started. Turn to 238.

9

As you prepare to leave, you see Martha running down the road towards you. She is waving her arms frantically.

'Stop her!' she cries. 'Stop her eating it! I've changed my mind!' She flings open the garden gate, tears streaming down her face. 'Please,' she begs. 'I feel awful. We can't let her eat that turnip – who knows what will happen? Please, we have to do something!'

You draw your weapons and agree to check out the cottage. Turn to 255.

10
Quest: Scarlet in the woods

In Tithebury, idle gossip travels fast. It isn't long before reports of a missing child reach your ears. Sensing an opportunity for some paid work, you head to the edge of the Tithebury woods, where a small wood cabin rests on a grassy knoll. A grizzled old man sits outside the building, sharpening the blade of his long sword with a notched stone. He looks up as you approach and offers a mumbled greeting. You notice that the man's right leg is heavily bandaged. A pair of crutches rest beside his stool.

You explain that you have heard news of a missing child. The man shakes his head, and looks away for a moment, his jaw clenching and unclenching.

'Yeah, my daughter,' he says at last, shaking his head. 'A spirited thing. Not seen hide nor hair of her for three days. Gave her some of my best brandy to take to her poorly grandma – lives right across the other side of the valley.' The man lowers his gaze to his injured leg. 'I fear the worst, stranger. Goblins have moved into those woods. I tried my best to find her ... I did.' He reaches out, gripping your arm tightly. 'Please, I have no gold or treasures to offer – but I still have a father's love for his daughter. Please, will you find her and bring her home safe?'

Will you:

Agree to help?	17
Ask about the woods?	23
Politely refuse?	Return to the map

11

The taproom of the 'Pie and Black Bird' is dark and muggy, the only light coming from a narrow window opposite the bar. The tables and benches are mostly empty – just a few customers sit sullenly over their mugs of ale, making little effort at conversation. At the bar, a group of elderly farmers are seated on stools, talking in hushed tones as they puff on their pipes. The barman listens in on their talk, fanning himself with a grime-stained dishcloth.

As you approach the bar, you notice a man sitting alone at the far side of the room. He appears to be watching you from beneath the brim of his hat, his long, pale fingers shuffling and reshuffling a deck of cards.

Will you:

Speak to the barman?	19
Talk to the farmers?	75
Walk over to the card player?	16
Leave and return to the village?	6

12

The man puts a hand to his back, emitting a loud and rather unconvincing groan.

'Pains, see. I got pains. Put my back out last season – no ways as I can keep up with those rats now. Fast little critters they are.' He shrugs his scrawny shoulders. 'I tried traps see, but they avoid them. It's like they're smart or something. Never seen their likes before. Bigger than your average rats too.' The man glances down at the weapon hanging by your side. 'I say, that pretty thing looks just about right for skewering those vermin. Make a nice tasty rat kebab with that, don't yer think?'

Will you:

Ask if there is a reward?	20
Agree to the quest?	34

13

You follow Martha into the shack – a cramped, stuffy room filled with dirt and cobwebs. A single pallet bed rests along one wall, lined with five grubby-faced children. One of them is rocking a wooden crib with her foot. Inside, two new-born babies fidget and squirm beneath a moth-eaten blanket.

Martha opens her larder, which you notice is almost bare – save for some dust and a scuttling beetle – and takes out a small sack of flour and a couple of eggs. She explains that this is all the food she has now, having killed the last of her chickens to feed her starving family.

'Henry, light the fire if you can, please,' says Martha, as she clears the table of broken dolls and gnawed chicken bones. One of the children, clearly the eldest, takes a tinder box from next to the mattress and proceeds to light the few sticks of dry wood in the stone heath.

'I have nothing,' explains Martha, breaking the eggs and adding them to the flour. 'But I ask for no charity. Certainly not from those stuck-up Tithebury villagers. They go too far with their petty games and superstitions.' She glances at the basket of turnip and grins.'But this time … this time I'm gonna make them eat their words!'

Will you:

Offer Martha 10 gold crowns?	200
Let Martha finish her cooking?	78

14

'Those vile things,' says the girl, wrinkling her nose. 'I fell foul of one of their silly traps while I was picking mushrooms. I could have been a goner I suppose, but in my heart of hearts I always knew that my handsome huntsman would find me eventually.'

She pauses, looking you up and down like a dirty piece of laundry.

'Shame you came along and spoiled everything. You don't even look like a hero. Not like the ones in the storybooks – not like my gorgeous huntsman.'

Will you:

Ask about the huntsman?	5
Demand she goes home immediately?	129

15
Quest: Curse of the cornfields

As you descend into the patchwork valley of farmsteads, you notice a flock of crows circling over the nearby fields. Below them, a fine white mist hangs like a shroud over the wilting, sun-beaten corn – its appearance looking slightly unnatural in the dazzling sunlight. An elderly man hurries towards you, a pitchfork held tightly in his hands. His expression looks panicked.

'Please! Will you help me?' he cries. 'My farm is cursed! It's the witch – the witch I tell you!'

Will you:

Ask about the strange mist?	31
Ask why the witch is to blame?	163

16

As you walk over, the man doffs his hat to you in greeting. You settle onto the bench opposite. 'Greetings, my friend,' he says. 'You care to make a little wager?'

Will you:

Agree to play cards?	54
Ask about local rumours?	128

17

The man offers you a grim smile. 'Thank you,' he says. 'And remember, be on your guard. Those goblins are cowardly creatures, but they're smart – smarter than they look.' He pats his bandaged leg, as if to drive home the point. 'Never underestimate them.'

The woodsman leans forward, and points to a small break in the nearby trees.

'You can find the path there; it will take you straight through to the other side of the valley if you want. Keep to the path, and only stray if you have to … no telling what you might find in those woods.'

After thanking the woodsman, you shoulder your backpack and head out into the Tithebury woods. Turn to 149.

18
Legendary monster: Mauler

A narrow trail takes you up into the rocky hills. Picking your way past boulders and scree, you spy a cave opening ahead. As you near, you hear an ominous, thundering growl coming from inside the cave. You ready yourself for combat as a huge black bear comes snuffling out of the darkness. With a snarl, it rears up onto its hind legs, its immense, muscled frame towering above you. Swiping its paws through the air, you catch sight of the beast's razor-sharp claws. Now you know why the locals call this bear 'the mauler'. It is time to defend yourself:

	Speed	Brawn	Armour	Health
Mauler	5	8	5	30

Special abilities
◖ Ferocity: If Mauler wins a combat round and inflicts health damage on your hero, the beast automatically raises its *speed* to 7 for the next combat round.

If you defeat Mauler turn to 26. If you are defeated, you have no choice but to return to the quest map.

19

The barman grunts as you approach, pushing himself lazily up off the counter.

'Wha' can I do yer for?' he asks, scratching his rotund belly. 'Need something to cool yer down? Ain't got nothing cold, I'm afraid. Warm beer's all yer getting here.'

Will you:

Ask if he has heard any rumours?	245
Ask about Avian Dale?	53
Talk about the weather?	42
Turn your attention back to the taproom?	11

20

The man shows you the pouch dangling from his belt. You are more than a little surprised to see that it is heavy with coin.

'Mercenary type, huh?' he grins. 'I got some gold to make you happy, if that's what you're after. It ain't much mind ... but this ain't a good year, not a good year at all.' He looks up into sky, shielding his eyes from the sun. 'Ne'er seen a spit of rain for weeks. It's the witch I hears them saying – she's the one brought this on us. Hard times for us all in Tithebury, very hard times.'

Will you:

Agree to the quest?	34
Politely decline?	Return to the map

21

You cut the girl loose, taking a small degree of satisfaction as she drops to the ground with a thud.

'Ouch!' she cries. 'You could have done that a little more graciously.' She gets to her feet, brushing the leaves and twigs from her clothes. 'All day I've been up that bloomin' tree, and not a single sign of him. Not a single sign.' She wanders over and picks up her basket. 'I was sure that handsome huntsman would come and save me. I screamed and screamed until I was hoarse. Oh, that would have been so perfect – for him to find me here, a maiden in distress.' She gives a long, wistful sigh.

Will you:

Ask about the huntsman?	28
Ask about the goblins?	14
Demand that she goes home?	129

22
Quest: Best in show

As you leave the village of Tithebury Cross, you pass a small row of thatched cottages. One of them catches your eye, its garden abundant with brightly-coloured flowers and sweet-smelling roses. An elderly woman is working in the garden, pruning a cherry tree with a small pair of shears. When she sees you watching her, she immediately straightens and waves you over.

'Good day to you traveller,' she says, her chubby cheeks bulging with a smile. 'I'm Beatrice Fletcher – how lovely to meet you. I see you're admiring my garden. Isn't it a marvel, despite this wretched weather?' The woman wipes her brow. 'I don't suppose you fancy some work, do you? Ha, don't worry – I don't see you as the type to have green fingers. No, I got other work in mind for you. See that?' She points to an area of the garden where several large turnips are starting to emerge from the soil. 'Those turnips ... they're prize-winners. Do you know I've won the prize for Best Root Vegetable in Tithebury five years running. Five years! People expect me to win ... but this year ... this year is different.' She sighs and shakes her head. 'My little beauties aren't doing so well. It's the heat you see. But Martha Weevil, you should see the size of her turnips. Witchery, I tell you. It's outright cheating!'

The woman places a hand in her apron pocket and pulls out a small earthenware pot. 'But this ... this will even up the odds. I got it off that kind old witch, the one that lives out in the woods – but don't tell a soul. Wouldn't want my good name to be associated with the likes of her. I'm sure you'll understand.' She holds out the pot to you. 'Look, it's simple. Do you fancy earning a bit of coin? I need someone … discreet – someone to accidentally spill a bit of this on Martha's turnips.' She shakes the pot and you hear the sound of liquid, sloshing around inside. 'What do you say?'

Will you:

Agree to the task?	63
Tell her it's cheating?	148

23

'The woods always been safe if you stick to the path. Liselle always knew that – can handle herself that girl, I tell you; always visiting her kind old grandma.' The man runs a finger along the edge of his sharpened blade. 'It's been three days now and not a word. She should have been back by now. Liselle knows I would be worrying. She's all I got now, see.' The man's steely eyes settle on your own. 'I'll wager she's still with her grandma. That old woman's a glutton for fanciful stories; fills my dear Liselle's head full of 'em. I daresay she may have tarried there. But goblins …' He sniffs at the air like a wizened old wolf. 'Their taint is on the breeze. If goblins have taken her, I fear the worst.' He looks down at the crutches, resting next to his stool. 'If I wasn't crippled so, I'd be out there now, scouring every inch of that blasted wood.'

Will you:

Agree to help?	17
Ask the woodsman about his injury?	30
Politely refuse?	Return to the map

24

You are at a stalemate. To proceed further with the game you must put more money on the table. Decide how much gold you will add – and the gambler automatically adds the same amount. You must bet at least one extra gold crown. (If you have no more money, then you have lost and lose all your gold. Turn to 11.) Then roll a die. If the result is ⚀ or less turn to 67, if the result is ⚁ or more turn to 259.

25

Quest: The stone circle

The sun beats down mercilessly, casting a shimmering haze over the fields and meadows. Feeling dizzy from the heat, you leave the trail and take shelter under a tree. As you begin to doze in the cool shade, a voice suddenly startles you back to wakefulness.

'Wake up! Wake up!' A bird lands by your feet in a flurry of brightly-coloured feathers. 'Please don't tell me you're as dim-witted as those farmhands. You look like an adventurer, am I right? Am I right?' Its head twitches from side to side, watching you with its beady black eyes.

Too stunned to speak, you settle for nodding instead. 'Good, good – well that's a start,' says the bird, flapping its wings. 'Come, my master is in danger and he needs your help. Something terrible has happened!'

Will you:

Ask the bird about his master?	39
Ask the bird how it can talk?	32
Agree to help the bird?	3

26

The giant bear gives a deep, bellowing cry, then crashes to the ground, dead. You may now take one of the following items as a reward for your heroism:

Mauler's maw	Savage pelt	Rage claw
(head)	(cloak)	(left hand: fist weapon)
+1 speed +1 armour	+1 brawn +1 magic	+1 speed +1 brawn
Ability: fearless	Ability: savagery	Ability: dominate

Once you have made your choice, return to the map to continue your adventure.

27

The man sniffs his clothes, looking surprised. 'Well, can't says as I ever had anyone telling me I pong before.' He catches your eye and gives a dry, cackling laugh. 'I'm just a simple farmer, see. Not pretending nothing different. All's me water used for crops and cattle feed. Think I can spare any for a bath?' He shakes his head, grinning. 'I do knows one thing, though. That is a very nice looking blade you sportin' there. Just about right for skewering those critters in me barn. You'll make a nice rat kebab with that, don't yer think?'

Will you:

Ask if there is a reward?	20
Agree to the quest and get started?	34

28

'Why, he's the only reason I'm here in these horrible woods,' says the girl, flicking a stray leaf from her shawl. 'He lives up on the hills, to the east of here. A traveller – and handsome ... so very handsome. My, when I picture those big arms of his ... all the better to hug me with.' Her eyes glaze over and she starts to sway from side to side, beaming like a love-sick child. It isn't until you cough loudly, that she comes out of her romantic reverie. 'Yes ... well, I'm in love. Isn't that obvious? Oh, poor daddy – he thinks I'm always visiting granny. But gosh, who would want to travel these woods just to see that wrinkly old goat? No, it's the huntsman I always come to see. He has such fascinating stories to tell. One day we'll leave Tithebury together and travel the world ... just think of that!' She looks at you intently, as if challenging you to say otherwise.

Will you:

Demand she goes home immediately?	129
Ask about the goblins?	14

29
Legendary monster: Humbaroth the giant

You head east along the gravelly track that winds through the foot-hills of the Blackthorn Mountains. You pass the splintered wrecks of several carts and caravans, and are immediately reminded of the tales of the giant that now holds sway over this stretch of Tithebury. To slay the deadly creature would be doing the locals an enormous favour.

You haven't travelled far into the rocky hills before the ground begins to tremble and shake beneath your feet. Steadying yourself against a nearby boulder, you turn to see a giant of a man stomp-ing purposefully towards you, his immense strides carrying him over the jagged rocks that litter the hillside. Dressed in filthy animal skins and a necklace of human skulls, the giant is a truly imposing sight. In his hands he carries a mighty stone club, which he now raises above his head as he bellows with rage. You glance down at your own weapons, which suddenly look small and insignificant by comparison. Can you really hope to best such a monster in combat? It's time to find out:

	Speed	Brawn	Armour	Health
Humbaroth	4	9	4	35

Special abilities

🔖 Punishing blows: Each time Humbaroth inflicts health damage, your *armour* is lowered by 1. (Your *armour* value is restored after the combat is over.)

If you manage to defeat the giant turn to **44**. If you are defeated, you have no choice but to return to the quest map.

30

'Got jumped by goblins. Three of the vermin – and fierce fighters too. I was lucky to escape with my life.' The woodsman raises his sword, the polished blade reflecting the afternoon sunlight. 'I've seen a fair bit of action in my time. I know how to handle myself. But those goblins ... they're something else. Never seen their likes in these parts before. It's a bad sign. A very bad sign.'

Will you:

Agree to help?	**17**
Politely refuse?	**Return to the map**

31

'It's been there two days, two days!' says the elderly farmer, pointing a trembling finger at the mist. 'And I seen strange things in there. Shapes ... and sounds ... horrible sounds! I won't go in there. No, I won't! Please don't make me.' He jerks his head round to look at you, his expression slightly crazed. 'The wife won't let me back in the house – not until I sort it out. But I can't go in those fields. I can't! The mist ... it's just not right. The witch did it, I know she did!'

Will you:

Agree to help the farmer?	**139**
Ask why the witch is to blame?	**163**

32

The bird ruffles its feathers angrily. 'Oh by the saints of Judah, if I had a nice juicy worm for every time some idiot asked me that question. Look – I'm a special bird, alright? My master trained me. I think some magic was involved – well, OK perhaps a lot of magic, but that's not important. What *is* important is that my master is in danger!'

Will you:

Ask the bird who his master is?	39
Agree to help the bird?	3

33

Inside the tower, it is a scene of destruction: shelves and cupboards have been smashed to pieces; tables and chairs have been flung on their sides; books, scrolls and potion bottles litter the floor … and at the centre of the circular room, spinning in a cracking maelstrom of electrical light, is a living whirlwind. With a booming thunderous rumble, it spins towards you, sending torn papers and pieces of wood hurtling up into the air. You must now defeat this fearsome magical creature:

	Speed	Magic	Armour	Health
Storm elemental	2	1	1	25

Special abilities

◗ Charged: Each time you inflict health damage on the elemental, you take 2 damage in return. This ability ignores *armour*.

If you defeat the storm elemental, turn to **94**.

You head off quickly down the track, pleased to have finally got away from the man's odorous stink. After several minutes, you veer off the track, joining a gravel pathway that leads into the nearby farmstead. As you approach the barn, you cast a curious glance at the other farm buildings. All of them seem eerily quiet, as if the place has long been abandoned. The shutters on the windows are closed, and the garden and surrounding outhouses show clear signs of neglect. The hairs on the back of your neck begin to prickle. Something isn't quite right here. You step into the barn and discover that it is just as empty as the rest of the farm. Instead of golden piles of hay, there are just a few oily rags and some rusty pieces of farming machinery. Scanning the ground you see no sign of any rats either. Across from you, a rickety-looking ladder leads up into the hayloft.

Will you:

Climb the ladder to the hayloft?	45
Return to the man at the roadside?	51

35

The moment you touch the stone there is a bright flash of light, followed by a dizzying sensation of movement. When the light fades, you find yourself in a large stone chamber, its walls lined with blazing torches. In the centre of the room stands a man, wreathed in flame. He watches you intently, the fire licking around his ember-red eyes.

'You trespass in the halls of ancient kings,' booms a voice, from somewhere above. 'Many have come here. All have failed. Fight my champions and prove your worth.'

The man points at you, then curls his finger, beckoning you to attack. Seeing you hesitate, he laughs to himself – then rushes forward, jets of flame streaking from the palms of his hands.

	Speed	Magic	Armour	Health
Malachi of fire	4	4	2	20

Special abilities

● Fiery aura: You automatically take 3 damage at the end of each combat round. This ability ignores *armour*.

If you are defeated, you find yourself back on the hilltop, turn to 153. If you defeat Malachi, his body turns to ash. All that is left is a stone rune, its glowing surface marked with the symbol of a flame. If you take the *Rune of Malachi*, make a note of it on your hero sheet. There is a sudden flash of light and you find yourself back on the hilltop (turn to 153).

36

The farmer scratches his greying hair. 'A reward? Well, yes I suppose yer did do me a favour. Thing is, I don't have a penny to me name – not a thing. Hey, wait! Perhaps I can give yer something.' He stuffs a hand in one of his pockets and pulls out a small, grime-covered key. 'I found this just the other week, when I was tilling me southern fields. Don't suppose it has much use really, but yer more likely to find the lock it fits than I am.'

If you decide to take the *grime-coated key*, simply make a note of it on your hero sheet (it does not take up a backpack space). You thank the farmer and then bid him farewell. Return to the map to choose a new quest.

37

Bursting out of the woods, you find yourself in a clearing, dominated by a large, gnarly tree. A young girl is dangling up-side down from one of its branches, her feet tangled in a rope. She is dressed in boyish breeches and a tunic, with a thick red shawl hanging loosely off her shoulders.

Below her, two spindly goblins are hunched over the girl's basket, rummaging through its contents. As you approach, one of them looks up, its black glassy eyes glinting in the dappled sunlight. The creature gives two hooting cries, then scurries towards you, pulling a rusty sword from its belt. The other goblin slides a knife from its boot and hurries to join the battle. You must fight the goblins as a single enemy:

	Speed	Brawn	Armour	Health
Goblin poachers	0	1	0	20*

* Once the goblins have been reduced to 10 *health* or less, turn to 77.

38

'Well, it is a fitting end of sorts,' says Martha, eyeing up the turnip with a thoughtful expression. 'Now, she'll win that silly competition after all.' You both exchange bemused glances.

If you gave Martha a gift of ten gold crowns, turn to 104. Otherwise, turn to 145.

39

'Why, he is the great Perinold the Magnificent – explorer and scholar to the king no less. Do you think I would travel around with just *anyone*? You must have heard of him – author of the award-winning History of Everything?'

You shrug your shoulders apologetically. The bird makes a snorting sound through its beak. 'Well, you don't strike me as the type to have ever opened a book, let alone know how to read. Humph!' The bird twitches its head disapprovingly. 'Look, it doesn't matter *who* he is – all you need to know is that he's gone and got himself in a pickle. He was doing research for a new book – investigating some old stones, up on the hill. Everything was fine until they started to glow. Then he touched one of them, there was a bright flash of light and he was gone! Gone! And I have no idea how to find him.'

Will you:

Ask the bird how it can talk?	32
Agree to help the bird?	3

40

The three ruffians lie dead at your feet. You search the bodies as quickly as you can, covering your nose from the stench of their unwashed bodies. You find five gold coins and can take any / all of the following items:

Crone's dagger	Gilbert's club	Moth-eaten blanket
(main hand: dagger)	(main hand: club)	(cloak)
+1 speed +1 magic	+3 brawn	+1 speed

You peer over the edge of the platform, scanning the hay barn below. There is no sign of the other ruffian – and the ladder he took is now firmly out of reach, propped up against the far wall. Turning back to the loft, you discover that your only route of escape is through a narrow window, leading out onto a sloping, tiled roof.

Perhaps you could pretend to be 'Gilbert' and call for the other ruffian – or escape by climbing out onto the roof.

Will you:

Do your best impression of Gilbert?	70
Leave the hayloft using the window?	83

41

The king falls to his knees, his head bowed. 'I yield ... now begone from this cursed place.' There is a faint serpentine hiss from somewhere in the darkness, then the spectral body of the king vanishes, leaving behind a golden casket, engraved with runes. As you watch, the lid creaks open of its own accord, revealing a series of magical treasures inside. You may now take one of the following before the chest closes and disappears:

Stone collar	Stone shield	Stone ward
(necklace)	(left hand: shield)	(talisman)
+1 armour	+1 speed +2 armour	Ability: might
Ability: charm	Ability: slam	of stone

When you have made your choice, turn to 170.

42

The barman whistles through his stumpy, yellowed teeth. 'I says it's magic – some kind of curse. I ain't seen rain around 'ere for months.' He dabs at his brow with the dirty cloth. 'We're all tired of the heat. If I wanted this weather I'd pack me bags and travel south. This ain't normal, I tell yer that.' The barman casts a nervous glance over his shoulder, then leans in over the counter. 'They say it's that witch,' he says, dropping his voice to a whisper. 'The old crone that lives out in the woods. Since she moved to Tithebury two summers ago, things been going wrong. Calves born with three legs, children with the pox ... I reckon this weather is all her doing. If I was you, I'd pass straight through Tithebury and be on your way. Safer.' He gives you a wink, then settles back behind the counter.

Will you:

Ask about Avian Dale?	53
Ask if he has heard any rumours?	245
Turn your attention back to the taproom?	11

43

With relief, you discover that your weapons and magic can harm the shadow. Dodging its snapping jaws and cold, piercing touch, you are finally able to overcome the nightmarish creature. As you deliver the killing blow, the shadow evaporates with an echoing hiss, leaving behind something small and round, which drops to the earth at your feet. You may now take:

Essence of shadow
(left hand: orb)
+1 speed +1 magic
Ability: chill touch

You pick your way past the last of the gravestones and approach the double-doors of the church. Turning the black circular handles, you push open the heavy doors and enter. Turn to 253.

44

They say the bigger they are, the harder they fall ... as you land the killing blow, the giant teeters back on its heels, then topples backwards, arms flailing in the air. The ground shakes as the mighty giant hits the ground, throwing up clouds of billowing dirt and dust.

Humbaroth the giant is dead. There will be much rejoicing in Tithebury when the locals hear the news. You may now take one of the following items as a reward:

Skullbreaker	**Trophy of bones**	**Boar-hide boots**
(main hand: club)	(necklace)	(feet)
+1 speed +2 brawn	+1 magic +1 armour	+1 speed +1 armour
Ability: pound	Ability: charm	Ability: steadfast

Return to the map to continue your adventure.

45

The rungs of the ladder creak in protest as you make your way towards the hayloft. As you near the top, you can make out a scuffling sound coming from above. Perhaps the man was right after all – there really are rats in the barn. As you pull yourself up onto the straw-covered platform, your eyes widen at the sight before you. Instead of a swarm of black-bodied rats, you find yourself facing three scruffy-looking ruffians.

Instinctively you draw your weapon, eyeing up the largest of the three, who you assume is the leader. An ugly scar cuts across the man's face, disfiguring his nose and mouth. He watches you intently, licking his lips as if planning his next meal.

At his side a spindly old woman cackles with delight. 'Ooh, this one looks delicious. What do you say, my beloved?' The third ruffian, an elderly man with a wild tangle of beard, giggles in a manner that suggests he has long since gone mad.

'Delicious! Delicious! Yes! Yes!' he barks, clapping his hands together.

The scarred leader begins to advance. 'About time we got some food sent up,' he growls. 'I'm famished.' His foot knocks into something, sending it skittering across the floor. You give a cry of revulsion when you catch sight of it – a half-eaten human hand.

'Careful, Gilbert,' says the crone, revealing a dagger from beneath her tattered shawl. 'This one looks smarter than the rest.'

The scarred man tightens his grip on the spiked club he is holding. 'Don't worry, ma. He won't give us any trouble.'

A scraping sound forces you to turn. Alarmed, you see that the ladder has been pulled away, leaving you trapped in the hayloft.

'Save some for me, my dears,' calls a voice from down below. You recognise it as belonging to the man you met on the road.

Slavering like animals, the three ruffians rush towards you. Turn to 62.

46

You pass under the cloth awnings to explore the village market. Three stalls immediately catch your eye. The first is crammed full of herbs, jars and bottles. Behind it, an elderly man is weighing ingredients on a small set of brass scales. On the stall next to him, an elegantly-dressed woman is sewing cloth. Displayed all around her are a number of fine-embroidered garments, all neatly folded in colourful piles. At the end of the row, a rickety table has been set up, covered in a bizarre assortment of odds and ends – from wooden toys to battered pieces of rusty armour. The stall-owner is currently rummaging in a box underneath the table.

Will you:

Visit the first stall (the apothecary)?	56
Visit the second stall (the clothier)?	68
Visit the third stall (the tinker)?	175
Leave the market?	6

47

You decide to leave your torch behind (remove the word *torch* from your hero sheet). Swinging your legs over the side of the pit, you take a deep breath and push yourself off, dropping into the darkness. The pit is deeper than you thought and your shoulders bang painfully against its rough walls several times as you tumble down the shaft.

Then, all of a sudden, you are swallowed up by a freezing torrent of fast-moving water. The shock of it knocks the breath from your body as you are brutally dragged under the surface. Caught in the river's tow, you are powerless to stop yourself as you are buffeted along through the cold, pitch blackness. Turn to 171.

48

You may collect some of the silk from Spindle's web to take with you:

Spindlesilk (2 uses)
(backpack)
Perhaps a master clothier
could do something
with this fine silk

Searching the rest of the cavern, you find little of interest. You decide to leave and return to the villagers at the well. Turn to 246.

49
Legendary monster: Zalladell the satyr

The path leads you down into a thickly wooded valley – the trees pressing in tightly on either side. You stop to examine the sheet of parchment that a passing traveller gave to you. It shows a map and the location of some ruins. Apparently, local archaeologists are excavating the site and could do with some paid muscle to help with the dig. Sounds like easy money ...

You leave the path, following a narrow trail into denser woodland. As you plunge deeper into the wilderness, you start to make out sounds coming from up ahead. They sound like cries for help ... and a scream, cut short by a gurgling cry. You quicken your pace, pushing your way past gnarly branches and stinging nettles.

You emerge in a large clearing dominated by a series of ivy-covered ruins. A number of men are fleeing towards the tree line – spades and other equipment left scattered around a half-dug hole. Wondering what has spooked the men, you enter the clearing.

At that moment, a creature steps out from behind an old crumbling tower. It is at least a head taller than a man, with curved horns and goat-like feet. Its hairy body is covered in black sigils that seem to writhe and change before your very eyes.

'You! You do not run,' hisses the bestial creature, pointing a taloned finger in your direction. 'At last, an opponent worthy of my attention.' You prepare yourself for combat as the nightmarish creature advances:

	Speed	Magic	Armour	Health
Zalladell	5	7	4	40

Special abilities
- Black sigils: At the end of every combat round, your hero automatically suffers 1 damage. This ability ignores *armour*.
- Bewitched: Re-roll any ⚀ or ⚁ dice results for Zalladell. The results of the re-rolled dice must be used.

If you defeat Zalladell turn to **80**. If you are defeated, you have no choice but to return to the quest map.

50

You drive your blade deep into the creature's body, watching as its pale form dissolves back into the mist. Before the grisly totem can summon any more guardians, you lunge forwards, slicing it in two. As the severed wood topples to the ground, the magical green light flashes, then is gone. A few seconds later, the mist begins to disperse. Soon, you can feel the warmth of the sunlight once again – its heat evaporating the last of the chill fog.

'Yer did it! Yer did it!' The elderly farmer skips and jumps through the corn towards you. 'Me fields – they're back! Thank you stranger, thank you!'

Will you:
Demand a reward?	**36**
Bid the farmer farewell?	**Return to the map**

51

You decide that the stranger must have made a mistake. Angry that your time has been wasted, you stride out of the barn and bump straight into the scruffy-looking man coming the other way. On seeing you, his eyes widen in surprise.

'They're alive! They're still alive! Boss! Boss!' He turns and starts sprinting towards the nearby farmhouse.

Will you:
Immediately take chase?	**144**
Let him go and leave the farm?	**Return to the map**

52

The king falls to his knees, his head bowed. 'I yield ... now begone from this cursed place.' There is a faint serpentine hiss from somewhere in the darkness, then the spectral body of the king vanishes, leaving behind a golden casket, engraved with runes.

As you watch, the lid creaks open of its own accord, revealing a series of magical treasures inside. You may now take one of the following before the chest closes and disappears:

Nightbringer	**Nightfall**
(main hand: sword)	(main hand: staff)
+1 speed +4 brawn	+1 speed +4 magic
Ability: might of stone	Ability: might of stone

When you have made your choice and updated your hero sheet, turn to 170.

53

The barman gives another grunt. 'Not heard that name for a while now. Strange fella, lives in that castle, across the gorge. Been there for as long as I remember, but he seldom comes 'ere.' He leans towards you, beckoning you to do the same. 'I'd stay away from the likes of him. Something ain't right when a man lives as long as I have, but doesn't look a day older.' The man taps his grey, balding pate. 'Look at me, fifty years to me name. But that Avian – still looks younger than my son. I smell magic there, and no good ever comes of magic.'

Will you:

Ask for directions to Avian's castle?	84
Ask if he has heard any rumours?	245
Talk about the weather?	42
Turn your attention back to the taproom?	11

54

The man nods and starts dealing out two hands of cards. He asks you how much you wish to gamble. (Choose how many gold crowns you would like to bet. These are placed in the middle of the table. The man then matches your bet with the same number of gold crowns.) Once the cards are dealt, the gambler explains the rules of his game. You pick up your cards and begin playing.

Roll a die. If the result is: ⚀ turn to 67, ⚁ turn to 24, ⚂ turn to 237, ⚃ turn to 226, ⚄ turn to 205, ⚅ turn to 259.

55

The ruffian lies dead – his corpse joining the rest of his cannibalistic family. You reach down and cut the man's purse loose. Inside you find 15 gold crowns. You may also take:

Rennie's slicer
(left hand: dagger)
+1 speed +1 brawn
Ability: first cut

After pocketing the man's gold, you ponder your next move.

Will you:
Explore the rest of the farm?	**96**
Leave the farm?	**Return to the map**

56

The elderly man looks up from his work, his expression one of surprise. 'A customer at last,' he says, pushing his glasses up his nose. 'Can I interest you in any of my wares?'

You may purchase any quantity of the following for 5 gold crowns each:

Pot of healing (1 use)	Pot of speed (1 use)	Pot of magic (1 use)
(backpack)	(backpack)	(backpack)
Use any time in combat to restore 4 *health*	Use any time in combat to raise your *speed* by 2 for one combat round	Use any time in combat to raise your *magic* by 2 for one for one combat round

When you have made your choices, you may visit another stall (turn to 46) or leave the market (turn to 6).

57

'Yes, yes,' says the man, nodding quickly. 'How could I forget.' He pats the leather carry-case hanging at his waist. 'Get me the book, and I will offer you a fine choice of rewards. After all, you *do* desire power and glory, do you not?'

Will you:

Ask why he can't get the book himself?	69
Agree to the quest?	164

58

You find Beatrice waiting expectantly for you in her garden, a basket of freshly-picked flowers in her hands. 'Gosh, I thought you were never coming back,' she grins, her rosy-cheeks bulging like apples. 'You do look a little flustered. Did everything go to plan?'

You recount what happened – that the witch's potion turned the turnips into deadly monsters! The woman merely chuckles to herself.

'Ah that witch – so she does have a sense of humour after all. Well, what's done is done, my dear, and I did promise you a reward didn't I?' She puts down her basket, and then fishes in her apron pocket. She pulls out two small glass bottles. 'I suppose you might find a use for these on your adventures; some herbal remedies that I made myself.'

You may take any / all the following items:

Healing salve (1 use)	Miracle grow (1 use)
(backpack)	(backpack)
Use any time in combat to restore 6 *health*	Use any time in combat to raise your *brawn* by 2 for one combat round

Beatrice also hands you 5 gold crowns. 'Thank you again, stranger,' she smiles sweetly. 'And remember, we never met or did business together – did we?' She gives you a sly wink then, picking up her basket, returns to tending her garden.

Pocketing your items, you resume your journey. Return to the map.

59

The snarling undead bound towards you. This will be a tough battle, as you prepare to take on all three opponents on open ground:

	Speed	Brawn	Armour	Health
Ghouls	5	3	2	30

Special abilities

♥ Piercing claws: The ghouls' attacks ignore *armour*.

If you manage to defeat the ghouls, turn to 127.

60

'What foolish insect dares set foot in the domain of Spindle? You will perish here – and your worthless blood will feed my brood!' The giant spider scuttles towards you, your panicked face mirrored in its bulging, black eyes. You must now defend yourself against this fearsome opponent:

	Speed	Brawn	Armour	Health
Spindle	5	5	3	30

Special abilities

🌑 Webbed: The spider's sticky webbing inhibits your movement. At the start of every combat round, roll a die. If you roll ⚀ or ⚁ then your *speed* is reduced by 1 for that combat round. (Note: Ignore this ability if you have used your torch to set fire to the web.)

🌑 Venom: Once you have taken health damage from the spider, at the end of every combat round you must automatically lose 2 *health*.

If you manage to defeat Spindle, turn to 91.

61

'Waste of bloomin' space if you ask me,' interjects the other woman, with an angry snort. 'He's supposed to help us, by bringing a little rain when we need it, or some fair wind.' She jerks a thumb over her shoulder. 'He lives in a tower, way up on the hills. My husband went up to see him only the other day – to convince the crazy old man to bring us some rain and end this drought. Well, you should have seen him. Scared out of his wits when he returned. He said that the tower was haunted and he weren't going back. Not sure what is going on up there, but I'm staying away too. It's a matter for the Speaker to decide what happens if you ask me.'

Intrigued, you ask for directions to the wizard's tower. Then, bidding the women farewell, you set off east along the river. Turn to 235.

62

You have no choice but to fight the three ruffians. They attack you as a single enemy.

	Speed	Brawn	Armour	Health
Ruffians	2	3	1	15

Special abilities

🌑 Crone's dagger: If the ruffians roll a ⚅⚅ for damage, the crone's dagger automatically inflicts an extra point of health damage.

If you win the combat, turn to 40.

63

Following Beatrice's directions, you head out of Tithebury Cross and soon find yourself on a seldom-used track that winds up the face of a craggy hill. At the summit, you discover an old shack, perched precariously on the cliff-edge. Like a house of cards, you could easily imagine the slightest gust of wind toppling it over at any second. From an open window, you hear the screech of a baby crying, and a woman's voice raised in anger. Next to the ramshackle building is an empty chicken coop and a small vegetable garden.

You take the earthenware pot out of your backpack and remove the stopper. A strong vinegary smell drifts up from the inside. Keeping the pot at arm's length, you approach the vegetable patch. Much of it is covered in straggly weeds and withered plants. But, astonishingly, along its furthest edge, three enormous turnips are growing – their pale rounded tops protruding from the soil.

You sprinkle the vinegary potion over the turnips, then step away, not entirely sure what the results will be. A minute or two later and you get your answer. The turnips start to shake and tremble – then, suddenly, one of them sprouts a pair of spindly arms and starts to push itself out of the ground! From a jagged mouth, the creature emits a rumbling growl as it squeezes itself free, staggering dizzily onto a pair of skinny legs. The other turnips are also pulling themselves out of the soil and within seconds you find yourself facing three of the monstrous creatures. Their root-like hands clench into fists as they stumble crazily towards you.

You must fight the turnips as a single enemy:

	Speed	Brawn	Armour	Health
Turnips	0	0	1	10

If you defeat the turnips, turn to 241.

64

The wolf lies dead at your feet. As you watch, the creature's body begins to shift and change – the bones cracking and reforming into a human shape. Within moments, the body of a man lies before you, the black liquid still coating his lips.

It is then that you hear a quiet sobbing coming from behind the wagon. You hurry to investigate, and find the woodsman's daughter huddled next to one of the wheels, trembling with fear.

'It was all my fault,' she gasps. 'I let him drink the potion. I said it was a gift from my father. Then he changed ... he changed!' She looks away, shivering. 'I did everything that the recipe said. Everything. And it turned him into that!' She points to the huntsman's corpse. 'I should have known not to trust the witch. Oh, what have I done?'

You help the girl to her feet. As it is now late evening, you decide it best that the two of you sleep in the wagon and head back to her father at first light. Turn to 82.

65

You start towards the totem, with the intention of smashing it apart with your blade. However, you have only taken a couple of steps when the mist in front of you suddenly twists and broils, forming itself into a phantom-like creature. Before you can react, a spectral fist slams into your chest, sending you sprawling backwards onto the flattened corn. With an ear-splitting howl, the phantom glides towards you, its green eyes glowing with a malevolent hunger. You scramble to your feet and prepare to fight:

	Speed	Brawn	Armour	Health
Mist Stalker	0	1	0	10

If you defeat the mist stalker, turn to 50.

66

Quest: Whatever the weather

The midday heat is almost unbearable. You leave the dusty track and head into the cool, dark woods, grateful for the shade. After resting beneath the tangled boughs of an ancient oak, you set off once again, keeping to the deep shadows cast by the trees. After a few minutes, you hear the rush and splash of water. Licking your parched lips, you head in its direction, quickly breaking into a run as the sound gets louder.

Slipping and sliding down a wooded slope, you find yourself on the banks of a river, its white waters churning around the rocks and stones that litter the river bed. Further up the bank you see a wooden cart and two women – who you guess are local farmers – filling a series of buckets with water from the river. Next to them a skinny-looking mule sips greedily from the waters.

The women wave to you as you approach, and greet you cheerily. They explain that the local wells have run dry and now they must collect water from the river to nourish their crops and feed their livestock.

'Wouldn't be surprised if this here river doesn't dry up next,' says one of the women, carrying another full bucket to the wagon. 'This weather shows no signs of stopping. If only that darned weather wizard would get down from his tower and help, then we might see some signs of a turn.'

Will you:

Ask about the weather wizard?	61
Help to fill the buckets?	79

67

You have an excellent hand and beat the gambler. You may take back double the amount of gold that you have bet. If you would like to play again turn to 54, otherwise you decide to leave the table. Turn to 11.

68

The woman puts aside her sewing, looking you up and down with interest. 'A traveller,' she says, nodding her head. 'So, I might sell something in this backwater village after all. Please, take a look at my fine silks. I use only the finest cloth and thread – from the deserts of the south, no less.'

You may purchase any of the following items, for 12 gold crowns each:

Silk robe	Embroidered gloves	Patchwork cloak
(chest)	(gloves)	(cloak)
+1 magic	+1 speed +1 magic	+1 speed

'My skills are the finest around,' says the woman. 'If there's nothing here that interests you, perhaps I can tailor you something a little more ... unique.'

Will you:

Ask about the unique items?	85
Explore one of the other stalls?	46

69

The man lifts a pale finger and waves it back and forth. 'Ah, no, no, no. That hill is still hallowed ground, my friend, and that makes it ... difficult for people like me.' He pauses for a heartbeat and then gives a dry, rattling laugh. 'I have done some bad deeds in this life, things I am not proud of. I have always had a fear of such holy places – that the One God, in his good grace, will strike me down for my sins. A silly superstition of mine, nothing more.' The man folds his arms, his fingers tapping impatiently on the sleeves of his robe. 'Now, I think I have answered your questions. So, what's it to be?'

Will you:

Agree to the task?	164
Ask what your reward will be?	57

You put your hands to your mouth and call out: *'Hey! Fancy something to eat? Ma and pa are already tucking in!'* Seconds later you hear a banging from down below.

'OK, OK. I was just going ta fetch the boss. He won't be happy if there's none left for 'im and his rats, I tell ya.' As you hoped, the ladder suddenly appears, followed by a series of creaks as the ruffian ascends. The moment his head comes into view, you step forward, grabbing him by the scruff of the neck and yanking him to his feet.

The grubby man gives a cry of alarm when he sees the dead bodies. Tears start to well up in his eyes. 'Please, no ... you didn't ... not the family ...'

You release him – no longer sure if you feel pity or anger for the wretched thief. The man drops to his knees beside the three corpses.

'Not ma and pa,' he sobs. 'Not ma and pa ...' He turns to face you, his tears forming dirty rivulets across his grubby cheeks. 'You killed 'em!' he cries, pointing a shaking finger at you. 'You did it!' With an animal-like snarl, he launches himself at you, taking you by surprise. Steel flashes, followed by a stabbing pain in your side. Stumbling backwards, you see a bloody knife in the man's hands – your blood. He licks the blade hungrily, then rushes to attack.

	Speed	Brawn	Armour	Health
Rennie	3	2	2	15

Special abilities

First cut: Start this combat having already lost 1 *health*.

If you defeat the ruffian, turn to **55**.

71

'Humph, how charming!' snaps the girl, sticking out her tongue. She reaches into her basket and pulls out a sharp-looking kitchen knife. 'Don't worry about me, I can handle myself thank you very much!' With a sniff, she turns and marches off into the woods.

You retrace your steps, to find yourself back on the main trail.

Will you:

Follow the trail to Grandma's house?	168
Head east into the hills?	181

72
Quest: Down the well

At the top of the hill, a crowd is gathered around the stone well. You see that several of the villagers are peering over the side, their faces looking both concerned and horrified. The rest are currently drawing lengths of straw from an elderly man in white robes. He turns as you approach.

'May the One God have mercy,' he says. 'Are you a sword for hire? Will you help us? Our well has dried up – first time in a hundred years. I sent my son down there, to see if it needed repairs. Then we heard … we heard …' The man puts a hand to his mouth, trembling. After taking a deep breath, he continues. 'We heard screaming … terrible screams and then, just silence. I fear something terrible has happened. Would you go down there and investigate. Please?'

The other villagers are all looking at you, nodding their heads eagerly. You notice one man, who clearly drew the short straw, nodding more enthusiastically than the others.

Will you:

Agree to help the villagers?	238
Ask the elderly man who he is?	86
Ask if there will be a reward?	8

73

The old woman shakes her head. 'It was a cleansing totem. Those spirits were there to spook the farmers and keep them away, while it did its work. I wasn't banking on someone like you to come along.' She continues to hastily pack items into her sack. 'That field had been tainted – by a summoning ritual. There is a demon loose in Tithebury, and that is why I came here. To root it out.'

Will you:

Accuse the witch of another crime?	113
Attack the witch?	137
Help her to escape?	101

74

You slide the key into the lock. To your surprise, you find that it fits perfectly. A quick twist and you are rewarded with a satisfying click. You eagerly push open the lid, expecting valuable treasures to be hidden inside. However, your excitement is short-lived. Inside the locker, all you find are a few gold coins and another key – this one fashioned from silver.

You have gained 20 gold crowns and may now take the *fine silver key*. If you decide to take the key, simply make a note of it on your hero sheet (it does not take up backpack space). With little else of interest in the room, you decide to leave via the archway. Turn to 154.

75

The farmers fall silent as you approach, looking you up and down suspiciously. You quickly explain that you are a traveller, and wonder if there is any work for a hired sword. The farmers glance at each other, then begin chuckling behind their pipes. One of them beckons you closer, blowing smoke out of the corner of his mouth.

'I tell yer wha' yer can do,' he says in a thick accent. 'Go kill the witch. She's the one tha' be bringing the curse to this land.' The other farmers nod, mumbling in agreement. Before you can ask any further questions, they turn their backs on you and resume their conversation. Turn to 11.

76

Fetch backs away from you. 'Fool,' he hisses, spitting blood. 'I expected better of you. Especially from one who carries the mark of shadow.' He points to your arm which has become partially exposed in the fight. The brand pulses with a purple light – the heat from it prickling your skin.

'What is this?' you demand angrily. 'Do you know what it means?'

Fetch simply raises his hands skywards, throwing back his head. There is a flash of black lightning then he is gone. On the spot where he was standing, there is a small charred crater – the smell of sulphur is strong in the air.

You kick at the blackened soil in frustration. What did he mean by 'the mark of shadow' you wonder. You cover it up quickly, before heading back to the village. Return to the map to continue your adventure.

77

Despite being short and ungainly, the goblins prove to be accomplished fighters. It takes all your skill just to fend off their frenzied attacks. At last, just as you are starting to tire, a sudden opening presents itself – allowing you to deliver a fatal blow. With a gurgling cry, one of the goblins topples to the ground dead. On seeing its companion fall, the other goblin gives a cowardly whimper, then turns and starts running for the nearby trees.

You start to follow when a voice brings you up short. 'Hey! Hey! Excuse me!' The young girl is glaring at you angrily from her up-side-down vantage point. 'Well, don't just stand there gawping like the village idiot,' she snaps. 'Cut me down from this tree, this instant!'

Will you:

Pursue the fleeing goblin?   95

Cut the girl down from the tree?   21

78

Martha spoons the turnip into a bowl and covers it with a thick layer of pastry. The pie is then placed in a small clay oven to cook. The gaunt children sit in silence, eyeing the pie hungrily as the smell of freshly baked pastry fills the room.

Half an hour later and the pie is ready. Martha takes it out of the oven and places it on the table. The children gather round it, watching it expectantly, as if something mysterious will suddenly happen. Martha catches your eye and begins to explain her plan. Apparently Beatrice makes a pie every afternoon and leaves it on her windowsill to cool. Martha wants you to sneak back to the woman's cottage and switch the pies. 'Whatever that potion did to those turnips, let's see what it does to her!' She smiles.

Will you:

Agree to switch the pies?   261

Refuse and return to Beatrice instead?   58

79

The women are grateful for your help. Soon, all the buckets are filled and loaded onto the wagon. One of the women begins tethering the mule, while the other rummages in her pack and pulls out a bottle.

'You might like to take this, as a thank you,' she says. 'It's a little something with a kick in it – good for putting some fire in yer belly after a hard day's graft.'

You may take:

Mercia's brandy (1 use)

(backpack)

Raises your *speed* by 3 for

1 combat round

As the women prepare to leave, you decide to ask them about the weather wizard that they mentioned earlier. Turn to 61.

80

'No, it can't be!' The satyr drops to its knees, cupping its hands to catch the black blood that flows from its many wounds. 'I am immortal ... like the forest. I will live for ... ever.' The creature's eyes glaze over and then, slowly, it falls backwards onto the freshly dug earth.

The satyr is dead. You may now take one of the following as a reward:

Circle of thorns	Duskleaf doubloon	Forest dew (2 uses)
(ring)	(chest)	(backpack)
Ability: thorns	+1 speed +1 brawn	Use any time in combat to
	Ability: charm	restore your *health* to full

One by one, the men return from the forest, relieved that the creature is dead. After tending to the wounded, the men offer you a day's work, digging at the site. You agree to help and earn yourself 20 gold crowns.

Thanking the archaeologists, you take the track that leads back to Tithebury Cross. You may now return to the map to continue your adventure.

81

The wizard heads into another room and emerges a few minutes later with a plain-looking staff in his hands. 'This one will do,' he says. 'But it's no good until we have a new water spirit to put inside. It's the water spirit that gives the rainmaker its power. Follow me.'

The old man leads you out of the tower and back down the stone steps. 'There is a lake just over here,' he says, striding purposefully over the crest of a hill. 'See, down there. That will do just nicely.' He heads down the hill, towards a small lake of still water, its surface shimmering in the bright sunlight.

At the edge of the lake, the wizard takes his staff and pushes it into the ground, twisting it deep into the earth. Then he raises his hands above his head. 'When the spirit appears,' he says, 'it will try and attack me. I want you to keep it busy – so it doesn't interrupt my spell. It will take me a few minutes to bind it to the staff. Understand?'

You nod, readying yourself for combat as the wizard begins chanting his spell. A couple of minutes pass, before you spot a disturbance on the surface of the lake. It starts out as a series of slow circular ripples, which soon become a swirling whirlpool of churning water. As it gains momentum, the water whooshes up into the air, forming a glittering column of spray. With a thunderous roar, the column curls into a wave, rushing towards the wizard at tremendous speed. Two powerful-looking arms spring out from its sides, forming themselves into watery fists. Quickly, you dash in front of the wizard, to protect him for as long as you can:

	Speed	Magic	Armour	Health
Lake spirit	4	5	2	50

If you survive to the end of 5 combat rounds, turn to 234.

82

The next morning, the girl is quiet and sullen. You eat a cheerless breakfast together then head back into the woods, following the trail back to her father's house. The girl walks in silence, huddled in her tattered red shawl.

Back at the cabin, the woodsman is overjoyed to see his daughter again. He asks what happened, and you take him aside to explain the sequence of events. The woodsman shakes his head.

'My daughter should have known better than to trust that witch. Been nothing but trouble since that old crone came to these lands.' Thanking you once again, the woodsman offers you his prized sword as a reward for returning his daughter safely:

Goblinhewer
(main hand: sword)
+1 speed +1 armour

You may now return to the map to continue your journey.

83

You climb through the window and out onto the sloping roof. As you slide towards the edge, your foot dislodges a tile, sending it skating off the roof to smash onto the ground below. You wince, cursing yourself for being so clumsy. A moment later you hear a voice from somewhere below.

'Who's there? Who ... wait! Boss! Boss! We got a live one here!'
You spot the man from the roadside, sprinting towards the farmhouse.

Will you:
Immediately take chase?   144
Let him go and leave the farm?   Return to the map

84

The barman raises an eyebrow. 'Yer want to pay Avian a visit do yer?' He grins, revealing two rows of rotted, yellow teeth. 'Good luck with that. The man keeps himself to himself – lives right across the gorge, south of 'ere. Only ways across is a bridge, and I hears that a troll moved in now, made it his own. Unless you pay the toll, it's lights out for yer ...' The barman slams his fist on the counter, making you jump. His face cracks into another grin. 'Truth is, I think Avian likes the troll – otherwise he would have done something about it. Keeps strangers away ... and I hear Avian don't like strangers.'

Will you:
Ask if he has heard any rumours?   245
Talk about the weather?   42
Return your attention to the taproom?   11

85

The clothier offers you a polite smile. 'Well I can't just fashion them from thin air, my dear. I need materials to work with. Bring me the following, and I will be able to create some fine clothing.'

If you have *ragged boots* and *spindlesilk*	110
If you have a *ragged cloak* and *spindlesilk*	132
If you have *bat leather* and *crocodile skin*	114
Otherwise, you promise to return at a later date	46

86

'I am sorry,' says the elderly man, offering out a hand in greeting. 'I am Father Grandolt, the village priest. I pray each day for the One God to deliver us from the terrible curse on our land.' He walks over to the edge of the well. 'I fear this is just a part of the ill luck that has befallen us. Perhaps we are being punished for some sin, some wrongdoing . . .' He shakes his head, sadly. 'My son . . . he didn't deserve this.'

Will you:

Agree to help the villagers?	238
Ask if there will be a reward?	8

87
Quest: The witch hunt

As evening falls, you head into the village of Tithebury Cross, eager for some hot food and a bed for the night. However, as you turn into the main square, you find yourself walking into the middle of an impromptu gathering.

You squeeze through the tight press of bodies to reach the front of the crowd. A thin, gaunt man wearing blue robes is stood on the steps of the village hall. From the resplendent gold chain around his neck, you assume he is the local Speaker. He is holding up a sheet of parchment for all to see. You edge forwards to take a closer look. On the parchment, there is a crudely drawn sketch of a witch. Underneath it, scrawled in red ink, is the single word: GUILTY.

'You don't need to stand for this anymore,' intones the Speaker, beating his fist against the parchment. 'You know – we all know – who is responsible for your hardships. You don't have to stand by and watch your crops fail, you wells dry up, your children suffer … it is time for you to take matters into your own hands! It is time for justice!' A loud cheer goes up from the crowd.

'For the first man, or woman, who brings me the head of the witch, I will award them a purse of gold.' The Speaker pats the bulging money pouch at his waist. A few oohs and aahs pass through the gathering.

'But,' and he suddenly drops his voice. Everyone pushes closer to listen. 'She is a trickster – a master of the dark arts. She will deceive you with her words, put thoughts into your head … make you doubt. But you must be strong. You must believe. Do you hear me? Do you believe?' The villagers give another deafening cheer, beating their weapons and stamping their feet.

'Come with me!' Someone tugs on your arm, forcing you to turn. It is Father Grandolt, the village priest. He quickly leads you away from the thronging mob.

'I need you to go to the witch,' he insists. 'Please, these people are angry. They are looking for someone – anyone – to blame for their hardships. But I need someone with a clear head, someone who is impartial, to confront the witch. I don't know if she is guilty or innocent, but she deserves a fair trial at least.' He stuffs a crumpled piece of parchment into your hand. 'That map will lead you to her cottage. Please, go. And let your heart judge her crimes.'

You thank the priest for putting his trust in you. After studying the map, you hurry out of Tithebury Cross – the cheers and cries of the angry mob echoing in your wake. Turn to **195**.

88

After several metres, the passage takes a sharp right turn, opening out into a small, low-ceilinged room. A stone tomb lies at its centre, bearing the effigy of a woman – her hands held together in prayer. In the far wall there is another archway, leading deeper into the catacombs.

Will you

Attempt to push aside the lid of the tomb?   173

Continue onwards?   1

89

As you step out of the cabin, you see the angry mob approaching, still jeering and egging each other on as they advance towards the witch's home. You hold up your grisly trophy for all to see. There are gasps of astonishment from the crowd as they halt at the edge of the clearing, mouths agape. Then a loud cheer echoes through the forest.

'The witch is dead!' shouts one of the women.

'The witch is dead!' calls another.

The chant is soon taken up by the whole crowd. Several of the farmers rush forward and hoist you up onto their shoulders.

Like a hero returning from a grand crusade, you are carried back into Tithebury Cross, where the Speaker is waiting for you on the steps of the village hall. He is rubbing his hands together in glee.

After being lowered to the ground, you drop the crone's head at his feet. 'You have served me well,' he grins, his gaunt features looking particularly skull-like in the flickering torchlight. 'This is a great victory.' He removes the money pouch from his belt and hands it to you. (You have gained 30 gold crowns).

'A drink!' roars a nearby villager. 'A drink for our hero!'

You soon find yourself in the crowded tap room of the 'Pie and Blackbird', its walls resounding with song and merriment. As you recount your tale of heroism to the spellbound audience, you notice the village priest watching you from the doorway. He shakes his head sadly, then turns and leaves.

'Come on!' insists one of the farmers. 'What did you do next?'

A fresh mug of ale is placed in your hands and within minutes you are back to sharing your impressive tale: 'Now, did I tell you the bit about the toad?'

Your quest is now complete. Return to the map to continue your adventure.

90

The passageway ends in a rectangular chamber, its walls lined with cobwebbed recesses. Within each one you can see piles of bones and skulls, glinting in the yellowy-green light that seeps from the cracked flagstones. Across the other side of the chamber, two passageways lead off into deeper sections of the catacombs.

As you step into room, you notice two decayed skeletons, leaning against the left-hand wall. Sensing your presence, they immediately jerk into life, raising their rusty swords and shields. With slow, faltering steps the skeletons amble towards you. You must now fight:

	Speed	Brawn	Armour	Health
Skeleton guards	4	4	3	25

Special abilities
🖤 Body of bone: The skeletons are immune to *bleed* and *venom*.

If you defeat the skeletons, turn to **166**.

91

You have defeated Spindle, the queen of spiders. You may now take one of the following rewards:

Venomous fang	Spindlesilk mantle	Spindle's eye
(main hand: dagger)	(chest)	(talisman)
+1 speed +1 brawn	+1 magic +1 armour	+1 speed
Ability: venom	Ability: spindlesilk set	Ability: charm

If you previously set fire to the web, turn to **270**. Otherwise, turn to **48**.

'So be it,' says the witch, with a hint of regret. 'You are not the first, and certainly won't be the last, to underestimate an old lady.' She raises her hands, and green lightning begins to flicker and crackle along the lengths of her wrinkled fingers. 'Can we do this quickly?' she insists. 'There is a mob on their way here, and I must be gone from this place.'

	Speed	Brawn	Armour	Health
Grey hag	6	6	3	40

Special abilities

Warts and all: At the end of each combat round, roll a die. If the result is a ⚀ then the witch has temporarily transformed you into a warty toad! As a toad, you can only roll 1 die to determine your attack speed at the start of the next combat round.

If you defeat the witch, turn to **155**.

93

The moment you step within range of the roots, they immediately come alive, whipping and thrashing through the air. To reach the footlocker you will have to fight your way past:

	Speed	Brawn	Armour	Health
Tree roots	5	4	2	30

You may leave the combat at any time by simply moving out of range of the roots. If you take this option, then you leave the room via the archway, turn to **154**. Otherwise, if you defeat the tree roots turn to **167**.

94

The elemental crackles and hisses, then is extinguished, becoming little more than a wisp of cloudy smoke. As you waft it away, your eyes settle on a door at the far side of the room. It swings open and the weather wizard emerges, tugging nervously at his white beard. After quickly scanning the room, he gives a hoot of laughter.

'At last! At last! You did it!' He rushes over and grabs you by the hand, shaking it so hard, you fear it may come off. 'Thank you! Thank you! Thank you!' he cries.

You ask the wizard to explain what happened. 'It was my rainmaker,' he says, rummaging through a pile of scorched papers. 'A-ha, here it is.' He picks up two pieces of charred wood. 'It got struck by lightning, right here in my tower. Broke in two, and released the water spirit that was trapped inside. The dratted thing went crazy – it was uncontrollable, so I had no choice but to shut myself away, in my upper rooms. Been stuck there for weeks now, living off magic bread. Have you ever tasted magic bread?' He sticks out his tongue, pulling a disgusted face. 'Horrible! Horrible!'

You tell the wizard that the local farms have been suffering because of the heat. The wizard nods. 'Yes, yes. I have been observing the weather – my speciality you see.' He taps his nose in a knowing fashion. 'That weather isn't normal ... some magic behind it I'm guessing, although why anyone would want to cause a drought, I just can't fathom.' He eyes the two broken ends of his staff thoughtfully. 'Hmm. I need a new rainmaker. Well, no time like the present. Come on, let's get cracking!' Turn to 81.

95

Ignoring the girl's protests, you race into the trees, in pursuit of the goblin. It isn't long before you realise the foolishness of your decision. The undergrowth is thick and knotted, pulling and clawing at your clothes. Floundering onwards, you try your best to keep up with the fleeing goblin but it is soon lost from sight.

Scratched and bleeding, you head back to the clearing. When

you re-emerge from the trees, you see the girl watching you with an amused expression.

'Well that was very brave of you, wasn't it?' she says in a mocking tone. 'Leave a poor defenceless girl behind while you go playing off in the woods. Now, do something smart for once and get me down. NOW!' Turn to 21.

96

You approach the door to the farmhouse, stepping over the straggly weeds and vines that snake across the cracked stone path. Trying the handle, you discover that it is locked. To break down the door, you must pass a *brawn* challenge.

	Brawn
Farmhouse door	5

If you are successful, turn to 119. If you fail, you are left with no choice but to leave the farm and return to the road. Return to the quest map.

97
Boss: Bridge troll

At the southern edge of Tithebury, the quiet woods and meadows give way to dusty, boulder-strewn slopes and craggy cliffs. After several tiring hours of navigating the maze-like valleys, you finally arrive at a wide ravine. You walk up to the edge and tentatively peer over the side of the vertiginous drop. Below there is nothing but clouds and water vapour, thrown up from the numerous waterfalls, which spill into the sheer precipice.

The only way across the ravine is by way of a rickety old rope bridge. With no other choice, you cautiously step out onto the bridge, clutching the sides for support as it sways alarmingly. After taking a deep breath, you begin to cross.

You have just passed the halfway point when you spot something clambering up the far side of the ravine. It moves quickly, using its long, muscled arms to pull itself onto the bridge.

You realise that this must be the troll the locals told you about; the one that guards the pass. It advances towards you, the bridge creaking and swaying with each heavy footstep. Standing a head taller than a man, the creature's leathery skin is brown and mottled, its face little more than an enormous snout, protruding between two yellowed tusks. As the troll nears, your attention focuses on the large, mean-looking club it is now tugging free from its belt.

'Oi you,' says the troll, stopping several paces in front of you. 'To cross da bridge ya gotta give me forty of those shiny fings or I gonna clobber ya. What's it to be?'

Will you:

Pay gold to cross the bridge?	135
Attack the troll?	156

98

You push aside the lid – the chamber echoing with the sound of grating stone. As you lean over the tomb to look inside, a rotted, skeletal hand suddenly shoots out of the darkness, grabbing you around the throat. Gasping for breath, you jerk backwards – your sudden movement snapping the hand from its limb. There is a wheezing cry from inside the tomb as something bangs and rattles to get free.

You rip the still-twitching hand from your throat, throwing it away with disgust. As you ready for battle, you watch as a mould-covered skeleton lurches out of the tomb. In its remaining hand it grips a mighty, rune-etched sword, its glowing blade untarnished by the rot and mould that seems to permeate every other surface of this room.

Clad in little more than a tattered cloak and some mildewed rags, the ancient warrior stumbles towards you, its mouldy bones creaking in their sockets. You must now fight:

	Speed	Brawn	Armour	Health
Ancient knight	5	4	2	25

Special abilities

♥ Body of bone: The knight is immune to *bleed* and *venom*.

If you are victorious, turn to 222.

99

This is your opportunity to choose the path you wish to follow – the warrior, the mage or the rogue. The warrior is a master of weapons and armour. Although slow in combat, the warrior compensates for this with a hardy endurance and mighty strength. If you have a high *brawn* or *armour* score, then the path of the warrior could be for you. If, on the other hand, you have a high *magic* score, then you may favour the path of the mage – mastering arcane magics to smite your foes or impede their abilities. Finally, the rogue is the master of speed and deception. Whilst weak and vulnerable in longer fights, the rogue excels in exploiting weaknesses and avoiding damage. If you have a high *speed* and *brawn* score, then the path of the rogue may be a wise choice.

Will you choose:

The path of the warrior?	214
The path of the mage?	256
The path of the rogue?	250

100

You quickly search through your pack, rooting around for the scroll. Just as you are about to tug it free, the ghouls are upon you, jabbering and howling with glee. You have no choice but to battle these three deadly opponents:

	Speed	Brawn	Armour	Health
Ghouls	5	3	2	30

Special abilities

♥ Piercing claws: The ghouls' attacks ignore *armour*.

If you manage to defeat the ghouls, turn to 127.

101

You grab the last of the witch's spell books and place them inside the open sack. She looks at you in surprise, then offers you a smile. 'Thank you,' she says. 'You have a kind heart.' After tying up the sack, you help the witch to load her belongings onto the horse. In the distance you can hear the jeering crowd, advancing through the woods.

'I must go,' says the witch, hoisting herself into the saddle. 'My time here is at an end.' She leans over to you, beckoning you closer. 'Listen to me. The Speaker is a changeling. He is the one responsible for the villagers' woes. He is the one that has brought the goblins here – and the dark things of the underworld. It has taken me many years to track down that demon-spawn. Now that I know the true nature of its form, it wants me dead.' She reaches into the pocket of her dress and pulls out a small phial. Inside the glass casing is a clear, blue liquid. 'If this potion comes into contact with its skin, it will reveal the changeling for what it truly is.'

You take the vial and thank the witch. She places a hand on your shoulder and whispers something – a blessing perhaps – then she kicks the flanks of her gelding and gallops away. As the angry mob descend on the clearing, you decide to make your own speedy retreat, back to the village. Turn to 142.

102

Avian takes the letter of introduction and studies it thoughtfully. 'Ah yes, the graduate from the academy. How splendid. I have been expecting you.' He rolls up the parchment and gestures towards the courtyard. 'I am anticipating great things from you. Shall we get started and see what you are capable of?' As you move forward, he stops you, placing a hand on your arm. 'Although, I should warn you. Honesty is one of the traits I value highly in my apprentice.' Turn to 126.

103

You make your way carefully down the passage, avoiding the deadly puddles of white gooey acid. After several minutes, you come to a junction – the passageway splitting into tunnels to the north and south. To the north, there has evidently been a cave-in, as the tunnel is blocked by rubble and stone. To the south, you notice the tunnel walls are glistening with big, fresh dollops of white goo. As the north tunnel is impassable, you decide to head south. Turn to 273.

104

Martha removes a ring from her finger and offers it out to you.

'Thank you, for all that you have done,' she says. 'I want you to take this. It is my wedding band. No – please, don't look so shocked. It hasn't brought me much luck in this life. Perhaps it will give you better fortune.'

You may take:

Widow's band

(ring)

+1 magic

Ability: heal

You thank Martha for the kind gift and then you both leave the cottage. Return to the map to continue your journey.

105

The moment you touch the stone there is a bright flash of light, followed by a dizzying sensation of movement. When the light fades, you find yourself in a flooded cave, its oily black waters lapping around your waist. At the centre of the cave is an island, illuminated by a shaft of pale green light. Its radiance outlines the figure of a woman, dressed in a trailing gown of weeds and lilies. Her emerald eyes watch you intently.

'You trespass in the halls of ancient kings,' booms a deep voice, from somewhere above. 'Many have come here. All have failed. Fight my champions and prove your worth.'

The woman draws a leaf-shaped sword from her belt, its blade flickering with magic. Patiently she waits for you. With few other options, you wade through the water and drag yourself up onto the island. The woman smiles and nods, then rushes to attack:

	Speed	Brawn	Armour	Health
Allura of water	5	4	1	25

Special abilities
♥ Healing touch: At the end of each combat round, Allura heals 2 *health*. Once her *health* has been reduced to zero, she cannot heal.

If you are defeated, you find yourself back on the hilltop, turn to 153. If you defeat Allura, her body turns to water vapour, which drifts away across the cavern. On the spot where she was standing, you find a small stone rune with three wavy lines cut into its surface. If you take the *Rune of Allura*, make a note of it on your hero sheet. There is a sudden flash of light and you find yourself back on the hilltop. Turn to 153.

106

It is a miracle, but you managed to defeat the three ghouls. You may now take any / all of the following items:

Grave dust ring	Ghoul hair	Ghoul claw
(ring)	(backpack)	(left hand: dagger)
+1 brawn	This may come in useful one day	+1 speed +1 brawn Ability: piercing

You decide not to risk the stairs in the pitch blackness, so you decide to head back to the pulpit and investigate the room behind the painted screen. Turn to 296.

107

The target dummy is soon reduced to a pile of straw and sack cloth. Avian claps his hands as he walks over.

'Impressive, very impressive. I see much potential in you.' He snaps his fingers and a sword flies out from one of the racks, landing in his outstretched hand. 'Now, fight me,' he says, raising his sword. 'And I'll teach you how to become an even better fighter.' Turn to 99.

108

'Ah yes,' grins the witch. 'You might have got me there. That woman was as heartless as they come. Although, I never thought she would go through with her plan. Beatrice was fond of her social standing in the community. She would never have risked been seen performing such a deed.' The old woman's eyes sparkle with mischief. 'I suppose she must have found someone who was ... hmm, less concerned with such things.' She gives you a knowing wink and then returns to her packing.

Will you:

Accuse the witch of another crime?	113
Attack the witch?	137
Help her to escape?	101

'I feared you would say that,' the old warrior wheezes. He reaches down to the scabbard at his waist and pulls loose his great, two-handed sword. 'It gives me no pleasure to take your life,' he rasps, shambling towards you. 'Although, your death will at least provide me with some company in this dark place.'

You must fight:

	Speed	Brawn	Armour	Health
Valadin Roth	5	4	3	35

Special abilities

- Faithful duty: For every ⚅ that Valadin rolls, he automatically heals 2 *health*. This ability cannot take him above his starting score of 35.
- Body of bone: Valadin is immune to *bleed* and *venom*.

If you manage to defeat the undead crusader, turn to 123.

You provide the clothier with the ragged boots and a length of spindlesilk (deduct these two objects from your hero sheet). Using these materials, the clothier creates the following item, which you may now take:

Spindlesilk boots
(feet)
+1 speed +1 magic
Ability: spindlesilk set

If you do not want the item, then the clothier agrees to pay you 20 gold crowns for the garment. Once you have made your choice, turn to 68 to look at more of the clothier's items, or turn to 46 to leave.

111
Quest: The black book

Night has fallen; the full moon shines brilliantly against a cloudless backdrop of stars. As you hurry along the rutted lane towards the welcoming lights of Tithebury Cross, you find yourself pausing outside the graveyard. A wooden sign has been tied to the old, rusted gate. It reads simply: DANGER. KEEP OUT. Peering through the spike-topped railing, you see a dark hill, tangled and overgrown with weeds. It leads up to a steepled church, standing silent and forgotten on the hill.

Suddenly, you catch something out of the corner of your eye. Turning, you see a hooded man standing by the side of the lane. You feel his eyes upon you, even though they are hidden deep within the shadows of his cowl. The hairs on the back of your neck begin to prickle. You never heard the man approach – glancing around, you cannot see any trees or undergrowth where he might have been hiding. The man walks slowly towards you, his boots making only the faintest whisper of noise.

'Good evening, stranger,' he says, in a thin velvety voice. 'Your reputation precedes you in these parts. A brave adventurer, to be sure. I was wondering if I could make use of your ... services.'

If you have already completed the quest: *The witch hunt* turn to 210. Otherwise, turn to 249.

112

You push aside the stone lid – far enough to reveal the interior of the tomb. To your surprise, you find that the hollow cavity is empty, save for a thin, grey funeral shroud and a silver necklace resting on top of it. You may take:

Clymonistra's sorrow
(necklace)
+1 magic
Ability: Clymonistra's
adornments

You find little else of interest in the room, so you decide to leave through the archway. Turn to 1.

113

Which of the following crimes will you accuse the witch of:

Giving Liselle the potion recipe?	223
Placing a totem in the farmer's field?	73
Causing drought and ruining the crops?	177
Giving Beatrice Fletcher the turnip potion?	108

114

You provide the clothier with the bat leather and the crocodile skin (deduct these two objects from your hero sheet). Using these materials, the clothier creates the following item, which you may now take:

Bat cape
(cloak)
+1 speed +1 armour

If you do not want the item, then the clothier agrees to pay you 20 gold crowns for the garment. Once you have made your choice, turn to 68 to look at more of the clothier's items, or turn to 46 to leave.

115

The book contains a history of Tithebury and the adjoining regions of Black Marsh and Mistwood. The corner of one page has been turned down. Flicking straight to it, you discover a page entry describing the stone circle. You quickly scan the text for any clues as to the purpose of the circle. You discover that it dates back over a thousand years and was built by a sect of druids to commune with 'rune spirits'.

Something has been written in the margin of the book. Turning the page around, you read the spidery writing. It says: *'Dwarf runes. Much older. Possibly dark age. Hill burial ground for king.'*

Will you now:

Look through the notes?	301
Return your attention to the stones?	153

116

You do your best, within the confines of the rubble-filled tunnel, to defend yourself against the enormous creature. At last, you manage to pierce its thick, bulbous skin. From the wound, a fountain of white acid sprays across the tunnel. It catches you, searing through your armour. (You must deduct 1 *armour* point from any one item you are currently wearing.)

The creature squirms and writhes in pain, then finally lies motionless – acid pouring out of its gaping mouth. You retrieve your torch, then walk cautiously past the dead maggot, coming to a halt at the edge of the newly-burrowed hole. Your torchlight picks out the craggy sides of the pit dropping away into darkness. From somewhere far below, you can hear the roar of an underground river.

Will you:

Continue along the tunnel?	254
Risk jumping down the pit?	47

117

A glowing white portal has appeared at the centre of the circle. The bird is flapping around it excitedly. 'This is it! This is it! It's just like the magic doorway that my master entered! Quick – get in before it closes again!'

You take a deep breath before stepping into the bright, glowing light. Turn to 207.

118

By some small miracle, you are able to defeat the frenzied crocodile. You may now take any / all of the following rewards:

Crock's tooth	Crocodile skin
(left hand: dagger)	(backpack)
+1 brawn	Perhaps someone can
	put this to good use

As you wipe the mud and pondweed from your clothes, you become aware of the girlish giggles coming from the far shore. The woodsman's daughter is hopping up and down, waving her arms above her head. 'Oh that was so exciting!' she gasps. 'You were almost as brave as my handsome huntsman!'

You wade back across the mire, muttering several obscenities under your breath.

'Come on! Give it to me quick!' demands the girl, holding out her hands. 'It's all I need for my potion!' Angrily, you fling open your pack and hand her the findlewort. 'Perfect!' she smiles. 'You're a hero after all!'

Suddenly, something hits you in the chest, sending you flying backwards into the swamp. Coughing and spluttering, you surface to find yourself face to face with a goblin – the same one that ran from you earlier. He holds a knife to your throat. Over the creature's shoulder, you see the woodsman's daughter sprinting into the forest, chased by another of the goblins.

Before you can hope to rescue her, you must defeat your foe:

	Speed	Brawn	Armour	Health
Goblin poacher	0	1	0	10

If you defeat the goblin, turn to 143.

119

You push open the farmhouse door and step inside. The musty interior is little more than a squalid mess of broken furniture and rotting debris. You note a number of gleaming bones lying amongst the waste – evidently picked clean by rats, or something far worse. Across the room, a staircase leads up to the second level. To your right there is a closed door, its green paint faded and peeling.

Will you:
Open the door?	**130**
Head up the staircase to the second level?	**151**

120

A wild swing connects with the bat creature, knocking it to the ground. Quickly, you step in and deliver the final, killing blow. You may now take the following item:

Bat leather
(backpack)
Perhaps someone can
put this to good use

You decide to ignore the other bundles and make your way across the cave to the tunnel opening. Turn to 266.

121

The changeling is a more powerful foe, thanks to the black book that it now reveals in its clawed hands. As it advances towards you, the infernal creature surrounds its body with a crackling ring of black fire. 'You will burn,' it snarls. 'Like all those who dare stand in my way!'

	Speed	Brawn	Armour	Health
Changeling	5	5	3	45

Special abilities

♥ Black fire: At the end of every combat round, your hero automatically takes 2 damage from the flames that surround this demon. This ability ignores *armour*.

If you defeat the changeling, turn to 133.

122

'Wha'? Ya clobbered me!' The troll teeters back onto its heels, then falls backwards onto the rope bridge with a thunderous crash. You grab hold of the sides as the bridge's wooden slats ripple and shudder. Several come loose, spinning off into the mist below, but thankfully the ropes tethering the bridge manage to hold.

You search the troll's body and find 30 gold crowns. You may also take one of the following items:

Troll's nose ring	Reed-woven sandals	Troll's blood (2 uses)
(head)	(feet)	(backpack)
+2 brawn	+1 speed +1 magic	Restores 2 *health* at
Ability: charm	Ability: charm	the start of every
		combat round for
		one combat

You edge past the troll and cross to the other side of the ravine. Turn to 140.

123

Valadin Roth drops to his knees, his sword rattling to the ground at his side. As the mighty warrior takes his last, wheezing breath, a pale white mist slips from between his parted lips and rises up into the sparkling moonlight. Then the withered, undead body crumbles to dust at your feet.

A second later and there is an angry rumbling sound, followed by a loud crack as the lid of the tomb shatters in two. You hurry over, peering into the hollow cavity that has now been revealed. There is no body or remains inside, only a plain black leather-bound book. You take it out of the tomb and open it up. Flicking through the pages, you find that it is full of strange runes and markings, but nothing that is intelligible.

A little disappointed, you slip the black book into your backpack and then leave the tomb. Turn to 146.

124

The huntsman raises his axe and prepares to meet you in combat. 'I fear I have done you some ill,' he says. 'Perhaps I misjudged you – as you have misjudged me.' You must now fight the huntsman:

	Speed	Brawn	Armour	Health
Huntsman	1	1	1	15

If you succeed in defeating the huntsman, turn to 228.

125

You step over the body of the ratling and approach the remaining ruffian, who is now back peddling towards the farmhouse. 'Yer killed the boss! Yer killed the boss!' With a cry, he turns and races into the house, slamming the door closed behind him.

You decide that the cowardly thief can wait. Returning to the dead ratling, you search the body. You find 5 gold crowns and may take any/all of the following items:

Leader's edge	**Studded leather**
(main hand: sword)	(chest)
+1 speed +1 brawn	+2 armour

Make a note of the word *leader* on your hero sheet.

Will you:

126

Avian leads you across the courtyard, into a large hall lined with weapon racks and suits of practice armour. A number of target dummies, fashioned from straw and sackcloth, hang suspended from the criss-crossing beams.

'Now is your chance to show me what you can do,' says Avian, nodding towards the nearest target dummy. 'If I am to train you, I need to observe your strengths and your weaknesses.'

You eye up the target dummy, wondering exactly what it is you are supposed to do. Noting your hesitation, Avian chuckles to himself. 'Don't be afraid of it. It's an equal match, don't you think?'

Drawing your weapons, you march towards the inanimate dummy, with the intention of beating the straw and stuffing out of it. However, as you approach, the dummy springs to life, kicking and flailing with its arms and legs. As you duck and dodge the flying limbs, you see that the dummy has come loose from its rope binding.

Avian's laughter fills the chamber, as the strange automaton glides towards you, seeking to pummel you with its spinning arms and legs.

	Speed	Brawn	Armour	Health
Target dummy	5	6	6	25

Special abilities

♥ Sack and straw: The target dummy is immune to *lightning, piercing, immobilise, venom, thorns* and *corruption*.

If you defeat the target dummy, turn to 107. Otherwise, turn to 136.

127

It is a miracle, but you managed to defeat the ghouls. You may now take any / all of the following items:

Grave dust ring	Ghoul hair	Ghoul claw
(ring)	(backpack)	(left hand: dagger)
+1 brawn	This may come in useful one day	+1 speed +1 brawn Ability: piercing

Once you have regained your strength, you turn your attention back to the door. Perhaps the scroll of opening that Fetch gave you will deactivate the glyphs. Turn to 197.

128

The man stops shuffling the cards and places them down on the table.

'Hmm, looking to make your fortune, eh?' He rests his chin on his hands, offering you a crooked smile. 'Well, if it's treasure you seek, that graveyard would be a good place to start. Haunted good and proper it is – the locals won't go near the place, even the priest. They say it's cursed. Something to do with an old legend about a book, buried beneath the church.' He chuckles to himself. 'Could all be nonsense stories. I mean, the heat is making the locals a little, you know,' he taps his forehead, 'crazy.' He picks up the cards again. 'But still, there has to be a reason why that place is always locked up tight. Protecting themselves maybe ... but when I sees a lock it usually means there's something important on the other side.' He gives you a mischievous wink. 'Now, enough ghost stories. Fancy a game of cards?'

Will you:

Offer to play cards?	54
Turn your attention back to the taproom?	11

'Home? I'm not going home!' snaps the girl, stamping her feet. 'I can't go home!' When you demand to know why, she lifts up her basket, revealing the freshly-picked mushrooms inside. 'I'm making a potion,' she says. 'A love potion. The witch gave me the recipe – all I need now is some findlewort then I'll have everything I need!'

She stomps off across the clearing, heading towards a tangled line of trees. You hurry after her, explaining that there isn't time for making potions. The sunlight is fading fast – it will be dark soon and the goblins could be back; not to mention her worried father waiting for her at home.

But the girl does not appear remotely bothered by your concerns. 'I'm not going home,' she declares. 'With the potion, I will get exactly what I want. The huntsman will fall in love with me and we will be together forever! Now,' she stops abruptly, pointing a finger under your nose, 'are you going to make yourself useful and help me find some findlewort, or what?'

Will you:
Agree to help the girl?	159
Tell her she is acting like a selfish brat?	71

The door swings open, releasing a horrible, eye-watering stench. By a sheer effort of will, you force yourself not to flee. Instead, you hold your ground and peer into the gloomy space beyond. Part of you wishes that you hadn't. The room is full of rats. Hundreds and hundreds of them, scuttling over tables and cupboards, riffling through rotted food and what looks like human remains. It takes only seconds for you to realise the terrible danger you are in. With a deafening rush of skittering paws, the black bodies swarm towards you:

	Speed	Brawn	Armour	Health
Rabid rats	3	1	0	30

If you defeat the rats, turn to 161.

131

The runes above the door begin to glow with a pale radiance. Then there is a deep rumbling sound as the door itself begins to lower into the ground, revealing a small room beyond, lined with shelves and wooden chests. Turn to 548.

132

You provide the clothier with the ragged cloak and a length of spindlesilk (deduct these two objects from your hero sheet). Using these materials, the clothier creates the following item, which you may now take:

Spindlesilk cloak
(cloak)
+1 speed +2 magic
Ability: spindlesilk set

If you do not want this item, then the clothier agrees to pay you 20 gold crowns for the garment. Once you have made your choice, turn to 68 to look at more of the clothier's items, or turn to 46 to leave.

133

The changeling is dead. As its immense, smoking body slumps to the earth, a peal of thunder echoes across the skies. You look up to see grey storm clouds starting to swirl and gather overhead. It appears that the demon's death has finally broken the spell of drought that once assailed the land.

You may now take one of the following rewards:

Hellfire robes	Blackfire ring	Demon's heart
(chest)	(ring)	(talisman)
+1 speed +1 magic	Ability: sear	+1 speed
Ability: trickster		Ability: trickster

As you leave the village, the first rains for many months begin to fall. Return to the map to continue your adventure.

134

After several metres, the passage turns sharply to the left, opening out into a small, low-ceilinged room covered in yellow mould and lichen. A stone tomb lies at its centre, bearing the effigy of a praying knight. In the far wall an archway leads through into another green-lit passage.

Will you
Attempt to push aside the lid of the tomb?   182
Continue onwards?   1

135

As you begin counting out the coins, a sudden thought occurs to you. This troll doesn't appear to be the most intelligent and quick-witted of foes. Perhaps you could trick it by only handing over some of the money.

Will you:
Give the troll 20 gold crowns?   192
Pay the full 40 gold crowns?   165

136

The target dummy knocks you to the ground, leaving you bruised and winded. Avian snaps his fingers and the dummy freezes in mid-air. He offers out a hand and helps you up.

'Well, I've seen better,' he says, evidently disappointed with your performance. 'Clearly you still lack focus. To master your powers you must concentrate on your strengths.' Avian snaps his fingers a second time, and a sword suddenly flies out from one of the racks. He snatches it from out of the air, performing a deft series of whirling moves as he spins to face you. 'Now, I want you to fight me – and I'll teach you how to become a true fighter.' Turn to 99.

137

You draw your weapon, declaring that you have found the witch guilty. The old woman's eyes widen in surprise. 'You're going to kill me? But it's the Speaker that is the cause of all this. He is the one you should be threatening!'

Will you:

Attack the witch anyway?	92
Help the witch to escape?	101

138

You sprint over to the stairs and start to climb them. The way is dark, almost pitch black. Slipping on a stone, you find yourself falling forwards, flat onto your stomach. You barely have time to right yourself before the ghouls are upon you. Thankfully, the confines of the staircase means that the ghouls can only fight you one at a time. Even so, this will be a tough battle. You must defeat this foe three times in a row. You are unable to restore your *health* between fights (except by using potions):

	Speed	Brawn	Armour	Health
Ghoul	5	2	2	15

Special abilities
🛡 Piercing claws: The ghouls' attacks ignore *armour*.

If you manage to defeat the ghouls, turn to 106.

'Oh thank you! Thank you!' says the farmer. He all but pushes you into the swirling, white mist. 'Good luck,' he says. 'And please ... be careful!' You assure him that you will, drawing your weapon as if to underline the point.

As you cross into the swirling banks of mist, the first thing that hits you is the cold. The wispy tendrils of fog are like ice, almost burning your skin with their freezing touch. Within seconds you are shivering, your breath forming clouds in the chill, damp air.

You press onwards, pushing your way through the blighted corn, no longer sure what direction you are headed in. Whichever way you turn, the mist is there – swirling around you like a cruel tormentor. Perhaps it is just your imagination, but you are convinced that you can see shapes moving through the insubstantial haze. Each time you try and focus on one, they are gone – drifting away like ghosts on the rolling currents.

As you head deeper into the mist, you stumble across a large, cross-shaped pole sticking out of the ground. It is frosted with ice, sparkling in the eerie white luminescence. For a moment, you ponder what the pole was used for. Then you realise ...

Something is moving towards you through the field, making a bee-line for your position. As the sound of snapping corn gets louder, you ready yourself for battle. From out of the mist lurches a creature of nightmare ... a man made entirely of straw, his ragged clothes coated in ice. With an inhuman howl, the creature raises its hands, revealing a deadly set of splintered claws. You must now fight the scarecrow:

	Speed	Brawn	Armour	Health
Scarecrow	0	1	0	8

If you defeat the scarecrow, turn to 204.

140

You join a dirt track, which takes you up into the cloud-tipped mountains. As you scale the edge of a ridge, you get your first glimpse of Avian's castle. The impressive structure stands grand and regal on a plateau of rock, its white-stone walls and blue spires gleaming in the afternoon sunlight. It is a startling, breath-taking view – and one that you wish the young knight from the academy had lived to see. His letter of introduction is now clutched firmly in your hands.

At your approach, the hinges of the drawbridge give a noisy squeal, then slowly the wooden platform begins to lower itself across the moat. Eventually, with a dull echoing boom, the bridge comes to rest across the murky waters. You cross to the gatehouse, where a man is waiting for you beside an open portcullis.

'Well, well. I am glad the troll didn't cause you too many problems,' he smiles. You see that he is a tall man, broad-shouldered and muscular. His age is indeterminate – the grey of his hair at odds with the youthfulness of his face. Clad in regal-looking robes and a feathered cloak, the man is as striking and imposing as his castle.

'I am Avian Dale,' he says. 'And you are?'

Will you:

Hand over the letter of introduction?	102
Tell Avian the truth?	196
Say you are a traveller, looking for lodgings?	188

141

Under pressure to escape the ravenous undead, you rush forwards and put your hand to the door. The moment you touch it, you are thrown backwards, as if a mighty wind had suddenly lifted you off your feet. With your arms flailing at your sides, you find yourself careering into the advancing ghouls. For a moment, the ghouls are caught off guard as you slam onto the stone floor between them. Then they pounce, jabbering and howling with glee.

You manage to dodge out of the way of their deadly claws, furiously kicking and punching at their filthy, dirt-covered bodies. At last, you are able to scramble to your feet and draw your weapon.

The ghouls circle around you, slavering and hissing.

Will you:

Fight the ghouls where you stand?	59
Fight the ghouls by the door?	157

142

The village is eerily quiet as you hurry along its winding lanes; nearly everyone is out in the woods, seeking vengeance against the witch. In the distance you can see smoke and flames rising into the clear night sky. You guess it is the witch's cabin, which has been torched by the angry mob.

Only one man remains in the village. The Speaker waits patiently on the hall steps, rubbing his hands together in gleeful anticipation. As you stride towards him, the witch's phial held tightly in your fist, he looks up in surprise.

'What is this?' he scowls. 'I want the witch's head! Where is it?'

'I don't have her head,' you say defiantly. 'But I do have this.' You remove the stopper from the glass phial and throw its contents into the Speaker's astonished face. He staggers back, clawing at his skin as it sizzles and burns. You back away, gagging as a sulphurous smoke fills the air.

Then the man's cries suddenly become a bestial roar as he begins to transform. His body widens, splitting out of the flimsy blue robes to reveal muscular black skin. From his back, two enormous leathery wings expand outwards, their veins pulsing with a hellish light. Finally, the Speaker removes his hands from his face, to reveal a demonic visage, contorted with rage.

'See me for how I truly am,' he snarls. 'Now, you will pay for your insolence!'

If you have the words *black book* written on your hero sheet, turn to 121. Otherwise, turn to 217.

143

You slay the goblin, its lifeless body sinking down into the mire. Exhausted, you pull yourself up onto the bank, your clothes sagging heavily from the mud and water. After taking a moment to recover, you clamber to your feet and begin your pursuit of the remaining goblin, following its trail through the undergrowth. Turn to 150.

144

In his haste, the ruffian trips and falls, sprawling onto his stomach. Before he can get back to his feet, you are on top of him, pinning him to the ground. 'Ger off me!' he shrieks. 'The boss made me do it! The boss! We ain't had any fresh meat for ages.'

Suddenly, the door to the farmhouse is flung open and a wiry man in a long open coat comes running out, brandishing a sword.

'Let him go!' he demands. You barely have chance to draw your weapon before the leader is upon you, his blade whipping through the air in a steel blur.

	Speed	Brawn	Armour	Health
Leader	2	3	4	25*

* Once you have lowered the leader's *health* to 12 or less, turn to 230.

145

'I should go,' says Martha anxiously. 'I don't want to be caught here with ... that thing.' She points to the giant turnip. 'You should too,' she adds. 'The villagers will not be forgiving if they suspect us both of dabbling in witchcraft.' Martha runs to the door, checks that the coast is clear and then departs without another word.

Finding yourself alone in the cottage, you wander over to examine the well-stocked shelves in Beatrice's kitchen. If you wish, you can help yourself to any of the following:

Healing salve (1 use)	Miracle grow (1 use)
(backpack)	(backpack)
Use any time in combat to restore 6 *health*	Use any time in combat to raise your *brawn* by 2 for one combat round

You stuff the herbal mixtures into your backpack, then give Beatrice Fletcher a final nod of farewell. Return to the map to start a new quest.

146

You return to the gate without incident. Fetch is waiting for you on the other side, pacing up and down impatiently. He jumps to attention as you approach.

'At last! At last!' he hisses, withdrawing the key from his robes and fitting it into the lock. 'I thought you'd become another addition to the graveyard.' With a dull click, the gate is unlocked. You pull it open and pass through, banging it shut behind you.

'Well?' asks Fetch, watching you intently from beneath the brim of his hood. 'Did you get the book?'

Did you:

Leave the book in the tomb?	280
Take the book from Valadin?	271

147

The spider drops onto its back, its hairy legs trembling and shaking in their death throes. You may now take the following item:

Spider's leg (1 use)
(backpack)
It may come in useful,
one day

You break through the rest of the webbing and leave the cave. Turn to 208.

148

Beatrice gives you a shocked glare. 'Do you realise what will happen to me if Martha wins? I'll be the laughing stock of the whole village. I've never lost – look!' She stabs a finger in the direction of her turnips. 'Look at them. My poor little beauties are suffering in this wretched heat and I've done everything – everything! Martha is using witchcraft to get the better of me. I always knew she was a bad apple. Lost her husband last year and with all those mouths to feed – seven little brats at the last count – I know she'll stop at nothing to win that prize. A nice medal it is too, been in the village for generations – and one that she'll melt down in a second for a few measly coins, I'm sure!' She takes a deep breath and then holds out the earthenware pot. 'I can't do this myself. If I was caught ... well, my reputation would be in tatters. But you – you could do it.'

Will you:

Agree to the task?	63
Refuse and leave?	Return to the map

149

After listening to the woodsman's gloomy warnings, you are initially surprised by the pleasant and inviting woodland. The path is easy to follow, leading you past gentle tree-lined hills and picturesque meadows of wildflowers. The sun casts dappled patterns over the leafy clearings, ringing with birdsong. You can't imagine these woods hiding any deadly monsters ...

Half an hour later and you find yourself grudgingly eating your words. Almost without warning, the trees have closed in on all sides, swallowing the sunlight and replacing the gentle sound of birdsong with the eerie rustle of leaves and creaking boughs. The path has narrowed, becoming little more than a game trail littered with rocks and wandering tree-roots. Picking your way carefully along the dark trail, you keep an anxious eye on the tangled knot of trees to either side. This is prime territory for an ambush.

The trail leads you along the crest of a hill, then plunges down into a wooded valley. The sound of a chuckling stream can be heard from somewhere off to your right, where the ground rises steeply into rocky hills. You are considering whether to leave the trail and refill your water skin, when a scream from up ahead shatters the silence. It sounded like a young girl.

Drawing your weapon, you break into a sprint, racing along the narrow, winding trail. After a few minutes, you skid to a halt, ears pricked for any further clues as to the girl's whereabouts. Then you hear another scream, coming from the trees to your left. You leave the trail and plunge into the undergrowth. Turn to 37.

150

You haven't gone far before you find the corpse of a goblin – a kitchen knife protruding from its chest. Perhaps the woodsman's daughter knows how to defend herself after all. You search the body and find 5 gold crowns. You may also take any/all of the following items:

Goblin leathers	Goblin grog (2 uses)
(chest)	(backpack)
+1 armour	Use any time in combat
	to restore 4 *health*

You push your way through the tight undergrowth, to find yourself back on the main trail. There is no sign of the woodsman's daughter.

Will you:

Follow the trail to Grandma's house?	168
Head east into the hills?	152

151

The wooden stairs are rotten. After only a couple of steps, your foot goes through the wood with a loud crack. Carefully, you withdraw your leg from the jagged splinters and continue up the creaking staircase.

Reaching the top, you find yourself on a narrow landing. Opposite you is a closed door, its surface scoured by a series of deep claw marks. At the end of the landing, a door stands open – the space beyond swathed in darkness.

Will you:

Open the closed door?	169
Enter the room at the end of the hall?	158

152

As you head east, the land rises sharply, becoming a series of rocky hills covered in gnarly vegetation. You quicken your pace, aware that the sun is already beginning to set, casting an auburn brilliance over your stark surroundings.

You haven't ventured far into the hills before you spot a thin column of food smoke rising into the darkening skies. Could this be the huntsman's camp that the young girl mentioned? You hurry towards it, the succulent aroma of freshly-cooking meat providing all the encouragement you need.

You finally reach the campsite, set in the sheltered hollow of a bleak, stony hill. A skinned rabbit slowly roasts over a roaring fire, the dripping fat causing the flames to spit and sizzle. Behind it, you can see a covered wagon and a straggly line of trees where a piebald pony is tethered. The beast looks agitated, tugging against its restraints.

There doesn't appear to be anyone around. Then you notice a straw basket lying on its side in the grass. Next to it is a broken bottle, from which a black bubbling liquid steams. Turn to 240.

153

Large tablet-shaped stones mark the north, south, east and west points of the circle. On each of the stones is a rune, carved into the grey rock. The north stone has a circular rune, the south stone has a crescent-shaped moon. To the east, the stone is marked with a flame symbol, and to the west the stone is marked with three horizontal wavy lines.

You feel as though you are drawn to touch each of the runes.

'Careful,' squawks the bird. 'My master touched those stones – and then a door appeared. Then he never came back!'

Will you:

Touch the north stone?	221
Touch the south stone?	244
Touch the east stone?	35
Touch the west stone?	105

If you have examined all four stones, turn immediately to 117.

154

You enter a large flag-stoned chamber. A solitary beam of moonlight breaks through a hole in the ceiling to illuminate a stone tomb at its centre. As you approach, you see that a figure of a knight has been etched in high relief on the lid of the tomb, his gauntleted hands grasping a mighty two-handed sword.

'You have come for the book, haven't you?' wheezes a voice from the darkness. You hear a scuffling sound to your right. Turning, you watch as an undead creature shambles into the pool of moonlight. You assume it was a man once, but now his sallow skin hangs in loose tatters from his exposed bones.

'My name is Valadin Roth,' says the man, his voice little more than a whisper. 'I am the crusader – sworn to protect the book until the end of days.' His ivory fingers tap the jewelled pommel of his sword. 'I implore you – do not take the book. It is a thing of evil and must stay here. If you wish to take it, then you leave me no choice but to fight you.'

Will you:

Ask about the book?	194
State that you are taking the book?	109
Leave the book under the crusader's protection?	160

With a screeching wail, the witch is knocked back into a high-stacked cupboard, which crashes down on top of her, burying the old woman under a pile of books, scrolls and bottles.

You have defeated the witch and may now take one of the following items:

Ruby slippers	Third eye	Hag's shawl
(feet)	(talisman)	(cloak)
+1 speed +1 armour	+1 speed	+1 magic +1 armour
Ability: click your heels	Ability: charm	Ability: charm

You may also take the *witchfinder's signet ring*. If you take this item, simply make a note of it on your hero sheet (it does not take up backpack space). After you have made your choices, you perform the grisly task of removing the crone's head, as evidence of your victory. Then, you leave the cabin. Turn to 89.

156

'I like da fightin' talk!' says the troll, giving a rumbling belly laugh. 'I is hungry and could do with some nice tasty 'uman. Come 'ere and let me clobber ya then.' You draw your weapon and prepare to defend yourself:

	Speed	Brawn	Armour	Health
Troll	5	6	3	60

Special abilities
- ♥ Knockdown: If your hero takes health damage from the troll, you must reduce your *speed* by 1 for the next combat round.
- ♥ Regeneration: At the start of each combat round, the troll regains 2 *health*. Once the troll's *health* has been reduced to zero, he cannot heal. (Note: This ability cannot take the troll's *health* above his starting value of 60).

If you defeat the troll turn to 122. If you are defeated, you have no choice but to return to the quest map.

157

You sidestep one of the ghouls and rush over to the glyphed door, planting your back against the wall next to it. You remember Fetch mentioning that the ward on the door was used to keep the undead in the catacombs from getting out. Perhaps it will work its magic on these ghouls as well.

Gibbering like hungry hounds, the ghouls spring at you. Your heart skips a beat as you watch the filthy undead creatures hurtle through the air towards you, their clawed hands ready to tear you to pieces ...

Suddenly, a sizzling bolt of light shoots out from the door, streaking into each of the ghouls in turn. With a howl of pain, the ghouls are sent reeling back into the far wall, their bodies writhing in a crackling white fire. You don't waste a moment and, taking your weapon, you finish off each of the ghouls in turn, backing away from the charred bodies once your work is done.

You may now take any/all of the following items:

Grave dust ring	Ghoul hair	Ghoul claw
(ring)	(backpack)	(left hand: dagger)
+1 brawn	This may come in	+1 speed +1 brawn
	useful one day	Ability: piercing

Pleased at your good fortune, you turn back to the glyphed door. Perhaps the scroll of opening that Fetch gave you will deactivate the glyphs. Turn to 197.

158

Warily, you step through the doorway. If you have the word *leader* written on your hero sheet, turn to 220. Otherwise turn to 201.

'Hmm, that's more like it,' she nods. 'Now, follow me. I assume you're capable of that, at least.' With a swish of her red shawl, the girl turns and heads back into the woods. You bite down on your tongue and follow, reminding yourself that you are here to protect her and return her home safely, no matter how rude and temperamental she is.

You have only gone a little way into the trees, when the ground starts to slope downwards, becoming moist and spongy underfoot. Soon you are squelching through thick mud, the air buzzing with black flies.

'Just up here,' says the girl, pushing her way through the low-hanging branches. 'Findlewort grows in bogs. And this looks just about perfect!' She stops and points through the tangled undergrowth. Ahead, you see a sludgy-looking mire and at its centre, a small island covered in root-like plants. 'There they are. Now, go get me some. I just need a little for my potion.'

Eager to get it over with, you push past her and wade into the thick mire – the dirty sludge reaching up to your waist. The girl watches you from the mire's edge, chewing nervously on a fingernail.

'Hurry up,' she shouts. 'And be careful!'

You reach the island and pull yourself up onto the bank. After taking a moment to catch your breath, you snatch up some of the findlewort and stuff it into your backpack. Just as you are about to slide back into the mire, you notice a series of ripples spreading out across the surface of the water. As you watch, the ripples start to move, forming an arrow-like pattern that is headed straight towards the island.

Suddenly, there is a blinding spray of mud and pondweed as something huge lunges out of the swamp. For a second all you can see is giant teeth and black scales. Then you are frantically fighting for your life:

	Speed	Brawn	Armour	Health
Giant crocodile	0	1	1	10

If you defeat the crocodile, turn to **118**.

160

'You have acted with honour,' wheezes the undead warrior. 'And for that you will be rewarded.' He raises a hand, and suddenly you hear a deep rumbling sound coming from the far side of the chamber. Hurrying around the tomb, you see a hidden panel in the wall slowly revolving to reveal a secret cubby-hole.

'I asked to be buried with all my belongings,' says the crusader. 'Now, choose one of my treasures as a gift.'

You may take one of the following items:

Crusader's mantle	Crusader's vestments
(cloak)	(chest)
+1 speed	+1 brawn +1 armour
Ability: charm	Ability: heal

'I will remain here,' rasps Valadin Roth. 'To protect the book from all who would seek to take it. Good luck, it warms my cold heart to know that there are still honourable heroes in this world.'

Thanking the knight, you decide to head out of the catacombs and return to Fetch. You wonder how he will take the news ... Turn to 146.

161

You step over the dead rats and enter the room. Covering your nose, you quickly rummage amongst the broken furniture and rotting remains. You can take up to two of the following items before the stench forces you to leave:

Ragged boots	Gourd of healing (1 use)	Rat-bitten gloves
(backpack)	(backpack)	(gloves)
Perhaps someone can repair these	Use any time in combat to restore 6 *health*	+1 brawn +1 magic

You may now take the staircase up to the second level (turn to 151) or leave the farm building (return to the quest map).

162

The stadium erupts into deafening applause as you stand over the body of your defeated opponent.

'I don't believe it,' gasps the wizard-announcer, his carpet grinding to a halt in a shower of sparks. 'Shara Khana is no more ... we have a new grand champion!' He throws his arms up into the air, jumping around in glee.

You may now take one of the following items as your reward:

Tiger's fury	**Tiger's heart**
(talisman)	(talisman)
+1 speed	+1 speed
Ability: berserker career	Ability: cat's speed
(see below)	
(requirement: warrior)	

If you take the *Tiger's fury* talisman and you are a warrior, you may now learn the berserker career (turn to 398 to find out more about your new abilities). When you are ready to continue, turn to 414.

163

The elderly man is visibly shaking, almost on the verge of tears. 'I told her to keep her mouth shut, I told her! But she never listens to me, never listens to a word I say.' He grabs your arm, gripping it tightly. 'You've got to believe me. It's the witch that done it. I saw it all – two days ago, down in the village. The wife, she stood nose to nose with the witch and gave her what for. She only went and accused her, didn't she – said the witch not doing her job, not doing a thing to help us poor farmers out.' He looks up, shaking his pitchfork at the blazing hot sky. 'It's the heat,' he whimpers. 'It's the darn heat that's doing us all in. Loosened the wife's tongue it did, made her say bad things. And the witch – she was furious she was. Never heard a woman go on so ... said she would put a curse on us. A curse on us all. And she's gone and bloomin' done it. Look!' He pulls on your arm, turning you to face the eerie, mist-laden fields. 'Tell me, that ain't natural. That ain't natural is it? Things have gone all strange. Things ain't what they meant to be!'

Will you:

Agree to help the farmer?	139
Ask the farmer about the strange mist?	31

164

'Good, good!' The man reaches into his robes and pulls out a large iron key. He fits it into the heavy padlock and twists it with a loud 'click'. Removing the lock, he pushes on the gate, which gives a grating squeal as it opens out onto the moonlit expanse of undergrowth and crumbling headstones.

'Good luck, my friend. And be on your guard. Oh wait ...' He puts his hand in a pocket and produces an old, rolled-up piece of parchment. 'Take this. It is a scroll of opening. You will need it to enter the catacombs.'

Make a note of the scroll on your hero sheet (it does not take up backpack space), then turn to 178.

165

'Shiny fings! Lots and lots of shiny fings. Give it 'ere,' demands the troll excitedly, holding out one of his big leathery palms. You drop the gold into his hand – then, while he struggles to count it all ('One and two and three and ... oh where woz I again?') you quickly inch past him and hurry across to the other side of the ravine. Turn to 140.

166

The skeletons are quickly reduced to a pile of bones and grave dust. If you wish, you may now take any/all of the following items:

Rusted helm	Dented buckler
(head)	(left hand: shield)
+1 speed	+1 speed +1 armour

Will you:

Take the passageway to the left?	134
Take the passageway to the right?	88

167

You manage to beat away the tree roots and grab the footlocker. Bruised and bleeding, you scarper through the remaining roots and make for the safety of the far side of the room. After taking a few moments to recover from your ordeal, you kneel down to inspect the locker. To your annoyance, you discover that it is locked.

If you have a *grime-coated key* turn to 74. Otherwise, you are unable to open the sturdy locker and must now discard it. You leave the room via the archway, turn to 154.

168

The trail meanders south and, to your relief, you find that it takes you out of the tight press of trees into wide, golden meadows and hills carpeted with hawthorn and blackberry.

At last, you come to the end of the trail, which leads up to the gate of a small thatched cottage. Everything about the place seems homely, from the neatly-tended garden to the white picket fence.

You walk up to the red front door and give several loud knocks.

'*Who is it?*' calls a high-pitched voice from inside. You state your name and explain that the woodsman sent you. '*Lovely. Just lift up the latch and walk right in!*'

You lift the latch and push open the door. Turn to 184.

169

The door opens a few inches, before it jams against something resting behind it. Peering through the gap, you see a number of objects piled up against the door, forming a barricade. To push it aside you will need to pass a *brawn* challenge.

	Brawn
Barricade	11

If you are successful, you can enter the room (turn to 180). Otherwise, you may explore the room at the end of the hall (turn to 158) or leave the farm (return to the quest map).

170

There is a bright flash – then you find yourself back on the hillside. 'Master! Master!' The bird is hopping around the body of the scholar, who is now lying on the grass, right next to his backpack. With a groan, he sits up and rubs his head.

'Wha ... what happened?' he asks.

The bird gives a warbling cry of joy. 'Look! He's alive!'

The man pushes himself onto his feet, swaying for a moment as he regains his balance. 'By the heavens, I don't know what happened. I just touched a stone and ...' He notices you and scratches his brow. 'Do ... do I know you? I'm Perinold, I think. Yes ... Perinold.'

'The magnificent!' injects the bird, strutting around proudly. 'Now, master, you should thank this adventurer for saving your life. You were a goner there – of that I am sure.'

Still a little befuddled by his experience, Perinold puts a hand to his belt and unfastens a pouch of money. 'If my faithful bird speaks the truth, then I owe you a debt of gratitude. Please take this.' He hands you the pouch. You accept it gratefully, before bidding the scholar (and his bird) farewell. You have gained 20 gold crowns and the following rewards:

Perinold's hipflask (1 use)
(backpack)
Use any time in combat
to boost your *magic* score
by 2 for one combat round

Scholars' circle
(ring)
Special ability: eureka

Return to the map to continue your adventure.

171

The flooded tunnel forms a narrow-sided chute, which suddenly flings you out into nothingness. For several desperate seconds you are in freefall, then you plunge into a deep pool of freezing-cold water.

You propel yourself back to the surface, to find yourself in a flooded cave. The walls are covered in thick clumps of glowing fungi, their phosphorescent light giving your surroundings an eerie, other-worldly glow.

You spot a muddy bank and swim towards it, pulling yourself up out of the pool. It is then that you notice the sparkling, glittering strands covering the nearby wall of the cave. As you lean back, tilting your head to take in the sight, you realise that it is a large web, and it is covering the only exit from the cave.

Will you:

Search the cave?	193
Attempt to cut through the webbing?	189

172

As Avian strides into the dining hall, the torches along the walls light up one by one, throwing their warm glow on the magnificent oak table that stretches the whole length of the room. Without slowing his pace, Avian clicks his fingers and there is a 'whoosh' as a wave of showering sparks washes across the table's surface. You blink in surprise as the once empty table is suddenly filled with an immense feast.

There are platters of roasted meats, a greased suckling pig, bowls of grapes and berries, mountains of cake and sweetbreads. It is like something from a child's fairytale.

'Please, I hope you will forgive the magic food,' says Avian, gesturing for you to take a seat on one of the high-backed chairs. 'It doesn't taste as good as the real thing, but it does save on kitchen staff.'

Eagerly, you slip into the chair and begin helping yourself to a plate of honey-roasted beef. Avian watches you with a smile. 'I see you are hungry. Good. Enjoy the feast.' He turns and heads back up the hall, towards a side door.

'You aren't joining me?' you ask in surprise – your mouth already full of food.

'I have some small matters to attend to,' says Avian. 'Please, eat your fill and then retire to your room. Just take those stairs up to the tower room.' He waves a hand towards an archway at the end of the hall. 'We will talk in the morning. Farewell.'

Once Avian has left, you tuck into the rest of the feast, amazed by the rich and succulent flavours of the food. Soon, you are leaning back in your chair, surrounded by piles of empty plates and platters. After pouring yourself another goblet of mead, you decide to head to your room – a large, circular chamber at the top of one of the towers. Surprised by how tired you suddenly feel, you find yourself making a beeline for the comfy-looking four-poster bed. Within minutes you are fast asleep. Turn to 252.

173

To push aside the heavy stone lid, you must pass a *brawn* challenge.

	Brawn
Tomb lid	8

If you are successful, turn to 112. Otherwise, you are forced to leave the tomb and take the passageway deeper into the catacombs. Turn to 1.

174

The ratling lies dead at your feet. You search the body and find 5 gold crowns. You may also take any/all of the following items:

Leader's edge	Studded leather
(main hand: sword)	(chest)
+1 speed +1 brawn	+2 armour

You may now:

Search the rest of the room   251
Leave the farm   **Return to the map**

175

'Wait up, wait up!' There is a thump as the man knocks his head on the underside of the table. 'Ugh, third time in as many minutes.' Rubbing his forehead, the man stands and holds out his hand. You shake it warmly, asking him what he has for sale.

'I'm a tinker,' says the man, stepping back and taking a bow. 'I find things and I repair them. Let's see ... you look like the adventuring sort. Guess I might have some armour you might like. Not the good stuff, like what those mighty inquisitors wear. Although,' he makes a point of eyeing up your current equipment, 'beggars can't be choosers, can they?'

He spreads out a choice of objects on the table. You may purchase any of the following, for 12 gold crowns each:

Notched blade	Simple coif	Buckled boots
(main hand: sword)	(head)	(feet)
+1 speed +1 brawn	+1 brawn +1 armour	+1 speed +1 brawn

'If yer got any bits and pieces on you, I may be able to knock something special together for you,' says the tinker.

If you have a *damaged shield* and *crocodile skin*   191
Otherwise, you thank the tinker and leave   46

176

You decide not to risk exploring the flooded tunnel. Planting your feet against the nearest wall, you push yourself upwards, swimming back towards the surface of the pool. At last, you break out of the water, coughing and spluttering for air. Wet and tired, you drag yourself onto dry land and rest. When you have finally recovered, you retrieve your torch and return to the first junction, choosing to take the other tunnel westwards. Write the word *torch* on your hero sheet, then turn to 103.

177

The old woman cackles to herself. 'Tell me, do I really look capable of commanding the weather? Yes, those bumbling weather wizards can sometimes bring a little rain or some wind, but to bring drought to the land ...' She begins filling another sack with spell books and bottles. 'The weather is the work of a higher power. A changeling no less. It wants the crops to wither – it wants to spread anger and resentment and chaos. That is what they do.'

Will you:

Accuse the witch of another crime?	113
Attack the witch?	137
Help her to escape?	101

178

You start up the hill towards the church, trudging through the scraggly grass and rank weeds. Behind you a loud grating squeal is followed by the click of a lock. Fetch has closed the gate and locked you in. You are now all alone in the eerie graveyard.

You stride briskly towards the double doors of the church, keen to be done with this unsettling task. However, your pace soon slows as you become aware of a patch of shadow by the wooden doors of the church. It appears to be moving ...

In horror, you watch as the shadow glides across the nettles and grass towards you, passing straight through the weed-choked headstones in its path. As it nears, the shadow begins to grow, spreading out like a giant net – and at its centre, an immense grinning mouth opens wide, lined with needle-sharp teeth. You must now fight:

	Speed	Magic	Armour	Health
Shadow	5	4	3	20

If you defeat the shadow, turn to 43.

179

The spiders have been defeated and their giant web has now been reduced to a few smoking cinders. You retrieve your torch and then search the bodies. You may take the following items:

Spider's leg (1 use)	**Spider's spinneret**
(backpack)	(left hand: unique)
It may come in useful,	+1 speed +1 magic
one day	Ability: webbed

You leave the cave, following the passageway north. Turn to 231.

180

You push open the door, toppling the pile of objects that had been stacked up to block the entrance. Stepping over the debris, you see that the rest of the room is bare – all of its furnishings have either been torn down or dragged over to the doorway, to bolster the barricade. Whatever the room's occupants wanted to keep out, they were clearly intent on doing so.

Sadly, it appears that the defences did not succeed. Three skeletons lie sprawled across the floor – two adults and a child. Around the bodies, you notice hundreds of tiny claw marks raked into the wood. Following the markings, you see that they emanate from a hole in the floor, where two floorboards have buckled upwards.

Rats, you quickly surmise.

As you turn to leave, something catches your eye. Walking over, you discover a ring, resting in the dust where a cupboard, or some other item of furniture, had once been. You may take the ring:

The missing link
(ring)
+1 magic +1 brawn

You may now:
Enter the room at the end of the hall   158
Leave the farm   Return to the map

181

You leave the trail, picking your way through the trees and undergrowth. The land rises sharply, becoming a series of rocky hills covered in gnarly vegetation. You quicken your pace, aware that the sun is already beginning to set, casting an auburn brilliance over your stark surroundings.

You haven't ventured far into the hills before you spot a thin column of food smoke rising into the darkening skies. Perhaps it belongs to the huntsman that the young girl mentioned. You hurry towards it, the succulent aroma of freshly-cooking meat providing all the encouragement you need.

You finally reach the campsite, set in the sheltered hollow of a bleak, stony hill.

A skinned rabbit slowly roasts over a roaring fire, the dripping fat causing the flames to spit and sizzle. Behind it, you can see a covered wagon and a straggly line of trees where a piebald pony is tethered.

As you watch, a man steps around the fire, adding more sticks to the flames. You see that he is dark skinned, dressed in the bright patchwork clothing favoured by the travelling folk. He pauses in his task, sniffing the air for a moment. Then he suddenly straightens, his hand going to the axe at his belt. 'Are you going to watch me all night, stranger?' he asks. 'Or do you wish to join me?'

Will you:

Say you are a friend? 190

Draw your weapon and attack? 203

182

To push aside the heavy stone lid, you must pass a *brawn* challenge.

Brawn

Tomb lid 8

If you are successful, turn to **98**. Otherwise, you are forced to leave the tomb and take the passageway deeper into the catacombs. Turn to **1**.

183

You kick your legs furiously, pulling your tired body along the rocky walls of the flooded passageway. Just as your lungs are about to give out, the walls of the passage vanish and you find yourself floating in what appears to be another pool. You propel yourself upwards, towards a faint light glimmering on the water's surface. At last, coughing and gasping for air, you break the surface of the pool.

Dragging yourself onto dry land you discover that you are in a small cave, illuminated by a soft phosphorescent glow. You notice that it is coming from the umbrella-shaped fungi growing along the walls. Ahead of you, a passageway winds away to the north.

Will you:

Search the cave? 206

Take the north passage? 225

184

You enter a low-ceilinged room, dominated by a wooden table, some cupboards lined with neat rows of crockery, and a large four-poster bed. There, tucked up under a bright patchwork blanket, is Grandma. At least, you think it is Grandma. You notice that her fingers are long and green, with claws instead of nails, and protruding from underneath the nightcap is a big, hairy snout!

'My, what big claws you have Grandma.'

With a snarl, the impostor rips off their bonnet, revealing an ugly, green-skinned hobgoblin! It leaps out from beneath the blanket, clutching a blood-stained sword in its hands. '*All the better to eat you with!*' it growls. You must now fight:

	Speed	Brawn	Armour	Health
Hobgoblin	0	1	1	12

If you defeat the hobgoblin, turn to 199.

185

You get to your feet, feeling more than a little awkward as Martha and her tribe of children glare at you intently. Even the two babies have stopped bawling and appear to be appraising you with interest.

Offering a weak apologetic smile, you brush a chunk of turnip from your hair, then quickly turn tail and run – slipping and sliding your way across the pulpy garden, and back down the hillside. Turn to 58.

186

The flooded tunnel is longer than you thought. With no end in sight, you start to panic, aware that you are running out of air. The next few minutes are a mad scramble, as you head back the way you came, desperately pulling yourself along the sharp, rocky walls.

Flailing amidst a sea of bubbles, you fight your way free of the tunnel. You twist round, frantically trying to gain your bearings. The dark waters are disorientating and you no longer have a sense of which way is up or down. Thankfully, you catch sight of a faint shimmering light. With a final determined effort, you swim towards it, coughing and gasping for air as you finally burst out of the pool.

Shivering with the cold, you drag yourself out of the chill water, your chest heaving as you greedily suck in great lungfuls of air. Once you have recovered from your ordeal, you retrieve your torch (add the word *torch* to your hero sheet) and then head back to the main junction, following the tunnel westwards. Turn to 103.

187

You push aside the painted screen to reveal a small, semi-circular room – nondescript save for the black-wood door in the facing wall. A number of strange glyphs are etched into its panels, each one glowing with a soft white light. Behind you, you can hear the ghouls closing in. You must make a quick decision:

Will you:
Search inside your pack for the scroll of opening?	100
Fight the ghouls by the door?	141

188

Avian folds his arms. 'A simple adventurer, you say?' He tilts his head to one side as he appraises you. When his eyes come to rest on your arm, you notice his expression change. Despite the fact that your mark is covered, you sense that he knows it is there.

'How odd,' he says, furrowing his brow. 'I have been expecting you. A friend of mine foresaw your coming – but ...' He shakes his head, clearly bemused by something. 'I would never have guessed ...'

Avian turns and gestures towards the courtyard. 'I am looking for a new apprentice. Perhaps someone of your talents would like to consider the post.' Turn to 126.

189

You attempt to break through the sticky tendrils. They are stronger than they look and it takes several attempts before you manage to sever the silken cords. As you start to widen the gap that you have made, you hear a skittering sound coming from above. Looking up, you see a giant spider clambering down the web towards you.

'My web!' hisses the spider angrily. 'No one touches my web!'

You must now fight:

	Speed	Brawn	Armour	Health
Giant spider	4	3	2	20

Special abilities

🛡 Venom: Once you have taken health damage from the spider, at the end of every combat round you must automatically lose 2 *health*.

If you defeat the spider, turn to 147.

190

You offer out a hand in friendship. With a smile, the man steps forwards and shakes it heartily. 'I am Manni,' he says. 'Please, join me. It would be a shame for good food to go to waste, don't you think?' The succulent smells emanating from the cooking rabbit make your mouth water. You keenly agree and take a seat around the fire.

'So, what brings you out in these woods?' he asks, placing a pan of water onto the fire.

You tell Manni the full story about the woodsman's daughter, and how she is intent on making a love potion to run off with her 'handsome' huntsman. Manni nods solemnly.

'I fear it is my fault,' he sighs. 'She has been visiting me – her company has been warmly welcomed.' He stops stirring the water and looks up at you. 'The locals don't trust my folk. My people are seldom welcome in the towns and villages. But she accepted me at least, and

I repaid her generosity by sharing stories of my travels. I had no idea that she ...'

At that moment you hear the baying of a horn. Manni jumps quickly to his feet, drawing his axe. 'Raiders,' he says grimly. 'The fire and meat must have attracted them.' He points down the hill, where you see four hooded figures emerging from a copse of trees. From their short stature and ungainly, shambling walk, it is obvious that they are goblins. One is slightly larger than the others, a thick animal pelt resting across its wide shoulders. In its hands it holds a rusty meat-cleaver, caked in dried blood. With hooting cries, the goblins charge. Turn to 242.

191

You provide the tinker with the damaged shield and the piece of crocodile skin (deduct these two objects from your hero sheet). Using these materials, the tinker knocks together the following item, which you may now take:

Scaled defender
(left hand: shield)
+2 brawn +1 armour

If you do not want this item, then the tinker agrees to pay you 20 gold crowns for the shield. Once you have made your choice, turn to 175 to have another look at the tinker's items, or turn to 46 to leave.

192

'Shiny fings! Lots of shiny fings. Give it 'ere,' demands the troll excitedly, holding out one of his big leathery palms. You drop the gold into his hand – then, while he struggles to count it all ('One and two and three and ... oh where woz I again?') you quickly inch past him and hurry across to the other side of the ravine. Your trick has worked! Turn to 140.

193

You cautiously search around the edges of the cave. You find little of interest other than lichen-covered rocks and glowing fungi. Just as you are about to give up, your foot knocks against something. You kneel down and pick up the object, brushing away the age-old dirt and dust. You are holding a fine gold necklace, its length sparkling with jewelled beads. Who it belonged to and how it got here is a mystery – but you may now take this special item:

Beads of brilliance
(necklace)
+1 brawn +1 magic

You cut through the webbing and leave the cave. Turn to 189.

194

The crusader leans against the tomb, his exposed ribcage rising and falling as he takes several long, wheezing breaths. 'The book was given to me long ago, by one of the Grand Viziers of See-Val. I was indebted to his family, so it was a matter of honour for me to do his bidding. The book is known as The Grimoire of Naraghost. A tomb robber found it in one of the pyramids, on the edge of the dune sea. They say it came from the sky, with the godless elves that built those accursed cities.

'The book is a thing of chaos, which cannot be destroyed by sword or magic. I tried … believe me I tried.' He gives a deep, rasping sigh. 'I took it north, seeking a sanctuary where it could be kept safe. But the longer I held onto the book, the sicker I became. Eventually I could go no further.' The crusader lowers his gaze to the stone tomb. 'I made the priest promise me he would bury me in these ancient catacombs – with the last of my possessions. I thought, at least here, the book would be safe.' He looks up, his hollow eyes burning into your own. 'The book cannot leave here – do you understand this?'

Will you:

State that you are taking the book?   109

Leave the book under the crusader's protection?   160

195

You follow the map, sprinting along the overgrown path that twists and turns through the dark forest. At last, you come to a clearing where a small wood cabin sits on the edge of the tree line. A grey gelding is tethered to a post outside, already saddled and laden with bags.

You hurry over to the door and contemplate knocking. Instead, you simply push it open and step inside. A plump old woman, with her white hair tied back in a bun, is in the process of stuffing books and scrolls into a sack. She looks up as you enter, her piercing blue eyes twinkling in the lantern light.

'Well, well. I wasn't expecting you so soon,' she says, squinting towards you. She puts a hand into the pocket of her dress and pulls out a pair of spectacles. She places them on the end of the nose, then looks you up and down. 'Hmm, you don't look like one of those witchfinders. They dress with a little more ... style.' She raises one of her hands, displaying a silver signet ring. 'This belonged to one of their kind, once upon a time. The fool underestimated me.' She returns to stuffing objects into the sack. 'Are you here to kill me?' she asks, almost matter-of-factly.

Will you:

Attack the witch?   137

Accuse the witch of her crimes?   113

Help the witch to escape?   101

196

Avian listens to your story with interest. For now, you leave out the part about your strange mark, although you notice the man's eyes flicking to your covered arm several times. 'I appreciate your honesty,' says Avian. 'In truth, a friend of mine foresaw your coming. Let's just say, he has a gift for that kind of thing.' He turns and gestures to the courtyard of his castle. 'If you are going to be my apprentice, then I suggest we get started. I want to see what you are capable of.' Turn to 126.

197

Unfurling the scroll, you read out the strange words that have been scratched into the parchment. As you utter the last word of the spell, the scroll suddenly bursts into flames. You hurriedly let go of it, watching as it floats away on the air, curling and blackening, until it is nothing more than ash.

When you turn your attention back to the door, you are relieved to see that the glyphs have vanished. You pull it open, revealing a steep spiral staircase descending down into the earth. Vein-like cracks in the wall emit a soft, greenish glow, lighting the way.

Cautiously, you make your way down the stone stairs. At the bottom, you find yourself in a cold, stone passageway, the walls scabbed with fungus and lichen. At the foot of the stairs is a small, iron chest.

Will you:
Open the chest?	209
Make your way up the passage?	90

198

Your lungs are already at bursting point. You grab the sides of the opening and propel yourself forwards – entering a narrower side passage. You will need to pass a *speed* challenge if you hope to continue.

	Speed
Flooded tunnel	10

If you are successful, turn to 183. If you fail, turn to 186.

199

The hobgoblin falls backwards onto the bed, its dark blood soaking through the patchwork blanket. You may now take one of the following items:

Goblin kickers	Granny's locket	Curved blade
(feet)	(necklace)	(main hand: sword)
+1 speed +1 brawn	+1 magic	+1 speed

You search the rest of the cottage, but find little of interest – except for some grey hairs, sizzling on the coals in the fireplace. You assume that is all that is left of poor Grandma. Leaving the cottage, you follow the trail back into the woods.

Will you:

Head east into the hills?	152
Return to the woodsman?	219

200

You take a handful of gold crowns from your purse and place them on the tabletop. Martha looks at the gold and gives a tiny gasp. 'No, please! No – I can't.' She pushes the coins towards you. 'I can't accept it. I'm sorry.'

You quickly explain to Martha that her children desperately need food. With the money she can buy a couple of chickens and some much-needed provisions from the village. Martha begins to argue, but stops when she catches the wide-eyed stares of her hungry, half-starved children.

'I suppose ... I could, just this once.' She scoops up the coins into her flour-smeared hands. 'I'll take it for the children. For them.' She gives you a smile. 'Thank you. I will remember your kindness.'

Deduct 10 gold crowns from your hero sheet and then turn to 78.

201

You enter the room, gagging as an acrid stench fills your nostrils. It takes only a few seconds to discern the cause – looking down, you see that the floor of the room is covered in a thick layer of rat droppings.

You draw your weapon and advance, picking your way with care between the broken furnishings that litter the dark space. To your right, a dirt-stained mattress rests on its side, covering the window and the room's only source of light. You pause, letting your eyes grow accustomed to the murky gloom. It is then that you see the man watching you from the shadows. He is sat on a plush, velvet chair, a long sword resting across his knees. His narrow eyes glitter in the dark.

'I see yer made it this far, stranger,' he drawls, his long fingers drumming against the arms of the chair. 'I do hopes the family didn't give yer too much trouble. Nice folk really, once yer get to knows them. They were so grateful that I let 'em move in. Even me rats seemed to like 'em – and that's rare for rats.' The man snatches his sword and jumps to his feet. 'There ain't much for common folk to live on around 'ere. A few tasty farmers and the odd traveller ain't much now is it?' He advances towards you, his lips curling back to reveal razor-sharp teeth. 'Yer will excuse me if I don't say grace, but I prefers to just tuck right in . . .' With a snarl, he leaps towards you.

You have no choice but to fight:

	Speed	Brawn	Armour	Health
Leader	2	3	4	25*

* Once you have lowered the leader's *health* to 12 or less, turn to 233.

202

For what seems like an age, you are lowered deeper and deeper into the well. At last, your flickering torchlight illuminates what appears to be the bottom of the shaft. You step out of the bucket, your boots sinking into the wet, soggy mud.

It is immediately apparent what has caused the well to dry up. One of the walls has crumbled inwards, revealing an earthen tunnel stretching away into darkness. With one hand resting on your weapon, you edge past the rubble and enter the tunnel.

After several yards, you come across a body lying against the tunnel wall. As you step closer, you realise that it must be the priest's son – or what is left of him. His body is covered in a glistening white slime, which has eaten through most of his leather clothing, exposing charred skin and bone.

You notice traces of the same glistening acid on the smooth tunnel walls. Curious as to what could have made the tunnel, you follow it deeper into the musty, dark earth. Soon, you arrive at a junction.

Will you:

Take the east tunnel?	248
Take the west tunnel?	103

203

You draw your weapon and advance. The man appears startled by your response. 'You look like no common thief or brigand,' he says. 'State your business here!' He nods his head towards the rabbit, cooking on the spit. 'There is food here for two, if you care to lay down your arms.'

Will you:

Attack the huntsman?	124
Agree to talk?	190

204

Your weapon cleaves through the creature's straw body with ease. As it falls to the ground, still jerking and shaking, you notice something around the creature's neck. It looks like a necklace fashioned from human finger bones. You cut the necklace loose. As you do so, the creature immediately stiffens and becomes lifeless.

You may now choose one of the following rewards:

Crow's feet	Murder of crows
(feet)	(left hand: fist weapon)
+1 speed +1 magic	+1 speed +1 brawn

With the scarecrow dead, you eye your surroundings, hoping that the strange mist will finally lift. However, the fog only seems to have thickened, reducing your vision still further. With little choice but to continue, you start across the field once again, your numb fingers almost frozen to your weapon.

After several minutes, you see a flickering green light ahead. You hurry towards it – the light shining like a beacon through the swirling banks of fog. As you near, you hear the cackle of ghostly voices from somewhere in the mist.

Entering an area of flattened corn, you soon discover the source of the light. A grim totem has been pushed deep into the frozen earth. Fashioned from dark wood and bone, its length crackles with a magical green light. This must be the source of the witch's curse. Turn to 65.

205

You are at a stalemate. To proceed further with the game you must put more money on the table. Decide how much gold you will add – and the gambler automatically adds the same amount. You must bet at least one extra gold crown. (If you have no more money, then you have lost and lose all your gold. Turn to 11.) Then roll a die. If the result is ⚅ or less turn to 259, if the result is ⚀ turn to 67.

206

Behind a clump of glowing fungi you discover the skeleton of an adventurer, his clothes coated in sticky strands of webbing. Searching the body you find 20 gold crowns and may take any/all of the following items:

Damaged shield	Web-coated jerkin	Dusty footpads
(backpack)	(chest)	(feet)
Perhaps someone can repair this	+1 brawn +1 armour Ability: webbed	+1 speed Ability: charm

You leave the cave, taking the passageway to the north. Turn to 225.

207

You step through the glowing doorway, to find yourself in a long pillared hall. Torches flicker in sconces along the wall, casting dancing shadows across the cracked, stone tiles. There is the musty smell of earth here – and things long dead. At the end of the hall stands a dark figure, shrouded in a ghostly fog.

'So, you dare challenge me!' booms the now familiar voice. The veil of fog lifts briefly, to reveal a rugged warrior clad in fur and leather. 'Puny maggot! You come looking for this worthless fool?' The warrior's narrowed eyes flick to a body lying sprawled beside one of the pillars – a pot-bellied man, dressed in fine-looking robes. At first you assume he is dead, but then you notice that the man's chest is rising and falling with shallow breaths. He is still alive ... for now.

'I will not waste my time with his kind,' growls the mist-cloaked warrior, his booming voice echoing in the vaulted chamber. 'I am Noldor. The First King. These are my hallowed halls and only death is welcome here.' The ghost strides down the hall towards you. As he nears, you see a black sword materialising in one of his gloved fists. With maddened laughter, the spectral warrior raises his black blade and charges. 'I am Noldor and I will carve my name on your soul!'

	Speed	Brawn	Armour	Health
Noldor	7	5	4	60

Special abilities
You may use your runes to help you against this powerful, ancient king. The runes (if you have them) do the following:

- Rune of Voldring: Increase your *armour* by 3 for the duration of this combat.
- Rune of Allura: Use once, any time in combat, to instantly replenish your *health*.
- Rune of Malachi: Use instead of rolling for a damage score, to instantly reduce Noldor's *health* by 30. This can only be used once.
- Rune of Talos: You may increase your *speed* by 2 for the duration of this combat.

If you defeat Noldor, turn to **41**. (Special achievement: If you defeat Noldor without using a single rune, turn to **52**.)

208

You find yourself in a rough-hewn passageway, lined with more of the glowing fungi. After following it for several minutes, you find that the way forwards is blocked by an impassable wall of rubble. Thankfully, a side-tunnel branches off from the main passageway, leading steeply upwards. You notice tell-tale traces of acid, smouldering in pools along its uneven floor.

With no other option, you follow the side-tunnel, clambering up several near-vertical sections as it cuts through the rock and soil. At last, you pull yourself out into a passageway. To your surprise you see your torch lying a few metres away. It appears that this freshly made tunnel has brought you back to where you started. Just ahead of you is the corpse of the maggot and the pit that led to the underground river.

You retrieve your torch (write the word *torch* on your hero sheet), before deciding on your next course of action.

Will you:

Continue east along the passage?	254
Return to the first junction and go west?	103

The chest is unlocked. Inside you find a mildewed pair of gloves, some stone-cutting tools and a couple of earthenware pots. You may take any / all of the following items:

Mason's gloves	**Pot of healing (1 use)**	**Pot of brawn (1 use)**
(gloves)	(backpack)	(backpack)
+1 speed	Use any time in combat	Use any time in combat
Ability: first cut	to restore 4 *health*	to raise your *brawn* by
		2 for one combat round

When you have made your choices, turn to 90.

210

If you killed the witch, turn to 249. Otherwise, turn to 257.

211

'Beatrice? Beatrice Fletcher?' Angry tears start to well in Martha's eyes. 'That cruel narrow-minded woman. She would see my family starve just because of a silly village competition. Bertrand, Emma, take the babies inside. Now!' The two children hurry to their mother's side and take one of the bawling babies into their arms. After giving you a suspicious look, they head back up the hill, towards the ramshackle building.

As you push yourself onto your feet, Martha strides over, shaking her head as she eyes the chopped-up pieces of turnip. 'A traveller gave me those turnips. They were to feed the young ones,' she says. 'It's been hard without my dear Frederick around. But those turnips ... they're the first thing that's ever grown in this wretched soil. A miracle they were.' She brushes away her tears, then fixes you with a cold, determined stare. 'Will you help me get my own back on Beatrice Fletcher? She should pay for what she has done, don't you agree?'

Will you:

Agree to help Martha Weevil?	236
Politely decline and return to Beatrice?	58

212

You clamber through the narrow fissure, emerging in a small cavern. Above you, dangling from the ceiling, are a series of web-like bundles. You notice that one of them is wriggling back and forth – as if whatever is inside is struggling to get out. Across the far side of the cave, you see a tunnel opening. Sticky strands of webbing criss-cross the ground between you and the cave exit.

Will you:

Cut open the wriggling bundle?	295
Cross the room to the tunnel opening?	266

213

'Can I 'elp yer matey?'

The voice at your side makes you jump. A young boy, around twelve years old, is looking you up at you with a curious expression. 'I bet a pretty penny yer new 'ere, ain't yer?' He doffs his cap to you, then swings his arm out to take in the sprawling settlement. 'This 'ere is No Hope. Wanna guided tour of our splendid establishment?'

Will you:

Agree to take the tour?	265
Politely decline and enter the town?	348
Ask if he knows Jenlar Cornelius?	282

214

You have chosen the path of the warrior. You may permanently increase your *health* by 15 (to 45). Make a note of this change on your hero sheet.

After an hour of sparring with Avian, you are relieved when he finally lowers his sword and steps away. 'Impressive,' he says, nodding his head. 'You are a mighty opponent. Perhaps there is something special in you after all. Come,' he starts towards a pair of double doors at the end of the room. 'You must be famished after your journey. A think a little banquet is in order, to welcome you to your new home.' Turn to 172.

215

Behind a mound of rubble, there is a wide vertical crack in one of the walls. It leads through into a tunnel, which slopes downwards, deeper into the earth. Across the other side of the chamber is a rectangular doorway leading out into daylight.

Will you:

Investigate the tunnel?	463
Leave the chamber by the open doorway?	475

216

The ground trembles as the mighty creature crashes to the ground, dead. You may take one of the following items as your victory spoils:

Breastplate of the bull	Braids of the bull	Horns of the bull
(chest)	(talisman)	(head)
+3 brawn +2 armour	+1 speed	+1 speed +2 armour
Ability: charge	Ability: charge	Ability: charge
(requirement: warrior)		

When you are reunited with Bart, he hands over a bulging bag of money. (You have gained 40 gold crowns.) 'That was some fight,' he grins. 'But I still think you're holding back. This is the arena – you can fight dirty, you know. Perhaps Knuckles here could show you some of his special moves. Might help you in the coming fights. What do you think?'

If you have taken the path of the warrior, you may now learn the gladiator career (turn to 307). Otherwise, turn to 293 when you are ready for your next fight.

217

The changeling surrounds its body with crackling flames. 'You will burn in hellfire,' it snarls. 'Like all those who dare stand in my way!'

You must now battle this fearsome foe:

	Speed	Magic	Armour	Health
Changeling	5	5	2	40

Special abilities

♥ Hellfire: At the end of every combat round, your hero automatically takes 2 damage from the flames that surround the demon. This ability ignores *armour*.

If you defeat the changeling, turn to 133.

218

You wedge your torch between some rocks. Then, taking a deep breath, you plunge into the flooded tunnel. (Remove the word *torch* from your hero sheet.)

The water is freezing cold; the shock of it almost forcing you to swallow water. With powerful strokes you dive deeper and deeper into the murky depths. Soon, you are blinded and disorientated by the darkness. Feeling along the walls, you discover what could be an opening in the rock.

Will you:

Risk exploring the opening?   198
Return to the surface?   176

219

You haven't travelled far before you spot a light, flickering between the dark trees. Curious as to what it might be, you leave the trail, pushing your way through the thick clinging undergrowth.

You round a copse of trees, and finally discover the source of the light – a small campsite, set in the sheltered hollow of a bleak, stony hill. A skinned rabbit slowly roasts over a roaring fire, the dripping fat causing the flames to spit and sizzle. Behind it, you can see a covered wagon and a straggly line of trees where a piebald pony is tethered. The beast looks agitated, tugging against its restraints.

There doesn't appear to be anyone around. Then you notice a straw basket lying on its side in the grass. Next to it is a broken bottle, from which a black bubbling liquid steams. Turn to 240.

220

You enter the room, gagging as an acrid stench fills your nostrils. It takes only a few seconds to discern the cause – looking down, you see that the floor of the room is covered in a thick layer of rat droppings.

You draw your weapon and advance, picking your way with care between the broken furnishings that litter the dark space. To your right, a dirt-stained mattress rests on its side, covering the window and the room's only source of light. As you reach over to pull it down, you catch a sudden flash of movement out of the corner of your eye. Something knocks into your shoulder, sending you flying backwards across the room. You land heavily, crying out in pain as a splinter of broken chair lances into your side. You pull it free and toss it away, as the ruffian from the roadside leaps towards you – his dagger glinting in the half-light.

'Yer killed the boss,' he growls. 'Now 'is rats are gonna feast on yer bones!'

You have no choice but to fight:

	Speed	Brawn	Armour	Health
Rennie	3	2	2	15

Special abilities
🛡 First cut: You must start this combat having already lost 1 *health*.

If you defeat the ruffian, turn to 247.

221

The moment you touch the stone there is a bright flash of light, followed by a dizzying sensation of movement. When the light fades, you find yourself on a rocky island, bobbing on a sea of bubbling hot lava. At the far side of the island is a man dressed in black plate armour, his face hidden behind the visor of his helmet.

'You trespass in the halls of ancient kings,' booms a deep voice, from somewhere above. Looking up, all you can see are thick clouds of steam and smoke. 'Many have come here. All have failed. Now, fight my champions and prove your worth.'

The knight suddenly lurches into life, drawing an elegant sword from the scabbard at his side. Raising the sword to his chest, the silent knight marches towards you, his armour creaking and clanking in an eerie, menacing manner. You prepare to defend yourself:

	Speed	Brawn	Armour	Health
Voldring of earth	4	3	5	20

Special abilities
🛡 Mighty blows: Voldring rolls 2 dice for damage.

If you are defeated, you find yourself back on the hilltop, turn to 153. If you defeat Voldring, the knight's body turns to ash. All that is left is a stone rune with a circle carved into it. If you take the *Rune of Voldring*, make a note of it on your hero sheet. There is a sudden flash of light and you find yourself back on the hilltop. Turn to 153.

222

The skeletal knight crumples into a pile of loose bones and dust. You may now take any/all of the following items:

Ragged cloak	Ancient sword
(backpack)	(main hand: sword)
Perhaps someone can	+1 speed +1 brawn
repair this item	Ability: bleed

You find little else of interest in this mouldy, decaying room, so you decide to head through the archway. Turn to 1.

223

'Ah yes,' grins the witch. 'Sweet, love-sick Liselle.' She reaches over and snatches a book from a nearby shelf. Flicking to a particular page, she hands the book to you. It appears to be a simple recipe book for cooking sauces. 'Look, is it really my fault the girl had cobwebs in her ears? The recipe I gave her was for a herb-and-mushroom garnish. Ha! Love potion indeed. I suspect she got the ingredients wrong. Substituted the greenwort for findlewort. Can I really be held accountable for a young girl's foolishness?'

Will you:

Accuse the witch of another crime?	113
Attack the witch?	137
Help the witch to escape?	101

224

You travel along several stone passageways before coming to the top of another set of stairs. You follow them down to a stone door covered in sigils and runes. Through your clouded vision, you watch as your hands pass over the strange inscriptions, lighting them up one by one. Then the stone door grates open with an echoing boom, revealing a dark chamber.

You walk forward, past shelves stacked with boxes and chests. Everything is illuminated by a dull purple light. You realise it is coming from the brand on your arm; the three entwined snakes giving off a strange, unearthly glow. At last, you come to a wooden box. Carved into its side are the words 'Artefact 51'. You open the box and take out the stone fragment that is held inside.

You are walking down more corridors – the edges of your vision obscured by a blurry fog. Turning down another passageway, you enter a large domed chamber. In the middle of the chamber is a stepped dais that leads up to a curved, stone arch. Again you pass your hand through the air, making a series of arcane gestures. Suddenly the archway begins to glow with a golden light. As you step closer, you see a scene slowly starting to form within the archway. It looks like a courtyard, bathed in moonlight. And a man is standing there . . . beckoning to you.

You clutch the stone to your chest and step through the portal. Turn to 263.

225

As you pass along the passageway, you notice that the walls are not as smooth as those you encountered earlier – nor is there any acid coating the floors and walls. You sense that you have entered a much older cave network. Turn to 231.

226

You are at a stalemate. To proceed further with the game you must put more money on the table. Decide how much gold you will add – and the gambler automatically adds the same amount. You must bet at least one extra gold crown. (If you have no more money, then you have lost and lose all your gold. Turn to 11.) Then roll a die. If the result is ⚂ or less turn to 259, if the result is ⚃ or more turn to 67.

227

You search through the backpack. There is little of interest, except for some dog-eared notes, scribbled hastily onto parchment, and a red leather-bound book.

Will you:

Look through the notes?	301
Examine the book?	115
Return your attention to the stones?	153

228

The huntsman was a skilled warrior – but no match for your prowess. You search the body and find 15 gold crowns. You also find the following items, which you may take:

Huntsman's axe	Huntsman's jerkin
(main hand: axe)	(chest)
+2 brawn	+1 armour

You settle down next to the fire to warm yourself as the chill of the evening settles around you. After helping yourself to some of the freshly-cooked rabbit, you spend the night in the huntsman's wagon.

You rise at daybreak. After washing yourself in a nearby stream, you leave the wooded hills and head back to Tithebury Cross. You decide to avoid a meeting with the woodsman, having failed to bring his daughter home safely. Return to the quest map to continue your adventures.

229

It is late evening when Beatrice finally appears at the window. 'Time for a nice slice of pie,' she declares, licking her lips. The old woman picks up the pie and takes it inside. You wait patiently in the garden, wondering what will happen to the woman when she eats it. Could it be worse than what happened to you on the hillside?

You creep towards the window, hoping to take a quick peek inside. At that moment, Martha comes rushing up to the garden gate, waving her arms around frantically. 'I've changed my mind! I've changed my mind!' she cries. 'We have to stop her eating it! Quick!' Turn to 255.

230

The leader backs away. 'Think yer can best me, huh?' he snarls. 'It's time to show yer what yer really up against!' In horror, you watch as the man's body begins to change. His face stretches outwards to form a pointed snout, his nails and teeth lengthening into deadly claws and fangs. Coarse black hair erupts from the man's flesh, bursting through the seams of his ragged clothing. Within seconds you are staring at a man-sized rat, its pink tail whipping back and forth through the air. With a high-pitched squeal, the ratling lunges forward, foamy saliva drooling from its jaws. With no time to heal, you must take on this foe with the *health* that you have remaining:

	Speed	Brawn	Armour	Health
Ratling	3	3	2	12

Special abilities

🛡 Tail lash: For every ⬚ you roll during this combat, the ratling's tail automatically hits you for 1 damage, ignoring *armour*.

If you defeat the ratling, turn to 125.

231

After several minutes, the passageway becomes a narrow ledge, overlooking a huge cavern. Its walls and columns are coated in forests of glowing fungi, their pale light illuminating a giant, glittering web that stretches from floor to ceiling. At the centre of the web, resting on the sticky criss-crossing strands, is the biggest spider you have ever seen, its massive fangs dripping with a deadly green venom.

If you still have the word *torch* on your hero sheet, you can choose to set fire to the web (turn to 7). If you don't have a torch or choose not to set fire to the web, you can:

Attack the spider	60
Flee and return to the well	246

232

As you proceed along the tunnel, you quickly become aware of a distant rumbling sound. It gets louder and louder, growing in intensity. Then, all of a sudden, the stone and rock beneath your feet is thrown upwards with tremendous force. You are sent sprawling onto your back, as a white bulbous head erupts from the soil. It looks like a giant maggot, eyeless and blind.

As you scramble to your feet, the beast swings its bloated head in your direction. Then it pulls its enormous, rippling body out of the pit and squirms towards you, its jaws snapping together hungrily. You will have to defeat this creature before you can continue down the tunnel:

	Speed	Brawn	Armour	Health
Burrower alpha	5	5	4	25

Special abilities

🖤 Acid: The burrower's mouth drips with a deadly, corrosive acid. Roll a die at the start of each combat round. If you roll a ⚀ or a ⚁ you automatically take 2 damage from the acid. This ability ignores *armour*.

If you defeat the burrower, turn to 116.

233

The man backs away, his shirt soaked with blood and sweat. 'Think yer can best me, huh?' he snarls. 'It's time to show yer what yer really up against!' In horror, you watch as the man's body begins to change. His face stretches outwards to form a pointed snout, his nails and teeth lengthening into deadly claws and fangs. Coarse black hair erupts from the man's flesh, bursting through the seams of his ragged clothing. Within seconds you are staring at a man-sized rat, its pink tail whipping back and forth through the air. With a high-pitched squeal, the ratling lunges forward, foamy saliva drooling from its jaws. With no time to heal, you must take on this foe with the *health* that you have remaining:

	Speed	Brawn	Armour	Health
Ratling	3	3	2	12

Special abilities
🖤 Tail lash: For every ⚀ you roll during this combat, the ratling's tail automatically hits you for 1 damage, ignoring *armour*.

If you defeat the ratling, turn to 174.

234

The lake spirit is powerful, knocking aside your flimsy weapons with its giant, watery fists. As you stagger backwards, losing ground to this fearsome foe, there is a sudden flash of white light. Risking a sideways glance, you see that the wizard's staff has started to glow. The lake spirit drifts towards it, like a moth attracted to a flame. The nearer it gets, the smaller and smaller it becomes, until it is little more than a gentle wave, lapping around the foot of the glowing staff. There is another flash and the light is gone.

The wizard lowers his arms, his chanting finished. Exhausted, he drops to his knees. You rush to his side, offering him support as he stumbles back to his feet. 'I'm OK, I'm OK,' he says, patting your arm. 'It is done. The lake spirit is now trapped in the staff. It is mine to command now – the rainmaker is complete.' He tugs the staff out of the earth and holds it up, admiring it as if it was suddenly made from solid gold. It looks much the same to you: just a length of ordinary polished wood.

'With this, I may be able to defeat the weather spell and bring some rain to this land.' He regards you for a moment, then he offers you a warm smile. 'You have done well. Come, let's go back to my tower. I'm sure I have something I can offer you as a reward. Turn to 243.

235

As you head east, the trees start to thin, the ground becoming steeper and more rugged. Soon you are picking your way between boulders and narrow wind-seared gullies. Following the directions you were given, you come to a series of worn steps, carved into the granite cliffs. These take you to the top of a high pinnacle of rock, where a tall stone tower stands stark against the azure-blue skies.

As you approach, you see that the tower is visibly shaking from side to side, dislodging dust and stone from its walls and crenellations. A booming, banging sound can be heard coming from somewhere inside the tower. You call out, asking if anyone is home. A pair of window shutters fly open from high up the tower, and a bald-headed man with a wispy white beard sticks out his head. 'Help me!' he cries. 'Please don't go! I have a problem and I need help!'

You draw your weapons and agree to hear him out. 'It's my tower. I'm trapped in my tower. One of my ... experiments has escaped and is now running loose. Please get rid of it so I can come down!'

You warily approach the front door, as the tower shakes and rattles on its foundations. Trying the door you discover it is locked. 'I can't get in,' you shout up to the wizard. Suddenly, the door is blown off its hinges by some powerful force, sending pieces of splintered wood hurtling past your head.

'OK, no longer a problem,' you add dryly. From inside the tower, you hear a roar – like a fierce, howling wind. Bracing yourself for what is to come, you step inside. Turn to 33.

236

'Good! Help me clear some of this up – we'll need it.'

You look at Martha quizzically, wondering what plan she has in mind. She re-enters the house and returns a few moments later with a basket. Several of her children follow at her heels, whispering excitedly to each other. Together, you gather up some chunks of the vinegary-smelling turnip. Once the basket is full, Martha starts back towards the house.

'What is it for?' you ask with interest. Martha turns and gives you a sly grin. 'I'm going to make Beatrice Fletcher eat humble pie.' Turn to 13.

237

You are at a stalemate. To proceed further with the game you must put more money on the table. Decide how much gold you will add – and the gambler automatically adds the same amount. You must bet at least one extra gold crown. (If you have no more money, then you have lost and lose all your gold. Turn to 11.) Then roll a die. If the result is ⚀ or less turn to 259, if the result is ⚁ or more turn to 67.

238

While one of the men winds up the bucket, the white-robed man walks over to your side. 'You will need a light, my friend,' he says. 'Edward, some wood please.'

One of the villagers, a boy of around thirteen, runs over and places a length of wood in the man's outstretched hand. Holding it aloft, the priest utters a short prayer. Suddenly, the end of the wood ignites, becoming a blazing torch. He eyes it with a smile of satisfaction.

You swing yourself over the side of the well and clamber into the water bucket. The priest hands you the torch, then slowly you are lowered inch-by-inch into the cold, murky darkness. Make a note of the word *torch* on your hero sheet, then turn to 202.

You are almost to the other side when your foot catches on one of the strands, causing it to wobble back and forth. You think nothing of it, until you hear the skittering sound coming from above. Almost too late, you spin round – to catch the two giant spiders swinging towards you on strands of webbing. One hits you squarely in the chest, its venomous mandibles sinking into your shoulder. You drop your torch with a cry of pain, its flame instantly igniting the flammable webbing.

'The web! The web!' hisses one of the spiders. 'Kill it! Kill it!' As the silken strands go up in smoke, the spiders leap at you, seeking to trap you in their deadly webbing.

	Speed	Brawn	Armour	Health
Giant spiders	4	4	2	25

Special abilities

◖ Venom: You have already been bitten! At the end of every combat round you must automatically lose 2 *health*.

If you defeat the spiders, turn to 179.

240

Alert for danger, you step warily around the camp fire and are amazed and horrified by what you see. A giant grey wolf watches you from the edge of the light, its amber eyes reflecting the dancing flames. You notice an oily black liquid dripping from its fangs – the same liquid you saw in the bottle.

With a bestial snarl, the wolf launches itself at you. You have no choice but to fight this ferocious creature:

	Speed	Brawn	Armour	Health
Big Bad Wolf	0	1	1	15

If you defeat the wolf, turn to 64.

241

Your sword slices through the last of the turnips, sending a spray of white fleshy pulp showering across the vegetable patch. The creature topples to the ground, its strange spindly legs kicking in the air for a few seconds, before finally becoming still. You drop to your knees exhausted. In every direction, chunks of turnip lie across the ground, each one giving off a strange, vinegary smell.

A child's cry alerts you to the fact that you are no longer alone. Spinning round, you see two young children watching you from the edge of the garden, mouths agape. A third has run back to the shack. Raised voices follow, then a young woman emerges from the building, striding angrily onto the hillside. A screeching baby is held under each arm – both carried along like a sack of potatoes.

'Henry, if you're playing games again, I swear I'll ...' Martha sees you and stops dead in her tracks. Her eyes scan the scene of turnip devastation.

'What ... what have you done?' she gasps. 'My turnips!'

Will you:

Reveal Beatrice's plan?	211
Blame the strange turnips?	289
Make a run for it?	185

242

Manni moves with startling speed, dispatching one of the goblins with a well-aimed swing of his axe. Two of the smaller goblins break away and attack him, leaving you to face the goblin chief alone. With a snarl, this larger goblin charges towards you, his meat cleaver raised high above his head:

	Speed	Brawn	Armour	Health
Goblin chief	0	1	1	15

If you defeat the goblin chief, turn to 260.

243

Back at the tower, the wizard rummages through the wreckage of his front room and produces three items. 'Thank you again,' he says. 'Please, choose one of these magical artefacts as a reward for your bravery.'

You may choose one of the following:

All-weather hat	Rain-soaked robe	Weather ring
(head)	(chest)	(ring)
+1 speed	+1 magic +1 armour	Ability: lightning

Thanking the wizard, you leave the tower and resume your journey. (Return to the map to begin a new quest.)

244

The moment you touch the stone there is a bright flash of light, followed by a dizzying sensation of movement. When the light fades, you find yourself on a narrow rock bridge, spanning a cloud-filled gorge. Warily, you advance along it, trying to ignore the vertiginous drop to either side.

You halt when you see a man approaching you from the opposite direction. All but his eyes are hidden behind swathes of blue cloth, that swirl and dance in the wind.

'You trespass in the halls of ancient kings,' booms a deep voice, from somewhere above you. 'Many have come here. All have failed. Fight my champions and prove your worth.'

The man shows no signs of stopping. In a blur of motion, he draws two steel blades from his belt and leaps into combat:

	Speed	Brawn	Armour	Health
Talos of air	4	4	2	20

Special abilities
- Wind-dancer: Talos moves like the wind. You cannot use any potions or special abilities during this combat.

If you are defeated, you find yourself back on the hilltop, turn to 153. If you defeat Talos, his body turns to dust. All that is left is a stone rune with the mark of a crescent moon on it. If you take the *Rune of Talos*, make a note of it on your hero sheet. There is a sudden flash of light and you find yourself back on the hilltop. Turn to 153.

245

'Rumours eh?' The barman spits into his cloth, then proceeds to rub the counter with it. 'Well, latest news I 'eard is that a giant is causing problems along the eastern pass. Cut off the only trade route to Kimsbrook. Yer can imagine some of the locals ain't happy with that.' He nods towards the elderly farmers seated at the bar. 'Unless the locals can get their produce to market, not much to be made.' He shakes his head. 'Tough times, I think yer'll agree.'

Will you:

Ask the barman about Avian Dale?	53
Talk about the weather?	42
Turn your attention back to the taproom?	11

246

You retrace your steps through the caves and tunnels, stopping to retrieve the body of the priest's son. Using a blanket from your pack, you carefully wrap the body and then lift it onto your shoulders. The water-logged mud squelches underfoot as you trudge back to the well shaft. After clambering into the bucket, you tug firmly on the rope several times. A moment later, it begins to rise, taking you back up the shaft towards the circle of daylight above. Turn to 2.

247

The ruffian lies dead at your feet. You reach down and cut the man's purse from his belt. Inside you find 15 gold crowns. You many also take:

Rennie's slicer
(left hand: dagger)
+1 speed +1 brawn
Ability: first cut

You may now:

Search the rest of the room   251

Leave the farm   Return to the map

248

Your footfalls echo as you pass along the wide tunnel, the glow of the torchlight illuminating more puddles of the white acidic goo. As the tunnel begins to angle downwards, taking you deeper into the earth, you begin to make out a slimy, squelching sound coming from the darkness to your right. You swing round – your torch revealing a narrower side-tunnel heading south.

Will you:

Investigate the side passage?   262

Continue along the main passage?   232

249

'My name is Fetch,' says the man, bowing his head to you in greeting. 'My master, a man of some influence in the affairs of Tithebury, is seeking an item of significant worth.' He raises a pale hand and gestures towards the dark church on the hill. 'Do you know the legend of this place? The reason the locals will no longer set foot on the hill?' You clear your throat, intending to answer, but the man carries on regardless. 'It's the black book. The Grimoire of Naraghost.' The man's voice trembles slightly at the mention of the name. Turn to 290.

250

You have chosen the path of the rogue. You may permanently raise your *health* by 5 (to 35). Make a note of this change on your hero sheet.

After an hour of sparring with Avian, you are relieved when he finally lowers his sword and steps away. 'Impressive,' he says, nodding his head. 'You are fast and agile. Perhaps there is something special in you after all. Come,' he starts towards a pair of double doors at the end of the room. 'You must be famished after your journey. I think a little banquet is in order, to welcome you to your new home.' Turn to 172.

251

You pull the mattress away from the window, allowing fresh air and sunlight to spill into the dark, stuffy room. As the shadows recede, the true extent of your squalid surroundings are revealed. Every inch of floor space is covered in rat droppings and refuse. Rotted food and bones lie next to mouldy rags and splintered, broken furniture. How the ruffians could have lived in such conditions you have no idea. Eager to now depart, you speedily rummage through the debris for any items of interest. You may now take any/all of the following:

Traveller's band	**Traveller's cloak**
(ring)	(cloak)
+1 brawn +1 magic	+1 brawn +1 magic
Ability: charm	Ability: charm

Return to the map to continue your journey.

252

You toss and turn in your sleep, tormented by dreams of darkness and shadow. Each one is the same – you are running from a nameless terror that hunts you across a plain of featureless black sand. You never see what it is, but you feel it, constantly at your back.

You trip and fall, your arm throbbing painfully. With trembling fingers, you pull back your sleeve to reveal the mark. It is burning as if newly branded, giving off a sulphurous smoke that forces you to turn away, choking. Then you see it – your hunter – a hooded giant with demon-like wings. Its features are indistinct, but you can see its eyes … a pair of bright crimson orbs that smoulder with an ancient evil.

'You will obey me,' booms a deep, thunderous voice.

In a flash, you find yourself awake, sitting up in bed with your eyes wide open. 'Obey me,' booms the voice once again. Your legs slide off the bed, your body twitching and jerking into a standing position. Like a macabre puppet, you begin to move across the room, your actions no longer your own. Furiously, you try and wake from this peculiar nightmare, but you can only watch, like a trapped prisoner inside your own body, as you are forced to descend the stairs into Avian's castle. Turn to 224.

253

Moonlight streams through the arched, glass windows, illuminating the wooden pews that line the nave. You move slowly down the aisle, your eyes flitting from one deep shadow to the next.

You are almost at the pulpit when a gargling, guttural cry forces you to turn. Bounding along the tops of the pews is a ragged, bony creature with a hairy, wolf-like face. It springs towards you at unnatural speed, using its spindly arms and legs to propel itself forward. As the creature leaps down into the aisle-way, its sharp claws throw up sparks as they rake against the stone. With no chance of evading this fast foe, you must fight:

	Speed	Brawn	Armour	Health
Ghoul	5	2	2	25

Special abilities
◗ Piercing claws: The ghoul's attacks ignore *armour*.

If you defeat this fearsome opponent, turn to 264.

254

The tunnel broadens out into a small cavern. You examine the rough-hewn walls but find no other side passages. In the middle of the cavern there is a bowl-shaped dip and, at its centre, a pool of dark water. Walking over, you see that the pool is in fact a flooded tunnel, heading deeper into the earth. You try to see what may be down there, but the water is murky and dark.

Will you:

Dive into the flooded tunnel shaft?	218
Return to the first junction and go west?	103

255

You push open the door of the cottage, to find Beatrice sprawled on the floor, gasping for breath. She is clutching at her throat with both hands, her once rosy-cheeks now a deathly shade of white.

'Oh what have I done?' cries Martha. 'This is terrible. We have to help her!'

You start towards the flailing woman, but draw back when you see the body start to shake and convulse.

'We're too late!' gasps Martha, backing up towards the door. 'It's the witch's magic. It'll do to her what it did to those turnips!'

All of a sudden, Beatrice Fletcher begins to expand, growing outwards like a giant balloon. Gnarly roots burst from the ends of her fingers and toes, followed by a flurry of green shoots growing out of her mouth and ears, to slowly form a tangle of leaves.

'She's ... she's turning into a ... no, it just can't be!' Martha is staring at the growing monster in horror. 'She's becoming a turnip!'

As you continue to watch, the old woman grows bigger and bigger, her root-like legs and arms shrinking into her bulging, round body. Seconds later and there is nothing that remains of Beatrice Fletcher ... only an enormous turnip resting on the floor of her living room.

You walk over and warily prod the turnip with your foot, fearing it might be another of those strange creatures that attacked you in Martha's garden. But this turnip appears ordinary. Turn to 38.

256

You have chosen the path of the mage. You may permanently raise your *health* by 10 (to 40). Make a note of this change on your hero sheet.

After an hour of sparring with Avian, you are relieved when he finally lowers his sword and backs away. 'Impressive,' he says, nodding his head. 'A practitioner of the magic arts, I see. You remind me of myself at your age. Perhaps there's something special in you after all. Come,' he starts towards a pair of double doors at the end of the room. 'You must be famished after your journey. I think a little banquet is in order, to welcome you to your new home.' Turn to 172.

257

'There have been some changes in these parts of late,' says the man. 'You could say that it has created some opportunities for those with the ... right ambitions.' He cackles to himself – a dry, heartless sound that makes you shiver. 'My name is Fetch. A collector, nothing more; someone fascinated in the relics of a bygone age.' He turns and points to the church, its angular features silhouetted against the full moon. 'There is something there that I desire. Something that I desire greatly.' Turn to 290.

258

You slice open the maggot's belly, moving quickly out of the way as a wave of gooey acid pours out of the squirming body. After a final, trembling spasm, the wurm lies still, its acid steaming and sizzling in the sudden silence. As you retrieve your torch, you notice several objects resting in the puddles of acid. The maggot obviously found the objects and ate them, but miraculously its acid has not harmed them ... too much.

You may take one of the following items before the fumes of the acid force you to retreat:

Half-digested gauntlets	Acid-coated battleaxe
(gloves)	(main hand: axe)
+1 brawn +1 armour	+1 speed +1 brawn
Ability: acid	Ability: acid

You return to the main passage and continue deeper into the tunnel network. Turn to 232.

259

You have a bad hand of cards and immediately lose the round. The gambler takes all the money, chuckling to himself. 'Another game?' he asks eagerly. If you would like to play again turn to 54, if you decide to leave the table turn to 11.

260

The goblin chief slumps to the ground dead. On seeing their leader defeated, the other goblins, both wounded from the fight, turn and flee into the woods. Manni turns and offers you a nod of approval. 'You handle yourself well. It was an honour to fight by your side.'

You search the goblin and find 5 gold crowns. You may also take any / all of the following rewards:

Meat cleaver	Chieftain's furs	Rat-skin boots
(main hand: sword)	(cloak)	(feet)
+1 brawn	+1 armour	+1 speed
Ability: bleed		

After the bodies have been disposed of, you both settle down to a hot meal of rabbit stew. As you are just tucking into your second helping, the crunch of approaching feet makes you both look up in surprise. It is the woodsman's daughter. She steps into the circle of light cast by the campfire, her shawl and clothes caked in mud. Manni immediately hops to his feet, and runs over to the girl.

'Liselle, dear Liselle. What happened to you?'

The girl starts sobbing. When at last, she can speak, she confesses to Manni about her plan to make a love potion, but her efforts to find the last ingredient proved in vain. Manni takes her aside to talk. When he finally returns to the campfire, he offers you a knowing smile.

'She will be OK. A little heartbroken perhaps – but she will survive. A tough one, that girl.' He reaches into his jerkin and pulls out a locket. 'This was given to me by my sweetheart, to always remember her wherever I roam. When I am done, I will return to her. I showed it to Liselle. I think she understands now.' He slides the locket back under his jerkin. 'Let us sleep, and tomorrow I will return to the woodsman and explain everything that has happened.'

The next morning, when you awake, you discover that Liselle and Manni have already left for the woodsman's hut. You help yourself to some porridge that Manni has left for you, then rejoin the trail. Return to the map to begin a new quest.

261

You wrap the hot pie in a blanket and tuck it into your backpack. Then you head back down the hill to Beatrice Fletcher's cottage. As Martha predicted, you find a freshly-baked pie resting on one of the windowsills.

You push open the garden gate and carefully creep up to the window. After a last check to make sure no one is watching, you remove your backpack and take out Martha's pie. Both are of similar size and colour – you doubt the old woman will notice much of a difference. Quickly, you switch the pies, placing the turnip pie on the windowsill.

Will you now:

Hide in the garden and wait?	229
Return to Martha?	9

262

You make your way carefully down the side passage, avoiding the puddles and dripping strands of gooey acid. You haven't gone far, before your torch illuminates the source of the squelching sound. A giant white maggot is chewing through the dirt and earth at the end of the passageway.

The creature must have sensed you, because it suddenly shuffles round, its bloated body rippling as it moves. Although appearing blind, the giant maggot clearly knows you are there – its wide maw opening to reveal serrated teeth, dripping with acid.

You put aside your torch and prepare to defend yourself:

	Speed	Brawn	Armour	Health
Burrower wurm	4	4	3	20

Special abilities

🗡 Acid: The burrower's mouth drips with a deadly, corrosive acid. Roll a die at the start of each combat round. If you roll a ⚀ or a ⚁ you automatically take 2 damage from the acid. This ability ignores *armour*.

If you defeat the burrower wurm, turn to 258.

263

You find yourself standing at the edge of a walled courtyard, lined with trees and flowers. Beyond the walls you can see a skyline of towers and minarets, soaring up into the dark, smoky skies. The man walks towards you, his grey robes rustling around his thin frame. You try to get a glimpse of his face, but it is hidden deep within the shadows of his gold-embroidered cowl.

'Give me the last piece,' he orders. It is the same deep voice that you heard in your dream.

You hold out the stone fragment without question. The man takes it and carefully slides it into a cloth bag hanging at his waist. Then he raises his hands, palms turned outwards. He makes a quick gesture – and suddenly you feel yourself being tugged backwards.

You find yourself back in the stone chamber. The archway continues to glow for several seconds, then the light flickers and is gone. You are left, standing alone, in a deep, impenetrable gloom. Turn to 299.

264

The ghoul's broken body flies back through the air, crashing into the nearest pew. It slumps to the cold stone floor, black blood oozing from its gaping mouth. You are about to breathe a sigh of relief, when you hear more guttural cries coming from the far end of the nave. Three more ghouls are slipping and bounding across the stones towards you, racing on all fours like hungry dogs.

Frantically, you scan your surroundings, looking for some kind of advantage. Behind you is the stone pulpit, and beyond that a painted screen that divides the chancel from a small room beyond. To your left you see an archway and a set of stairs leading up into darkness, and to your right you see a stone font, carved with the figures of angels.

Will you:

Investigate the room behind the painted screen?	187
Make for the stairs?	138
Run over to the stone font?	274

265

'Wise choice,' grins the boy, spitting into the palm of his hand and then offering it out in friendship. 'My name is Afty. A pleasure to make yer acquaintance.' After exchanging a hasty handshake, you both start towards the town.

The boy takes the lead, guiding you along the rickety walkways and swaying rope-bridges that connect the buildings. 'Bet yer wondering why this place even exists, yeah?' says Afty, looking back at you with a smile. 'Rubies and emeralds, big as yer hand. That's why.' He jerks a thumb in the direction of the marsh. 'Prospectors came 'ere long time ago. They discovered the waters of the swamp have all kinds of goodies. There's jewels to be sure, but there's also gold to be found – not to mention all those smelly weeds and other shrivelled up things that grow out in the swamp. Mages pay high prices for those back in the cities.'

The boy stops abruptly, and points to a large wooden amphitheatre on the edge of the town. Lanterns hang along its walls, illuminating the queues of people waiting outside its doors. 'That's the pit,' says Afty. 'It's what passes for good wholesome entertainment out here. Dangerous sport, the pit – but many fortunes been made in that place, if yer bet on the right fighter.'

He tugs your arm. 'Come on, I wanna show yer the warrens.' You follow Afty along another series of walkways, until you come to a shabbier end of town. Most of the buildings here have subsided into the marsh and many of the bridges look frayed and rotting. Nevertheless, it is still thronging with people – many of whom are eyeing the exotic wares of the street vendors, lined up along the dark, dingy lanes.

'The king ain't bothered about this place,' says Afty, pushing through the crowds. 'That's why you get smugglers and criminals, and all sorts coming 'ere. No king's troops would wanna risk making trouble – even those inquisitors know to keep their holy noses out of swamp business, know what I mean?'

He stops and turns, knocking into you. 'Ah, sorry mister. Clumsy of me.' He steps back, and to your surprise you see that he is holding your money pouch. 'Ah, this yours?' The boy shrugs his shoulders. 'Payment for the tour, eh? Well, thanking yer very much. Now, must be off!'

Before you can grab him, the boy races off through the crowded market – carrying all of your gold (deduct your gold from your hero sheet, but keep a record of how much you were carrying).

Will you:

Attempt to give chase?	278
Return to the main part of town?	348

266

You attempt to cross to the other side of the cave by stepping care-fully between the sticky strands of webbing. You must pass a *speed* challenge:

	Speed
Webbed cave	10

If you are successful, you cross the cave without incident and enter the new passageway, turn to 231. If you fail turn to 239.

267

'Ah, a shame. A terrible shame,' sighs the man. He fishes in one of his pockets and pulls out a business card. 'Look, if you change your mind then call back here any time. Show that card and someone will point you in the right direction to find me.' (Make a note of the number 286 on your hero sheet. If you wish to return to the gladiatorial pit and take up Bart's offer, then turn to that entry number when you are ready.)

Thanking Bart, you watch the rest of the show and then leave. Turn to 348.

268

You tell Lady Roe that you are searching for a man named Jenlar Cornelius. She puts a finger to her chin, her thin brows creasing together.

'Hmm, I am not familiar with the name. But I'm sure Papa would know.' Her eyes flash with a sudden excitement. 'Oh please come with me. You can meet him and I'm sure he will be more than happy to tell you everything he knows.'

The rain has grown stronger, soaking through your clothes and causing you to shiver. A night in a warm castle has started to sound very appealing. Turn to 284.

You push through the crowds, looking around frantically for the thief. Then you catch sight of him, hurrying down a narrow side-street. As you start towards it, a group of street children run out in front of you, begging for some food. You try and push past them, but whichever way you turn, their eager faces appear again – distracting you from the escaping child.

Realising that you have now lost the thief, you angrily jostle your way free of the orphans and head back to the centre of the town. Turn to 348.

270

The smoke and heat from the fire forces you back out of the cavern. With the giant spider defeated, you decide to leave the caves and return to the villagers at the well. Turn to 246.

271

You reach into your backpack and pull out the plain black book. The hooded man snatches it from your grasp the moment it is revealed. Giggling with insane glee he flicks through the pages.

'Oh yes, this is it! This is it!' He snaps it shut and slips it inside his robes. 'You have done well. We have both done well. Now, a reward for your bravery.'

Fetch unhooks the leather case from his belt and breaks the waxed seals that hold it closed. Lifting up the cover, he reveals its contents – two elegant-looking daggers, resting on a red velvet cushion. One is black and glows with a soft greenish light, the other is silver, its hilt inlaid with sparkling garnets and rubies.

You may take one of the following:

	Dirk of deceit	Silver silence
	(main hand: dagger)	(main hand: dagger)
	+1 speed +1 brawn	+1 speed +1 magic
	Ability: corruption	Ability: immobilise

If you do not wish to take either of these items, Fetch offers you a purse of gold instead, containing 20 gold crowns. After you have made your choice, Fetch closes the case, turns on his heel and silently walks away down the lane. Within moments, the dark hooded figure has vanished, becoming one with the shadows. Make a note of the words *black book* on your hero sheet. Then return to the map to choose another quest.

272

The markings on the stone table glow with a soft, blue light. Then suddenly, the two triangular panels lift open, accompanied by the whirr and click of hidden gears. Moments later and you are peering into a velvet-lined cavity, filled with sparkling treasure. Well done, you have solved the puzzle and opened the chest! Turn to 522.

273

At the end of the tunnel is a giant maggot, its bloated body almost filling the passageway. The creature appears to be chomping its way through the earth, using the acid that drips from its gaping maw to burn through the rock and stone.

As you approach, the maggot suddenly stops its activity and turns round to face you. With a series of squelching noises, the eyeless creature starts to wriggle and squirm in your direction, its wide mouth hanging open to reveal row upon row of diamond-sharp teeth. Quickly, you prepare to defend yourself:

	Speed	Brawn	Armour	Health
Burrower wurm	4	4	3	20

Special abilities

 Acid: The burrower's mouth drips with a deadly, corrosive acid. Roll a die at the start of each combat round. If you roll a $\boxed{\cdot}$ or a $\boxed{\cdot\cdot}$ you automatically take 2 damage from the acid. This ability ignores *armour*.

If you defeat the burrower wurm, turn to 285.

274

To your surprise, you find that the font bowl is still full of water – holy water. Perhaps it might help you in your fight against the ghouls. Quickly, you dip your weapons into the sparkling liquid. As the snarling undead bound towards you, you prepare to defend yourself from all three of these powerful foes. This will be a tough battle – but the holy water may tip the balance.

	Speed	Brawn	Armour	Health
Ghouls	5	3	2	30

Special abilities

 Piercing claws: The ghouls' attacks ignore *armour*.

 Holy water: You may add 2 to your damage score in this combat.

If you manage to defeat these three deadly adversaries, turn to 106.

You hurry back to your room and quickly gather your belongings. Before you leave, you take the white key that Avian gave you, and use it to unlock the small chest at the foot of the bed. Inside you find a pouch containing 40 gold crowns and the following items:

Gourd of healing (1 use)	Avian's crest	Gourd of speed (1 use)
(backpack)	(talisman)	(backpack)
Use any time in combat to restore 6 *health*	+1 brawn +1 magic Ability: charm	Use any time in combat to raise your *speed* by 4 for one combat round

With your final preparations complete, you leave the castle, taking a narrow pass through the mountains to emerge in the dark, tangled forest known as Mistwood.

Turn to the Act 2 map to continue your adventure.

276

Lady Roe looks mildly surprised. 'The traveller people? I ... well I believe Papa moved them on. These are his lands you see, extending all the way to that horrid, smelly swamp. He caught them hunting wolves – and Papa so loves the wolves of the forest.'

You shiver as the cold rain begins to soak through your clothes. Lady Roe pats the seat next to her. 'Come on, join me. We will be at Papa's castle in just a few minutes and then you can warm yourself by a nice fire. I promise you, you will find Castle Crookhollow more hospitable than anything the traveller people have to offer.'

As the cold, grey rain continues to fall, the idea of spending a night in a warm castle suddenly sounds very appealing. Turn to 284.

277

There is thunderous applause from the stalls. You may now take one of the following as your victory spoils:

Left hook	Tri-horned hat	Buccaneer's rapier
(left hand: fist weapon)	(head)	(main hand: sword)
+1 speed +2 brawn	+1 magic +2 armour	+1 speed +1 brawn
Ability: immobilise	Ability: charm	Ability: riposte

'Whoop! What a fight!' booms the announcer, as he swoops over the arena floor. 'Let's hear it again for our new rookie!'

The crowd roar their approval once again, as you head back into the side-tunnel. Bart and his ogre, Knuckles, are waiting for you. The thin man is hopping up and down in excitement, waving a pouch of money in the air.

'Oh, listen to that sweet jingle-jangle! Music to my ears!' He opens the pouch and spills some of the gold into your hands. 'A splendid performance and there'll be plenty more where that came from. Of that, I am sure.' (You have gained 30 gold crowns.) Turn to 367.

278

The boy is small and fast, weaving expertly between the tight crowds of shoppers. To catch up with him you will have to take a *speed* challenge.

	Speed
Town chase	10

If you are successful, turn to 354. Otherwise, turn to 269.

You search through the drawers, but find little of interest, except for some sheets of blank parchment and two pots of black ink. One item does catch your eye, however. It is an envelope addressed to a Lord Wellsbourne. The seal has already been broken.

You open the envelope and pull out the note. It reads:

My dear Wells,

I hope this letter finds you in good health after your long journey. It pains me to bring you sour news, especially as we both know the significance of the count's interest in the welfare of our estate. I urged you to attend the ball to further our relations with the count, however, in giving you this counsel I fear I may have put you in grave danger.

There is a talk of a wytchfinder in Mistwood. Reports say that he is one of the best, a confessor who answers only to the king. I urge you to be on your guard. There is no knowing when and how he might strike. Keep a guard with you at all times. Two or three if you can – we know what wytchfinders are capable of.

If we are clever, the king's meddling could work in our favour. If the count is removed from play, then Baron Greylock would be the rightful heir to Castle Crookhollow. Yes, my beloved – we both know he has shown a keen interest in our fair Gwendolyn. His rise to power would be a most advantageous situation ... for the both of us.

Feed well my darling and raise your glass high, a toast to the wealth and power that will soon be ours.

Your true love, J.

The note makes little sense to you; it sounds like the typical plotting and back-stabbing that is commonplace amongst the nobles. However, the mention of the witchfinder piques your interest. Perhaps he is already in the castle – and if so, that might make him a valuable ally.

Will you:
Examine the sleeping man (if you haven't already)?   291
Leave the room?   349

280

'What!' shrieks Fetch, when you tell him the news. 'You disobeyed me! Now you will pay for your foolish mistake!' The hooded man draws a knife from his robes and lunges at you. You must now fight:

	Speed	Brawn	Armour	Health
Fetch	5	4	3	35

Special abilities

🥄 Dark disciple: All your hero's rolls of ⚁ automatically become a ⚀ when fighting this sinister foe.

If you defeat Fetch, turn to 76.

281

You grab the nearest harness and saddle, and then enter one of the stalls. Inside, a chestnut mare is frantically struggling against its tether. The beast's nostrils are flared, its bulging eyes rolling nervously in their sockets. The raging storm has clearly panicked the beast.

A rumble of thunder shakes the stable walls. Rearing up onto its hind legs, the horse breaks loose, dragging its hitching post from out of the ground. You try and dodge out of the way of the frightened animal but you are struck by one of its flailing hooves.

Everything fades to black as you slump to the straw-covered floor, blood trickling down your face. In the distance you can hear gun shots … then you lose all consciousness. Turn to 424.

282

'Whoa, mister! You don't waste any time, do yer?' The boy removes his cap and scratches his scruffy, blond hair. 'Well, information like that is gonna cost yer.' He holds out his cap and gives you a cheeky grin. 'Five gold ones, and I'll tell yer all I know.'

Will you:

Pay the 5 gold crowns?	303
Decline, but agree to take the tour instead?	265
Leave the boy and enter the town?	348

283

The giant mud golem collapses, splattering you in a shower of rank-smelling sludge. After wiping the thick gloop from your face, you wade through the mud to the objects that you spied earlier. You may now take any/all of the following:

Ashen staff	Champion's blade	Mottled cloak
(main hand: staff)	(left hand: sword)	(cloak)
+1 speed +2 magic	+2 speed +1 brawn	+1 speed +1 armour
(requirement: mage)	Ability: bleed	

After you have made your choices, you clamber out of the mud pool and leave the cave, taking the passageway north. Turn to 361.

284

The moment you step inside the cabin, the driver cracks his whip and the carriage lurches into motion. You find yourself falling into the seat next to Lady Roe, who smiles at you as she pulls the door closed. It may have just been a trick of the light, but you were almost sure you saw fang-like incisors protruding from her gums.

Another lurch forces you to grab hold of your seat. Looking out of the window, you see the forest whipping by in a dark blur, its twisted branches illuminated by the staccato flashes of lightning.

The carriage sweeps round the base of a hill, taking a narrower path through the forest. You are soon hemmed in all sides by the trees, their branches and twigs scratching at the windows.

At last the trees start to thin, as the land rises abruptly towards a set of jagged peaks. And there, standing in isolation on the edge of a black pinnacle of rock, is a castle. It is fashioned from the same black stone as the surrounding mountains, its spindly towers looking like dark fingers clawing at the sky. There is nothing about the place that looks warm or inviting.

'Do you like it?' asks Lady Roe eagerly, her pale features momentarily lit by a flash of lightning.

You force a nervous smile as the coach rattles across a narrow bridge and passes into a cobbled courtyard, shrouded in a pale mist. Turn to 387.

285

You slice open the maggot's belly, backing away as green slime and white acid pour out of its body onto the floor of the tunnel. Eager to escape the noxious fumes, you retrace your steps and retrieve your torch. It is then that you notice a jagged fissure in one of the tunnel walls. Curious as to where it might lead, you decide to explore it further. Turn to 212.

286

Bart slaps you on the back. 'Splendid! Splendid! Follow me, no time like the present, eh?' You are ushered down a set of stairs and through a door into a small, stuffy backroom. Here, various fighters are kitting themselves out with weapons and armour.

Bart leads you through the room and into a tunnel. 'No need for those rusty old hand-me-downs,' he says, nodding back towards the equipment room. 'Now, put on a good show and give the audience what they want – blood, and lots of it! Preferably not your own, of course.'

After another slap on the back, Bart turns and hurries away. 'Oh I'll make a killing on this one,' he chuckles, rubbing his hands together in glee.

You step up to the portcullis – the only thing standing between you and the blood-thirsty roar coming from the pit. Peering through the grill, you see one of the previous combatants being stretchered off to a side door, to the accompaniment of angry boos and jeers. Several tense minutes later and the announcer's voice booms into life once again:

'Ladies and gentlemen – we have a last minute addition to our ranks. A new combatant from the ... from the ... well, they are so mysterious we don't know where they are from. But please put your hands together as we welcome our new challenger!'

The portcullis clatters open and you step out into the pit, your ears ringing with the deafening applause from the eager spectators.

It is time to face your first opponent. Turn to 320.

287

You chop the centipede down to size, each blow sending plumes of green gas billowing out into the cave. Finally, the creature lies dead in a smouldering pile of legs and body parts.

Heading deeper into the mushroom forest, you come across the body of a dead adventurer. It looks as though he tried eating one of the mushrooms and it poisoned him, as several chunks of the strange fungi lie next to his outstretched fingers. You search the body and find 20 gold crowns. You may also take any/all of the following items:

Deerskin boots	Shiny dirk	Skull cap
(feet)	(main hand: dagger)	(head)
+1 speed +1 brawn	+1 speed +2 brawn	+1 speed +1 armour

Determined not to share the same fate, you decide to keep your distance from the strange mushrooms. You quickly cross to the other side of the cave, where you take another tunnel heading north. Turn to 361.

288

The coach driver smirks. 'Look, it's the count's orders. He don't like his guests bringing weapons into the castle. All them dukes and nobles

... they each got their petty differences. Would be a blood bath if we let 'em all in one room with weapons to hand.' He nods to his open palms. 'So, come on, stranger. We don't want any trouble now, do we?'

Will you:

Hand over your weapons?	294
Explain that you are no feuding duke?	332
Try and leave the castle?	345

289

Martha shakes her head in bewilderment. 'They ... they just came alive? I always suspected they were magic ... but I never expected this.' She glances down at the squirming babies in her arms. 'Those turnips were to feed my family. Just think if we had tried to eat them. It's too horrible to consider!'

Will you:

Confess to the truth?	211
Leave the hillside and return to Beatrice?	58

290

The hooded man recounts a legend: 'Two hundred years ago, a crusader came to Tithebury Cross. He had a disease – a terrible affliction; some records say it was the plague. In his fever, he spoke of a book that he was protecting. The village priest did what he could, but the crusader could not be saved. He passed away ... but not before he implored the priest to obey his final, dying wish: to bury him in the old catacombs beneath the church, with all of his belongings. And so the wish was granted.'

Fetch walks over to the rusted gate, placing his pale hands against the iron bars. 'It was many years before the bad things started to happen. The noises, the whispering ... the dead walking. The land itself had become corrupted.' He turns to look at you, eyes glinting from beneath the hood. 'The locals keep this place under lock and key. They fear what lurks in the catacombs beneath their church. The priest put a spell of warding on its door, not to keep the villagers away, but to keep what was inside from getting out. That is where I need you to go. That is where you will find the book!'

Will you:

Ask why he can't get the book himself?	69
Ask about a reward?	57

291

You walk over and shake the sleeping man. To your surprise, you discover that he is dead. Blood has congealed on one side of his head, where an ugly gash is visible through his lank, wet hair. You guess that someone was hoping to knock him unconscious, but did a better job of it than they were probably intending. You search the body for some signs of who the traveller might have been. Sadly, there is nothing much of interest – just a purse containing 10 gold crowns and the following items:

Wayfarer's ring	**Silver cross**
(ring)	(necklace)
+1 brawn +1 armour	+1 speed +1 magic
Ability: charm	Ability: heal

As the traveller no longer has any use for these items, you may take them if you wish. After you have made your choices, you turn back to view your surroundings.

Will you:

Search the desk (if you haven't already)?	279
Leave the room?	349

292

'My name is Woad,' says the tree. 'For fifteen centuries I have been a guardian of this forest, protecting it from those who would bring ill to this land. Once, there was many of us – brothers and sisters of the wood – sworn to guard these borders and keep the land safe. Now there is only me.'

The tree gives a heavy, rumbling sigh. 'They are all dead now. Their spirits have flown, leaving bark and branch to wither away. That will be my fate also. My magic wanes and I have not the strength to battle this blight for much longer.'

Will you:

Ask what happened to the other trees?	325
Put the tree out of its misery and attack?	331
Offer to help the tree?	344

293

You enter the arena to face your third opponent. 'Ladies and gentlemen,' booms the announcer. 'It's time to welcome the pride of the western plains – the one and only, Nalsa the black lion!'

As the portcullis clatters open, you hear a thunderous roar from within the tunnel. You ready your weapons as the black lion steps out into the arena. It is huge, at least a head taller than yourself, with a thick mane that hangs down over its thickly-muscled shoulders and fore-legs. The beast twists its head, snarling at the jeering crowds. Then, with a roar, the lion bounds towards you, covering the distance in a matter of seconds. You must now fight for your life!

	Speed	Brawn	Armour	Health
Nalsa	11	10	6	50

Special abilities

♥ Mighty roar: If Nalsa wins two consecutive combat rounds and causes health damage in both rounds, at the start of the third round he issues his mighty roar. This increases his *speed* and *brawn* by 4 for the rest of the combat. Nalsa can only use this ability once.

If you manage to defeat the black lion, turn to 379.

294

You grudgingly hand over your weapons. (You must remove your main-hand and left-hand items from your hero sheet and make the necessary adjustments to your attributes. Keep a note of these, as they may be returned to you at a later date.)

The coach driver grins. 'Why, you are the obedient little cub, ain't yer.' He kicks open the lid of a chest and tosses the items inside, with little regard for their worth or well being. 'There. They'll still be waiting for yer if ...' He stops mid-sentence to clear his throat. 'Sorry, when you leave.' The smirk that settles across his face does little to put you at ease.

'Oi, this way,' calls the guard. He opens the door and gestures to the passageway beyond. 'Head down there and take the first door on yer left. Understand?'

You glower angrily at the two men. This was hardly the warm welcome you had been expecting. 'Thank you for your ... generosity, gentlemen.' You give them both a steely glare, before entering the passageway. Turn to 317.

295

You step over the strands of webbing and approach the wriggling bundle. Taking a knife from your backpack, you carefully slice through the silken cords to reveal the inside of the web-like cage. Tangled up in the sticky strands is something large and furry ... with pointed ears and sharp teeth!

Backing away, you watch as the creature struggles free of the webbing. It lands on the ground, shaking its black leathery wings. Then its blood-shot eyes fix on you ... With a deafening screech, the freed creature springs into the air, its fangs reaching for your throat:

	Speed	Brawn	Armour	Health
Batwing	5	4	2	25

Special abilities

 Bleed: After the batwing makes a successful attack that causes health damage, you must take a further point of damage at the end of each combat round. This damage ignores *armour*.

If you defeat the batwing, turn to 120.

296

The painted screen depicts a row of brown-robed monks, kneeling in prayer beneath a bright star. Pushing it aside, you enter the small stone chamber beyond. It is semi-circular, with a black door in the middle of the facing wall. Strange glyphs have been carved into the wood, glowing with a faint, white light.

This must be the door that Fetch spoke of – the one that has been warded to keep the undead from escaping the catacombs. You rummage in your backpack and pull out the scroll of opening. Turn to 197.

297

The giant ghoul lies dead at your feet. You may now help yourself to one of the following special rewards:

Iron-mane	Silverghast	Gorgis grip
(cloak)	(main hand: dagger)	(left hand: fist weapon)
+2 speed +3 armour	+2 speed +4 magic	+2 speed +4 brawn
Ability: second skin	Ability: quicksilver	Ability: rake

When you have made your decision, turn to 879.

Warily, you step through the doorway. If you have the word *leader* written on your hero sheet, turn to 220. Otherwise turn to 201.

You are roughly shaken awake. Opening your eyes, you discover Avian leaning over you. 'What happened?' he asks tensely. 'How did you get here?'

Still groggy with sleep, you allow yourself to be helped into a sitting position. As your surroundings slowly come into focus, you discover that you are still inside the stone chamber. Only metres away is the stepped dais and the strange, magical archway.

'I said, what happened?' insists Avian, shaking you once again.

'I'm ... I'm not sure,' you reply, rubbing your aching head. 'I remember falling asleep and then I was ...'

Suddenly, the archway begins to glow. Avian looks over his shoulder, surprised. 'What is this? Someone communicating ...' He rises to his feet, as a scene slowly starts to form at its centre – a scene of chaos and destruction.

A grey-bearded man, encased in thick plate armour stands facing you. He looks panicked, as crowds of people race past screaming and calling for help. Behind them you can see towers and buildings on fire – the ground shaking as further explosions rip across the skyline.

'General Ravenwing,' gasps Avian. 'What is this? We're being attacked?'

'It's an invasion!' bellows the warrior, raising his shield as shards of rubble shower across the paved street. 'The shadow gate has been opened. The legion is coming through!'

Avian runs back and grabs you by the arm, yanking you to your feet. 'Come on. We need to see what has happened to the city. If Talanost falls I dread to think what will become of us.' He pushes you roughly through the archway ...

In the blink of an eye, you find yourself on the paved street. Behind you, an archway, identical to the one in the stone chamber, is glowing with a pale blue light. Avian steps out of it, a white staff now gripped in his hands.

You scan your surroundings, staring in wide-eyed horror at the extent of the devastation. The entire city is aflame – most of its once-proud buildings reduced to charred shells of rubble. And hovering above them, framed against the hellish purple skies, is a swarm of creatures, like floating eyeballs with tentacles. From these bulbous orbs, bolts of black fire tear through the remaining buildings, sending stone and rubble flying in all directions.

'Someone opened the shadow gate,' says Ravenwing, shouting to be heard over the chaos. 'We think it was one of the magic students at the school. They broke into the reliquary last night.'

'But that's impossible,' replies Avian furiously. 'They would have needed the keystone . . . NO!' He spins to face you. 'It can't have been! I was sure!'

You back away, momentarily startled.

'But you passed the final test.' Avian shakes his head in confusion. 'The magic food . . . it would have poisoned you. How? How did you betray me?'

'Wait!' you implore hastily. 'I was made to do it. By this!' You tug down your sleeve, revealing the branded mark.

'Judah's light!' growls Ravenwing, drawing his sword. 'Avian. What are you doing bringing *that* here?'

Before Avian can reply, there are cries of alarm from further down the street. A dishevelled mob of soldiers are spilling out of an alley-way, their armour battered and smoking. Behind them the buildings buckle and shake – and then topple to the ground, as a giant creature stomps through them, snarling with rage. It looks reptilian, with black scales that seem to shimmer in the purple half-light. In one hand it carries a mighty black mace and, in the other, a whip – its length rippling with black fire.

'This is only the start of it,' cries Avian, raising his staff. 'Ravenwing, we need to gather the mages from the school. We need to form a perimeter.'

The general nods. 'Can they hold against the might of these forces?'

'We don't have any choice,' Avian replies. 'We need to buy time for the king's army to get here.' He turns to face you, scowling in disgust. 'I don't know who you are or what you have done, but if you have any shred of honour left inside of you, you will do what I ask.'

You nod frantically, the ground trembling and shaking as the giant behemoth advances towards you.

'Listen to me!' snaps Avian, gripping your shoulder. 'Go back to the castle. I need you to find a man. His name is Cornelius, Jenlar Cornelius. If anyone knows how to defeat this foe it is him.'

Avian presses something into your hand. Looking down, you see that it is a white key. 'This unlocks the chest at the foot of your bed. Now, go! Cornelius is a hermit – he lives south of the castle, on the edge of Black Marsh. Find him and bring me the information!'

He pushes you into the glowing portal. A heartbeat later, you are back in the castle chamber. You turn and watch as the giant creature bears down on Avian and Ravenwing. The behemoth gives an eldritch screech, then belches black flame from its nostrils. Avian raises his staff – a white light bursting from the gem in its crook.

Then the portal flickers and vanishes. The scene is gone … and there is silence. Turn to 275.

300

As you go to leave, you notice something glimmering beneath the lake. You drop to your knees, brushing away the loose snow, to reveal a gold chest suspended within the ice. If you wish to try and break through the ice and retrieve the chest, turn to 644. Otherwise, return to the quest map to continue your journey.

301

You flick through the parchment. Most of the spidery writing is indecipherable, however, a hastily-scrawled drawing of the stone circle grabs your attention. Four words have been written next to it – *Malachi, Talos, Allura* and *Voldring*. Each name is ringed in red ink and a single word scribed underneath them. 'Dangerous.'

Will you:

Will you:	
Examine the book?	**115**
Turn your attention back to the stones?	**153**

302

You rush to attack Lady Roe, while Eldias moves to intercept the baron. The vampiress raises a blood-coated sickle, then gives a hellish ear-splitting screech as she flings herself at you:

	Speed	Magic	Armour	Health
Lady Roe	8	8	5	50

Special abilities

🩸 Blood harvest: Each time you take health damage from Lady Roe, the vampiress can automatically heal 2 *health*. This cannot take her above her starting *health* of 50.

🩸 Vampire: You can use your *stake* and *reflect* abilities (if you have them) against this opponent.

(Note: You cannot heal after this combat. You must continue this quest with the *health* that you have remaining. You may use potions and abilities to heal lost *health* while you are in combat.)

If you defeat Lady Roe turn to 455. If you lose the combat turn to 424.

303

You deposit the gold in the boy's cap. He scoops it into his grubby hands, then stuffs it into the pocket of his breeches.

'Well, who was it again?' he asks, screwing up his face. 'Ah yeah – Cornelius. Well I told yer I'd tell yer all I know, and it ain't much. The locals call 'im the marsh man cos he lives out in that 'orrible swamp, all on his own. They say he's a bit crazy – all that marsh gas gone to his 'ed – but he sees things.' The boy shivers, clutching his cap to his chest. 'He knows the future. All of it. Those that find 'im … they get their fortunes told. And it ain't always to their liking.'

You ask the boy if he knows the current whereabouts of the 'marsh man'. He shakes his head. 'Can't 'elp yer there, mister. I stick to the town, where I knows I can make a decent living.' He gives you a wink as he slaps his cap back onto his head. 'Now, you want this tour or what?'

Will you:
Agree to take the tour?   265
Politely decline and enter the town?   348

304

Exhausted from your trek across the swamp, you are relieved when the mists finally begin to recede – scattering at the head of a salty sea wind. Through the thinning haze, a dark mangrove of tall trees and straggly vegetation is now revealed.

As you get closer to the mangrove, the water becomes steadily deeper, until you are wading up to your waist through the stagnant murk. The stilt-like roots of the trees quickly form an infuriating maze, making your progress slow and tiring. Several times you are forced to sink beneath the water and swim, in order to navigate past the thicker, winding roots.

Eventually, you spy a solid island of reeds and grass. Several clumps of wrinkled, tubular plants are growing along its banks, capped with small black flowers. You assume that these are the black mandrake that Bern spoke of. Quickly, you clamber up onto the hilly mound and tug one of the plants free.

'I hope this was worth it,' you muse, as you place the plant, complete with its long trailing roots, into your pack. Hoisting the bundle back onto your shoulders, you gaze down at the cold, wet murk of the swamp, and release a heavy sigh. It will be a long and tiring journey back to the wreekin village.

Suddenly, you are jolted out of your thoughts as the ground shakes violently from side to side. Unable to keep your balance, you fall backwards into the swamp, surfacing just in time to see the hilly mound that you were standing on, rise up into the air. Beneath it, sand and water drain in rivulets across a huge face chiselled into stone; a face that is alive and contorted with rage.

As the water swells and froths around you, two enormous shoulders and then two vast limbs tear themselves free of the swamp. Frantically, you grab onto the nearest branch and cling on for dear life, while boulder-sized rocks and giant clots of earth rain down from the sky.

When you finally dare to open your eyes again, you gasp in fear and disbelief at what you see. A gargantuan monster towers above you, its black eyes gleaming beneath a jutting, forehead of stone. Your instincts are screaming at you to run, but snagged by weeds and buffeted by churning swamp water, you realise that your chances of escaping are slim. Resigned to your fate, you draw your weapons and valiantly prepare to defend yourself against this colossal foe. Turn to 486.

305
Quest: The withered glade

You make your way through the deep undergrowth of Mistwood, clambering over the thick roots and logs that litter the forest floor. Above you, giant trees, gnarled and withered with age, stretch their branches across the sky – blotting out the sunlight and plunging your surroundings into a perpetual, murky twilight.

As you head further westwards, you find yourself wading into a green-tinged fog. The air has become thick and stifling, carrying with it the odour of rot and decay. Within moments, you have lost all trace of the path that you were following. Instead, the ground underfoot has become wet and boggy, sucking at your feet as you struggle onwards through the swirling mist.

Soon, you are wandering out into a wide open clearing, the bleak space punctuated with the rotted remains of dead trees. Most are little more than stumps, others lean sullenly over the blighted, black earth as if begging the land to finally take them.

At the centre of the clearing, one tree still stands proud, seemingly unaffected by the blight that surrounds it. As you near, however, you realise that even this tree is fighting for its very survival. Much of its lower bark is rotted and black, and many of its winding roots are now dried and shrivelled husks, belching a foul green smoke into the air.

You are about to turn and leave this sorrowful scene, when you hear a rumbling groan coming from within the tree. As you take a step back, you suddenly realise that the trunk is actually a wizened old face – a knobbly stump gives the appearance of a nose, a shabby growth of lichen forms a drooping moustache, and above the tree's deep set eyes rests a splintered crown of wood.

'Go! Leave this place,' croaks the tree, its lichen moustache rustling up and down. 'The land is lost. My brothers and sisters are gone … all gone!'

Will you:

Introduce yourself and ask the tree its name?	292
Ask about what happened?	325
Put the tree out of its misery and attack?	331

306

You rush to attack Baron Greylock, while Eldias moves to intercept the vampiress. The burly warrior gives a blood-thirsty roar, then charges towards you, sweeping his mighty battleaxe through the air:

	Speed	Brawn	Armour	Health
Baron Greylock	8	8	5	60

Special abilities

♥ Vampire: You can use your *stake* and *reflect* abilities (if you have them) against this opponent.

(Note: You cannot heal after this combat. You must continue this quest with the *health* that you have remaining. You may use potions and abilities to heal lost *health* while you are in combat.)

If you defeat Baron Greylock turn to **385**. If you lose the combat turn to **424**.

Knuckles, as it turns out, was a former fighter in the arena, but was forced to retire after a few too many knocks to the head. Nevertheless, he hasn't forgotten everything he learned out in the pit, so he offers to show you some of his best moves.

As a gladiator you have the following abilities:

Blood rage (mo): If you win two consecutive combat rounds and cause health damage in both rounds, you automatically go into a blood rage. This increases your *brawn* by 2 for the remainder of the combat.

Head butt (co): Use this ability to prevent your opponent from rolling for damage. This automatically ends the combat round. You can only use *head butt* once per combat.

When you are ready for your next fight, turn to 293. If you wish to tackle your next opponent at a later date, then make a note of the entry number and return to the quest map.

308

The blacksmith is relieved when he sees you running over to help. One of his adversaries turns and launches itself at you, its spindly body flying through the air. This time you are ready for it, and dodge aside as the creature goes crashing into a table. The blacksmith quickly dispatches the other vampire, driving a stake into its heart.

'Take them to the stables,' shouts the blacksmith. He nods towards the family, who are standing by the wall, paralysed by their fear. 'It's through that archway and down the hall. Hurry!'

You are about to insist that he comes with you, but then you see another group of vampires racing towards you. The blacksmith heads them off, raising his crucifix. 'Go!' he shouts. 'I can handle these!'

As more screams echo throughout the hall, you hurry over to the panic-stricken family. The husband looks at you, his face drained of all colour. 'Wha ... what's happening?' he gasps.

You grab him by the shoulder and shake him. 'Come on! We're moving. All of you come on!' You push the man and his wife towards the archway, their young children clinging to their mother's dress. You follow them into the passageway. Turn to 429.

309

Lowering your weapons, you turn to face the silent crowd of children. They flinch away, eyeing you with a newfound fear and respect. Afty pushes to the front and, with a humble-looking smile, holds out your money pouch.

'He weren't much cop anyway,' he says, glancing down at the dead thief. 'Probably did the boss a favour; she wanted to stick 'im in the back for a long time.'

You take back your pouch and hook it back onto your belt (you may restore all your lost gold). As you turn to leave, the boy puts a hand out to stop you. 'Hey, wait up,' he says. 'With Fargin gone, guess there's a position vacant if yer want it. Could use an extra pair of hands, if yer know what I mean.'

If you are a rogue you can now learn the pickpocket career (turn to 369). Otherwise, you politely decline the offer and leave (turn to 348).

310

The dirt path takes you through cool, dark forest, eventually bringing you out into a sunlit clearing. A number of tents have been set up around its perimeter – one of which houses a crude-looking laboratory. From inside, there is a series of bangs and flashes, followed by the acrid smell of ammonia and rotten eggs. A bald-headed man in white robes is hurrying from one workbench to another, adding chemicals and ingredients to a row of brass bowls, balanced over small magical flames.

'Bah, that's not right at all!' snaps the man, peering at one of his concoctions through thick glass spectacles. 'Tanner, get me more bronze filings from the crate.'

A short blond-haired girl in brown overalls leaps to attention, and hurries over to a set of crates, where she begins picking through a selection of packets. 'Are you sure we have some bronze left?' she asks worriedly, almost disappearing inside one of the crates as she roots through the contents.

The bald scientist is about to answer when he sees you approaching. He squints at you through his spectacles, the thick glass magnifying his eyes to twice their normal size. 'Good day, I'm Totsvig Hellen. Can I help you?' he asks, a little abruptly. 'I am rather busy. Very important work.'

Will you:

Ask what he is doing here?	504
Ask about Jenlar Cornelius?	334
Ask if he has anything for sale?	371
Hand over a corrupted seed pod if you have one?	516

311

The tinker turns the leather case to face you. To your surprise, you discover that the interior of the case is far bigger than its outward appearance suggests. Inside is a veritable treasure trove of armour and equipment.

Rummaging through the selection, the following three items catch your eye. Each is available for 150 gold crowns.

Ramrod helm	**Dark crystal**	**Rune-forged greaves**
(head)	(main hand: dagger)	(feet)
+1 speed +2 armour	+1 speed +2 brawn	+2 speed +2 magic
Ability: haste	Ability: venom	
	(requirement: rogue)	

Once you have made your purchases, you turn back to the tap room. Turn to 404.

312

You awake on a pallet bed, your head thumping with pain. Beside you, the wind and rain lash against a window, rattling its shutters. Then lightning flashes, casting a ghoulish glow over your austere surroundings.

You find yourself in a small room, furnished with a simple wooden desk and high-backed chair. Opposite you, next to the door, is another pallet bed. A young man lies face-down on top of it, his clothes sodden with rain water.

You swing your legs off the bed and sit up, wincing as fresh pain shoots across your brow. It is then that you notice the contents of your backpack, scattered across the floor. Quickly, you take a stock of your inventory. To your annoyance you discover that some of your equipment has been taken. (You must remove your main-hand and left-hand items from your hero sheet and make the necessary adjustments to your attributes. Keep a note of these, as they may be returned to you at a later date.) Thankfully, you still have all your backpack items and your clothing.

Will you:

Search the desk?	279
Try and wake the other traveller?	291
Leave the room?	349

313
Legendary monster: Logan

You are unprepared for the ambush. Your first warning is a rustle of leaves, off to the side of the track. Then you hear the twang of a bowstring. The arrow hurtles out of the undergrowth, slamming into your shoulder and sending you reeling back against a tree. As you try and move, a flash of agonising pain draws you up short. In alarm, you realise that the arrow has gone straight through your shoulder and pinned you to the tree.

A man steps out from the forest, his body and face wrapped in bindings of black cloth. In his left hand he carries a curved long bow, its dark wood pulsing with a spectral light. As you watch through your pain, the assassin slowly unravels the cloth that hides his face.

You give a sharp gasp of surprise. The man's skin is a clear, translucent white – completely devoid of pigment – and his eyes are a crimson red, like droplets of blood.

The albino tilts his head to one side, examining you closely. 'I thought I had killed you once. Perhaps I should be calling you the cat, for it is evident you have more than just the one life.'

You glance down at the shaft protruding from your shoulder. The black-feathered flight and smooth, dark wood are identical to the arrow that killed the young academy knight.

'You! You killed the boy,' you spit, angrily.

'And you killed my men,' snaps the assassin, dropping his bow to the ground and drawing two daggers from his belt. 'You killed all of them. An impressive display of power, I have to say.'

You grit your teeth, placing your free hand on the shaft of the arrow. In one swift movement, you snap it in two. Your screams echo through the forest ... screams that fast become sobs of agony.

'You have strength,' says the assassin, his eyebrows raised. 'You are not at all what you seem, are you?'

Tears of pain stream down your face as you teeter forwards, slowly sliding your shoulder along the broken length of the shaft. At last, you tear yourself free, the force of the pain driving you to your knees.

'I promised the knight ... I would ... avenge him.'

'How gallant of you,' the assassin sneers, twirling his daggers deftly in his hands. 'Honour, chivalry ... do you take me for a fool? The only code we live by is death! Do you know who I am?'

You wipe the blood from your lips. 'A killer. Nothing more.'

'I am Logan. Some call me the Reaper.' The albino starts towards you, his red eyes boring into your own. 'I'm now going to finish what I started. I hate loose ends – sloppy work. This time, I will make sure I do the job properly.'

You stumble back to your feet, blood coursing from your shoulder wound. Biting back the pain, you ready your weapons and prepare to fight. (You must begin this fight having already lost 4 *health*.)

	Speed	Brawn	Armour	Health
Logan	10	10	9	50

Special abilities

🔴 Poisoned arrow: At the end of each combat round, you must automatically lose 2 *health*.

If you defeat this expert assassin, turn to 394.

314

The hive queen and her bodyguards lie in curled heaps around you. However, there is little time to celebrate your victory as you can hear the frenzied hum of angry bees approaching. You make a quick search of the queen's lair and discover the following items, which you may take:

Amber-coated collar	Bees' wax	Diaphanous wings
(necklace)	(backpack)	(cloak)
+1 armour	This might come in	+1 speed +1 magic
Ability: heal	useful one day	Ability: haste

You squeeze into one of the tunnels and crawl back out of the hive, thankfully avoiding any encounters. As you cling onto the side of the wall, you realise that you will have to make the jump again – to cross the pit. This will be a much harder challenge, as you don't have the benefit of a run up beforehand.

	Speed
Pit jump	15

If you make the jump, then you are able to return to the main cave and take the other tunnel north, turn 472. If you fail, then turn to 528.

Quest: The unicorn's horn

You are drawn into the forest by the smell of smoke and the cries of battle. Hurrying through the thick undergrowth, you finally emerge in a grassy clearing. Dotted around a campfire are a dozen dead goblins. Most are riddled with arrows, looking like they died before they even had chance to arm themselves. Others made it as far as drawing their swords and daggers, but from the surprised expressions, now frozen onto their faces, it appears they accomplished very little.

The camp has already been ransacked and searched. As you wander through the scattered debris, you realise that the goblins must have been poachers. There are several half-broken wooden frames lying in the grass, with fresh animal skins still stretched across them.

You notice a money purse on one of the goblin's belts. You kneel down to take it, wondering why the attackers hadn't bothered to loot the bodies. (You have gained 20 gold crowns.) As you stand, you feel a sharp point pressing into your neck.

'One more move,' growls a woman's voice, 'and you die!'

From the edges of the clearing, you see figures start to appear from out of the forest. They are all female – clad in tunics of woven leaves and wildflowers. Their skin is the colour of the forest, mottled with patches of brown and grey. No wonder the goblins had no chance against them; the women are almost invisible as they stand against the forest backdrop. You count nearly thirty of them – each armed with a short bow and a quiver of green-fletched arrows.

One of the women strides towards you, her bow held in one hand and a sword in the other. Unlike the others, she is wearing a long cloak of golden-coloured leaves. You guess she is their leader.

'Why do you trespass here?' she sneers, her amber eyes flicking to the weapons you are carrying. 'Are you a hunter also?'

Will you:

Say that you are looking for Cornelius?	363
Ask why they attacked the goblins?	395
State that you can go where you please?	381

316

The man grumbles something beneath his beard. 'Yes, yes, if saving the life of a poor lassie ain't enough for you then I'm sure I might have something about my person that'll interest you.' He twists his head and points to a pack laying some metres away in the dust. 'Managed to save most of my belongings but my prize invention – my magic clockwork camera – fell into the rift. If you happen to come across it …' He sighs wistfully, his eyes coming to rest on the jagged fissure. 'Suppose it sounds odd for me to be talking about something so trivial, especially at a time like this. But I got to tell you, twenty years of work went into that camera – found the plans in one of those elven pyramids. Could have made me rich.' He shakes his head. 'Humph! It's probably lying in some dragon's den now.'

Turn to 538 to ask another question, or 526 to begin your quest.

317

You approach a door on your left. From the other side you can hear a multitude of voices, all seemingly talking at once. It sounds like a large gathering of people. With little to lose, you carefully lift up the door latch and push open the door.

As you predicted, the room is full to bursting point. But where you had been expecting richly-dressed nobles, instead, you are presented with a rag-tag crowd of commoners. Some are dressed in little more than peasants' clothing, others look like travellers, their cloaks and boots stained with mud and dirt. A family huddle together in one corner, the mother and father gazing at their opulent surroundings with the same wide-eyed amazement as their two young children.

You move around the room warily, listening to snatches of conversation. One woman is gleefully telling her attentive listeners of how she was specially invited to the meal by the count himself.

'I met him on the road, only today. I was so honoured when he asked me, I just didn't know what to say.'

Another gentlemen is explaining how his cart was set upon by wolves: '... then the count came and the wolves just left me alone. It was quite a relief, I can tell you. Thought I was a goner to be sure. Then he asked me to attend his ball. Well, I was so surprised I just nodded like a fool.'

It appears that all these people are guests, like yourself – and each has a tale to tell of how they met the count or one of his family, who invited them to the evening meal at a moment's notice.

As you ponder the situation, you notice a boy weaving between the crowd. He is tall and skinny, his movements looking stiff and awkward in the heavy black coat he is wearing. You notice that he is stopping by some of the guests and whispering something to them, then moving on through the crowd.

When he catches your eye, the boy walks over. 'Listen,' he says, dropping his voice so he isn't overheard. 'Join me by the statue. We don't have much time.'

Then he moves away again. Several of the other people are already making their way to the far corner of the room, where a black onyx statue of an angel stands in a torch-lit alcove. Intrigued as to what is transpiring, you cross the room to join them. Turn to 355.

318

As you start to climb, several of the roots that you are holding onto begin to split. You will need to take a *speed* challenge in order to avoid falling:

	Speed
Root climb	10

If you succeed, turn to 503. If you fail, turn to 514.

319

The queen smiles, though there is little warmth or comfort in the gesture. 'The man whom you seek is one of the Council of Nine – an order founded by a powerful human mage named Avian Dale.

'Cornelius has many gifts, but his most powerful is that of prophecy. He sees the future – all futures, which shift and change like the wind. Some paths are set, others can be altered. Cornelius sees them all. You will need his help if you wish to close the shadow gate. Yes. I know of what has befallen the city of Talanost. If the Legion of Shadow is not contained there, then all that we hold precious and dear will be lost ... forever.'

Turn to 376 to ask another question, or turn to 336 to end your audience with the queen.

320

'Ladies and gentlemen, show your appreciation for the one and only, "Left Hook" Luke. Former captain of the Betsy Blue and the most feared pirate of all the seven seas! Yee-hah!'

Your opponent strides confidently towards you, his bucket-topped boots squelching through the mud. He is ragged and thin, his greasy hair hanging in loose strands from beneath his tri-horned hat. With his one good eye (the other concealed by an eye-patch), he gives you the once over, his lips curling into a sneer.

'I asks for a champion and they send me a deckhand.' He circles around you, tapping the hook of his left hand against the blade of his cutlass. 'I hopes yer understand,' he says, grinning, 'I needs the money for a new ship. So, there ain't nothing coming between me and my bounty.'

You must now fight this deadly pirate captain:

	Speed	Brawn	Armour	Health
Left hook Luke	7	8	4	50

Special abilities

🥢 By hook: For each ⚀ that you roll for your hero (either for attack speed or damage), they immediately take 2 damage from Luke's left hook. This ability ignores *armour*.

🥢 And by crook: Once Luke's *health* is reduced to 20 or less, his attacks become more desperate. Luke only rolls 1 die for his attack speed, but rolls 2 dice for damage.

If you win the combat, turn to 277.

321
Quest: The seared scar

The forest gives way to a plain of black, scorched sand. A few shrivelled, charcoal stumps are all that remain of the once verdant wilderness. Warily, you wander alone through this brooding landscape, past crevices that gout smoke and steam into the red-tinged sky.

The scar widens as you progress southwards, eventually bringing you to the lip of a vast, bowl-shaped crater. Cutting across its centre is a jagged rift, where the ground has violently buckled and split apart. The flickering red glow of lava and flame dance along its steep sides, presenting a stark contrast to the grey-black ash that covers the rest of this wasteland.

You descend into the crater, half running and half sliding through the ash and dust. When you reach the bottom, you see that the ground is hard and smooth – the soil having been heated to such a degree that is now fragments of dark crystal. Each footstep you take forces the crystals to splinter like broken glass – the only sound to be heard in this grim silent place.

As you approach the rift, you spot a figure lying on their side in the dust. You hurry over, suspecting that they have been injured. As you near, you see that it is an elderly man; his narrow face encircled by a thick bush of wiry grey hair. He is dressed in simple leather clothing, with a skullcap resting lopsidedly on his head.

'By Judah's light, a traveller,' he gasps. 'Don't suppose you could spare a little healing tonic. I appear to have taken a bit of a tumble.'

If you have a healing potion in your backpack and wish to offer it the man, turn to 467. If you don't have a potion or do not wish to waste it on a stranger, turn to 483.

322

As you open the door at the top of the stairs, you are met by an icy blast of wind and rain. Ahead of you stretches a section of the castle battlements, its narrow walkway slick with rainwater. Not wishing to turn back, you race out into the fury of the storm.

The count follows you onto the battlements, his cloak whipping around his narrow frame. 'You think you can run from me?' he shouts. 'You can't escape your doom.'

Suddenly, you hear a screeching sound coming from behind you. Spinning around, you see a mass of black bodies sweeping down from the clouds. As the winged creatures near, you realise – to your horror – that they are giant, fang-toothed vampire bats! Fighting them on these slippery battlements is going to be a real test of your skill:

	Speed	Brawn	Armour	Health
Bat swarm	7	8	4	20

Special abilities
🦇 Watch your step: If you roll a ⚀ when rolling for your hero's attack speed then you are knocked off the battlements by the angry bat swarm and fall into the courtyard below. You automatically lose this combat. If you have a special ability that allows you to re-roll dice, then you may do so to avoid this happening.

(Note: You cannot heal after this combat. You must continue this quest with the *health* that you have remaining. You may use potions and abilities to heal lost *health* while you are in combat.)

If you defeat the bat swarm then turn to 505, otherwise turn to 424.

323

Weapons raised, you follow Bern into the pack of wreekin. The air rings with their warbling cries, as the creatures spin their nets about their heads, weighted with hook-like bones. Bern quickly becomes entangled in one of the nets, falling to the boggy ground. You try and go to his aid, but are brought up short by a bolt of green light, which rips into the swamp ahead of you, throwing up mud and water high into the air.

As you spin round, you see one of the wreekin holding a wand fashioned from strips of bone. It levels the wand at you again, preparing to fire another blast:

	Speed	Magic	Armour	Health
Wreekin mage	11	6	5	45

Special abilities

◗ Charge her up!: The wreekin mage does not roll for damage if it wins a combat round. Instead, for every two rounds of combat it wins, it launches a bolt from its wand. This automatically does 10 damage to your hero, ignoring *armour*. You cannot use *vanish, evade* or *sidestep* to avoid this.

If you defeat the mage, turn to 529.

324

The map leads you to a cave, set into the marshy hills. To your surprise, you discover that it is filled with treasure! You may now help yourself to 100 gold crowns. If you are a rogue or a warrior, turn to 333. If you are a mage turn to 446.

325

'Two moons ago, a black rock blazed across the sky. A dark splinter of it broke away and pierced the heart of our glade. I know not the nature of its evil, but now my magic is waning also. I can feel it … being drawn out of my roots. Once my magic has gone I shall become like the others.'

The tree sweeps a branch through the air, gesturing to the other withered trees that dot the wasteland. 'That will be my fate.'

Will you:

Introduce yourself and ask the tree its name?	292
Offer to help the tree?	344

326
Quest: The count's ball

A distant rumble of thunder announces the coming of a storm. As the skies darken towards evening, you find yourself hurrying along the narrow dirt path that winds through the forest. The patter of cold rain forces you to huddle deeper into your cloak, your mind conjuring up images of hot food and roaring fires. According to local rumour, there is a gypsy camp somewhere nearby. You are hoping that they will welcome a fellow traveller.

Your thoughts are interrupted by the pounding of hooves on the road behind you. You turn, just in time to see a horse-drawn carriage career around the corner of the track, its wheels rattling over the uneven bumps and troughs. The carriage is approaching at such speed that you are forced to throw yourself out of the way, as it hurtles past, missing you by scant inches.

Angrily, you step back onto the track, brushing the dirt and dust from your clothes. The carriage continues down the track for another hundred metres, then veers over to the side, coming to a screeching halt. The door of the riding cabin opens slightly and a white-gloved hand beckons you over.

Determined to give the driver a piece of your mind, you stride over to the carriage. Those horses could have trampled over you if it hadn't been for your quick reflexes. As you step up to the cabin, the door opens a little further – and you are surprised to see a young woman leaning forward on her seat, her face a mask of worry and concern. 'Are you all right?' she asks.

You find yourself lost for words as you gaze into the woman's brilliant blue eyes, framed by golden curls of blond hair. Her skin is perfect and exquisite, without line or blemish.

'I'm so sorry,' she says. 'I told my driver to pick up the pace. I didn't want to be late for Papa. He ... I'm sorry ...' She puts a gloved hand to her bosom, where you see a blood-red gem resting against her pale skin. 'How rude of me. I should introduce myself. I am Lady Roe. My father is the count. Count Kristoe.'

There is a flash of lightning, followed by a deafening peal of thunder.

'Oh where are my manners,' smiles the woman. 'Papa is having a little get-together this evening. Would you care to join us? It is the least I can do, to make up for my terrible indiscretion.'

Will you:

Accept the invitation?	284
Ask about Jenlar Cornelius?	268
Ask for the location of the gypsy camp?	276
Tell her to be more careful?	339

327

You search the bodies of the dead trogs. You may now take any / all of the following items:

Trog spear	My precious	Beetle-shell garland
(main hand: spear)	(ring)	(necklace)
+1 speed +3 brawn	+1 armour	+1 speed
(requirement: warrior)	Ability: vanish	Ability: charm

A quick examination of the creatures' camp turns up very little – just a few tatty blankets and some gnawed bones. If you have *Lorinwold's Field Guide to Roots, Herbs and Leaves* then you find 2 root grass growing at the side of the cave. You may pick these. (Make a note of the herbs on your hero sheet.)

Another tunnel leads out of the cave, heading north. You decide to take it, heading deeper into the underground network. Turn to 451.

Solandris is waiting for you when you step out of the cave. 'Well, are you going to help us, then?' she snaps, looking sullenly at Bern. Talandra looks about to reprimand her, but Bern interjects by raising a hand.

'It was your queen who granted me my powers. I swore to use them only in defence of the forest. Last night, she came to me in a dream and begged for my aid. And that is why I am here. I am a ranger and I can track your enemies to the ends of the world if I must. Now, I insist we do not waste time. Lead on.'

You are taken to the edge of the glade, where a patch of bloodied grass marks the site of the attack. Bern disappears into the trees – then returns only moments later. 'There are tracks here, leading south toward the marsh. They belong to wreekin; about seven in number by my estimate. They have about a day's lead on us.'

'Then what are we waiting for?' says Solandris, drawing her daggers. 'Let us go and kill them, and get the horn back. Before it is too late.'

Bern looks to you. 'I will go with this one,' he says. 'I have a charm that I can use to give us swift flight. The two of you should stay here and protect your queen until we return.'

Solandris looks to her leader, pouting angrily. 'I will not stay! I want to see justice done, by my own hands!'

Talandra shakes her head. 'No, Solandris. We are friends with the wreekin. What has happened here may not be an act of aggression or war – there may be more to this. Your anger will only make things worse.'

Solandris gives you a sulky glare, then turns her back on the gathering. 'So be it.'

Bern reaches into one of the pouches hanging from his belt. 'This is glimmer dust,' he explains, producing a vial of sparkling powder. 'Sprinkle some on your boots, then follow me. And,' he offers you a wry smile, 'try and keep up.'

You take the vial and dust some of the powder onto your boots. Suddenly, they start to glow, as a whoosh of magic spirals up around your legs, making them feel as light as air. Turn to **518**.

329

'Ah, new little gadget of mine,' grins the explorer. 'Clever use of smoke and mirrors – creates an image onto parchment. Here, look at these …' He digs into his jerkin pocket and pulls out a handful of small, square sheets of parchment. Each one has a picture on it, rendered in perfect detail. Most of the collection show sections of the crater, but a couple show a short, stocky woman with long ginger hair and a beaming smile.

'That's Belinda,' he says, his voice breaking. 'Poor little lassie. It's all my fault!' He snatches the pictures from you and stuffs them back into his pocket. 'Don't know what I'll do if something has happened to her.'

Turn to 538 to ask another question, or 526 to begin your quest.

330

You trudge through the brackish water of the fens, towards the homely lights of the nearby town. As the ground begins to rise, you pass a wooden sign staked into the boggy earth. It once read 'New Hope', but someone has painted a cross over the 'New' and written the word 'No' beside it instead.

'No Hope.' Somehow, this name seems more appropriate to the ramshackle settlement that sprawls across the marsh.

Built around a series of walkways, the town's rickety buildings rise high into the cold, grey mist. Most are little more than hovels, supported by a precarious webwork of stilts and planks. As you near, you can't help but marvel at the size and scale of the place. Its walkways and bridges extend as far as the eye can see, quickly becoming a confusing labyrinth of criss-crossing paths and tumbledown structures. Nearly all appear to be busy with people, hurrying through the chill fog as they go about their business.

If this is your first time visiting No Hope, turn to 213. Otherwise, turn to 348 to view your options.

331

You ready your weapons and charge at the tree. Fast as lightning, a branch swings down from above, striking you across the shoulder and knocking you to the ground.

'Don't be so hasty, youngling!' rumbles the tree. 'I mean you no harm, and I am not ready to give up the fight just yet.'

The deep, black eyes watch you intently. 'I admire your spirit, but I would ask that you channel your rage against something more deserving. My time will come eventually – but not by your hand, youngling.'

Will you:

Introduce yourself and ask the tree its name?	292
Ask about what happened here?	325

332

'No, you ain't,' sneers the coachman, reaching for the club at his waist. 'You're just some poor lonely traveller that got lost in the woods.'

The guard by the door strides over, his armour jingling. 'Do we have a problem 'ere?' he asks, looking you up and down with contempt. He stabs a finger into your chest. 'Hey, I asked yer a question dumb-dumb.'

Will you:

Draw your weapons and attack?	402
Hand over your weapons?	294
Try and leave the castle?	345

333

Amongst the mounds of gold and jewels, you find a number of interesting items. You may now choose one of the following:

Serpent's coil	Ivory	Band of conquest
(ring)	(left hand: sword)	(ring)
+1 brawn	+2 speed +2 brawn	+1 armour
Ability: immobilise	Ability: ebony and ivory	Ability: fortitude

Having searched through the cave and filled your pockets with gold, you decide that it is time to leave and continue your journey. Return to your original entry number.

334

'Why, I know Cornelius,' says Totsvig, his magnified eyes widening even further. 'The greatest scholar in his field. His musings on trans-mutation are absolutely second to none. Blew me away – and that research paper on petrification, the art of turning living tissue to stone – wow, compulsory bedtime reading. Yes, a bestseller that one. I may even have a copy of it somewhere ...' He glances around at the clut-tered workbenches, where books, scrolls and makeshift equipment cover every inch of space.

Not wishing to waste time searching for a book, you ask him if he can direct you to where Cornelius lives.

'Where he lives?' he asks, looking surprised. 'Well, I've never actu-ally met the man. I know his work, as does every scholar worth their salt. So, he lives around here? Gosh, if you do happen to cross paths with him ...' he puts his hands together pleadingly. 'Could you get his autograph for me? Please?'

You give him a reassuring nod, trying your best to hide your dis-appointment. Finding Cornelius is not going to be as easy as you first thought. To speak with Totsvig further, turn to 310. Otherwise, return to the quest map to continue your travels.

335
Legendary monster: Vesuvius

The column of flame moves quickly across the scorched earth, leaving a blazing trail of smoke and embers in its wake. The creature is headed straight towards you, gaining momentum as it blasts through the withered trees and shrivelled ferns that litter the crater basin.

Two angry molten eyes form within the column, narrowing to slits of rage as it closes in. 'All will burn by my hand,' hisses the elemental, spitting sparks and flame. 'I am Vesuvius – and nothing stands in my way!'

You brace yourself, as the infernal monster slams into you, plunging your surroundings into a searing maelstrom of fire and sulphur:

	Speed	Magic	Armour	Health
Vesuvius	10	13	9	45

Special abilities
- Molten armour: At the end of every combat round, your hero automatically takes 4 health damage from Vesuvius. This ability ignores *armour*.
- Body of flame: Your opponent is immune to *sear, fire aura* and *bleed*.

If you defeat your fiery opponent, turn to 377.

336

You awake to find yourself lying in a patch of long grass, your pack and belongings resting beside you. As you stumble groggily to your feet, you try and remember what happened. You were talking to the queen in the dryad grove and then . . .

'I see you're awake at last.'

You spin round, readying your weapons – then relax, when you see it is Bern. The ranger is sat watching you, chewing on a stem of grass. 'The queen asked me to do her a little favour,' he grins, standing. 'To take you to Cornelius. Are you ready?'

Looking around, you see that you are both standing in a meadow, surrounded by the dark trees of Mistwood. There is no sign of the dryads or their peaceful, idyllic grove.

'Was I dreaming?' you ask, scratching your head.

Bern gives a snort of laughter. 'Don't worry, the queen has that effect on most people. Now, do you want my help, or not?'

Still a little befuddled by what has happened, you find yourself agreeing to the ranger's kind offer. Turn to 430.

337

As you start to wade across the pool, you are suddenly thrown off balance by something pulling at your legs. You quickly realise that the entire mud pool has started to move – sliding past you at great speed. Within moments, you are standing on dry, stony ground, as the thick sludge is sucked up towards the centre of the pool.

Then, in one fluid motion, the sludge rises up, moulding itself into a humanoid shape. The objects that were once lying in the mud are now sticking out of the creature's body at various angles.

With a wet-sounding roar, the mud golem slithers towards you, clearly with the intention of smashing you to pieces with its enormous, sludge-dripping fists:

	Speed	Brawn	Armour	Health
Mud golem	6	5	3	35

Special abilities
- Mud pie: At the end of every combat round, the golem flings a mud pie at you. Roll 2 dice – if the amount is the same as or less than your *speed* then you take no damage. If the amount is higher than your *speed*, you take 2 damage. This ability ignores *armour*.

If you defeat the mud golem, turn to 283.

338

(You must pay a fee of 5 gold crowns to enter the guild.) The thieves' guild has the following items for sale for 40 gold crowns each:

Boots of swift flight	Footpad's cover	Blackjack
(feet)	(head)	(main hand: club)
+1 speed +2 brawn	+2 brawn +1 armour	+1 speed +3 brawn
		Ability: slam

As a pickpocket you may return to the guild at any time. (Make a note of this entry number on your hero sheet). If you wish to leave the guild and explore the rest of the town, turn to 348.

339

Still shaken by your encounter, you warn the woman to be more careful when using the roads. Lady Roe attempts to look serious as she listens to your heated speech, but you notice the corners of her mouth twitching, as if she is restraining herself from laughing.

'Oh I know – it was awful!' she says at last, her eyes twinkling mischievously. 'We should have taken more care. I was just so excited at the thought of seeing Papa again. I've been east, visiting my cousin at Fairwater View. I do so love the country – such simple ways ... but Papa's grand occasion, well I couldn't miss it for the world. He promised me it will be the best ever!'

The woman places a hand on your arm. 'Please, I would be honoured if you would join me.'

Will you:

Accept the invitation?	284
Explain your mission?	268
Ask the whereabouts of the gypsy camp?	276

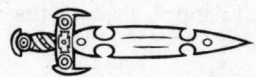

340

Ignoring the woman's grief-stricken howls, you continue onwards through the swirling fog. Roll a die. If you get 🎲 or less turn to 457. Otherwise, turn to 438.

341

You cleave through the tree's rotten trunk, releasing more of the noxious green smoke. With a final gasp, the tree creaks and shudders – then becomes still, its branches drooping by its sides. The pitiful creature is dead. You may now take one of the following as a reward:

Dryad's band	Barkskin greaves	Sprig of corruption
(ring)	(feet)	(left hand: wand)
+1 brawn	+1 speed +2 armour	+2 speed +3 magic
Ability: thorn armour	Ability: steadfast	Ability: corruption

You also find a pouch of 30 gold crowns nestled within the creature's decaying wood. Return to the quest map to continue your adventure.

342

As you enter the cave, your eyes widen further in amazement. Instead of being a damp, gloomy space, the cavern is filled with colour and light. From the holes and spaces in the rocky ceiling, amber columns of sunlight stream down across a carpet of rose petals and woven reeds. They form a natural pathway, leading up to a bed of purple blossom at the centre of the cave. And there, lying on top of it, is a magnificent white stallion. The beast's eyes are closed, as if in sleep; its ragged breathing the only sound in the still, silent cave.

'Follow me,' says Talandra, leading the way up the path. 'The queen is here, also.'

At first you wonder who or what she is referring to – then, as you get closer to the horse, you see a woman lying perfectly still next to it, her eyes closed and her own breathing stilted and irregular. She is like all the other dryads you have met – green-skinned with mottled patches of grey and brown. But her beauty surpasses all. As she lies in slumber, her blond hair cascades around her thin body like spun gold, mirroring the delicate leaves that adorn her robes.

'My queen,' gasps Bern, rushing to her side. 'What happened here? How long has she been like this?'

'Since the unicorn's horn was lost to us,' says Talandra. She walks over to a carved wooden table set beneath a natural overhang of rock. From it, she takes an arrow and hands it to Bern, who studies it with interest.

'That was the arrow that brought down the unicorn,' says Talandra, her face hardening. 'The hunters took the horn. Without it, the grove will lose its magic. The queen already weakens ... trapped in a slumber from which she cannot awake. Their magic, their fates, are intertwined. Without the horn, the unicorn will pass away and our dear queen will ...' She stops, taking a deep breath to compose herself. 'Bern, can you help us?'

The warrior studies the arrow. 'This is not the work of goblins. The wood is weak – marsh wood from the mangroves. And look, this fletching is oiled. The wreekins are responsible.'

'No!' gasps Talandra. 'But they are a peaceful race. They honour our borders as we do theirs. Why would they take the horn? They know it is precious to us!'

Bern gets to his feet. 'I intend to find out. Can you take me to where you found the unicorn? I can pick up the trail from there.'

As you are led out of the cave, Bern stops beside you. 'I'm afraid the answers you seek will have to wait. The queen's life is now in the balance. Unless we find the horn, everything you have just seen will be gone forever.' Turn to 328.

343
Quest: The sunken city

You come to the shores of a vast blue lake, where a camp has been set up within the shadows of the mountains. There are over a dozen rich pavilion tents, arranged in a rough circle, with armed guards patrolling the perimeter. Each guard is wearing a blue tabard over their chain mail, with a circle and a white rose emblazoned at the centre.

On seeing you approach, several of the guards head over in your direction, drawing swords from their sheaths. Behind them, you see inside an open tent, where a woman in similar getup is leaning over a table, scrutinising a map.

'What you sniffing around 'ere for?' growls one of the guards, his scarred face visible beneath his helm.

'Perhaps we got another deader,' grins one of his companions. 'Coming 'ere thinking they gonna get some treasure.'

The scar-faced guard raises the point of his sword. 'Shall we see if this one's got anything to show?'

'Gentlemen, please.' The woman from the tent strides over. She has long brown hair, tied back in a ponytail. From her trappings and the way she moves, you can tell she is an accomplished warrior.

'Stand down, Merik,' she snaps, addressing the scarred-face guard. 'Back to your duties. All of you.'

The guards oblige, leaving the two of you alone. The woman folds her arms, her eyes fondly appraising your gear and weapons. 'Well, well. You don't look like the ordinary kind of treasure seeker we get down here. I'm Sahna.' She tilts her head back, gesturing towards the ring of tents. 'I work for Raolin. So, let me guess – did old Marcus at the Pisa's Rest send you down here?' She arches an eyebrow. 'We are kind of desperate for volunteers, if the truth be told.'

Will you:

Ask if she has heard of Jenlar Cornelius?	427
Ask why the guard referred to you as a 'deader'	440
Ask about Raolin?	448
Ask why she needs volunteers?	476

344

The guardian places a branch on your shoulder, the twig-like fingers curling round to grip it tightly. 'Thank you,' says the tree, its eyes misting with sap. 'I had given up hope ... but perhaps, I was wrong to be so hasty. See, over there.' The tree gently turns you to face the far side of the clearing. Ahead, billowing out of a deep crater, is a plume of green smoke.

'That is where the dark splinter landed,' explains the tree. 'It was the black rock that brought the evil and menace to this land. I have seen things … the creatures of the forest, corrupted and mutated by its power. I fear that it was one of these creatures – a parasite – that has eaten away at my brothers' and sisters' roots. Even now, I feel my own magic seeping away. Soon all my magic will be gone and I, the mighty Woad Brightbough, will cease to be.'

The tree gives a shaky, wavering breath. 'If you would investigate the black rock for me, then the forest would forever speak your name.'

You promise the tree that you will do all you can. Turn to 409.

345

You turn to leave, having had enough of this foolish charade. Suddenly something strikes you from behind, sending you toppling forward onto your knees. The room starts to spin as white flashes of pain explode across your vision. You try and turn, to see what hit you, but your muscles are no longer doing what you ask.

'Sorry, but I can't let yer leave,' growls the coach driver, his face swimming through the dizzying, white haze. 'Lady Roe picked you out specially, and she ain't one to have her evening ruined.'

'Yeah, you said it,' chuckles the guard. 'She got quite an appetite on her for one so young. That'll be a real treat …'

The voices fade, replaced by a roaring white noise in your ears … you can feel your limbs stiffening, growing numb. Then you lose consciousness, falling into a deep dark sleep. Turn to 312.

346

You sever the stem in two, sending the plant's snapping head flying across the clearing, to squish against a nearby tree. The creeping vines give a shudder and suddenly start to recoil, winding their way back into the marshy ground.

You have defeated the deadly snapjaw plant. You may now take one of the following as your reward:

Spine tooth	Wreath of woe	Barbed bracers
(left hand: dagger)	(head)	(gloves)
+2 speed +2 brawn	+1 speed +3 magic	+1 speed +2 armour
Ability: critical strike	Ability: barbs	Ability: barbs
(requirement: rogue)		

If you are an alchemist, you may also take a *corrupted seed pod* from the base of the plant. Make a note of this item on your hero sheet (it doesn't take up backpack space). When you have made your choices, return to the quest map to continue your adventure.

347

'Gosh, yes how rude of me!' she gasps, her cheeks suddenly flushed with colour. 'If you're going to be risking your life for me, then I suppose it is the least I can do. Here …' Shay fishes inside various pockets and after several minutes of feeling around, manages to gather together a small handful of dirt-covered coins. She hands them over, chewing her bottom lip nervously. 'I do hope that is OK.'

You have gained 20 gold crowns. After pocketing the money you offer out your hand and shake on the agreement. 'How splendid!' she grins excitedly. 'Shall we get started then?' Turn to 353.

348

You find yourself standing on a wide promenade, which cuts through the centre of the town. To your left you see a lop-sided building, its lower-storeys sloping backwards into the murky swamp water. A sign outside the crooked front door reads, 'Pisa's Rest'.

To your right, street vendors are touting their wares to the steady stream of passers-by. One in particular catches your eye – an elderly woman selling mushrooms from a squeaky wheel-barrow.

Finally, ahead of you, rising high into the pale mist, looms a large wooden amphitheatre, its lofty heights glowing with lantern-light. Outside, crowds of people are pushing and shoving to get through the open doors.

'Come on, move it!' shouts one of the mob. 'The first fight of the season is about to begin!'

Will you:

Visit the tavern?	404
Talk to the mushroom seller?	362
Enter the amphitheatre?	373

349

The door opens out onto a steep, spiral staircase. You follow it down into a torch-lined passageway. Turn to 317.

350

Legendary monster: Hydra

Having lost your way in the murky fog, you find yourself wading through a treacherous quagmire of mud. Every step you take becomes an effort of will as you struggle to lift your feet out of the clinging, boggy earth.

With your attention focused solely on your predicament, you don't see the huge swamp monster until it is too late. Three snapping heads lunge out of the pale mist, each attached to a long scaly neck. In horror, you realise you have waded into the den of a hydra. You must now fight for your life against its many, snapping jaws:

	Speed	Brawn	Armour	Health
Hydra	12	15	10	60

Special abilities

🝰 Many heads: If the hydra is still alive at the end of three combat rounds, it automatically heals back to full *health* at the start of the fourth round.

🝰 Venom: Once you have taken damage from the hydra, at the end of every combat round you must automatically lose 2 *health*.

If you defeat the hydra, turn to 389. (Special achievement: If you defeat the hydra before it can heal, turn to 418.)

351

As you approach the dark line of trees, you see that they are growing alongside a brown, stagnant pool. Their thick, gnarly roots creep out like fingers into the muddy water, forming a makeshift bridge that leads across to a small island. There, crouched on the bank, is an old grey-haired woman huddled in a black shawl. She sobs and wails, as she gazes upon her reflection in the still waters.

Will you:

Cross to the island?	462
Leave and continue your journey?	340

352

The crowds are chanting your name as you stride out into the arena, ready to face your next opponent. 'Welcome, ladies and gentlemen, to our quarter-final match-up!' The announcer zooms overhead like a bright, trailing comet. 'Facing our challenger today, is one of the

deadliest fighters ever to set foot in the arena. From across the scorching sands of the dune sea, I bring you Nasareim!'

The stadium shakes with the roar of applause as a tall figure steps
out from the tunnel. He is dressed in a loose-fitting poncho and flared
silk leggings, decorated with embroidered suns. Most of the man's
face is hidden behind wraps of cloth, leaving only his dark eyes and
curved nose visible. You notice that he moves with a quick-footed
grace, his sandalled feet barely making an impression in the wet earth.
Drawing a black-bladed scimitar from his belt, the silent assassin stalks
towards you. It is time to fight!

	Speed	Brawn	Armour	Health
Nasareim	12	10	12	60

Special abilities
- Dervish: This fighter's deadly attacks ignore your *armour*.
- Whirlwind: Each time Nasareim rolls a ⚅⚅ for damage, he may roll
  an extra die for damage. If Nasareim rolls another ⚅⚅ then he may
  roll another die – and so on.

If you defeat Nasareim, turn to 370.

353

You lead the way down the tunnel, with Shay following behind. You
make slow progress, as the narrow passage is choked with thick roots.
They break out of the walls and ceiling, filling the tunnel in crisscross-
ing patterns. Shay stops several times to take samples.

'These roots seem healthier,' she comments, holding up her latest
sample in its glass bottle. 'Interesting.'

As you struggle onwards, weaving between the roots, you finally
emerge in a huge bowl-shaped cavern. A narrow ledge leads around
the dip to another tunnel opening, covered in more snaking tree
roots. However, your attention is drawn instantly to the bottom of
the crater-shaped hole, where a series of stone ruins are protruding
from out of the soil.

'Dwarf ruins,' gasps Shay, her hand going to her mouth. 'I never thought we would stumble on those down here. How utterly fascinating!'

Will you:

Investigate the ruins?	380
Leave via the tunnel?	393

354

You've almost caught up with the boy, when he suddenly swerves to the side, dodging your grasping hands. 'Don't give up, do yer,' he shouts, darting into a shadowy alleyway. You follow him in – realising a moment later, the foolishness of your hasty pursuit.

You skid to a halt, facing a rag-tag crowd of children, all armed with clubs, knives and other dangerous-looking weapons. Afty stands in the middle of the group, grinning at you. 'Sorry friend, but I can't lets yer catch me. No one catches Artful Afty.' A couple of the children nod in agreement, their small hands tightening around their makeshift weapons.

As you ponder your next move, a soft, well-mannered voice breaks the silence. 'Well, well little ones. What we caught in the net today then, eh?'

You look round, to see a scruffy-looking man standing in the mouth of the alleyway. He bows to you, his mud-flecked coat opening to reveal the hilts of several daggers, tucked into his waist band.

'Now, under normal circumstances, I'd be a gentleman,' says the stranger, rubbing his stubbly chin. 'But as it is – you have some nice gear there. And, as you're new to town, no one will miss yer, will they?'

In a flash, he has drawn two daggers and is lunging towards you, his weaselly eyes full of greed and envy. You must now fight this thief:

	Speed	Brawn	Armour	Health
Fargin	6	5	4	25

If you defeat this desperate vagabond, turn to 309.

From glancing at the other people gathered around the statue, it is clear that the boy is cherry-picking those from the group who look like they can handle themselves. The man opposite you has the appearance of a blacksmith, with broad shoulders and thick muscular arms. Next to him is a stern-faced woman, dressed in a thick riding cloak and leather armour. You see an empty scabbard and knife-holder hanging from her belt.

The boy suddenly appears, sweating heavily. You imagine it must be hot underneath the thick, black coat he is wearing. 'Listen,' he says, leaning in towards the group. 'Now don't show alarm to the others. We can't have any ... panic. Do you understand?'

A few uncertain looks are passed around the circle, then everyone nods.

'Good.' The boy proceeds to unfasten his coat, then, with a flourish he holds it open. To your surprise, you see a veritable armoury of items tied into the lining of the coat. 'I want you all to take what you need. What we are going up against ... well... you'll soon see.'

'What possible use are these?' asks the blacksmith, wrinkling his brow. He points to a string of garlic. The boy gives him a wry smile – suddenly looking much older than his years.

'You don't get it, do you? The count is no ordinary man. And his ...'

The boy is interrupted by the creak of the double doors at the end of the room. Two servants enter. One is holding a small brass gong, which he proceeds to hit. The room echoes with the resonating boom.

'Ladies and gentlemen,' the other servant announces. 'The Count Kristoe cordially invites you all to his banquet.'

A wave of excitement washes across the crowd as people start to make their way through the double doors. The boy turns back to your group, his face looking panicked.

'Come on, there isn't much time. Arm yourselves and keep them hidden from view. You'll know when the time is right to use them.'

One by one, the members of the gathering choose from the odd assortment of items in the boy's coat. At last, it is your turn to choose. Turn to 405.

356

You follow Bern and Talandra deeper into the forest. Solandris, now freed from her bonds, walks beside you, occasionally casting a dark glance at yourself and Bern. Her fingers are continually tapping the pommels of her daggers, tucked into her garland belt. It is clear that her defeat in the clearing has only served to intensify her desire for revenge.

The thin, almost invisible trail meanders south, taking you across streams and over steep, muddy banks. At last, you pass beneath an archway of blossoming roses, to find yourself in an area of forest more beautiful than you could ever have imagined.

Golden light streams through the tree tops in brilliant beams, casting an otherworldly hue over the hills and glades. From a rocky cliffside, carpeted in climbing roses, a marvellous waterfall plunges down into a wide, crystal-blue pool – its many rivulets and streams sparkling in the sunlight.

Everywhere you look, there is something that steals your breath away, from the ancient trees that soar impossibly high to the intricate marble statues bedecked in garlands of red and gold. You walk through this paradise as if in a dream, the fragrant air and melody of cricket song and cascading water, making you feel both relaxed and light-headed.

'Come, the unicorn is this way.' Talandra leads you to a cave, its entrance almost hidden from view by trailing foliage. Pulling the vines aside, she gestures for you and Bern to enter. Turn to 342.

357
Legendary monster: Barkrot

On the edge of the withered glade, a single rotting tree stands alone, surrounded by a blackened patch of blighted earth. As you approach, the tree springs into life, its immense black branches forming themselves into gnarly fists.

The creature's mouth falls open, belching clouds of green, noxious gas. 'Back! Go back!' chokes the tree. 'I have suffered enough! I will not suffer anymore!' Before you have a chance to act, the tree's roots wrap themselves around your legs, their barbed thorns puncturing your armour and digging painfully into your skin.

Rooted to the spot, you have little choice but to defend yourself against the corrupted tree's flailing branches:

	Speed	Brawn	Armour	Health
Barkrot	10	10	10	30

Special abilities

🔻 Tangled roots: Roll a dice at the start of every combat round. If you roll a $\boxed{\cdot}$ or $\boxed{\cdot\cdot}$ you automatically lose 5 *health* from the deadly thorns. This ability ignores *armour*.

🔻 Air of corruption: You cannot use any special abilities in this fight. You may still use potions and other backpack items.

If you defeat this mighty opponent, turn to 341.

358

You barely have a moment to recover before the giant queen is upon you, the thunderous beat of her immense wings whipping up a tornado:

	Speed	Magic	Armour	Health
Hive queen	6	6	4	35

Special abilities

🔻 Wing buffet: You must reduce your *speed* by 1 for the duration of this combat.

🔻 Venom sting: Once you have taken health damage from the queen, at the end of every combat round you must automatically lose 2 *health*.

If you defeat the hive queen, turn to 314.

359

The arena echoes with the beast's final bellow of pain ... then there is silence. A heartbeat later and the stadium erupts into wild applause.

'The king is dead!' cheers the announcer, spinning through the air on his magic carpet. 'Long live our new champion!' You may now take one of the following as your reward:

Winter pelt	Diamond of the Tundra	Simian crown
(cloak)	(necklace)	(head)
+2 speed +2 armour	+1 speed	+1 speed +2 brawn
Ability: savagery	Ability: piercing	Ability: chill touch

Bart is waiting for you at the entrance to the tunnel. 'You did it! You did it! I never thought I'd see this day! We're in the final!' He flings his arms around you and gives you a big hug. 'Here! Take this. You deserve every shiny golden penny.' He places a bulging money pouch in your hand. (You have gained 100 gold crowns.) 'Now, let's get you ready for the final show. I suggest you stock up on some potions – you're going to need all the help you can get. Trust me!'

When you are ready to take on your final opponent, turn to 386.

360

You race over to help Spink, pushing your way past the snapping vampires and their frightened, bewildered victims. As you near, you see that two of the vampires have wrestled the boy to the ground. One of them has bitten deeply into his arm, forcing him to cry out in pain. As you pass a table, you grab a silver platter, tipping the leftover food onto the floor. Raising it like a club, you hurtle into the two vampires, swinging it with all the force you can muster. There is a satisfying clang, as the platter connects with one of the vampires, knocking it away. The other suddenly explodes in a ball of fire, sending black ash showering across the hall. Spink leaps to his feet, magic crackling in the palm of his hand.

'Just a little trick I learned from my master,' he grins. 'Come on, cover me. I need to get the holy water.' He runs over to the bottle, snatching it up into his hands.

The surviving vampire is groggily getting back to its feet. It is an elderly woman, dressed in a plush black velvet gown. With a hiss, she advances towards you, raising her long, pale fingers. In horror, you watch as her painted nails begin to stretch – becoming animal-like claws.

You toss the platter aside, and ready the special equipment that Spink gave you. Screeching like a banshee, the woman springs at you, her claws reaching for your throat:

	Speed	Brawn	Armour	Health
Clymonistra	7	5	4	40

Special abilities

◗ Piercing: This opponent's attacks ignore your *armour*.

◗ Vampire: You can use your *stake* and *reflect* abilities (if you have them) against this opponent.

(Note: You cannot heal after this combat. You must continue this quest with the *health* that you have remaining. You may use potions and abilities to heal lost *health* while you are in combat.)

If you defeat this vampire, turn to 460. Otherwise, turn to 424.

361

The passageway winds through the earth, eventually ending in a wide cavern.

Again, the ceiling is covered in a tangle of withered tree roots, which leak a thick green smoke into the air. You spot several black beetles scuttling amongst them, chewing at what is left of the rotted wood.

Underneath this smoky canopy, you see a group of grey, hairless humanoids seated around a camp fire. They are licking their lips hungrily as they watch a line of skewered beetles slowly cook over the flames.

As you enter the cavern, one of them looks up, sniffing the air. Quickly, it grabs a flint-tipped spear and starts towards you, its companions following suit. Although spindly and slow-moving, the creatures are clearly accomplished hunters. They spread out, cautiously forming a circle around you. Then they attack, jabbing at you with their spears:

	Speed	Brawn	Armour	Health
Cave trogs	6	7	3	40

If you defeat the trogs, turn to 327.

362

The elderly woman looks up as you approach. 'Care to take a look at my wares, young one?' she asks, gesturing to the bundles of mushrooms and other fungi packed into the wheelbarrow. 'All of these are fresh – oh yes. Picked them myself only yesterday.'

You may purchase any of the following for 40 gold crowns each (Note: You can only use one glittercap mushroom and one mottled marshstick per combat):

Glittercap mushroom (1 use)
(backpack)
Use any time in combat to raise your *magic* score by 3 for two combat rounds. Afterwards, you must reduce your *magic* by 1 for the remainder of the combat.

Mottled marshstick (1 use)
(backpack)
Use any time in combat to raise your *speed* score by 3 for two combat rounds. Afterwards, you must reduce your *speed* by 1 for the remainder of the combat.

When you have made your purchases, you return to the main square. Turn to 348.

'Cornelius?' the leader stops, her eyebrows raised. 'What do you know of Cornelius?'

Suddenly, a foot slams into your back, knocking you forward onto your stomach. 'Enough!' snarls the woman behind you. 'This one must have seen something. Let me get the truth out of them – my way!'

You roll over onto your elbows, to see another of the green-skinned females standing over you, a curved knife held in each hand. From the cold-hearted glare she is giving you, you suspect her method of interrogation is not going to be pleasant.

'Hold! All of you!'

To your surprise, it is a man's voice. You turn your head, to see a warrior in forest green leathers emerge from the trees. He has long blond hair, braided with feathers and cords, and about his neck hang a number of beaded charms. 'Since when do the dryads hunt so openly,' he scowls, 'and without judgement or mercy?' He starts forward into the clearing, a yellow glow cascading down his arms to gather along the tips of his fingers.

'Bern Farstrider,' sneers the knife-woman. 'This is none of your concern. Stand down or face the consequences.'

From around the circle, there is the creak of bowstrings as the archers nock arrows and take aim at the warrior.

He shakes his head sadly. 'Has it really come to this – that my return is welcomed with an arrow in the back. Well, so be it.' Turn to 474.

364
Legendary monster: Snapjaw

A wet mist rolls in across the forest, coating the tangled trees in a sheen of glistening dew. As you stumble blindly through the haze, you suddenly become aware of a creaking, scraping sound coming from behind you. In a flash, you are thrown forwards as something whips across your back. Rolling onto your front, you turn to see a giant vine thrashing through the air. Another is slithering out of the undergrowth and begins to wrap itself around your feet. Within moments you are being lifted up and carried through the air, towards a hungry pair of snapping jaws.

Frantically, you bash and tear at the vine, severing it in two. You fall to the ground, landing heavily on your side. Looking up, you see a gigantic plant towering above you, its bulbous head splitting open to reveal two sets of spine-like teeth. All around you, more vines are sliding across the boggy earth, seeking to entrap you in their deadly embrace.

You must now fight for your life against this fearsome carnivorous plant:

	Speed	Brawn	Armour	Health
Snapjaw	12	12	10	60

Special abilities

♥ Strangle vines: Your hero automatically loses 2 *health* at the end of the first combat round from Snapjaw's constricting vines. As the combat continues, these deadly vines wind tighter and tighter around your hero – increasing their damage by 2 each round. (Your hero takes 4 damage at the end of the second round, 6 damage at the end of the third and so on.) This ability ignores *armour*.

If you manage to defeat the mutated plant, turn to 346.

365

You take a long run up, sprinting towards the edge of the ledge. At the last possible second you launch yourself into the air, kicking your legs to power yourself across the yawning chasm. It is a miracle, but you make it to the other side, grabbing hold of the hive wall to stop your fall.

After taking a moment to catch your breath, you begin to explore the strange hive. You discover that the honey-combed holes are actually narrow tunnels that lead deeper into the structure. You duck down into the nearest tunnel and begin crawling into the clammy darkness.

After several minutes you find yourself entering a large chamber, lined on all sides with glowing green eggs. At the centre of the chamber is a gigantic bee, with immense diaphanous wings that glitter with magic. You guess that this is the queen – and she isn't happy that you have invaded her hive. The queen beats her wings and immediately, as if in answer to her unspoken command, a swarm of drones sweep towards you from out of one of the tunnels. You must fight this deadly swarm as a single enemy:

	Speed	Brawn	Armour	Health
Drones	7	3	4	40

Special abilities

♥ Stingers: The bees' stingers can punch through anything. Your *armour* is useless in this fight.

If you manage to defeat the drones, turn to **358**.

366

Instead of following Bern, you make a bee-line for the escaping wreekin. You guess that the stolen horn could be inside the sack that it is carrying. As you get closer, a ball of golden light whistles past your ear, slamming into the ground ahead of the wreekin. Suddenly, a wall of thorns rises up out of the boggy earth, cutting off its escape route. A quick glance over your shoulder confirms that it was Bern – the palm of one hand flickering with yellow magic.

However, before you can catch the stunned creature, a barbed net whips around your legs, slicing into your skin. As you desperately try and cut it away, there is a warbling cry as one of the wreekin pounces on you with its pronged trident:

	Speed	Brawn	Armour	Health
Wreekin hunter	8	8	5	40
Wreekin net	-	-	2	15

Special abilities

♥ Entrapment: You can only roll 1 die to determine your attack speed while you have the net around your legs. If you win a combat round, you can choose to attack the wreekin hunter or the net. If the net is destroyed then you can roll 2 dice for your speed as normal. If the hunter is killed first, then you can simply cut yourself free of the net.

If you defeat the wreekin, turn to 491.

367

'Now, here's the real deal,' says Bart, his expression turning solemn. 'The good news is that you're through to the next round. The bad news is that, from here on in it gets a lot tougher. Knuckles here has been checking out your opposition.' He gestures to the ogre, who gives a rumbling belch in response. 'There are some big names in this tournament – best fighters we've ever seen. I suggest you get some rest before the next round. You're going to need it.'

If you are ready for the next fight turn to 382. Otherwise, make a note of this entry number and return here when you are fully prepared for the next round.

368

You slice open the beetle's stomach, backing away as its gooey entrails pour out of the wound. Hobbling on its spindly legs, the beetle attempts to reach the glowing tree roots, seeking to draw more of the magic into its shattered body.

'Stop it!' shouts Shay. 'If it feeds it will heal!'

You have no intention of letting that happen. Springing onto the beast's back, you look for a soft spot between the creature's armoured wing cases. Then you drive your weapon deep into its fleshy skin. The beetle jerks backwards onto its hind legs, then, with a deafening screech, it collapses to the ground, sending a shockwave of dust and soil billowing out across the chamber.

The beetle has finally been defeated. You may now help yourself to one of the following rewards:

Bone scythe	Chitinous carapace	Sap-filled gland
(main hand: sword)	(chest)	(talisman)
+1 speed +2 brawn	+1 speed +2 armour	+1 speed
Ability: retaliation	Ability: charm	Ability: heal

If you have *Lorinwold's Field Guide to Roots, Herbs and Leaves* then you may also pick 4 root grass from this cavern. Make a note of these on your hero sheet. Then turn to 461.

369

'I ain't no good at it, as you could probably tell – but Mouse here, he'll show yer the ropes.' Afty nudges a younger child standing next to him, who beams at you excitedly.

If you decide to learn the pickpocket career you will gain the following abilities:

Patchwork pauper (pa): When replacing an item of equipment in your chest, gloves, cloak or feet locations on your hero sheet, you can keep the special ability from the old item but replace its name and attributes with those of the new item.

Loot master (pa): If you do not wish to choose a reward when you defeat an enemy, you may award yourself an extra 20 gold crowns instead.

While you are a pickpocket, you also have access to the thieves' guild. You can visit the guild at any time, at the cost of 5 gold crowns per visit (the guild likes to take a cut of your ill-gotten gains!). Once inside, you can purchase special items. To visit the guild, turn to 338. Remember, you can only access the guild if you are a pickpocket.

Make a note of your new abilities on your hero sheet. Thanking the children, you head back into the town. Turn to 348.

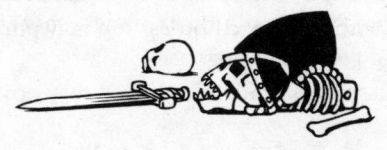

370

There is wild applause as the speedy, agile dervish is finally brought down. You may take one of the following items as a reward:

Desert keffiyeh	Ebony	Agal of shifting sands
(head)	(main hand: sword)	(head)
+1 speed +2 brawn	+2 speed +3 brawn	+2 magic +2 armour
	Ability: ebony and ivory	

As you exit the tunnel, you find a jostling crowd of people waiting for you, all eager to meet the great warrior of the arena. Some are begging for autographs (the quill and parchment already in their hands), whilst others pester you to show off your best moves. Soon, you are surrounded on all sides by a deafening crescendo of voices, all asking or demanding something from you. (If you have a *photograph* in your possession, then you can sign this and hand it over to an eager fan for 50 gold crowns.)

You are relieved when Bart and Knuckles finally put in an appearance. The burly ogre pushes the crowds aside as Bart ushers you into a private room.

'Well, well. Getting quite a reputation around here,' he smiles, handing over your latest winnings. (You have gained 80 gold crowns). 'We're through to the semi-finals. Just two more fights and you'll be crowned the champion!'

When you are ready for your next fight, turn to 391.

371

'Yes, yes of course,' says Totsvig, brightening up suddenly. 'All donations to the Botany Society will be gratefully appreciated.' He rummages underneath one of the benches, then reappears moments later with a case filled with flasks and bottles. You may purchase any of the following for 40 gold crowns each:

Gourd of healing (1 use)	Elixir of invisibility (1 use)
(backpack)	(backpack)
Use any time in combat to restore 6 *health*	Special ability: vanish

'My assistant, Tanner, is a promising young herbalist,' says Totsvig, smiling proudly at the small girl. 'You might find her skills useful, also.'

Will you:

Ask Totsvig a question?	310
Talk to Tanner and view her wares?	421

372

As you get closer, you become aware of an irregular humming sound coming from the black rock. On each hum, a green light pulses along the veins that branch through the rock, moving from the top of the stone to its jagged, half-buried tip. Warily, you place a hand against the side of the rock – and snap it back quickly, surprised at how deathly cold it is to the touch.

Will you:

Take a sample of the rock?	415
Leave the rock and follow the tunnel?	428

373

Inside, you find people milling around a row of booths, where gold is being exchanged for coloured tickets. Next to the booths, a large chalk board provides the odds on the upcoming fight:

Left Hook Luke 2-1   *Samson the Small 20-2*

Taking a nearby set of stairs, you emerge onto a balcony overlooking a circular pit. The floor of the pit is wet and marshy, littered with skulls, bones and other human (and half-human) remains. All around this makeshift arena, people are crowding into wooden stalls and booths – pushing and shoving to get the best vantage points.

Then, from out of an archway overlooking the pit, a wizard on a magic carpet swoops out over the assembled crowds. 'Ladies and gentlemen – it's that time you've all been waiting for. Yes, it's the five hundred and eleventh gladiatorial games!'

The crowds cheer and holler as the wizard-announcer soars above their heads. 'Now, please put your hands together for the first of our brave competitors. On the red side, from the exotic pirate islands of Barbica, we have the enigmatic ...'

You miss the rest of the announcement, as you are roughly spun around – to face the leering visage of a fat, bald-headed ogre. Standing next to him is a thin man, dressed in fine-embroidered clothes.

'Good day my friend,' he says, lifting a monocle to his left eye to inspect you better. 'You look a fine specimen, yes, a fine specimen indeed.' He offers out his hand, covered in a plethora of sparkling rings. 'I am Bart Murkrock and this is my business associate, Knuckles.' The ogre gives an unsettling growl. 'I noticed you coming in and I hope you don't mind me pointing this out, but you really should be down *there*.' He points to the pit, where two fighters are now entering the circle. The cries and shouts from the crowds are almost deafening.

'Look, I'll keep this simple. My prize fighter is ill – she's got the marsh fever. A terrible sickness ... doubt she'll make it through. So, if you're brave enough to step up to the mark, you could make yourself a household name. Not to mention,' the man licks his lips greedily, 'substantially richer. So, what do you say?'

Will you:

Agree to take part in the gladiatorial games?	286
Decline the offer?	267

374

The undead jester has been defeated, his body crumbling into a fine black dust. You may now help yourself to one of the following items:

Jester's cap	**Patchwork jerkin**
(head)	(chest)
+1 speed +1 brawn	+1 speed +1 brawn
Ability: last laugh	Ability: evade

All around you, you see the panicked faces of men, women and children, struggling to defend themselves from the blood-hungry vampires.

A scream draws your attention to the near wall. You see the blacksmith trying to defend himself from two vampires. Behind him, the family that you saw in the entrance hall are huddled against the wall. It was the mother who screamed, her children's faces buried in her dress. The blacksmith is trying to protect them but he is wounded and needs help.

Then, over to your right, you see Spink dodging between the slashing claws and biting teeth of a crowd of vampires. He is headed for a big cauldron of soup positioned between two of the tables. Reaching into his coat pocket, he produces a bottle. Suddenly, two vampires pounce on top of him, knocking him to the ground. The bottle skitters across the floor.

Will you:

Help Spink to recover the bottle?	360
Help the blacksmith and the family?	308

375

The tunnel broadens out, becoming a huge cavernous chamber filled with giant, peak-topped mushrooms. You haven't travelled far into this peculiar forest, before you become aware of a drumming, skittering sound coming from up ahead. It sounds like hundreds of fast-moving legs, beating and scuffling against the earth. As you scan your surroundings, your eyes come to rest on something black and snake-like, zigzagging between the mushrooms.

As it nears, you see that it is a giant centipede – its long, segmented body giving off the same sickly green hue as the black rock and the withered tree roots. With startling speed, the multi-legged creature is upon you, its serrated mandibles clicking together hungrily:

	Speed	Brawn	Armour	Health
Centipede	6	5	3	60

Special abilities

♥ Downsized: For every 10 *health* that the centipede loses, one of its body segments is destroyed, reducing its *speed* and *brawn* by 1 each time.

If you manage to defeat this multi-legged foe turn to 287.

376

You sit alone in a lattice-walled gazebo, facing one of the dryads' quiet wooded glades. It has been an hour since you returned with Solandris and the unicorn's horn. Since then, you have received no news from the cave. You wonder if, perhaps, you were too late to save the queen and the unicorn after all.

Tired from your journey, you start to close your eyes, your head nodding forward onto your chest. As you shake yourself awake, you catch sight of a silver-gold radiance at the far side of the glade. In an instant, all your thoughts of sleep are gone as you gaze upon the captivating majesty of the dryad queen and her unicorn.

You rise hurriedly to your feet, suddenly feeling awkward and ungainly as you bow before them. The unicorn bows its head in answer – its spiral horn glittering in the sunlight.

Your attention shifts to the queen, who is walking gracefully towards you, her long gown of leaves sparkling in a dazzling radiance of hues. When she stops next to you, her face is impassive and unreadable.

'You have saved my life,' she whispers. 'You have protected my sisters and saved our grove. If you wish to become one of our own, then take my hand and the power of nature will be yours. Otherwise, ask of me what you will, shadow walker, and then be gone from our lands.'

Will you:

Learn the ranger career (requirement: warrior)?	417
Ask about Jenlar Cornelius?	319
Ask about the shadow gate?	425
Ask about the mark on your arm?	383

When you wish to end your audience with the queen, turn to 336.

377

The fire elemental is finally extinguished, its blazing form reduced to a pile of smouldering ash. You may now take one of the following items as a reward:

Flame mantle	Molten gauntlets	Firebrand
(cloak)	(gloves)	(main hand: wand)
+2 speed +1 armour	+2 brawn +1 armour	+2 speed +2 magic
Ability: fire aura	Ability: fire aura	Ability: fire aura
	(requirement: warrior)	(requirement: mage)

If you are a mage, turn to 407. Otherwise, return to the quest map to continue your adventure.

378

'Treasure hunter, eh?' nods the barman. 'Everyone around here's looking for treasure. This marsh used to be full of gold and precious jewels, but it's all been picked clean now. You've got about as much chance of finding anything out there as I have of becoming the next king of Valeron.' He gives a snort of amusement. 'Look, if you're really serious about finding some treasure, then there's an old local legend that might give yer some hope. When the original prospectors came here, they spoke of a cave, out in those mangroves – and inside it, a treasure hoard of gold and jewels; enough to make anyone a king or queen. Only thing is, the explorer who found it never managed to find it a second time.' The barman shrugs his shoulders. 'Never heard of anyone losing a cave before. Sounds like nonsense if you ask me, but doesn't stop the treasure hunters coming in their droves. If it's good for business, it's all good by me.'

Will you:

Ask if he knows Jenlar Cornelius?	411
Ask if there is any work going?	420
Turn your attention back to the taproom?	404

379

Your mighty blows silence the beast once and for all. The crowd go wild as you raise your arms in the air, in a victory salute. You may now claim one of the following as your reward:

Mane of the black lion	**Nalsa's claws**	**Hunter's hide**
(cloak)	(main hand: fist weapon)	(chest)
+1 speed +3 brawn	+1 speed +2 brawn	+1 speed +2 armour
Ability: fearless	Ability: piercing	Ability: immobilise

After the match, Bart hands over your winnings. (You have gained 60 gold crowns.) To face your next opponent, turn to 352. If you wish to return to the arena at a later date, make a note of the indicated entry number on your hero sheet.

380

You take Shay's hand and help her down into the bowl-shaped depression. 'Look! This is dark age architecture,' she gasps, hurrying over to the nearest ruined pillar. Along its length are a number of strange runes and symbols. 'This must date back to the culling. Yes, these markings here – I think they are Illumanti.' She shakes her head sadly. 'How a people could destroy such beauty.'

Will you:

Ask Shay to tell you more?   478

Explore the ruins for yourself?   465

381

'Oh is that so?' A foot slams into your back, knocking you forward onto your stomach. 'You are a trespasser!'

You roll over onto your elbows, to see another of the green-skinned females standing over you, a curved knife held in each hand. 'This one must have seen something,' she snarls. 'Let me get the truth out of them – my way!' From the cold-hearted glare she is giving you, you suspect her method of interrogation is not going to be pleasant.

'Hold! All of you!'

To your surprise, it is a man's voice. You turn your head, to see a warrior in forest green leathers emerge from the trees. His long blond hair is braided with feathers and cords, and about his neck hang a number of beaded charms. 'Since when do the dryads hunt so openly,' he scowls, 'and without judgement or mercy?' He starts forward into the clearing, a yellow glow cascading down his arms to gather along the tips of his fingers.

'Bern Farstrider,' sneers the knife-woman. 'This is none of your concern. Stand down or face the consequences.'

From around the circle, there is the creak of bowstrings as the archers nock arrows and take aim at the warrior.

He shakes his head sadly. 'Has it really come to this – that my return is welcomed with an arrow in the back. Well, so be it.' Turn to 474.

382

The portcullis rises and you step out into the arena. The announcer swoops overhead, his flying carpet leaving a trail of glittering stars hanging in the air. 'And in the red corner, from the blighted coast of Cretaria, we have a mighty gladiator. His savage race know no pain, no mercy, no forgiveness. Put your hands together folks for Zen the Minorian!'

The portcullis at the opposite end of the arena rattles open. For a moment there is a hushed silence. Then you hear the clatter of hooves as a giant, armoured creature charges out of the tunnel. It has the upper body of a man and the lower-body of a bull. Wielding a barbed spear, the Minorian dashes towards you, sending muddy water showering in all directions.

You must now fight this deadly adversary:

	Speed	Brawn	Armour	Health
Zen	10	10	8	60

Special abilities

🭬 Charge: Zen can roll 3 dice for speed in the first round of combat. He is immune to any abilities that reduce his speed dice for this first round.

🭬 Trample: If Zen gets a 🎲🎲 when rolling for his damage score, your hero is trampled under the beast's mighty hooves. This adds an extra 5 to Zen's damage score.

If you defeat Zen, turn to 216.

383

You start to pull back your sleeve, to reveal the mark, but the queen recoils, looking fearful for the first time. 'Please, I do not need to see it. I feel its presence and it is a dark thing. That is why I would ask that you leave our lands. I will not have the taint of shadow here.'

'But what is it?' you implore, anger edging into your voice. 'I don't remember anything. I woke with this on my arm – and since then, everyone has judged me, the moment they see it.'

The queen raises an eyebrow. 'Yes, unfortunate – or perhaps fortunate that your past has been taken from you. That mark is what all the shadowborn carry. It means that you obey the legion and would give your life for it. It also grants you many powers, although I imagine these are now forgotten to you.'

It takes several moments for the queen's words to sink in. 'Wait – I am to obey the legion. You mean, I am just like those *things* I saw in the city – the monsters that came through the shadow gate? Are you saying that this mark on my arm … makes me a monster?'

The queen looks you straight in the eye. 'I don't see a monster standing before me. You saved my life and the dryad grove. You are only a monster, shadow walker, if you choose to become one.'

To ask the queen another question, turn to 376. Otherwise turn to 336.

384

The barman looks busy, scurrying from one end of the bar to the other. When you finally manage to grab his attention, he hurries over, rubbing his hands on his greasy apron. 'What yer want?' he asks gruffly.

Will you:

Ask about Jenlar Cornelius?	411
Ask if there is any work going?	420
Ask about local rumours?	378
Turn your attention back to the taproom?	404

385

You silence the vampire with a killing blow, watching as the giant man topples backwards, his body exploding into plumes of black ash as he hits the ground.

Baron Greylock has been defeated. You may now take one of the following items:

Cloak of white winter	Winter's bite	Baron's boots
(cloak)	(main hand: axe)	(feet)
+1 speed +2 brawn	+2 speed +2 brawn	+1 speed +1 armour
Ability: piercing	Ability: bleed	Ability: dominate
	(requirement: warrior)	

Eldias is still sparring with his foe, agilely dodging the vampire's attacks. She makes a hasty lunge, throwing herself off balance. Eldias takes the opportunity to dart over to a broken table. Ripping one of the wooden legs free, he makes several cutting motions with his sword. A second later, he is holding up a sharp-ended stake. As Lady Roe clambers to her feet, hissing and spitting like a venomous snake, Eldias throws back his arm and hurls the stake straight through her heart. The vampire's horrified scream is cut short as she disintegrates into a fine black dust.

Eldias sheaths his sword and flashes you a cocky smile. 'Now that, my friend, is how you do it in style.'

You can't help but marvel at the man's self-assured skill. He makes killing these deadly foes look like child's play. It seems you are not the only one to appreciate his performance.

'Bravo!'

The sound of clapping forces you to turn. The count is standing amidst the wreckage of his hall, watching you both with dark, hungry eyes. At his side stand two guards, dressed in heavy chain mail armour.

'It is time,' hisses the count, his lips curling back over his fanged teeth, 'for you to die.' Turn to 392.

386

You nervously pace up and down, waiting to be called into the pit. Through the portcullis grill, you can see the wizard zipping around the crowded stalls, performing his pre-match warm-up. Finally, you hear your name called, and the portcullis rattles open. Taking a deep breath, you walk out into the pit to be greeted by a tumultuous roar from the crowds.

The opposing portcullis lifts open and, for the first time, you glimpse the other fighter. It is a woman, dressed in black leathers. As she steps out into the murky light, you give a gasp of astonishment. Instead of a human face, the woman has the striped head of a tiger. You notice that she carries no weapons on her person, only vicious claws that protrude from her tiger-like paws.

'Ladies and gentlemen, this distinguished fighter needs no intro-duction. Hailing from the steamy jungles of Terrall, we have the heart of darkness itself ... the savage, the deadly and the ever-so-slightly sexy, Shara Khana!'

The crowd cheer and stamp their feet as the woman takes a bow. 'I am Shara Khana,' she announces with pride. 'And no man, woman or beast, has ever bested me in combat.' She turns to face you, her piercing, lambent eyes filled with a hungry malice. 'Such a hapless cur. I look forward to feasting on your still-beating heart!' With astonishing speed, the tigress springs towards you, her sharp claws fully extended to rip and rend.

It is time to battle your toughest foe yet:

	Speed	Brawn	Armour	Health
Shara Khana	10	12	12	60

Special abilities
♥ Cat's speed: Shara Khana rolls 3 dice to determine her attack speed. Your hero's special abilities can be used to reduce this number, if available.

If you manage to defeat Shara Khana, turn to 162.

387

You step down from the carriage, wincing as the cold wind and rain lashes against your face. Lady Roe seems unperturbed by the stormy elements. She throws back her head, spinning round on the spot with glee.

'Oh, how I love a good storm,' she gasps, lifting her hands to catch the rainwater. 'My dear papa couldn't have asked for better weather.'

She starts towards a pair of black-wood doors at the base of one of the towers.

You follow her but are brought up short by the coach driver, who blocks your way. His grizzled features look almost bestial in the flickering storm-light, his long black beard dripping with water.

'Yer can't go thata way,' he says, his rancid breath forcing you to recoil. 'Yer can see Lady Roe later. At the meal.' He stabs a finger in the opposite direction, towards a smaller door set underneath an arch.

Outside of it are several barrels and boxes, with piles of rotting left-overs heaped inside. A scraggly dog is currently sniffing at the contents. 'It's the servant's entrance for you,' grins the coach driver.

For a moment, you wonder if a mistake has been made. You turn back, but Lady Roe has already entered the castle – the oaken doors banging closed behind her.

'Come on, move it,' he growls. 'Yer wanna catch yer death out here?'

The driver pushes you towards the other door. You reluctantly oblige, wrinkling your nose as you pass the rotted food. Surely, Lady Roe never meant for you to take the servant's entrance, did she? You open the door and step inside. Turn to 396.

388

You find yourself back in the rift, facing a pathway of stone that winds down the side of the crevice. Following it, you soon find yourself outside another cave opening. Turn to 426.

389

You hack and slash your way through the creature's many heads. At last, after an exhausting battle, the beast finally lies dead, its immense body slowly sinking into the mire. You may now take one of the following rewards:

Hydra-scaled gloves	Hydra's wing	Marsh striders
(gloves)	(left hand: shield)	(feet)
+2 magic +2 armour	+2 speed +2 armour	+2 speed +2 brawn
Ability: regrowth	Ability: deflect	Ability: sideswipe
(requirement: mage)	(requirement: warrior)	(requirement: rogue)

You also find the decayed bodies of several other unfortunate travellers, lying in the bog. From their remains, you are able to loot 30 gold crowns. Return to the quest map to continue your adventure.

390

The moment you apply pressure to the wall panel, it swings outwards revealing a small, candlelit landing. There are two sets of stairs here – one set leads up to a door of banded black iron and the other spirals downwards, past cobwebs and flickering torches.

Will you:

Head up the staircase?	322
Head down the staircase?	493

391

'Good luck,' says Bart. 'This time you're going to need it.'

As you walk out into the arena, you are met by a roar of applause and cheers. The stadium is full to bursting point, and to your relief, most of the crowd are chanting your name, waving their blue-coloured tickets in the air.

'Welcome one and all, to the first of our semi-final match-ups,' announces the wizard, zipping around the stadium on his flying carpet. 'In the red corner today, we are honoured to have the self-proclaimed king of the frozen tundra – King Louis the Sixteenth!'

Two enormous white fists shake and rattle the portcullis. There is the sound of grating, squeaking metal, then, to your surprise and alarm, you see the portcullis ripped free of the wall. You dodge aside as it goes careening past you in a ball of twisted metal. With a roar, a giant white ape bounds out of the tunnel. Rising up onto its hind legs, the creature beats its broad chest, its savage snarls revealing a mouth filled with inch-long teeth.

'Well that's a grand entrance and no mistake,' laughs the wizard, his carpet lurching rapidly to a safe distance.

The white ape drops back onto all fours, and then charges towards you, the ground shaking and trembling underfoot. This will certainly be a fight to remember:

	Speed	Brawn	Armour	Health
King Louis	12	12	12	50

Special abilities

♥ King of the swingers: The white ape's swinging fists are hard to avoid. At the end of every combat round, you automatically take 15 damage. *Armour* can be used to absorb this damage.

If you manage to defeat this powerful opponent, turn to 359.

392

The two guards charge towards you, their gleaming swords held high above their heads. Eldias intercepts them, his own swords cutting a skilful dance through the air. One of the guards goes down in seconds, his armour dropping empty to the ground as his body is turned to ash. Ducking beneath the remaining guard's swing, Eldias kicks him backwards. Then, sheathing one of his blades, he summons yellow fire into the palm of his hand.

'I judge you,' he shouts, his voice suddenly taking on a frightening intensity. 'And I find you guilty!' He hurls the fire at the guard. It hits him squarely in the chest, lifting him off his feet and slamming him against the far wall. The guard crumples to the ground, his body turning to dust.

With a snarl, the count spins on his heel and makes a run for it, his black cloak billowing out behind him. You are about to pursue when a scream echoes around the chamber. It came from the far end of the hall, where the last survivors are defending themselves from a mob of vampires. You can see Spink and the blacksmith with their backs to a pillar. The scream must have come from one of the vampires, as you spot an explosion of black ash billowing across the room.

'They need help,' scowls Eldias. 'There are too many of them.'

He draws a pistol and starts running towards the crowd of vampires. 'Go after the count,' he shouts back. 'I'll handle these. Go!'

Without a moment's hesitation, you hurry after the escaping count. Turn to 450.

393

The tunnel ends abruptly in a large, rough-hewn chamber. Knotted roots hang down from the ceiling, glowing with a bright yellow light. Beneath them, chewing at the ends of the roots is the largest beetle you have ever seen.

The moment you enter the cave, the insect stops feeding and turns to face you. Between a pair of stag-like antlers, its enormous mandibles click back and forth, dripping with glowing tree sap.

'That's it!' gasps Shay in horror. 'That is what has been feeding on all the trees. It has been absorbing their magic ... growing bigger and stronger, while the trees wither away.'

You realise that the roots hanging above you must belong to Woad – the only tree left standing in the withered glade. To save Woad you will have to defeat this monstrous bug.

The creature's wing cases snap open, revealing pale, translucent wings. As they hum into life, the giant beetle flies towards you, its razor-sharp antlers looking to run you through. You push Shay to safety, then prepare to take on this mighty mutated insect:

	Speed	Brawn	Armour	Health
KerKlick	7	5	7	40

Special abilities

🖤 Pincer movement: If you roll a ⚀ when rolling for your hero's attack speed, you are immediately caught in KerKlick's pincers and must lose 2 *health*. This ability ignores *armour*. If you have an ability that lets you re-roll dice then you may use it to try and avoid this.

🖤 Unnatural growth: At the end of every combat round, KerKlick raises its *brawn* by 1, up to a maximum of 10.

If you manage to splat this over-sized bug, turn to 368.

Despite your wound, you are able to expertly weave between the assassin's flashing blades. At last, you strike him down. In his final moments, the albino grabs your arm and pulls you close.

'You are shadow born,' he rasps. 'I was hired to kill you ... to stop you ... you were following the knight ... to kill him.' His grip tightens, his gloved fingers digging into your branded flesh. 'His death ... the arrow ... it was meant for you. The fool died trying to protect you!'

With a final gasp, the assassin's eyes close and his body becomes limp.

You drop to your knees, exhausted and sick from pain. For what seems like an eternity, you sit hunched in silence, dwelling on the assassin's words. Were you really intending to kill the knight? Was it your plan all along to steal his documents so you could enter Avian's castle? You peel back your sleeve and gaze down at the purple brand. You wonder if it is the mark of a killer. An assassin, perhaps?

You struggle to your feet, more determined than ever to find the truth about who you are – what you are. Perhaps Jenlar Cornelius will be able to provide the answers that you seek.

For defeating Logan, you may now take one of the following as your reward:

Death strike	**Logan's runners**	**Magpie's mischief**
(left hand: bow)	(feet)	(ring)
+1 speed +3 brawn	+2 speed +1 brawn	+1 armour
Ability: bull's eye	Ability: sidestep	Ability: steal
	(requirement: rogue)	

If you are a rogue, turn to 410. Otherwise, after you have rested and bandaged your wounds, you resume your journey. Return to the quest map.

'They are poachers,' says the leader, eyeing the corpses with contempt. 'They are trespassers in the grove and their foolish actions may have harmed the ...'

'Enough! Do not speak of our secrets!' This comes from the woman behind you. She presses her knife deeper into your neck. 'This one must have seen something. Let me get the truth out of them – my way!'

The leader looks displeased at being spoken to in such a way. There is a heated exchange in a dialect that you have never heard before. It ends with you taking a kick in the back, which forces you down onto your knees. 'There will be no grove and no magic unless we take action.' The woman behind you grabs hold of your head, pulling it back – then places the blade of her knife against your throat.

'Hold! All of you!'

To your surprise, it is a man's voice. From the corner of your vision, you see a warrior in forest green leathers emerge from the trees. He has long blond hair, braided with feathers and cords, and about his neck hang a number of beaded charms. 'Since when do the dryads hunt so openly,' he scowls, 'and without judgement or mercy?' He starts forward into the clearing, a yellow glow cascading down his arms to gather along the tips of his fingers.

'Bern Farstrider,' snaps the woman standing at your back. 'This is none of your concern. Stand down or face the consequences.'

From around the circle, there is the creak of bowstrings as the archers nock arrows and take aim at the warrior.

He shakes his head sadly. 'Has it really come to this – that my return is welcomed with an arrow in the back. Well, so be it.' Turn to **474**.

396

You find yourself in a kitchen, filled with noise and steam as a number of cooks hurry around a set of bubbling pots. Your arm is grabbed by the coach driver, who proceeds to lead you through the hot, noisy kitchen into a quieter side passage. You follow it into a small room where a number of chests and boxes are lined up along the walls. A guard in heavy chain mail, stands by the far door. He glares at you from beneath his helmet, a halberd held across his chest.

'Yer weapons,' says the coach driver, holding out his dirt-stained hands. 'Hand 'em over.'

Will you:

Do as the man says?	294
Refuse to hand over your weapons?	288

397

Inside, you find a sack containing 50 gold crowns and a selection of rare treasures. If you wish, you may now choose one of the following:

Majestic shoulders	**Abyssal brimstone**	**Dour fury**
(cloak)	(ring)	(necklace)
+2 speed +2 armour	+1 magic	+1 speed
Ability: royal regalia	Ability: cauterise	Ability: savagery
(requirement: warrior)		

You also find a small *stone tablet*, which you may take:

Stone tablet
(backpack)
Its surface is covered in
strange symbols

If you wish to take the *stone tablet*, then make a note of it on your hero sheet along with the number 19. Once you have updated your hero sheet, turn to 482.

398

You must have the *Tiger's fury* talisman equipped if you wish to learn the berserker career. As soon as this item is unequipped or you learn a new career, you lose the abilities associated with this career.

The berserker has the following abilities:

Seeing red (pa): If your *health* is reduced to 20 or less, you may add 2 to your *speed*. If you are healed and your *health* rises above 20, you lose your bonus.

Raining blows (mo): Every time you get a ⚅ result when rolling for your damage score, you may automatically roll another die to add further damage. If you roll a ⚅ again, you may roll another die – and so on.

Turn to 414 to return to the arena.

399

The count's great hall stretches out before you, its long tables groaning with a succulent array of wild meats and fruit. The diners, all dressed in extraordinary finery, are laughing and joking with each other – drinking wine and mead from large golden goblets. High above their heads, colourful banners and ribbons hang down from the ceiling, swaying back and forth like hypnotic pendulums.

On a stage in one corner of the room, a group of musicians are playing to an attentive audience. Elsewhere, a jester is capering madly around the tables, his face covered in white paint and rouge. He laughs and giggles as he juggles a set of knives with practised ease.

You scan the room for Lady Roe. At last you spot her, seated at the top table with several other gentlemen and ladies. Next to her sits a regal-looking man in a high-collared black cloak. His thin, gaunt face is partly concealed behind a golden mask. On seeing your group enter the hall, he stands and claps his hands together.

Immediately, a hush falls over the room. The musicians stop playing – a few discordant notes hanging in the air – and the jester freezes in mid-step. All the diners put down their knives, forks and goblets and rise to their feet. You notice that they are all looking at you and the other members of your group with an intense interest.

'Distinguished guests,' says the count, his deep voice carrying the full length of the room, 'I promised you a night to remember.'

Your hands go to your concealed weapons as you quickly eye up the nearby tables. The diners standing around them all look tensed, as if awaiting a command.

'Now is the time, my dear friends.' The count raises his arms into the air. 'I give to you ... dessert!'

There is a howl and then a scream. Before you can register what is happening, you see the count's diners descending on your group like a pack of wild animals. There are snapping fangs and claws ... a jet of crimson arcs through the air. More screams follow. Then a woman's face swings into view, her fanged incisors dripping with blood. It is then that you realise the shocking truth – the count's diners are all vampires!

'This is it,' says Spink, drawing a stake. 'This is war!'

You watch dumbfounded as he races towards the nearest diner, expertly staking the man through the heart. The vampire screeches in pain before exploding in a cloud of black dust.

Then you are hit by something. You are flung into a table, knocking over plates and food. Desperately you snatch up a nearby knife, as a vampire duke attempts to bite your neck. You wrestle free, sinking your knife into its leg. But the vampire isn't registering any pain. Of course, these creatures can only be harmed by the items that Spink gave you.

You draw out your concealed weapons, just as the vampire gives a shriek of pain. It falls forward, landing on top of you, the back of its head a smouldering ruin. As you push him away, you see a man in a black coat and hat sliding down one of the banners. In one of his hands is a smoking flint-lock pistol.

Before you can thank your mysterious rescuer, you are swung round to face a fresh adversary. Turn to **435**.

The flame giant has been defeated. Its roaring body of flames are silenced forever as it vaporises into a cloud of black ash and smoke, blackening the sky.

Around the island you find the charred remains of several less fortunate adventurers. You have gained 200 gold crowns and may now help yourself to one of the following items:

Crimson cuffs	**Firewalker's faceguard**	**Burning heretic**
(gloves)	(head)	(main hand: sword)
+1 speed +4 magic	+1 speed +3 armour	+3 speed +3 brawn
Ability: sear	Ability: overpower	Ability: critical strike
(requirement: mage)	(requirement: warrior)	(requirement: rogue)

Elated with your victory, you head back across the stepping stones to the black-stone island. From here, you take the pathway eastwards, into the dark cave. Turn to 426.

401

Totsvig sets you to work – to test some fragments of the black stone with a number of different chemicals. He watches you intently as you record the results of your investigations. It appears that the rock reacts strongly to anything it comes into contact with, giving off a foul-smelling green smoke. It also appears to introduce mutations into the compounds that are created.

Totsvig is clearly impressed by your findings. So much so, that he offers to teach you some of the basics of his profession. As a mage, you may now learn the alchemist career.

The alchemist has the following abilities:

Good taste (pa): Each time you use a backpack item that raises *magic* in combat, roll 1 die and add the result to the item's benefit. For example, if you use a pot of magic (+3 to *magic*) and you rolled a 🎲, you would benefit from +8 to your *magic* instead.

Midas touch (pa): Every time you destroy an item of equipment (by replacing it with a new item) you gain 30 gold crowns. This ability does not work on backpack items.

Once you have updated your hero sheet, turn to 310 if you wish to talk to Totsvig further, or return to the quest map to continue your journey.

402

In less than a heartbeat your weapons are in your hands. You swing at the guard, taking him by surprise. A glancing blow knocks him backwards, sending him toppling over one of the chests.

The coach driver gives an animal-like snarl. 'Vermin! Yer really shouldn't have done that!' He tugs a club loose from his belt and then lunges at you, his teeth bared.

	Speed	Brawn	Armour	Health
Jenkins	7	8	5	30

If you lose the combat, turn to 312. If you manage to defeat Jenkins, turn to 413.

403

The tunnel ends in a circular cave filled with a bubbling pool of mud. Several items of equipment are floating in the thick gooey sludge, including a longsword and a white polished staff. Across the other side of the cave is another tunnel opening.

Will you:

Try and retrieve the items?	337
Continue onwards?	361

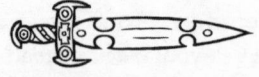

404

The taproom of Pisa's Rest is almost full to bursting point. As you make your way through the smoky haze, you spot a woman weaving between the crowded tables. She is carrying an open leather case, which she passes under the noses of the curious patrons. One man lifts a pair of metal gauntlets from out of the case, inspecting them thoughtfully. Gold exchanges hands, and the woman moves on to another table. You suspect she is a tinker, selling odds and end of armour and equipment.

Where the sloping floor has sunk into the marsh, a make-shift bridge of wooden planks has been erected, forming a pathway to the bar. Behind it, a skinny man in a greasy apron, is serving drinks to the waiting clientele.

Will you:

Talk to the barman?	384
View the tinker's wares?	311
Leave the tavern?	348

405

'Hurry,' says the boy, looking back over his shoulder. Most of the crowd have already left the room. 'Take what you need and let's go.'

You may select a main-hand and a left-hand item from the selection on offer:

Crucifix	Stake	Garlic	Magic mirror
(main hand)	(main hand)	(left hand)	(left hand)
+1 speed	+2 brawn	Reduce enemy	+1 speed
Ability: heal	Ability: stake	*brawn* by 1	Ability: reflect

When you have made your choices and updated your hero sheet, turn to **416**.

406

The eagle veers around in a tight arc, before swooping down to land next to you on the moss-covered rock. Solandris turns in the saddle, eyeing you with a newfound respect.

'That was nice work back there – for a human. Now, did you get the mandrake root?'

You pat the side of your backpack, wary of the dryad's intent. After all, it wasn't that long ago that Solandris was holding a knife to your throat.

'Don't worry,' she says, reading your expression. 'I followed you to the wreekin village.' She glances back, towards the corpse of the giant. 'Bern convinced me of the urgency of your quest. I suppose it's the ranger you have to thank for saving your life. Now, let's get back to the village. Their leader doesn't have long.'

You accept Solandris' hand, climbing onto the saddle behind her. Then, the giant eagle takes to the air, its enormous wings rising and falling as it ascends out of the murky swampland. Turn to 525.

407

As a mage you may also take the following item:

Core of flame
(talisman)
+1 magic
Ability: pyromancer career (see below)

You must have the *core of flame* talisman equipped if you wish to learn the pyromancer career. As soon as this item is unequipped or you learn a new career, you lose the abilities associated with this career.

The pyromancer has the following abilities:

Ignite (co): If you win a combat round, instead of rolling for a damage score, you can cast *ignite*. This automatically inflicts 2 damage dice to *all* your opponents, ignoring *armour*. It also causes them to *burn* (see below). *Ignite* can only be used once per combat. (Note: You cannot use modifier abilities to increase this damage.)

Burn (pa): All opponents who have suffered health damage from *ignite* automatically lose 1 *health* at the end of every combat round. This ability ignores *armour*.

Once you have made your decision, return to the quest map to continue your journey.

408

When you re-enter the hall, you find yourself confronted by a scene of chaos. Bodies lie everywhere, sprawled like rag-dolls over broken tables and chairs. Fights still continue in small pockets around the room as the last of the vampires seek to destroy the remnants of the resistance.

You see the man in the black coat and hat weaving dextrously through their ranks, spinning twin swords in an elaborate pattern of swirling blades. Wherever he moves, vampires are cut down, reduced to dust the moment they come into contact with his magical swords. Behind him, Spink follows, a flint-lock pistol in one hand and a crucifix in the other.

You hurry to join the fight but skid to a halt when you see two vampires striding purposefully towards you. One you recognise instantly. It is the Lady Roe, her long white gown splattered with blood. Next to her walks a tall, barrel-chested man. A thick fur cloak is flung back across his shoulders, making them appear even wider than they already are. In his massive hands, he carries a double-headed axe.

Suddenly, the black-coated stranger appears at your side. 'I'm Eldias Falks,' he says, his eyes twinkling beneath the brim of his hat. 'Glad you could make the party.' He watches as the two vampires approach, bowing to them with exaggerated flourish. 'Ah, the Lady Roe and Baron Greylock. An honour to make your acquaintance. A shame it will be such a brief meeting.'

Will you:

Attack Lady Roe?	302
Attack Baron Greylock?	306

409

You scramble down into the crater, your eyes stinging from the thick green smoke. At the bottom, you discover a jagged splinter of black rock sticking up out of the charred soil. It glows as if alive, each pulse giving off more of the green, putrid-smelling smoke.

The rock is far too large for you to pull out of the ground. It also looks too thick and strong to break. As you ponder your next move, you suddenly notice a large burrow-like tunnel to the north, winding away into darkness.

Will you:

Examine the black rock further?	372
Enter the earthen tunnel?	428

410

Searching through Logan's belongings, you discover a number of powders and poison vials, wrapped in tattered cloth. As a rogue, you may now learn the assassin career.

The assassin has the following abilities:

First strike (pa): (requires a dagger in the main hand.) Before combat begins you may automatically inflict 1 damage dice to an opponent, ignoring *armour*. This will also inflict any harmful passive abilities you have, such as *venom* and *bleed*.
Deadly poisons (mo): If you have the *venom* special ability, its damage is increased by 1 (causing 3 points of damage instead of only 2).

Once you have made your decision, return to the quest map to continue your journey.

411

'Who?' snaps the barman, cupping a hand to his ear. 'Cornelius, yer say? The only Cornelius I ever heard of is the marsh man. A crazy old hermit who lives out in the swamp. Never set eyes on 'im myself, but he's something of a local legend. They reckons he can see the future.' He snorts dismissively. 'Like I said, crazy old man. Now, I got work to do so hurry it up.'

Will you:

Ask if there is any work going?	420
Ask about local rumours?	378
Turn your attention back to the taproom?	404

412

The crumbling walls and weed-choked flagstones offer up a wide selection of different herbs. If you have *Lorinwold's Field Guide to Roots, Herbs and Leaves* then you may add 2 bramble thorn, 1 thimble sage and 1 taponica bulb to your collection. (Make a note of the herbs on your hero sheet.)

Finding little else of interest amongst the outbuildings, you make your way over to one of the larger, colonnaded temples. Most of its ceiling has caved in, littering the cracked mosaic-floor with dusty piles of stone and rubble. Whatever furniture or items of worth this place once contained, they have long since been buried or looted by thieves. You are about to leave and continue your journey, when you spot a black-stone chest resting against one of the walls. You hurry over to inspect it – discovering that it is still locked. There is no keyhole or any other obvious way of opening the chest. Perhaps the strange angular runes that are etched into the lid, might provide a clue.

If you have *The Compendium of Dwarven Lore* then turn to 471. Otherwise, you cannot understand the complex markings. Turn to 482.

Jenkins is dead. You turn to face the guard, who is still struggling back onto his feet, encumbered by his heavy armour. 'Yer killed Jenkins,' he blusters, a tremor of fear in his voice. 'The count will be really mad at yer – he hates good blood going to waste.' He glances down at the dark pool forming around the body.

'Good blood?' you ask quizzically. 'What do you ...?'

Suddenly something strikes you from behind, sending you toppling forward onto your knees. The room spins, as white flashes of pain obscure your vision. You try and turn, to see what hit you ... but your muscles are no longer doing what you ask.

'Is this one causing you problems?' says a gruff voice, from somewhere amongst the white haze. 'Well, no matter. They'll get their just desserts soon enough.'

'Ah yeah, desserts,' laughs the guard. 'That's a good one that is ... desserts ... yes ... good one.'

The voices fade, replaced by a roaring white noise in your ears ... you can feel your limbs stiffening, growing numb. Then you lose consciousness, falling into a deep dark sleep. Turn to 312.

A delighted Bart rushes over to you, a silver casket held in his hands. Flipping open the lid, he reveals its contents – a pile of sparkling gold coins.

'Here are your winnings!' he exclaims excitedly. 'That was the best fight I ever saw. You're a hero!' (You have gained 150 gold crowns.)

The wizard swoops down to the arena floor, and hops off his carpet. 'Congratulations,' he says. 'You're the Grand Champion of the five hundred and eleventh gladiatorial games!' Another wave of applause sweeps across the stadium. 'It is with great honour that I now present to you the champion's chest ...' He makes a series of quick gestures and suddenly a sparkling gold chest appears, hovering in mid-air. As you watch, the lid creaks open, revealing rare treasures inside.

You may now choose one of the following rewards:

The cage	**Brawler's shiv**	**Battlemage's fists**
(chest)	(main hand: dagger)	(gloves)
+2 speed +3 armour	+2 speed +4 brawn	+3 magic +3 armour
Ability: iron will	Ability: venom	Ability: dominate
(requirement: warrior)	(requirement: rogue)	(requirement: mage)

Congratulations, you are now the arena Grand Champion! Return to the quest map to continue your adventure.

415

You attempt to chip away at the black rock. However, the moment your weapon comes into contact with the rock, it begins to vibrate, sending your weapon spinning out of your hand. When you go and retrieve it, you see that it is now blackened and charred, giving off a faint green smoke. (You must lower either the *speed, brawn* or *magic* of your main-hand weapon by 1 point.)

Shaken by your experience, you decide to keep your distance from the infernal rock. Clearly it is not something of this world and you can't even begin to fathom how to destroy it. Perhaps, by exploring the tunnels beneath the glade, you will learn more about this peculiar rock. You head into the northern passageway. Turn to 428.

416

You quickly conceal the items about your person and then join the back of the crowd. Passing through the double doors, you are led down a wide corridor lined with paintings and tapestries. Ahead of you is a golden archway, beyond which you can hear the sound of music and revelry.

You notice the boy walking at your side. His face is grim-set, his hands stuffed in his pockets. 'Who are you?' you whisper to him.

He looks at you and smiles proudly. 'Why, I'm Spink. Apprentice to the great Eldias Falks.'

You shrug, giving him a confused expression. The name doesn't sound familiar, but then so much seems unfamiliar these days. As you start to frame your next question, you find yourself passing beneath the golden arch. Turn to 399.

417

You take the dryad queen's hand. Suddenly, you feel a surge of power flow into your body, surrounding you in a halo of golden light. 'I put my trust in you,' whispers the queen. 'Use your powers wisely and nature will always be your ally.'

The ranger has the following abilities:

Lay of the land (sp): You can now use the natural features of the land to your advantage. Add one extra die when rolling for your attack speed, for one combat round only.
Nature's revenge (co): Use this ability instead of rolling for a damage score, to automatically bind a single opponent in deadly thorns. This inflicts 2 damage dice to your opponent, ignoring *armour*. It also reduces their *speed* by 1 for the next combat round. This ability can only be used once per combat.

When you have updated your hero sheet, return to 376.

418

You skilfully behead the beast – again and again, until its many headless necks are pumping black blood into the mire. At last, after an exhausting battle, the beast finally lies dead. You may now take one of the following special rewards:

Hydra-scaled fists	Hydra's guard	Marsh stalkers
(gloves)	(left hand: shield)	(feet)
+3 magic +2 armour	+2 speed +3 armour	+2 speed +3 brawn
Ability: regrowth	Ability: deflect	Ability: sideswipe
(requirement: mage)	(requirement: warrior)	(requirement: rogue)

You also find the decayed bodies of several other unfortunate travellers, lying in the bog. From their remains, you are able to loot 30 gold crowns. Return to the quest map to continue your adventure.

419
Boss: Shadowstalker

You find the trail at dawn: a series of scorched craters blasted deep into the boggy earth. Many are still smoking, the air reeking of brimstone and magic. A little further on, pockmarked impressions in the mud suggest a scuffle and someone falling into the mire, wounded. Blood still stains a rock.

You continue southwards, into the foothills of the mountains. Somewhere up ahead you can hear the thunderous boom and crackle of magic. You pick up the pace, convinced that you are getting closer to the mysterious Jenlar Cornelius.

The tracks take you higher into the mountains, where the air is cold and the wind howls through the gullies and across the weatherbeaten slopes. They eventually bring you to a set of stairs, carved into a pillar of rock. Without hesitation, you start up them, taking the stairs two at a time.

You wind your way around the pillar, following the stairs to its lofty summit: a plateau of smooth rock, bordered by flecks of white cloud. Here, resting atop a tiered dais, is an archway of stone.

At the foot of the dais, an old man in mud-spattered robes is lying on his side, his hands clasped to his chest in a vain effort to stem the flow of blood. Standing over him is a hooded figure, dressed in black and grey cloth. As you approach, the figure turns to face you, their gloved hands tightening around a pair of swords.

'Well, well, you finally made it.' The figure hooks a thumb under their hood and pulls it back. Your blood runs cold when you look upon the assassin's features, staring back at you with a cruel smile. It is your face – identical in every aspect.

'What ... how?' You take a step backwards, shaking your head in dismay. 'Is this some trick?'

The assassin twitches an eyebrow. 'Oh, so much has been forgotten, hasn't it, my shadowkin.' Turn to 433.

420

'If I could afford to pay yer, I'd have you working behind here,' the barman grins, tapping the counter. 'Yeah, I know – you ain't looking for tap work, are yer? Well, I hear talk there's some mercenaries moved in down south. Think they're planning on exploring those sunken ruins at the foot of the mountains. You might want to join them. I understand they were asking around for some talented treasure-hunters.'

Will you:

Ask if he knows Jenlar Cornelius?	411
Ask about local rumours?	378
Turn your attention back to the taproom?	404

421

The young girl beams at you excitedly. 'Hello! I'm Tanner,' she says. 'You're looking for things to buy, right? Let's see – I do have a couple of interesting books for sale. I've read them both six times already!'

You may purchase any of the following for 20 gold crowns each:

Lorinwold's Field Guide to Herbs, Roots and Leaves (backpack) This handy guide will allow you to pick herbs for use in potion-making	The Compendium of Dwarven Lore (backpack) This pocket-sized tome will help you decipher Dwarf runes

Tanner points to one of the workbenches, which contains a jumble of glass vessels, tripods and mixing bowls. 'If you find any herbs on your travels then I can mix up some potions for you. I'll even do it for free, as its great practice. One day I want to be the best potion-maker in all of Valeron!'

If you have herbs or wish to view what Tanner can make, turn to 459. Otherwise, return to 310 if you want to talk to Totsvig again.

422

Your final blow sends the count's golden mask skittering across the floor, revealing his scarred, disfigured face. It begins to wither and age before your very eyes. 'No! I will not die!' hisses the vampire. He tries to grab you, but the count's legs give way beneath him. He collapses to the ground, his body crumbling into a pile of grave dust.

Congratulations! You have defeated the vampire lord. You may now take one of the following rewards:

Vampire's kiss	Vermilion rage	Mask of deceit
(left hand: dagger)	(ring)	(head)
+1 speed +2 brawn	+1 magic	+1 speed +2 armour
Ability: leech	Ability: bleed	Ability: deceive
(requirement: rogue)		

'A good show,' rasps a voice. 'Carry on like that and you'll put me out of business.'

You hurry over to the witchfinder, who is clutching a scrap of black cloth to his wounded neck 'Don't worry friend, I'll be fine. Just a flesh wound.'

You help to support him as he stands.

'My apprentice has plenty of healing draughts,' he says, noticing your look of concern. 'Nothing that can't be fixed. Let's head back to the hall and see what's left of the place, eh?' Turn to 515.

423

Beyond the doorway, a short passageway leads out onto an open plateau of rock, jutting out from the wall of the ravine. The area nearest the wall is covered in a high mound of broken stone and rock. South of it, along the edge of the plateau are a number of cone-shaped protrusions, belching steam into the air.

'Oh, what am I going to do?' says a dispirited voice, from somewhere behind the haze of steam. A moment later, a woman steps into sight – her ginger hair pushed back behind a pair of smog-stained goggles. She notices you and gives a gasp of surprise.

'Belinda?' you ask.

She nods her head. 'How … how did you know?'

Suddenly, there is a deafening explosion. You are thrown to the ground, your ears ringing, as fragments of rock and dust rain down about you. Turning towards the source of the blast, you see that the pile of rock and stone has gone and in its place is a giant throne fashioned from black marble. Seated on it is an armoured knight. Smoke and flames billow from the holes in his visor and between the dark plates of his armour.

'What is it?' cries Belinda, running over to you. 'I didn't do anything – I promise!'

The giant knight gets to his feet, flames flickering beneath his helm. 'I awaken,' he booms. 'The long sleep is over. Your power calls to me!'

Raising his gauntleted hands, the knight summons a sword of blazing fire into each palm, then starts towards you, as more flames ripple across the surface of his armour to coat it in fire.

If you gave Hal the health potion, turn to **578**. Otherwise, turn to **527**.

424

Something warm and syrupy fills your mouth, clogging at the back of your throat and forcing you to gag. All of a sudden you are awake, coughing and spluttering.

'Why thank you for that,' grins the black-coated man, kneeling beside you. He produces a handkerchief and proceeds to mop up the syrup from his face. 'Come on, drink some more. It is a healing draught.' He holds a flask to your lips, allowing you to take another gulp of the potion. Slowly, you feel your strength returning. (You may restore your *health* to its starting value.)

'You're probably still dazed and confused,' says the man, placing his black hat back onto his head. 'I'm Eldias Falks, one of the king's witchfinders.' He rises to his feet. 'My apprentice Spink is tending to the other wounded. The count has escaped – but I know exactly where he is headed: his personal crypt beneath the castle. Are you up for joining me?' He holds out a gloved hand. You grab it and clamber back onto your feet.

'OK, I'm ready,' you nod. 'Just lead the way.' Turn to **535**.

425

'The gates were built long ago, as a means of travelling between worlds. The people who crafted them were a heathen race – elves, whose dark magic and infernal machines once tainted this land.' The queen is silent for a moment, before continuing. 'The shadow gate was the last of their great works. When they created it, they had no idea what they would find on the other side. They dreamed of power and glory and knowledge ... but what they awakened instead was a vast and deadly evil. When they stepped through the gate, they didn't find a land of splendour and riches ... instead, they found a vast army waiting for them; an army brutally fashioned to fulfil one single purpose – to destroy everything in its path.'

'The Legion of Shadow,' you interject, nervously.

'Yes. Like a plague of locusts, it turned the land to ash and desert. It was an unstoppable force – for every shadowborn that fell in battle, there were hundreds more to take their place, pouring through the shadow gate like a relentless tide.'

Your arm tingles as the mark beneath your clothing begins to grow hot. 'You mentioned the shadowborn. Did they ... Did all the shadowborn fight for the Legion of Shadow?'

'The shadowborn *are* the legion. They take their name because they were born in that other place – that place of shadow and death, beyond the gate.'

You look down at your concealed mark, your mind suddenly racing with thoughts and questions.

'The legion was defeated,' continues the queen, regarding you impassively. 'A group of mages managed to close the gate by removing one of its keystones. This device, known as the Nexus, was separated into four pieces and entrusted to a group of guardians to safeguard with their lives. As for the gate itself, it was moved to Talanost – to the reliquary beneath the University of Magic – where it could be better protected. Since then, the survivors of the shadow have been searching for the pieces of the keystone, to create the Nexus anew and unlock the shadow gate.'

Your eyes widen in sudden realisation. 'The Nexus,' you gasp. 'Avian Dale had the final piece and I ... I ...' You look away, the full weight of what you have done finally hitting home. 'I stole it ... I was *made* to steal it! I am the one responsible for the legion returning to this world.'

The queen nods. 'A charm of submission. All shadowborn have it. It means they can be commanded by a superior – remotely if necessary.'

You find yourself leaning against the bench, suddenly feeling sick and nauseous. 'Then, if I am one of these ... shadowborn ... why does Avian trust me? Why would he ask me to do this task – to stop the legion's invasion?'

The queen raises a hand and lightly touches your brow. 'Perhaps, destiny has granted you a second chance, shadow walker.'

To ask the queen another question, turn to 376. To end your audience with the queen, turn to 336.

426

You pass through the opening, to find yourself in a large square chamber chiselled from black rock. A circular pit, filled with smouldering coals, dominates the centre of the chamber. Beyond it, a set of stairs leads up to rune-bordered doorway.

You start towards the pit, but come to a halt when you see three sparkling balls of light zoom out of a crack in the floor. They spin around the edge of the pit before throwing themselves against the glowing coals. There is a sudden whoosh of heat as the coals ignite, sending a swirling torrent of flame high into the air.

As the flames die down, you see a woman standing barefoot on the coals. She is clad in a black gown that hangs in scorched tatters over her shimmering, yellow skin.

'You may not pass,' she commands, her voice deep and sonorous. 'This is the domain of Inferno – the master of the eternal flame.' The woman summons fire into her hands and then advances towards you.

'Prepare to have your ashes scattered to the wind!'

	Speed	Magic	Armour	Health
Cinders	9	9	6	45

Special abilities

🟣 Vortex of fire: At the end of each combat round, Cinders transforms into a spinning vortex of fire. To avoid her spinning flames you must roll 2 dice. If the amount is the same as or less than your *speed* then you take no damage. If the amount is higher than your *speed*, you must lose 4 *health*. This ability ignores *armour*.

🟣 Body of flame: Your opponent is immune to *sear*, *bleed*, *fire aura*, *burn* and *ignite*.

If you defeat Cinders, turn to 655.

427

Sahna furrows her brow. 'No, don't think I can place the name. A prophet, you say? Well, we've had quite a few crazies down here, it has to be said. Mention the words treasure and gold, and you got to expect them. People just want to make a fast penny. But when there's real danger involved,' she smirks. 'That soon sorts the wheat from the chaff.'

Return to 343 to ask Sahna another question.

428

The rough-hewn tunnel slopes downwards, opening out into a small cave. Above you, breaking through the ceiling of the cave, you can see the withered roots of the trees, forming a natural roof of snaking tentacles. Most of them are split and cracked, their insides glowing with a sickly-green luminescence.

Two tunnels lead out from the cave. One heading north and the other heading east.

Will you:

Take the north tunnel	403
Take the east tunnel?	375

429

You hurry along the hallway, towards an open doorway that leads you out into the lashing rain. A flash of lightning illuminates the castle stables, situated at the far side of the cobbled yard. You can hear the horses whinnying and snorting nervously in their stalls.

Seeing their chance to escape, the family pick up their pace, sprinting towards the stables. You are about to follow when you feel something cold and icy wrapping around your leg.

'Not so fast,' crows a voice.

You are thrown off balance, falling to your knees. Twisting around, you see a woman watching you from the shadows. A black thread of mist extends from her outstretched fingers and is now curling around your leg. You try and tear it away, but your efforts prove futile – the coil of mist simply tightens its grip, biting through your armour and into your flesh.

The woman gives an insane cackle of delight. For a brief moment, a flash of lightning illuminates her gaunt features. She is tall, dressed in a long trailing gown of midnight black. Curtains of dark hair frame her pale face, shot through with a single lock of white.

To buy the family time to escape, you must fight this powerful undead witch:

	Speed	Magic	Armour	Health
Elvera	7	6	5	35

Special abilities

🟣 Black coils: The witch's black magic coils around you. At the end of every combat round, you must automatically lose 2 *health*. This ability ignores *armour*.

🟣 Vampire: You can use your *stake* and *reflect* abilities (if you have them) against this opponent.

(Note: You cannot heal after this combat. You must continue this quest with the *health* that you have remaining. You may use potions and abilities to heal lost *health* while you are in combat.)

If you defeat Elvera turn to 445. If you are defeated, turn to 424.

430

You follow Bern back into the forest, following a narrow trail that takes you up into the black mountains. After an hour of trekking through the barren, rocky foothills you arrive at a small stone cabin, almost invisible against the dark cliffs that loom behind it.

'Cornelius likes his solitude,' grins the ranger. 'Can't say as I blame him. Nice vacation spot, I suppose.' He points to the breathtaking view, that takes in the whole of Mistwood and the misty fenlands to the south.

However, your attention doesn't waver from the cabin. Something is wrong. Your arm is tingling, where the mark is concealed beneath your clothing. It grows stronger, the closer you get to the small building. Bern appears to have sensed something also. He is sniffing the air, his eyes scanning the nearby rocks.

'Do you ...?'

Bern puts a finger to his lips, stopping you in mid-sentence. Stealthily, he approaches the door of the cabin, which you notice is standing slightly ajar. Golden light flickers along his arms to pool in the palm of his hands. He is preparing a spell. You follow suit, readying your own weapons with an increasing feeling of unease. Turn to 466.

431

When you awake, you find yourself on a pallet bed inside a smaller tent. Sahna is sat by your side, a basin of water and a cloth resting on her knees. 'How do you feel?' she asks tensely.

'Like I just swallowed a lamprey worm,' you scowl, sitting up on your elbows.

'I know,' she says, putting the basin and cloth aside. 'I hope you forgive me. The truth is, without that thing inside you, you would never make it down to the city.'

'Wait a moment.' You slide your legs off the bed, suddenly alarmed. 'How long was I out?'

Sahna grins. 'Don't worry. Only half an hour. You still have plenty of time to make it there and back. Are you ready?'

You nod and agree to get going. The more time wasted, the less time you will have to find the crown and get back before the worm . . . You wince, not wanting to think about that.

Sahna escorts you to the shoreline. 'The lake is deeper than it looks. We think there might be channels that lead out into the western ocean – it's the only explanation for some of the things reported down there. Big sea monsters.' She shivers. 'Good luck. I hope, for all our sakes, that you're the one to finally make it.'

You strap on your pack and then wade out into the chill water. 'Yeah, me too,' you mutter under your breath. Turn to 569.

432

The old man's eyes twinkle. 'Why yes – yes I do. Bah, forget those old things,' he waves his hands dismissively at the junk that litters the room. 'I'll show you some real beauties; treasures that I found in these here halls.' He reaches underneath his pallet bed and pulls out a small, gilt chest. Opening the lid, he holds it out to you.

'Take your pick,' he grins, licking his toothless gums. 'But for these beauties I want 300 gold crowns a piece, or no deal.' When he catches your look of surprise, he scowls. 'Hey, don't gawp like a gutter fish. I gotta save for my retirement ain't I? This is my personal pension fund right here.'

The following items are available for 300 gold crowns each:

Splintered band	Abyssal blade	Black pearl
(ring)	(main hand: dagger)	(necklace)
+2 brawn	+2 speed +3 brawn	+2 magic
Ability: retaliation	Ability: deep wound	Ability: curse
(requirement: warrior)	(requirement: rogue)	

When you have made your choices, return to 626.

433

'You don't remember anything do you,' sneers the assassin, circling around you like a predatory wolf. 'I thought you would have worked it out by now.' The assassin's face begins to ripple and change, shifting into the pale features of a young man. Then they shift again, becoming a woman's face, with angular cheeks and almond-shaped eyes. The body follows suit, narrowing around the waist and broadening at the chest. 'There,' says the now-female assassin, admiring her new slender form. 'Always did prefer this one. It was one of your favourites too, once upon a time.'

The assassin sheaves her weapons, before pulling back the sleeve of her left arm to reveal a branded mark identical to your own. 'We are the Nevarin,' she says, spitting out the words with gusto. 'The shadowborn generals who led the legion into this world a thousand years ago.'

'That's impossible,' you snap angrily. 'A thousand years ...?'

The assassin's expression sours. 'We are immortal. We do not age like the humans on this primitive planet. Have you never stopped to wonder why you cannot die? Why your body heals faster than any normal human's? Why others fear you?'

'But ...' You shake your head, not wanting to hear the truth.

'When the gate was closed, we were cut off from our kin. Since then we Nevarin have searched for the Nexus. It has been a mission that has spanned a thousand years ... but at last the keystone has been remade. No thanks to you!' She gives a snort of derision. 'A shame that a little blow to the head gave you a conscience all of a sudden. If the master hadn't stepped in and taken control of you at Avian's castle, all would have been lost.' The assassin raises a finger in the air and extends it out towards you. 'You know, I can remove that little memory blockage if you want me to.'

'No!' you growl between clenched teeth. 'I don't want to remember. I don't want to know what I am ... what I was.'

'So be it.' The assassin draws her twin swords with a ring of steel. 'Please tell me you haven't forgotten how to fight as well.' In a blur of grey and black, the woman dives past you. You can barely keep up with her speed as she rolls and then somersaults back onto her feet, landing in a battle-ready stance. Turn to 442.

434

You find the body of a dead mage, lying amongst the refuse at the bottom of the pit. Some of the man's items and clothing are still salvageable. You may take up to two of the following:

Channeler's robes	Quicksilver boots	Ebenezer's spell book
(chest)	(feet)	(left hand: spell book)
+3 magic +2 armour	+2 speed +1 magic	+2 speed +2 magic
Ability: focus	Ability: quicksilver	Ability: sear

You also find a purse of gold. (You have gained 50 gold crowns). As you scan the rest of the pit, looking for any other chance treasures, you discover a small circular grill in one of the walls. A quick examination reveals that it is protecting a pipe outlet. Relieved that you have finally found a way out, you tug the grill free and then enter the tight crawl-space. Turn to 453.

435

To your surprise, you find yourself face to face with the jester. His painted lips pull back, revealing long white fangs. As he reaches forward to bite your neck, you lift up the items that Spink gave you. The jester draws back, emitting a chilling, high-pitched laugher.

'Oh, you want to play do you!' he cackles.

	Speed	Brawn	Armour	Health
Jester	7	6	4	40

Special abilities

💧 Itchy and scratchy: At the start of each combat round, roll a die. On a result of ⚀ the Jester sprinkles itching powder on you, reducing your *speed* by 1 for that combat round.

💧 Vampire: You can use your *stake* and *reflect* abilities (if you have them) against this opponent.

(Note: You cannot heal after this combat. You must continue this quest with the *health* that you have remaining. You may use potions and abilities to heal lost *health* while you are in combat.)

If you defeat the jester, turn to 374. If you are defeated, turn to 424.

436

You quickly show the gold ring to the old man. His eyes widen with surprise and then recognition. 'My ring ... you are the one!' he gasps. 'Help me up. There isn't much time. You must warn them ... they are all in great danger!' Turn to 604.

437

Whoever came before you has used magic or some powerful explosive to blast through the foundations of the building. The narrow tunnel you are following twists and turns past jutting stones and bent metal bars, to finally bring you out into a wide pool. Above you, light is playing across its surface like liquid gold. You push yourself upwards, finally surfacing in a small stone chamber. This part of the building has not been flooded – magical torches splutter along three of the walls, casting a golden sheen over the two giant statues facing you. Each one depicts a giant bearded warrior, armed with a two-headed axe. Between them, in an alcove in the wall, is a pedestal. And resting on it is a sparkling crown.

You pull yourself up out of the pool, relieved to be finally breathing air once again. As you approach the pedestal, you suddenly pause mid-step, your eyes coming to rest on the stone statues either side of you. Something tells you that this might be a trap. You back up, scanning your surroundings. At the other side of the room, beneath the carved face of a leering dwarf, you notice a stone door, standing slightly ajar.

Will you:

Try and take the crown?	**701**
Leave the chamber via the open door?	**520**

438

As you continue across the swamp, you spot a pale watery-yellow orb gleaming through the mist. Having lost all sense of direction, you decide to head towards it in the hope that it might be a fellow traveller, or at least some building that will provide a helpful landmark on your journey.

The land quickly begins to rise, becoming a series of boggy hills covered in boulders and patches of crab grass. Relieved to be out of the brackish water, you trudge across the soggy ground towards the light. It is coming from inside a rock cave, resting on top of one of the hills.

You step inside, the light hovering just ahead of you. It appears to be a strange ball of magical light, which is bobbing up and down as if on a string. As you near, you see that it *is* on a string; the globe is attached to a greeny-brown tendril that dangles from the dark ceiling. You go to touch it – and suddenly, there is a deafening roar as something lurches out of the darkness. Stumbling back, you realise, in horror, that the light is simply a lure, attached to the forehead of an immense fish-like creature. As it crawls towards you on slippery fins, your eyes become fixated on its immense, cavernous maw. Inside, you see row upon row of hooked teeth, forming a deadly tunnel of gnashing death, that leads all the way back into the creature's stomach. Determined not to become its next meal, you draw your weapons and prepare to defend yourself:

	Speed	Brawn	Armour	Health
The angler	11	10	16	60

Special abilities

 Indigestion: The creature's rubbery skin is difficult to penetrate. If you win an attack round, you can either strike the angler fish as normal (against an armour value of 16) or run into the creature's stomach and attack it from the inside! If you decide to enter the stomach, then you automatically lose 5 *health* from the fish's teeth, but you can roll for damage as normal, and the damage you inflict ignores the creature's *armour*. The fish then spits you out – meaning you must win another attack round to decide whether to attack as normal or enter the stomach again.

If you defeat the angler, turn to 452.

439

To the east of the island, a pathway leads across another lake of bubbling lava and then passes into a cave set into the rock. To the north, you see a series of loose stones bobbing in the lava, forming a makeshift pathway over to a crescent-shaped island. Towering over this island is a huge giant of living flame, surrounded by flickering sprites of fire that dance and pirouette around its blazing form.

Will you:

Take the pathway over to the cave?	426
Cross the stepping stones to face the giant?	502

'Deaders.' Sahna grins, nodding her head. 'They're what the guards call our volunteers. Treasure seekers, mercenaries, adventurers ... call them what you will, but the truth is – so far, hardly any of them have returned from that lake. The few that have, well ... perhaps death was the better option. Raving and mad for the most part. There really hasn't been much of a success rate. So far.'

Return to 343 to ask Sahna another question.

441

You quickly explain your story, that you were at Talanost with Avian Dale when the legion was attacking. Avian had asked you to find a Jenlar Cornelius, believing that he would have information to help them close the shadow gate.

The man nods impatiently as he listens to your story. Before you have even finished, he is struggling to gain his feet. 'Yes, yes – I believe you. I have no choice in this matter ...' He leans into you, grabbing your arm. 'Now, help me up. There isn't much time. You need to warn them – warn them all that they are in grave danger!' Turn to 604.

442

'What can you possibly hope to gain by this?' you scowl, drawing your weapons. 'Power, destruction. For what? To turn these lands to ash and ruin?'

The assassin throws back her head, laughing. 'Oh, Nevarin. To think that you were once such a devout follower of the shadow. You were one of the best – I looked up to you. I wanted to be you. And now,' her smile fades, replaced by a cold mask of loathing, 'I will take your life and absorb your power, Nevarin. At last, you will finally taste death!'

The assassin leaps into the air, spinning and twisting gracefully as her swords perform a deadly dance of flashing steel. With an answering flurry of deft moves, you press your own attack:

	Speed	Brawn	Armour	Health
Shadowstalker	12	12	12	75

Special abilities

🌢 Deadly venom: Once you have taken health damage from the shadowstalker, at the end of each combat round, you must automatically lose 3 *health*.

If you defeat the shadowstalker, turn to **558**.

443

After a gruelling battle, the giant finally staggers and then topples backwards. Its immense body smashes into the side of the chamber, sending cracks branching through the stone. As they begin to widen, water starts to gush into the chamber.

You put the crown safely into your pack, before approaching the body of the downed giant. Amongst the rubble there are a number of treasures, which must have been hidden within its stone form. You may now take one of the following:

Stone crescent	Avatar's circle	Kaggadour's cloak
(left hand: shield)	(ring)	(cloak)
+2 speed +2 armour	+1 magic	+2 speed +2 brawn
Ability: slam	Ability: overload	Ability: savagery
(requirement: warrior)	(requirement: mage)	

The cracks in the wall continue to expand, until there is a white torrent of water pouring through from the lake beyond. You battle against the surging flood, forcing yourself through one of the larger cracks. At last, kicking off from the jagged walls, you propel yourself out into the lake. At last, you are free of the building with the precious crown of kings in your possession! Turn to **637**.

With teeth clenched, you struggle against your compulsion to absorb the magic. As the swirling tendrils of magic dissipate, a ringing cry draws you back to the situation at hand. 'Bern!' you gasp. Turn to 539.

445

The undead witch crumbles into a black powdery dust, which is blown away by the howling wind. You may now help yourself to one of the following items:

Book of Black Deeds	Gown of midnight	Gourd of healing (1 use)
(left hand: spell book)	(chest)	(backpack)
+2 speed +2 magic	+1 speed +2 magic	Use any time in combat
(requirement: mage)	Ability: evade	to restore 6 health

The stable doors are flung open as two mounted horses gallop out into the courtyard. On the back of each horse, a small child clings desperately around their parent, their rain-slick faces still trembling with fear. The husband reins in his horse next to you.

'Thank you, traveller,' he says. 'There are more horses in the stables, I suggest you leave this cursed place while you still can.' He shivers as he looks up at the tall, dark spires of the castle. 'Judah's light protect us.'

He kicks his horses flanks and races out of the courtyard. His wife follows, her head bowed to the wind and rain.

Will you:

Saddle up a horse and leave the castle?	281
Return to the great hall to help the others?	408

446

Amongst the mounds of gold and jewels, you find a number of interesting items. You may now choose one of the following:

Magician's crook	Scarab sandals	Steadfast ring
(main hand: staff)	(feet)	(ring)
+2 speed +3 magic	+2 speed +2 armour	+1 armour
Ability: radiance		Ability: steadfast

Having searched through the cave and filled your pockets with gold, you reluctantly decide that it is time to leave. Return to your previous entry number.

447

It appears that the pieces of cloth and wood are the remains of Hal's balloon. Amongst the charred splinters, you find a box-shaped object made of brass. Picking it up, you see that it has a number of gears, cogs and buttons along one side, and a strange protruding lens on the other. If you wish, you may now take this item:

Clockwork camera
(backpack)
An engraved panel reads:
Property of H. Arbuckle

There is no sign of Hal's companion, Belinda. She must have dropped down elsewhere in the rift, although you imagine her chances of surviving long in this hellish place are slim. Turn to 439.

448

'Raolin Storm?' Sahna wrinkles her nose, derisively. 'Humph! He's a powerful mage and a rich one. My chapter have been in his employ now for several months, though I never thought this was going to be on the cards. I've lost two good men to that lake already and I'm starting to wonder if this so-called expedition of his is really worth the gold.' She glances over at one of the guards, who is doing his routine march around the camp. 'I can't blame the guys for getting a little testy. It's been no fun stuck here with only marsh flies for company. Unless we see some results soon,' she whistles. 'Oh boy, might even have a mutiny on my hands. Wouldn't that be fun?'

Return to 343 to ask Sahna another question.

449

Quickly and skilfully, you down the mage. You may now take one of the following items:

Ring of the marshes	T-bone wand
(ring)	(left hand: wand)
+1 brawn +1 armour	+1 speed +1 magic
Ability: swamp legs	Ability: bolt
	(requirement: mage)

Meanwhile, Bern has dispatched the last of the wreekin warriors, his glowing blade now coated with green blood. Grimly, he eyes the dead bodies. 'Let's search these and see what we can find.' Turn to 479.

450

You see the count slipping behind a red velvet curtain. Jumping over the bodies and broken furniture in your way, you reach the curtain and pull it aside. Behind it is an open doorway and a set of stairs leading upwards. Taking them two at a time, you race up the steps – to find yourself in a narrow hallway lined with paintings. The door behind you slams shut of its own accord.

The count is stood at the end of the hall. Behind him hangs a large solemn painting, depicting a sour-faced woman in a white-lace wedding dress.

'Fool,' hisses the count, his golden mask reflecting the light from the nearby candles. 'Only Eldias is worthy of my attentions. You are no witchfinder!' He turns to face the painting. 'Countess,' he calls. 'I call you forth. Come to me now, at the time of the witching hour ...'

Suddenly, the painting comes alive. The bride throws herself forwards, her malign face stretching out of the canvas. She opens her mouth, sucking in a great lungful of air ... then she screams. It is a shrill, piercing wail that drives you to your knees. You try and cover your ears, but the eldritch noise is deafening – sapping at your resolve, eating away at your courage. Every inch of your pained body is screaming at you to flee – to run from this place and never come back.

The count strides towards you. There is a flash of steel as he unsheathes his rapier. 'Come, my love. Let us dine on this one's flesh!'

Will you:

Fight the count in this hallway?	464
Use something from your backpack?	532
Try and open the door behind you?	473
Look for an alternative escape route?	480

451

The circular tunnel ends in another wide cavern. Along one side of the cave, a forest of tangled roots hangs down from the ceiling, as dried and withered as all the other roots you have seen. To the north and to the east, you see more tunnel openings.

As you contemplate your next move, you become aware of a wet, slurping noise coming from the eastern tunnel. You creep cautiously forward, intrigued as to what it could be. Then you see it – a giant brown blob of ooze, moving slowly along the tunnel. Everything it comes into contact with gets sucked up inside its gelatinous body – rocks, stones ... you can even see several skeletons hanging in the mass of ooze, as well as some swords, helmets and other odds-and-ends of equipment.

The creature is slow-moving. It wouldn't be difficult to cross the cavern and take the northern passageway, avoiding the ooze before it even reaches the cave.

Will you:

Hurry across the cave and head north?	472
Wait for the ooze and then attack it?	481

452

The giant fish-like beast collapses to the cave floor, its bobbing light flickering for a second before winking out into darkness. As your eyes slowly become accustomed to the gloom, you spot an area of the cave littered with the remains of the creature's many meals. Searching through these scraps, you find 30 gold crowns. You may also take one of the following items:

Lucky fishing rod	Twin furies	Scaled vest
(main hand: rod)	(left hand: pistol)	(chest)
+2 speed +1 brawn	+1 speed +3 brawn	+1 speed +2 magic
Ability: charm	(requirement: rogue)	Ability: swamp legs

You also find a *treasure map*, scratched onto a tattered piece of parchment. Make a note of the entry number 512. Any time you wish to view the map, turn to that entry number (keep a record of the entry you were on previously).

Concerned that this distraction may have cost you valuable time, you delay no further in leaving the cave and continuing your journey. Turn to 304.

453

You wriggle along the circular pipe on your elbows, the sound of your breathing amplified in the narrow space. After passing several vertical openings, you come at last to another grill plate. This one is tougher than the last, but with much pulling and tugging, it finally comes loose.

You slide out of the pipe to find yourself in another black-stone chamber. Turn to 725.

454

You stride up to the dragon and issue your challenge. Lazily, the beast opens one eyelid and examines you with interest. A reptilian hiss escapes from its mouth as it lifts up its enormous head.

'You challenge *me*?' it booms. The power of its voice dislodges stones from the ceiling and sends more branch-like cracks snaking across the ground.

The beast rises onto its clawed feet, its immense black wings filling the cavern.

'Puny human,' hisses the dragon. 'It is time for you to discover the true might of dragonkind.' Opening its jaws wide, the dragon breathes a roaring column of flame in your direction:

	Speed	Brawn	Armour	Health
Kindle	12	11	9	90

Special abilities
- Dragon breath: At the end of every combat round, the dragon breathes fire. To avoid being hit, roll 3 dice. If the result is equal to or less than your *speed*, then you have avoided it. If the result is higher, you have been hit and must take 5 damage, ignoring *armour*.
- Dragon hide: Kindle is immune to *piercing, impale, thorns* and *barbs*.

If you manage to defeat this epic foe, turn to 708.

455

You silence the vampire with a killing blow, watching as the woman's delicate, porcelain features crumble into a fine powdery dust. Lady Roe has been defeated. You may now take one of the following items:

Vermillion heart	**Blood harvest**
(necklace)	(main hand: sickle)
+1 speed	+2 speed +1 magic
Ability: life spark	Ability: leech
	(requirement: mage)

Eldias is still sparring with his foe, appearing to take delight in dodging the baron's slow and heavy swings. At last, the black-coated man sheathes his blades and pulls out two flint-lock pistols. Aiming them towards the ceiling, he fires two shots in quick succession. There is a grinding, ripping sound – then the huge crystal chandelier hanging above the baron's head, plummets to the ground, its spear-like tip staking him straight through the heart.

As the dust settles, Eldias spins his pistols and then holsters them. He flashes you a cocky grin. 'Now that, my friend, is how you do it in style.'

You can't help but marvel at the man's self-assured skill. He makes killing these deadly foes look like child's play. It seems you are not the only one to appreciate his performance.

'Bravo!'

The sound of clapping forces you to turn. The count is standing amidst the wreckage of his hall, watching you both with dark, hungry eyes. At his side stand two guards, dressed in heavy chain mail armour.

'It is time,' hisses the count, his lips curling back over his fanged teeth, 'for you to die.' Turn to 392.

456

Using the book, you are able to translate the symbols. They represent a series of numbers, arranged within a square-like pattern. Around the edge of the stone is an inscription, written in angular Dwarven script:

Three become one, if you obey the laws
Speak the answer and the chest is yours.

Shay wanders over and looks at the markings. 'Ooh, puzzles! I love puzzles!' She takes your book and flicks through the pages. 'Hmm, a Dwarven treasure chest. I wonder what the answer could be.' After several minutes of studying the numbers she snaps the book shut in irritation. 'Those show-off dwarves. Why couldn't they just use a key and a lock like any normal person!'

If you are able to work out the answer, then 'speak your answer' and turn to the corresponding entry number. If you can't solve the puzzle, then after much head-scratching, you decide to leave the cave, taking the tunnel north. Turn to 393.

457

The wet banks of fog surround you on all sides, plunging the featureless landscape into a cold, murky twilight. After what feels like an eternity of trudging through a constant veil, the mists finally begin to thin, affording you a rare glimpse of your surroundings.

Ahead of you, stretching across a low line of hills, is a set of black-stone ruins. They stand in stark contrast to the gleaming white fog, which curls around the dark columns and crumbling temple-like structures. As you near the ruins, you cannot help but wonder who, or what, would have chosen to live out in this treacherous, bleak marsh.

Will you:

Search the ruins?	412
Ignore them and continue your journey?	304

458

You allow your mark to absorb the shadow magic. The moment the magic comes in contact with the squirming snakes, your feel a rush of powerful energy flowing through your body. You may raise your *brawn* and *magic* score by 2 for the next two combats that you fight. Turn to **539**.

459

Tanner runs through the potions that she can make, and the ingredients she will need to make them. If you have the ingredients written on your hero sheet, then Tanner will make the potion for free. However, you must remove the relevant herbs and ingredients from your hero sheet afterwards. All potions are backpack items and have 1 use only:

Ingredients:	**Potion:**
Bramble thorn and *root grass*	Restore 6 *health* in combat
Bramble thorn and *thimble sage*	Restore 10 *health* in combat
Bramble thorn and *taponica bulb*	+4 *brawn* for 1 combat round
Spider leg and *fire grass*	+4 *speed* for 1 combat round
Ghoul hair and *black orchid*	+2 *armour* for 1 combat.

Make a note of this entry number. Return here at any time to turn your herbs and ingredients into useful potions. Remember, you will need *Lorinwold's Field Guide to Herbs, Roots and Leaves* to identify and collect the herbs that you need. Turn to 421 if you wish to view Tanner's other items, or 371 to examine Totsvig's potions.

460

You turn away as the vampire disintegrates into powdery black ash. You may now take one of the following items:

Clymonistra's folly (ring)	Gourd of healing (1 use) (backpack)	Sanguine gown (chest)
+1 magic +1 armour Ability: Clymonistra's adornments	Use any time in combat to restore 6 *health*	+1 speed +2 magic Ability: evade

Spink is standing over the cauldron of soup, pouring the bottle's contents into the oily-looking liquid. Once the bottle has been drained, he turns to you and beckons you over. 'Come on – help me with this!'

The boy grabs hold of the cauldron and attempts to tip it over. You join him and add your strength to the task. Within moments, the cauldron is on its side, spilling its contents across the floor of the hall. As the sizzling liquid comes into contact with the vampires, they immediately scream and screech – then explode into thick clouds of dust.

'Holy water,' smiles Spink. 'What a kick!'

As you turn back to the fight, you see the man in the black coat and hat weaving dextrously through the ranks of vampires, spinning twin swords in an elaborate pattern of swirling blades. Wherever he moves, his enemies are cut down, reduced to dust the moment they come into contact with his magical swords.

Elsewhere you see the blacksmith, crucifix in one hand and bloody stake in the other, valiantly defending himself against a wave of undead. You start across the room to join him, but skid to a halt when you see two vampires striding purposefully towards you. One you recognise instantly. It is the Lady Roe, her long white gown splattered with blood. Next to her walks a tall, barrel-chested man. A thick fur cloak is flung back across his shoulders, making them appear even wider than they already are. In his massive hands, he carries a double-headed axe.

Suddenly, the black-coated stranger appears at your side. 'I'm Eldias Falks,' he says, his eyes twinkling beneath the brim of his hat. 'Glad you could make the party.' He watches as the two vampires approach, bowing to them with exaggerated flourish. 'Ah, the Lady Roe and Baron Greylock. An honour to make your acquaintance. A shame it will be such a brief meeting.'

Will you:

Attack Lady Roe?	302
Attack Baron Greylock?	306

461

Shay is examining the tree roots, her face alight with fascination and excitement. 'These are elder roots! You know what that means, don't you? There must be an elder tree that is still alive.'

You nod, offering her a knowing smile. 'Yes, there is. Do you want to meet him?'

Her eyes widen further. 'What? You've met a tree elder? Why yes. Yes!'

Together, you backtrack through the network of caves and tunnels, until you arrive back at the withered glade. It is a sad and sobering moment as you walk through the bleak landscape, littered with the stunted remains of the dead trees. All their magic has gone – taken by the giant beetle to feed its insatiable hunger.

Woad is the only tree left standing, his mighty branches stretching high into the sky. Shay gives a giggle of delight as you both approach the last of the elders.

'Thank you,' says the tree, his deep-set eyes now glittering with a newfound vigour. 'I can feel my magic again – I can feel myself healing at last.'

You describe to the tree what you saw in the caves. The tree listens intently. When you have finished your tale, he gives a heavy sigh, blowing out the tips of his lichen moustache.

'It is as I thought,' he says. 'The rock has mutated the wildlife. It has turned them into things that nature never intended. While the splinter remains in our side, I fear this glade will never fully recover.'

Shay steps forward and gives a nervous bow. 'Great elder, I am Shay Blackwell, of the Royal Botany Society. You have my word that I will return here with my team, and we will remove that horrid thing as soon as possible. Something like that should not be allowed to wreak further havoc to this beautiful woodland.'

The elder looks pleased. 'You are most gracious,' he says. 'Please, accept my blessing as a token of my gratitude.' There is the creak and rustle of branches as the tree begins to sway. Then, all of a sudden, you feel a tingling rush of magic course through your body. (You have received Woad's blessing. For your next combat, you may temporarily raise your *brawn* or *magic* score by 1.)

After thanking the tree elder, you leave the withered glade to continue your journey. Return to the quest map.

462

You cross to the island, using the thick roots as a makeshift bridge. The old woman is still huddled over the water, continuing to sob and wail. You ask if you can help, but she shows no signs of having heard you. Tentatively, you put out a hand, to touch one of her scrawny shoulders and announce your presence. Suddenly, with a heart-stopping scream, the woman swings round, tossing her shawl aside. You stagger backwards in shock. The creature that is now revealed is no old lady! It is a fang-toothed monster – its body coated in black oozing slime. You barely have a chance to ready your weapons before this shape-shifting beast is upon you:

	Speed	Brawn	Armour	Health
Boggart	11	8	5	60

Special abilities

● Dread: This opponent causes fear, reducing your *brawn* and *magic* score by 2 for the duration of this combat.

If you defeat the boggart, turn to 497.

463

You follow the tunnel as it slopes downwards into the under-earth. Someone or something must still use this passage, as the walls are lined with torches – their magical blue flames casting eerie shadows against the smooth stone walls.

Eventually, the tunnel opens out into a vast cavern, the size of which is truly breathtaking. The ceiling, if indeed there is one, is lost to sight in the smoky darkness high above you. Similarly, the two nearest walls sweep away into the distance, with no sign of meeting an adjoining wall. Ahead of you, the ground is cracked and broken – revealing veins of molten lava that crisscross this vast space with heat and flame.

And there, reclining on a mound of gold and jewels, is a huge black dragon. From its snout to the tip of its long, spiked tail, the creature is over a hundred metres long. Thick black smoke spirals out of its nostrils and flames lick along its forked tongue, dangling from the side of its mouth.

This would be a mighty opponent to battle, but one that is likely to be far beyond your powers to defeat. If you do not wish to battle this foe yet, make a note of this entry number and return here at any time during Act 2 when you feel up to the challenge. If you wish to fight the dragon, turn to 454. Otherwise, you head back up the tunnel. Turn to 215.

464

The countess's deafening screams sap at your strength and willpower. This will be a tough fight – particularly as the count looks to be an accomplished fighter. His rapier slices through the air in a dizzying whirlwind of cuts and thrusts:

	Speed	Brawn	Armour	Health
Count	9	8	5	40
Countess	-	-	-	35

Special abilities

◗ Wailing bride: At the end of each combat round you must lower your *speed*, *brawn* and *magic* score by 1. (Your attributes are automatically restored at the end of the combat.)

◗ Painted veil: The countess cannot be harmed by *venom* and *bleed*.

◗ Vampire: You can use your *stake* and *reflect* abilities (if you have them) against the count.

In this combat you roll against the count's *speed*. If you win the round, you may choose to strike against the countess or the count. If you reduce the countess's *health* to zero, then the painting is slashed to pieces and the *Wailing bride* ability no longer applies (your attributes are instantly restored back to their original values). If you defeat the count first, then the painting immediately falls silent and no longer attacks.

If you defeat the count, turn to **487**. If you are defeated, turn to **424**.

465

At the centre of one of the ruined temples you discover a large, flat-topped stone. A number of intricate symbols have been carved into its surface. If you have *The Compendium of Dwarven Lore* then turn to **456**. Otherwise, you cannot understand the complex markings. Finding little else of interest, you rejoin Shay and together you head out of the cavern, taking the tunnel north. Turn to **393**.

466

The moment Bern puts a hand to the door, there is a deafening explosion of black light, sending him reeling through the air. The ranger slams into a rock, then crumples to the ground, his body flinching and jerking as black magic crackles about his body.

Paralysed by shock, you watch as a dark shape begins to coalesce in the doorway. As the shape grows and solidifies, it quickly becomes a writhing mass of black tentacles, each one ending in sharp, snapping teeth.

'Shad ... shadow magic,' croaks Bern, his voice weak with pain. 'Someone trapped the door ...'

To your surprise, the tentacled horror glides past you, heading straight towards Bern – its black body growing larger by the second. As a creature of shadow, the beast has not attacked you. However, in order to save Bern, you will have to fight it. Issuing a battle cry, you charge in with your weapons blazing:

	Speed	Brawn	Armour	Health
Shadow terror	10	9	6	50

Special abilities

💜 Fed from fear: The shadow terror feeds off fear, growing larger all the time. At the end of each combat round, the shadow terror's *armour* is increased by 1.

If you defeat the shadow terror, turn to 513.

467

You offer a healing potion to the wounded stranger, who takes it and gulps it down in one go. (Remove one healing potion from your backpack.) After wiping his mouth with the back of his hand, the man gives a noisy belch of appreciation.

'Why, thank you,' he smiles. 'Hopefully that'll get to work on my injury.' With a groan, he pushes himself up into a sitting position. Turn to 538.

468

As you wade deeper into the marshland, the humming drone of the cicadas is joined by a woman's wailing cry. Disorientated as you are, it takes several minutes for you to pinpoint the direction of the sad, mournful noise. It is coming from an area to your right, where the thick fog swirls around a dark line of stunted trees.

Will you

469

When you push against the wall panel, you hear a loud click. It is followed, moments later, by a sharp stabbing pain in your hand. As you pull away, you quickly realise that the secret door was trapped. In the palm of your hand is a single pinprick of blood.

Your legs give way beneath you. Then your body begins to shake and convulse. The last thing you see, before your vision fades, is the count standing over you.

'What a shame,' he sighs, sheathing his blade. 'I hoped for so much more.' His chilling laughter joins his wife's tormented screams. You have been defeated. Turn to 424.

470

You swim through the blast hole, to find yourself in a vast hall covered in stone pillars. Each one has a series of Dwarven faces carved into the rock, one above the other. As you swim past, you notice that all the bearded faces are leering or scowling at you in some manner. It is almost as if they are expressing their silent anger at you for daring to enter this sacred hall.

But you are not the only one to intrude here. Something large and ungainly is moving through the murky waters, heading straight in your direction. Its thick, rubbery skin is coated in barnacles, which scrape noisily past the pillars, leaving flakes of stone swirling in their wake. Within seconds, the beast's barnacled head is in full view. It has the appearance of a giant, bloated fish with a black gaping chasm for a mouth.

However, it isn't just the creature's size you need to worry about. The beast has allowed a number of parasitic creatures to take residence on its body, boosting its natural defences. From the poisonous horn-like anemones on its head, to the writhing tubular spines growing between its teeth, this beast is a living battleship. You ready yourself for combat, watching in silent alarm as the leviathan reveals another of its deadly weapons – a shoal of razor-toothed snapper fish. They emerge from the beast's mouth, streaking towards you like a volley of silver arrows:

	Speed	Magic	Armour	Health
Leviathan	11	10	8	50
Snappers	-	-	-	20
Poison needles	-	-	-	20
Thorn spines	-	-	-	20

Special abilities

◖ Snappers: At the end of every combat round, the snapper fish automatically deal 2 damage, ignoring *armour*.

◖ Poison needles: The spiked anemones on the beast's head are laced with a deadly venom. At the end of every combat round you must automatically lose 2 *health*.

◖ Thorn spines: These deadly spines release a crippling poison, reducing your *speed* by 1.

If you win a combat round against the leviathan, you can choose to apply your damage to the sea beast or one of its three parasites. If you kill any of the parasites (snappers, poison needles or thorn spines), their relevant ability no longer applies. If the leviathan dies, any remaining parasites will cease fighting and you win the combat.

If you defeat the leviathan and its army of parasites, turn to 544.

471

Using the guide, you are able to translate the runes. They all represent numbers, aligned along a series of pathways that meet at a raised centre. Some Dwarven script has been carved into the side of the chest. Again, referring to the guide, you are able to translate the strange markings:

Build and raze, ruin and blaze
Speak your answer to the Dours' maze

If you know the solution to the puzzle then 'speak your answer' by turning to the relevant entry number. If you cannot solve the puzzle, then turn to 482.

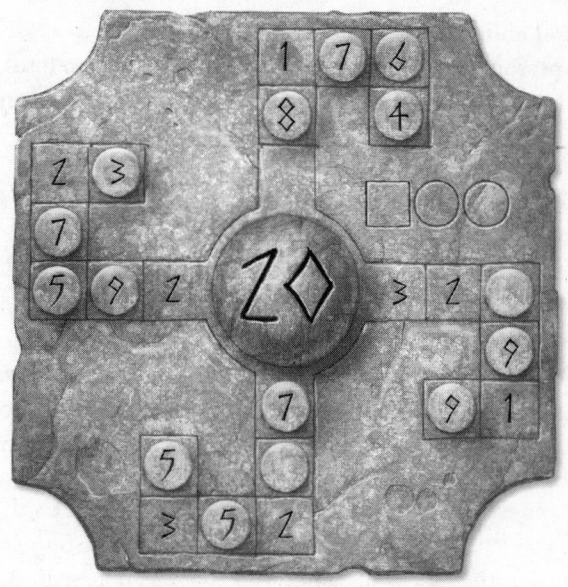

472

The tunnel spirals upwards, eventually widening out into a wedge-shaped cave. Long, spindly roots hang down from the ceiling, forming a dense curtain that stretches the full length of the cavern. As you push your way through the roots, you hear a cry and the scrape of metal as a weapon is drawn. Quickly, you hurry towards the noise, pulling back the roots to reveal a woman dressed in dirt-stained robes. She has her back to the cave wall, defending herself from the snapping jaws of a giant purple worm. Clutched in her hands is a rusty-looking short sword, which she clearly doesn't know how to use, as she proceeds to make ineffectual stabs at the beast.

Without a moment's hesitation, you race to the woman's defence, your first attack drawing the beast's attention:

	Speed	Brawn	Armour	Health
Purple worm	5	5	5	40

Special abilities

♥ Split personality: For every 10 *health* that the worm loses, its severed body splits into another worm, increasing its *speed* and *brawn* by 1.

If you defeat the purple worm, turn to 508.

473

The door is held fast by some supernatural force. No matter how hard you pull at it, the door will not budge. With the countess's screams still ringing in your ears, you turn to face the count. You have no choice now, but to fight the vampire in this haunted hallway. Turn to 464.

474

You don't see who fired the first arrow, but within seconds the air is humming with their flight as their steel-tipped heads streak towards the warrior. Calmly, he raises his hands and utters an arcane command. Suddenly, the ground around his feet cracks open, as thorn-covered vines burst up out of the soil. They whip through the air, snapping or deflecting the arrows from their path.

As the archers reach for fresh arrows, the warrior utters another word of command, his fingers crackling with a yellow light. There are answering flashes from around the circle as the archers' bows burst into flames. With shrieks of surprise, the archers drop their weapons, leaving them to smoulder and blacken amongst the grass.

'No!' snarls the knife-woman, stalking towards the warrior. 'We do not trade words with your kind – not any longer!'

'Solandris, wait!' cries the leader, raising her sword high in the air. 'We are not savages. I command you to stop!'

The knife-woman leaps at the warrior, hissing through her sharpened teeth. He makes no move to counter her. Instead, the writhing vines snap to attention, forming a wall between the dryad and her prey. As she attempts to cut through them, smaller shoots erupt from the vines, wrapping quickly around her wrists and binding them together. Similar shoots weave a net around her ankles, rooting her to the spot.

It is all over in a matter of heartbeats. The warrior steps around the wall of vines. Ignoring Solandris, who is cursing and struggling against her bonds, he approaches the leader. His sword remains in its scabbard, although the golden glow still dances across his fingers. He stops in front of the leader and then, to your surprise, he goes down on one knee, his head bowed low.

'Your queen summoned me, Talandra,' he says softly. 'I bring no malice or ill to your lands. I know of your loss and I give you my word that I will do all I can to put right this terrible wrong.'

The leader's face softens. 'Bern. I am sorry. My sisters are ... we ... are not ourselves. This is a time of war. Our precious lands grow smaller and smaller. Evil encroaches on our borders and now, with the loss of the horn, I fear we will diminish and the grove will be no more. We cannot afford to be weak – not now, not in the face of this danger.'

The warrior rises to his feet. 'Then, take me to the unicorn.'

'And what of this one?' asks Talandra, pointing her sword-tip towards you. 'Do we let it go? It has the taint of shadow about its person.'

Bern walks over to you and places a hand on your shoulder. His clear, blue eyes fix on your own, staring intently as if gazing into your very soul. Feeling uncomfortable, you flinch and look away – a cold tingle running along your branded skin. Bern nods to himself, as if something has just been confirmed.

'The queen will want to see this one I think,' he says. 'You're coming with us.'

Will you:

Demand your freedom?   489

Show him your mark?   495

475

You find yourself back in the rift, facing a pathway of stone that winds down the side of the crevice. Following it, you soon find yourself outside another cave opening. Turn to 426.

476

Sahna turns to face the lake. 'You've heard of the dwarves and their big war, right?' Happened thousands of years ago according to Raolin. Well, one group of them built a big city – one of many – here by the mountains, long before this place became a rotting marsh.

'The dwarves were at war with each other. Don't know the ins and outs, but what I do know is that one faction, the Illumanti I think, used sappers to tunnel underneath the cities and then use explosives to create vast cave-ins. That's how they sunk the city. All you see now is a big lake, but it's under there. And all its treasures are there too.'

Sahna kicks at the briny salt, which forms a thick white tide along the shore. 'Raolin is looking for something. A crown that once belonged to one of the great Dour kings. He believes it is still down there.' She looks at you, a weight of expectation in her eyes. 'It would be dangerous – very dangerous. But you would be well rewarded.'

Will you:

Agree to help find the crown?   549

Ask Sahna another question?   343

477

'My camera!' Hal gasps, his eyes going wide. 'Oh, thank the spirit of Judah, you are a hero! Here, give us a hand with this.' Hal starts to remove his pack, wincing as he shifts his balance to his injured leg. Belinda helps him to struggle out of the straps.

'Thank you,' he wheezes. 'Would you do the honours?' Belinda opens the pack and pulls out a selection of odd-looking contraptions. 'Don't suppose any of these take your fancy. You know – as a reward?' he asks.

If you wish you may take one of the following items:

Gold detector	Shrink ray
(backpack)	(left hand: wand)
Ability: beep, beep!	+1 speed +2 magic
	Ability: zapped!

Afterwards, you escort Hal and Belinda out of the seared scar.

'Thank you once again,' says Hal, as you prepare to part company. He rubs his eyes, sniffling sadly. 'Bah! Look at me, blubbering like a fool!'

Belinda kisses you on the cheek. 'Yes, I owe you my life stranger. And don't worry, I'll keep a close eye on this one.' She pinches Hal, giggling.

You wish both the explorers the best of luck, before heading back into Mistwood. Return to the quest map.

478

'The dwarves were the first born – the oldest race on Dormus,' says Shay, tracing her fingers along the edge of a carved statue. It depicts a squat, bearded humanoid dressed in rune-covered robes. 'They were scholars – experts in science and arithmetic. It allowed them to build great underground cities, sculpturing breathtaking architecture out of the minerals and stone that they mined.'

She gives a heavy sigh. 'But there were those amongst the dwarves who were not content with such feats of intellect and beauty. They were warriors, expansionists – who saw the stones and metals of their land as merely tools to make war with the other races. They wanted to conquer the world – to live in cities above the earth, where their strength and power would be seen and admired by all.'

Shay walks over to the crumbling remains of a temple. Along one wall is a mural showing dwarf fighting dwarf. 'There was a war. On one side was the Illumanti, those who were sworn to uphold the original ideals of their society – truth, justice and enlightenment. And then there were the Dours – the warlike dwarves who had given in to their bloodlust. As you can imagine, the Dours were unstoppable. After all, they were warriors; masters of their craft. Some say they had been tainted … warped by the demonic magics that they sought to master. The few Illumanti who survived the culling, fled to the surface, leaving their underground cities to be pillaged and destroyed by the Dours.'

You look around at the half-buried ruins. This must have been part of one of the dwarf cities, which was destroyed long ago in this great war.

'Few now remain,' says Shay, kicking at the loose dirt and rock. 'It is a sad end for such a great people.'

Will you:

Explore the ruins further?	465
Leave and take the tunnel north?	393

479

You search the bodies and find 10 gold crowns and the following items, which you may take:

Wreekin net	**Trident of the south seas**
(left hand: net)	(main hand: trident)
+1 speed +2 brawn	+1 speed +3 magic
Ability: webbed	

If you have *Lorinwold's Field Guide to Roots, Herbs and Leaves* then you may pick 2 bramble thorn and 1 thimble sage from the swamp. (Make a note of the herbs on your hero sheet.)

Bern sheaths his blade and turns to view the misty horizon. 'As I suspected – the one that fled probably has the horn. Hmm, he won't have got far. Come on, let's go finish this.' Turn to **501**.

480

There are paintings hanging on the walls to either side of you. One of them depicts a white-walled castle set in sunny meadows. A plaque beneath it reads: Fairwater View. The painting opposite shows a dusty track winding up the side of a bleak, wind-scoured crag. Its plaque reads: Road to Perdition.

You notice a thread of light running between the wall panels next to each of the paintings. You guess that the light is coming from a hidden room behind the walls, which means the panels themselves could be secret doors.

Will you:

Push on the panel next to 'Fairwater View'?	390
Push on the panel next to 'Road to Perdition'?	469

481

You ready yourself for combat as the ooze slithers into the cave. Clearly the creature has some sentient intelligence, as the moment it comes close to you, it suddenly spreads out, forming a slimy net to swallow you up. This ooze could prove to be deadlier than it first appeared:

	Speed	Brawn	Armour	Health
Giant ooze	6	6	6	40

Special abilities

♥ Glutinous maximus: Every time you win a combat round, you are reduced to using one speed dice for the next round of combat while you pull your weapons free from the slime. You can't use abilities to avoid this.

If you defeat your sticky foe, turn to 494.

482

With your attention focused solely on the Dwarven chest, you fail to notice your attacker until it is almost too late. A skittering rock alerts you to their presence, allowing you to throw yourself aside as a barbed spear strikes the ground, missing you by scant inches. You spin round, to find yourself facing a giant, nightmarish creature. Its head and torso are human, but its lower body is that of a black, armoured scorpion. The creature's venomous tail arches high above its head, its pointed tip dripping with the same black venom that coats the wickedly-barbed spear:

	Speed	Brawn	Armour	Health
Scorpios	10	7	4	60

Special abilities
 Black venom: After Scorpios makes a successful attack that causes health damage, you must lose a further 2 *health* at the end of each combat round, for the remainder of the combat. This damage ignores *armour*.

If you defeat this deadly predator, turn to 506.

483

The elderly man grunts with pain. 'Bah, just my luck to find the one adventurer who doesn't carry a healing potion.' He looks down at his injured leg. Blood has soaked through his breeches, where a rip in the fabric has exposed a nasty jagged cut. 'Can't put any weight on this,' he grimaces. 'I'm next to useless until I get a healer.' Turn to 538.

484

Three columns of runes are set into the stone on the door. Above it, carved into a cross-section of rock, is a message in an angular script. If you have *The Compendium of Dwarven Lore* then turn to 530. Otherwise, you cannot decipher the strange markings, so you decide to leave the chamber. Turn to 496.

485

The foul stench of decay wafting out of the cave makes your decision an easy one. Not wishing to meet whatever is inside, you return to the clump of tree roots and carefully climb back down into the cave.

Will you:

Take the tunnel north?	472
Take the tunnel east?	524

486

The swamp giant lurches forward, knocking aside trees and roots in its efforts to reach you. Then, from out of the dark skies, you see a feathered body swoop down in front of the monster, forcing it to take a teetering step backwards. Your eyes strain to follow the rapidly-moving object as it darts and wheels around the confused giant – then, as one of its dives brings it closer towards you, you see that the creature is in fact a large golden eagle, and riding on its back is one of the dryads.

'Wasn't going to let you have all the fun now, was I?' she shouts, as the eagle blazes past in a flurry of grey feathers and claws. It is Solandris, and she is armed with a magical, glowing bow. The dryad's arrows already pepper most of the giant's upper body, and her relentless attacks have succeeded in drawing its attention away from you. With the giant distracted, you now have a chance at defeating it:

	Speed	Brawn	Armour	Health
Swamp giant	10	10	7	70

Special abilities

⬥ Knockdown: If your hero takes health damage from the giant, you must reduce your *speed* by 1 for the next combat round.

⬥ Body of rock: Your opponent is immune to *piercing, impale, bleed, venom, thorns, barbs* and *lightning*.

If you defeat the swamp giant, turn to **509**.

487

Your final blow sends the count's golden mask skittering across the floor, revealing his scarred, disfigured face. It begins to wither and age before your very eyes. 'No! I will not die!' hisses the vampire. He tries to grab you, but the count's legs give way beneath him. He collapses to the ground, his body crumbling into a pile of grave dust.

Congratulations! You have defeated the vampire lord. You may now take one of the following special rewards:

Silk cut	**Cloak of shadows**	**Velvet slippers**
(main hand: sword)	(cloak)	(feet)
+2 speed +2 brawn	+1 speed +2 armour	+1 speed +3 magic
Ability: riposte	Ability: feint	Ability: haste
(requirement: rogue)		

'A good show,' says a voice.

You look up to see Eldias Falks watching you with a grim smile. 'Carry on like that and you'll put me out of business.' Removing his hat, the witchfinder walks towards you, offering out his hand. 'Well done, my friend. Truth and justice have triumphed this day.'

If you are a rogue and have the *witchfinder's signet ring* turn to 498, otherwise turn to **515**.

488

To your surprise, a hairline crack of light appears across the lid of the chest, splitting it in two. The newly-revealed halves slide back with a scraping rumble, revealing a soft, velvet-lined cavity. You lean over and take a look inside the chest. Turn to 397.

489

Having being held at knife point and then ordered to obey these strangers, you are feeling more than a little testy. You state that you wish to leave, explaining that you have your own important matters to attend to.

Bern places a hand on your shoulder. 'Friend, I may need your help. All will be revealed to you when we get to the grove.' His eyes stray to your covered arm, where the brand is burning beneath your skin. 'I know what you are. You are shadow born. A survivor from the shadow war. The queen will want to meet with you.'

You ask the warrior if he can tell you more about the strange mark. He scowls, stepping away from you. 'I don't wish to talk of it here. What your people did ... what they are capable of ...' He visibly shivers. 'I should kill you, stranger. I would have every right. And yet,' he cocks his head to one side, his eyes narrowing, 'there is something about you. My instinct tells me that you have no malice in your heart. That I do not understand ... but the queen will be your judge, not I. Now, come with us. Time is pressing. If you wish to learn more, then the queen will give you your answers – if you are deserving of them.'

You agree to accompany the warrior. If the queen really can help you to understand more about your former life, then perhaps it will throw light on what happened that fateful night at Avian's castle. Turn to 356.

490

You have barely set foot in the cave before you hear something moving towards you from the fetid darkness. It is impossibly large, its chitinous sides scraping along the walls. As it nears, you catch a glimpse of spider-like legs and a head of squirming, translucent tentacles. Quickly, you back out of the cave, the stench and the size of the creature overwhelming your senses. But there is no escape. The mutated insect follows you out onto the ledge, its massive bloated body squeezing out of the hole. Every inch of its skin is covered in thick black plates, each one giving off a green smoky hue. As it raises its tentacled head, the insect opens its mucus-filled mouth and gives a knee-trembling wail, soaking you in spit and the half-digested remains of its last meal.

You have no choice but to fight this deadly adversary:

	Speed	Brawn	Armour	Health
Wormwood	7	7	4	50

Special abilities
🖤 Soft spot: If you win a combat round, you must immediately roll 1 die. If you get a ⚀ or ⚁ result then your blow glances off the creature's armoured exoskeleton and you cannot roll for damage.

If you defeat Wormwood, turn to 517. (Special achievement: If you defeat Wormwood in five combat rounds or less then turn to 533.)

491

You struggle free of the net and clamber back to your feet. Suddenly, there is a whoosh of crackling magic followed by a loud explosion. When you turn, you see that part of the thorny wall has been blasted apart – and the wreekin leader is now fleeing through it. Before you can give chase, there is another explosion right in front of you, sending torrents of water and mud high into the air.

You spin round, to see one of the wreekin holding a wand fashioned from strips of bone. It levels the wand at you again, preparing to fire another blast. Quickly, you charge towards it:

	Speed	Magic	Armour	Health
Wreekin mage	11	-	5	50

Special abilities

◗ Charge her up!: The wreekin mage does not roll for damage if it wins a combat round. Instead, for every two rounds of combat it wins, it launches a bolt from its wand. This automatically does 10 damage to your hero, ignoring *armour*. You cannot use *vanish*, *evade* or *sidestep* to avoid this.

If you defeat the mage, turn to **449**.

492

The chest is an extraordinary piece of craftsmanship, sculptured to look like two dragons, entwined in each other's wings. You settle down onto the ice, wiping the dripping water from the jewel-encrusted lid. Worryingly, you notice a large keyhole staring back at you. After trying the lid of the chest, you discover that it is locked.

If you have a *rune key*, turn to **777**. Otherwise, no matter how hard you try, you cannot break open the chest. After kicking it several times in frustration (and getting a very sore foot!), you head back to camp. Return to the quest map.

493

At the bottom of the stairs is a cold, gloomy crypt, its walls lined with wooden coffins. The steady drip of water is the only sound in this silent, unsettling chamber. As you look around for an exit, the count appears at the foot of the stairs.

'Fool!' he laughs, his voice echoing from the cold, stone walls. 'Did you think you could run from me?'

Suddenly, the lids of the coffins are thrown back and from each, a skeleton emerges. There is the hideous scraping of bones, as they shamble towards you, their jaws cracking open to reveal sharp, serrated teeth.

'Feast my ancestors,' commands the count. 'There is plenty for you all!'

With nowhere to run, you must now battle these undead foes:

	Speed	Brawn	Armour	Health
Ancient ancestors	7	8	8	30

Special abilities
♥ Body of bone: The ancestors are immune to *bleed* and *venom*.

(Note: You cannot heal after this combat. You must continue this quest with the *health* that you have remaining. You may use potions and abilities to heal lost *health* while you are in combat.)

If you defeat the skeletons, turn to 505. If you are defeated, turn to 424.

494

As you deliver your final blow, the ooze collapses – its gloop cascading down around you to form lots of separate puddles. Floating in these puddles are various items of equipment. You may now take any/all of the following:

Great helm	Sludge waders	Ardent edge
(head)	(feet)	(left hand: sword)
+1 speed +1 brawn	+1 speed +1 armour	+1 speed +2 brawn
		Ability: parry

With your enemy defeated, you now have more time to examine the cavern. If you have *Lorinwold's Field Guide to Roots, Herbs and Leaves* then you may pick 2 root grass. Make a note of these on your hero sheet.

You also notice a high ledge leading around the edge of the cavern. To reach it you will need to try and climb up the rotted roots hanging down from the ceiling.

Will you:

Try and reach the ledge?	318
Take the north tunnel?	472
Take the east tunnel?	524

495

You peel back your sleeve, revealing the branded mark. Without looking at it, Bern quickly snatches your hand. 'Do not show that here,' he whispers, through clenched teeth. 'Don't you understand what that is? What you are?'

You shake your head, explaining that you have no memory of your former life. Bern leans in close to you, ensuring that he is not heard by Talandra or the others. 'That is a shadow bond. It means you are a survivor from the shadow war – and that makes you dangerous. What your people did ... what they are capable of ...' He visibly shivers. 'I should kill you, stranger. I would have every right. And yet,' he cocks his head to one side, his eyes narrowing, 'there is something about you. My instinct tells me that you have no malice in your heart. That I do not understand ... but the queen will be your judge, not I. Now, come with us. Time is pressing. If you wish to learn more, then the queen will give you your answers – if you are deserving of them.'

You agree to accompany the warrior. If this queen really can help you to understand more about your former life, then perhaps it will throw light on what happened that fateful night at Avian's castle. Turn to 356.

496

The next chamber is filled with stony rubble, where a section of the ceiling and one wall have toppled inwards. As you step foot into the room, some of the rocks and small boulders begin to tremble and shake. Then, all of a sudden, they lift up into the air and begin hurtling towards the centre of the room, where they clash and scrape together, forming themselves into the body of a giant humanoid creature.

The monster's arms start to revolve around its body, until they are a spinning blur of grey stone. With a rumbling howl, it starts towards you, throwing up dirt and rubble as it speeds across the ground:

	Speed	Brawn	Armour	Health
Rumbler	8	8	5	40

Special abilities
- Knockdown: If your hero takes health damage from Rumbler, you must reduce your *speed* by 1 for the next combat round.
- Body of rock: Your opponent is immune to *piercing*, *impale*, *bleed*, *venom*, *thorns*, *barbs* and *lightning*.

If you manage to defeat Rumbler, turn to **540**.

497

Your final blow sends the creature reeling backwards into the murky swamp water. It lurches and sways for several moments, then its slimy, black body turns to a liquid sludge, oozing back into the pool.

The boggart has been defeated. Searching the small island you find the remains of several of its unfortunate victims. You have found 30 gold crowns and may take one of the following items:

Bright greaves	**Nightwalker tunic**	**Sanguine slippers**
(feet)	(chest)	(feet)
+1 speed +2 brawn	+1 speed +2 brawn	+2 speed +2 magic
Ability: steadfast	Ability: nightwalker set	Ability: charm
	(requirement: rogue)	(requirement: mage)

If you have *Lorinwold's Field Guide to Roots, Herbs and Leaves* then you may pick 2 bramble thorn and 1 root grass from the island. (Make a note of the herbs on your hero sheet.)

You then continue your journey through the swamp. Turn to **304**.

498

As Eldias goes to shake your hand, he gives a gasp of astonishment. 'That ring! Where did you get it?' He draws back, looking at you uncertainly. 'That was my brother's ring.'

You explain how you came upon it, having killed the witch that was terrorising Tithebury Cross. The man listens to your account in silence. When you have finished, he plants his hat back onto his head and then folds his arms.

'It takes years to perfect my craft, but perhaps – if you are willing – I could pass on the rudiments of my profession. What do you say? Do you wish to become the embodiment of justice – to punish all witchcraft, vile sorcery and evil that walks this land?'

If you wish to learn the witchfinder career turn to 521. Otherwise, you politely decline Eldias' offer. Turn to 515.

499

'Ah good, good.' The old man places a filleted fish onto the hot stove and then adds a variety of spices and peppers. Soon, the chamber is filled with the succulent aroma of grilled, peppery fish. 'This will put hairs on your chin and your chest,' he chuckles, dishing you out a plate (which looks suspiciously like it was once the top of a broken stool) and serving you a generous portion. You tuck in hungrily, your quest and its burdens momentarily forgotten. It isn't until your stomach makes an unsavoury rumbling sound that you are reminded of the lamprey worm and the urgency of finding the crown.

Getting to your feet, you thank the old man for his time and generosity. 'The crown you seek is back the way you came, through the flooded room,' he says, nodding to the blast hole. 'I did tell you about the stone giant didn't I? Tall as a ship's mast and twice as wide. You be careful with that one.'

Heeding the man's advice, you make your way back through the blasted tunnel. After climbing down the kelp ladder, you wade across the chill waters of the flooded chamber and enter the passageway. Turn to 619.

500

The camp is deserted. Redguard and his soldiers are now stationed at Ravenwing's camp, under the command of Inquisitor Bovis. You check the infirmary tent for any supplies that may have been left behind in the army's haste to leave. Most are locked away in magically-sealed boxes, but you do find a few potions left on the shelves. You may take any of the following, however once these items are taken, you cannot return here again.

Pot of mending (1 use)	**Elixir of swiftness (1 use)**
(backpack)	(backpack)
Use any time in combat to	Increase your *speed* by 4
restore 12 *health*	for one combat round

When you have updated your hero sheet, return to the quest map.

501

You track the fleeing wreekin across the swamp, to a small settlement of mud huts on the banks of a stagnant lake. A crowd of the creatures have gathered outside one of the larger huts.

As you approach, a pair of sentries hurry towards you, armed with spears. Bern doesn't slow. Instead he raises his hands and summons roots of thorny vines to trap the sentries in place. 'That is the last of my magic,' he says, his face looking pale and drawn. 'I hope we don't face much more resistance this day.'

Thankfully, the wreekin in the village are so intent on pushing and jostling each other to see into the mud hut, that they don't even notice your arrival. As you make your way through the crowd, there are a few warbling cries of alarm, but when Bern draws his glowing sword and raises it high into the air, the wreekin cower away, covering their eyes. Most of them appear to be simple fishermen and hunters, unlike the fierce warriors that you fought in the swamp.

Unhindered, you follow Bern into the hut. The single large room is dominated by a large pallet bed and sprawled on top of it is a giant toad, its brown-green skin glistening with moisture. From his size and appearance, you can only assume that this is the leader of the village – and he looks as though he is dying. From between his rubbery lips comes a moan of pain, as his bulging, glassy eyes roll back and forth in a feverish delirium.

The wreekin in the headdress has already unwrapped his pack, revealing a glowing ivory horn. He now holds it over a bowl of steaming liquid, a knife held ready to begin cutting into it.

'No! Wait!' demands Bern, rushing forwards. He snatches the horn from the surprised wreekin's grasp, and clutches it protectively to his chest. He speaks something in a guttural language. The wreekin answers, stabbing a finger towards his dying leader. Their exchange continues for some minutes, before the wreekin finally appears to concede. Bern walks over to the bowl, rolling up his sleeves.

'They took the horn for its magical properties,' he says to you. 'Their leader has a fever. He could die unless he gets a cure. It looks to me like a rare strain of the marsh fever. I can cure it, I think – but I will need your help.' Turn to 523.

502

The stones bob and tilt dangerously as you hop across them to reach the island. As you get closer, there are shrieks from the fire sprites, who stop their dance and turn to eye you – their flaming bodies sparking angrily. Behind them, the giant gives a thunderous grunt of displeasure. The immense beast stands over three hundred metres tall – its conical head of flames almost lost from sight amongst the clouds of smoke and steam. The heat from its body is like a raging furnace, drawing you to a halt at the edge of the island, as you feel it burning your exposed skin.

This would be a mighty opponent to battle, but one that is likely to be far beyond your powers to defeat. If you do not wish to battle this foe yet, make a note of this entry number and return here at any time during Act 2 when you feel up to the challenge. If you wish to fight the giant, turn to 738. Otherwise, you head back to the previous island. Turn to 439.

503

You expertly swing yourself to the side, grabbing hold of stronger roots as the previous ones crumble to rotted dust. With a final burst of speed, you clamber up the tangle of roots and pull yourself up onto the ledge.

The first thing that hits you is the stench – a sickly aroma of death and decay. All along the ledge, the dirt is littered with bones. In alarm, you notice that several look distinctly human. As you proceed along the ledge, weaving between the thick gnarly roots, you spy a cave opening. Outside, there are more gnawed bones and the rotting carcasses of several animals.

Will you:

Enter the cave?	490
Climb back down to the main cavern?	485

504

'I work for the Royal Botany Society,' explains Totsvig, clearly looking delighted to be able to talk about his work. 'I moved here with my team two weeks ago to study the local flora and fauna.'

He lifts up one of his copper bowls, which contains tiny fragments of black rock. 'A meteorite hit down here, just south of the forest,' he says, poking at the contents. 'The devastation was fairly significant, but of greater concern to the society are the changes that have been occurring since. I've observed and recorded several cases of mutations. The rock appears to have brought with it some kind of reactive agent. In all the areas where we have found traces of the rock, we have seen the localised wildlife changing – and not for the better. One of my assistants is currently investigating a hotspot to the west. In fact, I'm starting to grow a little concerned. She should have been back by now, although she is easily distracted from her studies.'

Will you:

Offer to help (requirement: mage)?	401
Continue to question Totsvig?	310

505

'Impressive, very impressive,' grins the count. With a swish of his cloak, he unsheathes his bright-bladed rapier. 'It's time we finished this,' he hisses, his fanged teeth gleaming beneath his golden mask. 'It will be a fine pleasure to drink your blood!'

At last, it is time to face the count – a powerful vampire lord:

	Speed	Brawn	Armour	Health
Count	9	8	5	40

Special abilities

🦇 Blood drinker: If the count rolls a ⚁ for damage, his fangs latch onto your throat and he sucks your blood! He can immediately roll an extra die for damage. If he successfully bites you, he also restores 2 lost *health*.

🦇 Vampire: You can use your *stake* and *reflect* abilities (if you have them) against the count.

If you defeat the count, turn to 487. If you lose the combat, turn to 424.

506

You defeat the scorpion, dodging its twitching tail as the giant creature crashes to the ground, dead. If you wish, you may now take one of the following items:

Dark malice	Scorpion stinger	Marsh pendant
(main hand: spear)	(main hand: dagger)	(necklace)
+2 speed +3 brawn	+2 speed +1 brawn	+1 magic +1 armour
Ability: impale	Ability: venom	Ability: steadfast
(requirement: warrior)	(requirement: rogue)	

Having tarried here longer than you intended, you leave the ruins and continue your journey through the swamp. Turn to 304.

507

The key fits the lock perfectly. You twist it and unlock the box, eagerly flipping open the lid as your mind races with images of all the possible treasures you might find inside. Your face drops, however, when you discover that the box is empty – except for another small key, resting within a velvet-lined cavity. This one is made from gold, inlaid with silver runes. If you wish to take the *rune key* then make a note of it on your hero sheet (it does not take up backpack space). After shaking the chest repeatedly, in the hope that something more interesting might fall out, you give up on it and throw it aside, turning your attention back to the chamber. Turn to 215.

508

You chop up the purple worm until there is nothing remaining but a heap of sliced worm meat. The woman lowers her short sword, still trembling from her ordeal.

'Thank you,' she says, sheathing her blade. 'I don't know what I would have done if you hadn't come along. I am Shay Blackwell, a researcher from the Botany Society.' She walks over and retrieves her pack, which you notice has several glass bottles and vials attached to it.

Shay takes a small knife from her belt and cuts a chunk out of the nearest tree root. She turns it around thoughtfully in her hands. 'I really don't understand it. These are elder roots, and as such they should be positively full of magic. Look, it isn't healing at all.' She puts her fingers in the fresh cut that she has made. 'Something has just simply sucked all the life out of it. But what . . .?'

Her eyes settle on the worm remains. 'The creatures here seem changed. My tutor, Totsvig Hellen, thinks it is the sky rock. It dropped down in the forest just over a month ago. Since then, very peculiar things have been happening. The wildlife has been mutating . . . becoming much more aggressive.'

She deposits the root sample into one of her bottles, then straps on her pack. When your eyes finally meet again, the woman gives you an awkward smile. 'I don't suppose ... well, now that you're here, you would mind accompanying me deeper into the caves? As you can see, I am no fighter. I could use your protection.'

Will you:

Accept the offer?	353
Demand a fee for your service?	347

509

While Solandris and the eagle hold the giant's attention, you slice, cut and blast away at its enormous legs. After a tiring battle, the colossal creature finally gives a thunderous roar of pain and then begins to topple forwards. In horror, you realise that you are standing directly beneath it and, without any chance of moving aside quickly enough, you are going to be squashed!

Suddenly, you feel a rush of wind as something grabs your shoulders and lifts you up out of the water, just as the giant smashes down into the swamp, sending a tidal wave of mud and weed rushing out across the mangroves.

'I would say that was good-timing on two accounts,' grins Solandris as her eagle drops you beside the body of the defeated giant. To your surprise, you notice several items of treasure tangled up in the monster's vines and roots. You may now help yourself to one of the following rewards:

Vigilant chestguard	**Blackout**	**Sparkcraft mantle**
(chest)	(left hand: mace)	(cloak)
+1 speed +3 armour	+2 speed +2 brawn	+2 speed +2 magic
(requirement: warrior)	Ability: stun	Ability: life spark
		(requirement: mage)

If you have *Lorinwold's Field Guide to Roots, Herbs and Leaves* then you also find 1 thimble sage, 1 taponica bulb and 1 black orchid growing on the giant's body. Make a note of the herbs on your hero sheet, then turn to 406.

510

You swim through the blasted hole, emerging in a square chamber with a vertical shaft in the middle of its floor. As you make your way towards the shaft, you see something move at the corner of your vision. Treading water, you twist around to see an immense sea creature with a body of writhing tentacles, detach itself from the wall. It propels itself towards you, using its tentacles to push through the water. When it is almost upon you, it swings around, extending its suckered limbs to grab hold of you. You furiously bat them away, aware that they are trying to pull you in closer to the creature's parrot-like beak. In a swirl of air bubbles and squirming tentacles, you quickly draw your weapons and prepare to fight:

	Speed	Brawn	Armour	Health
Kalimari	11	10	9	60

Special abilities
🌶 Ink bombs: If your hero gets a $\boxed{\cdot}$ when rolling for attack speed, they are hit by an ink bomb. This temporarily blinds your hero, causing them to lose the round. You cannot use any abilities (other than passive abilities) until the start of the next combat round. You may re-roll dice if you have an ability that lets you do so.

If you defeat the Kalimari, turn to 716.

511

'They say it was a sky rock,' says the explorer. 'Must have hit down here with quite a force. Caused that rift to appear and, since then, all kinds of things been spilling out of the earth.' He leans forward, grunting as he tries to reposition himself into a more comfortable position. 'Fool that I am, I thought I'd take a closer look – you know, see what was happening.' He shakes his head. 'Wasn't expecting to get blasted out of the sky.'

Turn to 538 to ask another question, or 526 to begin your quest.

512

You examine the treasure map, which consists of a selection of directions and measurements:

FOUR LEAGUES WEST
THREE LEAGUES EAST
TWO LEAGUES SOUTH

When you have finished viewing the map, return to your previous entry number.

513

The strange creature explodes, releasing whirling tendrils of shadow magic into the air. Without thinking, you raise your arm and pull back your sleeve, revealing your branded mark. The three snakes writhe and twist beneath your skin, as if suddenly alive. Mesmerised, you watch as the floating shadow magic starts to spiral towards them, like a moth to a flame.

Will you:

Absorb the shadow magic? 458

Quickly conceal your mark? 444

514

You are not fast enough to secure another handhold. The roots you are holding onto break apart, sending you tumbling down the face of the wall to land in a bruised heap back in the cave.

The lower roots are now broken, making the ledge unreachable.

Will you:

Take the tunnel north? 472

Take the tunnel east? 524

515

You return to the grand hall where Spink is tending to the wounded survivors. From your original group there is only a handful remaining. One of them is the blacksmith, who grins and waves at you, his face and hair caked in matted blood and vampire dust.

If you have any of Spink's items still on your person, you can hand them back as they will be of no further use. If you wish, you may now retrieve your original main-hand and left-hand equipment before leaving the castle. Return to the quest map.

516

'Oh, what a splendid specimen!' Totsvig takes the seed pod from you and carefully hands it over to his assistant, Tanner. 'Put this beauty in some of the special compost, will you? – the one with the ogre dung in it. I can't wait to observe the results!' Tanner nods obediently, carrying the pod over to one of the tents where a number of odd-looking plants are growing inside clay tubs.

'Thank you for making such a valuable contribution to the Botany

Society,' grins Totsvig. 'Please, take one of these as a token of our appreciation.'

You may choose one of the following rewards:

Gardener's gloves	Field kit	Ogre dung compote (2 uses)
(gloves)	(backpack)	(backpack)
+1 speed +2 armour	Can hold two	Use any time in combat
Ability: thorns	potions inside	to raise your *magic* by 2
		for one combat round

Once you have made your choice and updated your hero sheet, you can talk to Totsvig further (turn to 310), or return to the quest map.

517

The creature gives a wet, gurgling cry as its bloated body crashes to the ground. Its legs kick and squirm for several seconds, then with a final trembling shudder, they curl up and lie still.

Congratulations – you have defeated Wormwood. You may now help yourself to one of the following rewards:

Ridgeback	Black fang	Wyrm crest
(left hand: shield)	(main hand: sword)	(head)
+1 speed +2 armour	+1 speed +2 brawn	+1 magic +2 armour
Ability: slam	Ability: parry	
(requirement: warrior)		

You contemplate searching the creature's cave, but the smell is so overpowering that you are forced back out onto the ledge. Keen to get away from the foul reek of decay, you clamber back down the trailing roots, to the cavern below.

Will you:

Take the tunnel north?	472
Take the tunnel east?	524

518

The forest whips past you in a blur of brown and green, as you race at breakneck speed through the undergrowth. Bern is at your side, matching you step for step as he leaps and bounds over logs and fallen branches. Incredibly, despite the unnatural speed that you are both travelling at, he appears to be studying his surroundings with a keen eye. He gestures to the left, veering off in that direction in a blazing trail of glittering light. You follow suit, the tight-press of trees whipping past you as the wind roars in your ears.

Within seconds the blurred wall of trees is gone, replaced by a wide expanse of boggy marshland. Your feet skim the surface of the water as you hurtle onwards, across the grey-green swamp. Eventually, you begin to slow; your feet sinking deeper and deeper into the brackish water. Soon you are wading through it, upto your knees, Bern only a few metres ahead of you.

'That powder will have helped us close the distance,' he says, surveying the featureless landscape. 'Over here. Come on.' He points to a swelling of hills, that rise up like some hump-backed creature from the scrubby wetlands.

Arriving atop the hill, you spot your prey. A number of creatures, that look like man-like frogs in reed skirts, are scurrying across the marsh. One of them is wearing a headdress made from animal bones. Across his back is slung a palm-leaf sack.

'There they are,' says Bern. He loosens his sword in his scabbard. 'I do not imagine they will give up the horn without a fight. Are you ready?'

You nod, readying your own weapons. Then, together, you race after the fleeing wreekin. Turn to 534.

519

You pass through the opening, to find yourself in a rectangular, stone-carved chamber.

All its surfaces are perfectly smooth; its floor covered in a mosaic of tiles. You notice that several of the tiles have cracked and buckled, where straggly weeds have forced themselves up out of the earth. If you have *Lorinwold's Field Guide to Roots, Herbs and Leaves* then you may pick 2 bramble thorn and 1 fire grass from this area. (Make a note of the herbs on your hero sheet.)

Set into one of the walls is what appears to be a stone door. A number of strange markings and runes adorn its surface. At the opposite side of the chamber is an open doorway, leading through into another area.

Will you:

Examine the stone door?	484
Pass through the open doorway?	496

520

Beyond the door is a short passageway, ending in a large rectangular chamber. Along its side walls are a number of winged statues, perched on pedestals. They look like dwarves, save that their features appear even more scowling and malign than the previous statues that you have seen.

Next to each pedestal is a stone chest, covered in faintly glowing runes. You assume that this is one of the king's treasure rooms, although it could also be a trap. As you walk between the statues, you can't help but feel that their narrow eyes are watching you. You pause, mid-way through the room, wondering if you should simply continue through and leave by the arched doorway at the far end, or try one of the chests.

Will you:

Attempt to open one of the chests?	563
Pass through into the next room?	725

521

You have the honour of learning from one of the grandmasters of the profession.

'Remember my friend,' says Eldias, his eyes blazing with a fierce zealotry. 'The destruction of evil is our life's task. We cannot rest until we have cleansed the world of the foul existence of sin and corruption.'

The witchfinder has the following abilities:

Judgement (co): When you take health damage from your opponent's damage score, you can inflict damage back to your opponent equal to half your *speed* score, rounding up. This ability ignores *armour*. You can only perform *judgement* once per combat.

Execution (sp): (requires a sword in the main hand) Once an opponent's *health* is equal to or less than your *speed* score, you may automatically 'execute' them at the start of the combat round, reducing their *health* to zero. (Note: You can only execute a single opponent in each combat round.)

Once you have updated your hero sheet, turn to **515**.

522

You search through the many treasures contained in the chest. You may now help yourself to one of the following items:

Channeler's prism	Rock biter	Stone fists
(necklace)	(left hand: pick)	(gloves)
+1 magic	+1 speed +2 brawn	+2 brawn +1 armour
Ability: focus	Ability: piercing	

You also find a sack containing 50 gold crowns and a *large ruby*. (If you wish to take the gem, simply make a note of it on your hero sheet. It does not take up a backpack space.) After helping yourself to the many treasures, you rejoin Shay and then head out of the cavern, taking the tunnel north. Turn to **393**.

523

Bern issues orders to the wreekin, who hurriedly leaves the hut, returning a few minutes later with a reed basket filled with herbs. The ranger begins adding some of these to the steaming liquid.

'I can slow the onset of the fever,' he says, his brow furrowed with concentration. 'But to heal it completely I will need some black mandrake. It grows out in the swamp, on the edge of the mangroves to the east. I need you to go and get me some – I must stay here and do what I can.' He looks up from his work, his eyes settling on the unicorn's horn, resting next to the bowl. 'I promised them that I would save their leader, in return for the horn. There is very little time – now go!'

The wreekin scatter out of your way as you hurry from the hut. With your eyes set firmly on the mist-shrouded horizon, you set out into the marsh. Turn to 537.

524

You make your way down the tunnel that the giant ooze appeared from. After several minutes, the tunnel ends on a ledge overlooking a deep pit. At the other side of the pit, the wall is honey-combed with natural looking holes and undulations.

The air hums with a relentless buzzing sound. Scanning the ceiling, you see several tunnels leading out into daylight. A number of giant-sized bees are using these to fly into and out of the cave. You realise that the wall opposite must be a hive.

If you wish, you could try jumping across the pit to reach the hive (turn to 536). Otherwise, you can head back to the cave and take the other tunnel north (turn to 472).

525

Back at the village, the solemn crowd is still gathered around their leader's hut. On seeing your arrival, there is a sudden wave of excited chatter as the frog-like creatures push and jostle with each other to get a better view of what you are carrying.

With the mandrake root clutched tightly in your hands, you hurry through the crowd of wreekin and enter the hut. Inside, Bern is standing over the pallet bed, his face worn and tired. The toadish leader looks in a worse condition, his skin now dry and cracked, and his breath coming out in ragged gasps. Bern snaps to attention as you enter, his eyes coming to rest on the mandrake root.

'You got it! Excellent! Over here!' He gestures to a pot of white liquid that is bubbling in front of a fire. Taking the mandrake, he uses a knife from his belt to add shavings of the root to the liquid. It froths and hisses as each piece sinks into the mixture.

Solandris appears at your side, her own face etched with concern. However, her attention is focused solely on the unicorn's horn resting on the table, not the dying wreekin leader. 'Hurry,' she says, her voice strained. 'We must get the horn back to the glade. We don't have much time.'

Bern takes a cloth and uses it to lift the pot from the flames. Then he pours out some of the bubbling mixture into a bowl. Carefully, he moves to the leader's side, gesturing for one of the wreekin to lift up the patient's head. Bern then forces a little of the mixture past the leader's dry, parched lips.

'It is done,' he says. 'It will only take a few hours to run its course.' He turns and says something to one of the nearby wreekin in their strange, warbling language. The creature hops up and down, looking happy and relieved. It then waddles out to the waiting crowd. A moment later, there is a loud cheer from the gathered villagers.

Solandris moves forward and snatches up the horn. 'If this is done then I am returning to the grove.'

Bern nods. 'The wreekin will let you leave. I have promised them I will stay here, until their leader is well again.' He looks to you and smiles. 'Thank you for your help, friend. Now return with Solandris; I know you seek answers that only the queen can give. Farewell. I will join you when I can.'

You leave the hut and follow Solandris over to the waiting eagle. Within seconds you are airborne again, soaring high above the misty wetlands. Turn to 376.

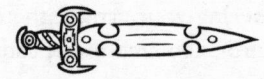

526

The weathered explorer appears to relax for the first time. 'Thank the saints of Judah,' he says. 'My name is Hal Arbuckle; an honour to make your acquaintance. If you find that poor lassie of mine, then tell her I sent you – and that I'm waiting for her.'

After reassuring Hal that you will do all you can, you head over to the scar's edge. Through the smoky haze, you see rivers of lava, hissing and steaming at the bottom of the ravine. To your relief, you also spot a number of rocky islands and ash-covered paths, that will provide a helpful route through this molten nightmare. Turn to 560.

527

You draw your weapons and advance, to take on this deadly adversary:

	Speed	Brawn	Armour	Health
Inferno	9	8	7	50

Special abilities
◖ Blazing armour: Your opponent is immune to *piercing, impale, sear, bleed, burn* and *ignite*.

If you defeat Inferno, turn to 568.

528

You fall short of the other side of the pit and plummet into the darkness. Cold air rushes past you as you desperately seek to grab some kind of handhold. Then you land with a lancing shock of pain – your right leg splintering against the jagged floor of the shaft.

Surrounded on all sides by an inky, impenetrable blackness, you begin to despair. Is this how it will end, dying alone at the bottom of this dark pit? Desperately, you try and crawl through the darkness, scrabbling along the uneven ground. After what feels like an eternity, you finally reach the cave wall. You grit your teeth as you try and stand. It takes several attempts, but at last you are able to pull yourself up onto your one good leg.

It is then that you feel a prickling along your arm. You quickly tug back your sleeve, to see the purple mark glowing beneath your skin. The three entwined snakes look almost alive, their diamond patterns standing out in vivid detail.

Then, to your surprise – and horror – you feel the bones and muscle in your wounded leg sliding back into place. Within moments, your leg, that was once twisted and broken, is perfectly healed. Tentatively, you place your weight on it and find that it is strong and healthy again. The mark continues to glow for several more seconds, then blinks back into darkness.

Your mind is racing with what has just happened. The strange markings on your arm have just saved your life. Why would Avian Dale and General Ravenwing regard it as something evil? Marvelling at this sudden reversal of fortune, you feel your way back to the wall. It is a simple effort to find suitable hand and footholds in the pock-marked rock face. After taking a deep breath to calm your nerves, you start your long climb back out of the pit.

The going is slow but you persevere, finally reaching the ledge. With a final grunt of exertion, you pull yourself back onto solid ground. It takes you some minutes to recover from your ordeal, but once your strength has returned you get to your feet and head back down the tunnel. When you reach the cave with the ooze, you decide to take the passageway north. Turn to 472.

529

Quickly and skilfully, you dispatch the mage. You may now take one of the following items:

Ring of the marshes	T-bone wand
(ring)	(left-hand: wand)
+1 brawn +1 armour	+1 speed +1 magic
Ability: swamp legs	Ability: bolt
	(requirement: mage)

You turn your attention back to Bern. The ranger has got back to his feet; two wreekin now lie dead in the swamp around him. As he battles with a third, you feel something whipping around your legs, dragging you to the ground. Startled, you look down to see one of the wreekin's nets snagged around your legs. Before you have a chance to cut your way free, the net's frog-like owner is upon you, stabbing with its pronged trident:

	Speed	Brawn	Armour	Health
Wreekin hunter	8	8	5	40
Wreekin net	-	-	2	15

Special abilities

♥ Entrapment: You can only roll 1 die to determine your attack speed while you have the net around your legs. If you win a combat round, you can choose to attack the wreekin hunter or the net. If the net is destroyed then you can roll 2 dice for your speed as normal. If the hunter is killed first, then you can simply cut yourself free of the net.

If you defeat the wreekin, turn to 542.

530

Using the book you are able to decipher the runes and markings. The door contains three columns of numbers, which lead up to a raised circular stone. Above it, the message reads:

> No key, no lock
> Three riddles on the rock.
> Speak and you may enter.

If you know the solution to the puzzle on the next page then 'speak your answer' by turning to the relevant entry number. If you cannot solve the puzzle, then you reluctantly give up and decide to leave the chamber. Turn 496.

531

Your aim is perfect. The nearest crow crashes to the ground in a flurry of feathers, crushing its rider beneath its immense black body. You take aim again, hitting another as its archer prepares to fire. Again the bird is brought to the ground in a whirling cloud of dust – however, this time the archer leaps clear of the body, landing in an agile roll. She springs back to her feet, throwing aside her bow and drawing her longsword from its scabbard.

'For the legion!' she cries, charging towards you.

 Village, town or camp

 Green quest (easy)

 Orange quest (average)

 Blue quest (hard)

 Red quest (hardest)

 Boss monster

 Legendary monster

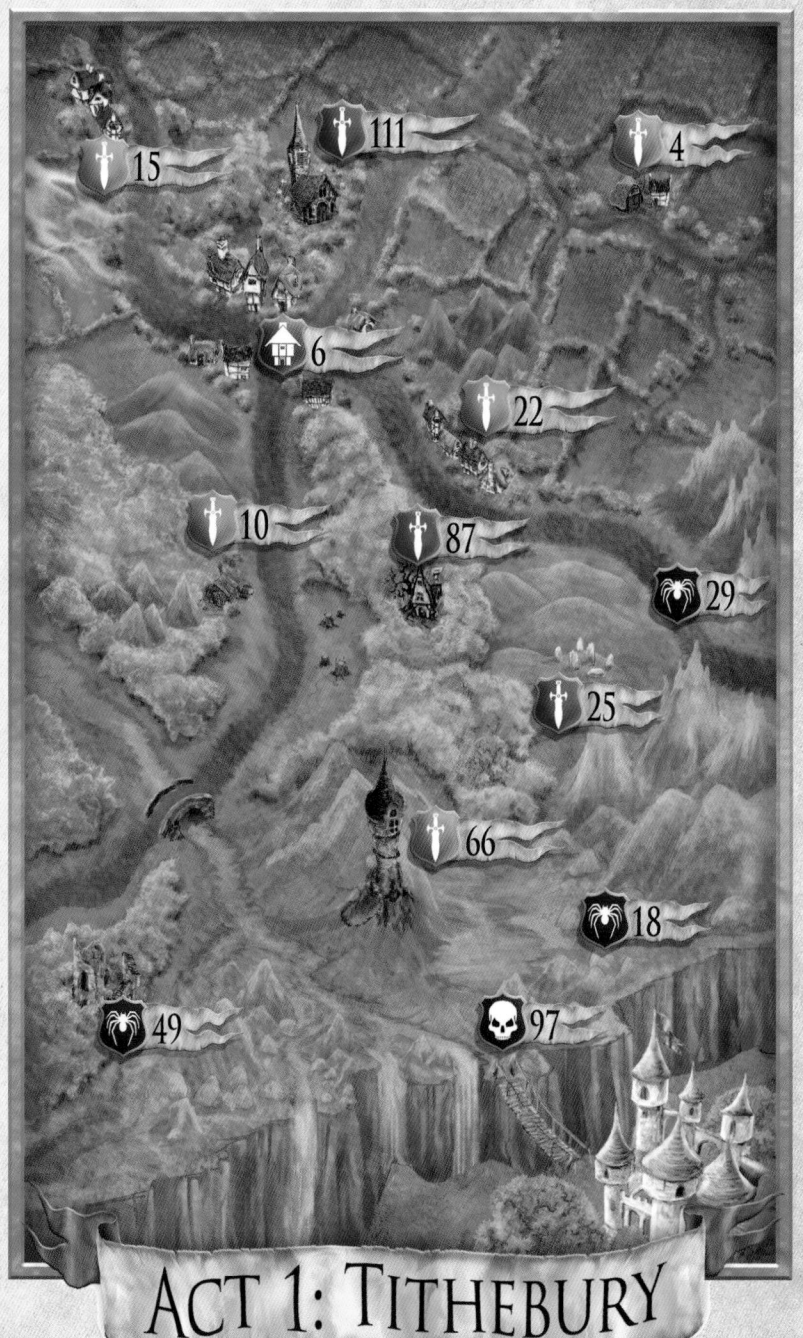

ACT 1: TITHEBURY

ACT 2: MISTWOOD & BLACKMARSH

ACT 3: THE BONE FIELDS

Fourth Ullir, Faolan, 1384 of the Ascendant

By the grace of the One God,
we lay down our lives for those we are sworn to protect.

Avian Dale,
High Seat of the Council, Grand Master of the Dawn

I pray for thee to accept this knight of House Carney, child of
Gore Thrain Carney and heir to the estate of Beringal Hall.
In brief, as of my previous missive, I pass the bearer of this
document on to thee for apprenticeship, in accordance with the
third agreement of the Lexicon Acadmius and by binding vote of
the Stone Cast.

    I impart our everlasting gratitude for your generous support
of the academy and keen interest in the welfare of the young
knights. Of this distinguished graduate, decorated with the
Star of Valour and the Knight's Rose, I have no hesitation in
their recommendation. They doth honour the legacy of the
grandfather, Godfrey Raith Carney, paladin of the Seventh Circle
and veteran of the fifth holy crusade. I am proud to be blessed
with this charge, to pass on a faithful student who hath every
intention of rewarding you with many years dutiful service.

    I beseech your Grandness does not take offence that I cannot
meet with thee at Tithebury. I appeal for your forgiveness in
this matter, as my attentions are duly directed to the capital in
troubled times.

By the grace of the One God, may our good friendship prosper
by the future deeds of this venerable knight and apprentice.

The Holy Light seal my words.

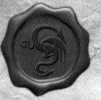

Malon Tulane
Master of Arms, King's Academy.

	Speed	Brawn	Armour	Health
Scout	14	15	14	85

If you defeat the scout, turn to 762. If you are defeated, turn to 732.

532

If you have the *bees' wax* then you can use it to plug your ears (turn to 545). Otherwise, rummaging around in your backpack has cost you time. You must now fight the count in this haunted hallway. Turn to 464.

533

The creature gives a wet, gurgling cry as its bloated body crashes to the ground. Its legs kick and squirm for several seconds, then with a final trembling shudder, they curl up and lie still.

Congratulations – you have defeated Wormwood. You may now help yourself to one of the following special rewards:

Razorback	**Lacerator**	**Wyrm crown**
(shield)	(main hand: sword)	(head)
+2 speed +2 armour	+1 speed +3 brawn	+2 magic +2 armour
Ability: slam	Ability: parry	
(requirement: warrior)		

You contemplate searching the creature's cave, but the smell is so overpowering that you are forced back out onto the ledge. Keen to get away from the foul reek of decay, you clamber back down the trailing roots, to the cavern below.

Will you:

Take the tunnel north?   472
Take the tunnel east?   524

534

The creatures are slow-moving, their bow-legged gait not designed for speed. You close with them fast, but not before one of the party has noticed you. It gives a warbling cry of alarm, drawing the wreekin to a halt. The one in the headdress barks guttural orders to its companions, then hurries away, heading further into the marsh, while the rest of the wreekin turn to face you, tridents and barbed nets held ready in their frog-like hands.

'So much for the diplomatic approach,' Bern grimaces.

In a singing blur of steel, the warrior draws his sword, its blade bursting into yellow light. With a thunderous war cry he charges into the pack of wreekin.

Will you:

Help Bern fight the wreekin?	323
Run after the wreekin in the headdress?	366

535

You follow Eldias along a series of black-stone passageways, lined with expensive paintings and tapestries. Eventually, you arrive at a set of stairs.

'Be on your guard,' whispers the witchfinder, drawing his swords. 'The count is a vampire lord. Do not underestimate him.'

Eldias leads the way down into a small, stone chamber, chiselled from the dark rock of the mountain. In the centre of the room is a stone coffin, its wooden lid pushed partially aside. The count is currently lowering himself inside.

'Not so fast,' growls the witchfinder, marching towards him. 'There is no hiding from judgement, Count. Prepare to finally meet your maker.'

With a snarl, the count leaps on Eldias, his black cloak engulfing the witchfinder. You hear a muffled scream – then, as the count opens his cloak, you see Eldias drop to the ground, blood pouring from his neck.

Licking his lips, the count turns to face you. He unsheathes his rapier, the bright blade reflecting a band of light across his golden masque. 'No one can stand against me,' he hisses. 'Your death will be swift ...'

	Speed	Brawn	Armour	Health
Count	9	8	5	40

Special abilities

🩸 Blood drinker: If the count rolls a ⚁ for damage, his fangs latch onto your throat and he sucks your blood! He can immediately roll an extra die for damage. If he successfully bites you, he also restores 2 lost *health*.

🩸 Vampire: You can use your *stake* and *reflect* abilities (if you have them) against the count.

If you defeat the count, turn to 422.

536

This will be a difficult jump. To make it across the pit you will need to pass a *speed* challenge:

	Speed
Pit jump	14

If you succeed, turn to 365. If you fail, you fall into the pit, turn to 528.

537

The further into the swamp you go, the thicker the swirling mist becomes. Soon you are stumbling through an impenetrable white haze, with little sense of which direction you are headed in. Roll a die. If the result is ⚀ or ⚁, turn to 468, ⚂ or ⚃, turn to 457, ⚄ or ⚅ turn to 438.

538

'I was a fool and it's all my fault,' says the man, grimacing with pain. 'We were taking pictures of the scar – me and my companion, Belinda. It was her balloon, you see – she's an aeronaut. Poor lass never wanted to come, but I talked her round in the end. Like the clot I am, I never admitted that the real reason was so I could spend more time with her.' The man's cheeks redden beneath his grey beard. 'It was all going without a hitch, then there was this big gout of flame – came right up out of the scar like dragon's fire. And it hit us! Next thing I know I'm falling and I hear Belinda screaming. Oh it was terrible!'

He tries to stand, but sags back to the ground with a grunt. 'Belinda fell right into the scar. Yes, right down into it. And our balloon went with her.' He shifts around, to look upon the jagged rift that cuts across the ashen wasteland. 'I don't suppose you would go down there and see if she is still alive? I can't do anything with this darned wound – but I'll join you as soon as I can.'

Will you:

Ask what 'taking pictures' means?	329
Ask how the crater was made?	511
Ask if you will get a reward?	316
Agree to enter the scar and find his companion?	526

539

You hurry to Bern's side and help the ranger to sit up. Although you can see no physical wounds, the magic has clearly caused serious injury to the warrior.

'Don't worry,' he wheezes, his face ashen. 'I paid for my mistake, but it won't happen again. Help me up.'

Bern leans on you for support as he struggles back to his feet. You ask him what that thing was, and why it attacked him when the door was touched.

'Someone or something put a magical trap on the door,' explains Bern, eyeing the cabin warily. 'It was activated the moment that I tried to enter. If it hadn't been for you, I would have been a goner. Thank you, friend.'

'So, will it be safe now?' you ask.

'Perhaps it's best you go on ahead,' says the ranger, settling down on a rock to catch his breath. 'You won't set off any more traps, if there are any. You are shadowborn; the traps will simply think you are a friend, not a foe.'

You grimace – finding little comfort in the man's words. Leaving Bern to rest, you carefully approach the cabin door and pull it open. Turn to 550.

540

The stone elemental breaks apart in a shower of stone and dust. You may now help yourself to one of the following rewards:

Diamond gauntlets	The rock	Elemental dust
(gloves)	(main hand: club)	(talisman)
+2 brawn	+4 brawn	+1 magic
Ability: piercing	Ability: slam	Ability: might of stone
	(requirement: warrior)	

Where the stones and rocks had originally lain, you spot the skeleton of an adventurer. Evidently they were crushed when the ceiling caved in. Kneeling down beside the corpse, you notice that they are gripping a small steel box to their chest. You peel their bony fingers away from it and lift it free. Trying the lid you discover that the box is locked. If you have a *fine silver key* then turn to 507. Otherwise, no matter how hard you try, you cannot prise open the lid. Angrily, you discard the box and turn your attention back to the chamber. Turn to 215.

541

The mage gives a gasp of astonishment as your blow penetrates his defences. Black energies spill out of his broken body, twisting and swirling into the air.

'No! I will not be defeated!' His grey robes crumple in a heap at your feet, the magic from his body spinning like a whirlwind, up into the air.

You kneel beside the body, searching the mage's remains. You find 50 gold crowns and may now help yourself to one of the following rewards:

Pot of mending (1 use) (backpack) Use any time in combat to restore 12 *health*	**Inner circle** (necklace) +5 health Ability: curse	**Zul's zapper** (ring) +1 brawn +1 magic Ability: zapped!

When you stand, the dark magic begins to pour into your exposed shadow mark.

You drink it in – all of it – feeling it healing your wounds, feeding your tired and aching muscles. And still it comes ... surging into you, forcing your head to snap back as you open your mouth in a silent scream. You want it to stop, but you are powerless, as the mage's dark magic flows like a river through your senses, filling you with an unimaginable power. Turn to 750.

542

You hack away at the reed netting, finally clambering free of its painful barbs. Meanwhile, Bern has dispatched the last of the wreekin warriors, his glowing blade now coated with green blood. Grimly, he eyes the dead bodies. 'Let's search these and see what we can find.' Turn to 479.

When you reach the bottom of the ravine, the steam and heat is almost overpowering. All around you, pools and rivers of magma flow sluggishly through the black rock, occasionally throwing up steam and gas into the air. Struggling to see through the smoky heat haze, you manage to spot a narrow pathway of rock leading across the molten sea.

You make your way along the path; the stone cracking into glass splinters beneath your feet. At last, you arrive at a circular island of black rock. From this island, another pathway winds further out into the smoke and fire.

At the centre of the island, within a circle of stones and ash, rests a nest of thorny brambles. As you approach this curious oddity, the nest suddenly erupts into flames. There is a screeching cry as a giant bird, made of pure fire, rises up out of the blazing bonfire. The creature spreads its wings – its gold and scarlet plumage rippling with fire. You realise, in alarm, that you have awoken a phoenix. It emits another piercing screech from its sharp, serrated beak, then launches itself at you:

	Speed	Magic	Armour	Health
Phoenix	8	7	5	30
Risen Phoenix*	7	6	5	30

Special abilities

- From the ashes: * When the Phoenix has been slain, it immediately rises again from the ashes. Use the stats for the Risen Phoenix to continue the battle. Once the Risen Phoenix is slain, the combat is over.

- Body of flame: Your opponent is immune to *sear, bleed, fire aura, burn* and *ignite*.

If you defeat the phoenix, turn to 565.

544

You split open the fish's gargantuan belly, back-pedalling to a safe distance as rotting meat and bones spew out into the water. As the putrid miasma of half-digested food begins to settle, you spot a number of items floating amongst the debris. You may now take one of the following:

Betsy Blue anchor	Navigator's waistcoat	St Elmo's fire
(main hand: anchor)	(chest)	(left hand: orb)
+1 speed +4 brawn	+2 speed +2 armour	+2 speed +2 magic
Ability: stun	Ability: charm	Ability: lightning
(requirement: warrior)		

You swim to the other side of the hall, where a set of stairs lead through into another chamber. Turn to 587.

545

With the plugs of bees' wax blocking your ears, you are now immune to the countess's wailing. (You can remove the *bees' wax* from your hero sheet.) With the odds a little more in your favour, it is time to finally face the count:

	Speed	Brawn	Armour	Health
Count	9	8	5	40

Special abilities

🖤 Blood drinker: If the count rolls a ⚅⚅ for damage, his fangs latch onto your throat and he sucks your blood! He can immediately roll an extra die for damage. If he successfully bites you, he also restores 2 lost *health*.

🖤 Vampire: You can use your *stake* and *reflect* abilities (if you have them) against the count.

If you defeat the count, the infernal screaming stops and the painting of the countess becomes still once again. Turn to **487**. If you lose the combat, turn to **424**.

546

You feel a rush of wind above you. Looking up, you see a regiment of red-robed mages streaking overhead. As their magic carpets sweep past the bone giants, they release their powerful spells. You are thrown to the ground as the horizon explodes in a fiery maelstrom of light and heat. A wave of ash washes over you, causing you to cough and choke. When at last you can see clearly again, you discover that the bone giants have now been reduced to a few fragments of scorched bone, sticking up at irregular angles from the burnt earth.

Ravenwing is already on his feet and charging forwards again. Wiping the dust from your eyes, you follow his lead, sprinting across the cratered ground. Turn to **728**.

547

A lucky blow cracks into the knight's head, sending his helm flying through the air. The face that is now revealed is one of black smoke and ghostly red eyes.

'Finish it!' hisses the knight. 'Free me!'

You drive your weapon into his exposed body, extinguishing the knight's unholy life. If you are a warrior, turn to **719**. Otherwise turn to **726**.

548

Inside the treasure trove you find 100 gold crowns. You may also help yourself to one of the following special rewards:

Nightguard cover	Golden fleece	Illumanti rod
(head)	(cloak)	(main hand: staff)
+1 speed +2 armour	+1 speed +2 armour	+2 speed +1 magic
	Ability: radiance	Ability: overload
		(requirement: mage)

Finding little else of interest, you leave and take the other doorway, through into the next chamber. Turn to 496.

549

You offer to help find the crown. Sahna lifts her eyebrows, nodding appreciatively. 'So, you like a challenge, huh? Good. Follow me and I'll brief you.'

The warrior leads you into a nearby tent. Inside, a single table dominates the space, covered in numerous maps and charts. Sahna points to one of the larger maps, which looks as though it has undergone numerous corrections and revisions. Between all the markings and crossings-out, you can see a pattern of squares and rectangles, arranged along a grid of lines.

'This is the city,' she explains. 'It took a while for us to get this accurate. Some of the earlier scouts gave us conflicting reports, so I used one of my own men, who I trust.' Her finger travels across the map, stopping at one of the larger squares on the western side. 'The few treasure hunters who did make it back,' she glances up at you, grimacing. 'There wasn't a huge amount to get out of them. They raved about sea monsters and ghosts, and refused to set a foot in the lake ever again. However, Raolin has talents. He used magic to ... well, not sure what he did exactly but it was like he was drawing out their memories – seeing what they saw.' She shudders at the thought. 'Anyway, we've pieced together the reports, sketchy though they are, and we have established where the king's treasure house is. It is here.' She taps the square building with her finger. 'I sent two of my best men in there, hoping to find the crown so we can pack up and leave. But they never came back. Then some mercenaries offered their skills. They looked the business and all, but not seen hide or hair of them since.'

The crunch of dirt and gravel announces a visitor. You both turn to see a dark-haired, dark-eyed man with a waxen beard standing at the entrance to the tent. Sahna bows respectfully. 'Master Raolin,' she says. The man glares at you stubbornly, until you follow suit.

'Do we have a fresh volunteer for the lake,' he asks, in a greasy-sounding voice. 'I am getting tired of waiting for results.'

Sahna nods quickly. 'Yes. This adventurer has agreed to the mission.'

The mage pulls an unimpressed sneer. 'Hmm, a weak-looking specimen but then we are getting desperate. OK, fetch the worms.'

Your eyes widen in surprise. Sahna gives you an apologetic look as she hurries out of the tent. Moments later, she returns with two guards flanking her, and a big jar held in her hands. Sloshing around in the briny water are two black, flat-bodied worms, the size of your hand.

'Hold them down,' orders Sahna. 'Let's make this quick.' Turn to 572.

550

Inside the cabin, you are met by an unsettling scene. Furniture lies in broken ruins, papers and scrolls litter the floor, and blood covers one of the walls. As you wander through the debris, it becomes obvious that a fight took place here. There are areas of the walls where the stone has been nocked by sword blades or burnt away by fire. One cupboard, still left standing, is sliced entirely in half, from top to bottom

Searching through the papers and scrolls you find little that provides any insight into what happened. Then you notice a loose floorboard, raised slightly above the other panels. You kneel down and pull it loose, revealing a small cavity underneath. A roll of parchment and a bag lie inside. You take the parchment and unroll it. To your surprise you find that it is written to you.

I knew you would find this. Call it a little gift of mine, for seeing things that have yet to happen. You are looking for me, as are many others. The vision doesn't tell me your motives although I see Avian Dale's destiny entwined in your own. He is a good friend and as such, I will put some trust in you.

I must hurry and leave this place. One of the stalkers is headed here as I write and I cannot afford to battle against such a foe. I must head south if I can. Something of great import has been made clear to me. I have a seen a most dark future, if the events that I have witnessed come to pass. The greatest threat to us is not the Legion of Shadow – no, the attack will come from elsewhere. I can't say more in case this paper falls into the wrong hands. There is a bag with some of my possessions. When we meet again, show me the ring and I will know it is you.

Cornelius.

You open the bag and discover a *plain gold ring* inside (make a note of this on your hero sheet). You pocket the ring before turning your attention to the other objects, which you may take:

Pendant of foresight	Tome of deep thought	Prophet's handwraps
(necklace)	(left hand: spell book)	(gloves)
+1 speed	+2 speed +3 magic	+1 brawn +1 armour
Ability: evade	(requirement:mage)	Ability: trickster

Looking around at the chaotic ruin, it is clear that Cornelius failed to make it out of the cabin before the stalker arrived. However, there is no sign of a corpse – unless it was buried or taken. Confused, you exit the cabin. Turn to **562**.

551

Belinda throws her arms around you. 'Oh thank you! I was so scared. I had no idea how I was going to get off this rock. All I could hear from that doorway was horrible laughter – and those strange dancing lights. I was just too afraid to ...'

'Belinda!'

You both turn to see Hal tottering through the doorway, using a length of wood as a crutch. 'Sorry I missed all the action,' he wheezes. 'I tried to get here as soon as I could.'

'Oh Hal!' Belinda rushes over and attempts to pick him up in one of her hugs.

'Easy, lassie. Easy!' he chuckles, as she squeezes him tightly. 'I'm a wounded soldier.'

If you have Hal's *clockwork camera* then turn to 477. Otherwise, Hal rewards you with a purse of gold from his pack. (You have gained 30 gold crowns). Then together, you head out of the seared scar.

'It was an honour,' says Hal, as you prepare to part company. He rubs his teary eyes, sniffling into his beard. 'Bah! Look at me, blubbering like a fool!'

Belinda kisses you on the cheek. 'Yes, I owe you my life, stranger. I'll certainly be more careful where I fly in the future. And don't worry, I'll keep a close eye on this one.' She pinches Hal, giggling.

You wish both the explorers the best of luck, before heading back into Mistwood. Return to the quest map.

552

'So we meet again,' hisses Zul. He raises the palm of his left hand, then clenches his long fingers. You feel a sudden flash of pain, starting in your arm and then rushing up across your whole body. It drives you to the ground, forcing you to claw at your mark as it burns like fire beneath your skin. Mathis slows, looking down at you uncertainly.

'What is it?' he growls.

'Oh didn't you know, inquisitor,' says Zul, speaking in soft dulcet tones. 'That is a shadow spawn. Just like myself. A Nevarin who helped me to find the last piece of the Nexus and open the gate.'

'What?' Mathis' eyes widen, his face seething with rage. 'It can't be true.'

'Oh it is,' chuckles the mage. He makes a quick gesture with his fingers. Still wracked with pain, you watch through your tears as your sleeve is pulled back, revealing your mark.

'NO!' Mathis bares his teeth, his whole body shaking with anger. 'This ... this is the true betrayer!'

Suddenly, you feel yourself being pulled to your feet. In horror, you realise that your body is no longer your own, you are being controlled by Zul. The mage is making gestures with his hands, chuckling all the time, as he plays you like a marionette.

'Stop this!' you shout, watching helpless as your hands raise your weapons. You begin to advance towards Mathis. 'No, wait! I am not your en ...' Your mouth snaps shut, held together now by some invisible force.

'Showing your true colours, eh,' sneers Mathis. 'May the One God have mercy on you, shadow spawn!'

Controlled by Zul, you find yourself meeting the inquisitor's charge, your weapons meeting in a blazing flash of magic and energy. Turn to 700.

553

(If you have already participated in the quest, *The battle of the bone fields*, then turn to 500. Otherwise read on.)

Redguard's garrison is smaller than you thought. As you walk the perimeter of the crumbling tower, you count only a smattering of guards – all looking sullen and deeply uncomfortable to be stationed in this outlandish camp.

The tower itself houses supplies and sleeping quarters for yourself and the rest of the garrison, whilst the area to the north of the building has been put aside as a training yard. Here, Nyms and Caeleb spend most of their time, sparring with each other or working with the guards on their stances and moves.

Near the edge of the camp, within the shadows of the stone wall, two large tents have been set up. One houses an infirmary, where Lansbury is tending the sick and the wounded. The other is a make-shift war room, with maps and charts covering various benches and tables. At its centre is a stone table, with a floating map of the bone fields hovering above it. You assume that this is some leftover magic or device from the time of the shadow war, which Redguard has now pressed into fresh service.

Will you visit:

The training yard?	588
The war room?	607
The infirmary?	597

554

As you pass through the runes they suddenly start to glow red. You snatch the crown from the pedestal and begin running back towards the stairs. However, to your dismay, you see a stone slab sliding down to seal off the exit. There is no way you will be able to get through in time.

A thunderous cracking sound forces you to turn. The statue of the king is now rising up off its throne, its crowned head almost touching the ceiling of the vast chamber. Behind it, the throne begins to break up into spinning stone shards, which quickly rearrange themselves into humanoid shapes. With ground-trembling steps, the stone giant advances towards you, with its golem army marching at its heels. Trapped and with nowhere to run, you must now make a final stand:

	Speed	Brawn	Armour	Health
Stone giant	10	10	12	50
Stone golem	-	-	6	15
Stone golem	-	-	6	15
Stone golem	-	-	6	15
Stone golem	-	-	6	15

Special abilities

◗ Knockdown: If your hero takes health damage from the giant, you must lower your *speed* by 1 for the next combat round.

◗ Body of rock: Your opponents are immune to *piercing, impale, bleed, venom, thorns, barbs* and *lightning*.

◗ Stone golems: At the end of every combat round, you automatically take 1 point of damage, ignoring *armour*, from each golem that is still alive.

If you win a combat round against the stone giant, you can choose to direct your damage towards the giant or one of the stone golems. If you defeat the giant, all remaining stone golems immediately crumble into dust.

If you manage to defeat this colossal foe, turn to 443.

555

'For the king! For Valeron!' shouts Redguard. Together, the four of you charge into the bone giants, each of you pairing off against one of the immense constructs of bone:

	Speed	Brawn	Armour	Health
Bone giant	15	14	12	140

Special abilities

◗ Knockdown: If your hero takes health damage from the giant, your *speed* is lowered by 1 for the next combat round.

◗ Body of bone: Your opponent is immune to *bleed* and *venom*.

If you defeat the bone giant, turn to 722. If you are defeated, turn to 732.

556

You climb the make-shift ladder and pull yourself up onto the narrow ledge. The wall in front of you has been blasted open, its edges scorched with black spears of soot. Beyond, you can see a rubble-strewn passageway sloping away into a twisted network of metal beams and charred rock.

Will you:

Enter the blasted-out tunnel?	603
Climb back and follow the flooded tunnel?	619

557
Legendary monster: The blob

The foetid smell of evil permeates every stone of the old mausoleum. You pass warily along its dark corridors, towards the glow of lights and the sound of chanting. Arriving in a large, circular chamber, you see a ring of black-robed necromancers surrounding a raised stone slab. Lying across it is a huge, zombie-like creation, its bulbous body sewn together from various limbs and other body bits. At the head of the circle is a wild-haired man in a blood-splattered white coat. He is giggling insanely, rubbing his hands together as he watches the beast.

Your foot knocks into one of the bones littering the floor. It skitters across the stone tiles, alerting the necromancers. On seeing you, their chanting takes on a frenzied urgency. Suddenly, black lightning flares from each of their hands. It arcs through the air, striking the metal plates that have been sewn into the monster's flesh. The body spasms and jerks, the enormous legs and arms twitching as the lightning crackles back and forth across its corpulent form.

'It's alive!' gasps the mortician, hopping up and down with insane glee. 'It lives!'

The hulking monster pushes itself off the stone table, scattering the necromancers. As it steadies itself on its squat, trunk-like legs, you see the true horror of its foul existence. The creature is a chaotic mishmash of human and giant body parts. Thick purple stitching criss-crosses its puffy flesh, holding together the monster's bloated, patchwork form.

'Go my beauty! Destroy this intruder!' commands the white-coated mortician, spittle flying from his lips. 'Show me what you can do!'

The giant zombie takes hold of a spiked mace and then starts lumbering towards you. 'Me destroy!' he booms. 'Me make master happy.'

	Speed	*Brawn*	*Armour*	*Health*
The blob	14	15	12	120

Special abilities

- Knockdown: If your hero takes health damage from the blob, you must lower your *speed* by 1 for the next combat round.
- Bloated body: The blob is immune to *piercing, impale, barbs* and *thorns*.

If you manage to defeat this hulking brute, turn to 616.

558

The shadowstalker may be fast, but she proves no match for your powers and abilities. As she staggers and falls, you feel a sudden tingling sensation in your arm. You draw back your sleeve to reveal the mark, its three entwined snakes writhing and twisting beneath your skin.

'No! Spare me!' The shadowstalker gives a startled cry as her body begins to slowly unravel, becoming ribbons of shadow magic that curl through the air.

Without thinking, you raise your arm. Almost immediately, the swirling tendrils of magic flow towards it. As each one comes into the contact with the mark, there is a crackling flash of purple light as they are absorbed into the skin. You feel a cold, rushing sensation as the magic surges through your body, filling you with a newfound strength and vigour. (You may now increase your maximum *health* by 10.)

Once the last of the shadow magic has been absorbed, the snakes cease their agitated motion and the tingling sensation stops. You lower your arm, bewildered and amazed at what you have just experienced. If you are a rogue, you can now learn the shadowstalker career (turn to 586). Otherwise, turn to 729.

559

As the giant crows soar overhead, you take aim and prepare to fire. You will need to take a *speed* or *magic* test (using whichever of your attributes is the highest).

	Speed/Magic
Headshot	24

If you are successful, turn to **531**. If you fail, turn to **579**.

560

You walk along the sheer-sided ravine for several hundred metres, before finding a suitable route into the scar: an overhang of rock that slopes down onto a narrow ledge. Perspiring from the heat, you start to make your way carefully down the slope. The loose ash and gravel underfoot is treacherous, and within moments you are slipping and sliding through a choking black cloud.

You land in a heap on the ledge, your hair, skin and clothing caked in ash. After scrubbing the stinging dirt from your eyes, you take stock of your new surroundings. To your left, the ledge snakes around the upper edge of the ravine, before dipping down into a cave-like opening. To your right, the same ledge descends steeply towards the bottom of the ravine and the rivers of lava.

Will you:

Enter the cave?	**519**
Follow the ledge down to the lava?	**543**

561

There is the noisy clatter of steel as the swords fall to the ground, their dark magic finally extinguished. With the guardians of the chamber defeated, you can now help yourself to the best that the king's armoury has to offer.

If you are a rogue, turn to **567**. If you are a mage, turn to **598**. If you are a warrior, turn to **581**.

562

Outside the cabin, you are shocked to see that Bern has gone. Worried that something may have happened, you ready your weapons and scan the nearby rocks, fearing that whoever laid the trap has returned.

You are relieved when the ranger finally reappears, rounding the side of a large boulder. He looks to have recovered from his ordeal, although he still walks with a slight limp.

'I was checking for tracks,' he explains. 'What did you find inside?'

You tell him that it appears a fight has taken place, but there was no clear victor. The blood on the wall suggests that someone was wounded.

The ranger nods. 'Yes, that would seem to make sense. I found two sets of tracks. The first are about a day old. The second are fresher and are following the first, although I found no traces of blood. Both were headed south.'

You thank Bern for his help.

'Good luck finding Cornelius,' he says. 'He is a good man and I would hate for him to come to harm. As for me, I must return to the grove. The queen has other assignments for me.' He walks over and takes your hand, shaking it firmly. 'I think I misjudged you,' he says, smiling. 'It was an honour to have fought by your side.'

With that, he turns and heads back towards the dark forest, leaving you alone on the cliffside, deep in thought. Return to the quest map to continue your journey.

563

Your curiosity gets the better of you. Striding over to the nearest chest, you put your hands to the stone lid. The moment your hands come into contact with the glowing runes there is a thunderous crack. You step back, wondering if the sound came from the chest itself – but then you become aware of movement.

The stone statues are coming alive. The cracking sound is coming from their huge wings, as they slowly begin to beat, freeing clouds of age-old dust from their surface. The nearest statue throws back its head and emits a bone-chilling howl. Then it takes off into the air, its wings lifting its squat body with ease. The other statues follow suit, their eyes now glowing with the same light as the runes on the chests.

You ready your weapons and prepare to fight as, one by one, the gargoyles swoop towards you, their dagger-like claws and fingers raking the air:

	Speed	Brawn	Armour	Health
Gargoyles	11	10	9	50

Special abilities

♥ Body of rock: Your opponent is immune to *piercing*, *impale*, *bleed*, *venom*, *thorns*, *barbs* and *lightning*.

If you defeat the gargoyles, turn to 571.

564
Legendary monster: Chilblain

A piercing wind blows across the frozen lake, scattering the flakes of snow that drift down from the grey sky. This strange place, trapped in a permanent winter, is a magic anomaly, or so Lansbury had called it – some strange fusion of nature and the leftover residue of powerful magic.

As you head out across the lake, you notice the ice ahead of you cracking and splintering. Something appears to be forcing its way out. You start to back away, but lose your balance and fall, slamming down onto your back. Only metres away, clawing its way free of the lake, is a creature made entirely of ice. It is humanoid in shape, with a pointed, half-moon face crowned with icicles, and long spindly arms ending in frost-dripping fingers.

You quickly find your feet again, as the beast cracks open its jaws and gives an ear-splitting wail. As if in answer to its cry, four giant pillars of ice burst up out of the lake, glowing with blue fire. At first you wonder what purpose they could serve, then you notice that the creature appears to be drawing in their energy – the cold fire settling over its frozen body to form a suit of sparkling, spiked armour.

You must now fight this deadly, magical monstrosity:

	Speed	Brawn	Armour	Health
Chilblain	13	13	20/10*	80
Ice pillar	-	-	8	20
Ice pillar	-	-	8	20
Ice pillar	-	-	8	20
Ice pillar	-	-	8	20

Special abilities

- Ice armour: * While all four ice pillars are standing, Chilblain has an *armour* of 20. If the pillars are destroyed, his *armour* is lowered to 10.
- Frost bite: Your hero takes 4 damage at the end of every combat round. This ability ignores *armour*.
- Body of ice: Chilblain and the ice pillars are immune to *venom*, *disease* and *bleed*, but take double damage from *sear*, *fire aura* and *burn*.

If you win a combat round against Chilblain, you can choose to apply your damage to Chilblain or an ice pillar. If Chilblain dies, all surviving ice pillars are automatically destroyed.

If you manage to overcome this frosty foe, turn to **584**.

565

The phoenix consumes itself, adding its ashes to those that already fill the nest. You may now take one of the following items as a reward:

Phoenix claw	Phoenix feathers	Phoenix ashes
(main hand: dagger)	(cloak)	(talisman)
+1 speed +2 brawn	+1 speed +1 armour	+1 magic
Ability: immobilise	Ability: charm	Ability: heal

If you have *Lorinwold's Field Guide to Roots, Herbs and Leaves* then you may pick 1 bramble thorn and 2 fire grass from this area. (Make a note of the herbs on your hero sheet.)

You cross the island and take the other pathway, which winds through the bubbling, hissing lava. After several minutes you come to another rocky shelf, littered with stone debris. Amongst the rocks you spot some long, tattered strips of cloth and pieces of scorched wood.

Will you:

Search the rocks?	**447**
Continue onwards?	**439**

566

'All eyes are on Talanost,' whispers Jenlar, blood now coating his lips. 'The legion is contained there, for now. But ... the resistance is not seeing the real danger, the real threat. They are weak ... exposed. Their true enemy will strike from the rear. They will be crushed. I have seen it!'

The man starts shaking, his hands grasping like claws. 'A necromancer, a powerful mage with power over the dead, is amassing an army. His name is Zul Ator. He was the traitor who opened the gate.'

You find yourself picturing the hooded man who you met in your strange dream – the one who took the last piece of the Nexus from you. 'I know him,' you mutter, under your breath.

Jenlar is now gripping you tightly, his fingers digging into your skin – into your mark that now buzzes and tingles with its own unearthly energies. 'Zul is creating an army that will march south and crush the last remnants of Talanost's resistance. The king's army won't get there in time ... the city will fall and then ...' The old man becomes silent. For a moment you fear he has already passed away, then his eyes suddenly flick open, focusing intently on you.

'You must stop this army. You must warn the resistance, warn them that Zul is the real threat.' Again he waves away your attempt to ask questions. 'Listen! Listen to me and don't speak. Avian is in grave danger. He thinks he can close the gate. But he can't ...' Jenlar breaks off into a fit of coughing. It is several minutes before he is able to speak again, his voice hoarse and almost inaudible. 'In the last war, the mages closed the shadow gate by removing its heart, the Nexus. Avian thinks he can do the same again. But if he does ... he will die.'

'Then how can we close it?' you ask, your own grip on the frail man tightening. 'I must know how we can close it!' Turn to 580.

567

The weapons and armour are some of the finest you have ever seen. If you wish, you may now take one of the following:

Vorpal sword	Spellbreaker	Nightguard gloves
(left hand: sword)	(main hand: mace)	(gloves)
+2 speed +3 brawn	+2 speed +4 brawn	+1 speed +2 armour
Ability: vanquish	Ability: disrupt	Ability: steadfast

After casting a final, wary glance at the Dour king's statue, you exit the chamber, taking a wide staircase down into a flooded annex. Turn to 610.

568

Gouts of whistling steam billow out from between the knight's armour. Then the giant topples to the ground, his armour falling into disparate pieces as they hit the stone floor. There is no sign of a body. Instead there is just a cloud of ash hanging in the air.

You may now help yourself to one of the following rewards:

Scorched tunic	Vambraces of might	Destroyer's drape
(chest)	(gloves)	(cloak)
+1 speed +2 armour	+1 speed +2 armour	+2 speed +1 armour
Ability: charm	Ability: parry	Ability: backfire

If you have *Lorinwold's Field Guide to Roots, Herbs and Leaves* then you may pick 2 bramble thorn and 1 fire grass from this area. (Make a note of the herbs on your hero sheet.)

If Hal is with you, turn to 573. Otherwise turn to 551.

569

You dive down into the turquoise-blue waters of the lake. With powerful strokes, you are soon passing over the dead city, lying at the bottom of the basin. Most of the ruined buildings are covered in coral and kelp, making them look almost indistinguishable from their surroundings. Others, like wedge-shaped pyramids, still retain their magnificent grandeur, looking other-worldly in the dappled, rippling light.

The size of the city is almost overwhelming. As you turn in the water, looking down at the sprawling expanse, you marvel at the scouts and adventurers who have helped map this place for Sahna. Your thoughts also wander to those who didn't make it back – for those who gave their lives for Raolin's cause. The twitch in your stomach reminds you that the next 'deader' could be you.

Regaining your focus, you swim down towards the building that was marked on Sahna's map – the treasure house of the king. On the map it was a small square; one amongst hundreds of other small squares. But here, in reality, it is a huge triangular building, not dissimilar to a shark's fin. Its sloping side is covered in plates of black metal, which shimmer in rainbow hues beneath the ever-shifting light.

You make several circuits of the building, looking for an obvious door or entrance. All you find, instead, are two irregular holes with scorched blast marks around the edges. You assume that your predecessors used some kind of magic or explosive to blow their way inside. One hole is near the base of the building and the other is nearer the top, just below the pointed tip.

Will you:

Swim into the hole at the top?	510
Swim into the hole at the bottom?	470

570

Searching the necromancer's body, you find a purse containing 40 gold crowns. You may also take one of the following rewards:

Grimoire of entropy	**Wand of lightning**	**Silleer's robes**
(left hand: spell book)	(main hand: wand)	(chest)
+3 speed +4 magic	+2 speed +4 magic	+1 speed +3 magic
Ability: sear	Ability: shock!	Ability: curse

All around you, the battle continues to rage. Turn to 743.

571

You step over the gargoyles' shattered remains and approach the nearest chest. The runes have stopped glowing, so you assume that they are now safe to open.

If you are a rogue, turn to 744. If you are a mage, turn to 713. If you are a warrior, turn to 706.

572

The guards close in quickly on both sides. One backhands you, knocking you to the floor, while the second drags you back to your feet, wrenching one of your arms behind your back. Roughly, you are pushed down on the table, while your head is pulled backwards.

'Oh, I do wish they wouldn't struggle,' says Raolin. 'It just makes it so much more difficult.'

Sahna steps forward and lifts up your chin. There is genuine remorse in her eyes as she fishes out one of the black, wriggling worms. 'I promise, this will be real quick,' she says. 'Now open your mouth.'

You breathe out a curse. One of the guards, you don't see which, punches you in the side of the gut. You cry out in pain – and as you do so, Sahna stuffs her fingers in your mouth, holding it open. With her other hand, she pushes the black, squirming worm into your mouth.

You try and bite down, gagging – but the thing is already slipping down your throat, moving with such speed that Sahna can barely maintain a grip on it.

You kick and thrash to free yourself, knocking maps from the table. Then a white-hot shooting pain explodes behind your eyes. Your head is released and you slump forward onto the table, spitting and coughing.

'Oh, not over the maps,' tuts the mage. 'Help him up will you?'

You feel yourself being lifted again, your legs dragging uselessly along the ground. Raolin moves to stand in front of you, stroking his beard. 'Now, that was just a precaution,' he explains. 'That is a lamprey worm, native to the rivers of the Terrall jungle. They allow you to breathe underwater – a rather crucial ability for your upcoming task, wouldn't you say?' He gives you a smug and self-satisfied smile. 'There is a drawback, however. In twenty-four hours it will begin to react to the digestive fluids in your stomach. That is when it will try and eat its way out. Nasty, but there you go.'

Rage swells in you like a mountainous wave. You wrestle and buck against the guards that are holding you, but there is no longer any strength left in you. The movement leaves you feeling sick and nauseous.

'Let's call this a bond of trust,' smiles Raolin, folding his arms across his flabby chest. 'You bring me the crown and I'll remove your little guest. If you find the crown, but decide to keep it for yourself . . . well, then in twenty-four hours you will be in a lot of pain. And I do mean that, most fervently.' The mage gives a greasy-sounding laugh before turning and leaving the tent.

'I'm sorry,' says Sahna, once the mage is out of earshot. 'He made them all swallow one of those things. They're his way of making sure you keep to the bargain. He wants that crown – I mean, really wants it. So, just do your job and then we all go home, OK?'

You nod your head weakly and then black out. Turn to 431.

573

'Good to do battle with you,' grins Hal. 'That healing tonic sure set my leg to rights.' He hops up and down, beaming through his beard.

All of a sudden there is a shriek, followed by a rush of feet. 'Oh my hero!' Belinda throws her arms around a surprised Hal, lifting him off his feet as she squeezes him tightly.

'Why ... er ... thank you,' he grins meekly, his cheeks glowing red. 'It was really nothing. This one did all the hard work,' he nods in your direction. 'All I had to do was follow the smoking trail of destruction.'

If you have Hal's *clockwork camera* then turn to 585. Otherwise, Hal rewards you with a purse of gold from his pack. (You have gained 30 gold crowns). Then together, you head out of the seared scar.

'It was an honour,' says Hal, as you prepare to part company. He rubs his teary eyes, sniffling into his beard. 'Bah! Look at me, blubbering like a fool!'

Belinda kisses you on the cheek. 'Yes, I owe you my life, stranger. I'll certainly be more careful where I fly in the future. And don't worry, I'll keep a close eye on this one.' She pinches Hal, giggling.

You wish both the explorers the best of luck, before heading back into Mistwood. Return to the quest map.

574

In the wall facing you, are a number of plain square tiles forming a grid. As you touch one, it slides into the wall then slides back out again. You wonder if this is some form of puzzle.

Above you, there is another blast hole in the ceiling. It leads through into a narrow tunnel that winds away into the innards of the building.

If you have a Dwarven *stone tablet* on you, then you will also have a number associated with it written on your hero sheet. Add this number to 574 and turn to the resulting entry number. Otherwise, unable to decode the puzzle you have no option but to leave the room via the blast hole. Turn to 437.

575
Quest: The warning

As the dull grey light darkens towards evening, you notice a gathering of guards at the southern tip of the camp. You hurry over to join them, wondering what it is that has caught their attention. Then you see it for yourself – a green halo of light flickering over the horizon. Every now and again there is a distant boom, as if of thunder, and for an instant the light flares brighter.

'What is happening?' you ask to the guard next to you. He is young, little more than a boy. His hand rests on the pommel of his short sword, and you notice it is shaking.

'That's ... that's the shield ... the mage shield over Talanost. It's what keeps the legion from breaking out of the city.' He jumps as another thunderous boom echoes across the plains. 'It's the legion. They're trying to break through ... testing the defences.'

Suddenly, there is the piercing clamour of a bell. You all leap to attention, turning towards the source of the sound. One of the guards on the eastern wall is waving a lit torch in the air.

'Oh no,' sighs the young guard next to you. 'That can't be good.'

When you reach the wall, a number of guards have already assembled there, led by Captain Redguard. You spot Nyms and Caeleb amongst their ranks, still hastily strapping on their armour.

'Tell me again what you saw,' demands Redguard, speaking to the guard that raised the alarm.

'It was a flare: a ... a yellow light that shot up into the sky,' he says nervously.

Redguard nods. 'It's my ranger. She's in trouble.'

There is a disgruntled murmur from the guards as a tall, burly man barrels his way to the front. He is dressed in white and gold armour, the thick shoulder plates almost a man wide. His hair is like a lion's mane, thick and golden, held back from his eyes by a silver band. Redguard snaps to attention, saluting the man, who you assume is his superior.

'Inquisitor Mathis,' he says, with an obvious trace of resentment in his voice.

'What is this? What is going on?' the plated warrior demands gruffly.

Redguard gives a heavy sigh. 'I was given information ... rumour sir, that there may be an army gathering out in the bone fields.' His eyes flick to you for a second.

The inquisitor raises an eyebrow. 'Go on.'

'So I sent Janna out to scout. She was a ranger before she joined the garrison, sir. It appears she may be in trouble ... my guard saw her signal flare.'

The inquisitor snorts. 'Of course she will be in trouble. The bone fields are a dangerous place.'

'Then what are we waiting for,' scowls Nyms, adjusting his sword belt. 'We better get out there.'

Redguard nods and looks about to assign orders, but stops when the inquisitor raises his hand. 'No, I forbid it,' he declares loudly. Turn to **600**.

576

When you come round, you find yourself lying on a set of stairs. You head is still banging with pain. With a groan, you clamber to your feet and attempt to get your bearings. Ahead of you is a flooded high-ceilinged chamber and behind you is the king's armoury. The old man has brought you back to where you started.

Entering the flooded chamber once again, you see that the kelp ladder has been drawn up, stopping you from reaching the ledge. You now have only one option left – to cross the room and take the flooded passageway, heading deeper into the king's halls. Turn to **619**.

577

Searching the necromancer's body, you find a purse containing 40 gold crowns. You may also take one of the following rewards:

Pot of mending (1 use) (backpack) Use any time in combat to restore 12 *health*	Witchwood thorn (ring) +1 brawn Ability: thorns	Seven stars (ring) +2 brawn Ability: heal

All around you, the battle continues to rage. Turn to **743**.

578

A defiant battle cry echoes around the ridge. 'Behold my wrath, you fiend!' There is a blur of grey hair and leather, as Hal charges past you, a pen knife held in each hand. 'No one threatens my lassie!'

Belinda goes to grab him but it is too late. 'Wait! Don't Hal, it's too dangerous!'

The ragged explorer and the knight collide – sparks and flame flying in all directions. Quickly, you draw your own weapons and charge into the fray:

	Speed	Brawn	Armour	Health
Inferno	9	8	7	50

Special abilities

🌢 Crazy Hal: When you roll for damage, Hal adds one extra point to your damage score.

🌢 Blazing armour: Your opponent is immune to *piercing, sear, bleed, fire aura, burn* and *ignite*.

If you defeat Inferno, turn to **568**.

579

You have no means of attacking these ranged foes. In frustration, you watch as they launch more missiles into the thronging melee, showing little remorse for whether it is friend or foe who are caught in their blasts. Ravenwing's forces are taking heavy losses from the barrage – you can only hope that the flying mages are able to rally and press their attack. For now, your concern is the ground battle. You slip out from the cover of the rocks and hurry onwards. Turn to **591**.

580

'The legion has learned from the past,' explains Jenlar weakly. 'The keystone is now warded with shadow magic – it will ensnare anyone who attempts to tamper with it. Avian will not see the danger. He will try and remove the stone and when that happens he will become a prisoner of the legion ... enslaved forever.'

'Then I have to stop Avian!'

The old man nods, his breathing becoming shallower by the second. 'Avian yes ... warn them of Zul ... the attack is coming.'

You can barely hear Jenlar as his eyes flutter closed and his arms go limp by his side. Leaning in close, you beg him to reveal more – to explain what you must do.

'You are the chosen one ... the one who will betray the legion ... find Redguard ... warn him ... tell him the angels must awaken.'

'What do you mean?' you ask between clenched teeth, gripping the old man as if willing him to stay alive.

But Jenlar now lies still, his eyes closed and his chest unmoving. The assassin's poison has finally run its course and taken the prophet's life. You gently lay his body to the ground, before turning your attention to the glowing portal. Already it is beginning to fade. You have only seconds to make your decision.

You are the chosen one.

The old man's words ring in your ears. You rise and approach the glowing portal – the doorway that will take you a step closer to discovering your destiny.

'So be it.' Steeling yourself, you step into the light, uncertain as to what it is you will find on the other side. Turn to **599**.

581

The weapons and armour are some of the finest you have ever seen. If you wish, you may now take one of the following:

Frenzy	**Majestic greaves**	**Vanquisher's helm**
(main hand: axe)	(feet)	(head)
+2 speed +4 brawn	+2 speed +2 brawn	+2 brawn +2 armour
Ability: cleave	Ability: royal regalia	Ability: vanquish

After casting a final, wary glance at the Dour king's statue, you exit the chamber, taking a wide staircase down into a flooded annex. Turn to 610.

582
Legendary monster: Flay

South of the road, the ash of the bone fields becomes scorched, red sand. According to legend, this was the site of a great battle between powerful mages. The sand is all that remains of that conflict – heaped in great banks, which swirl and ripple in the wind.

As you trudge through the desolation, you notice that the wind is picking up speed, quickly becoming a buffeting gale. You cover your face as best you can, eyes narrowed to the stinging sand. Ahead of you, the wind-tossed dust is starting to take on shape, forming itself into a whirling column. It spirals across the dunes, heading in your direction. As it nears, you notice that it is pulling up stones and other debris as it moves. Soon, you are faced by a thundering whirlwind of rock and sand – and within its swirling form, you can make out a face. Formed by the twisting particles of dust and dirt, the face stretches out to form a gaping, wide maw.

Then the monster speaks to you, its voice as powerful and humbling as the stormy elements that surround you. 'Dust. Dust. All will become dust.'

	Speed	Magic	Armour	Health
Flay	15	15	16	100

Special abilities

🦇 Maelstrom: For each ⊡ that you roll for your hero (either for attack speed or damage), they are automatically thrown up into the air for 8 damage, ignoring *armour*. (If you have an ability that lets you re-roll dice, you may use this before determining the result.)

🦇 Body of air: Flay is immune to *bleed*, *venom* and *disease*.

If you manage to defeat this whirling elemental, turn to 754.

583

You find the body of a dead witchfinder, lying amongst the refuse at the bottom of the pit. Some of the rogue's items and clothing are still salvageable. If you wish, you may take up to two of the following:

Witching hour	Night watch	Skulker's coat
(left hand: pistol)	(head)	(chest)
+2 speed +3 brawn	+1 speed +2 brawn	+1 speed +3 armour
Ability: bull's eye	Ability: steadfast	Ability: evade

You also find a purse of gold. (You have gained 50 gold crowns.) As you scan the rest of the pit, looking for any other chance treasures, you discover a small circular grill in one of the walls. A quick examination reveals that it is protecting a pipe outlet. Relieved that you have finally found a way out, you tug the grill free and then enter the tight crawl-space. Turn to 453.

584

You pierce the monster's armour, shattering its body into tiny fragments. The jagged splinters rain down across the surface of the lake, tinkling like glass as they slide across the ice.

You may now help yourself to one of the following special rewards:

Frost burn	Glacial shards	Ice splinter
(main hand: wand)	(necklace)	(left hand: sword)
+2 speed +4 magic	+1 speed +1 brawn	+2 speed +4 brawn
Ability: piercing	Ability: piercing	Ability: piercing
(requirement: mage)	(requirement: warrior)	(requirement: rogue)

If you are a mage, turn to 761. Otherwise, turn to 300.

585

'My camera!' gasps Hal, his eyes going wide. 'Oh, by the light of Judah, you are a hero!' Hal fishes in his pack and pulls out a selection of odd-looking contraptions. 'Here,' he says, laying them out on the ground. 'Don't suppose any of these take your fancy. You know – as a reward?'

If you wish you may take one of the following items:

Gold detector	Shrink ray
(backpack)	(left hand: wand)
Ability: beep, beep!	+1 speed
	Ability: zapped!

When you have made your choice and updated your hero sheet, turn to 592

586

The newly-absorbed shadow magic courses through your veins, heightening your senses and filling you with a furious new energy. As a rogue, you may now learn the shadowstalker career.

The shadowstalker has the following abilities:

Shadow speed (sp): When rolling for your attack speed, all results of ⚀ automatically become a ⚁.

Shadow fury (co): Use this ability to add the *speed* of both your weapons (main hand and left hand) to your damage score. This ability can only be used *once* per combat.

Once you have made your decision, turn to 729.

587

In the middle of the chamber, a huge stone pillar rises up to the ceiling. On each of its faces is carved the figure of a dwarf, dressed in various attire, from rune-covered robes to plated armour. Each of the four incarnations is wearing a jewel-studded crown. You assume that this must be the Dour king and the carved crown is a replica of the one that you are seeking.

There is little else in this room, save for clumps of fluorescent anemones and some swaying fronds of seaweed. You swim over to a passageway in the north wall and follow it through into a small, flooded room. Turn to 574.

588

The training yard rings with the sound of steel on steel as Nyms and Caeleb spar with one another. A crowd of eager young guards have gathered around them, cheering and applauding as the two expert warriors put on a startling display of sword-work.

Nyms spots you in the crowd and lowers his swords, nodding in your direction. Caeleb pauses in mid-step, twisting round to see what has caught his opponent's attention.

'Well, well,' says Nyms, twirling his blades expertly in his hands. 'Have you come to show us what you can do?'

There is a hushed silence as everyone looks to you expectantly. Caeleb bangs his sword against his shield, grinning through his teeth. 'Shall we see if those weapons of yours are just for show, eh?' he asks, looking you up and down.

Nyms walks over and stands by his companion's side. 'If you beat us, we may even teach you some of our best moves. What do you say?'

Will you:

Challenge Nyms?	753
Challenge Caeleb?	676
Politely decline and leave the yard?	553

589
Quest: Winter's hill

The bang of a door wakes you from your slumber. Still befuddled by sleep, your hand reaches out to the table beside your bed, fumbling for your weapon. You notice that the rest of the barracks is empty. A pale morning light filters through the shutters over the window.

Lansbury is marching down the aisle between the pallet beds. She stops at the foot of yours, her face red with rage. Under one arm is a collection of books, and in the other is a sack. 'Of all the pig-headed, stubborn ...' She drops onto the end of the bed, looking about to cry. She takes a moment to compose herself, then glances over at you.

'I'm sorry,' she apologises. 'It is rather indecent of me to just barge in here, but I need your help.'

You run a hand through your dishevelled hair. 'What happened?' you ask.

'Inquisitor Mathis, that is what happened,' she snaps, her rage rising again. 'He won't listen to a word I say. And now he has Redguard running rings around him – I can't get a straight answer out of either!' She opens one of her books and turns it to face you. 'Look, see that?'

You lean forward, examining the page. It appears to be a journal, and sketched on the page is a picture of an angel, with its arms and wings outstretched.

'It's an angel,' you state, scratching your head.

Lansbury rolls her eyes. 'Yes. Since you mentioned to Redguard about the message that Jenlar gave you – that the angels must awaken – I've been researching through the books I found in those ruins. Those statues are referred to several times in that text as guardians. And here,' she fumbles for another book, opening it out to a marked page. 'Here they are also referred to as the arcs of light.'

'Arcs of light?' you repeat, handing the journal back. 'Jenlar never mentioned that.'

Lansbury gets to her feet, stuffing the books back under her arm. 'I'll explain on the way. You will come with me, won't you?'

'Come where?' you ask, already sliding off the bed.

'We're going out into the bone fields. I want to examine one of those statues.' Turn to **656**.

590

You find the body of a dead ranger, lying amongst the refuse at the bottom of the pit. Some of the warrior's items and clothing are still salvageable. If you wish, you may take up to two of the following:

Lincoln green	Scout's longboots	Deliverance
(chest)	(feet	(left hand: sword)
+2 speed +2 brawn	+1 speed +3 brawn	+1 speed +3 brawn
Ability: charm	Ability: sideswipe	Ability: deep wound

You also find a purse of gold. (You have gained 50 gold crowns). As you scan the rest of the pit, looking for any other chance treasures, you discover a small circular grill in one of the walls. A quick examination reveals that it is protecting a pipe outlet. Relieved that you have finally found a way out, you tug the grill free and then enter the tight crawl-space. Turn to **453**.

591

You press on, making for a line of bone giants who are slowly advancing at the rear of the army. As you bat away the skeletons that seek to frustrate your progress, you become aware of three others making for the same position. You recognise Redguard and Mathis – both are now fighting on foot, their faces grim-set as they battle against the endless horde. The third warrior is a grey-bearded man in thick plate armour. In one hand he holds a shield, riddled with dents and splintered arrows. In his main hand is a broadsword, glowing with magical runes.

He catches your eye and for a moment the battle recedes into the background, as you both try and place how you know each other.

'Ravenwing!' you gasp, recognition dawning.

The man offers you a tight smile. 'Still fighting for us I see. Long may it last.' He swings his blade in a deadly arc, lopping the heads off the surrounding skeletons. 'Follow me, we're going for Zul.'

You cut your way through the skeletons to join Ravenwing. Together you fight side by side, heading steadily northwards. Mathis and Redguard are doing likewise. A few minutes later and the four of you are stumbling free of the surging tide, the area ahead of you clear. And marching towards you are four of the biggest bone giants you have ever seen. If you have *air superiority* turn to 546. Otherwise, turn to 555.

592

You escort Hal and Belinda out of the seared scar. As you prepare to part company, Hal takes out his camera. 'Here, can I get a picture of you? Do you mind? Might be worth a bob or two in the future, you never know.'

You watch with fascination as the old explorer presses various buttons on the brass box. The cogs and gears begin spinning and then, all of a sudden there is a bright flash, followed by a jet of steam escaping from one of the camera's nozzles.

'There you go!' he grins. He whips out a square of parchment from the underside of the camera and then begins flapping it back and forth in the breeze. Intrigued, you walk over and take a look. To your surprise, an image of you is slowly starting to appear on the parchment.

'Wow. Do I really look that ugly?' you ask, feeling at your face.

'Camera never lies,' says Hal, chuckling into his beard. 'Hey, why don't you keep it. Little memento of your adventure.'

You take the *photograph* (make a note of this on your hero sheet. It does not take up backpack space). After thanking Hal and Belinda, you head back into Mistwood. Return to the quest map.

593

You press the tiles into the wall, following the sequence shown on the stone tablet. This time, as each tile slides back, they remain in place. When the final tile is pressed, there is a grating rumbling sound from somewhere behind the wall. Suddenly, the grid begins to rearrange itself, some tiles sliding into secret recesses, others moving into the newly created spaces, to end up forming a small hole at its centre.

From this secret cavity a number of gold crowns, jewels and glowing talismans spill out into the water. You try and collect as many of the treasures as you can. (You have gained 40 gold crowns and a *perfect diamond*. If you wish to take the gem, simply make a note of it on your hero sheet. It does not take up backpack space.) You may also choose one of the following special items:

Dour's whetstone	Seal of war	Lodestone
(talisman)	(talisman)	(necklace)
+1 speed	+1 speed	+2 magic
Ability: piercing	Ability: fearless	Ability: rust
(requirement: warrior/rogue)		

After pocketing your treasures, you swim up through the blast hole in the room's ceiling. Turn to 437.

594

You deliver a fatal blow, silencing the evil mage. Stepping over her body, you watch as several more of the knights topple from their black steeds, their now-empty armour rattling to the ground. If you are a mage, turn to 570. Otherwise turn to 577.

595
Legendary monster: Malcontent

The creature is perched on a broken colonnade of stone, its black wings outstretched like an angel of death. Tattered black cloth hangs over its skeletal body, rippling in the bleak wind. Perhaps it was a man once, before it was twisted and reshaped by dark magics. From the depths of its black hood, you feel the creature's eyes upon you – watching and waiting.

Redguard was right. This is the undead monster that has been preying on the scouts and messengers along the Talanost road. You make towards the bone-covered hill, weapons drawn and glinting in the evening twilight. As you near, the creature flaps its enormous wings, sending black shapes whirling into the air. They coalesce in a dark cloud above the creature's head, cawing and screeching. Crows, you realise, grimly.

In silence, the creature kicks off from the colonnade, its immense wings carrying its hunched form towards you. From its decaying robes, two scythe-like claws whip outwards, long and wickedly sharp. Then the sky goes dark as the crows fall upon you, pecking and biting at your exposed flesh.

	Speed	Magic	Armour	Health
Malcontent	15	15	13	100
Carrion crows	-	-	8	40

Special abilities

- **Leech:** Whatever health damage Malcontent inflicts on your hero (after *armour* has been taken into account), he automatically heals himself for the same amount. This ability cannot take him above his starting *health* of 100.
- **Carrion crows:** At the end of every combat round, you automatically take 4 damage (ignoring *armour*) from the crows' raking claws and piercing beaks.

If you win a combat round against Malcontent, you can choose to apply your damage to Malcontent or the carrion crows. If Malcontent dies, the carrion crows will immediately scatter and no longer attack, winning you the combat.

If you manage to defeat this deadly opponent, turn to 765.

596

Anticipating your attack, the old man leaps to the side with a startling agility. Rather than countering you with his trident, he tugs on a silken rope that is hanging from the ceiling. Before you can react, a weighted net falls on top of you, dragging you to the ground. The more you struggle to free yourself, the tighter and more restrictive the net becomes, until you are thoroughly caught up in its woven strands. After several minutes of kicking and squirming, you finally lie still, admitting defeat.

The old man scratches his long green beard thoughtfully. 'Humph. Humans. They just get more and more stupid.' Raising his trident, the old man brings the heft-end down across your forehead, knocking you unconscious. Turn to 576.

597

Inside the tent, every inch of space is covered in pallet beds, laid out in regimented rows. Most are occupied, with young soldiers displaying various ailments and wounds.

Lansbury is perched on a stool at the end of the tent, next to a cabinet filled with bottles, pots and ointments. She has a book open on her lap, using the light from a candle to illuminate the small writing. She looks up as you approach, removing her spectacles.

'Can I help you with something?' she asks with concern.

Will you:

Ask if there are any helpful potions?	697
Ask about the sick and wounded?	686
Ask how Lansbury came to be in this camp?	672
Ask about the book?	659

598

The weapons and armour are some of the finest you have ever seen. If you wish, you may now take one of the following:

Swordbreaker	Spellplate	Warder's collar
(main hand: mace)	(chest)	(necklace)
+2 speed +3 magic	+1 speed +3 armour	+1 magic +2 armour
Ability: retaliation	Ability: focus	Ability: might of stone

After casting a final, wary glance at the Dour king's statue, you exit the chamber, taking a wide staircase down into a flooded annex. Turn to 610.

599

When the light fades, you find yourself standing on a paved square of cracked stones, surrounded on all sides by ruined buildings. A grey pall hangs heavy in the air – caused, you suspect, by the thick ash that seems to coat everything in sight.

You twist round, expecting to see a portal archway looming above you, but instead there are just two crumbling columns, choked with black thorny roots.

From one of the buildings to your right you hear a commotion. A woman in white robes hurtles out of the dark interior, a staff held aloft in her hands. The tips are glowing with white crackling flames. Behind her you can see small dark shapes skittering in her wake.

When she reaches the square, she pivots and sends a ball of white fire from her staff towards the doorway. You hear shrieks and cries from inside the building as black smoke drifts out into the chill, grey air.

Then, to your surprise, she turns and aims her staff directly at you. As your eyes meet each other, you realise – too late – that she has seen you as an enemy. 'Shadow spawn!'

She releases a ball of white fire. You try and dodge aside at the last moment, but the magic slams into you, throwing you back against the ruined arch. Crying with pain, you look down at your smoking armour and charred flesh. There is a flash from your exposed mark and, as if in answer to the pain, you feel a cold calmness wash over you, blocking out the agony.

When you look up again, you see the woman fending off a wave of ghoul-like creatures, with bony arms ending in sharp claws. Behind her, two men have now emerged from the building. One is tall and pale, armed with two glowing swords. The twin blades move like quicksilver, rapidly cutting a swathe through the ghouls. At the swordsman's side a shorter, broader-shouldered warrior is fending off attacks with his shield, while he wrestles with a heavy sack that is dragging in the dirt.

As you watch the battle, you see more and more ghouls pouring out of the building. The endless tide has pinned the two warriors against one of the ruined walls, where they are frantically dodging and parrying the incoming claws. Meanwhile, the robed woman is struggling to gain ground to reach them – her staff now proving ineffective in knocking away the creatures' frenzied attacks.

You draw your weapons and rush into the battle, gritting your teeth against the occasional twinge of pain coming from your side. The woman looks up as you approach, her eyes going wide. For a moment she thinks you are going to strike her – but instead you wade into the ghouls, your weapons rising and falling as they beat back the tide of undead. Turn to 628.

600

'You forbid it?' repeats Redguard, visibly shaking with anger. 'On what grounds? She is king's army. She is one of my best soldiers.'

The inquisitor is already turning, to head back down into the camp. 'I will not have men's lives wasted. It was an ill decision to send a lone guard out into the fields, chasing rumours of all things.' He stops, and looks back towards Redguard. 'I forbid any member of this garrison to leave their post.'

'Wait!' Nyms slides through the assembled guards to reach the inquisitor. For a moment they stare, eyeball-to-eyeball with each other. 'I'm not army,' he says defiantly. 'And neither are these two.'

He gestures towards Caeleb and yourself. 'So, you can't stop us. Your word has no authority over us.'

The inquisitor opens his mouth to protest, but closes it when he sees the assembled crowd nodding with approval. Redguard is smiling to himself as he looks to the three of you. 'I can't authorise this. If you go, it is your own decision.'

'Look there! There it is again!' shouts one of the guards, pointing. This time you all see it: a bright arrow of light arching up into the grey twilight.

'Come on,' says Nyms. 'Enough talking, I want some action.'

You and Caeleb follow him down the steps, ignoring the pouting inquisitor who is glaring at everyone with a furious anger. 'They will not return,' he growls, raising his voice so that it carries after you. 'They are fools to risk the bone fields. No good will come of this!'

As you head out into the grey ash-covered hills, littered with the bones of the dead, you wonder if the inquisitor may have a point. Turn to **605**.

601

It appears that Ravenwing's forces are making headway into the bone army. You can see their signal flags and pennants nearby, slowly pushing northwards through the masses of skeletons. Above you, a barrage of explosions light up the sky. A moment later and you are running for cover as a giant bone wyvern smashes into the ground, leaving a smoking crater on impact. A red blur flashes by overhead. To your surprise you see that it is a red-robed mage, standing astride a magic carpet. He is rapidly followed by a whole squadron of mages, twisting and weaving through the air as they battle the wyverns.

'Nevarin.'

The voice forces you to turn. A black-clothed warrior is striding towards you, his body flickering with shadow magic. He is tall and lean, his eyes hidden by a black band of cloth. In either hand he carries a large runed sword, already bloodied. 'I see you fight for them,' he spits – the last word said with loathing.

You realise that this is a shadowstalker, one of the generals of the Legion of Shadow. Weapons raised, you fall into a battle stance, watching your opponent closely as you both circle each other. Despite the man's blindfold, it appears that he can see you perfectly.

'When I kill you,' hisses the stranger, 'I will enjoy absorbing every last shred of your pitiful existence.' His body blazes with dark energy as he speeds towards you, his swords moving impossibly fast:

	Speed	Brawn	Armour	Health
Budak	14	14	12	110

Special abilities

♥ Lightning reflexes: You cannot use *sidestep, evade* or *vanish* in this combat.

♥ Poison: Once you have taken health damage from Budak, at the end of each combat round, you must automatically lose 2 *health*.

If you defeat Budak, turn to 740. If you are defeated, turn to 732.

602

The remaining swarm wheels away to attack another area of the camp. You hurry onwards, relieved to see that the magic shield is now intact once again. Nevertheless, the camp is still being overrun by the elements of the legion that made it through.

Explosions are ringing out to either side of you as the defending mages let loose barrage after barrage at the legion. You catch up with Ravenwing, who is barking orders to his men as a wave of black-clothed assassins charge through the camp, swords glowing with shadowy magic.

'Stalkers!' shouts Ravenwing. 'Fight them with a mage!' He catches sight of you and, for a moment, a grim smile plays across his lips. 'They heal.'

Then the forces clash, swords and magic forming a whirlwind of ringing steel and flaring energy. Ravenwing dispatches one of the stalkers, its body turning into wisps of purple light. A second later and the shadowy energy ignites in a ball of bright flame. A red-robed mage runs past you, his hands flickering with fiery light. 'Don't let them heal!' he cries. 'Destroy their energy. Focus, mages!'

You are drawn to the left flank where some of Redguard's men are fighting a small band of shadowstalkers. Nearby, one of the assassins has a hand raised to the air, his long fingers covered in black markings. He is attempting to absorb the energy from one of his defeated comrades to heal his wounds. Turn to 741.

603

You make your way through the jumble of stones and metal, at times having to squeeze through small gaps or lower yourself carefully down high walls of stone. At last, exhausted from your trek through this crude passageway, you come to another blast hole, leading through into a large square room.

Unlike the other chambers, that have all been cold stone and statues, this one is cluttered with furniture and objects. As you look around, you see that most of the items are salvaged junk that has been turned to other uses. A huge ship's wheel is now resting on its side, covered with planks of wood to form a table. Elsewhere, a mast and several tattered tapestries have been shown together to form a canvas-style awning, stretched over a pallet bed. Next to it, a giant oyster shell has been cleaned and used as a chest for clothing. The rest of the room is littered with mounds of junk, from old boots to barnacle-encrusted anchors.

A metallic clink forces you to turn. In the corner of the room, an old man with a long, green beard, is glaring at you intently from beneath his bushy brows. In his hands, which you notice are webbed like a frog's, he holds a rusty-looking trident.

'What yer want here?' he growls, stepping towards you warily. 'I ain't meaning you no harm, but don't wants you thinking this old merman is an easy push over.'

Will you:

Explain your mission and ask for help?	626
Draw your weapons and attack?	596

604

You slide an arm underneath the man's shoulder, helping him to his feet. He gives a cry of pain, his hands moving to his side where blood soaks through his blue robes. When he catches your worried expression, he gives a ragged gasp. 'I saw this end for me. The assassin's blade was coated with poison. It is just a matter of time now ...'

You start to ask a question but the man waves you to silence, his concentration focused on the stone archway. Muttering under his breath, the old man makes a series of motions with his fingers. There is an answering glow from the runes that have now appeared in the white stone. The old man nods with satisfaction, before making another series of gestures. You can see that each one brings pain to the wounded man, but he is clearly determined to finish his ritual.

Finally, he slumps into your arms exhausted, as a sparkling golden light appears beneath the archway, spreading out to form a glowing doorway. 'It is done,' he gasps. 'You must go through the portal. It will take you to the bone fields outside of Talanost. There you will find Captain Redguard.' He takes a deep, shuddering breath before continuing. 'I have seen it all – the fall of Avian Dale, the march of the legion, the destruction ... I have seen a most dark future. But it can be changed. Yes, now it makes sense ... you are the one who has been chosen ...' He breaks off into a fit of coughing.

You lower him gently to the steps of the dais. 'What must I do?' you ask intently.

The man closes his eyes and when next he speaks, his voice is little more than a whisper. You lean in close, hanging on his every word. Turn to **566**.

605

Nyms and Caeleb set a gruelling pace, sprinting at full pelt across the hills and valleys. You do your best to keep up, your eyes focused intently on the ground. The bones and rocks are proving treacherous, threatening at any second to twist an ankle or trap a leg.

Then your attention shifts to the sky, as it is lit up by another flare of yellow light. Nyms immediately changes course, swerving to the right.

'Over here!' he shouts back.

You follow him down into a steep-sided gorge. In the walls to either side, you can see doorways cut into the grey earth. Some are blocked by tablets of stone, others are open, revealing nothing but impenetrable darkness.

Up ahead, you see a woman racing towards you. From the green tabard she is wearing over her shirt of chain mail, you assume this must be Redguard's ranger. She has a short bow clutched in one hand, with a quarrel of arrows bouncing at her hip.

'Janna!' shouts Nyms, waving to her. 'Are you all right?'

The ranger is out of breath when she reaches you, her skin and hair caked in grey dust. 'I saw them ... I saw them,' she gasps.

From above, there is a deafening shriek. Looking up, you see four monstrous creatures sweeping down from the sky. They look like giant birds, save that they have no skin or feathers – their bodies are simply bone and sinew.

'Bone wyverns,' growls Caeleb, drawing his sword and raising his shield.

'Yeah, and they're not our only problem,' adds Nyms, his own swords leaping into his hands.

Each of the bone wyverns is carrying something in their claws. As they pass above you, they let go of their packages. The four of you scatter, as the 'things' thump to the ground. For a moment, they look like piles of bones. Then suddenly they start to animate – the bones sliding and cracking into place to form giant, humanoid creatures with bony claws and horned skulls.

'Bone constructs!' yells Nyms.

'Heads up!' orders Janna, nocking an arrow to her bow. Her eyes are following the path of the wyverns, who are already sweeping back to join the attack. Turn to 612.

606

If you have a *borehole charge* in your backpack then now might be the time to use it. You can choose to plant it on the statue, the throne or one of the walls of the chamber. Make a note of which option you have chosen before going to grab the crown. Turn to **614**. If you don't have a *borehole charge* then you will have to grab the crown and run. Turn to **554**.

607

As you enter the tent, your eyes become fixed on the floating map of the bone fields. Everything on it has been picked out in the minutest detail, from the hills and valleys to the sprawling city of Talanost to the south.

Redguard is observing the map with a furrowed brow. 'Things could go ill for us, if what you say is true,' he grumbles.

You walk around the map, following the line of a road that leads through the bone fields to the walls of the city. There, arranged in a loose circle, is an army encampment. You can even see the banners atop the tents, fluttering in an unseen wind.

'That is Ravenwing's camp,' explains Redguard. 'The last of the city defenders are holed up there with the mages. They're trying to hold out until the king's army arrives from the east. It could be four days or more before that force comes within sight of the walls – until then, we're on our own.'

You lean closer over the map, noticing a faint dome of light glittering above the ruined city. 'What is that?' you ask, puzzled. 'It looks like some kind of shield.'

'It is,' nods Redguard. 'The mages in the camp have created it. It's a barrier that keeps the legion trapped and contained within the city. I don't know how much longer they can hold it though.'

As your eyes trace the rest of the map, they come to rest on two statues, standing atop jagged hills of rock. A closer inspection reveals that they are angels, with flowing robes and swan-like wings. 'The angels must awaken,' you mutter to yourself.

Redguard looks up. 'What was that?'

'Something Jenlar told me before he died. He said the angels must awaken. What do you think that means?'

The captain cups his chin, looking perplexed. 'They're just statues I thought; some kind of marker left over from the war. Not investigated them myself, but I'll see what Lansbury knows. She always has her nose in a book.'

Will you:

Ask about Zul Ator?	737
Leave and explore the rest of the camp?	553

608

The passageway opens out into a square chamber. The air is stale and heavy with the reek of damp earth. Within moments, Janna has lit a set of torches, resting in sconces on the walls. As the chamber fills with a warm, golden glow, your eyes come to rest on the large stone tomb at its centre. Etched onto its lid is the figure of a helmed knight, with sword and shield resting on his chest.

'What a wonderful plan,' growls Nyms, who is pacing up and down like a caged lion. 'Now, we're trapped. There is no way out of here.'

Janna gives him a narrowed look. 'Sorry, I missed the part where you were full of ideas, Nyms.'

'Guys! Guys! Come here.'

It is Caeleb, who has stopped to study a mural, which covers the entire length of one of the walls. It is a masterpiece of artwork, depicting a battalion of mounted knights, charging across a battlefield in wedge-shaped formation. Facing them is a chaotic-looking mass of shadowy creatures, more teeth and claw than anything else.

'The Legion of Shadow,' gasps Janna, observing the grisly detail.

'Who are the knights?' asks Nyms, his brow furrowed.

'The Tor Knights,' states Caeleb, his voice filled with wonder. 'They fought in the last battle against the shadow. That's Arthurian, the king's son.' He points to the armoured knight, leading the charge. 'They were slain in that battle, to the very last man. They gave their lives to hold off the legion, buying time for his father's reinforcements to arrive.'

'Is this a Tor Knight, then?' you ask, glancing back to the tomb.

Caeleb nods reverently. 'Arthurian and the knights were all buried here, in the bone fields.'

'Enough of the guided tour,' interjects Nyms. 'We've got company.'

Back down the tunnel, you can see the ghouls clawing and tearing at the wall of thorns. It won't be long before they are through and into the tomb. Turn to 630.

609

Suddenly, from out of the portal, four tentacles of dark light streak outwards, wrapping themselves around Avian and yanking him back off his feet. The mage snarls with rage as he struggles to free himself, but the tentacles have his arms pinned to his sides, his magic sparking uselessly in the palms of his hands.

Then, in another dizzying blur of motion, the tentacles draw back into the portal, taking Avian with them.

'No!'

Frantically, you climb back up through the innards of the machine, your way quickly becoming an infuriating maze of pipes and steam. At last you reach the gantry and pull yourself up onto the bridge. Sprinting to the podium, you falter as you approach the black floating scar. This, you realise, is the shadow gate – the portal that will take you back to your home-world ...

'Home ...' You clench your teeth and step into the portal. For a moment you are blinded by a white light. Then, all of a sudden, you feel yourself being dragged forward, your stomach left somewhere far behind. Turn to 638.

610

The vaulted chamber is waist-deep in water, which spills from cracks in the walls and ceiling. Opposite you is a doorway leading through into a flooded passageway. To your right, a ladder of woven kelp hangs down from a rock shelf jutting out of the wall.

Will you:

Enter the flooded passageway?	619
Climb the kelp ladder?	556

611

'Your swords are an extension of your thoughts,' explains Nyms, his twin blades blurring into ribbons of grey as he dances about the circle. 'Once you understand that, your physical movements will flow from form to form.' He pivots and spirals, performing a deadly whirlwind of strikes and cuts – his weapons moving with a life and energy of their own.

You try your best to follow his example, finding that meditative state where you and the swords are one, acting in perfect unison.

The swordmaster has the following abilities:

Swift strikes (pa): (requires a sword in the main and left hand) For each ⚁ that you roll for your attack speed, you can inflict damage to *any* opponent, equal to the *speed* of your fastest weapon (either main or left hand). This ability ignores *armour*.

Ambidextrous (pa): You can equip main-hand swords in your left hand, and vice versa.

Once you have updated your hero sheet, turn to **553** to leave the training yard and return to the camp.

612

Nyms and Caeleb charge into the monstrous bone constructs, agilely dodging their raking claws. However, they are outnumbered two to one; you wonder how long they will be able to fend off the creatures' savage attacks.

Meanwhile, Janna is firing arrow after arrow into the flock of wyverns. As each arrow takes flight, they burst into magical flames – slamming into the wyverns and sending them reeling back through the air. Yet, despite the ranger's best efforts, one of the wyverns has peeled away from the group and is swooping in to attack.

Will you:

Help Nyms and Caeleb?	772
Help defend Janna?	681

613
Quest: Battle of the bone fields

'Orders have come through,' announces a soldier as he races into the barracks. You recognise him as Tulcas, one of the more promising young warriors under Redguard's charge. 'Assemble outside the tower – five minutes!'

This is the news you have been waiting for. For the last two days, the mood in the camp has been tense. With no word from Ravenwing, there has been little to keep you and the rest of the garrison occupied. Instead, your thoughts have been increasingly turning to Jenlar and the warning he gave you about Avian Dale.

Avian is in grave danger. He thinks he can close the gate. But he can't …

Every night, you have stood at the edge of the camp and listened to the thunderous barrage of the legion's spells, as they break against the magical barrier that keeps them imprisoned. If that barrier should fall … would Avian finally make his bid to enter the city and destroy the gate?

'Hey, wake up!'

You snap out of your reverie to see Nyms grinning at you – his rakish smile has been a rare sight these last few days. 'What're you waiting for, Ravenwing to come in person and deliver his orders with fireworks and a troupe of minstrels?'

You slip off the bed and begin strapping on your belt and weapons 'What's the orders, do you know?'

Nyms shrugs. 'I suspect, my good friend, we're going to war.' Turn to 647.

614

You step through the runes and grab the crown. As you do so, there is a rumbling sound from behind you. Turning, you watch as a black stone slab drops down across the exit, sealing you in.

The moment the stone slab falls into place, the ground begins to tremble and shake. There is a thunderous cracking sound as the stone giant rises up off its throne, its crowned head almost touching the ceiling of the vast chamber. Behind it, the throne begins to break up into spinning shards, which quickly rearrange themselves into humanoid shapes. With ground-trembling steps, the stone giant advances towards you, with its golem army marching at its heels. Holding the fuse wire in your hand, you light the end using a tinder box from your pack. Then you quickly back away, as the flame eats its way along the wire towards the borehole charge.

If you planted the charge on the giant statue, turn to 652. If you planted it on the throne, turn to 658. If you chose to plant it on one of the walls, turn to 643.

615

The flesh golem lumbers forward, its hulking mass almost filling the chamber. Janna looses arrow after arrow at its sinuous hide, but the golden bursts of magic appear to only enrage it further. The golem sweeps its clawed hands through the air, one of which hits Caeleb, launching him across the room. He slams into the far wall, where he slumps to the ground, stunned.

With Nyms busy fending off the ghouls, you realise it is now up to you and Janna to defeat this fearsome undead monster:

	Speed	Brawn	Armour	Health
Flesh golem	13	13	12	80

Special abilities

🟣 Distraction: Janna is firing a barrage of arrows into the creature. If you lose a combat round to the golem, roll a die. On a roll of ⚀ or ⚁ the golem doesn't roll for damage, having been forced back by Janna's magical arrows. Instead, the combat round ends.

If you manage to overcome this deadly adversary, turn to 759.

616

The beast stares at you dumbly, its slow-brain struggling to register that most of its vital organs are spilling out onto the cold, stone floor. Then, with a baby-like whimper, the monstrous zombie topples backwards, smashing the stone slab to smithereens as it crashes to the ground.

You may now help yourself to one of the following rewards:

Rumble thumpers	Pacemaker	Belching bludger
(feet)	(chest)	(main hand: mace)
+1 speed +3 brawn	+1 speed +4 armour	+2 speed +4 brawn
Ability: knockdown	Ability: kick start	Ability: disease
	(requirement: warrior)	

When you have updated your hero sheet, turn to 752.

617

You finally manage to pierce the knight's armour. There is a roar of pain from beneath the helm as the armoured warrior drops to its knees, the sword and shield clattering noisily to the ground.

Caeleb starts forward, intending to finish the task with the point of his blade. However, he draws back when the knight raises its gauntleted hands. It places them either side of its helm and lifts it free. You find yourself looking down at the ghostly face of a young man, his hair hanging in tangled strands over his translucent skin. He smiles up at you and whispers something. You lean in, struggling to catch his last words as he slowly fades to nothingness . . .

'I rest in peace. Thank you.'

The armour then rattles to the floor, empty and lifeless. If you are a rogue or a mage, then turn to 677. Otherwise, you may now help yourself to one of the following rewards:

Tor shield	Gauntlets of the fallen	Herald's spurs
(left hand: shield)	(gloves)	(feet)
+2 speed +2 armour	+3 brawn +2 armour	+2 speed +1 brawn
Ability: deflect	Ability: finery	Ability: charge
	of the fallen	

You glance over to see Nyms standing over the body of the defeated necromancer. 'That'll put an end to his tricks,' he mutters. Turn to 710.

618
Quest: Against all odds

(Note: You must have participated in the quest *Winter's hill* before starting this quest.)

The warning bell sounds before dawn. You hastily pull on your clothes and grab your weapons. All around you, the soldiers are doing the same – moving with the speed and efficiency of drilled army men. No words are spoken as you race from the barracks, following the soldiers out into the yard.

Redguard is already there, fastening his sword belt around his waist as he hurries towards the southern entrance of the camp. Lansbury emerges from the infirmary tent, looking around with a concerned expression.

'What's happening?' she asks, catching your eye. 'Is it an attack?'

'No! Reinforcements, I think,' interjects a guard, pointing to the dust cloud that is fast approaching the camp.

When you reach the southern entrance, you see three horsemen and several riderless horses, hurtling out of the grey dust. Their leader is clearly an inquisitor, dressed in the white and gold armour of his order. At his right hand is a thin man with pointed features. A broad-brimmed hat is pulled down low over his face, his white lacy shirt spilling out from a high-collared black coat. Behind them is a younger man, swathed in red-and-black robes. An ornate staff rests across his saddle.

'Hail!' Redguard salutes the riders as they pull up in a swirl of dust. 'Inquisitor Laine, glad you could make it.' He peers behind the rider, his brow wrinkling at the sight of the riderless horses.

'What … where are the reinforcements?' asks Redguard.

Inquisitor Laine removes his helm, revealing a weathered face framed by grey hair and stubble. 'We were attacked on the road. Undead. They have slain five of our number, including Artorius and Bale.'

'Laine!' Everyone turns at the thunderous boom of Mathis' voice. The sour-faced inquisitor shoves past the soldiers in his way, grumbling. 'Report. Where are the men that I asked for?'

The mounted inquisitor bows his head to Mathis, but you notice a muscle twitching in his jaw as he clenches his teeth. 'Mathis. A pleasure as always.' By his tone, it is evident that there is no love lost between the two. 'This is Witchfinder Gull,' Laine gestures to the man in the black coat and hat, 'and this is Klaret Pace, a pyromancer of the fifth order.' The red-robed youth nods in greeting.

'And let me guess – those things are what attacked you,' states Lansbury, pointing to the south. There are gasps of alarm from the assembled crowd as all eyes come to rest on the black swarming clouds that are drifting towards the camp.

'What are they?' asks Mathis squinting.

'Bone wyverns,' says Witchfinder Gull, speaking in a high scratchy voice. 'There are a hundred of them. Maybe more. And they are all headed straight for your camp.' Turn to 639.

619

The passage turns sharply to the left, before ending in a row of wide stairs. They lead up, out of the water, into a vast stone chamber. Braziers along the walls flicker with magical blue fire, which cast an eerie sheen against the cold black walls. At the centre of the triangular room, there is a circle of glowing runes hovering several inches from the ground. In the middle of this circle you can see a stone pedestal and resting on top of it is a magnificent crown of black obsidian. There is no doubting that this must be the real crown of kings; the crown that you have come all this way for.

However, your eyes are drawn from the crown to the huge ten-metre high statue of the Dour king, seated on a throne of black stone. The blue light from the braziers makes the scowling face look even more malign and evil.

You have a sneaking suspicion that the moment you break the circle of runes to get the crown, some form of trap will be triggered. And looking up at the immense statue of the king you have some inkling as to what it will be.

Will you:

Grab the crown and run?	554
Use something from your backpack?	606

620

As the packmaster falls, you notice that the remaining ghouls appear to lose their bestial vigour. It takes only a few moments for Nyms and yourself to pick off the stragglers, one by one.

With the last of the ghouls defeated, you walk over and search the packmaster's body. You find 50 gold crowns and may help yourself to one of the following rewards:

Vagabond boots	Bestial gloves	Lasher
(feet)	(gloves)	(main hand: whip)
+2 speed +2 armour	+2 brawn +2 armour	+3 speed +3 brawn
Ability: steadfast	Ability: adrenaline	Ability: bleed

When you return to the chamber, you see that Caeleb and Janna have skilfully downed the flesh golem. However, your problems are far from over. Turn to 654.

621

Together, you race between the fingers of rock, which form a winding pathway up the side of the snow-drenched hill. Several times you lose your footing and fall, slipping in the wet snow, but the baying horn in the distance drives you quickly back to your feet.

At the top of the hill, Lansbury points to the sack you are carrying. For several seconds she is too out of breath to speak. 'Rods ... get the rods. Quick!'

You drop the sack to the ground and pull out the three metallic rods. Each one has a different set of gems embedded along its length. 'OK, what do they do?' you ask hurriedly.

'Each rod has a different power,' explains Lansbury. 'Look, if they attack they can only reach us by these three pathways.' Her hand points to the winding formations of stone, that lead up to the summit. 'Place a rod at the mouth of each of these pathways,' she says. 'They will help you fend off any attacks.'

'What about you?' you ask, glancing up at the huge statue.

'I'm going to have to work out how to fix this,' she says, sounding less sure of herself than before. 'Otherwise, we could be done for.'

The baying horn has got louder. In the distance you can now see plumes of ash as a huge force advances across the wasteland. You spot several bone giants leading the way, their mismatched armour glinting in the pale light. Around them, a pack of ghouls are scampering through the dust, with men armed with whips driving them forwards.

'We can't hope to win this,' you gasp.

Turning, you see that Lansbury has already started some spell or incantation, as her arms are outstretched and her concentration is focused solely on the angel. It looks like it is now up to you to defend the hill from the advancing horde. Turn to 704.

622

You search the body of the two-headed giant. In a pouch around its waist is a bag containing 50 gold crowns. You may also help yourself to one of the following rewards:

Black death	Gloom shade	Grimm ichor
(left hand: sword)	(cloak)	(talisman)
+2 speed +4 brawn	+2 speed +3 brawn	+1 speed
Ability: critical strike	Ability: steal	Ability: poison mastery
		(requirement: assassin)

Special achievement: If all four heroes – Gull, Laine, Janna and Klaret – are still alive, you may receive an extra reward. Turn to 735. Otherwise, turn to 731.

Sahna escorts you to the edge of the camp. 'You saved us,' she says, her eyes flicking back towards Raolin's tent. 'At last, we can all bid farewell to this forsaken swamp.' She reaches into her pocket and pulls out a purse of gold. 'Here, take this. You deserve it.' (Inside the purse is 100 gold crowns.) You thank Sahna for her generosity.

'Good luck with your adventures,' she smiles. 'I have a feeling we will meet again, one day.' The warrior salutes you, before turning and heading back into camp. Return to the quest map to continue your journey.

Darkness falls suddenly, the grey sky blotted out by the dense clouds of bone wyvern. There are hundreds of them, more than you had possibly imagined – all shrieking and cawing as their featherless wings drive them through the air towards Redguard's camp. A few have peeled off, diving down towards you – twenty or thirty wyverns, screeching to each other, as if already celebrating a quick kill.

But Janna has her bow drawn, firing a volley of magic arrows into their ranks. The leading wyverns drop from the sky, their bodies blazing – but there are countless others to take their place. Beside you, Witchfinder Gull pivots in his saddle, bringing two flint-lock pistols to bear on the nearest wyverns. There is the flash of gunshot as his glowing bullets tear through bone and sinew, bringing down more of the beasts.

As you gallop onwards, you hear explosions behind you and a fierce heat at your back. Glancing over your shoulder, you see the young mage firing bolts of flame into the remaining wyverns. Their charred, scorched bodies form a smoking trail behind you.

You turn back in the saddle, focusing on what is ahead. With relief, you see the hill and the statue of the angel coming into view.

'We're going to make it,' you hear Lansbury cry. 'Look, there it is.'

But then you catch something moving at the foot of the hill; the ground itself is rising and falling like waves on the ocean. Light catches on bone and claw, and then you realise what it is you are seeing. Ghouls. Hundreds of them, scampering across the grey wasteland. There is no way past them and they are charging at full speed towards you. Turn to 771.

625

While Nyms and Janna battle the necromancer, you and Caeleb take on the undead knight. Its grey-and-black armour is thick and plated, making it difficult to penetrate.

'I must obey!' snarls a voice from deep within the helm. 'My new master commands me.'

As you and Caeleb continue to press the attack, you can't help but marvel at the knight's speed and agility. The undead creature dodges and deflects your blows with ease, seemingly unencumbered by the heavy shell of armour that it is wearing:

	Speed	Brawn	Armour	Health
Tor knight	13	12	24	50

Special abilities

- Dismantle: If you win a combat round, instead of rolling for damage you can choose to lower the knight's *armour* by 4. You can do this as many times as you wish, lowering its *armour* by 4 each time.
- Steel yourself: The knight is immune to *piercing, impale, barbs* and *thorns*.

If you manage to defeat this heavily-armoured foe, turn to 617.

626

The old man lowers his trident and offers you a toothless grin. 'The crown of kings, eh? You do realise it's guarded by the biggest stone giant I ever saw. Ah well, wish you luck with that one. Perhaps I could fix you up a last supper, before you head off to your foolish and somewhat untimely demise.' He tosses his trident onto the nearest pile of junk, then wanders over to a small stove.

'My name is Steverwellida Blartvaarti.' He pauses and glances over his shoulder. 'That's my mer name. My friends just call me Steve. Sea Shanty Steve.' He clicks his fingers and a small blue flame appears beneath the stove. 'You like fish? I have plenty of fish.' The old man clambers over a mound of junk to reach the silver-scaled fish dangling from a rope line. 'You won't find better silverbacks anywhere else this time of year; I'd bet all five feet of me ridiculous beard on it.'

Will you:

Ask what he is doing here?	633
Ask about lamprey worms?	640
Ask if there is anything for sale?	432
Try the fish and then continue your quest?	499

627

You hack and blast your way through the tide of shadow spawn, quickly reaching the ring of soldiers that have surrounded the giant creature. Despite their best efforts, the soldiers' swords and spears are proving no match for the beast's scaled hide.

'Move aside!' you order, barrelling past the soldiers. With your magical weapons raised, you dodge the snap of the beast's whip and hurl yourself against its scaled might:

	Speed	Magic	Armour	Health
Lord of Pain	15	14	13	100

Special abilities

🩸 Disease: Once you have taken health damage from the Lord of Pain, at the end of every combat round you must automatically lose 2 *health*.

If you win the combat you may restore your *health*, then turn to 711. If you are defeated, then you must begin this boss encounter

from an earlier point (although you cannot choose rewards from enemies that you have already defeated). Restore your *health*, then turn
to 748.

628

'You fight for us?' asks the woman in astonishment, as you both stand
side-by-side, striking down the endless surge of ghouls. You give her a
cursory glance. Up close, she is older than you expected, her bobbed
blond hair streaked with grey. A green tabard hangs over her white
robes, displaying the gold insignia of a crouching dragon.

At last, the ghouls lie dead, smoking in a crumpled heap around
you. Likewise, the two warriors have dispatched their own enemies.
The tall swordsman bares his teeth as he strides over the corpses
towards you.

'No wait!'

Before the woman can intervene, the man barrels into you, knocking you to the ground. 'Shadow spawn,' he growls, his cold blue eyes
flicking to your exposed mark. You begin to protest your innocence,
but the man is already bringing the pommel of one of his blades
across your forehead. You feel a hot burning flash of pain, then there
is blackness. Turn to 651.

629

You emerge from the lake, shivering in the cold evening light. As you
pull yourself up onto the banks of the lake, you feel another painful
twinge in your stomach. It must be the lamprey worm, you grimace
with disgust.

If you have the *jar of night creeps* turn to 679. Otherwise turn to
674.

Nyms races towards the wall of thorns, as one of the ghouls breaks through. His swords whip through the snarling creature, severing it in two. Already, more of the ghouls are clawing at each other to be next through the breach. Nyms angles his swords, scraping one against the other and sending a flurry of sparks towards the thorns. Within seconds, the sparks have lit the dry weed, sending flames marching along its wiry limbs.

The creatures screech and recoil as the whole wall of thorns finally bursts into flame, burning those ghouls still struggling to get past. Nyms retreats down the tunnel, putting distance between himself and the blinding, black smoke.

Back in the chamber, there is a sound like thunder, as dirt and stone rain down from the ceiling. Your eyes are drawn upwards, as a pair of serrated claws break through the soil, raking through the earth and cracking stone.

'What is it?' you gasp, readying your weapons.

'I'm not sure,' replies Caeleb, raising his shield to cover himself from the flying fragments. 'But it's big!'

There is another thunderous crack and then part of the ceiling gives way, opening up a jagged hole. You move back around the tomb, as grey light spills into the chamber, framing an immense hulking creature. Its body is without skin – just a grisly mass of muscle and sinew, stretched tight over a frame of bone. As it hunches forward, the creature's beady eyes rove back and forth. Then it proceeds to slide its wickedly-clawed hands through the hole. They find purchase and with a bellowing roar, the giant hurls itself into the chamber, splintering the stone beneath its feet as it lands.

'A flesh golem,' calls Caeleb. 'Back ... get back!'

'Yeah, they *really* want us dead,' growls Nyms, turning to face the pack of ghouls, which are now scampering down the tunnel.

Will you:

Help Nyms fight the ghouls?	781
Help Caeleb and Janna fight the flesh golem?	615

631

The monstrous creation collapses to the ground, its clawed appendages making a last effort to grab you. With skilled ease you sidestep
the raking talons and sever them with your weapons. Black poison
oozes onto the ground as the monster finally lies still, its mouth hanging open in a rictus snarl. You may now help yourself to one of the
following rewards:

Blood crescent	**Mages' tears**	**Shadow bindings**
(main hand: sword)	(necklace)	(chest)
+3 speed +5 brawn	+1 armour	+2 speed +3 brawn
Ability: cleave	Ability: disrupt	Ability: evade
(requirement: warrior)		(requirement: rogue)

Checking the line, you see that fresh mages have arrived to replace
their fallen comrades. With arms outstretched, they each stand in a
magical trance as they work fast to repair the faltering shield. Behind
you, the defenders have now broken through the ranks of shadow
spawn and are starting to outflank them. As your hopes of victory
begin to rise, you feel the ground tremble beneath your feet. Turn to
718.

632

Your progress through the city is swift. The tentacled monsters and
other abominations that you come across are more intent on scavenging through the rubble than showing you any interest. A few regiments of mages and shadowstalkers pass you by, their faces hidden
beneath dark cowls. With your shadow mark openly exposed, you go
unchallenged.

At last you come to the centre of the city, where the University of
Magic stands in a circle of walled gardens – or at least, what is left of
it. Only two large cylindrical buildings remain standing. The rest of
the university has been reduced to ash and rubble.

Of the remaining two buildings, the one nearest to you has had its entire northern face seared off. As you approach, you see that some kind of explosion from below ground level was responsible for the damage, ripping open the promenade and exposing an underground chamber. From it you can hear an incessant rumble, accompanied by a screeching, grinding sound.

You clamber down a slope of rubble into the blast hole. At its bottom, you find yourself in what was once an elegant hall. One of its walls has been blown away entirely to reveal an expansive chamber beyond. The rumbling, grating sound is coming from somewhere up ahead – its thunderous beat shaking the very walls. Drawing your weapons, you make your way past the scorched rubble and enter the chamber. Turn to 766.

633

'Perfect place for a scavenger like me,' he smiles, unhooking one of the silverbacks. 'This lake goes all the way out into the ocean, if you follow the valleys and channels to the west. All kinds of flotsam and jetsam finds its way into this lake – and yes, some big critters too, which is why I got this place. Safe as a fortress.'

He draws a knife from his belt and then sets about skinning the fish. 'I found some borehole charges in the wreck of an old schooner. I think it may even have been one of the king's own. Anyway, those little beauties will blast their way through anything. Allowed me to burrow my way in here, safely away from any danger I can't handle.'

Flipping over the fish, he proceeds to skilfully ease the back bone from out of the soft pink flesh. 'I spend my days fishing and scavenging. It's what I always done – and what I do best. There's no end to the things you can find around here. Like this.' He holds up the fillet of fish with a satisfied smile. 'Hope you're hungry!'

Will you:

Ask if he has any borehole charges left?	648
Ask him another question?	626

'Your shield is a weapon,' explains Caeleb. 'As cavaliers we make a few modifications to the grip. It allows us to do this . . .' He spins his shield, making cuts and slashes with its tapered end, as if it was a blade. Coupled with the quick thrusts of his own sword, the two move in perfect harmony. Rather than being a piece of metal to block with, the shield has become a versatile weapon, as deadly as any sword.

Caeleb hands you his shield, allowing you to practise the complex hand movements that allow you to spin, reverse and then strike with the shield, mimicking the fatal efficiency of a blade.

The cavalier has the following abilities:

Shield spin (pa): (requires a shield in the left hand) Each time your opponent gets a ⚀ when rolling for attack speed, they are hit by your shield, taking 1 damage dice, ignoring *armour*. They cannot use a re-roll to avoid this.

Shield wall (co): (requires a shield in the left hand) Use this ability to double your *armour* score and inflict 1 damage dice to your opponent, ignoring their *armour*. You can only use this ability once per combat.

Once you have updated your hero sheet, turn to **553** to leave the training yard and return to the camp.

635
Boss: The Legion of Shadow

(Note: You must have taken part in the previous quest, *The battle of the bone fields*, before continuing with this encounter.)

You make your way through Ravenwing's camp, your eyes scanning the endless rows of white tents. Soldiers scamper out of your way, muttering under their breath as you march past. You pay them no heed, having grown tired of their whispered comments and distrustful glares.

Lansbury appears at your side, struggling to keep pace. 'What do you think you are doing?' she asks breathlessly, her tone carrying a hint of annoyance. 'I thought we had decided it was best for . . .'

'You decided,' you cut in, changing course down another avenue of tents. 'You and all the others decided that it was best I stay hidden.' Your eyes catch the stares of the surrounding soldiers. All are looking to your arm, where your mark is vividly on display.

'But some of the men . . . Ravenwing's . . . they don't understand,' protests Lansbury. 'I think that you should stay with Nyms, at least until . . .'

You come to a halt, your fists clenched at your side. 'Where is Avian Dale? Have you seen him?'

Lansbury shakes her head. 'No . . . I haven't, but I . . .'

You continue walking, forcing the medic to hurry to catch up. 'I need to find him,' you insist. 'It's important.' For a moment, you turn your gaze to the immense green shield, surrounding the ruined city of Talanost. 'I have a message for him.'

'Perhaps the command tent,' sighs Lansbury. She takes your arm, drawing your attention to a circle of pavilion tents at the centre of the camp. 'Although, I should warn you that . . .'

You are already making for the circle, both hands going to your weapons as you approach the largest tent, surrounded by armed guards. Turn to 749.

636

The wounded man has started to drag himself up the stairs of the dais, leaving a trail of blood smeared across the stone. You hurry to his side, kneeling to offer your support.

'Jenlar? Jenlar Cornelius?' you ask, tentatively.

The old man turns towards you, his pale eyes roving with fever. For a moment he struggles to focus, then he gives a strangled gasp, pulling away from you. 'No! Why do you still hound my steps, shadow spawn?'

'But I'm not here to harm you,' you protest. 'I was sent to find you.'

As the old man continues to cower away, you suddenly realise why he is acting in such a manner. He must be assuming that you are the body-shifting assassin that was sent to kill him. After all, the stalker had the exact same appearance as you, when you first arrived. If you have the *plain gold ring* from Jenlar's cabin, turn to 436. Otherwise, turn to 441.

637

You emerge from the lake, shivering in the cold evening light. As you pull yourself up onto the banks of the lake, you feel another painful twinge in your stomach. It must be the lamprey worm, you grimace with disgust.

If you have the *jar of night creeps* turn to 663. Otherwise turn to 696.

638

You hit the ground so quickly that you lose your balance, pitching forwards onto your stomach. Putting out your arms, you try and cushion your fall as you slam down onto cold, black sand. For several moments you can't move, your head ringing with white noise. As the sickness and dizziness subside, you push yourself up off the sandy ground.

To either side of you, stretching as far as the eye can see, is a vast army, equipped and ready for battle. There is little uniformity to its ranks – beasts and monsters stand next to mages and warriors, giant four-legged creatures tower over spindly, bird-like abominations – everywhere your eye settles there is something new, different and equally horrifying.

To your relief, they are making no move to attack you. Instead they simply stare ahead impassively, as if under some spell.

Suddenly, a pained cry shatters the silence.

You spin round, your eyes sliding along the ranks of shadow spawn, to finally come to rest on a grisly, grotesque monster. It has the appearance of a giant snail – its body bulging out of a black shell that glows with purple light. From the gash that passes for a mouth, black ooze dribbles down over its pallid, rubbery skin.

Floating in front of it, bound by circles of black light, is Avian Dale.

The mage is crying and whimpering with pain as lightning flickers over his body, spitting and crackling from the surrounding bands of magic that hold him prisoner.

'So you return,' the snail-like monster speaks, spitting black drool onto the ground. 'I see you still remember the way home, Nevarin.'

'Don't listen!' cries Avian. 'Just run! Run!'

'Ah, Avian – let's not be too hasty,' spits the creature. 'After all, we're only just getting reacquainted.' On the top of the monster's head, two giant eyestalks lean forward. 'I am Sharroth, third of the seventh brood of Borellin-var. It is I who has been given the honour of leading the legion. When the pitiful mage shield falls, and fall it will, we will march through the portal and lay claim to a new world.'

You raise your weapons and start forward towards the monster, the mark on your arm flaring with a hellish light. 'You will not take my world!' you growl challengingly.

'Your world,' hisses Sharroth, its bulbous sides shaking with laughter. 'But this is your world, Nevarin. At least … it was.'

Will you:

Attack Sharroth?	769
Ask Sharroth about the 'Nevarin'?	742
Ask Sharroth about the mark on your arm?	641

639

'Guards, man the walls – move!' orders Redguard. 'Crossbows at the ready!'

The soldiers leap into action, bolting immediately for their posts.

'We don't have enough firepower to see off that many wyverns,' states Mathis grimly. 'The camp will be overrun.'

'Oh wyverns are not your only problem, Inquisitor,' says the witchfinder softly, leaning forward in his saddle. 'Behind the wyverns is a band of undead, four-hundred strong. Ghouls, wights … it's quite an impressive sight.'

Redguard lets out a heavy sigh. 'We're finished. We can't repel a force of that size.'

'Yes – yes we can.' All eyes turn to Lansbury. She clears her throat before continuing. 'There is a statue to the south – an angel. We have already seen what they can do. I suggest we ride south and attempt to head off the undead there. I can activate the statue.'

'Those statues are weapons?' asks the witchfinder, his blue eyes sparkling with interest.

Lansbury nods. 'It's our only chance.'

Redguard looks to be considering the plan. 'It's too dangerous. The wyverns would just rip you to shreds.'

'They're coming here to this camp,' states Laine matter-of-factly. 'They may not attack a few of us heading south. If we made it through then perhaps we can use this ... statue against the force that is following. I see no other alternatives. Mathis?'

The inquisitor spits on the grey, ash-covered ground. 'Take Lansbury with you – the rest of us will stay here and defend the camp.'

'I would like to go.' Janna hurries over, sliding her bow across her shoulder. 'I can hold off some of those wyverns if they get close.'

Redguard nods. 'And you too,' he says, looking in your direction. 'You've had more experience than most against this foe.'

'Yes, sir.' You hurry over to one of the waiting horses, aware that Witchfinder Gull is watching you with a keen interest. Pulling yourself into the saddle, you take the reins. Already, you can hear the shrieks and cries of the approaching wyverns.

'Let's not delay,' says Laine, pulling his helm down over his face. 'Good luck, Redguard. I hope when next we meet it is under better circumstances.'

With that he turns his warhorse and urges it southwards at a gallop. You follow his lead, joining the other four riders as they dash across the wasteland towards the thronging black swarm. Turn to 624.

640

'Oh those things. Yes, nasty.' He glances down at your stomach, then his eyes widen in surprise. Quickly, he walks over and puts a hand to it, feeling around with his fingers. 'Well, shake me sideways with a length of seaweed, I see now why you asked. Got one suckered in there, good and proper. Now, let me see.'

You watch as the old man hurries across the room and begins

rummaging through a pile of objects. After examining the insides of an old boot, a doll's half-chewed head and a copper kettle, he mutters something under his breath and then starts on a fresh pile. 'Got to be here somewhere ... ah yes!'

He lifts up a small glass jar, with what looks like an old sock as a stopper. Inside you can see a squirming mass of black maggots, wriggling to get free. You instinctively draw back, grimacing.

'Oh settle down,' he grins. 'They won't hurt you – well, nothing like what that thing will do when it decides to chew through your insides.' He offers you the jar. 'These are night creeps. Swallow a couple of 'em and your problem is solved. They're covered in an acid that is deadly to lamprey worms but harmless to humans and merfolk. Which is lucky.'

You take the jar and hold it up, watching with revulsion as the slimy maggots crawl around the face of the glass. 'Now, I don't advise you trying it until you're good and ready, or else you won't be able to breathe water again and – unless I have the brains of a pickled crab – I'd say that's why you swallowed one of those things in the first place. Ain't I right?'

You may now take the following item:

Jar of night creeps
(backpack)
They're slimy!

Return to 626 to continue your conversation with the merman.

641

'That is the price of failure,' hisses Sharroth. 'All Nevarin wear the mark, to remind them of who they are; who they serve.'

'I serve no one.' You glower defiantly. 'I am no slave.'

'Oh, you are a slave to many things, Nevarin.' The creature inches closer, its body making sickening, squelching noises. 'You are a slave to yourself ... to your thirst for power. Look at you. Do you think you would be standing here, with armaments that reek with magic, if you did not desire power and reward.'

'I'm here to end this ... to end *you*.'

'I would like to see you try,' Sharroth sneers. Black tendrils of drool slip from the sides of its mouth. 'You are Nevarin – and you are sworn to serve me!'

Will you:

Attack Sharroth?	769
Ask Sharroth about the 'Nevarin'?	742

642

The mortician slumps to the ground with a groan of pain. Slowly, he drags himself across the stone tiles, to lie next to the remains of his zombie creation.

'My beauty,' he whispers. 'My poor beauty.' He rests his hand inside the giant palm of the monster, then finally lies still.

With the mad mortician defeated, you may now help yourself to one of the following rewards:

Abattoir gloves	**Brain infusers**	**Mortician's scalpel**
(gloves)	(head)	(main hand: dagger)
+1 speed +4 magic	+2 speed +3 armour	+3 speed +4 brawn
Ability: bleed	Ability: lightning	Ability: disease
		(requirement: rogue)

When you have updated your hero sheet, return to the quest map to continue your adventure.

643

You cover your head as a deafening explosion rocks the chamber, sending fragments of stone showering across the room. Looking up, you see that you have blasted a sizeable hole in the wall – and now torrents of churning water are pouring into the chamber. The force of its passage knocks you off your feet, hurling you backwards into the advancing army of golems. One tries to take a swipe at you, but its own balance has been thrown by the rushing maelstrom of water. Unable to stay on its feet, it is knocked over, slamming into the golem behind it. In a tangle of bodies they go careening past you, as the water continues to fill the chamber.

As the momentum of the water begins to dissipate, you start to swim against it – towards the hole. It is then, and only then, that you realise that you have dropped the crown. Frantically you look around, but you can see no sign of it. The rushing water could have carried it anywhere. The stone giant, still staggering on its feet, sees you and advances through the swirling waters. With no choice left, you swim out of the hole and into the lake, cursing your misfortune at having lost the crown. Turn to 629.

644

To break through the sheets of ice you will have to take a *brawn* or *magic* test (using whichever attribute is highest).

	Brawn/Magic
Break the ice	25

If you are successful, you break through the ice and retrieve the chest. Turn to 492. Otherwise, after many attempts you are forced to give up. The chest is buried too deep for you to reach it. Return to the map to continue your journey.

645

As the giant crashes to the ground, there is a grating squeal from the statue. You look over to see the angel start to turn on its pedestal, grinding against centuries of dust and dirt as it forces itself into motion.

Then there is a flash of light followed by an explosion. As the statue spins round, it throws white beams of light out over the hilltop and the surrounding plains. Each sizzling bolt finds a target, punching through ranks of undead, hurling ghouls high into the air, slicing through shades and wights ... everywhere the beams land the sky is filled with giant clouds of ash as mighty explosions rip into the barren landscape.

You scramble over to Lansbury's side. The woman looks pale and drawn, but she is smiling through her exhaustion. 'We did it,' she gasps. 'We did it.'

You watch awestruck as the statue does its tireless work, destroying the undead and sending the scattered remnants of the force into a full scale rout. The battle has been won. If you are a rogue, turn to 622. If you are a mage, turn to 664. If you are a warrior, turn to 727.

646

You are led inside a small tent, filled with crates and boxes. The warrior walks over to one of the smaller boxes and pulls out a jar of wriggling maggots. You take a step back in surprise.

'These are night creeps. Harmless but the lamprey worms hate them. Swallow a couple of these and your problems are over.'

You take the jar and remove the lid. Then, holding your breath, you tilt back your head and deposit the squirming maggots into your mouth. Trying to ignore the slimy sea-salt taste, you swallow them as quickly as you can. After several seconds you feel a queasy, churning sensation in your stomach, then a hot flush of burning pain as something shoots up through your chest, forcing its way into the back of your throat. Your eyes bulge as you begin to choke, gasping for air. Then, suddenly you feel the pressure in your throat ease as your mouth is filled with something wet and slimy.

Bending over, you watch in horrified revulsion as the lamprey worm drops out of your mouth onto the muddy soil. The creature is writhing from side-to-side, its skin blistered and raw.

Sahna hands you a canteen. You grab it from her and take a long drink of water, your hands shaking from the ordeal.

'See, that wasn't too bad was it?' she grins wryly, grinding the worm beneath her boot heel. If you delivered the crown to Raolin, turn to 623. If you lost the crown, turn to 667.

Outside, the air is chill and damp. A rumble in the distance suggests thunder. Redguard and Mathis approach quickly from the tower, both deep in conversation. You notice a man following behind, in a red cloak and feathered helm. You assume that he is the messenger, newly arrived from Ravenwing's camp to the south.

They halt in front of the lined ranks. It is a paltry gathering, you observe with some concern. The garrison now numbers less than thirty – having taken heavy losses in previous skirmishes with the undead forces. A glance to your side confirms that Nyms is coming to a similar conclusion as he looks around at the assembled guardsmen.

'Soldiers and friends,' announces Redguard. 'We now have word from the south. Ravenwing suspects that Zul's strike is imminent. His scouts have reported that a large army of undead are moving south, using the valley for cover. He has asked that we abandon this post and join his forces outside of Talanost. There we will link up with the eleventh brigade under Inquisitor Bovis.'

There are murmurs of approval amongst the soldiers. It appears that the man is a well-liked and respected warrior.

'We leave now. Saddle up and gather outside the south wall. Full armour and weapons ready, we don't know what we may encounter on our way there. Dismissed.'

As the soldiers break off, you follow Nyms and Caeleb towards the stable building. 'How big is our force to the south?' you ask.

'About four hundred apparently,' replies Caeleb grimly. 'Guardsmen from Talanost, and a few mercenaries and refugees. Rest are mages, but most of them are being used to maintain the shield.' He shakes his head. 'We will need luck on our side if Zul's army is as big as we suspect.' Turn to 763.

'Oh yeah, still got a few of those beauties left. Just over there, take a look.' The merman gestures towards a large wooden crate, which has the words – WARNING: HANDLE WITH CARE stamped over every inch of space. Having noted the 'subtle' message, you very carefully lift off the lid. Inside, resting on a bed of straw, are two disc-shaped metal cases, attached to long rolls of fuse wire.

'I'll sell you one for 30 gold crowns,' he says, scratching his beard. 'Fair price considering it'll blow a hole in just about anything. Might be useful to you.'

If you wish you may purchase the following for 30 gold crowns:

Borehole explosive
(backpack)
Warning: handle with care

When you have made your decision, turn to **626** to ask the merman another question.

649

All around you, the shades shriek and holler as Nyms expertly slays them one by one. Meanwhile, your attacks have forced the necromancer back against the wall of the tomb. The mage makes a last desperate stab with his dagger, but you are ready for it, dodging aside and delivering the killing blow. As the necromancer's lifeless body slides down the wall, the last of the shades vanishes into thin air.

Searching the mage's remains, you find 50 gold crowns and one of the following rewards:

Spite	Hood of night	Ebon boots
(left hand: dagger)	(head)	(feet)
+2 speed +3 brawn	+2 speed +3 magic	+2 speed +1 brawn
Ability: venom	Ability: deceive	Ability: fearless
(requirement: rogue)		

If you are a mage, turn to **692**. Otherwise, turn to **710**.

650

The giant creature emerges from the east passage. (Remember which rod you placed here, as it will help you with this battle.) Moving on four bowed legs, the giant barrels its way past the last of the stones, its elongated tail whipping back and forth across its broad shoulders. The beast's body is fashioned from spiny bones, knitted together by a grotesque assortment of bulging muscles. As it opens its mouth, the creature vomits a swarm of black skittering beetles, which rush toward you like a black tide, their mandibles clicking together hungrily:

	Speed	Brawn	Armour	Health
Rottaghast	14	14	15	100
Carrion beetles	-	-	10	40

Special abilities

🛡 Carrion beetles: At the end of every combat round, you automatically take 2 damage, ignoring *armour*, from the swarm of biting beetles.

🛡 Body of bone: Rottaghast is immune to *bleed* and *venom*.

If you win a round of combat against Rottaghast, you can choose to strike against Rottaghast or the beetles. Once Rottaghast is dead, the beetles will scatter and no longer attack you.

If you manage to defeat your monstrous adversary, turn to 770. If you are defeated, turn to 723.

651

When you regain consciousness, you find yourself propped up against a stone wall, your hands tied behind your back. The three strangers are huddled close, clearly discussing what to do with you. You take your time to study each in turn, trying to discern their loyalties.

'I say hand them over to the inquisitor,' snaps the swordsman. He is tall and lean, with a long angular face and hooked nose. His black hair has been spiked and a pony tail hangs down his back, braided with gold bands. The two swords now rest in their scabbards, but his hands impatiently tap their hilts, as if he is eager to draw them once again.

'Shadow spawn or not, they tried to help me,' implores the woman. 'The least we could do is give them a fair chance to explain themselves.' From her age you assume the robed woman might be their leader – both men are looking to her for guidance, although seem reluctant to believe her story.

'They could be a spy,' says the shorter warrior, scowling. He is dressed in heavy plate armour, his shield now strapped to his back. The sack that he was carrying lies at his feet. You see that it contains a number of odd-looking metal rods and a collection of books. The plated warrior glances in your direction and gives a start when he sees you watching them. 'Nyms, they're awake.'

The swordsman immediately walks over, his face blank and unreadable. 'You have some explaining to do,' he says. 'I've killed your kind before and one more wouldn't make a difference.' He draws one of his swords and holds it to your throat, its runed steel glimmering with magic. Turn to 767.

652

You cover your head as the deafening explosion rocks the chamber. Fragments of stone and dust rain down about you, as the ground gives another thunderous shake. Looking up, you see that you have blasted a sizeable hole in the side of the giant. It staggers slightly, but continues to advance. At least you have seriously weakened your foe before the titanic battle begins:

	Speed	Brawn	Armour	Health
Stone giant	10	10	12	40
Stone golem	-	-	6	15
Stone golem	-	-	6	15
Stone golem	-	-	6	15
Stone golem	-	-	6	15

Special abilities

🝰 Knockdown: If your hero takes health damage from the giant, you must lower your *speed* by 1 for the next combat round.

🝰 Body of rock: Your opponents are immune to *piercing, impale, bleed, venom, thorns, barbs* and *lightning*.

🝰 Stone golems: At the end of every combat round, you automatically take 1 point of damage, ignoring *armour*, from each golem that is still alive.

If you win a combat round against the stone giant, you can choose to direct your damage towards the giant or one of the stone golems. If you defeat the giant, all remaining stone golems immediately crumble into dust.

If you manage to defeat this colossal foe, turn to 443.

653

The ground trembles and shakes beneath your feet. Turning, you see a monstrous hulk of a creature advancing on Lansbury, who stands defenceless in her magical trance. With effort, you throw yourself into the path of the beast, struggling to maintain your balance as it stomps closer, sending tremors rippling out across the hilltop.

The hulk stands seven metres tall, its thick body covered in knotted muscle. In each of its four arms is a cruel weapon of some description, from a serrated blade to a wide-headed axe. As your eyes are drawn upwards, you give a gasp of horror – the giant has two enormous heads, each one displaying an ugly mishmash of teeth and eyeballs. You raise your weapons and prepare to take on this unnatural abomination, buying Lansbury the time she needs to finish her ritual:

	Speed	Brawn	Armour	Health
Brothers Grimm	13	13	10	120

Special abilities

🝰 'Got ma eyes on yer': You cannot use *sidestep, evade* or *vanish* in this combat.

Helping hand: For each remaining hero that is still alive (Janna, Gull, Laine and/or Klaret) you can add an extra point of damage to your damage score.

If you defeat the Brothers Grimm, turn to **645**. If you are defeated, turn to **661**.

654

There is a rumbling crack as the lid of the tomb shatters. From the broken shards, an armoured knight rises to its feet, a tower shield grasped in one hand and a rune-etched sword in the other. From the narrow slit in the knight's visor, you see two red-glowing eyes.

'Ugh, why does everything want to kill us?' groans Nyms.

'Up there, look!' Caeleb points to the hole in the ceiling of the chamber. Crouched at its edge is a black-cloaked man, his face partially concealed by a hood. Both his hands are pointed towards the knight, their tips crackling with black magic.

'A necromancer!' gasps Janna.

Before you can act, the hooded stranger drops down from the shattered ceiling. He lands in a crouch, his tattered cloak rippling from his thin shoulders. 'Fools,' he hisses. 'You cannot stand against the might of the bone army!'

The mage reaches for his belt, his black cloak shifting to reveal the hilt of a jewelled dagger. With a scrape of steel, he draws out the hooked blade. As he holds it aloft, a murky ochre light spreads from the hilt to its tip. 'Your bones will rise again,' he cackles. 'And you will fight loyally by my side, as my eternal champions!'

Will you:

Attack the undead knight?	625
Attack the necromancer?	662

655

With a shriek, Cinders explodes. From the billowing cloud of soot, three sparks of light appear, crackling and hissing angrily. Then they speed back into the floor, leaving thin trails of smoke in their wake.

As the soot above the pit clears, you discover a number of charred items resting on the still-glowing coals. You may now choose one of these as a reward:

Finger of fire	Cinder's gown	Flame-bathed cowl
(ring)	(chest)	(head)
+1 brawn	+1 speed +3 magic	+2 brawn +1 armour
Ability: sear	Ability: sear	Ability: sear
	(requirement: mage)	

With the room's guardian defeated, you are now able to pass around the pit and take the stairs to the exit. Turn to 423.

656

You find Lansbury waiting for you at the edge of the camp. Together, you head out into the grey expanse of the bone fields. You glance her way, waiting for her to explain the reason for this impromptu expedition – but the woman has her eyes fixed on the horizon, the sack trailing in the dust behind her.

'Do you want me to take that?' you offer, indicating the sack.

Lansbury looks at you confused, her thoughts clearly on something else. 'Oh ... this? Yes.'

As you take it from her, you can't help but take a peek inside. 'What are these?' you ask, inspecting the three metallic-looking rods. 'You found them in ruins, didn't you?'

Lansbury nods. 'They're for protection – in case we run into anything ... hostile.'

You hoist the sack over your shoulder, then hurry to catch up. 'So, you going to fill me in on what this is all about?'

Lansbury gives you a sidelong stare. 'I think those angels, those statues, are weapons.'

'Weapons?' you ask incredulously.

She nods quickly. 'Reading between the lines, it's what the records seem to be suggesting. They were weapons built by the mages, to help them win the shadow war.'

You blow out your cheeks in wonderment. 'I would never have thought ... so, what do we do? Press a switch or something?'

Lansbury shakes her head. 'I think I will need to repair the magic weaves.' Noticing your look of confusion, she attempts to explain. 'Magic is like a tapestry – the threads and cords all interweave to make a whole. Sometimes the magic gets broken or frayed, and needs to be repaired so that it works again. Do you understand?'

You shrug your shoulders, not entirely convinced. 'So, you repair the angel and I watch?' You grin. 'Sounds good enough to me.'

'You may need to do more than that,' replies Lansbury, coming to a halt. She points to several specks, hovering in the grey sky. You squint, trying to discern what type of creature they are. Then you hear a devilish shriek carrying on the air.

'Bone wyverns,' you declare with a grimace.

'Lucky for us, they aren't attacking,' she says. 'They're heading north.'

As the flying creatures speed away, you pick up the pace again, hurrying through the silent wasteland. Turn to 673.

657

The defeated creature explodes into a whirling maelstrom of shadow magic. As it does so, the spell that held the legion in thrall breaks – and the inhuman monsters screech and holler as they rush forward. You quickly turn to Avian, who is struggling back to his feet. 'Shield us! Shield us now!' you order.

The mage throws up his hands, uttering the words of a spell. Suddenly a green dome of magic settles over you. Outside of it, the legion's howling, angry screams can be heard as their claws and weapons pummel harmlessly against the shield.

Lifting up your arm, you turn your glowing shadow mark towards the magic.

'No!' gasps Avian. 'You cannot do this!'

'It's our only chance.' You step forward, towards the whirling tornado of black magic. Your shadow mark suddenly blazes into life, writhing and twisting around your arm. There is an answering flash from the cloud of shadow magic, before it starts to spiral towards your outstretched arm. As it touches your skin, the mark greedily sucks in the energy, filling you with its power.

'It will kill you!' shouts Avian. 'You cannot hold that amount of magic.'

A mad peel of laughter escapes your lips as the magic continues to flow into your body. You can feel the air around you sizzling with magic ... When you look down you see that your whole body is glowing with purple light. You can't help but revel in the ecstasy of the power which is now yours, making you stronger, faster ... godlike.

'I can't hold the shield,' wheezes Avian. 'Too weak ...' The mage drops his arms. As he does so, the shield flickers and then is gone. With frenzied howls of bloodlust, the shadow spawn surge forward to attack.

But you are ready for them. Raising the palms of your hands you send a wave of shadow energy sweeping outwards from your position. It slams into the army, sending them flying backwards as if hit by the force of a tornado. As they try and charge once again, you send another wave of magic out, throwing them back through the air like they were nothing but straw dolls.

'I never saw power like that,' whispers Avian, looking at you in awe.

'The gate.' Your voice booms like thunder. 'Run!'

Together you sprint towards the glowing portal, aware that the recovered shadow spawn are rushing forward once again, weapons and claws glinting in the half-light.

You push Avian through the portal and then follow, your body still pulsing with Sharroth's absorbed magic. Turn to 688.

658

The charge is now attached to one of the lumbering golems. As the wire burns down, the golem stops, looking dumbly at the glowing thing stuck to its side. 'Uh-oh.' Suddenly, there is a deafening explosion. The golem and one of its nearby companions are blasted to smithereens, sending fragments of stone and dust in all directions. The remaining two golems and the giant continue to advance towards you:

	Speed	Brawn	Armour	Health
Stone giant	10	10	12	50
Stone golem	-	-	6	15
Stone golem	-	-	6	15

Special abilities

🌑 Knockdown: If your hero takes health damage from the giant, you must lower your speed by 1 for the next combat round.

🌑 Body of rock: Your opponents are immune to *piercing, impale, bleed, venom, thorns, barbs* and *lightning*.

🌑 Stone golems: At the end of every combat round, you automatically take 1 point of damage, ignoring *armour*, from each golem that is still alive.

If you win a combat round against the stone giant, you can choose to direct your damage towards the giant or one of the stone golems. If you defeat the giant, all remaining stone golems immediately crumble into dust.

If you manage to defeat this colossal foe, turn to **443**.

659

'Oh this?' Lansbury lifts up the book, turning it over in her hands. 'This is just one of the books I found in those ruins, when we met you. They're from the shadow war – yes, this is a thousand years old.' She opens the book again, smoothing down one of the yellowed pages.

'The parchment is enchanted so it will never age. This one in particular is an account of the war from a mage's apprentice. Fascinating reading.'

She looks down at the other books resting next to her chair. 'Finding these was a perilous business. But it was worth it. Some of what they contain may even help us in our upcoming struggles.'

Turn to 597 to ask another question, or 553 to leave the tent.

660

'Let me give you a gift,' hisses Sharroth. 'A taste of what is to come.'

You give a choking gasp, as something – a fierce, burning cold – races up the base of your spine and into your skull. There is a momentary flash of pain, like knives stabbing deep into your very being, then you open your eyes.

And you remember.

Memories come flooding back. You see yourself as a general – a mighty warrior and mage, leading regiments of shadow spawn across countless battlefields. Everything that lies before you is laid to waste by your power. You had respect ... you were feared.

'Yes, Nevarin,' rasps Sharroth. 'Remember who you were. Who you are.'

'No!' you grit your teeth as rage and anger build inside you. The images have shifted to ones of pain and misery. The gate has been closed and you have been cut off from your world. You see yourself running – always running – a fugitive, a monster that nobody trusts. Fists and weapons have all been turned against you ... angry faces, accusations. 'Shadow spawn!'

Power crackles from the mark along your arm, fuelled by your anger and resentment. 'A thousand years, I have been hunted,' you spit, advancing on Avian in cold fury. 'I have been judged.'

The mage backs away, shaking his head. 'Do not do this, Nevarin! Don't let the anger overtake you. I trusted you. I still trust you. You can change!'

For a moment your steps falter. Avian's look of sincerity, of honesty, has disarmed you. Then an image of Mathis flashes before your eyes. The inquisitor is staring at you with loathing and scorn. The inquisitor who would see you burnt at a stake for the mark that you carry.

Rage courses through your veins once more, pumping crackling energy into your shadow mark. It spits and hisses as it begins to change ... distending outwards to form a set of curved spectral claws.

You have gained a new special ability:

Dark claw (pa): For every double that you roll (before or after a re-roll), your hero automatically inflicts 4 damage to their opponent. This ability ignores *armour*.

When you have updated your hero sheet, turn to 682.

661

You awake to find yourself partially buried beneath the rotting carcasses of the undead. Grimacing with disgust, you push the corpses aside and get to your feet. Your head is still buzzing with pain, although a quick examination of your body finds no sign of a wound. You suspect that your shadow mark has healed you once again.

Everywhere you look, there are undead corpses – most of which are blackened and charred. Lansbury is propped up against the side of the statue, holding a hand to her bloody shoulder.

She looks up as you approach, smiling through her obvious discomfort. 'I really must examine you closer, shadow born,' she says, arching an eyebrow. 'Not a blemish on your skin. They say, when your kind dies you turn to shadow energy for a short time. That energy then remakes your body.' She gives a bemused snort. 'Immortality ... what I wouldn't give for that.'

You glance around at the remains of the battle. With regret, you note that none of the others survived the conflict. Laine's warhorse is the only mount remaining, standing loyal guard at his fallen master's side.

'The statue activated just in time,' explains Lansbury, as you help her to stand. 'Although, if I had just been a little quicker ...' She sighs, shaking her head. 'No use regretting what might have been. The living need us now – we should return to the camp.' The hand pressed to her shoulder glows brightly for a second. When she removes it, you see that the wound has healed.

'A shame I can't use my powers to bring back the dead,' she grumbles, as you pass the fallen bodies of your comrades. 'We will return and give them a hero's burial.'

You help Lansbury onto the warhorse, then slip into the saddle behind her. With a flick of the reins, the healer guides the horse down from the hill, now under the watchful protection of the stone angel. Turn to 731.

662

The necromancer throws out his left hand, his fingers grasping at the air. From the darkest corners of the room, tendrils of shadow began to move – swirling and twisting as they are drawn along the ground.

You jump aside as a black shadow brushes past your legs, to join the others that are swirling around the mage, forming a dense circle of darkness. Then, from out of this shifting gloom, shapes began to form ... like devilish silhouettes.

'Shades!' growls Nyms. 'He is summoning shades.'

The dark phantoms grow long, thin arms – each one ending in a frightening array of black-curved claws. Between their broadening shoulders, tentacles of fog ooze into ghostly faces with hollow eye sockets and toothless mouths.

In a heartbeat, there are six of the creatures surrounding the necromancer.

Suddenly, one gives a horrible banshee-like wail. It springs forward, its sharp talons raking through the air. Nyms reacts instantly by ducking beneath its blow and thrusting his twin blades through its middle. With a howl of agony, the shade is blown apart – sending whirling ribbons of shadow flying in all directions.

'Take the mage,' orders Nyms. 'I'll handle the shades.'

As the swordsman spins his blades into the mass of dark bodies, you charge the necromancer:

	Speed	Magic	Armour	Health
Necromancer	13	10	10	70

Special abilities

♥ Heightened magic: You cannot use *sidestep, evade* or *vanish* in this combat.

♥ Venom: Once you have taken health damage from the mage, at the end of every combat round you must automatically lose 2 *health*.

If you manage to defeat this powerful mage, turn to **649**.

663

You open the jar and stick your hand inside, pulling out a handful of the slimy, squirming maggots. 'I know medicine is never tasty, but this …' You bring the maggots closer to your mouth, trying not to choke from the wretched smell.

Will you:

Swallow the maggots?	679
Head into Raolin's camp instead?	696

664

You search the body of the two-headed giant. In a pouch around its waist is a bag containing 100 gold crowns. You may also help yourself to one of the following rewards:

Grasping grimm	Devourer's grips	Diadem of mastery
(left hand: wand)	(gloves)	(head)
+3 speed +3 magic	+1 speed +4 magic	+2 speed +3 magic
Ability: rake	Ability: rust	Ability: dominate

Special achievement: If all four heroes – Gull, Laine, Janna and Klaret – are still alive, you may receive an extra reward. Turn to **735**. Otherwise, turn to **731**.

665

There are cheers from the surviving fighters as the orb smashes into the ground, spraying gooey black slime in a wide radius.

'Nice work,' grins the mage, lowering his carpet to the ground. 'We'll make an airborne regular out of you yet.'

You hop off the carpet, thanking the mage for his help. Surveying the gooey wreckage, you notice a few salvageable rewards. You may now help yourself to one of the following items:

Cerebral helm	Lens of blasting	Orb stinger
(head)	(left hand: shield)	(main hand: dagger)
+2 speed +3 magic	+2 speed +3 armour	+3 speed +4 brawn
Ability: overload	Ability: lightning	Ability: shock!
(requirement: mage)	(requirement: warrior)	(requirement: rogue)

Elsewhere on the battlefield, Ravenwing and his soldiers have brought down the other monstrous creation. The remaining ranks of shadow spawn collapse into a full-scale rout, outnumbered and out-fought by the defenders. The pursuing soldiers make short work of the fleeing remnants and soon cries of victory are echoing around the camp. Turn to 757.

666

Nyms and Caeleb have made short work of the bone constructs, while Janna has dispatched the wyverns using her magical arrows. However, there is little time for celebration. Echoing from the valley walls comes a gibbering, chattering crescendo. As you regroup, you turn to see a horde of ghouls scampering around the corner, scattering ash and dust as they race towards you. Behind them, almost matching their pace, is a man dressed in fur and leather. In one hand he holds a whip, which he cracks constantly, driving the bestial ghouls to greater feats of speed.

'Ghouls and a packmaster,' grins Nyms. 'You must have really made 'em angry, Janna.'

'We can't fight them here,' snaps Caeleb. 'They'll overrun us.'

'In here!' Janna starts sprinting towards a nearby doorway, cut into the side of the cliff wall. Raising her right hand, she calls up a golden flame, to light the way as she rushes into the darkness.

You follow her into the earthen passageway. Once you are all inside, Janna turns and begins chanting a spell. The light in her hands turns to green fire, which she hurls at the tunnel entrance. The moment the magic hits the ground, a wall of black thorns bursts up out of the soil.

'That should hold them for a while,' she says. Turn to 608.

667

Sahna escorts you to the edge of the camp. 'I fear Raolin will not give up his search. He will send more good people down there to find that rotten treasure. I can only pray that fortune favours us – or else I fear the worst.

'Good luck with your adventures,' she says. 'I have a feeling we will meet again, one day.' The warrior salutes you, before turning and heading back into camp. Return to the quest map to continue your journey.

668

'The inquisition is a sacred order,' explains Laine. 'We are the king's finest – carrying the sacred flame of truth and honour in our hearts. It is our mission to root out evil in all its forms and to uphold the laws of the land. Our methods can be seen, by some, as,' he licks his lips, choosing his words carefully, 'direct. But we are dedicated to the cause, as are our faithful spies and agents, the witchfinders.'

The inquisitor has the following abilities:

Cleansing light (pa): Automatically heals the hero for 2 *health* at the end of each combat round.

Avenging spirit (co): When you take health damage from your opponent's damage score, you can inflict damage back to them equal to your *armour*. This ability ignores your opponent's *armour*. (Note: you cannot use modifier abilities to increase this damage.) You can only perform *Avenging spirit* once per combat.

Once you have updated your hero sheet, return to the quest map to continue your adventures.

669

With your hands still tied, you follow your captors out of the ruins. The land beyond is an endless plain of grey ash, littered with bones. The sky above is almost the same shade of grey – heavy and ominous. It is almost impossible to tell where one meets the other.

'What is this place?' you ask, as you trudge across the silent wasteland. To your left, there is the enormous skull of some ancient creature, grinning at you as if in mockery.

'The bone fields,' explains the plated warrior, who is carrying the sack of items from the ruins. 'I guess you don't remember anything, do you?' When he looks back, you see pity in his eyes. 'Perhaps you better explain, Lansbury.'

The woman nods, dropping back to walk beside you. 'This is where the last battle took place,' she says. 'When the shadow gate was closed, a thousand years ago, the last of the legion faced the mages of Talanost here. There was an epic battle. The accounts say it lasted forty days and forty nights.' She waves her staff across the grey expanse before you. 'This is what was left. The wreckage of a terrible war.

'The legion was defeated,' she continues. 'Many heroes were made in that war. Most of them mages. They were the ones who proved instrumental in ending the legion's reign of terror. That is why the gate was dug up and moved to Talanost – where it could be kept safe beneath the university, under the watchful eyes of the Arcane Circle.'

Nyms gives a dismissive snort. 'Yeah and that worked out just great, didn't it.' He gives you a sideways glance, scowling.

'Ah, here we are,' says Lansbury, breaking the tense silence. 'Home, sweet home.'

You crane your neck over the next rise to see the grey ash turn to red, scorched sand. It drifts in lazy swirling clouds around a series of rocks, arranged to form a wall or barricade. Behind it is a tall crumbling tower. Several parts of it have already broken loose – but instead of having toppled to the ground, the fragments hang suspended in mid-air, as if trapped in time and space.

'What is *that*?' you ask in wonderment.

'A relic left over from the war,' explains Nyms. 'Caeleb, you're the engineering expert – tell him.' You look to the plated warrior, who you assume he is referring to. The older warrior nods.

'The mages built a number of towers like this. They used their magics to pull the stone up out of the earth.' He motions with a finger, tracing the line of a deep rift, cutting across the ground. 'Took a day to build, if the records are true. Fine craftsmanship too … for mages.' He arches an eyebrow in Lansbury's direction. The woman smiles at the comment.

'Come on,' she says. 'Let's see what Redguard makes of our new visitor.' Turn to **683**.

670

You bring up the small matter of the lamprey worm, which you can still feel wriggling around inside your stomach. The mage frowns impatiently, as if such matters are now beneath him. 'Oh, Sahna, take this vagabond from my tent now. I will not have my valuable time wasted.'

You start forward angrily, your fists clenched. After all that you have gone through, the least you expected was to be treated with some respect. Sahna intercepts you, grabbing your arm and gripping it tightly. She leans in close to you, speaking between clenched teeth.

'Don't do it,' she says. 'Just come with me.'

You relax your muscles, glowering at the mage who has already turned his attention back to the crown. Sahna leads you out of the tent and across the camp. 'It's best you don't cross him,' she explains quickly. 'Raolin is a powerful mage with powerful friends. Trust me, you can't afford to get on the wrong side of that one. Come on, in here.' Turn to **646**.

You meet up with the riders at the edge of the rubble-strewn gardens.

'You're alive!' laughs Nyms, jumping down from his saddle. 'Which life is it this time? I'm losing count now.'

You stop and take a deep breath of fresh, morning air. 'I feel alive for the very first time, my friend.'

'Your mark,' he leans back in surprise. 'What happened?'

You glance down, to see that the purple mark has grown bigger – stretching from the tips of the fingers to your chest and neck. Its purplish light seems to glow brighter than before, thumping with newfound power. 'I guess there's no hiding what I am now,' you smirk dryly.

'What you are is what saved us,' he grins. 'Come, you're to be the guest of honour at the king's feast.'

'We won then?' you ask, arching an eyebrow.

'All thanks to you,' nods the swordsman, patting you on the back. 'All thanks to you. Look.'

Above the jewelled spires of Talanost, a squadron of mages soar through the skies, their magic carpets trailing rainbow hues that sparkle in the sunlight. As they pass overhead, bright fireworks burst from their raised staffs. The dazzling shards rain down across the liberated city, while in the distance the blare of horns sing of a triumphant victory.

Congratulations, hero! You have overcome the challenges set before you and have earned yourself the title *The Betrayer*. Thanks to your efforts and decisions, you have helped save the kingdom of Valeron from the sinister Legion of Shadow! (Bonus: A special quest has now been unlocked! Turn to **798** to join the resistance and help rid Talanost of the last remaining shadow spawn.)

672

'I've been stationed here for twenty years now,' says Lansbury, with a hint of pride in her voice. 'Yes, a long time – some would say too long. Oh, I know this is a dead-end garrison, but for me this is a once in a lifetime opportunity. The bone fields have barely been explored or studied in any great detail. Those plains are filled with relics from that great war, not to mention magics that are now long forgotten.'

She glances down at her tabard, displaying the golden dragon on a field of green. 'I have always been proud to serve the king at this outpost. Little did I know that another war is looming here. If what you say is true,' she looks up, her bright eyes catching the candlelight. 'Then it was fate I came here. I will serve the king in whatever manner I am able.'

If you are a mage and wish to learn the medic career, turn to 680. Otherwise, turn to 597 to ask another question or 553 to leave the tent.

673

The air grows colder as you travel eastwards, until you find yourself huddling into your cloak, your breath steaming in front of you.

'Why is it so cold?' you ask, shivering.

'A magic anomaly,' explains Lansbury, seemingly unaffected by the freezing conditions. 'In the war, a lot of magic was discharged over the bone fields. Some of it remains ... sort of like a magical echo. Winter's Hill is just one such place.'

'Winter's Hill?' you ask – then you see it for yourself as you pass over the next rise. The hill is a peaked mound of grey earth, surrounded by a winding maze of jagged stones, similar in size and shape to those that surround Redguard's camp. Thick snow coats most of the hilltop, including the statue of the angel. She towers high into the sky, her head crowned with ice and her giant wings glistening with rime frost.

'That's ... impossible,' you gasp, rubbing your eyes as if to clear them of some illusion.

'Magic makes all things possible,' grins Lansbury.

Suddenly, you can hear a baying horn in the distance. Lansbury stiffens, her eyes scanning the northern horizon. 'I think those wyverns were scouts. We've been found. Come on!' She starts sprinting towards the hill. You follow, drawing your weapons. Turn to 621.

As you approach the camp, you see Sahna standing at its edge, looking out over the waters of the lake. Sensing you, she turns quickly, drawing her sword. Then her eyes widen when she recognises you.

'You're back! You made it back.'

She sheaths her blade and hurries over to you. 'What happened? Did you find it?' she asks hopefully.

You shake your head sadly, explaining what happened in the Dour king's chamber. 'Finding the crown will now be impossible,' she says bitterly. 'I dread how Raolin will react to the news.' The warrior glances down at your stomach. 'I suppose we still have your little problem to sort out, don't we? Come, let's do this quick – I think it best Raolin doesn't know you made it back. You'll just be another "deader" as far as he is concerned.'

You quietly follow Sahna into the camp, receiving some lingering stares from her men. But none dare to challenge you, moving aside quickly to let you pass. Turn to 646.

675

Ravenwing secures two horses from the camp and soon you are both riding around the perimeter of the city walls. Every hundred metres a mage is positioned at the foot of the shield, their arms outstretched, brow furrowed in concentration.

'The majority of the legion are situated to the north,' explains Ravenwing. 'They see us as their only immediate threat.' He reins in his horse next to one of the mages. 'Entering here, they won't see the breach – if they do, they'll think it's a glitch, nothing more. The wall here is ruins – easy for you to slip inside.'

Together you dismount. Ravenwing walks over to the mage and gently places a hand on their arm. The mage jerks as if suddenly coming awake. For a moment, the shield in front of him wavers, flickering like a dying flame. Ravenwing explains something to the mage who nods, glancing at you with interest.

'You will have a second, nothing more,' states the mage in a cold, impassionate voice. 'I suggest you move quickly.' He throws back a hand, gesturing to the shield. You look up, to see a small hairline crack appearing along its length.

Without hesitation, you race forward, stopping inches from the shield as it slowly parts before you.

'Good luck, friend.' You see Ravenwing mirrored in the shield, his hand raised to his forehead in salute. Then the gap widens and you find yourself looking out on a scene of devastation. Smoke hangs heavy over the blackened shells of the city's buildings. The streets that stretch ahead of you are little more than smoking rubble, the once idyllic avenues and promenades torn up and shattered.

'How could they do this?' you gasp, your mouth falling open.

'Move it! Hurry!'

The mage's words bring you back to your senses. Quickly, you step through the narrowing gap, just seconds before the two sides of the shield snap back together again behind you. When you turn, you are faced by a perfect wall of shimmering green magic, arching up to form a dome, high above the city.

You put out your hand and touch its surface. The magic ripples slightly at your touch, but feels as hard and impenetrable as stone. A prison, you realise grimly, and now you have become its latest inmate. Turn to 632

676

You offer to challenge Caeleb, much to the surprise of his companion, Nyms. The tall swordsman moves away, looking disgruntled that this fight will not be his own. Instead, all attention turns to the warrior armed with sword and shield.

'I should warn you,' says Caeleb, as you both circle each other. 'I was once one of the king's cavaliers.'

You shrug, implying that the title means nothing to you. Drawing your weapons, you maintain eye contact with the burly warrior, who is hunkering down behind his shield, his sword arm held back and to his side.

'You haven't heard of the cavaliers!' heckles Nyms from the

sidelines. There are amused sniggers from the crowd. 'Sounds like you better knock some brains into this one, Caeleb.'

You take your attention away from the warrior for a second – and suddenly you feel an almighty blow to the stomach. The crowd cheer as you are brought to the ground in a cloud of dust. Caeleb laughs to himself as he shakes his shield at you.

'They're not only for defence, you know,' he grins. 'Now, get up and concentrate. I want to see what you can do.'

	Speed	Brawn	Armour	Health
Caeleb	13	16	14	65

Special abilities

♥ Shield slam: If you roll a ⊡ when rolling for your attack speed, you are automatically caught by Caeleb's shield. This does 6 damage, ignoring *armour*. You cannot use a re-roll to avoid this.

If you manage to defeat Caeleb, turn to 691. If you lose the combat, then you promise Caeleb you will return when you have had more practice. Turn to 553.

677

For defeating the knight, you may now take one of the following rewards:

Tainted striker	Enchanted coif	Leap of faith
(main hand: sword)	(head)	(necklace)
+3 speed +3 magic	+2 speed +2 armour	+1 speed
Ability: corruption	Ability: charm	Ability: radiance

When you have made your choice, turn to 710.

The first of the slavering ghouls reaches the top of the hill. You charge towards it, knowing full well that this could be your last battle. Then, all of a sudden, there is a blinding white flash. You lose your footing, temporarily dazed by the light. When sight returns, you see white bolts of light streaking through the air above you. As you twist round, to follow their path, you see that they are ripping into the ranks of undead, sending their bodies flying in all directions.

'Now that is more like it!'

You look back to see Lansbury punching the air in triumph. Next to her, the immense statue is pivoting around on its stone pedestal. From its eyes, white bolts of light are arcing out across the wasteland, striking the advancing undead and blasting them to smithereens.

For a moment you are too stunned to react, then you give a whoop of joy. Jumping to your feet, you race to the edge of the hill, watching as the white bolts continue to streak across the bone fields, decimating the giants, tearing the wyverns to shreds and blowing large holes into the ranks of skeletons. Within seconds, the army that had once threatened to overwhelm you, is now little more than a smoking ruin.

'How ... what?' You turn back to Lansbury, your mouth making a failed attempt at words.

She pats the side of the statue, which has now ceased its erratic motions. 'I told you it was a weapon,' she says, beaming with joy. 'Any undead that comes near it ... boom!'

As your attention shifts back to the wasteland, you see a few surviving necromancers making a run for cover. 'They will be back,' you sigh, heavily.

Lansbury shakes her head. 'I doubt it. This angel will guard the hill and destroy anything that comes within reach. Even if the necromancers try and deactivate it, they will find a few little surprises of my own.' She gives you a mischievous wink. 'Come on, I expect Redguard and Mathis will want to know what just happened.' Turn to 715.

Holding your breath, you tilt back your head and deposit the squirming maggots into your mouth. Trying to ignore the slimy sea-salt taste, you swallow them as quickly as you can. As the last one slides down your throat, you quickly reach for your canteen of water from your backpack, swilling out your mouth and spitting the foul taste away.

Then you feel a sharp stabbing pain in your stomach. You drop the canteen, falling to your knees as another wave of agony forces you to gag. Suddenly, there is a rush of stinging hot pain as something shoots up through your chest, forcing its way into the back of your throat. Your eyes bulge as you begin to choke, gasping for air. Then, suddenly you feel the pressure in your throat ease as your mouth is filled with something wet and slimy.

Bending over, you watch in horrified revulsion as the lamprey worm drops out of your mouth onto the muddy soil. The creature is writhing from side-to-side, its sides blistered and raw. Then it finally lies still.

You snatch up your canteen and take a long drink of water, your hands shaking from the ordeal. At last, you feel your stomach settling back to normal. You look down at the worm with a smile of triumph. The merman's cure worked – you are now free of Raolin's deadly leech.

If you have the Dour king's crown, turn to **685**. If you lost the crown, then with no reason or desire to return to Raolin's camp, you head back out into the swamp. Return to the quest map to continue your journey.

680

'When you fought those undead, that was an impressive display of magic' says Lansbury, smiling with admiration. 'I could really use an extra pair of hands around here – ones that know the healing arts.'

If you wish, you may now accept the following item:

Lady of the lamp
(talisman)
+1 armour
Ability: medic career

'I can't promise to teach you all that I know,' states Lansbury. 'But you look a quick study, and even the basics will be enough to help make a difference.'

The medic has the following abilities:

Mend (mo): You can cast this spell any time in combat to automatically heal yourself or an ally for 15 *health*. This ability can only be used once per combat.

Tourniquet (mo): This spell can be cast at any time to remove any *bleed, venom* and/or *disease* effects that you or an ally have been inflicted with. This ability can only be used once per combat.

As soon as the *lady of the lamp* talisman is unequipped or you learn a new career, you lose the abilities associated with the medic career.

Once you have updated your hero sheet, turn to 597 to ask Lansbury another question or 553 to leave the tent.

681

You draw your weapons and head off the wyvern, as it dives towards Janna. The ranger thanks you, scurrying away to find a safer vantage point to rain arrows on the remaining wyverns.

Dodging past the creature's clawing talons, you press home your attack:

	Speed	Brawn	Armour	Health
Bone wyvern	13	12	10	70

Special abilities

🌑 Snapping beak: At the end of every combat round, you automatically take 2 damage, ignoring *armour*.

🌑 Body of bone: Your opponent is immune to *bleed* and *venom*.

If you defeat the bone wyvern, turn to **776**.

682

You circle around Avian. The mage is weak; you can sense his magic failing him. He will be an easy fight – the last step on a road that has led you back home to the shadow legion. With that vast army at your side, you can return to Valeron, and then you can take revenge on a world that has branded you a monster.

'Yes! Yes!' hisses Sharroth. 'Use your anger. Destroy Avian. This fool dared to call you his apprentice. Show him who the true master is. Do it now!'

But your weapons remain at your side. Fresh memories, fresh faces are now flashing through your mind. You remember the adventures that you have had, the battles that you have fought, the companions that you have made: Nyms, Caeleb, Lansbury. You see Redguard, standing before you, his firm hand resting on your shoulder.

I will believe that fate has brought you to us . . .

You see Jenlar, gripping onto you with pain and hope in his eyes.

You are the chosen one . . . the one who will betray the legion . . . absorb the magic . . . the shadow magic will make you powerful.

You remember the sacrifice of others; those who fought and gave their lives on the battlefield to fight for what they believed in. Not for power – but for freedom.

'Please,' begs Avian. 'There is goodness in your heart.'

You turn to Sharroth. The vile, grotesque creature is watching you uncertainly, sensing a shift in your thoughts.

'I am not a monster,' you state firmly. 'What future can you offer me? There is no future in pain and destruction.'

'The legion is your future, Nevarin!' spits the creature.

You shake your head. 'I don't think so ...' Turn to 782.

683

Beyond the stone barricade you see a number of guards, armed with swords and shields. Over their vests of chain mail, you notice that each one is wearing a similar tabard to Lansbury – displaying a gold dragon on a field of green. You also observe that they all look young and decidedly nervous, as if this is their first posting.

Inside the tower, you are led through a series of stone chambers, mostly filled with crates and boxes, and up several flights of stairs, before coming to a small office. Seated behind a desk, littered with papers and books, is a pepper-haired man in a green tunic. His broad frame and muscled arms speak of a warrior still in his prime, despite his advancing years.

'Captain Redguard,' says Lansbury, by way of introduction. She takes a knife from her belt and cuts your bonds, releasing your hands. Nyms and Caeleb bow their heads and leave, closing the door behind them.

The captain looks at you with interest, his brow creasing as his eyes come to rest on the shadow mark. 'What is this?' he asks gruffly.

Lansbury explains how you came to meet and your story. You are impressed that she remembers every detail of it. When she has finally finished, you find that you can add very little.

'You have no reason to trust me,' you state nervously. 'But I have seen what the legion can do. I was in Talanost when the city was attacked. I saw monsters ... terrible things that had no remorse, no guilt for the destruction that they were causing.' You raise your arm, openly displaying the branded mark. 'Yes, I have been told that I am one of them – that I come from their world and as such I should glory in such pain and destruction. But ...' You take a deep breath, composing yourself and ordering your thoughts. 'I have no memory of that life. My past has been erased. And because of that, I hope my actions ... my choices now ... are what others will judge me by.'

You bow awkwardly then take a step back, awaiting Redguard's verdict. The captain smiles, his fingers absently tapping the table top. 'I can't say as I like having one of your kind around – but if Lansbury's account is a true testimony to your prowess, we could use you around here.' Turn to 739.

684

Suddenly, the sky is lit up by a bright series of explosions. A small squadron of mages are sweeping across the camp, mounted on flying carpets. They twist and weave around the floating monster, firing off a dazzling array of magic spells. However, the beast's giant tentacles simply bat their efforts away with ease.

As one of the mages hurtles past, you call out – beckoning him over. He veers away from his companions, his carpet spitting a trail of black smoke. 'Think I took a hit,' he shouts, screeching to a halt beside you.

You hop onto the carpet next to him. 'As long as it still flies . . . now, get me in close. We need to get past those tentacles!'

The mage's carpet lurches forward, taking you up into the midst of the aerial dogfight. Several of the mages have already been hit by the orb's deadly ray and are now plummeting to the ground, their carpets spewing flames and smoke.

'Steady, steady!' you order, as the mage guides the carpet closer to the orb, dodging its whirling tentacles. At last you find yourself whizzing past the beast's exposed back. 'That's it! Here goes!' Balancing on the edge of the carpet, you skilfully launch your own flurry of attacks against the giant orb:

	Speed	Magic	Armour	Health
Death orb	15	12	11	100

Special abilities
♥ Eye beam: At the end of every combat round, the death orb rakes the sky with a beam of scorching magical energy. To avoid being hit, roll 3 dice. If the result is equal to or less than 10, then you have avoided it. If the result is higher, you have been hit and must take 2 damage, ignoring *armour*.

If you win the combat you may restore your *health* and then turn to 665. If you are defeated, then you must begin this boss encounter from an earlier point (although you cannot choose rewards from enemies that you have already defeated). Restore your *health* and then turn to 748.

685

You lift the crown from out of your backpack and look upon its intricately carved stone work. With the lamprey worm defeated, you could keep this remarkable treasure for yourself. Alternatively, you could hand over the crown to Raolin. After all, Sahna was depending on you.

Will you:

Take the crown for yourself?	**689**
Give the crown to Raolin?	**696**

686

Lansbury looks over at the men under her charge. 'Yes, the bone fields are a dangerous place, particularly for those who are inexperienced. You see, the undead aren't the only problem. We still have the anomalies – areas of magic that are volatile and dangerous to the unwary. Most just cause a bout of sickness or fever, others can do worse things ... freeze you like ice, burn you like fire ... even turn you inside out.' She shudders. 'Don't worry, my healing arts are sufficient for most, but I do prefer more traditional remedies at times: bed and rest.'

Turn to 597 to ask another question, or 553 to leave the tent.

687

The south of the hill is overrun with black, multi-legged insects, their long snaking bodies moving with frightening speed. As several attempt to slip past Janna's guard, the ranger chants words of magic, summoning thorny spikes from the earth to skewer their segmented bodies. The remaining crawlers attempt to surround her, but Janna is a skilled swordswoman, fending off their sharp mandibles with her rune-etched blade.

You must now fight the following battle between Janna and the crawlers:

	Speed	Brawn	Armour	Health
Crawlers	13	14	10	150
Janna	14	14	10	50

Special abilities

- Thorn armour: Janna can cast this spell any time in battle, to raise her *armour* by 5 for one combat round. It also inflicts 1 damage dice, ignoring *armour*, to her opponent. This ability can only be used once.
- Field medic: If you are a medic, you can cast *mend* on Janna once during her combat. You may still use this ability on yourself, if you engage in combat afterwards (see below).

If Janna falls in battle, you must take her place, fighting the crawlers with the *health* they have remaining. If you defeat the crawlers, turn to 721. If you are defeated, turn to 661.

688

Back through the portal, you find yourselves on the bridge spanning the infernal whirring machine. You stagger and fall, the magic that you have absorbed now burning like molten fire beneath your skin. Avian goes to help you, but you push him away.

'I can't ... contain it,' you gasp. 'It's burning ...'

Already tendrils of the magic are seeping from your fingers, whirling through the air and slamming into the machine where they spark and hiss. 'I have to destroy the gate ... I have to stop them getting through.'

Avian shakes his head frantically. 'The machine is indestructible – only the Nexus ...'

You follow his gaze to the stone cog, set amidst the jigsaw of cogwheels. With your magically-heightened senses you can now see the coils of magic that are bound around it – the trap that Jenlar warned you about.

Now you have the power to defeat it.

You struggle to your feet, tears streaming down your face as the magic lances through your body, engulfing you in waves of scorching agony. Raising your hands, you make a series of gestures. There are answering sparks from the weaves of magic around the Nexus as, one by one, they are pulled away. Then, with a grating squeal, you rip the Nexus from the machine, sending it spinning through the air into Avian's hands. All around you the machine steams and grates in protest, its cogs slowly winding down. The lightning rods grow dim and the black portal closes.

'Take it and go,' you gasp, dropping to your knees. The power is too much to contain now, your body is screaming at you to release it. Avian grips the Nexus to his chest.

'I can't leave you here,' he protests.

'GO!' you snap fiercely. 'It will kill us both . . . now RUN!'

Avian looks at you in dismay as you beat your fists against the ground, crying out with pain. Already you can feel the magic burning through your body, blistering every inch of your skin.

'You will not be forgotten, Nevarin.' The mage touches his forehead in salute, before turning and fleeing the chamber.

With Avian gone, you raise your hands and point them to the ceiling. Then, with all the remaining strength left in your broken body, you hurl the magic – every last shred of it – at the ceiling of the chamber. Stone and rock rain down around you, the vast splinters smashing into the machine. As the last of the magic leaves your body, you bow your head to the wave of stone and dust that washes over you, encasing you and the shadow gate in darkness. Turn to 690.

689

You feel it is only fair that you get to keep this rare treasure – after all, you did all the hard work. As you place the crown on your head you feel a cold tingle running throughout your body. If you wish to keep this magical artefact, it bestows the following:

Crown of command
(head)
+1 brawn +1 magic
Ability: command

There are two empty sockets on either side of the crown. If you have a *large ruby* and a *perfect diamond* in your backpack, you discover that these fit inside the sockets. For each jewel that you place in the crown, you can raise the item's *brawn* and *magic* by 2.

You may now return to the quest map to continue your adventure.

690

You open your eyes to daylight. Above you, thin slivers of cloud drift across a bright azure sky. Lifting your head, you see that your body is perfectly healed. There isn't a single scar or blemish on your skin.

You clamber to your feet, feeling loose stones and rock shift under your weight. As you regain your balance, you find yourself standing atop a vast mountain of rubble. Of the university, nothing now remains. A few traces of shadow magic still hover amongst the scorched stone, serving as a grim reminder of the power that finally brought this place to ruin.

'The gate ...' You look down, imagining the vast, ancient machine buried deep beneath the debris. With the gateway closed, the legion will have had no reinforcements to aid them against the king's army. Victory would have been assured.

You shift your attention to the streets of Talanost. Shielding your eyes from the sun, you spot a patrol of knights riding towards you, pennants billowing from their lances. A smile crosses your lips when you see Nyms and Caeleb amongst their ranks. Both are waving and pointing in your direction. You return the gesture then make your way down the slope to meet them.

If you have the *dark claw* ability turn to 671. If you have the *bright shield* ability turn to 780.

691

It is a tiring and frustrating combat. Caeleb appears to have some kind of sixth sense, reading your moves before you have even performed them and deflecting them against his shield. As your attacks become more and more desperate, you start to lose ground to the burly warrior, who is battering you towards the edge of the circle. Moving onto the defensive, you begin to study his moves. Caeleb clearly favours his shield, using it to press his attack more often than his sword. You patiently wait for his next shield slam, this time sidestepping the blow ahead of time and moving inside his guard. From there, it is a simple matter of disarming and then shouldering him to the ground. As the warrior goes to lift up his shield, you bring your foot down, trapping it beneath your heel.

There is a cheer from the crowd as they acknowledge your win. Nyms is the most vocal, whistling and hooting as you help up the defeated warrior. 'He showed you what's for,' the swordsman taunts. 'Back to the academy for you, rookie!'

Caeleb retrieves his sword, breathing heavily. 'That was quite a work out you gave me there,' he smiles. 'I'll keep to my promise, though – if you want to learn to use this,' he shakes his shield, 'then I can show you a few special moves.'

If you are a warrior, you may now learn the cavalier career (turn to 634). Otherwise, you politely decline, deciding that you both deserve some well-earned rest. To the cheers and applause of the guardsmen, you leave the training yard. Turn to 553.

692

As a mage you may also take the following item:

Bone fetish
(talisman)
+1 armour
Ability: necromancer career (see below)

You must have the *bone fetish* talisman equipped if you wish to learn the necromancer career. As soon as this item is unequipped or you learn a new career, you lose the abilities associated with this career.

The necromancer has the following abilities:

Shades (pa): At the start of combat, you automatically summon a group of shades to aid you. The shades add 2 to each dice of damage you roll, for the duration of the combat. Once the shades have been summoned, they remain in play until you *sacrifice* them (see below).

Sacrifice (co): You may use this ability after an opponent has rolled their damage dice/damage score, to instantly *sacrifice* your shades. The shades absorb all the damage instead and you are unharmed. This destroys your shades instantly.

Once you have made your decision, turn to 710.

693

Redguard turns to face you, placing a firm hand on your shoulder. 'I will believe that fate has brought you to us and in these dark times we need whatever aid we can muster.' He glances over at Lansbury, sharing something unspoken as their eyes meet. 'I should warn you, however, we have an inquisitor in our midst and he may be less … forgiving of your past than I.'

Lansbury winces, her expression displaying her obvious distaste for the inquisitor. 'We asked for reinforcements,' she adds tersely. 'And they sent us an inquisitor. I suspect he is here to assess if there is any need for this garrison at all. If he pulls us to the front then the bone fields will be undefended.'

Redguard nods grimly. 'Make this place your home. I may have need of your skills sooner than you think.' Turn to the Act 3 quest map to continue your adventure.

694

As soon as the winged mounts touch down on the hill's summit, Laine is out of the saddle and barking orders. 'Lansbury – the statue. Do whatever you need to do.' The woman nods and hurries over to the grey-stone angel, which is identical to the one on Winter's Hill. You also notice that the rocks serve a similar function, forming a maze of pathways, that lead up to the top of the mound.

'Gull, Klaret, Janna – take those.' Laine points to where the north, south and east pathways open out. 'Kill anything that tries to get through. I'll take the west passage.' He grabs your shoulder as he moves past you. 'And you! Defend Lansbury – anything that gets past us, kill it. We're the expendable ones – Lansbury has to survive and get that statue …' His words catch in his throat as he scans the surrounding wasteland. 'Hell, would you look at that.'

There are hundreds of undead now swarming towards the hill and in the hazy distance, you see even more hastening to bring up the rear. If this is only one small part of Zul's army …

'Do what you can,' sighs Laine, drawing his sword from its scabbard. 'Do not give up hope.' With that, he moves to take up position on the western side of the hill. Turn to 703.

695

The construct breaks apart, its separate pieces falling to the ground in a pile of bones and dust. You quickly pivot around, to concentrate your attacks on the wyvern, but it has already wheeled away, heading back towards Janna.

From the remains of the bone construct, you may now help yourself to one of the following rewards:

Bone claw	**Knuckle head**
(main hand: fist weapon)	(head)
+2 speed +3 brawn	+1 speed +2 brawn
Ability: rake	Ability: slam
	(requirement: warrior)

As the dust settles, you quickly scan your surroundings, taking in the current state of the battle. Turn to 666.

696

As you approach the camp, two guards hurry over with the intention of stopping and questioning you. However, they swallow their swift retorts when recognition dawns on them.

'It can't be,' gawps one, his eyes bulging like boiled eggs.

You continue past them into the camp, where more guards catch sight of you and drop what they are doing. Within moments there is an excited crowd following you through the camp, towards Raolin's tent. Inside, the burly mage is slouched on a gaudy throne of gold, sipping greedily from a goblet of wine. As you enter, he coughs and splutters, wiping his mouth with the back of his sleeve.

'I don't believe it.'

The voice is Sahna's. The warrior is leaning against a table, covered in tattered scrolls and charts. She stands abruptly and moves closer, her eyes gleaming as she looks upon the crown. 'You found it.'

You walk up to the throne and hold out the precious treasure with a self-assured smile. 'I believe you wanted this?'

'Give it to me!' Raolin snatches the crown from out of your hands, inspecting it closely. After several minutes he appears satisfied that you have presented him with the real thing. 'Well, well. You really did find the Dour king's crown. You have succeeded where so many other fools have failed.'

He makes a quick, flicking motion with his wrist. Sahna responds by moving over to a wooden cabinet, where she retrieves a small box. She walks over to you and opens the box, presenting you with three jewelled rings.

'Take one of those and be gone with you,' snaps the mage, not removing his greedy gaze from the crown.

You may now take one of the following items:

Lupine lapis	Cutter's cornelian	Mender's marcasite
(ring)	(ring)	(ring)
+1 brawn	+1 armour	+1 magic
Ability: bleed	Ability: piercing	Ability: regrowth

If you still have the lamprey worm inside you, turn to 670. Otherwise, you leave the tent with Sahna close on your heels. 'How did you ... ?' she begins to ask, then shakes her head grinning. 'There really is something special about you, isn't there?' You stop at the edge of the camp, looking out across the boggy marshland.

'You saved us,' she says, with a relieved sigh. 'At last, we can bid farewell to this forsaken swamp. I owe you, stranger.' She reaches into her pocket and pulls out a purse of gold. 'Here, take this. You deserve it.' Inside the purse is 100 gold crowns. You thank Sahna for her generosity.

'Good luck with your adventures,' she smiles. 'I have a feeling we will meet again, one day.' The warrior salutes you, before turning and heading back into camp. Return to the quest map to continue your journey.

697

Lansbury puts aside her book and gestures to the nearby potions. 'I do have some regulation healing potions. There's also a few swiftness potions there – useful when the old muscles start to flag.'

You run your finger along the row, lifting several from the shelf. Lansbury looks at them and nods. 'Each of those will be 50 gold crowns. Yes, I know – I'm sorry, but you must understand, all that stock is for the army. I have a limited inventory and with that inquisitor sniffing around, I can't afford to be seen giving away vital supplies.'

You may purchase any quantity of the following for 50 gold crowns each:

Flask of healing (1 use)	Elixir of swiftness (1 use)
(backpack)	(backpack)
Use any time in combat to	Increase your *speed* by 4
restore 10 *health*	for one combat round

When you have made your choices, turn to **597** to ask Lansbury another question, or **553** to leave the tent.

698

The swordsman is one of the most skilled opponents that you have ever faced. However, by studying his technique you notice that he often over stretches himself in his eagerness to push his attack. On one such occasion, you manage to sidestep him, bringing your foot behind his and pulling him across your body to throw him to the ground. Nyms hurriedly tries to regain his footing but it is too late

– your main weapon is already held to his throat, your knees pinning down his arms.

'I believe that makes it a win,' you grin triumphantly.

There is a cheer from the crowd. Even Caeleb is joining in, banging his sword against his shield. 'Bravo!' he calls. 'A magnificent win!'

You climb off Nyms, allowing him to get back to his feet. The swordsman brushes himself down with a sour expression. 'Yeah, OK, you got lucky.'

'Come on Nyms,' laughs Caeleb, walking over and slapping his friend on the back. 'It was a good fight – acknowledge that at least.'

Nyms grudgingly offers you a nod of approval. 'Well, I did say I would teach you some new moves,' he glowers, raising his twin swords once again. 'You ready?'

If you are a rogue, you may now learn the swordmaster career (turn to 611). Otherwise, you continue to spar with Nyms until you are both exhausted from the work out. Having gained valuable experience, you thank the warrior, before leaving the training yard. Turn to 553.

699

You ride east at a furious pace, the horses' hooves leaving billowing plumes of dust in your wake. At last, you find yourself reining in at the edge of a bone-littered ridge. The rest of the force are gathered along its length, their faces struck with fear and awe.

Below you, across a grey plain of ash, a mighty battle is raging. To the far south you can make out the banners and standards of Ravenwing's army – a tiny force already outflanked by the undead horde that is spilling out of the valley. There are thousands of skeletons making up its front lines. Amongst their ranks, you can see bone giants and immense abominations of flesh, created by the dark magics of Zul and his mages. Above them, buzzing like flies, are bone wyverns. They shriek and holler as they wheel through the sky, dodging the fireballs and other artillery that are flung their way from the beleaguered defenders.

Redguard raises his sword high into the air. 'Courage and honour. For the king! For Valeron!'

The chant is taken up by his soldiers. You join in, raising your weapons to the sky. There is an answering rumble from the gathering storm clouds, as if the heavens themselves are adding their own voice to your impassioned cry.

Then, you are riding forth, following the others as they gallop towards the nearest flank of the undead army. The odds stacked against you are vast, but you realise what is at stake. If Zul's army destroys the resistance and the shield over Talanost, then nothing will be able to stop the Legion of Shadow from obliterating everything in its path. Turn to 705.

700

Mathis is convinced that you are now his enemy. Unable to control your actions, you trade blows with the mighty inquisitor, the two of you performing an elaborate dance of thrusts, parries and blocks:

	Speed	Brawn	Armour	Health
Mathis	15	14	19	250

Special abilities

♥ Snap out of it!: You cannot possibly hope to defeat this powerful opponent. At the end of every combat round, roll a die. If you roll a ⚁ then make a note of this on your hero sheet. Once you have rolled three ⚁s you have broken control of Zul's spell. (Note: If you are wearing the *crown of command* you only need to roll one ⚁.)

If you break control of Zul's spell, turn to 745. If you are defeated, turn to 732.

701

When you try and grab the crown, you curse angrily as your hand passes straight through the clever illusion. It was a trap – just as you had suspected! You hear a creaking sound and immediately turn, fully expecting the stone statues to have come alive, ready to attack. Instead, the floor gives way beneath you, dropping you ten metres into a murky-smelling pit.

There is a rattling hiss from the darkness. As you quickly clamber to your feet, you notice a large pair of snake-like eyes circling around you. There is another hissing snarl … then a reptilian beast leaps out of the shadows, landing on its bowed legs only inches from you. You reel back, tugging your weapons loose, as the tall lizard makes a number of clicking sounds at the back of its throat. An answering call comes from behind you. Spinning around, you see another of the creatures baring its gleaming fangs. You sprint to the nearest wall, putting your back against it as the two predators stalk towards you, their clawed feet clicking against the stone:

	Speed	Brawn	Armour	Health
Raptors	12	6	8	60

Special abilities
◖ Piercing: The raptors' attacks ignore your *armour*.

If you manage to defeat these deadly predators, turn to 709.

702

The beast rears up onto its hind legs, then topples backwards, crushing scores of skeletons beneath its spiked carapace. You may now help yourself to one of the following rewards:

Ghoul's collar	Bracelet of power	Heart of the beast
(head)	(gloves)	(talisman)
+2 speed +3 armour	+1 speed +3 magic	+1 speed +1 brawn
Ability: piercing	Ability: focus	Ability: savagery
	(requirement: mage)	

You turn your attention back to the battle, which continues to rage around you. Turn to 601.

There are several minutes of tense silence, then you hear the rising din of the approaching undead, their snarls and howls echoing along the stone-lined passages. It gets louder and louder, until it breaks against the hilltop in wave after wave of undead.

To the north, Witchfinder Gull is facing off against a force of sinewy white creatures with haggard, drooping faces and grey spiky hair. With a pistol in one hand and a sword in the other, Gull weaves gracefully between the clawing monsters, driving them back with the fast dance of his sword and the force of his smoking gun.

You must now fight the following battle between Witchfinder Gull and the wights:

	Speed	Brawn	Armour	Health
Wights	13	14	10	120
Gull	13	12	10	60

Special abilities

- Retribution: If Gull rolls a ⚁ when rolling for his damage score, he engulfs the wights in magical fire. This allows Gull to add an extra 10 points of damage to his score.
- Field medic: If you are a medic, you can cast *mend* on Gull once during his combat. You may still use this ability on yourself, if you engage in combat afterwards (see below).

If Witchfinder Gull falls in battle, you must take his place, fighting the wights with the *health* they have remaining. If you defeat the wights, turn to 712. If you are defeated, turn to 661.

704

Lansbury has given you three rods. Each rod has a different magical effect. These are:

Type:	Effect:
Rod of enfeeblement	reduces all opponents' *brawn* and *magic* by 2.
Rod of slowing	reduces all opponents' *speed* by 1.
Rod of rending	reduces all opponents' *armour* by 4.

The army can only reach you by taking one of the three winding pathways up to the top of the hill. There is one to the north, east and west of where you are standing. By placing a rod in front of each of these pathways, you can use them to help defend each one.

Make a note on a piece of paper of which rod you are placing at which pathway exit (north, east or west). You must have one rod positioned at each exit. Also make a reminder note of what each rod does. Once you have made your decisions, you wait tensely for the assault to begin. Turn to 717.

705

You charge into battle, your ears ringing with the thunder of hooves and the roar of the wind. Ahead of you, the undead army surges across the barren plain, unaware of Redguard's force now galloping into their exposed flank. Bones crack and splinter as you spearhead through the ranks of skeletons, your weapons flailing at your sides as you beat back their futile efforts to strike back.

Then the momentum of your charge is halted by the sheer weight of the enemy force, bearing down on you from all sides. For what seems like an eternity, you are battling to remain in the saddle as the skeletal warriors seek to knock or drag you to the ground. You hear the cries of several of your comrades, who have been unhorsed and overwhelmed by the undead masses.

Things are starting to look bleak, when suddenly a loud explosion sends bones and ash showering across the battlefield. A second blast rips into the skeletons ahead of you, throwing their burning bodies up into the air. You glance over your shoulder to see Inquisitor Mathis and Lansbury hurling balls of magical flame into the undead ranks. Already sizeable holes have started to appear where their magic has blown away the skeleton defenders. But there are still more, spilling into the gaps like an endless tide.

'Back! Back!' shouts Redguard, struggling to be heard over the tumultuous din. 'We're being flanked!' He turns his horse and makes for the edge of the battlefield. You follow suit, battering away the wall of skeletons that seek to hamper your retreat. Once free of the tight press of bodies, you see the reason for Redguard's concern. A cloud of smoke is drifting down from the bone fields, thrown up by a regiment of plate-armoured knights astride nightmarish steeds.

Redguard is already charging towards them, to head off their attack. Nyms, Caeleb and most of the other soldiers have followed. Turning in your saddle, you look back to see Lansbury, Tulcas and the remaining guardsmen cut off by a dense mass of skeletons. With their attention focused solely on defending their position, the small force is oblivious to the huge lumbering beast that is fast approaching. It looks like a gigantic ghoul, its rotting flesh hanging off its thick, bony limbs. The creature is trampling across everything in its path to reach Lansbury and the small knot of defenders. Moving to head it off is Inquisitor Mathis. The burly warrior is battling his way through the skeletons, his mighty warhammer crackling with magical energies.

Will you:

Charge the undead knights?	773
Help Mathis to defeat the ghoul?	714

706

Each chest contains a number of items from the king's treasury. If you wish, you may now choose up to two of the following rewards:

Dour claws	Stone coat	Pulveriser
(left hand: fist weapon)	(chest)	(main hand: hammer)
+1 speed +4 brawn	+2 speed +2 armour	+2 speed +4 brawn
Ability: rake	Ability: might of stone	Ability: knockdown

After brushing the stone dust from your clothing, you take the archway through into the next chamber. Turn to 725.

707

It is late evening when you receive the summons to Laine's temporary quarters. You find the grey-haired man seated behind a small desk, wearing a woollen shirt and breeches in place of his armour. He stands as you enter and, to your surprise, salutes you.

'Sir, I am honoured but I don't ...'

The inquisitor raises a hand, interrupting you. 'You fought a fine battle out there. Indeed, Redguard speaks highly of your abilities.' He walks around the table to stand in front of you. 'Unlike many of my battle brothers, a soldier's past is of no consequence to me. It is what they do – their actions – that make them what they are.'

His clear blue eyes bore into your own, as he takes your arm and pulls back your sleeve. You flinch as your shadow mark is exposed. 'If Mathis knew of this, he would kill you without a second thought, without remorse. To him, you represent the enemy – everything we are sworn to destroy.' He removes his hand from your arm, which tingles and burns where the brand marks your skin.

'I may be judged for what I am about to do, but I have always gone with my heart. If you wish, I would like to make you an inquisitor. You won't be officially recognised as such – that I cannot do. The abbots in the capital bestow the true title of inquisitor to those who have proved themselves through years of testing and hardship. But I can gift you some of our powers. I think you have earned them.'

If you wish to learn the inquisitor career, turn to **668**. Otherwise, return to the quest map to continue your adventure.

708

The mighty dragon crashes to the ground at your feet, sending a shockwave around the cavern. There is a deafening, splintering sound from above, then stones and rock start to rain down from the darkness. In horror, your realise that the cavern is collapsing.

Quickly, you dive onto the dragon's hoard and begin filling your pockets. (You have gained 100 gold crowns.) You may also help yourself to one of the following items before you are forced out of the cavern by the raining debris:

Dragonslayer	**Dragonscale mail**	**Dragonscale cloak**
(left hand: sword)	(chest)	(cloak)
+2 speed +4 brawn	+2 speed +3 armour	+2 speed +2 armour
Ability: deep wound	Ability: second skin	Ability: second skin
	(requirement: warrior)	

You flee back along the tunnel, emerging in the rubble-strewn chamber where you fought the stone elemental. Eager to see daylight once again, you take the doorway opposite, which leads out into the seared scar. Turn to **475**.

709

With a rattling shriek, one of the raptors is sent sprawling across the pit in a spray of dark blood. The remaining predator fights with vigour, snarling and hissing as it attempts to bite at your shoulder. In your effort to back away, you stumble over the skeleton of a previous adventurer. As you crash to the ground, the raptor pounces, but you are ready for its attack, delivering a perfect killing blow to its exposed scaly stomach. The beast teeters back on its clawed feet, then crashes down, its legs feebly kicking in the air.

You breathe a sigh of relief as you pull yourself back onto your feet. The pit raptors have been defeated – one problem solved at least, but now a second one presents itself. How do you get out of here?

Although it isn't deep, the sides of the pit are sheer stone. There is no chance that you will be able to climb out. Besides, the false floor panel is already starting to swing back into place, sealing you inside.

Determined not to panic, you turn your attention to the base of the pit. All around you, the floor is covered in gnawed bones and tattered clothing. It would appear that you were not the only adventurer to be lured here by the illusionary trap.

If you are a rogue, turn to 583. If you are a mage turn to 434. If you are a warrior, turn to 590.

710

With your foes defeated, the four of you hurry from the tomb. Nyms takes the lead, guiding you out of the valley and back onto the dusty hills of the bone fields. From somewhere above you, there is a hellish, piercing shriek. You look back, scanning the grey-black clouds, but see nothing.

'Probably a wyvern tailing us,' says Janna, sprinting alongside you. 'It won't attack us if it is alone.'

At last, you see the welcoming lights of Redguard's camp ahead. As you come within sight of the walls you hear the clamour of the guards' bell. Minutes later and you are standing outside the tower, surrounded by an eager crowd of soldiers. Redguard joins you, smiling broadly.

'Janna, you're safe,' he says, his eyes misting with relief and happiness.

She nods, hooking her bow over her arm. The ranger looks solemn, despite the warm welcome. 'I think we should talk,' she says seriously.

Redguard shrugs. 'You may report, Janna. We have no secrets here.'

The ranger looks around at the faces of the young, fresh-faced troops then nods. 'Very well. The rumours that you spoke of are true. I saw an army – they're camped in the eastern section of the valley. I estimated about a thousand troops, but there could have been more.'

There are gasps from the assembled soldiers. Redguard visibly pales, shuffling his feet nervously. 'Those necromancers have been busy. Are they undead?'

Janna nods. 'I saw bone giants, skeletons, ghouls with packmasters – we got chased by some wyverns and a flesh golem. It's a serious force and I imagine it will only grow with time. These fields are covered in bones; all the building blocks those mages need to create an unstoppable force.'

'So, you made it back.' All eyes turn, as Inquisitor Mathis strides over. His steely tone contains no hint of pleasure. 'Come here, child.' He beckons Janna to move closer. She complies, glaring at the man with open contempt. Pushing back her hair, the inquisitor places a hand on her forehead and closes his eyes. Janna immediately winces, trying to pull away, but some force has her rooted to the spot. When the inquisitor finally removes his hand, she stumbles back, looking pale and drawn.

The inquisitor opens his eyes, his own expression haggard. 'So, it is true,' he says, a new note of fear in his voice. 'We will need reinforcements. Redguard, with me.' He turns and marches into the tower, with the captain following close on his heels. Return to the quest map to continue your adventure.

711

There are cheers from the surrounding soldiers as the hellish creature is defeated. You may now help yourself to one of the following rewards:

Torment	Cranium plate	Trickster's maul
(left hand: whip)	(head)	(main hand: mace)
+2 speed +4 magic	+2 brawn +3 armour	+3 speed +4 brawn
Ability: disease	Ability: fortitude	Ability: trickster

Elsewhere on the battlefield, a squadron of mages have brought down the floating orb. As its smoking body crashes to the ground, the remaining ranks of shadow spawn collapse into a full-scale rout, outnumbered and outfought by the defenders. The pursuing soldiers make short work of the fleeing remnants and soon cries of victory are echoing around the camp. Turn to 757.

712

To the west of the hill, the mighty inquisitor is slicing through rank after rank of ghouls. These ones, you notice, are different to those you have seen previously. They are bigger and broader-shouldered, their rotting bodies covered in haphazard pieces of bone armour.

You must now fight the following battle between Laine and the ghouls:

	Speed	Brawn	Armour	Health
Bone ghouls	13	10	12	100
Laine	13	17	-	80

Special abilities

- Holy light: If Laine rolls a ⚁ when rolling for his damage score, he also restores 10 *health*. This ability cannot take him above his starting *health*.
- Piercing claws: The ghouls' attacks ignore *armour*.
- Field medic: If you are a medic, you can cast *mend* on Laine once during his combat. You may still use this ability on yourself, if you engage in combat afterwards (see below).

If Inquisitor Laine falls in battle, you must take his place, fighting the ghouls with the *health* they have remaining. If you defeat the ghouls, turn to 687. If you are defeated, turn to 661.

713

Each chest contains a number of items from the king's treasury. If you wish, you may now choose up to two of the following rewards:

Torturer's rod	Mantle of spite	Tome of intellect
(main hand: wand)	(cloak)	(left hand: spell book)
+2 speed +2 magic	+2 speed +3 magic	+2 speed +2 magic
Ability: stun	Ability: curse	Ability: focus

After brushing the stone dust from your clothing, you take the archway through into the next chamber. Turn to 725.

714

You turn your horse and urge it back into the thronging mass of undead, aiming to reach Mathis. The inquisitor is using his mighty warhammer to pummel his way through the ranks of skeletons. As the giant ghoul nears on Lansbury's position, Mathis throws back his arm and then hurls his warhammer through the air. There is a blast of light as it slams into the side of the ghoul. The creature skids around, snarling with rage – then immediately starts towards the inquisitor, trampling over everything that stands in its way.

At last you reach Mathis, who is struggling to unsheathe his sword. Your horse whinnies and snorts with fear as the huge beast bears down upon you. The ghoul is huge, bigger than you first thought – its spiked carapace tapering back into a long ridged tail. Around each of its limbs are a set of golden bracelets, glowing with black magic. You assume these might be bonds of some sort, controlling the beast.

There is a grating ring of steel as Mathis tugs his sword free, its point flaring into a burst of white magical light. The ghoul opens its jaws, emitting a blood-curdling howl. Then, in a grey-white blur, the creature swings its tail in a savage swathe. You see skeletons smashed to pieces as its immense length whips out towards you ... then your mount is hit and you are flung up into the air.

You throw your arms around your horse's neck, clinging on for dear life. Then the danger of your situation hits home. Quickly, you slip free of the stirrups and push away from the flailing animal. You land in a roll, as the panicked beast crashes down amongst a group of skeletons. Narrowly, you avoided being crushed beneath your own mount.

There is no sign of Mathis or the others. The ghoul is now charging towards you, crunching the bones of the fallen skeletons beneath its splayed hands and paws. You ready yourself to take on this immense undead creature alone. Turn to 720.

715

Back at the camp, you are quickly swamped by a crowd of young soldiers, full of questions. You give a piecemeal account of the battle as you hurry past, following Lansbury into the war tent. Word of your return has clearly reached the ears of your superiors also. Inquisitor Mathis is leaning over the map table, with a face like thunder. Beside him, Redguard is pacing nervously.

'Ancient relics will not win this war,' Mathis roars, before either of you have even had a chance to speak.

Redguard quits pacing and glances over at you. His disappointment is clear. 'You disobeyed my order to stay within the camp, Lansbury. Explain yourself.'

'Sir, I had to try,' she implores, stepping up to the map. 'Look, with both of these statues operational, we could dominate the bone fields. The undead would not be able to get a foothold here.'

Redguard's brow wrinkles as he studies the map. 'What is their range?'

'I can't say for sure,' she shrugs. 'A couple of miles, maybe more.'

The captain gives a start. 'A couple of *miles*?' He glances over at Mathis. 'That would seriously restrict the enemies' movements. It would mean Zul's army would be forced to use the cover of the valley. We could dictate where they strike.'

The inquisitor snorts, thumping the table with a gloved fist. 'Zul is a genius. What is there to stop him from turning these weapons back on us?'

Lansbury raises a hand, shaking her head. 'Nothing I have read has suggested they are capable of harming anything other than undead. In the shadow war, the legion raised them in their thousands during the final assault. Those weapons were the mages' answer.'

'Fortuitous for us,' adds Redguard, his eyes fixed on the inquisitor.

Mathis grinds his teeth together, his fingers tightening their grip on the table. 'I already have reinforcements on their way. Until then, no one is leaving this garrison. Understand?'

Lansbury bows her head and nods glumly. 'As you wish,' she mutters. 'I just hope, by the time they arrive, it isn't already too late.' Return to the quest map to continue your adventure.

716

The creature writhes and twists, its tentacles slamming against the stone floor and ceiling as it enters its death throes. You duck beneath its flailing limbs, pushing yourself back through the water to avoid getting knocked unconscious. Finally, the tentacles stop moving, hanging lifeless in the water amidst a black cloud of ink and blood.

After scanning the room for any further signs of danger, you proceed to the edge of the shaft. Manoeuvring yourself around, you take hold of the sides and push yourself down into the murky darkness. As you head deeper into the structure, your eyes start to adjust to the dim light. Amongst the reeds and algae that have attached themselves to the walls, you see a number of floating objects. You may help yourself to one of the following:

Ink-stained vest	Pirate bandana	Captain's boots
(chest)	(head)	(feet)
+2 speed +1 brawn	+1 speed +2 brawn	+2 speed +1 armour

After several hundred metres, the shaft angles to the right, depositing you in a large round chamber. Turn to **587**.

As the undead horde reaches the base of the hill, it quickly fragments, clearly looking to assault the hill from different sides. Thankfully, it looks as though no one is commanding the force or issuing orders – therefore, it quickly descends into a confused rabble, with separate regiments scrambling to attack at their own pace and speed.

The pack of snarling ghouls are the first to make it to the top of the hill, appearing from the north exit. (Remember which rod you placed here, as it will help you with this battle.) The creatures scamper forward, using their arms and legs to propel themselves along the ground. Behind them, packmasters dressed in furs and leathers, crack their whips, driving their beasts into a frothing rage:

	Speed	Brawn	Armour	Health
Packmasters	13	12	10	60
Ghoul pack	12	9	10	45

Special abilities

🛡 Frenzy: While the packmasters are still alive, the ghouls can roll 2 dice for damage and choose the single highest result each time.

🛡 Piercing claws: The ghouls' attacks ignore your *armour*.

At the beginning of each combat round, choose the opponent that you wish to fight, rolling against their attack speed. If you win the combat, you must direct your damage against your chosen opponent (unless you have an ability that can strike more than one opponent, such as *ignite*). If you lose the combat, both opponents get to strike against you. If it is a draw, the round ends as normal.

If you manage to defeat this first wave of attackers, turn to 778. If you are defeated, turn to 723.

The tremors are the result of a giant creature, which is stomping through the tight press of soldiers, snarling with rage. It stands on two enormous hoofed feet, its scaled body shimmering with purple light. In one hand it carries a spiked black mace and in the other a whip.

'A Lord of Pain!' you hear one of the men shout. 'Stand firm! Stand firm!'

You start towards the beast, intending to help Ravenwing's men, but then you skid to a halt as an immense black shadow passes overhead. Looking up, you gasp in horror as an orb-like monster floats towards the battlefield. It has the appearance of a giant eyeball, surrounded by tentacles. From its single eye a beam of black light lances through the air, slamming into the defenders and sending bodies hurtling in all directions. You must now decide which boss monster you will fight.

Will you:

Attack the Lord of Pain?	627
Attack the Death Orb?	684

719

Before the body slides from its saddle, you may help yourself to one of the following rewards:

Plate of the fallen	**Dark tower**	**Thunder hammer**
(chest)	(left hand: shield)	(left hand: hammer)
+2 speed +4 armour	+2 speed +4 armour	+2 speed +4 brawn
Ability: finery of the fallen	Ability: impale	Ability: shock!

All around you, dust continues to choke your vision as Redguard and his men battle the remaining knights. Turn to 734.

720

The ground trembles as the enormous ghoul hurtles towards you, its powerful claws leaving deep trenches in the dirt. You suspect that the glowing bracelets around each of its limbs are what the necromancers are using to control the beast's movements:

	Speed	Brawn	Armour	Health
Ghoulash	14	13	15	100
Bracelet	-	-	8	25
Bracelet	-	-	8	25
Bracelet	-	-	8	25
Bracelet	-	-	8	25

Special abilities
🖤 Unleash the beast: If you win a combat round against Ghoulash, you can choose whether to direct your damage against the creature or one of its magical bracelets.

🖤 Iron clad: The bracelets are immune to *bleed, disease, impale, piercing* and *venom*.

If you manage to destroy all four bracelets before the creature is dead, turn to 736. If you defeat Ghoulash first, then turn to 702. If you are defeated, turn to 732.

721

To the east, a black fog has drifted in, twisting and swirling around the jagged peaks of stone. From this unnatural fog, you can see ghostly bodies slipping free, their hands stretching out to form demonic claws.

Klaret faces them without fear, his staff spinning in his hands as he cuts them down in a fiery display of explosive magic.

You must now fight the following battle between Klaret and the shades:

	Speed	Magic	Armour	Health
Shades	13	12	12	120
Klaret	13	16	10	60

Special abilities

🌑 Grave chill: The shades automatically inflict 2 damage to their current opponent at the end of every combat round, ignoring *armour*.

🌑 Fire storm: If Klaret rolls a ⚅⚅ when rolling for his damage score, he unleashes a firestorm. This allows him to add an extra 10 points of damage to his score.

🌑 Field medic: If you are a medic, you can cast *mend* on Klaret once during his combat. You may still use this ability on yourself, if you engage in combat afterwards (see below).

If Klaret falls in battle, you must take his place, fighting the shades with the *health* they have remaining. If you defeat the shades, turn to 653. If you are defeated, turn to 661.

722

Bones snap and splinter as the immense giant is brought toppling to the ground. You may now help yourself to one of the following rewards:

Pain in chains	Shield of bones	Razor fists
(main hand: morning star)	(left hand: shield)	(gloves)
+2 speed +4 brawn	+4 brawn +2 armour	+1 brawn +3 armour
Ability: pound	Ability: piercing	Ability: rake
	(requirement: warrior)	

You look over to see how the others are faring. Mathis' opponent is already a smoking heap of dust and bone. His sword blade is now turned on Ravenwing's giant. Together they bring it down, at the same moment as Redguard fells his own opponent, severing its spine and sending its over-sized skull spiralling across the battlefield. Turn to 728.

723

You feel a wash of warmth spilling through your body, knitting your wounds and broken bones together. With a gasp, you awaken, coughing and gasping for air. Lansbury is kneeling at your side, rubbing the palms of her hands, which still sparkle with magic.

All around you are the charred, smoking remains of the undead.

'What ... happened?' you manage to croak.

'I'm afraid you missed all the fun,' smiles Lansbury, helping you to your feet. She points to the statue atop the hill. You notice that it is now glowing with a white radiance.

'The statue did this?' you ask, looking around at the devastation. You can see piles of smoking bones that were once giants, tattered remains of a flock of bone wyverns, even a whole pack of ghouls, their bodies thrown like rag dolls across the hilltop.

'I told you it was a weapon,' beams Lansbury, patting the side of the statue. 'Any undead that comes near it ... boom!'

As your attention shifts back to the wasteland, you see a few surviving necromancers making a run for cover. 'They will be back,' you sigh, heavily.

Lansbury shakes her head. 'I doubt it. This angel will guard the hill and destroy anything that comes within reach. Even if the necromancers try and deactivate it, they will find a few little surprises of my own.' She gives you a mischievous wink. 'Come on, I expect Redguard and Mathis will want to know what just happened.' Turn to 715.

724

You find a purse containing 50 gold crowns. You may also choose one of the following rewards:

Pot of mending (1 use)	Band of elements	Budak's signet
(backpack)	(ring)	(ring)
Use any time in combat	+2 magic	+1 brawn +1 magic
to restore 12 *health*	Ability: lightning	Ability: steal

You step over the remains of the shadowy assassin and head back into the fray. Turn to 747.

725

The high walls of the chamber are covered in shelves and racks, containing a dazzling array of armour and weapons. A statue of the Dour king dominates the centre of the room, its cold eyes and cruel smile making the hairs on the back of your neck prickle. You almost feel as though this ancient warden is watching you, his expression one of scornful amusement at your efforts to steal his prized treasures.

Wrenching your gaze from the statue, you turn instead to the king's impressive armoury. You notice that some of the weapons have started to glow with a dull reddish light. As you watch, they suddenly lift themselves off their racks and begin to float towards you. In alarm, you realise that these must be the magical guardians of this place. The weapons slice and cut through the air, forming a deadly maelstrom of pointed steel:

	Speed	Brawn	Armour	Health
Animated weapons	12	12	9	40

Special abilities
- Whirling blades: At the end of every combat round, the fast-moving blades inflict 2 damage, ignoring *armour*.
- Sinister steel: The weapons are immune to *barbs*, *bleed*, *thorns*, *impale*, *piercing* and *venom*.

If you manage to defeat the king's animated armoury, turn to 561.

726

You may now help yourself to one of the following rewards:

Pot of mending (1 use)	Spider sapphire	Serpentine spiral
(backpack)	(ring)	(ring)
Use any time in combat	+1 magic +1 armour	+1 brawn +1 armour
to restore 12 *health*	Ability: webbed	Ability: immobilise

All around you, dust continues to choke your vision as Redguard and his men battle the remaining knights. Turn to 734.

727

You search the body of the two-headed giant. In a pouch around its waist is a bag containing 50 gold crowns. You may also help yourself to one of the following rewards:

Grimm reaper	Tooth 'n claw	Pauldrons of might
(main hand: axe)	(ring)	(cloak)
+3 speed +5 brawn	+1 speed +1 brawn	+2 speed +3 brawn
Ability: brutality	Ability: sideswipe	Ability: fortitude

Special achievement: If all four heroes – Gull, Laine, Janna and Klaret – are still alive, you may receive an extra reward. Turn to 735. Otherwise, turn to 731.

728

Beyond the smoking bodies of the giants, the steep-sided walls of the valley rise up to either side. Within its lengthening shadows you see a floating palanquin of bone, hovering several feet off the stony earth. Standing atop the grisly platform is a hooded man, his grey robes edged with gold.

Black lightning flares from his outstretched fingers, sizzling into the mages that dart and soar overhead. Expertly he fends off their attacks, both shielding himself from their fireballs and picking them off one by one. Their blackened bodies and frayed carpets crash to the ground around his floating palanquin. A dark laughter echoes within the valley.

'It's Zul,' scowls Ravenwing, raising his shield. 'We must be cautious.'

'We have bigger problems,' adds Redguard.

Two flesh golems are lumbering towards you, previously hidden by an overhang of rock.

'We'll take these,' says Ravenwing, nodding towards Redguard. 'You two, take out the mage'.

You glance over at Mathis. The inquisitor gives you an answering glare, full of distrust and unanswered questions. 'So be it,' he says grimly. The two of you advance, while Ravenwing and Redguard block off the advancing golems. Turn to 552.

729

With the shadowstalker defeated, you may now help yourself to one of the following rewards:

Shadowblade	Velocifero	Eye of shadow
(left hand: sword)	(main hand: sword)	(necklace)
+2 speed +3 magic	+3 speed +3 brawn	+1 speed
Ability: retaliation	Ability: riposte	Ability: haste

When you have made your decision and updated your hero sheet, turn to 636.

730

The giants may be powerful, but they are slow. You dart past their clumsy attacks, slicing and cutting through their animated bones. At last, the four mighty warriors lie dead at your feet, the dark magic that once held their bones together, now shattered and routed.

Amongst the remains you find 40 gold crowns and one of the following rewards:

Titan plate	Blinding dust	Bone gavel
(chest)	(talisman)	(main hand: hammer)
+1 speed +2 armour	+1 speed	+3 speed +4 brawn
Ability: fearless	Ability: deceive	Ability: knockdown
		(requirement: warrior)

As you look back towards the statue, you see that it has started to glow, surrounding itself with a pale radiance. Lansbury is still deep in concentration, her lips soundlessly forming words as she moves her hands through the air. You assume she is getting closer to fixing the statue's magic.

In the meantime, you have more pressing problems to deal with. The ground shakes beneath your feet as the biggest bone monster you have ever seen stomps into view. Turn to 650.

731

Despite your victory, the ride back to Redguard's camp is a solemn affair, your thoughts turning to what you might find on your return. As you near, you see a black pall hanging in the sky. At first you assume it is wyverns, still harassing the beleaguered garrison – then you realise it is smoke, curling up into the sky from a pyre outside the camp's walls. Riding past, you see wyvern bodies heaped high amongst the crackling flames and more being added to it as a line of sullen-looking soldiers file out of the camp, dragging or carrying the undead remains.

You dismount, with Lansbury at your side, and enter the camp. There are wyvern corpses everywhere, littering the ground like a grisly carpet. Lansbury rolls up her sleeves and makes straight for the infirmary tent, barking orders to a nearby guardsman who hurries after her.

Redguard approaches from the tower, his armour caked in dust and blood; thankfully, not his own. 'We saw the flashes and the explosions,' he says, still able to smile despite the carnage around him. 'You did well. We have struck a significant blow to Zul's army. I doubt he will try and raid our garrison again – although, I fear his attention will now turn to Talanost and Ravenwing's camp.'

You spot Nyms and Caeleb carrying a wyvern body towards the pyre. The cocky swordsman looks uncommonly morose. He glances up at you and nods as they pass by.

'We took heavy losses,' sighs Redguard, acknowledging the mood of the camp. 'But every last one of my soldiers accounted well for themselves. I fear more will be asked of them before the end.' He pats you on the shoulder. 'Now, get some rest. I'm sure we will be receiving fresh orders soon.' You follow his gaze to Inquisitor Mathis, who is seated on a boulder at the foot of one of the walls, silently gazing at the ash and blood on his gloved hands.

If you are a warrior and Laine survived the battle, turn to 707. Otherwise, return to the quest map to continue your adventure.

732

You open your eyes and give a start when you see a woman's face close to your own. She jerks backwards, covering her mouth in shock. 'This one's alive!' she shrieks, getting to her feet.

You push yourself up, your head still groggy and your limbs aching. All around you, there is scorched earth and the charred remains of skeletons and ghouls. As more of your surroundings come into focus, you see the woman now talking with a group of soldiers.

'There's one still alive,' she says, pointing to you.

The soldiers belong to Ravenwing's militia. On seeing you they draw their swords and start to advance. You glance down at your exposed shadow mark, pulsing with a faint purple light.

'Don't worry, we'll finish 'im off,' mutters one of the guards.

You stumble to your feet, your hands raised in surrender. 'No wait, I am with Captain Redguard ...'

'Yeah, likely story,' says their leader; a grizzled veteran with a face full of scars.

'Gentlemen, please.'

You turn to see Nyms stepping over the smoking bodies of the undead, his swords now sheathed at his sides. 'This one is with us.'

The guards look to him and then back at you, their scowls

remaining. 'Then he's your responsibility,' spits the leader. 'I'll have nothing to do with it.'

Nyms grabs your sleeve and tugs it down, covering the mark. He offers you a thin smile. 'I guess they're not quite ready to trust one of your kind, yet.'

You turn, looking out across the scene of devastation. Broken skeletal bodies litter the plain as far as the eye can see. 'We won?' you ask weakly, rubbing your aching head.

Nyms gives a hesitant nod. 'There were losses, but yes – once Zul was defeated the army kind of fell apart. Quite literally.'

'And the others?' you ask, scanning the nearby pockets of soldiers.

'Lansbury and Caeleb are fine – Redguard too,' says Nyms. 'You may want to give Mathis a wide berth though.'

You glance over at Nyms, your expression urging him to say more.

The swordsman sighs. 'He knows what you are now. He saw your shadow mark ... when you ... you died you know.' He shifts his feet nervously. 'There was all this glowing black stuff – magic. It was all Redguard could do to stop Mathis wading in and ... Well, you're OK now. Quite a gift you have there. Coming back from the dead.'

'Or a curse perhaps,' you add darkly, rubbing your sleeve.

'Come, on friend.' Nyms pats you on the back, smiling to lighten the mood. 'I hear the celebrations are already in full swing – that was quite a victory we won. I wonder if the bards will sing of it one day? Always wanted to be in a song. The great Nyms and his dancing blades!'

You laugh, but there is little feeling behind it. Your eyes keep wandering to the soldiers. Their nervous glances speak volumes to you. Clearly they are not ready to trust a shadow born, despite everything that you have done to fight for their cause. In silence, you accompany Nyms to the defenders' camp. Return to the quest map.

733

You find a purse containing 50 gold crowns. You may also choose one of the following rewards:

Budak's blindfold	Serenity	Stalker's jerkin
(head)	(main hand: sword)	(chest)
+2 speed +3 brawn	+2 speed +4 brawn	+2 speed +3 armour
Ability: second sight	Ability: deep wound	Ability: evade

You step over the remains of the shadowy assassin and head back into the fray. Turn to 747.

734

Half-blinded by the dust, you almost trample over one of the downed knights. As you wheel round, you see his armour rattling together as it reforms itself around his ghostly body. Slowly, the knight stumbles back to his feet, his dropped weapons lifting up off the ground to settle in the palms of his hands.

'They're healing,' cries Nyms, riding past you in a flurry of ash. 'Follow me!'

You gallop after the swordsman, who is headed out of the cloud of dust, towards a nearby hilltop. There, a row of black-robed necromancers have their hands raised, black magic curling around their fingers.

'They're the ones we need to kill,' orders Nyms, his twin blades glowing brilliantly in the grey gloom. 'They're using their magic on the knights – keeping them alive.'

Several of the necromancers break from the others, pulling wands from their belts and aiming them in your direction. Black fire blazes through the air – streaking into the ground and sending chunks of earth spraying across your vision.

You dodge and weave around the blasts, finally hurling yourself from your saddle to land on the nearest mage. Punching and kicking, you both tumble in a tangled mass down the hillside. You end up on top, pinning the mage's wand to the ground. With your other hand you take up a rock and bring it down ... ending the dark mage's life. Nearby, you hear the rattle of armour as several of the knights topple lifelessly to the ground.

You regain your feet as another mage charges towards you, a wand raised to blast you to smithereens. This one is female, with long raven-black hair spilling out from her pointed cowl:

	Speed	Magic	Armour	Health
Silleer	14	13	12	120

Special abilities

❤ Deadly charge: When Silleer causes *health* damage, she also electrocutes you with her wand. You immediately lose 1 extra *health* for every 2 points of *armour* you are wearing – rounding up. (If you have an *armour* of 12, you would take an extra 6 damage.)

If you defeat the necromancer, turn to **594**. Otherwise, turn to **732**.

735

Congratulations! For surviving the battle with all four heroes, you may choose one of the following special rewards:

Redguard's tabard	**Survivors' pennant**	**Martyr's blood**
(chest)	(talisman)	(ring)
+2 speed +4 armour	+1 speed +1 brawn	+1 magic +1 armour
Ability: iron will	Ability: fortitude	Ability: martyr

When you have made your choice, turn to **731**.

736

As you sever the last of the glowing bracelets, the creature suddenly pauses in its frantic attack, its bellows of rage petering out into a confused whine. Then, the ghoul's momentary confusion passes and it

gives another thunderous roar as it charges into the nearest rank of
skeletons. No longer under control, the ghoul is now running amok –
stampeding through anything and everything that gets in its way. One
of the necromancers' prize weapons has now been turned against its
own army.

You may help yourself to one of the following rewards:

Bracelet of fury	Bracelet of fire	Bracelet of iron
(gloves)	(gloves)	(gloves)
+1 speed +4 brawn	+1 speed +3 magic	+2 brawn +3 armour
Ability: adrenaline	Ability: embers	Ability: might of stone
	(requirement: pyromancer)	

All around you, the battle continues to rage. Turn to 601.

737

'Zul was a great man – a genius. He served in the army for many years
as a battle mage. That is when I knew him – we fought side-by-side
on many occasions.' Redguard traces a thin scar along his left cheek,
clearly remembering some past encounter. 'Then Zul left the army to
take a teaching post at the university. It was there that they discovered
...,' he stops, glancing up at you nervously. 'They discovered he was
shadow born.'

Your eyebrows arch in surprise. 'You never knew?'

Redguard shakes his head. 'Not all shadow born have the mark on
their arms,' he says grimly. 'Zul was caught practising the dark arts –
dabbling in things he shouldn't. So he was sentenced and imprisoned.'
The captain snorts, shaking his head. 'Like four walls would ever stop
him. I think it was a month later that he escaped. He was never seen or
heard from again – until now. Sound's like he's been busy ... plotting
the end of us all.'

You think back to your brief encounter with the hooded mage
– the man who had used you as a puppet to gain the last piece of
the Nexus. Would he use that same power again to control you? The
thought sends a cold shiver up your spine. Turn to 553 to continue
your exploration of the camp.

738

Undaunted by the size of your foe, you ready your weapons and rush into battle. The sprites streak towards you like fireballs, screaming and shrieking – whilst the giant throws back its enormous arms and begins hurling crackling bolts of fire in your direction:

	Speed	Magic	Armour	Health
Magmageddon	11	11	9	60
Fire sprite	-	-	5	15
Fire sprite	-	-	5	15
Fire sprite	-	-	5	15

Special abilities

- Heat exposure: At the end of every combat round you automatically take 2 damage from Magmageddon's raging flames. This damage ignores *armour*.
- Fire sprites: At the end of every combat round, each surviving sprite automatically inflicts 2 damage, ignoring *armour*.
- Body of flame: Your opponents are immune to *sear, bleed, fire aura, burn* and *ignite*.

If you win a combat round against Magmageddon, you can choose to apply your damage to Magmageddon or a fire sprite. Once a fire sprite is destroyed, you no longer take damage from it. If Magmaggedon dies, all surviving sprites are automatically reduced to ash.

If you manage to defeat this epic foe, turn to 400.

739

Redguard pushes back his chair and gets to his feet. 'You say that Jenlar mentioned an attack, an army that will be raised from the bone fields to crush the resistance?'

You nod. 'Yes, he mentioned a name. Zul Ator.'

The captain flinches, as if the name means something to him. You also notice Lansbury shifting uneasily at your side. 'I have suspected trouble from this quarter for a while now,' he says solemnly. 'You see, we are alone here. We are the only defence if things go ill. To the south of us is Talanost and the encamped remnants of the city guard; the resistance.'

He walks over to the window and beckons you over. You join him, looking out onto a training yard where a few young soldiers are sparring. 'We have seen increased skirmishes with the undead out in the fields. Their numbers are growing. You speak of an army – I have seen no such thing, but that doesn't mean it isn't out there. The fields are big, dangerous. I would need an army myself ...' He gives a heavy sigh. 'Most of my men – my best men – have been pulled back to the front, to Talanost, to help with the defence. Now I am left with my youngest troops. They are novices, fresh-faced and inexperienced.'

He points to Nyms and Caeleb, who you see walking out into the yard, inspecting the men's training. 'I was lucky to catch those two. Ex-army. They were passing through on their way to Talanost to sell their swords. Luckily I had enough in the coffers to pay them to stay. They're good at what they do – and if what you say is true, we'll need good fighters.' Turn to 693.

740

As you deliver the killing blow, the shadowstalker's body turns to wisps of shadow magic, leaving his clothes and weapons to fall useless to the floor. Instinctively, you draw back your sleeve to reveal your glowing mark. You can feel it pulsing and tingling beneath your skin, as if it can sense the nearby magic and craves its sustenance. The floating wisps spiral towards the branded skin, filling you with energy as they come into contact with the mark.

Enthused with Budak's dark magic, you throw back your head, laughing in ecstasy as the air crackles around you, charged with your newfound power. (You may increase your *brawn* or *magic* score by 2 for the next combat only).

Around you lies a scattering of Budak's clothing and equipment. If you are a rogue, turn to 733. Otherwise turn to 724.

741

You pull back your sleeve, revealing your own mark, burning with magical energy. The shadowstalker gives a gasp when he sees you, then his face lengthens into a cruel sneer. Between you, the shadow energy twists and coils, caught in an invisible tug-of-war as each of you attempts to absorb the energy.

You must take a challenge test using either your *speed* or *magic*, whichever is highest:

	Speed/Magic
Tug of war	20

If you are successful, then you absorb the magic. You may heal 12 *health* and restore 2 lost *armour* points. If you fail, the stalker absorbs the energy instead. Then turn to 746.

742

'This world was once yours,' spits the creature. 'Before we came and took it from you. You created us, with your dark magics and corrupted dreams of power. We were to be your servants, slaves to your will.'

Sharroth shakes its head, sending black drool showering across the sand. 'Fools! You brought us here and in doing so you sowed the seeds of your own destruction. We waged war and we won, destroying every last trace of your civilisation, wiping the planet clean of your taint. There is nothing left, only ash and shadow ... and the shattered, broken spirits of your people.'

You glance along the ranks of the army, noting a number of men and women just like yourself, their arms glowing with their own shadow marks.

'Yes. You surrendered,' continues Sharroth. 'You begged us for a second chance. You had seen what the legion was capable of – what power could be yours. And so, you joined us and became the Nevarin; the enslaved, for that is exactly what you are.'

Will you:

Attack Sharroth?	769
Ask Sharroth about the mark on your arm?	641

743

Nyms has taken out the last of the necromancers and is already headed for another group further along the ridge. Meanwhile, Redguard and his remaining cavalry have defeated the undead knights. They ride past you in a wedge-shaped formation, heading back into the thronging mass of the undead host.

You tag along behind them, fighting on foot as you wade through the masses of skeleton warriors. Their rusty swords and age-old shields shatter as your mighty weapons and powers beat them away. You have lost all sense of the bigger battle now – all that matters is the immediate space around you and destroying everything that gets in your way.

Above you, a barrage of explosions light up the sky. A moment later and you are running for cover as a giant bone wyvern smashes into the ground, leaving a smoking crater on impact. A red blur flashes by overhead. To your surprise you see that it is a red-robed mage, standing astride a magic carpet. He is rapidly followed by a whole squadron of mages, twisting and weaving through the air as they engage with the wyverns. Turn to 747.

744

Each chest contains a number of items from the king's treasury. If you wish, you may now choose up to two of the following rewards:

Cover of darkness	Nightwalker gloves	Shadow treads
(head)	(gloves)	(feet)
+1 speed +2 brawn	+1 speed +2 brawn	+1 speed +2 brawn
Ability: evade	Ability: nightwalker set	Ability: sidestep

After brushing the stone dust from your clothing, you take the archway through into the next chamber. Turn to 725.

'Stop!' You duck beneath one of the inquisitor's hasty swings and back away, raising your guard. 'It is not what you think, he was controlling me!'

'A likely story,' growls Mathis, advancing once again.

In desperation, you spin away from the inquisitor and charge towards Zul. Your only chance to convince Mathis of your innocence is to defeat this shadowy sorcerer. As you leap onto the palanquin, Mathis skids to a halt, confused by your actions.

'So, it has come to this,' grins the mage, meeting your gaze calmly. 'You cannot hope to defeat me, you do know this, don't you?'

You give your answer, in a flurry of magic and steel:

	Speed	Magic	Armour	Health
Zul Ator	14	15	12	100

Special abilities
- Black lightning: At the end of each combat round, you automatically take 4 points of damage from the mage's lightning attack. This ability ignores *armour*.
- Heightened magic: You cannot use *sidestep*, *evade* or *vanish* in this combat.

If you defeat Zul, turn to 541. If you are defeated, turn to 732.

The shadowstalker charges towards you, a magical sword in one hand and a curved dagger in the other. From the black markings along his fingers you see a set of black claws quickly distend, forming a third deadly weapon.

You must now battle this powerful assassin:

	Speed	Brawn	Armour	Health
Snaide	14	12	12	80

Special abilities

- Shadow infusion: If Snaide absorbed the shadow magic, he can increase his *brawn* by 2 for the duration of this combat.
- Dark claw: If Snaide rolls a double (before or after a re-roll) then he can use his claw special attack, immediately inflicting 4 damage, ignoring *armour*.

If you win the combat, turn to 751. If you are defeated, then you must begin this boss encounter from the start. Restore your *health* and *armour*, then turn to 764.

747

You cut, blast and pummel your way through the skeletons that block your passage. They are slow and cumbersome fighters, their reactions no match for your abilities and prowess. Soon, you find yourself on a rocky series of crags. To your left you can see Nyms, expertly twisting and dodging the attacks of a band of necromancers as he slices them down with his twin blades. To your right, you can see Lansbury and Tulcas. The latter is now holding the battle standard of Redguard's battalion, while the medic blasts the surrounding undead with her powerful magics.

Then the ground shakes as more powerful explosions rip into the earth. You turn your attention skyward, to see a flock of giant crows soaring over the battlefield. On their backs are archers, firing black-glowing arrows towards the surviving defenders. You look around desperately for the flying mages, but they are still fending off the bone wyverns to the east of your position.

You scramble for cover as another blast hits the ground nearby, leaving a smouldering black crater where you had once been standing. If you are a mage or have a bow or flint-lock pistol equipped, turn to 559. Otherwise, turn to 579.

The monstrous beast turns to face you, its half-human, half-demonic visage contorted with rage. 'Nevarin!' it snarls. 'Destroy the mages – now!'

You do not slow as you charge forwards, your grim expression a clear indicator of your intent.

'What is this!' hisses the hunter. 'Stand down, now!'

With the nearby mages now forgotten, the beast moves to meet you, its blades forming a deadly blur of steel as they spin expertly in its hands.

'Traitor!' it growls. 'Your betrayal is a sign of weakness!' From the hunter's back, its taloned appendages claw hungrily at the air, their serrated lengths dripping with black poison. 'Prepare to die, traitor!':

	Speed	Brawn	Armour	Health
Mage hunter	14	14	14	90

Special abilities

❥ Whirling blades: You cannot use *sidestep, evade* or *vanish* in this combat.

❥ Black poison: Once you have taken health damage from the mage hunter, at the end of every combat round you must automatically lose 2 *health*.

If you win the combat, you must continue this quest with the *health* that you have remaining. Turn to 631.

749

The guards move to intercept you, but your angry stare is enough to force them to reconsider. They edge back warily, letting you pass straight through and into the large pavilion tent. Inside, a number of men and women are gathered around a table of charts. The largest has a number of wooden markers placed on top of it, showing troop movements.

Ravenwing is speaking at the head of the table, with Mathis at his side. 'The king's army is only a day's march away. Once they arrive we will have a force nearly two thousand strong. At least then we will have a better chance of taking back the city.'

'Take it back?' protests one of the female officers. 'But there is nothing left to take. Some ruins? The surviving civilians are already evacuated and headed for Merino.'

'An assault will be futile,' interrupts Mathis, his deep voice carrying the length of the table. 'As long as the shadow gate remains open then ... You!' He stops mid-sentence, his hand going straight for his sword. 'How did you get in here?'

You step up to the table, ignoring the astonished gasps and glares. 'Where is Avian Dale?' you demand, making no attempt at formality.

'Shadow spawn!' hisses Mathis. He starts towards you, but Ravenwing places a hand on his arm, restraining him.

'Avian isn't here, as you can see,' states Ravenwing guardedly. 'This is a private meeting – if there was anything else?'

'Anything else?' You glower. 'As a matter of fact, there is. I have a message for him. Avian himself sent me on a mission, as well you know. I completed that mission – and I have an important message for him from Jenlar Cornelius.'

There are agitated mutterings from around the table.

'Jenlar, who is now dead I understand,' snaps Mathis darkly. 'And you think that I ...?'

'Avian has gone,' interjects Captain Redguard, stepping around the table to stand by your side. 'He left before the battle against Zul.'

'Gone! Gone where?' You look around furiously at the assembled soldiers, your eyes coming to rest on Ravenwing.

'I tried to stop him,' states the grey-bearded warrior with a heavy sigh. 'But he insisted. The mages were able to drop the shield, for just a moment – enough for him to slip inside and ...'

'He has gone into the city?' you balk in surprise. 'Jenlar said that he would try and close the gate ... but it will fail! I should have got here sooner!'

'To stop him, I suspect,' growls Mathis, his voice raised. 'It would not be in your best interests would it – for Avian to prevent more of your precious legion coming through the gate?'

You draw your weapons, fury washing through you. The mark

along your arm flares into purple life, flickering and pulsing with dark energies. 'I told you I am not ...'

From outside the tent you hear a commotion – voices raised and the sound of a horn blowing three times in quick succession. Then a guard races into the tent, his whole body trembling with fear. 'It's the legion! The ... the shield is down ... they've broken through!' Turn to 755.

750

When you open your eyes, you look around as if seeing the world for the first time. Your entire body is crackling with energy, and you feel it growing inside you – becoming something you can no longer contain.

You spring from the palanquin, gliding effortlessly over Mathis, Redguard and the others, who are watching you in both amazement and horror. They seem so small to you now, so insignificant ...

But a small part of you remembers – remembers what it is you came here to do. When you land, you see shadow energy radiating out in a circle from your point of impact. It slams through the lines of skeletons and ghouls, turning them to grey ash. You are dimly aware of Ravenwing's soldiers, fleeing from you as you advance towards the remaining masses of Zul's army.

'Get out of my way,' you scream, with a voice that no longer sounds your own.

You raise your hands and from their palms black fire spirals out into the ranks of undead, blasting them, crushing them, lifting them up into the air and driving them into the ground. This is power ... this is true power.

Then you stagger and fall. The magic is too much to contain, it is spilling out from your body now, rippling in tentacle-like waves as it is released back into the air.

'GET AWAY!' you scream.

You see regiments of men throwing down their standards and weapons, and running full pelt for safety – the undead now forgotten.

Then you open up your arms and release the magic – all of it. You feel a rushing wave of power flowing out across the battlefield.

Then there is silence. You fall backwards, your head hitting the hard-packed earth. The last thing you remember is a single bolt of white light arrowing across the sky. A victory flare perhaps ... Turn to 732.

751

You absorb the defeated warrior's shadow essence, feeling the wash of energy healing your wounds and knitting together your damaged armour. You may restore your *health* and *armour* to their starting values. You may also help yourself to one of the following rewards:

Duellist's blade	Duellist's shiv	Duellist's band
(main hand: sword)	(left hand: dagger)	(ring)
+3 speed +5 brawn	+2 speed +4 brawn	+2 magic
Ability: hamstring	Ability: expertise	Ability: ensnare
(requirement: warrior)	(requirement rogue)	(requirement: mage)

When you have made your decision, turn to 760 to continue the battle.

752

The necromancers have fled the chamber, however the mortician has remained behind, watching the battle from the sidelines. With a maddened screech he rushes towards you – a bloody scalpel held in one hand and a syringe in the other.

'My beauty! You killed my beauty!' he hollers insanely. 'You'll pay for what you did – you'll pay in body parts! It's operation time!'

	Speed	Brawn	Armour	Health
Dr Lichenstein	15	14	10	120

Special abilities

♥ Mad scientist: Before Dr Lichenstein rolls for damage, roll a die to determine the nature of his attack:

⚀ or ⚁: The doctor accidentally stabs himself with his own syringe. The sedative slows him down, meaning that he doesn't roll for damage this round and his *speed* is reduced by 1 for the next combat round.

⚅ or ⚅: The doctor stabs you with his syringe. He rolls for damage as normal, but in the next round of combat your *speed* is reduced by 1.

⚅ or ⚅: You are cut by the doctor's deadly scalpel. He can roll 2 dice for damage instead of only one.

If you manage to overcome your mad assailant, turn to 642.

753

You step into the ring to face the tall swordsman. He watches you intently with his cold blue eyes, his thin features twisting into a grim smile. 'I should warn you,' he says. 'I won't go easy on you.'

'I wouldn't expect you to,' you reply, drawing your weapons. There are gasps from the assembled crowd as they eye up your rare and hard-earned battle gear.

Nyms raises an eyebrow in approval. 'Flashy weapons are all well and good,' he says as you both circle each other, 'but it's what you do with them that counts.'

In a lightning-fast blur, he spirals through the air, spinning his blades in a deadly cutting arc. You barely have chance to block the attack, stumbling backwards from the force of his blows. Baring his teeth, the swordsman follows up with another flurry of attacks, giving you no quarter in his desire to defeat you:

	Speed	Brawn	Armour	Health
Nyms	13	13	12	65

Special abilities
◆ Double danger: Nyms attacks with his twin magical blades. When he wins a combat round he rolls 2 dice for damage instead of only one.
◆ Lightning reflexes: You cannot use *sidestep*, *evade* or *vanish* in this combat.

If you manage to defeat Nyms, turn to **698**. If you lose the combat, then you promise the swordsman you will return when you have had more practice. Turn to **553**.

754

As you land your final blow, the elemental breaks apart – the furious wind that once held its spinning form together, dying down to a faint breeze. The rocks and other debris that previously formed its body scatter across the scorched sand, including a number of rare treasures that must have been picked up by the whirling tornado.

You discover 50 gold crowns – and one of the following rewards:

Tempest's fury	Sands of time	Fall of angels
(main hand: staff)	(talisman)	(left hand: mace)
+2 speed +5 magic	+1 speed	+1 speed +5 brawn
Ability: windblast	Ability: time shift	Ability: windblast

Once you have updated your hero sheet, return to the quest map to continue your journey.

755

You hurry outside, accompanied by Redguard and the other leaders. To your horror you see that a section of the magic shield has gone and spilling out of it is a howling mass of shadowy creatures.

'How the hell did that breach happen?' shouts Ravenwing, grabbing the nearest passing soldier.

'One of the m ...mages collapsed sir. Fr ...from exhaustion,' he stutters.

All around you, the camp is mobilising as guards stumble out of tents, strapping on armour. Already you can see that a mob of the shadow creatures have piled into the camp – their savage cries mingling with those of the frantic defenders.

'We have to get that shield restored, as soon as possible!' commands Ravenwing, hurrying towards the breach. Turn to **764**.

756

As you clear a space around you, Nyms points down the tunnel. 'The packmaster! Get the packmaster!' he shouts.

You look up to see the man you saw earlier, standing at the entrance to the tomb. He has a whip in one hand and a knife in the other. He snarls, revealing jagged teeth as sharp as the ghouls'. Then he charges towards you, hissing with a bestial rage:

	Speed	Brawn	Armour	Health
Packmaster	13	12	12	70

Special abilities

🗡 Whiplash: For each ⚃ result that the packmaster rolls for attack speed, his whip lashes around you, causing 2 damage. This ability ignores *armour*.

If you defeat the packmaster, turn to 620.

757

You approach Ravenwing, who is wiping the blood from his blade. He looks up and offers you a smile. 'I saw you fighting,' he says. 'We're lucky to have you on our side.'

You brush aside his comment with an intent glare. 'I need you to drop the shield.'

The general starts in surprise. 'Excuse me?'

'I need to go after Avian. I may already be too late.'

Ravenwing makes to turn away, but you put out a hand out to restrain him. 'Listen. You said that the mages were able to drop the shield, for just a second, to let Avian through. I need to follow him – to stop him. He'll try and close the gate ... and if he does he'll set off a trap, some kind of spell.'

Ravenwing turns back, his brow creasing. 'Is this what Jenlar told you?'

You nod.

'And what makes you think you can reach him in time?'

'This.' You raise your arm, turning your shadow mark to face him. 'I will be able to pass through the city unharmed – they will think me one of their own.'

The general gives a grudging nod of approval. 'OK – I'll admit it could work. Besides ...' He glances over at a group of his men. 'No disrespect, but having you around is making everyone a little uneasy, Mathis especially. It would be in your best interests to ...'

'Disappear,' you add, with a wry smile. 'I understand.' You pull your sleeve down to cover the shadow mark. 'I will always be judged because of this. I accept that.'

Ravenwing studies you in silence, then places a hand on your shoulder. 'I am proud to have fought with you. Thank you.' He looks over to the mages, standing like silent sentinels around the shield. 'Come, let's get this plan of yours underway.' Turn to 675.

758

Four bone giants march out of the *north* passageway. (Remember which rod you placed here, to help you with this battle.) Each one is over six metres tall, made from the animated bones of a myriad of creatures. One has the skull of a giant lizard, another has curling bull horns and thick spikes; the largest, who could be the leader, has four arms and two ridged tails. Each one presents a different nightmarish mixture of bone and magic. However, they do all have one thing in common – they are all strong and menacing, wielding dull blades and mighty hammers:

	Speed	Brawn	Armour	Health
Bone giants	13	14	14	100

Special abilities

- Knockdown: If you take health damage from the giants, your *speed* is reduced by 1 for the next combat round.
- Body of bone: The bone giants are immune to *bleed* and *venom*.

If you manage to defeat the bone giants, turn to 730. If you are defeated, turn to 723.

759

The walls of the room shake, as the fearsome giant topples to the ground dead. Before the dust has even settled, you are at Caeleb's side, helping him to stand. Thankfully, apart from his injured pride, the burly warrior appears unharmed.

'Thank you,' he says, getting back to his feet.

Nyms returns to the chamber, his twin swords dripping with ghoul blood. 'Did you miss me, people?' he asks, with a wry grin. When he sees the dead corpse of the golem, he gives a low whistle. 'By the looks of it, I guess not.'

You may now help yourself to one of the following rewards:

Spinal tap	Spiked bone guards	Bone bracers
(main hand: spear)	(cloak)	(gloves)
+3 speed +4 brawn	+2 speed +2 armour	+1 speed +2 brawn
Ability: impale	Ability: piercing	Ability: bleed
(requirement: warrior)		

'I don't think we're out of this yet,' adds Janna, nocking an arrow to her bow. Turn to 654.

760

You reach the front line of the battle, weaving and dodging between the claws and snapping jaws of the shadowy monsters. There are hundreds of them, each one a different creation of vile sorcery.

Nyms appears alongside you, his twin blades making short work of the enemies in his way. 'To the shield,' he shouts, nodding towards the dome of magic. 'They have a mage hunter!'

You look around in confusion, then a momentary gap in the legion's ranks reveals a monstrous giant of a man, armed with two crescent-bladed swords. From his ridged back, four spine-like appendages arch over his shoulders, each ending in an unsettling array of claws and talons.

Nyms' warning suddenly hits home. The monster is moving along the ranks of mages, lined up around the shield. Already several have fallen to the monster's attacks and areas of the shield are starting to flicker and fade.

You look back to Nyms, but the tide of battle has carried the swordsman away from you, his blades rising and falling angrily as he attempts to break through the surging mass and help the mages.

Taking matters into your own hands, you throw yourself forwards, towards a tentacled creature with a ridged black carapace covering its back. You land on its shoulders, then leap again – agilely springing from one tentacle to another, your movements now fuelled by the magic flaring and spitting from your shadow mark. Within moments you are on the other side of the legion's frontlines. Breaking into a sprint, you head for the mage hunter, intending to bring its savagery to a swift end. Turn to 748.

761

As a mage you may also take the following item:

Winter's heart
(talisman)
+1 armour
Ability: Icelock career (see below)

You must have the *winter's heart* talisman equipped if you wish to learn the icelock career. As soon as this item is unequipped or you learn a new career, you lose the abilities associated with this career.

The icelock has the following abilities:

Ice shards (co): If you win a combat round, instead of rolling for a damage score, you can shower a single opponent with ice shards. This automatically does damage equal to your *magic* score, ignoring your opponent's *armour*. *Ice shards* can only be used once per combat.

Ice shield (mo): Use this ability to add 1 die to your *armour* score for one combat round. This ability can only be used once per combat.

Once you have made your decision, turn to 300.

762

The scout fights with a berserk frenzy, but your calm and precise attacks win the day. She slides to the ground at your feet, a scowl still etched deep into her face even in death. You may now take one of the following rewards:

Archstrike	Cloak of the wind	Spit fire
(left hand: wand)	(cloak)	(left hand: pistol)
+3 speed +3 magic	+3 speed +1 armour	+2 speed +4 brawn
Ability: dominate	Ability: surge	Ability: sear
(requirement: mage)	(requirement: mage)	(requirement: rogue)

You continue to fire into the flock of crows, bringing down more of their number and scattering the remaining few. Thanks to your efforts you now have *air superiority*. Make a note of this on your hero sheet, then turn to 591.

763

Having being issued with a steed, you follow the garrison south along the dusty road that winds through the bone fields. Redguard rides at the head of the force, resplendent in his plate mail armour and green tabard. On his right is Inquisitor Mathis, his blond mane of hair flowing out from beneath a white conical helm, and riding on Redguard's left is Lansbury. The medic has swapped her trailing robes for a suit of intricate silver armour, its runed neck-guard rising up to form a high collar. In one hand she carries a white staff, in the other is the battle standard of Redguard's force – proudly displaying a golden dragon on a field of green.

To the south you can see the glittering dome of magic surrounding

Talanost. As it gets nearer you can't help but marvel at the sheer scale of it and the mages who must be tirelessly working to keep it maintained. The shield stretches over the entire length of the city, sealing it in a magical prison from which there is no entry or escape. It is a sobering thought to think that the shield is all that stands between the legion and its destruction of Valeron – and perhaps, even the world.

'Flares! Look!' Tulcas is pointing eastward, across the grey barren plains. A number of red pulsing lights are arcing through the darkening skies.

'They're not flares, that's battle magic,' gasps Lansbury.

As if in answer to the medic's claim, there is a sudden barrage of light explosions, rippling across the horizon. They hang in the air like a sparkling strand of beads before slowly fading out, one by one.

'The war has started!' shouts Redguard, drawing his sword from his scabbard. 'Let's ride!' He urges his horse off the road, kicking up plumes of ash as he charges across the grey plain. Without a moment's hesitation, the rest of the force follow his lead, galloping towards the glittering frenzy that is lighting up the sky. Turn to 699.

764

As you race through the camp, you see a dense black cloud moving across the sky. It is only when you get nearer the battle that you see it is made up of thousands of black locusts. Columns of them are streaking down into the camp, engulfing soldiers in a whirling swarm of black bodies. One soldier races past you, his armour reduced to a few rusted fragments as the strange locusts nip and bite at his exposed skin.

Following the swarm are a pack of purple-scaled monsters running on splayed legs. Their beak-like faces are a mass of writhing, suckered tentacles. They bowl into the soldiers, knocking them to the ground – their stinging tentacles crackling with magic as they latch onto their stunned victims.

As you hurtle into their ranks, you realise that the tentacled creatures are not attacking you. Instead, they are concentrating their attacks on the soldiers. You glance down at your shadow mark and quickly realise the reason; these creatures must think you are an ally and not an enemy.

Turning this to your advantage, you move behind the packs of creatures, cutting and swiping at their exposed flanks. Soon, your weapons are slick with their slimy ichor, the ground around you littered with bodies.

Then darkness clouds your vision as you are hit by the swarm. Evidently the beasts have some rudimentary intelligence and have realised you are now a threat. You swing out with your weapons, trying to bat away the buzzing locusts, but they are everywhere, chewing and biting into your armour. Several of the tentacled monsters are now headed in your direction, evidently looking to join the fight. You must now fend off both of these deadly adversaries at once:

	Speed	Brawn	Armour	Health
Horrors	14	12	10	100
Locusts	-	-	8	40

Special abilities

🌑 Sucker punch: Once you take health damage from the horrors, you must lose a further 2 *health* at the end of every combat round. This ability ignores *armour*.

🌑 Nasty nibblers: The swarm of locusts are chewing through your armour. At the end of each combat round, roll a dice. On a result of ⚀ or ⚁ you must lower your *armour* by 1.

If you win a combat round against the horrors, you can choose to direct your damage against the horrors or the locusts. Once the horrors have been killed, the locusts will immediately swarm away to find an easier opponent.

If you win the combat, you must continue this quest with the *health* and *armour* that you have remaining. Turn to 602.

765

In a cloud of feathers and tattered black cloth, the undead beast is finally brought down. Amongst its rotting remains you find 50 gold crowns and one of the following rewards:

The morgue	Nemesis shroud	Funeral wraps
(head)	(cloak)	(chest)
+2 speed +4 magic	+2 speed +3 brawn	+2 speed +3 brawn
Ability: leech	Ability: dark pact	Ability: bleed
(requirement: mage)		

Return to the quest map to continue your journey.

766

The shadow gate. You had always imagined it to be some kind of door or a magical archway, similar to the portals that you have used to travel the lands of Valeron. But what you see before you, filling the immense chamber, is something entirely alien.

It is a machine – a vast misshapen mass of cogs and wheels, all moving and spinning in a frenzied dance. Plumes of whistling steam belch out into the chamber, forming a dense haze through which more pulleys and wheels can be seen, clattering and humming with life.

In the middle of this chaotic contraption is a set of rods, hanging suspended from an arched frame. Lightning crackles from their tips, converging at the centre of a raised podium where a black shape hangs suspended in the air. It looks like a rip or a tear in the very fabric of space ... a black gash, beyond which you can see a vast, infinite void.

A gateway to another world.

You make your way along a gantry that spans the enormous machine. To either side of you, the air hums with the motion of the cogs and wheels. As you near the central podium, something catches your eye, drawing your attention to a higher scaffold. There, a man in white plate armour is clambering up onto a narrow walkway, his feathered cloak hanging in scorched tatters from his back.

'Avian!' you call.

The man whirls round, his hands raised to summon a spell. When he sees you he hesitates, his eyes narrowing. 'Nevarin,' he growls hoarsely. 'Don't try and stop me!'

'Wait! It's me – your apprentice!' you implore, lowering your weapons. 'I come with word from Jenlar.'

Avian turns his back on you and starts limping towards a wall of spinning cogs. 'I must remove the Nexus,' he wheezes. 'I've come too far now ...' In the middle of the complex jigsaw you see one large, stone wheel, its surface covered in glowing runes.

'The Nexus!' you gasp. 'Avian, no!'

The mage summons white flames into the palms of his hands. 'I must finish this!' he declares fiercely. 'Before I am too weak.'

'It's a trap! The Nexus is trapped!'

You leap over the side of the gantry, landing on one of the spinning cogwheels. Leaping from cog to cog, you try and make for Avian's position, but you stumble, mistiming your step from one rotating island to the next. Unable to regain your balance, you tumble backwards. For several heart-stopping moments you are in freefall, then you slam down onto another cog, the breath knocked from your body. High above you, Avian draws back his arms to fling his magic against the Nexus. Turn to 609.

767

'I need to find Captain Redguard,' you explain weakly. 'I must find him, it's important.'

The swordsman looks back to the others. 'I told you he was a spy.'

'Enough!' the woman comes forward, pushing past the swordsman to stand in front of you. She drives her staff down into the ash-covered dirt at your feet. 'Tell me all. Why do you seek Redguard?'

'Jenlar Cornelius gave me a message – a warning.' You squint up at her in the grey light. 'I am not your enemy.'

The woman appears to recognise the name Cornelius. She lifts her staff and prods your arm. 'This is a shadow mark. Why would you not be our enemy?'

With a sigh, you explain your story – from the moment you awoke in the knight's camp to the fight with the shadowstalker and Jenlar's last words. When you have finished there is a heavy silence. Nyms, the swordsman, finally whistles through his teeth.

'Well that was an impressive story,' he admits. Something has changed in his expression, you notice. You sense there is a newfound respect there – and perhaps even fear.

'Help them up,' orders the woman. 'We're taking this one with us.' Turn to 669.

768

A horde of skeletons spill out of the west passage. (Remember which rod you placed here, as it will help you with this battle.) Most are armed with crude spears and rusty swords but a few have more impressive-looking weapons and shields. Behind them, you can see a group of black-robed necromancers. Their hands crackle with dark magic, as they raise up more skeletons from the ground, to bolster their ranks.

	Speed	Magic	Armour	Health
Necromancers	14	12	12	60
Skeleton horde	13	12	12	80

Special abilities

◗ Raise dead: At the end of each combat round, the necromancers use their magic to raise more skeletons. This raises the *health* of the skeleton horde by 10. (Note: This can take the skeleton horde above their starting *health*, increasing their *health* by 10 each round.)

◗ Body of bone: The skeleton horde is immune to *bleed* and *venom*.

At the beginning of each combat round, choose the opponent that you wish to fight, rolling against their attack speed. If you win the combat, you must direct your damage against your chosen opponent (unless you have an ability that can strike more than one opponent, such as *ignite*). If you lose the combat, both opponents get to strike against you. If it is a draw, the round ends as normal.

If you manage to defeat the horde, turn to 775. If you are defeated, turn to 723.

769

'Enough talk!' You run at the monster, looking to drive your weapons into its saggy grey flesh. However, the moment you begin your charge, the mark on your arm flares angrily, sending hot pain lancing through your body. You stagger, almost falling to the ground as you grit your teeth against the waves of agony.

Sharroth's mouth curls into a garish smile. 'Have you learnt nothing, Nevarin. Your people are slaves to the legion – you surrendered so that you could join us ... so that you could become immortal and save yourselves from death. That mark is a reminder of your weakness, your enslavement.'

The magical bonds that surround Avian suddenly fade and disappear, dropping the mage to the sandy ground. He looks weak and exhausted, his face twisted with pain.

'I will show you what you are capable of,' hisses Sharroth.

The mark flares again, jolting your body into motion. With slow, faltering steps, you advance on Avian, your weapons raised. Despite your efforts to stop yourself, you find that you can no longer control your own body – Sharroth is directing your actions as if you were a puppet.

'No!' you cry out. 'Stop this! Stop!'

Avian looks up at you, his eyes widening as he realises what is happening.

'Kill him!' orders Sharroth. 'Kill him, slave!'

As you go to strike the mage, Avian raises his hand and sends a bolt of white light into your arm. It hits the glowing snakes, forcing them to hiss and sizzle. Fresh pain wracks your body, driving you to the ground.

'No!'

The cry comes from Sharroth who is rocking back and forth in rage. When you open your eyes, you see your mark is now surrounded by a halo of white light. A coolness slowly washes over you, taking away the pain.

'That will ... protect you,' gasps Avian, the effort clearly having taken most of his remaining strength. 'The charm of submission will no longer work.'

You rise up off the ground, realising that your movements – your actions – are now your own again. Turn to 779.

770

The ground shakes as the giant bone monster crashes to the ground, its enchanted bones scattering across the snow. You find 50 gold crowns and one of the following rewards:

Horn of courage	Tenacity	Deathgrip robes
(necklace)	(main hand: dagger)	(chest)
+1 speed +1 brawn	+2 speed +5 brawn	+2 speed +3 armour
Ability: courage	Ability: deep wound	Ability: corruption
(requirement: warrior)	(requirement: rogue)	(requirement: mage)

The fight is far from over. You look up see a pack of snarling ghouls racing towards the foot of the hill. In the air, wheeling in circles above them, is a flock of bone wyverns. They screech and holler, their piercing cries making your blood run cold. Then your eyes catch another dust cloud, moving in from the east. You count seven bone giants marching across the wasteland, leading a fresh horde of reinforcements.

You realise that you cannot hope to defend the hill from such an immense army. Raising your weapons, you take a deep breath, preparing yourself for what is to come. You can only hope that your valiant last stand will buy Lansbury the precious seconds she needs to complete the ritual. Turn to 678.

771

To your surprise, Laine urges his horse onwards. He shows no signs of slowing down or changing course – he is charging straight for the ghouls. With no other option, you fall in behind him, wondering how any of you will survive the fast-approaching wall of death.

'Hold on!' shouts Laine. He raises his right hand and suddenly it flares with a halo of white light. From the sides of his horse, a pair of ghostly white wings appear, beating as fast as the beast's hooves. Then, it takes off into the air, soaring high above the snapping, howling ranks of undead.

You lower your head, bracing yourself for impact – but a sudden lurching motion forces you to lift your eyes. With a whoop of joy, you realise that your own horse has been affected by the same spell and is now climbing skywards. Behind you, your companions are uttering similar exclamations of surprise and relief, as their mounts rise up on glittering wings.

'A nice display of magic,' says Lansbury, watching as the ghouls below her snap and hiss in anger, making futile leaps into the air.

'They're not giving up though,' sighs Janna.

Indeed, when you look down, you see that the ghouls are swarming back around, as if answering some unspoken command, and are now chasing after you.

'The hill is defensible,' calls back Laine, guiding his flying mount over the jagged stones that surround the hill. 'We can hold them off while Lansbury does her work.' Turn to **694**.

772

As you sprint towards the bone constructs, there is a piercing shriek from behind you. The wyvern that had been diving towards Janna has altered its course to tail you instead.

You contemplate halting your charge, but one of the bone constructs is already turning to face you, its fanged mouth opening to emit a bone-chilling roar. Too late, you realise that you are pinned between these two enemies, and will have to suffer the attacks of both:

	Speed	Brawn	Armour	Health
Bone construct	13	12	10	70

Special abilities

- Raking claws: The bone construct rolls 2 dice for damage and uses the highest roll for its damage score.
- Wyvern's talons: At the end of every combat round, you automatically take 2 damage, ignoring *armour*, from the creature's talons.
- Body of bone: Your opponent is immune to *bleed* and *venom*.

If you defeat the bone construct, turn to 695.

773

You dig your heels into your horse's flanks, urging it towards the armoured knights. Ahead of you, Redguard and the others have already met them head on. You catch sight of swords and shields clashing with a thunderous din, men toppling from their saddles, the flash of magic … then there is just swirling dust, obscuring the combatants from view.

You gallop into the dust cloud, dimly aware of frenzied melee to either side of you. A cry forces you to twist round, as a black hammer – crackling with magic – almost knocks you from your horse. You parry the attack, turning your horse to meet the knight's next deadly swing.

As your weapons clash, you realise that your opponent is no earthly knight. Between the thin slit in his helm's visor, you see two red burning eyes, glowing with hellish fury:

	Speed	Brawn	Armour	Health
Tor knight	13	14	24	80

Special abilities

- Dismantle: If you win a combat round, instead of rolling for damage you can choose to lower the knight's *armour* by 4. You can do this as many times as you wish, lowering its *armour* by 4 each time.
- Steel yourself: The knight is immune to *piercing*, *impale*, *barbs* and *thorns*.

If you defeat the Tor Knight, turn to 547. Otherwise, turn to 732.

774

You shake your head in defiance. 'No! I will never join you!' As you advance on the monster, your shadow mark blazes angrily with dark fire. There is a bright flash as the shadow energies spark against Avian's white magic – then you feel a strong jolt of power race up your arm, turning the halo around your mark into a bright glittering shield.

You have gained the following special ability:

Bright shield (mo): Use this ability to raise your *armour* by 4 for one combat round. You can only use *bright shield* once per combat.

When you have updated your hero sheet, turn to 782.

775

Piles of mouldy bones litter the mouth of the passageway as you cut a swathe through the skeleton horde. As the final necromancer goes down to your mighty weapons, a silence settles over the hilltop. Exhausted, you drop to your knees in the blood-splattered snow, wondering how long you will be able to keep up the fight. Already you can hear the thunderous footsteps of the bone giants approaching.

Struggling to your feet, you take a moment to catch your breath before searching the bodies. You find 50 gold crowns and may help yourself to one of the following:

Iron curtain	Forked crest	Bag o' bones
(left hand: shield)	(head)	(talisman)
+3 brawn +2 armour	+1 speed +3 brawn	+1 magic
Ability: iron will	Ability: charge	Ability: curse
(requirement: warrior)		

With your heart pounding in your ears, you hurry back to the stone angel, where Lansbury is still in a magical trance. Your eyes scan the hilltop, wondering where the next attack will come from. Turn to 758.

776

The creature beats its wings furiously, struggling to keep up as you dodge and weave about its body. Despite its strength, the wyvern is an ungainly fighter and it isn't long before the beast is finally brought crashing to the ground in a heap of bones and dust.

From its remains, you may now help yourself to one of the following rewards:

Wyvern jaws	Wicked claw
(head)	(main hand: dagger)
+3 magic +2 armour	+1 speed +3 brawn
	Ability: critical strike
	(requirement: rogue)

As the dust settles, you quickly scan your surroundings, taking in the current state of the battle. Turn to 666.

777

The key fits the lock perfectly. Trembling with excitement, you lift open the lid and look inside. Your face soon drops with disappointment, however. Instead of gold and rare treasures, you find yourself looking down at three peculiar items, resting on a silver cushion. One is a small white bottle containing a glowing liquid. Next to it is a winged locket, fashioned from polished wood. You open it up to discover a lock of black hair curled up inside. Lastly, you find a pair of fluffy dice, tied together with string – the significance of which baffles you.

You may take any of the following items:

Elixir of life (1 use)	Winged locket	Fluffy dice
(backpack)	(necklace)	(backpack)
Use any time in combat	+5 health +1 armour	The ultimate in
to restore your *health*	Ability: courage	backpack accessories
to full		

Once you have updated your hero sheet, return to the quest map to continue your journey.

778

You are surrounded by the steaming corpses of the ghouls and their packmasters. Searching the bodies you find 50 gold crowns and may take one of the following rewards:

Bone headdress	Chains of binding	Leader of the pack
(head)	(left hand: chains)	(ring)
+3 magic +2 armour	+2 speed +3 magic	+1 brawn
Ability: charm	Ability: shackle	Ability: dominate
	(requirement: mage)	

You barely have a moment to catch your breath before you hear another force approaching up the hill. Turn to 768.

779

'Fool!' snarls Sharroth, fresh ooze billowing from its mouth. 'I promise you power. Why do you fight for their cause? What have you got waiting for you through that portal? They distrust you – they despise you. You are, and always will be, one of us.'

'Do not listen,' gasps Avian, struggling to stand. 'It isn't true.'

'Look at you,' hisses Sharroth. 'Look at what you have become, Nevarin. You thirst for power and reward. I can give you those things. I can give you whatever you desire. Here, with the shadow legion, you will not be judged. You will only stand proud, at the head of your very own army.'

Your eyes flick between Avian and Sharroth.

'Prove yourself to the legion; strike down this mortal fool and take your rightful place at my side!'

'No, don't listen.' Avian summons flames into his hands. 'Come, apprentice. If we die here, we die as heroes – with honour.'

You look around at the regiments of shadow spawn, line after line of them, trailing back as far as the eye can see. What force could ever hope to overcome such a vast, monstrous army?

'Make your decision, Nevarin,' hisses Sharroth. 'Death or power, it is your choice.'

Will you:

Join with Avian and attack Sharroth?	774
Choose power and the path of shadow?	660

780

You meet up with the riders at the edge of the rubble-strewn gardens.

'You're alive!' laughs Nyms, jumping down from his saddle. 'Which life is it this time? I'm losing count now.'

You stop and take a deep breath of fresh, morning air. 'I feel alive for the very first time, my friend.'

'Your arm,' he leans back in surprise. 'What happened?'

You look down at the mark, which now glows like veins of silver beneath your skin. 'Avian's magic. Somehow I think it fused with the mark.'

'So, a Nevarin no longer, eh?' he grins. 'Come, you're to be the guest of honour at the king's feast.'

'We won then?' you ask, arching an eyebrow.

'All thanks to you,' nods the swordsman, patting you on the back. 'All thanks to you. Look.'

Above the jewelled spires of Talanost, a squadron of mages soar through the skies, their magic carpets trailing rainbow hues that sparkle in the sunlight. As they pass overhead, bright fireworks burst from their raised staffs. The dazzling shards rain down across the liberated city, while in the distance the blare of horns sing of a triumphant victory.

Congratulations, hero! You have overcome the challenges set before you and have earned yourself the title, *The Champion of Light*. Thanks to your efforts and decisions, you have helped save the kingdom of Valeron from the sinister Legion of Shadow! (Bonus: A special quest has now been unlocked! Turn to 798 to join the resistance and help rid Talanost of the last remaining shadow spawn.)

781

The ghouls are everywhere, filling the passageway like a swarm of ants. Some have leapt onto the walls and ceiling, using their powerful claws to dig into the earth.

'Watch out! Above you!' shouts Nyms.

Almost too late, you dodge aside as one jumps down, its claws missing your shoulder by inches. Even as you fend off its continued attack, you can see more of the spindly creatures out of the corner of your eye, skilfully using the walls and ceiling to outflank you.

	Speed	Brawn	Armour	Health
Ghoul pack	13	7	12	80

Special abilities

◗ Piercing claws: The ghouls' attacks ignore your *armour*.

If you defeat the ghoul pack, turn to 756.

782

Sharroth rears back, its shell-like armour crackling with magic. 'Then you have chosen death.' From the creature's mouth, a series of black drooling tentacles spew forth. One slams into Avian, knocking the mage to the ground. The rest attempt to wrap themselves around you, their lengths dripping with acidic venom.

	Speed	Magic	Armour	Health
Sharroth	14	14	12	100
Tentacle	-	-	6	20
Tentacle	-	-	6	20
Tentacle	-	-	6	20
Tentacle	-	-	6	20

Special abilities

🛡 Oozing tentacles: At the end of each combat round you automatically take 2 points of damage from every tentacle that remains in battle. This damage ignores *armour*.

If you win a combat round, you can choose to strike Sharroth or one of the tentacles. If you defeat Sharroth, all remaining tentacles are also defeated.

If you are victorious, turn to 657.

783

(If you have already met Waldo, turn to 830. Otherwise read on.)

There is a commotion at the edge of the camp. You lower your weapons, tired from the morning's sparring with Nyms.

'Trouble?' you ask, peering past the swordsman.

Nyms cocks his head, watching as soldiers hurry past. 'Looks like something's stirred up the ants ...'

A wooden cart is rattling its way through the camp, led by a single piebald pony. The driver has removed his cap and is waving it through the air in greeting.

You fall into step beside Nyms as you head over to the new arrival. 'Perhaps it's a tinker.'

Nyms spins the grips of his swords with a smile. 'Hope so. They may bring word from the south. And a lot more besides.'

Soldiers are jostling each other to get a better view inside the cart, but one by one, with much grumbling, they break away and return to their duties.

The driver pats his cap down on his head as he brings the cart to a squeaking halt. 'Ah, some more discerning customers,' he smiles, watching you approach.

'Perhaps,' states Nyms, sheathing his blades. 'You come from the south?' He nods towards the glittering dome of magic that surrounds the ruined city.

'Yes, from Talanost,' says the driver, hopping down from his seat.

'Talanost? That's impossible!'

You turn to see Lansbury, Redguard's medic, striding towards the cart. 'The city is taken. The mage's have it guarded. No one can enter or leave.'

The driver shrugs. 'Where's there a will, there's a way.'

'Not when it comes to the Arcane Circle,' says Lansbury suspiciously.

'Ain't that the truth.' Nyms walks around the side of the cart and starts to examine its contents. You join him, scanning the clutter of objects.

'This is junk!' scowls Nyms.

For once, you find yourself in agreement. The wagon is filled with all manner of bric-à-brac, but none of it valuable – pots and pans, musty-smelling rags, a rusty spade, part of an old cabinet ... there is even someone's front door in there.

The man shrugs. 'Times are hard, what can I say?'

Nyms start back towards the trader, drawing one of his swords. 'How did you pass through the city unharmed? The shadow spawn would have torn you to pieces.'

The driver shuffles round nervously, watching the swordsman warily. 'Perhaps they took me for a fool, just like ...'

There is the scuffling of boots as Nyms surges forward, grabbing the trader by the front of his coat and pushing him down into the grey-black ash. The tip of his blade rests against the man's throat.

'Hey, I meant no disrespect!' The panicked man raises his hands beseechingly. 'My name is Waldo. I'm just a trader.'

'Just a trader ...' Lansbury passes her hand along the side of the cart. At her touch, glowing runes and sigils blossom into being, revealing a dazzling pattern that covers every inch of the dark wood. 'These are not Dwarf runes,' she says, pausing to watch as the symbols glow and then dim to nothing once again, ' ...and certainly not the work of an inscriber. What manner of magic ...'

'I found it!' interjects Waldo quickly. He tries to sit up but Nyms forces him back with the edge of his blade. 'Or it found me. I know nothing of magic. Just that it has its uses. Makes me go unnoticed ...'

'Really?' Nyms offers the trader a sceptical frown. 'Not working now is it?'

Waldo looks to you pleadingly. 'Talanost is in ruins. The legion destroys everything in its way ... but they have no interest in the spoils of war. I have ... things ... items that I found amongst the rubble. I got a knack for finding it, see'. He looks back, towards his cart. 'It would be worth your while to see what I got for you. Could decide the fortunes of this war.'

Nyms snorts dismissively, but steps back from the trader. 'A cart load of broken junk is hardly what we need to win this war.'

Waldo stumbles back to his feet, brushing the dust from his weather-beaten coat. 'Have it your way, swordsman.' He gives you a sideways glance. 'But appearances can be deceiving.'

Will you:

Ask Lansbury about the strange runes?	860
Ask Nyms for his opinion on the trader?	898
Ask to see the trader's wares?	795

784

Your opponent is a wild-haired man, dressed in a mud-spattered coat. In one hand he holds a black short bow, its arched length glowing with purple runes. As he draws back the bowstring, you see another bolt of black fire forming from thin air ...

You roll beneath the shot as it goes sizzling overhead. Springing onto to your feet, you barrel into the archer, knocking the bow from his grasp and sending you both tumbling into a fist-flailing tangle.

With a bestial snarl, the warrior tugs a knife from his belt. At that same moment you notice the shadow mark glowing on the back of his other hand. You roll away, as a jagged set of black thorns burst out of the mark, wrapping around the man's fist and pounding the ground where you had been lying.

'That's a neat trick,' you grin, turning your arm to reveal your own shadow mark. 'Want to teach me that one?'

There is a flicker of surprise on the warrior's face. Then his grubby face settles into another rictus snarl. 'You are no Nevarin!'

Before you can answer, the ragged man is surging forward, his deadly thorns pulsing with a dark and unnatural magic:

	Speed	Brawn	Armour	Health
Baalim	12	10	10	80

Special abilities

🛡 Thorn fists: Each time your damage score/damage dice causes health damage to your opponent, you must take 4 damage in return. This ability ignores *armour*.

🛡 Heightened senses: You cannot use *evade*, *sidestep* or *vanish* in this combat.

If you defeat the shadow ranger, turn to 925. If you are defeated, turn to 862.

785

Forced back against the shield, you are uncertain how long you will be able to hold off against these fearsome adversaries. Suddenly, a bright flash of light draws your attention skywards. From out of the smog, you see white shapes swooping down over the ruined city, their vapour trails blazing bright like comets. Beneath them, a series of explosions swell out across the square, cutting a vicious swathe through the tightly-packed ranks of shadow spawn.

'The airborne regulars!' You punch the air as the mages hurtle past on their flying carpets.

Then, at the far side of the square, you hear the resonating blast of a horn. From your vantage point, it is difficult to see through the thronging masses, but it looks like a battalion of Ravenwing's militia have made it across the city. You catch the glimmer of polished armour and a fluttering standard, proudly displaying the black raven. Aid has finally arrived.

For your victory over the scarrons, you may now help yourself to the following reward:

Scarron bile (2 uses)
(backpack)
It smells bad. Very bad.
Ability: vitriol

When you have updated your character sheet, turn to 828.

You enter a small square chamber, hewn from the bare rock. The low ceiling peaks into a natural shaft, which angles upwards through stone and roots to reveal a narrow band of daylight above.

In a corner of the room, lies the skeleton of an adventurer. Their clothes are rotted with age, brushed with a carpet of tangled cobwebs. A jewelled dagger is still clutched in the bony fingers of one hand.

Lansbury kneels beside the skeleton, her brow creased. 'I wonder what happened here.'

'Tomb robber,' snorts Nyms, looking up at the narrow shaft. 'Probably climbed down here hoping for some easy loot. I guess they found more than they bargained for.'

Lansbury frees a loose bone from the cobwebs, turning it over in the light from her staff. 'This arm was severed,' she states grimly, tracing the uneven edge with a finger. 'I think they may have done it themselves.' The medic nods to the dagger in the other hand.

'Why would someone do that?' asks Caeleb.

'An infection perhaps.' Lansbury lets the bone drop from her hand. 'It doesn't really matter now. I think they are beyond helping.'

'No, I meant ... this.' Caeleb is stood facing one of the walls, his head craned back. You move to join him, your jaw falling open in bewilderment when you see what has caught the warrior's attention.

The entire wall is covered in hundreds of marks, cut deep into the rock by a blade or stone. Most are purely random symbols, but some are clearly an attempt at communication. You edge closer, the light from Lansbury's staff casting flickering shadows over the crude engravings.

Not me. Not me. One God punishes. I punish. Punish. Not me! I die for him. Not me. Not me. The rest descends into gibberish, the marks becoming more erratic.

Lansbury looks back at the skeleton. 'Perhaps they were trapped in here. That anomaly could have existed a very long time.'

You feel a sudden prickling along your skin. Instinctively, you spin round – to face the far wall. There, hanging like a glimmering curtain, is another anomaly. Whereas the previous one had been a glutinous mass of mould and decay, this one is sparkling like dew on a spider's web, its thin strands rising and falling on an unfelt breeze.

'What is it?' asks Nyms, trading confused looks between yourself and the far wall.

You glance at your companions. 'Don't you see it?'

Lansbury's face hardens. 'Another anomaly ...'

'Then why can't we see it?' growls Caeleb, raising his shield as he turns slowly on the spot. 'It's something to do with that thing you absorbed, isn't it?'

Nyms has started backing up, edging towards the entranceway. 'This could be very bad. I think it's time to leave, don't you?'

Will you:

Agree and leave the stone chamber?	831
Investigate the anomaly?	825

787

A short passage opens out into a long rectangular room, dominated by a stone tomb. An image of a knight is carved in high relief on its surface, his gauntleted hands folded in silent prayer. Around the edges of the room are a number of rune-bordered alcoves. Within each rests an item of equipment, from ornately-decorated weapons to highly-polished pieces of armour.

'Jorvic!' gasps Arthurian rushing to the side of the tomb. 'By Judah's light ...' He makes the sign of the cross in the air as his eyes rove around the chamber. 'This was a good man.'

You walk over to the nearest alcove, studying the fine sword that rests within the dusty recess. 'And this is a fine weapon,' you comment, reaching out to touch it.

'No!' Arthurian's voice echoes around the chamber.

You hesitate, looking back at him with surprise.

'Do not touch his belongings!' he snaps. 'They are protected.' He stabs a finger at the runes above the alcove. 'Holy magic.'

You immediately back away, reminded of the strange circle in the previous chamber.

'Come,' hisses Arthurian. 'I will not tarry here!' He strides across the room, taking an archway through into a magic-lit corridor. You follow close on his heels, fascinated by the blue flames that flicker in the iron sconces along the walls.

At the end of the corridor, another passageway branches to the left, ending in a statue of a knight, his head bowed. In the wall facing you is an immense door, fashioned from ivory and gold. Each of its panels has been intricately decorated, depicting a number of embossed scenes. As you edge closer, you see that they all feature a knight on horseback, battling a nightmarish menagerie of fearsome monsters.

In the centre of the door is a gold circle and inset within it is an ivory chalice.

'Where does this lead to?' you ask in wonderment.

Arthurian removes the crucifix from around his neck. Holding it up, he unscrews the base, pulling it away to reveal a miniature key. 'This is a perfect copy.' His bright eyes regard you through his ragged strands of hair. 'You have no idea how hard it was to get this.'

He steps forward and places the key into a small cavity at the centre of the chalice. As the key slots into place, there is a deep rumbling sound. Suddenly, piercing strands of white light radiate outwards from the chalice, spilling along previously unseen cracks and trenches. Within seconds, a spider's web of light has branched across the entire surface of the door, splitting it into sections, which suddenly start to revolve. You watch, mouth agape, as the door folds in on itself and then slides aside, revealing a small, dust-shrouded room beyond. (Make a note of the word vault on your hero sheet.) Turn to **886**.

789

Waldo closes the chest and locks it with the silver key. When he straightens, he claps you on the shoulder with a wide smile. 'Guess I'll be sticking around for a while, unless those inquisitors move me on – so, come seek me out if you need anything else.'

You glance down at the strange chest. Its glittering, embossed design now displays a winged dragon – identical to the one displayed on Redguard's fluttering standards. 'Hmm, appearances can be deceiving,' you mutter.

Waldo doffs his cap to you. 'I'll let others be the judge of that.'

Bidding the trader farewell, you head back into the camp. Return to the map to continue your adventure.

790

Warily you step through the archway, to find yourself in a circular chamber with a high-domed ceiling. At the centre of the room is a stepped dais leading up to a stone tomb. The lid has been smashed to pieces, its shattered stonework lying in jagged pieces around the base of the dais.

'Oh, this doesn't look good,' mutters Nyms, his swords spinning nervously in his hands.

Hovering above the open tomb is a man in rune-plate armour. He hangs suspended in the air, his head tilted back and his arms outstretched to either side, palms turned upwards.

Stood around him are four black-robed necromancers. They are chanting arcane words as streams of magic arc from their fingers, pouring into the warrior who basks in its purple glow.

'More ... give me more!' he snarls, his head snapping forwards.

One of the necromancers falls to his knees, clearly with exhaustion. The dark warrior turns to face him, his scowl deepening.

'Is this the best that Zul could send me?' He raises his left hand, tightening it into a fist. The mage begins to choke, gripping his throat.

'Something wrong with this picture?' asks Nyms worriedly, shooting Caeleb a hurried glance. 'Thought Arthurian was on our side?'

Caeleb looks equally confused. He starts forward into the room, his hand resting on the pommel of his sword. 'Great Arthurian, we seek your aid.' He drops to one knee, his head bowed. 'My lord. My protector – these are dark times. We ask that you help us to conquer this evil.'

The dark warrior looks down with derision, as the lifeless body of the necromancer slumps forward.

'Fools! Arthurian is not here.' The man's voice booms in the chamber, shaking its very foundations.

'But this ... this is his tomb,' implores Caeleb, stumbling to his feet.

The warrior shakes his head, his long mane of dark hair shifting across his purple-glowing eyes. 'This is his body,' snarls the knight.

'But I'm afraid Arthurian is no longer home.' He throws back his head, a cold and chilling laughter echoing back from the high stone walls.

Caeleb draws his sword with a flourish. 'Demon! I will send you back to the shroud!'

As he charges forward, the dark warrior drops to the floor of the tomb, splintering the stone beneath his plated feet.

'Ah yes, I have waited a long time for this!' Purple magic blazes from the warrior's runed gauntlets, forming two mighty axes – sparking with magic:

	Speed	Magic	Armour	Health
Dark Arthurian	13	12	13	80
Necromancer	-	-	6	20
Necromancer	-	-	6	20
Necromancer	-	-	6	20

Special abilities

◗ Dark mending: At the end of every combat round, Dark Arthurian is able to restore 2 *health* from each necromancer that is still alive. This ability cannot take him above his starting *health* of 80.

◗ 'Heal me!': Lansbury can heal you for 15 *health* any time during this combat. This ability can only be used once per combat.

◗ Team effort: Nyms' sweeping strikes add 2 to your damage score. Caeleb uses his shield to defend you from harm. Your *armour* is raised by 2 for this battle.

If you manage to overcome this sinister imposter, turn to 929. If you are defeated, then turn to 862.

791

Just like the tinker's chest in the town of 'No Hope', the interior of this chest is larger on the inside, filled with a myriad of weapons, armour and trinkets. It is a far cry from the battered pots and pans in the trader's cart.

'Now do you believe me,' grins Waldo, leaning over your shoulder. 'I got a knack for finding treasure. And rare stuff, too.'

'I suspect these don't come cheap,' you say with a wry grin, as you lift out a rune-etched shield.

'That depends. I got my rare items ... real beauties those, then I got my special deals.'

Will you:

Ask to see the special deals?	815
Ask to see the rare items?	803

792

Fetch leans back, folding his arms across his chest. 'Are you going to ask me any more foolish questions?'

Will you:

Ask how Fetch came to meet Avian Dale?	837
Ask about his magical ability?	829
Ask him what he was doing in the tomb?	800
Ask him to return you to the others?	915
Ask what is in all the crates and boxes?	853

793

Caeleb carefully places the weapon he was inspecting back onto its rack; a poignant but futile gesture, as the rest of the room still remains a cluttered mass of upturned chests and trunks. 'They will pay for what they have done,' he mutters, casting an angry glare around the room. 'Come on.'

He leads the way back down the corridor. As you near the inscribed room, you feel the air growing thick again ... your limbs weakening. The shadow mark hisses beneath your clothing.

Nyms gives you a worried glance as you stumble into the room, your head pounding with pain. Without pause, Caeleb crosses the chamber, taking the north passage. You follow, your concentration focused solely on putting one foot in front of the other. Turn to 857.

(Make a note of the word *rival* on your hero sheet.)

Forced back against the statue, you are uncertain how long you will be able to hold off against these fearsome adversaries. Suddenly, a bright flash of light draws your attention skywards. From out of the smog, you see white shapes swooping down over the ruined city, their vapour trails blazing bright like comets. Beneath them, a series of explosions swell across the square, cutting a vicious swathe through the tightly-packed ranks of shadow spawn.

'The airborne regulars!' You punch the air as the mages hurtle past on their flying carpets.

Then, at the far side of the square, you hear the resonating blast of a horn. From your vantage point, it is difficult to see through the thronging masses, but it looks like a battalion of Ravenwing's militia have made it across the city. You catch the glimmer of polished armour and a fluttering standard, proudly displaying the black raven. Aid has finally arrived.

For your victory over the ghasts, you may now help yourself to the following reward:

Spirit tincture (1 use)
(backpack)
Use any time in combat to lose
4 *health* but increase your *brawn*
or *magic* by 2 for the remainder
of the combat

When you have updated your hero sheet, turn to **884**.

795

'A-ha, I see you have a nose for a bargain!' Waldo grabs hold of the old riding blanket that covers his seat and, with a flourish, pulls it away to reveal an ornate chest. Putting the blanket aside, he takes the chest and lifts it down onto the ground.

You kneel beside it, entranced by the silver patterns that have been embossed onto its metallic surface. For a moment, they make no sense to you – but then the lines appear to shift and take on form. You lean back, scrutinising the scene that is materialising before you. It shows a vast city, crowned by towers and minarets. The bodies of three snakes form an arched entranceway, their bodies covered in glistening runes.

'What is this?' You cannot tear your eyes away from the intricate scene. 'Where did you find it?'

Waldo squats down beside you, hands resting on his knees. 'Does it mean something to you?' he asks hopefully.

'It is ... familiar.' You trace the raised patterns with your fingers. 'This city, have you seen it before?'

'Is it your home?' he ventures.

You shrug your shoulders. 'I wish I knew ... I have no memory of that place.'

'Well, I always say ... it's what's on the inside that counts, eh?'

Waldo puts his hand inside his shirt and pulls out a silver chain. On the end of it is a small sparkling key. Lifting the chain over his head, he takes the key and inserts it into the lock of the chest. A turn and a click later, and you find yourself staring into its velvet-lined cavity ...

If you are a warrior, turn to 791. If you are a rogue, turn to 875. If you are a mage, turn to 852.

796

Your eyes flutter open, the rain-drenched hills of the bone fields swaying before your blurred vision. Ahead of you, an indistinct shape moves quickly across the uneven terrain. As colours and detail swim into focus, you discern flowing robes and a bright staff of light.

You try and speak but the words clog at the back of your throat, producing little more than a guttural croak. The ground sways once again.

'They're awake,' mutters a voice close to your ear.

You are dropped to the earth, landing in the sodden ash. As you struggle for breath, you look up to see Caeleb standing over you, sweat and dirt staining his face. 'You aren't so light to carry, now get up.'

Nyms paces into view, looking around warily. 'We need to keep moving. Can you walk?' He glances your way, a grimace etched deep into his pale, narrow face.

'Get up!' snaps Caeleb, kicking ash in your direction. 'You have already slowed us down!'

In the distance you hear the shriek of some infernal creature.

'What happened?' you rasp, aware of a throbbing pain coming from your arm.

'Good question,' says Nyms, nervously tapping the pommels of his swords. 'You vanished into thin air, right in front of us, and then ... then you were back again. There was all this shimmering magic ...' He shrugs his shoulders. 'It didn't look good.'

'Demon magic!' Caeleb scowls, turning away.

'But the tomb ... our mission.' You push yourself back onto your feet, swaying slightly as you try and regain your balance.

'We ran into more of Zul's mages,' states Lansbury, looking back to survey the dark skies. 'We were lucky to escape – but now they have scouts looking for us. We must hurry.'

Another deafening shriek dashes the uneasy silence. You take a tentative step forward, relieved to find that your strength is slowly starting to return. 'I'll be fine. Lead the way.'

Lansbury nods, before starting down into a narrow ravine. You follow, slipping on the loose stones and bones that litter the ground. As you catch sight of a skull, grinning back at you from a mound of ash, you find yourself pondering your strange gift for immortality. Return to the Act 3 map to continue your adventure.

797

'Frontal assault it is!' Caeleb starts the charge, racing forward with his shield held high. Nyms and Lansbury fall in behind him, the latter uttering words of holy magic. A second later and the medic's staff flares into white brilliance, its shining light settling around the group like a glowing shroud.

You follow, aware that the bone creature has already spotted you. It throws back its enormous head and from its steel-encased beak it gives a series of sharp, guttural calls.

'Whoa, someone's happy to see us,' smirks Nyms, spinning the grips of his blades.

The undead creature takes to the air, pushing off from its rocky perch and sending jagged cracks branching through the stone. It isn't until you near that you see that the tablet is some kind of memorial – its surface etched with hundreds of neatly-scripted names.

Before you can ponder its significance, Nyms breaks away from the group. He has spotted four necromancers advancing towards you, their wands and staves crackling with dark magic.

'Nyms, wait!' Lansbury calls after him, but the swordsman shows no sign of slowing, his magical blades deflecting the necromancers' incoming blasts. 'We need to stay together!'

Another guttural screech draws your attention skywards. Above you, the bone creature wheels in the air, its immense body blotting out the sky and drowning you in shadow. Caeleb moves in front of Lansbury, raising his shield as the beast dives towards them.

Will you:

Help Nyms battle the necromancers?	823
Help defeat the bone angel?	849

798
Bonus quest: The betrayed

You crouch at the edge of the rooftop, studying the ashen wasteland that was once Talanost. The city lies utterly still. Only smoke moves, curling between the charred rafters of the burnt out buildings. In the street below, a lone knight appears from a rubble-choked alley, guiding his steed with care through the ravaged ruins. The beast's hooves clatter on the loose stone and masonry, its breath snorting clouds into the cold, morning air.

You turn away, your gaze shifting across the formless wreckage, to finally rest on the mansion – its white-washed walls untouched by the devastation that surrounds it. Your shadow mark tingles, its icy fingers crawling beneath your skin. Since you absorbed Sharroth's power, the mark has been a constant irritation – an itch that refuses to be scratched. You glare down at it angrily, knowing what it wants. What it desires.

'I can't wait any longer,' you state grimly. 'They're here; I feel them.'

Your companion shifts nervously beside you. His usual garb has been replaced by wraps of grey and black cloth, turning him near invisible against the wasted backdrop of the city.

'We were told to wait,' he replies, his hood shifting to reveal a thin face, pointed and angular. 'It's not wise to upset Mathis.'

You grunt with derision, the buzzing from your arm becoming more insistent. 'The fool will only get in the way.'

Nyms sighs. 'I know. Once your course is set, you seldom give ear to counsel.' He pauses for a moment. 'In truth, your nature has rarely led us awry.'

'Nor will it.' Your eyes remain rooted to the mansion. Every shred of evidence, every clue that you have scavenged over the last few days, has led you to this place – the last bastion of the enemy. 'But why here?' you mutter to yourself, frowning. The building is nothing special, save that it is perfectly intact. Around it, the other estates have fared less well, their broken remains stabbing like claws into the ashen sky.

'I've seen worse neighbourhoods,' grins Nyms. 'Real shame the king didn't stick around to enjoy the sightseeing.'

You favour him with a bitter laugh. 'Ah yes, the king ...'

A week has passed since the king's army broke camp and rode home, leaving yourself and Ravenwing's militia to pick up the pieces. 'Cleansing the city,' Mathis had called it, making it sound a noble and grandiose task. But the reality quickly proved otherwise – long days scrabbling across rubble, wading through miles of stinking sewers and dark catacombs, hunting for every last shadow spawn that survived the battle. Some of them talked, before their life was ended. Those that still had some humanity, at least.

Cleansing the city. Not the great heroic ending that you had imagined – but then, your disappointments have been many. After closing the gate, you assumed you would be heralded a champion, given a seat at the king's side, showered with gold and glory – and respect. But at the feast, the king never deigned to acknowledge you; his men treated you with the same suspicion and contempt as the others.

A Nevarin. Stained by the past. By what you were…

What you still are.

'I'm tired of waiting.' You rise to your feet, finding balance on the shattered rooftop. Across the avenue, the spiked wall of the mansion looms arrogantly before you, an imposing height of sheer stone and barbed iron. It might deter some thieves, perhaps. But not you.

Magic sparks at your fingertips as you contemplate blasting your way through, ripping each and every spike from their very foundations. But you clench your fist, letting the magic dissipate. 'Let's do it your way, Nyms.'

'Ah, appreciated at last.' He levels a crossbow, aiming for the gnarled yellowwood tree that dominates the courtyard. A click of the trigger sends the bolt streaking through the air, its course marked by the glittering rope that trails behind it. There is a thud as the bolt embeds itself deep into the body of the tree, stretching the rope taut. You follow its length to where the rope has been securely knotted around an exposed gable post. 'Is that thing seriously going to hold our weight?' you ask, scratching your chin.

'Providing you laid off the king's pies,' smiles Nyms, slapping your stomach with the back of his hand. 'Watch and learn.'

Nyms grabs the rope, swinging beneath it to hook his boots over the top. Then he proceeds to scurry across, moving hand over hand with practised ease. You watch tensely as the rope and wood creak in protest. But the make-shift bridge appears to be holding.

The nimble swordsman passes over the spiked wall and then drops into the courtyard below with barely a whisper of noise. You follow suit, hooking both legs over the rope and shimmying along its length. A minute later and you have joined your companion in the courtyard, weapons drawn and ready.

A set of stairs lead up to a pillared porch, where a pair of cedarwood doors offer an obvious route inside the mansion. You are about to start towards them, when you feel a touch on your arm. Nyms nods towards the second storey, where a wrought iron balustrade juts out from the wall. Between its bars, you see what the sharp-eyed rogue has spotted: a half-open window leading though into the interior of the house.

Will you:

Enter the mansion through the main doors?   932

Climb up to the second floor balcony?   835

799

You enter a vast pillared hall, bathed in a pale white light. Squinting up, you see that the light is coming from a cluster of crystals suspended from the ceiling. Below them, the paved floor is smashed and broken, as if something heavy has repeatedly pounded against the stonework. Amongst the jagged rubble, a few tiles remain unbroken, their surface covered in a spidery script. Had the stones been left undamaged, these decorative runes would have formed a perfect circle.

'Holy inscriptions,' says Lansbury. 'Much of their magic is broken, but you still feel it, don't you?' Her eyes remain forward, but it is obvious who she is speaking to.

'Yes,' you grimace. The pain from your shadow mark has intensified, forcing you to stagger. Caeleb puts out an arm to stop you.

'What is it?' he asks worriedly.

You shake your head, confused.

'I mean that.' Caeleb nods towards the curtain of light, where a dark shape is moving at the far side of the shattered flagstones. A guttural growl echoes in the hall.

'Why is nothing ever easy,' sighs Nyms, casting a wary glance towards the pillars either side of the room. 'Watch for an ambush, Nevarin.'

'I don't think we need worry about subtlety,' says Lansbury grimly.

The dark shape shuffles forward into the light. The radiance picks out its huge hunched shoulders and thick arms. Even from a distance you can see that the creature is a giant, at least seven metres tall. Its pale, almost translucent skin, is covered in purple runes – sharing a stark similarity to those that now burn bright along your arm.

'Well, that's a new one,' mutters Nyms, spinning his blades. 'Something from your world, Nevarin?'

You take an uncertain step back as the creature lurches forward on bowed legs, its wide gash of a mouth drooling spit onto the shattered floor.

Suddenly, with a speed that belies its ungainly form, the creature snatches up a broken tile and sends it hurtling towards the group. Caeleb raises his shield just in time – the stone breaking against its surface sending fragments showering in all directions.

Then the ground trembles as the giant beast charges forward.

Quickly, your party breaks for cover, moving aside as the beast thunders past. Skidding to a halt, the giant spins round with startling quickness, its enormous fists swinging through the air.

Caeleb rushes to meet it, blocking its powerful blows against his shield. Nyms and Lansbury circle the creature's flanks, preparing to deliver their own offensive. As you move to aid them, something leaps out from the darkness and slams into your side. Startled, you are flung against one of the pillars, as an agile shadowstalker, clad in night-black leathers, swings twin swords in your direction. You duck beneath the attack, the swords slashing through the stone as if it was paper.

Rolling to the side, you spring to your feet, as the shadowstalker advances.

'You are the one who has turned away from shadow,' hisses a woman's voice from behind the black, polished mask. 'You are not worthy to bear the shadow mark.'

'Then try and take it from me,' you growl. Turn to 904.

800

Fetch clenches his fists angrily. 'I was too late! Avian sent me there to find an artefact – a talisman. He was fearful it might fall into Zul's hands. The necromancers must already have it!'

Fetch lowers his shaking hands with a heavy sigh. 'It is no matter. Zul will be crushed. Avian will see to that.'

'He sent me on a mission also,' you state, remembering back to that fateful moment in Talanost, amidst the chaos and destruction. 'I have to stop him from closing the gate. If he tries, he will fail.'

Fetch's eyes widen. 'Really? How interesting. I'll deliver your message myself, if I am not already too late. Although, Avian is rarely turned from a course of action, once he sets his mind to it.'

Turn to 792 to ask another question.

801

Searching the ogre's filthy belongings, you find a leather pouch containing 50 gold crowns. You may also help yourself to one of the following special rewards:

Wrecking ball	Primal gauntlets	Beast's harness
(left hand: club)	(gloves)	(chest)
+2 speed +5 brawn	+1 speed +4 brawn	+2 speed +4 armour
Ability: demolish	Ability: merciless	Ability: knockdown

When you have made your decision, turn to 824.

802

Lansbury's warning forces you to hesitate. A second later and the dark-robed assassin has vanished, leaving behind a scorched circle on the ground where he was once standing.

'Who was that?' asks Nyms suspiciously. 'You knew him?'

You shake your head. 'Our paths have crossed, but, as for his motives ... I wonder what he was searching for?'

'We should have stopped him!' snaps Caeleb angrily, stepping over the debris. He bends down and picks up a sword, turning it over in the flickering light. 'They have no respect for the dead or the living.'

You turn to Lansbury with an accusatory stare. 'Why did you stop me?'

The medic looks startled by your tone. 'Why else – he reeked of the old magic. Whatever that creature is, it is no concern of ours.'

'Well, he clearly wanted something badly enough to fight for it.' You pick your way over to the black-robed bodies, lying amongst the knight's ransacked belongings. Searching the mages you find 50 gold crowns and may help yourself to one of the following:

Dark therapy	Ghoulish gloop (2 uses)	Bewitched boots
(talisman)	(backpack)	(feet)
+1 speed	Use any time in combat to	+2 speed +2 magic
Ability: regrowth	raise your *armour* by 2	Ability: dominate
	for the duration of	
	the combat	

When you have made your decision, turn to 793.

803

'Really?' The trader gives a low whistle. 'Want to be a great warrior of legend, eh? Well, I reckon these are exactly what you need.' He reaches inside the chest and produces three items, which he lays carefully before you. 'Now, in the right hands,' he catches your eye, his mouth twisting into a smile, 'they could win you a war. Tell me, how can anyone put a price on that?' He rubs his jaw thoughtfully. 'It pains me but, 900 gold crowns? Yes, that's a fair price. Risked my life for those little beauties.'

You may purchase any of the following items for 900 gold crowns each:

Raider's tunic	Talanost's wall	Mortuary gauntlets
(chest)	(left-hand: shield)	(gloves)
+2 speed +4 brawn	+2 speed +5 armour	+1 speed +3 armour
Ability: retaliation	Ability: deflect	Ability: acid

After you have made your decision, you can ask to see Waldo's special deals (turn to 815) or bid the trader farewell (turn to 789).

804

You race along the tunnel, passing the broken remains of Arthurian's lantern. As the passageway widens into a circular chamber, you suddenly experience a wave of nausea. You stagger, falling to your knees, your vision blurred.

'What's happening?' you croak hoarsely.

From somewhere up ahead you hear the crack of magic and someone crying out in pain. Gritting your teeth, you push yourself back to your feet. A white light lurches into view as you stumble onwards, its radiance is almost blinding.

You stagger and fall, your strength rapidly ebbing away. From your mark, you feel a terrible burning. Again, you struggle to rise, another flash of magic illuminating the space around you.

As you regain your feet, you see that you are standing in a large runed circle. At its centre is a glowing white figure – an angel, with immense wings arching out from its flowing robes. The face is that of a wizened old man, his features drawn into a scowl of rage. 'Be gone, infidels!'

Arthurian is on his knees, gasping for air. 'These are holy inscriptions,' he rasps. 'They are weakening us. Try and break ... the seals.'

'You cannot trespass here!' booms the angel, its pale form flickering like a ghostly flame.

'What is this?' you wheeze, struggling to focus.

'It's the master architect,' pants Arthurian. 'Part of him, part of his soul remains here to guard the tomb ...'

The angel throws backs its arms, summoning white flames into the palms of its hands. 'By holy light, I smite thee!'

You throw yourself into a dive, as the flames smash into the ground, sending stone fragments flying through the air. As the dust clears, you catch sight of a raised rune, glowing with white light. You notice two more, gleaming at the edges of the circle.

'Break the seals,' cries Arthurian, stumbling breathlessly to his feet. 'It is the only way!'

	Speed	Brawn	Armour	Health
Architect	12	13	15	80
Holy flame	-	-	4	15
Holy circle	-	-	4	15
Holy shield	-	-	4	15

Special abilities

💀 Holy flame: The seal of flame adds 4 to the architect's damage score.

- Holy circle: At the end of every combat round, the circle heals the architect for 4 *health*. (Note: This ability cannot take the architect above his starting *health* of 80.)
- Holy shield: Once the seal of the shield has been reduced to zero *health*, the architect's *armour* is lowered to 8 for the remainder of the combat.

If you win a combat round, you can choose to strike the architect or one of the seals. If you destroy a seal, its ability no longer applies.

If you defeat this ghostly guardian, turn to 812. If you are defeated, turn to 796.

805

With the golem defeated, your attention turns to Fetch, who is struggling to unlock a wooden door at the end of the room. He is cursing and muttering to himself, casting desperate glances over his shoulder. With a grim smile, you advance on the assassin.

'Going somewhere, Fetch?

There is the click of a lock. But it is too late . . .

You rush forward, slamming into the black-robed man and pinning him against the door.

'Don't try any of that magic business,' you growl in his ear. 'I'm done with the little excursions.'

'I couldn't if I wanted to,' spits the assassin. 'My magic is spent . . .'

'Good.' You spin him around to face you, peering intently into the shadows of his black hood. 'Now, I want some answers, Fetch'.

If you have the words *black book* written on your hero sheet, turn to 913. Otherwise turn to 810.

806

The endless rain drums against the floor of the cavern, splashing on the uneven rocks and forming ever-deepening pools of muddy water. You huddle in your cloak, shivering uncontrollably. You wish it was just the cold that was making you tremble, but deep down you know it is the result of your craving – the need to absorb more magic.

At the other side of the room, the shadow energy has started to coalesce, moulding itself back into a human shape. Once formed, the ghost drifts back into the robber's clothing, fleshing out its grime-stained folds.

There is a staccato flash of lightning.

When the brightness abates, you see that the robber is now lying on the ground – perfectly healed. With a gasp, he sits up, reaching instinctively for his throat.

You step forward, holding up his silver crucifix. 'Looking for something?' you ask.

The robber stumbles to his feet, his expression confused. 'Why do you still haunt me?' he mutters, shaking his head. 'Why do you test me?'

You throw the crucifix at his feet, watching as he scrabbles in the muddy water to retrieve it. 'Show me your arm.'

The robber looks up, a single crazed eye peering at you through long tangles of hair. 'What?'

'Your arm,' you insist angrily. 'You must have a mark!'

The robber straightens, regarding you thoughtfully. Slowly, he places his crucifix back over his head, tugging it down to lie over his chest. Then he proceeds to remove his coat. Holding it out at arm's length, he lets it drop into the mud. The military jerkin is short-sleeved, revealing a purple brand running up the entire length of his right arm. It is identical to your own.

'Are you one of them?' he asks, his voice trembling. 'This is not my body. I am not … a shadow spawn!'

'Then tell me everything,' you insist, folding your arms. Turn to 920.

807

At the foot of the stairs, two spluttering torches frame a grotesque creature, its back hunched over to allow its hulking form to fit under the low ceiling. It is humanoid, with coarse black hair covering much of its body. Tendrils of gooey saliva drip from beneath its fanged muzzle, as it drags a whetstone back and forth across a black-bladed sword. The beast appears to be guarding an iron door, set into the earthen wall behind it.

'Wha ...?' The beast looks up, its beady-yellow eyes squinting towards you.

Without slowing, you raise your hands and release a blast of shadow magic. The beast is blown backwards, smashing the door off its hinges and taking part of the wall with it. The air fills with the stench of brimstone and burnt hair. Wrinkling your nose, you step past the charred body and enter the room beyond.

Through the dust and smoke, you see that you have entered a large cave. Dark shapes are silhouetted by a bright golden light, pulsing from a circular object that rests on an ornate podium. There is something in its design that reminds you of the shadow gate; perhaps the steam that belches from holes around its edge or the glyphs that shimmer and crackle with magic.

For now, the dark shapes are of more immediate concern – a horde of misshapen creatures, each one a different aberration of nature. They clutch a makeshift assortment of mean weapons, their snarls and hisses echoing in the chamber.

But they hold their ground. Uncertain. A few eyes dart sideways, looking back towards the rear of the cave, where a black figure stands guard next to the strange machine. This one looks human, clad in black plates of armour, their face hidden in the shadows of their cowl.

'You cannot stop us, betrayer!' The voice is rasping, weak-sounding, its words carried on short, ragged breaths. 'Did you really think the legion could be defeated – that the black guard would be denied its revenge?' Armour and leather creak as the warrior raises an arm, pointing a finger towards you. 'Forward my fiends. Bring me its head!'

The monsters break ranks, rushing forward in an undisciplined mob. As their stinking bodies descend on your position, you feel the shadow mark blossom into life, relishing the battle to come.

You weave in amongst the beasts' clumsy strikes, moving with uncanny speed. Your weapons slice through armour and hide, leaving a deafening clamour of pained cries in your wake. A reptilian creature hefts a claymore above its head. You dodge aside as the weapon is brought down, with enough strength to have hewn a man in two.

Stepping onto the blade, you leap into the air, kicking the beast backwards into a crowd of its brethren. You land in a spin, cutting down more of the infernal creatures, your laughter mingling with their howls and roars.

You edge slowly towards the back of the cave, where the hooded warrior presides over the battle, his thick arms folded across his chest. 'You cannot stop us,' wheezes the voice in your ear.

Suddenly, the flat of a blade catches you across the back. You stagger, knocked forwards by the strength of the blow. Turning, you see a mountain of muscle bearing down on you, a sword held in each of its four hands. You dodge the first strike, catching the next and turning it away with your weapon. But the other blows hit home, drawing blood and beating you back against the wall.

Then you hear the crackle of magic and a hollering cry. Something is moving quickly through the ranks of shadow spawn, glowing swords exploding through weapons and armour. 'Nyms!' you call with relief. 'A welcome sight.'

The swordsman fights with a brutal efficiency, his quick arcs and jabs downing his stunned opponents. 'Hate to see you have all the fun,' he grunts, vaulting off the back of one of the creatures, to spin into your four-armed adversary. 'Get the hooded one!' he shouts. 'I've got your back.' He cuts down the giant, his magic swords blazing trails through the air.

You advance on the leader, smashing through the remaining shadow spawn that get in your way. As you near, you realise the warrior is a veritable giant, standing over two metres tall. His entire body is encased in thick sheets of shadow-forged armour; even his face is masked by an iron plate, its surface carved with intricate runes.

'So it comes to this,' wheezes the voice. The warrior uncrosses his arms, revealing a metal disc embedded in his chest. 'You know nothing of power, Nevarin.' He puts a gloved hand to the disc and then turns it. Suddenly his whole body changes, shifting into a ghostly shadow of purple light. With dark laughter echoing all about you, the warrior summons crackling flames to his hands. 'The black guard will have its victory,' he hisses. 'And all of Valeron will fall!'

You must now fight this dark general:

	Speed	Magic	Armour	Health
Daarko	15	-	-	140
Shadow form	-	11	12	-
Flame form	-	16	10	-
Rock form	-	13	20	-

Special abilities

 Elemental master: Daarko can change his form, giving him different abilities and strengths. At the start of each combat round roll a die. If the result is `⚀` or `⚁` he assumes his shadow form, `⚂` or `⚃` the flame form, and `⚄` or `⚅` the rock form. Daarko starts the first round of combat in his shadow form.

 Shadow form: Each time you take health damage from Daarko you must lower your *brawn* or *magic* (whichever is highest) by 2.

 Flame form: At the end of every combat round, you must take 4 damage from the flames that surround Daarko. This ability ignores *armour*.

 Rock form: If your hero takes health damage from Daarko, you are knocked to the ground. You must reduce your *speed* by 1 for the next combat round only.

If you defeat Daarko, restore any lowered attributes and then turn to 935.

808

On seeing their leader defeated, the necromancers scramble for the exit, the remnants of their magic sparking uselessly in the air. With a cry of triumph, Arthurian drops to the ground, shaking off the last of his magical shackles.

Caeleb kneels before the knight, his head bowed. 'Arthurian, My lord. My protector.'

Ignoring ceremony, you stride over to Arthurian and put out your hand. The warrior meets your gaze and smiles. He takes your hand and shakes it firmly. His touch is cold, like ice ...

'Soul and body are back together again,' you smirk, looking over his ghostly features. The eyes are the same as you remember, but they now stare back at you from a handsome face, framed by bright locks of long curling hair.

'This life is fading,' states the knight, glancing back towards his tomb. 'Take my horn. Do it quickly.'

Without hesitation, you hurry to the open tomb. Inside the cavity, lined with plush white cloth, you find an ivory horn. Carefully, you lift it out of the tomb and carry it over to the waiting knight.

'Good ... I can bind my essence to this.' He puts out a pale hand to touch the horn. 'When you need me, I will come to your aid – just as the bards always said I would.' His eyes meet your own, his lips forming a knowing smile. 'I suppose one part of my legend should stay faithful to the truth.'

Before you can answer, there is a sound – like a long drawn-out sigh – which echoes around the chamber. The ghostly form of Arthurian vanishes, his runed armour clattering to the ground. For the briefest second, the horn glows with a pale radiance ... then the light is gone.

You have now gained Arthurian's horn – a sacred relic:

Arthurian's horn (1 use)
(backpack)
Use any time in combat
to summon Arthurian. He
will automatically inflict 20
damage to a single opponent,
ignoring *armour*

Caeleb slowly gets to his feet, tugging off his helm to reveal eyes wide with astonishment. 'The horn ...' he gasps, reaching out and touching it with reverence.

Nyms walks over and examines the runed armour with his foot, pushing the breastplate over to reveal an engraved insignia – a chalice, surrounded by a circle of seven stars.

'Arthurian's coat of arms ...' Caeleb's expression hardens, his eyes coming to rest on the shattered remains of Arthurian's tomb. 'Zul will pay for this sacrilege.'

Lansbury places a comforting hand on the warrior's shoulder. 'We did a good deed this day. Be content with that, Caeleb, at least.'

You take the horn and place it in your backpack. It could prove to be a vital weapon in the upcoming battle against Zul. With little else of interest in the chamber, you leave Arthurian's tomb and head back into the bone fields. Return to the Act 3 quest map.

809

The general jumps free of her mount, somersaulting through the air on currents of magic. As she touches down at the base of the crater, tendrils of smoke begin to curl around her fists, forming themselves into two deadly scimitars.

'You chose the wrong side,' she states coldly, striding purposefully towards you. 'The black guard will win this day. We will reclaim the Nexus – and all will kneel before the legion!'

Your weapons clash, sending dark waves of magic rippling out across the battlefield. 'Your gate got destroyed,' you hiss between blows. 'The invasion is over!'

'No, you fool,' the general kicks you back, following up with another flurry of strikes. 'There is another way.' Before you can reply, the warrior's blades come at you again. It is time to fight:

	Speed	Brawn	Armour	Health
Sanrah	15	10	11	140

Special abilities

◗ Retaliation: Each time your damage score / damage dice causes health damage to Sanrah, she immediately retaliates by inflicting 1 damage die back to your hero, ignoring *armour*. (Note: if your blow reduces Sanrah to zero health, you do not take damage from *retaliation*.)

◗ Inquisitor's wrath: If you have the word *rival* on your hero sheet, then Mathis will wade into the combat at the start of round 3, adding 2 to your damage score for the remainder of the combat.

◗ Healer's gift: If you have the word *companion* on your hero sheet, then Lansbury will heal you once, any time during this combat, restoring 12 *health*.

If you manage to defeat this dark general, restore your *health* and turn to **855**. If you are defeated, then you must return to an earlier point. Restore your *health*, then turn to **905**.

810

Your shadow mark flares brighter as your grip on the assassin tightens.

'Tell me about the book. The Grimoire of Naraghost. Why was it so important?'

Fetch gives a wheezing cough. 'It does not concern you. Now release . . .'

'TELL ME!' you growl, shaking him angrily. 'I deserve to know. I risked my life for it.'

'Yes,' hisses the assassin, 'and you chose to leave it behind with that rotting crusader.'

'It was a thing of evil. It needed to remain there.'

'No,' sneers Fetch, staring hard into your eyes. 'It needed to be taken from there.'

'Why?' Your brow furrows with suspicion. 'What's so special about a book?'

'It belonged to a navigator,' hisses the assassin. 'One of the elves. My master had been searching for it for a very long time. Little did he know it had been right under his nose all along.'

'And your master? Who do you serve, Fetch?'

The man's pale lips curve into a smile. 'Avian Dale. I think you know him.'

You shake your head, scowling with contempt. 'Lies! That can't be true. Avian is a good man.'

'Know him so well do you? Let me tell you something about Avian. He has a special talent – a talent for finding people like us. Those who are broken and need fixing; those he can breathe new life into . . . give them fresh purpose.'

You release the assassin and back away, no longer certain if what he says is the truth or just more poison. 'And the book,' you ask, your voice little more than a whisper. 'Why did he need it? The crusader said it was evil.'

Fetch's glittering eyes fix on your own. 'It is evil, Nevarin. And that is why it had to be taken, far away from Tithebury.'

Your confused expression urges Fetch to say more.

'The book is a set of charts, to navigate through the shroud. It is how the elves used to travel between worlds, before they built the gates.'

'The shroud.' The word is familiar. You sift through your memories, trying to remember ... 'Lansbury. It has something to do with old magic.'

Fetch snorts. 'It is the birthplace of magic. It *is* magic. Anything that touches or passes through that place is changed ... and not always for the better.'

'And that's what happened to the book?' you ask intently. 'It was corrupted by this magic?'

Fetch gives a rasping laugh. 'You are learning fast, Nevarin. Yes, the book is dangerous – something that will always draw unwanted attention.'

You smirk, shaking your head. 'So you and Avian were doing the locals a favour. Never had you down as the altruistic sort.'

Fetch leans in close, fixing his eyes on your own. 'There is much you don't know about me, Nevarin.' Turn to 792.

811

You approach the strange podium, its whirring and clicking almost deafening in the sudden silence. Occasionally, whistling jets of steam belch out from the many cavities around its side, expelling a foul-smelling gas into the air. Warily, you lean over, to inspect the glowing orb that rests on top of the pedestal. Through the clouded glass, you glimpse a ball of fleshy tissue, beating rhythmically like a heart. Metal hooks dig into its fatty folds, anchoring it to a metal base where glyphs and runes glimmer with magic.

'That looks pretty. What's it do?' asks Nyms, picking his way over to the machine.

'It reminds me of the shadow gate,' you reply, noting the strange tubes that extend from the base of the podium. They snake across the cavern floor, disappearing into the ground at various points, like the roots of a tree.

'It looks… alive,' says Nyms, tapping the side of the glass. 'I suppose we should go find the others.'

'No need,' you reply with a grimace. There is the crunch of boots on the stairs, accompanied by clinking armour and muffled voices. A second later and Mathis marches in through the blasted hole, his white enamelled armour streaked with blood and dust. In his hands he grips a mighty warhammer, its stone head rippling with holy magic.

Behind the inquisitor, you recognise Redguard's medic, Lansbury, and Avian Dale, your master. Both are clad in similar armour to the inquisitor, the polished white plate spattered with mud. Finally, bringing up the rear, is a group of nervous-looking guards, their white tabards stitched with the black raven of Ravenwing's militia.

'You started without us,' scowls Inquisitor Mathis, glaring at the piles of corpses that litter the room.

'They weren't that keen on waiting,' you retort, meeting his cold glare with one of your own. 'Glad you could finally make it.'

'Indeed,' sniffs the inquisitor. 'And what have you found?' He strides over to the glowing podium. 'Avian?'

The mage hurries forward, his eyes wide with interest. 'It's elven,' he gasps, running his hands over the glyphs that adorn the side of the podium. 'I've seen their like before, but this is new. Zul must have found it in the Dune Sea. I can't believe…' He moves around the glass sphere, inspecting the beating organ trapped inside. 'This is a magic anomaly. Pressed into service… but for what I can't fathom.'

Lansbury appears at your side. She places a hand on your own and squeezes it tight. 'Good to see you,' she whispers. You glance her way, noting her tired expression. The past week has been trying on the elderly medic's reserves of strength, healing those who have fallen foul of the shadow spawn. But she has never complained or faltered from her duty. She grins with mischief, as she flicks her eyes towards Mathis. 'I'm afraid the company has been a little trying of late.'

'Lansbury!' snaps the inquisitor. 'Your thoughts please.'

The medic quickly releases your hand and moves forward. 'Yes, Inquisitor Mathis. Hmm, I'd say, these are not unusual.' She taps one of the tube-like tentacles with the end of her staff. 'A distortion of druidic practice. They're anchoring this thing to ley lines, tapping into deep magic.' She looks up at the ceiling of the cavern, bathed in the golden glow from the machine. 'This whole place is acting as a fount of power – but for what?'

Mathis raises his warhammer, its inscribed headpiece crackling with lightning. 'I have heard enough. Any fool can see this is the work of demons. It is a thing of evil – and must be destroyed!'

'No!' Avian tries to intercede, but the inquisitor shrugs him aside, bringing his weapon down hard onto the machine. There is a deafening boom as the orb shatters, dispelling its magic out into the cave. The force of the blast blows you backwards, slamming you into the far wall. The golden light winks out and then there is darkness.

The cavern begins to shake, dislodging rock and dust from its ceiling.

'What's happening?' cries a voice – one of the guardsmen.

Suddenly, a cold blue light flashes into being, glimmering around Avian's outstretched palms. The mage is still standing, although blood from a cut streams down one side of his face.

'A good question,' snarls Mathis, pushing himself up from the rubble. He turns to the machine, which is now a twisted carcass of metal and flesh. 'At least this abomination is dead.'

From somewhere above, you hear a noise – loud and powerful enough to loosen more rocks from the ceiling. 'We have to get out of here,' you shout, helping Lansbury to her feet. 'Or we'll be buried alive!' Lansbury stoops to pick up her staff, then follows you towards the stairs. Ravenwing's guards are already scrambling to get out of the cave, jostling each other in their haste to escape.

'You fool, Mathis!' barks Avian, his voice echoing in the chamber. 'We needed to study it – to understand why it was being guarded. I fear this was a grave mistake ...' Turn to **866**.

812

With a shriek of anguish, the angel flickers and is gone. Wearily, you drop to your knees, exhausted from the energy-sapping encounter.

'I thought the angels would be on our side,' you pant.

When you look up, you see that Arthurian is watching you with interest. He looks about to say something, but catches himself. Instead, he turns to face the doorway at the other side of the room.

'Yes. We are close. Come, the place I seek is just past the next chamber.'

Stumbling to your feet, you cast a last wary glance at the shattered circle of magic, before following him through the doorway. Turn to 787.

813

(Make a note of the word *rival* on your hero sheet.)

Overcome by a dark frenzy, you throw aside your weapons and turn to the statue. Black fire blazes in your hands as you grab the stone and rip it free from the plinth. As the remaining ghasts scramble towards you, hissing with rage, you swing the statue like a giant club, smashing their screaming bodies across the square.

The weight and momentum of your swing spins you around, throwing you face-to-face with the final ghast. Its lips pull back to emit a piercing shriek, blasting you with its noxious breath. Balking in disgust, you kick the creature away, then bring the remains of the crumbling statue down on top of it, smashing it to pieces. '*Now* you're history,' you grimace, kicking away the statue's goo-stained head.

Congratulations! The ghasts have been defeated. You may help yourself to one of the following rewards:

Drape of shadow	Scissor hands	Lexicon of bones
(cloak)	(gloves)	(left hand: spell book)
+2 speed +4 brawn	+1 speed +4 brawn	+2 speed +5 magic
Ability: chill touch	Ability: piercing	Ability: haunt
		(requirement: mage)

When you have made your decision, turn to 863.

814

The newly-absorbed magic twists beneath your skin, winding its way past muscle and sinew. When it reaches your heart, you feel its icy coils tighten ... extinguishing the warmth and light of the dryad queen's enchantment. In its place there is now something darker – something borne of that same magic, but corrupted somehow to serve a more wicked purpose.

If you choose to accept this new power, the shadow ranger has the following abilities:

Black rain (co): (requires a bow in the left hand.) Instead of rolling for a damage score after winning a round, you can use *black rain* to shower your enemies with dark magic. Roll 1 damage die and apply the result to each of your opponents, ignoring their *armour*. You can only use *black rain* once per combat.

Thorn fist (co): When your opponent's damage score causes health damage, you can immediately retaliate using your thorn fist, inflicting 2 damage dice back to them, ignoring *armour*. You can only use *thorn fist* once per combat.

Once you have made your decision, turn to 834.

815

'Yes, my special deals. Well let's take a look ...' he reaches inside the chest and produces three items, which he lays out on the ash-covered ground. 'For you, 450 gold crowns. I can't say fairer than that.'

You may purchase any of the following items for 450 gold crowns each:

Barbarous boots	Khana's revenge	Valiant spaulders
(feet)	(ring)	(cloak)
+2 speed +3 brawn	+2 brawn	+2 speed +2 brawn
Ability: savagery	Ability: bleed	Ability: overpower

After you have made your decision, you can ask to see Waldo's rare items (turn to 803) or bid the trader farewell (turn to 789)

816

The robber rushes forward, looking to stab you in the chest. You lean to the side, shouldering into him as he oversteps his lunge. The man stumbles away, his wildly-tilting lantern casting whirling ribbons of light around the chamber.

'You can't kill me,' he snarls, righting his balance. 'I can't die.'

'Me neither,' you add dryly. You turn your arm, to allow him a glimpse of your shadow mark.

The man gasps, drawing back. 'No, no it can't be. You mock me! You mock me!'

With a shriek he charges once again, his jewelled dagger flashing in the lantern light. You must now fight:

	Speed	Brawn	Armour	Health
Tomb robber	12	11	8	70

Special abilities
- Keen edge: If the robber rolls a 🎲 or 🎲 for their damage score, they can add 4 to the result.

If you defeat the tomb robber, turn to **888**. If you are defeated, turn to **796**.

817
Legendary monster: Gorgis Iron-mane

The crypt has become your hunting ground. Stepping over the bodies of the black-robed necromancers, you plunge onwards – the cold fire from your shadow mark illuminating the narrow, claustrophobic passageways. Ahead you can hear chanting, echoing from the dark.

More of Zul's followers.

Your hands clench around your weapons, sending magic sparking along the runes that writhe and twist along your arm. Your senses are heightened, your body pulses with shadow energy. All fear has gone – replaced now by a hungry, insatiable need to find more victims.

You are not disappointed.

As the next chamber opens up, you see seven necromancers gathered in a tight circle around an open tomb. Black magic pours from their fingers into the exposed body of a knight, seeking to put life back into its rust-spattered armour.

Then your attention shifts.

From the edge of the room, four black figures detach themselves from the shadows and start towards you. They appear to be assassins, their faces hidden behind black masks. There is the ring of steel as curved blades are drawn, catching the eerie purple light flickering along your branded flesh.

The nearest assassin slows, as if uncertain. You glance down at the shadow mark and then look up smiling.

'You wonder if I am a friend or a foe?' you nod wryly.

The four masked assassins share a sideways glance.

'Or perhaps it is fear that stays your attack?'

You raise your weapons, the cold fury of the mark coursing through your body, thumping in your ears, crying out for release ...

'And so you should fear me!'

You spring forward, meeting the leader head on. Your weapons clash, teeth gritted, as you both strain against each other's murderous intent. You can hear his ragged breathing from behind the polished mask ... then you are moving, twisting and turning in a dreadful dance.

Steel sparks.

Magic crackles.

There are cries and screams – a body flies back through the air, crumpling to the ground. You jerk backwards, as a poisoned blade slices the air next to your face. Leaning to the side, you meet the next attack with the guard of your weapon. Then your magic flares once again, your weapons sweeping around in a deadly arc.

It is over in seconds. The assassins' smoking bodies lie around you, broken and lifeless.

The chanting stops and a heavy silence settles over the chamber.

As one, the necromancers turn to face you.

'Betrayer! The legion will not be stopped!'

Your eyes settle on the speaker – possibly the leader. His hand is already pulling a dagger from his belt. The others form up around him, readying spells.

There is a quiet calmness to their movements, almost an overconfidence. They have strength in numbers, yes. But they should never underestimate a Nevarin.

Magic is thrown towards you – sizzling through the air – but you are already moving, dizzyingly fast, leaving their futile barrage to smash harmlessly into the stone flagstones. Then you are cutting, slicing, burning, stabbing ... you have lost yourself to whatever nightmarish fury lies in that branded mark, that part of yourself that connects you to a past now long forgotten.

There are snarls from the dark.

As the last necromancer falls before you, your eyes settle on the archway at the far side of the chamber. Ragged shapes are now pouring out of the darkness – running on all fours like hounds. You glimpse knife-like claws and shaggy, black manes of fur.

Ghouls.

The baying creatures surge towards you, snapping and biting. You somersault over the first wave of attackers, landing agilely behind them. Surrounded on all sides by the undead host, you fall into a spin of whirling steel and magic ... your movements flowing from one form to the next.

Bodies press against your own, the air humming with snapping jaws and clawing talons. Steadily, you force them back, your weapons sweeping into a familiar rhythm – rising and falling, blocking and parrying.

Within minutes you stand alone. Your arms are slick with ghoul blood ... and maybe some of your own. You look down to see a knife sticking out of your thigh. You wonder how it got there ... and why it doesn't cause you pain.

Then a rumbling growl snaps you back to attention.

From beneath the archway, a gigantic ghoul is shuffling towards you. Its mane is thick and grey, spreading out across its massive shoulders and tightly-knotted arms.

Your eyes meet and in that quiet moment something is shared.

Then the beast's face twists into a snarl. You answer in kind, emitting an animal-like roar. Then you pounce:

	Speed	Brawn	Armour	Health
Gorgis	14	8	13	100

Special abilities

- Fatigue: You are exhausted from your previous battles. You must reduce your *brawn* and *magic* by 2 in this combat.
- Piercing: This powerful creature's claws ignore your *armour*.
- Iron-mane: The ghoul's hide is covered in a thick mantle of iron-like hair. You cannot use *piercing* or *impale* in this combat.

If you manage to defeat this savage foe, turn to 297.

818

As you approach the anomaly, your shadow mark starts to burn. You tug back your clothing to expose the branded serpents. Their purple runes are pulsing with their own dark life, mirroring the rhythmic beating coming from the strange growth.

'Do not go near it!' cries Lansbury. 'It will kill you!'

You glance over your shoulder. 'It doesn't look that dangerous ...'

Suddenly, you hear a sickening series of squelches. The growth has started to move, its long tendrils of rotted fungus ripping themselves free from the crumbling stone.

'Oh, that's not good,' cries Nyms. 'That's really not good.'

From the creature's mould-encrusted centre, a noxious steam escapes into the air, reeking of death and decay.

You raise your arm, covering your face from the eye-watering stench. As you do so, an agonising wail fills the room. In horror, you realise it is coming from the anomaly. It is trying to draw away from you, its bloated fungal body seeking to drag itself across the stone wall.

You glance over at your arm and the shadow mark that is burning with an intense heat, sending dark smoke curling up into the earthen chamber. Your eyes flick back to the anomaly. A sudden hunger, a longing for its power, overwhelms your senses. You take a step forward, arm outstretched, to try and absorb the magic.

The air ripples as some invisible force grips the anomaly and attempts to drag it towards your mark. In a desperate effort to defend itself, the anomaly sends thrashing tentacles whipping out through the air, seeking to knock you away:

	Speed	Magic	Armour	Health
Sentient anomaly	12	16	-	-

Special abilities

🌑 Absorption: You cannot harm this magical foe. If you win a combat round, roll one die. If you roll a ⚄ or greater then the anomaly's *magic* is reduced by 4. Once the anomaly's *magic* is reduced to zero then it has been successfully absorbed into the shadow mark.

🌑 Concentration: You cannot use potions or special abilities in this combat.

If you defeat the magic anomaly, turn to 922. If you are defeated, turn to 862.

819

'It was an experiment,' nods the mage. 'And we were the chosen. The black guard.' He lifts his head proudly, his eyes focusing on something distant, some other place and time. 'We were the first through the gate. We led the legion – a thousand to our name.' He blinks, his fingers caressing the scar on his cheek. 'Daarko built the machine. A genius. A master maker. Better at building than destroying. Always in that tower – the high, high, high tower.'

'So, the elves didn't create it?' you ask, surprised.

'It was built from what we found. The salvaged odds and ends from the elves, yes. From the first invasion.' He purses his lips, looking thoughtful. 'It could have worked. Zul's plan. But the mage shield. It blocked us. Wouldn't bring us here in time. Wouldn't let us back from the shroud ...'

'Why not use the shadow gate?' you shrug.

Lorcan sneers. 'Are you not listening to me? We were the first – the first to go to the shroud.' He waves a hand in an arc through the air. 'We didn't even know it was possible. To exist there. The elves

... the elves did it, dragging their pyramids, their cities through it. Through... through... but not *existing* there. Not like us.' He pauses for a moment, letting the echo of his words reverberate throughout the chamber. Then he continues. 'The man who speaks. He told me it would fail. That the machine would be broken. Daarko would have waited ... waited until the city was quiet. Dark of night. Then we would come. But it was broken. Broken.' He heaves a sigh. 'I must go back ... I must.'

Return to 928 to ask Lorcan another question, or turn to 939 to attack this deranged mage.

820

You are thrown against a stone wall, hitting it with force. There is the taste of blood and something wet against your face, as you crumple to the ground, moaning with pain.

'Look!'

You hear a cry from your left and the sound of booted feet.

Dizzily, you open your eyes, feeling nauseous as the stone chamber spins around you in a blur of colour.

'They're bleeding. It looks bad.'

The voice belongs to Nyms. You feel strong arms about your shoulders, helping to support you as you mumble groggily. 'Where am I?'

You feel a cold palm against your forehead. Struggling to focus, you can make out a white shape. Then there is a flash of white light. You flinch away from it, fearful that you are being transported once again. But instead, you feel a comforting warmth flow through your body, taking away the pain and restoring your vision.

Lansbury straightens, looking down at you with a petulant expression. 'What happened?' she asks briskly. 'One minute you were there and then ...' The medic snaps her fingers.

With Nyms' help you struggle back to your feet. Caeleb is watching you from the other side of his room, his helm removed and held under his arm. His eyes are narrowed, his expression one of distrust. 'We deserve an explanation,' he adds sternly. 'We were about to leave you here.'

You glance over, to see that the anomaly has drifted away to the other side of the room, its sparkling sheen barely visible in the pale light from Lansbury's staff.

'I think I moved back in time ... to the past ... Wait!' Your attention immediately shifts to the skeleton of the tomb robber, still lying sprawled amongst the dust and cobwebs.

'I don't understand.' You frown, walking over and kneeling beside the skeleton. 'Why hasn't this changed? ' You look up at Lansbury, begging for an explanation. 'I absorbed the magic. He was a Nevarin.'

The medic shrugs her shoulders. 'Time is a complex weave – it is not a single thread but many. If your story is true, your meddling may have changed one aspect, altered a single thread, maybe others, but the weave will still follow its course.'

Nyms blows out his cheeks. 'I think I preferred it when I was just hitting things. Can we do that again, please?' Spinning his blades, he follows Caeleb out of the chamber.

You get back to your feet, still frowning. 'I wonder why he was here – what he was looking for.'

'We rarely get the answers we seek,' sighs the medic, prodding the skeleton with the end of her staff. 'Even less so from the dead.'

Nodding, you give the skeleton a final cursory glance before leaving the room. Turn to 902.

821

You kick off from the rooftop, spinning and twisting over the glittering sea of bodies, firing bolts of black fire into their ranks. As bodies are blown aside in a rising crescendo of shrieks and snarls, you come to a perfect landing in front of Avian's shield. The creatures surrounding him pay you no mind – their black chitinous bodies a chaotic mishmash of scorpion and spider. Curved, barbed tails pummel against the glowing shield, whilst their giant mandibles spit sizzling globules of venom over its surface, attempting to burn their way through.

'No, you must run!' gasps Avian, his eyes going wide. 'There's too many of them!'

With a snarl of fury, you dive into the creatures' midst, hoping to buy time until aid can arrive. You must fight:

	Speed	Brawn	Armour	Health
Scarron	16	15	10	30
Scarron	15	12	8	25
Scarron	15	14	10	30
Scarron	15	12	8	25
Scarron	15	14	10	30
Avian's shield	-	-	-	100

Special abilities

🛡 A siege of scarrons: At the end of each combat round, each surviving scarron inflicts 5 damage to Avian's shield.

At the start of each round, choose the scarron you will be attacking. If you win, you can roll for damage against that scarron (or multiple scarrons, if you have an ability that lets you do so). If you lose the round, then your chosen scarron will strike back as a single opponent.

If you manage to survive to the start of the *seventh* combat round, with Avian's shield still intact (i.e. it still has *health*), then turn to **785**. (Special achievement: If you defeat all the scarrons before the end of the *sixth* combat round, then turn to **868**). If you are defeated, then you may return to an earlier point. Restore your *health*, then turn to **885**.

822

At the end of the corridor, another passageway branches to the left, ending in a statue of a knight, his head bowed. In the wall facing you is an open doorway, leading through into a small high-ceilinged room.

'Arthurian's treasure vault,' you state dourly, stepping through into the cobwebbed space. All of its treasures are now gone, stolen by thieves or by Zul's minions.

'This is a dead end,' growls Caeleb, gesturing to the statue at the end of the passageway. 'We'll have to go back.'

'Hmm ...' Lansbury raises her staff and walks forwards towards the knight. Her white light picks out its detailed features – a young man, with a fringe of hair curling out from beneath a chainmail coif. His eyes are closed, his hands resting on the pommel of his sword. Lansbury leans closer, then reaches forward with a finger, pushing the stone at the centre of the sword's guard. There is a click followed by a deep rumbling, as the statue slides back into a hidden recess, revealing a secret archway in the wall.

'Good find,' grins Nyms, nodding with approval.

Caeleb shoulders through the group. 'Let's finish this,' he murmurs. Turn to 842.

823

You follow Nyms, knowing that the swordsman is worryingly outnumbered by the necromancers. However, a blast of black light sears down from the sky, slamming into the ground and sending you reeling backwards. Another series of blasts pepper the courtyard, spraying you with dirt and black ash.

'Look to the roof! There's a ranger!'

Through the rain and dust, you see Nyms cutting his way through a group of shades, summoned by one of the mages. You tear your eyes away, quickly scanning the roof of the tomb ... as another blast of black fire hurtles in your direction.

You dodge aside, as the spell rips past you and slams into the stone tablet, leaving a charred fracture running across its base. Turning back to the fray, you notice that the blasts are coming from a small balcony set above the door of the tomb.

Quickly, you race towards the steps that lead into the building, but are drawn up short when you see that the pillars either side of the entrance are now glowing with purple light, casting a flickering barrier across the doorway.

There is a cry from behind you. Turning you see that Nyms is now surrounded by shades. Two of the necromancers have already fallen to the rogue's blades, but the remaining two have now retreated behind a pillar of stone, summoning further spells to bring down the swordsman.

More blasts tear into the ground; one of which hits Nyms and sends him sprawling backwards into the ash. He is quickly on his feet again, wincing with pain, as the shades rush in to attack.

'Any help would be appreciated!' he scowls, slicing his magical blades through the ghostly apparitions.

Your shadow mark courses with dark magic, heightening your senses and bolstering your strength. In an agile blur of cold fury, you charge into the black-robed mages, cutting them down before they have a chance to retaliate.

Leaping over their smouldering bodies, you hurtle onwards, towards the stone tablet. Its base is now fractured and crumbling; the neat inscriptions broken by zigzagging cracks. Throwing your strength and magic against the stone you break through the last of its shaky foundations.

You dodge out of the raining rubble, as the immense tablet topples forward towards the domed building. Swiftly, you leap onto its top-side and race forward along its length. At the last possible moment, you kick off from your makeshift bridge and dive through the air – landing agilely on the narrow balcony to face your surprised assailant. Turn to 784.

824

Ravenwing rallies his men, pushing them deep into the ranks of the shadow spawn. Their dark general has fallen – and already they seem to have lost their edge, their ranks becoming confused and ill-disciplined. They are no match for Ravenwing's militia: drilled to the limits of perfection, flowing from defensive shield formations into penetrative wedges of whirling death in an instant, giving the black guard no mercy, no chance for retaliation.

You are about to rejoin the battle when a deafening boom rips out across the sky, throwing you to your knees. For a moment, you cower, as the noise continues to bear down on you, almost a physical thing that pummels against your body, throbbing in your ears.

Then black snow begins to fall, settling across the blood-streaked ground. You look up to see that the doom orb is no more – where it had been hanging in the sky, there is now only a huge black cloud of ash, as big as an entire city.

'The mages did it,' you gasp. 'They destroyed the orb.'

There are cheers from all around you, as the resistance realise that their victory is now assured. For the shadow spawn, it appears they have arrived at a similar conclusion. Shrieking and wailing, the demoralised rabble turns and runs, scrabbling across the square like a dark plague of rats. Ravenwing's men are already finding their feet, quickly forming up again and ready to give chase. If you have the word *rival* on your hero sheet, turn to 858. If you have the word *companion*, turn to 918. If you have the word *apprentice*, turn to 907.

825

The anomaly's sparkling strands are almost hypnotic, blurring into intricate patterns of light as they dance before your vision. Mesmerised by its gentle radiance, you find yourself moving closer and closer, until you are almost touching its glowing, rhythmic form.

Then, in an instant, the web-like strands wrap around you, encasing you in a suffocating prison. There is a scream from somewhere behind you – then you are enveloped in a white light. You feel yourself falling forwards. Frantically, you put out your hands to cushion your fall, but there is nothing to hold on to – the space is empty, featureless. Then there is a rush of cold air followed by another flash.

You land heavily on your stomach, the air punched from your lungs. Rolling onto your back, you gasp for air, your whole body trembling.

'Lansbury?' you croak.

There is no answer.

Something is wrong ... different.

As you push yourself up, you realise that you are in the same chamber, but it has somehow changed. It is darker, night time – the rough-hewn walls cut by shadows of flickering torch light. Rain pours in torrents from the open shaft, the rain glittering as lightning flashes overhead.

You catch the sound of dirt being scraped beneath a boot heel ...

Agilely, you spring to your feet, your weapons drawn and ready.

In the corner of the room, a figure is watching you. They have one hand around a lantern and the other gripping a jewelled dagger.

'Who are you?' he snarls, his voice shaking with anger. 'Are you more spirits to punish me?' A peal of maddened laughter echoes around the chamber. 'Yes, yes. You are here to test me. Test my faith.'

He cautiously circles around you, a flash of lightning picking out his grime-stained features. The man is thin and wan, clad in a tattered black coat. It hangs open, revealing the faded remnants of a military uniform. Between his long and ragged hair, you catch a cruel smile.

'Did you think I would fail?' he spits with scorn. 'I am a great man. I was not born to this.' He holds out his dagger, his hand shaking. 'I can cut you, yes – yes. Do you bleed, spirit?'

You glance past the stranger, towards the entranceway in the far wall. It appears to be blocked by something. There is no sign of the skeleton or your companions.

Will you:

Attack the stranger?	867
Try and convince him you mean no harm?	889
Demand to know what he is doing here?	910

826

Your magic spears into the brain, sending its grey matter spraying in all directions. Then the chamber begins to shake violently, throwing you from side to side. Desperately, you struggle back to Avian's side, slipping and sliding as the ground continues to tremble. Taking hold of the unconscious mage, you summon a shield with the last reserves of Daarko's stolen magic...

Then the chamber explodes, throwing you out into empty space.

All around you, black smoke and debris whirl through the air, accompanied by a deafening boom of thunder. Then you are falling at tremendous speed, buffeted by strong winds – and the giant wads of charred flesh that slam against your shield. For several minutes you are caught in a spin. When you finally manage to right yourself, you see the city of Talanost stretching far, far below, like a grimy black stain across the landscape.

Your shield stutters and fails, winking out in a flurry of sparks. Clinging to Avian, you continue to drop through the smoggy clouds, plummeting towards the ruined rooftops. Even with your supernatural abilities, you doubt you will survive such a fall.

Below you, the market square tilts into view. The shadow spawn appear to be routing, scampering like a plague of rats through the narrow streets of the city. Ravenwing's men follow close on their heels, slashing and blasting at their fleeing enemy. It is a sight that brings some small satisfaction – the legion's attempt to wrest control of the city has clearly failed.

The buildings are rising towards you now at an unsettling speed. You close your eyes, bracing for impact, wondering – in these final moments – if Avian is the lucky one, not to have witnessed this ignoble end. The mage is still slumped in your arms, his head lolling against your chest.

Then some force hits you with the power of a sledgehammer. You are dragged sideways, away from the jagged rooftop that would surely have spelled your end. Twisting round, you try and see what has a hold of you, but there is nothing there. And yet, you can feel something pressing in on you, holding you in a constricted bubble. Then the force is gone and you are falling the rest of the way, slamming down into the dusty street. From your shadow mark, a purple light flows quickly across your broken body, mending the splintered bones and torn muscle.

You slide out from beneath Avian, staggering back to your feet. Amongst the smoking mounds of rubble, you spy some of the doom orb's pulpy remains. You may now help yourself to one of the following rewards:

Thalamus tiara	Cortical bulb	Stria of Genna
(head)	(left hand: wand)	(ring)
+2 speed +5 magic	+3 speed +5 magic	+1 magic +2 armour
Ability: haste	Ability: brain drain	Ability: shock!

A rattle of armour forces you to turn. Someone is stumbling through the mist towards you. If you have the word *rival* on your hero sheet turn to 896. Otherwise, turn to 901.

827

You absorb the tomb robber's essence, delighting in the wave of ecstasy that washes over you. (You may raise your *brawn* or *magic* score by 2 in your next combat.) Kneeling beside the robber's empty clothes, you search through his meagre belongings. You find

50 gold crowns and the following items, which you may take:

Shallow grave	Oil flask (2 uses)
(left hand: dagger)	(backpack)
+2 speed +3 brawn	Set alight and throw at your
Ability: savagery	opponent, causing 2 dice of
	damage ignoring *armour*. Use
	instead of rolling for a damage score

As you straighten, your eyes catch on the magic anomaly lurking across the other side of the room. Somehow, the creature must have brought you back in time. Looking over to the room's exit, you see the mould-covered anomaly covering the other side of the doorway, exactly as it had before. The robber had obviously been trapped here, unable to escape – his skeleton was the one that you found in the room.

Up above, the storm vents its fury, the rainwater bouncing and spraying from the walls of the rough-hewn shaft. Pulling your hood down low over your face, you step through the curtain of water and approach the time-shifting anomaly.

As before, the magical creature suddenly springs to life, its silken threads snapping around you. You cry out in pain, as the air is crushed from your lungs, the powerful tendrils gripping you tightly as they drag you forwards, towards a brightening white light. Turn to 820.

828

Avian drops his shield with a pained gasp. You rush to his side, putting an arm out to support him. He bats you away impatiently. 'I'm fine, I'm fine.' Frantically, he begins rummaging around in his robes, his gaze fixed on the gargantuan doom orb which still floats above the city.

'Ah, yes!' The mage pulls out a small square of patterned cloth. With a flick of the wrist, he sends the cloth billowing outwards – its length rapidly unfurling into a full-sized magic carpet. 'We can't leave the doom orb unchallenged!' He steps onto the carpet, then offers out his hand. 'If your magic is strong, I could use your aid.'

If you have a *magic* score of 24 or above, you may accompany Avian Dale. (Turn to 921.) Otherwise, you decline Avian's offer, wishing to focus your efforts on the ground battle. (Turn to 890.)

829

Fetch brushes the dust from his robes. 'I am the only one of my kind, as far as I know. My gift is unique – I was born with it.'

'You can travel wherever you want?' you ask in wonder.

'Not exactly,' he says, looking up and meeting your gaze. 'I must have a connection with the place.'

'But if you travel through the shroud, then aren't you ...'

Fetch nods, offering you a knowing smile. 'Yes, I am more demon now than man. Each time I travel I lose a little more of my humanity. But it is a small price to pay. I think you will agree?' His eyes flick to your shadow mark, a cruel sneer visible beneath the shadows of his hood.

Turn to 792 to ask another question.

830

You find Waldo at the edge of the camp. He is sitting on a stool beside his tethered pony, picking stones from its hooves with a hooked knife. When he sees you approach, he quickly gets to his feet, brushing himself down.

'Can't keep away, can you? Let me guess, you traded in that annoying swordsman at last?'

You pat the jingling pouch hanging at your belt. 'Ha, you really think I'd get this much for him?'

Waldo's eyes widen. 'The spoils of war, eh?' He quickly hops onto the seat of his cart to retrieve the magical chest.

To view the trader's special deals, turn to 815 if you are a warrior, 839 if you are a rogue or 914 if you are a mage. For the rarer and more expensive items, turn to 803 if you are a warrior, 903 if you are a rogue or 881 if you are a mage.

At the end of the corridor, another passageway branches to the left, ending in a statue of a knight, his head bowed. In the wall facing you is an immense door, fashioned from ivory and gold. Each of its panels has been intricately decorated, depicting a number of embossed scenes. As you edge closer, you see that they all feature a knight on horseback, battling a nightmarish menagerie of fearsome monsters. In the centre of the door is a gold circle and inset within it is an ivory chalice.

'Where does this lead to?' you ask in wonderment.

Lansbury moves her light closer to the door. 'These panels depict scenes from Arthurian legend. This could be the entrance to his tomb – or a treasure vault perhaps.'

Nyms places a hand against the centre of the door and pushes against it. Nothing happens. He looks back at the group with a meekish smile. 'OK, it was worth a try.'

'How does this open?' snaps Caeleb impatiently, glancing at Lansbury. 'Some magic?'

Lansbury steps back, her eyes quickly roving across the door's surface. 'I sense magic here – very old magic. But clearly Zul's followers couldn't open it ... or they never made it this far.'

'Then this is a dead end,' growls Caeleb, gesturing to the statue at the end of the passageway. 'We'll have to go back.'

'Hmm ...' Lansbury raises her staff and walks towards the knight.

Her white light picks out its detailed features – a young man, with a fringe of hair curling out from beneath a chainmail coif. His eyes are closed, his hands resting on the pommel of his sword. Lansbury leans closer; then reaches forward with a finger, pushing the stone at the centre of the sword's guard. There is a click followed by a deep rumbling, as the statue slides back into a hidden recess, revealing a secret archway in the wall.

'Good find,' grins Nyms, nodding with approval.

Caeleb shoulders through the group. 'Let's finish this,' he murmurs. Turn to 790.

832

(Make a note of the word *companion* on your hero sheet.)

Forced back against the shield, you are uncertain how long you will be able to hold off against these fearsome adversaries. Suddenly, a bright flash of light draws your attention skywards. From out of the smog, you see white shapes swooping down over the ruined city, their vapour trails blazing bright like comets. Beneath them, a series of explosions swell out across the square, cutting a vicious swathe through the tightly-packed ranks of shadow spawn.

'The airborne regulars!' You punch the air as the mages hurtle past on their flying carpets.

Then, at the far side of the square, you hear the resonating blast of a horn. From your vantage point, it is difficult to see through the thronging masses, but it looks like a battalion of Ravenwing's militia have made it across the city. You catch the glimmer of polished armour and a fluttering standard, proudly displaying the black raven. Aid has finally arrived.

For your victory over the decayers, you may now help yourself to the following reward:

Spore bombs (1 use)
(backpack)
Sporelicious destruction!
Ability: spore cloud

When you have updated your character sheet, turn to **895**.

833

The rain falls in relentless grey sheets, pounding the ash-covered ground and spattering off your cloak and hood. The mist that once afforded you cover has now dispersed, forcing your party to use the cover of the outlying tombs.

Minutes later, huddled cold and shivering beside the crumbling statue of some long-forgotten hero, you find yourselves looking out on a cracked stone square. At its far side stands the domed building, looking more like a temple than a tomb. A staircase leads up to its main entrance: an open doorway, flanked by two pillars of rune-covered stone.

'We're too late,' growls Caeleb.

You follow his gaze to a tall tablet of rock, rising several hundred metres into the chill grey sky. Perched on the rock's summit is a huge demonic creature.

Nyms sucks air through his teeth. 'Judah's light . . .'

The creature's skeletal body and tattered wings share a passing resemblance to a bone wyvern, but this monster is at least four times their size, its serrated-beak and talons covered in spiked iron plates.

'What is that?' you gasp.

'Some mockery of life,' hisses Lansbury, her grip tightening around her staff. 'Zul's forces are already here. We should go back.'

Caeleb turns in surprise. 'But their presence here only lends our task a greater urgency. We have to stop them raising Arthurian and more of his knights!'

Your eyes haven't left the undead creature, marvelling at the dark magics that have given it life. 'Are you suggesting that we try and slip past that?' A red fire burns in the creature's hollow eye sockets, forming a gleaming trail as its head roves back and forth. 'It's a sentry. It will alert others.'

'Bah, it's nothing worse than we've faced before,' says Nyms, drawing his twin blades. 'I have no fear of it. Besides,' he cocks his head to one side, his eyes flicking to Lansbury, 'we have a healer.'

The medic purses her lips. 'Don't be foolish. There is always another way. Look.' Lansbury points to a row of smaller outbuildings that form a ring around the temple. 'We can use those for cover and go around the other side. I'm sure this place will have another entrance of some sort.'

'What do you think?' asks Caeleb, his narrowed eyes peering at you through the visor of his helmet. 'If we don't make a decision soon I'll be standing here in fifty pounds of rusted steel.'

Will you:

Risk a frontal assault on the temple?	797
Look for a back entrance?	894

834

The ranger's belongings are now yours for the taking. You may choose one of the following:

Raven eye	Sinister shadows	Dark queen
(left hand: bow)	(ring)	(necklace)
+2 speed +3 brawn	+1 brawn +1 magic	+2 magic
Ability: bolt	Ability: vanish	Ability: heal

You move to the edge of the balcony and survey the rain-soaked courtyard below. The immense bone creature is now lying in a crumpled heap of tattered flesh and bone. Lansbury is administering healing to a wounded Caeleb. Meanwhile, Nyms has defeated the last of the shades.

He looks up and waves to you, then starts towards the entrance of the building, spinning his bloodied blades in his hands. Turn to **859**.

835

You follow Nyms, whose practised eye quickly spots a route up to the balcony. From a running start, you rely on speed to carry you up the side of a buttress, to where a gargoyle-like decoration provides a suitable hand-hold. From here, you leap across the face of the building, springing off the porch roof to propel yourself higher, grabbing the railings of the balustrade. With a grunt, you pull yourself over the side, where Nyms waits by the window, weapons drawn.

'Blasting through the wall would have been easier,' you grimace, pushing yourself back to your feet.

Nyms rolls his eyes at you, before ducking through the window. You follow, drawing your weapons in readiness. The room beyond appears to be a library, with dozens of shelves filled with books and scrolls. Nyms has already crossed the space, taking position next to a half-open door. You hear voices coming from the other side.

At your bidding, your shadow mark pulses into life, flooding you with its power. You reach out, sensing for signs of shadow magic. The place reeks of it, as if every stone of the building is emanating a dark presence. But not as strong as the creatures outside this room. You see the outline of their bodies through the wall, marching along what you assume is a corridor. There are three of them, one shimmering more radiantly than the others. The most powerful – a Nevarin, perhaps.

You realise you must act quickly, before they sense your presence. You look to Nyms, raising three fingers. The swordsman nods, indicating his readiness.

You move to the door, waiting for them to move past. But the brightest one has slowed.

'Wait!' You hear a woman's voice – cold and commanding. 'Something is wrong.'

She turns back to the door. Then kicks it open.

You see an arm and grab it, pulling the woman into the room. She is clad in dark robes, shimmering with purple glyphs. With a snarl, she raises a gloved hand, a spell starting to form at the tips of her fingers. You slap it away, bringing your weapons down faster than she can react. From the other side of the door, you hear weapons clashing and sparking.

You leap over the woman's body, ignoring the glimmering shadow magic that is starting to coalesce around it. Through the door, you find yourself on a balcony, stretching around the edges of a large, rectangular hall. Nyms is battling a shadow spawn, an ugly beast with a face full of fanged teeth. It wields twin axes which hiss and flare with an angry red magic. Its companion already lies dead, slumped against the wall.

'Nevarin!'

There is the sound of wood splintering. You spin round, to see three black snakes springing towards you from the other side of the balcony. Their scaled bodies wrap around you, pinning your arms to your side and dragging you off your feet. Then you are flying across the hall, to where a grinning warrior has his arm extended. The snakes are flowing out from his shadow mark, pulling you within range of his venom-dripping dagger. You must fight:

	Speed	Brawn	Armour	Health
Viprus	14	13	10	100
Snakes	-	-	8	50

Special abilities

🛡 Tight spot: You are entangled in the snake's shadowy coils, restricting your movement and sapping at your strength. Until the snakes are defeated, you must lower your *speed* by 1 and take 5 damage, ignoring *armour*, at the end of every combat round.

🛡 Deadly venom: Once you have taken health damage from Viprus, you must automatically lose 3 *health* at the end of each combat round.

In this combat you roll against Viprus's *speed*. If you win the round, you may choose to strike against Viprus or his snakes. Once Viprus is reduced to zero *health*, the combat is won.

If you are able to defeat this mutated monster, turn to **938**.

836

The passageway is swathed in darkness. Lansbury utters a word of command, summoning a white light to the head of her staff. Holding it out before her, the medic takes the lead down the narrow corridor, the magical light dancing along the smooth stone walls.

You stumble after her with your head bowed. Each step is a challenge – your limbs ache and your vision is blurred. The mark on your arm spits and hisses, as if enduring its own private battle with the strange aura that surrounds this place.

The further you progress from the inscribed room, the better you start to feel. As the passageway angles downwards, deeper into the earth, you find yourself catching up with the medic.

'What did you mean ... old magic?' you ask, rubbing your sleeve where the shadow mark still burns.

Lansbury gives you a sideways glance. 'The Dwarves ... they were the first to discover the shroud. They were the first to commune with the spirits of that other place.'

'The shroud?'

Lansbury takes a sharp intake of breath. You follow her gaze, to where the passageway ends in a decorative archway. Sprawled on the ground in front of it is a dark-robed mage. They are lying on their back, their gloved hands gripping a dagger that protrudes from their chest.

Blood is smeared across the stone floor.

Next to the body, set back within a cobwebbed recess, is the statue of a man – a broad-shouldered warrior, encased in elaborate plate armour. The detail is almost lifelike.

Nyms races over to the mage and kneels beside them. After several seconds, he looks back and shakes his head. As you near, you see that the mage is indeed dead – his eyes stare up at the ceiling; his face frozen in an agonised contortion.

'Valentine D'Azzuro.'

Caeleb whispers the name, etched into the base of the statue.

'Who was he?' you ask, studying the stone figure closely. He was clearly a great warrior of some description – the hard solemn face is crisscrossed with a myriad of ugly scars.

'He was an inquisitor, before he became a Tor Knight,' says Caeleb. 'This must be his final resting place.' He turns to the archway, where a trail of blood snakes away into the dark.

'Several resting places,' adds Nyms darkly, prodding the body of the mage with one of his boots. 'Work of an assassin, by the looks of it. That blade was poisoned.'

From somewhere up ahead you hear a noise, like the smashing of pottery, followed by an angry muttering. Drawing your weapons, you follow Caeleb's lead as the warrior ducks underneath the archway and continues into the tomb. Turn to 900.

837

With a grimace, Fetch pulls back his hood – to reveal a face that is burnt and scarred. Veins stand out like cords across his pulpy, ruined flesh, branching past dark bruises and jagged scar tissue. You instinctively draw back, unable to speak.

'Not a pretty sight is it?' he hisses. 'Avian found me in the dungeons of the inquisition. I was there for ... questioning.' He tugs his hood back over his head, hiding it once again in shadow.

'What happened?' you ask hoarsely, still shaken by what you have seen.

'I have a unique gift,' states Fetch with a hint of bitterness. 'You have seen it. The ability to move between places,' he clicks his fingers,

'...instantly. And like all unique gifts, the inquisition want it – they want to study it, learn about it, punish it ...'

'And Avian rescued you?'

Fetch snivels with amusement. 'I would hardly call him a knight in shining armour, but yes – he has connections. He is very powerful – and he always gets what he wants, eventually.'

Return to 792 to ask another question.

838

You are thrown against a stone wall, hitting it with force. There is the taste of blood and something wet against your face, as you crumple to the ground, moaning with pain.

'Look!'

You hear a cry from your left and the sound of booted feet.

Dizzily, you open your eyes, feeling nauseous as the stone chamber spins around you in a blur of colour.

'They're bleeding. It looks bad.'

The voice belongs to Nyms. You feel strong arms about your shoulders, helping to support you as you mumble groggily. 'Where am I?'

You feel a cold palm against your forehead. Struggling to focus, you can make out a white shape. Then there is a flash of white light. You flinch away from it, fearful that you are being transported once again. But instead, you feel a comforting warmth flow through your body, taking away the pain and restoring your vision.

Lansbury straightens, looking down at you with a petulant expression. 'What happened?' she asks briskly. 'One minute you were there and then ...' The medic snaps her fingers.

With Nyms' help you struggle back to your feet. Caeleb is watching you from the other side of his room, his helm removed and held under his arm. His eyes are narrowed, his expression one of distrust.

'We deserve an explanation,' he adds sternly. 'We were about to leave you here.'

You glance over, to see that the anomaly has drifted away into another corner of the room, its sparkling sheen barely visible in the pale light from Lansbury's staff. After taking a deep breath, you recount your adventure, aware that it must sound as far-fetched as a children's bedtime story.

'You met Arthurian?' Nyms gawps, his head jutting forward on his narrow shoulders. 'Why does that never happen to me?'

'Because you are not of the shroud, Nyms,' states Lansbury, eyeing you up with a grimace. 'I suspect that none of us could have interacted with the anomaly in such a way – or at least, survived to tell the tale.'

'What's the shroud?' you ask, confused.

Lansbury gives a sigh. 'Yes, I guessed you would be ignorant of such matters. The shroud is the place between worlds, the place where the old magic is drawn from.'

'It is a place of evil – of demons,' states Caeleb darkly. 'And demons tell lies.'

Your eyes widen. 'Do you not believe my story?'

'That Arthurian never led the final charge?' he snaps angrily. 'That the stories and songs are a lie?' He laughs softly, shaking his head. 'I believe that you ... you took a blow to the head.' The warrior taps his forehead. 'Now, I think we have wasted enough time here.'

You watch as the warrior tugs his polished helm over his face, before striding out of the room. As your eyes follow him, your attention shifts to the skeleton of the tomb robber, still lying sprawled amongst the dust and cobwebs.

'I don't understand!' you gasp, walking over and kneeling beside the skeleton. You push aside the tattered remnants of the leather coat, revealing a silver crucifix. 'Why hasn't this changed?' You look up at Lansbury, begging for an explanation.

The medic shrugs her shoulders. 'Time is a complex weave – it is not a single thread but many. If your story is true, your meddling may have changed one aspect, altered a single thread, maybe others, but the weave will still follow its course.'

Nyms blows out his cheeks. 'I think I preferred it when I was just hitting things. Can we do that again, please?' Spinning his blades, he follows Caeleb out of the chamber.

You take the crucifix, turning it over in your palm. You notice that the key-piece is missing. 'Do you believe me?' you ask Lansbury, lifting your eyes to meet her stare.

'Time will tell,' she says, gesturing towards the exit. 'Now, after you ...'

Nodding, you place the crucifix in your pocket before leaving the room. Turn to 902.

839

'Yes, my special deals. Well let's take a look ...' He reaches inside the chest and produces three items, which he lays out on the ash-covered ground. 'For you, 450 gold crowns. I can't say fairer than that.'

You may purchase any of the following items for 450 gold crowns each:

Sliver of shadow	Ghoul's teeth	Total eclipse
(main hand: sword)	(necklace)	(head)
+2 speed +4 brawn	+1 speed	+2 speed +3 brawn
Ability: chill touch	Ability: piercing	Ability: vanish

After you have made your decision, you can ask to see Waldo's rare items (turn to 903) or bid the trader farewell (turn to 789).

840

Arthurian nods, his gaze falling on the magic anomaly that blocks the exit. 'A wizard gave me the plans for this tomb. He was one of those responsible for building it.' He steps warily towards the mould-encrusted growth. 'The rope I used was severed. I've been trapped in this room for days, weeks ...' He stops a short distance from the creature. 'I cannot defeat this thing. It keeps me prisoner. I have died many times ...' His body shudders, as if reliving painful memories. 'I cannot die. Not by my own hand, not by this creature ... not by starvation ...'

You pull back your sleeve, aware that your shadow mark is pulsing with a purple glow, filling you with its familiar craving.

Confidently, you stride up to the anomaly. With a snarl, you lunge forward, driving your arm into its saggy flesh. The anomaly gives a shriek of pain, its body blistering as it begins to unravel, forming thin shreds of green magic. You throw back your head, breathing in the power of the magic as it pours into your mark.

You stumble back, gasping – aware that your whole body is now glowing with a soft purple radiance.

'What are you?' scowls Arthurian, shrinking away. 'You are not the work of the One God.'

A flicker of amusement turns the corners of your mouth. 'My companions and I are here to save you. Trust me, the world is not safe from the Legion of Shadow. They are not defeated!'

You step through the entranceway, the glow from your body illuminating the chamber beyond. There is the scuff of boots as Arthurian moves to join you. 'What are we here for?' you demand, warily scanning the chamber. In the wall opposite, a set of stairs lead back to the surface.

To your right is an archway – the one that Caeleb had originally suggested you take.

'There is a talisman here,' states Arthurian, his fingers tracing the silver crucifix that rests against his chest. 'If I destroy it then the curse will be lifted.'

'And you will die,' you add, looking intently into his eyes. 'Why would you trade your life for that?'

Arthurian glowers with anger. 'I am a warrior, the first knight of the realm. I have led thousands in battle. I found the golden chalice, I fought in the crusades against the heathen lords of Mordland. I am the king's son, heir to the throne of Valeron! I have proven myself – I was not born to this!' He beats a fist against his chest. 'This is a lie!'

You take a step back, startled by the vehemence of his words. Despite the man's ragged appearance, you see a fierce strength in his steel-grey eyes ... Arthurian's spirit, trapped in the body of a Nevarin.

'I know something of what it is like,' you state grimly, 'to find yourself in a body that does not feel your own.'

Arthurian turns away, heading for the side passage. 'You know nothing of what it is like, shadow spawn.'

For a moment, you remain behind, lost in your own troubled thoughts. It is only when you see a flash of light down the passageway, and hear a raised cry of alarm, that you draw your weapons and hurry after your companion. Turn to 804.

You join Nyms at the foot of the stairs, leading up to the building. The swordsman has skilfully despatched the necromancers – but is now confronted by a new obstacle. The pillars either side of the entrance-way are glowing with a purple light, casting a flickering barrier across the doorway.

'Perhaps the front door wasn't the best choice after all,' says Nyms, warily approaching the magic wall. 'The necros did it. Any ideas?'

Lansbury shoulders past you, her staff raised. 'They have tried to reweave the magic that once protected this place. It is weak ...' The tip of her staff glows briefly as she utters a simple arcane command. A second later and the barrier has disappeared, the light of the runes dimming and then winking out entirely. 'Amateurs,' sniffs the medic.

'Nice work, Lans.' Nyms nudges you and gestures towards the open doorway. 'After you ...'

With a grin, you ready your weapons and enter the building: the tomb of the great hero, Arthurian. Turn to **848**.

842

You enter a vast high-domed chamber. At the centre of the room is a stepped dais, leading up to a stone tomb. The lid has been smashed open, its shattered stonework lying in jagged pieces around the base of the dais.

'Oh, this doesn't look good,' mutters Nyms, his swords spinning nervously in his hands.

Hovering above the open tomb is a man in rune-plate armour. He hangs suspended in the air, teeth gritted with determination as he struggles against a magical assault.

'Arthurian!' you gasp.

Stood around the undead warrior are four black-robed necromancers. They are chanting arcane words as black streams of magic arc from their fingers, slamming against Arthurian and surrounding him in a whirling frenzy of dark light.

Suddenly, you feel a sharp tingling from your shadow mark.

Something is wrong ... Quickly you throw yourself aside, as spears of ice rip through the air, shattering against the wall behind you.

'Interlopers!'

You turn to see a female mage striding towards you, her blue gown coated with rime frost.

'Well, well ... a Nevarin and a cavalier. How quaint.'

'Witch!' Caeleb springs forward, sword raised to strike. The mage makes no move to dodge his attack. Instead she narrows her wintry-blue eyes, watching as the air shimmers and crackles before her. There is a bright flash followed by a rush of cold air. When you are able to focus again, you see that Caeleb is now encased in ice – frozen in mid-step.

'No!' Lansbury summons white flames to her hand and hurls them at the icelock. The blast of magic breaks against an unseen shield, fizzing and sparking as it disperses in the chill air.

'Is that all you've got?' she hoots with delight.

You look to Nyms, who nods – then the two of you rush forwards, throwing your weapons and magic against the icelock's shield:

	Speed	Magic	Armour	Health
Sammain	13	10	20	90

Special abilities

◆ Wrath of winter: Your hero automatically loses 2 *health* at the end of the first combat round. As the combat continues, this cold damage increases by 1 each round. (Your hero takes 3 damage at the end of the second round, 4 damage at the end of the third and so on.) This ability ignores *armour*.

◆ Shatter shield: If you win a combat round, instead of rolling for damage you can choose to lower Sammain's *armour* by 4. You can do this as many times as you wish, lowering her *armour* by 4 each time.

If you defeat Sammain, turn to 869. (Special achievement: If you defeat Sammain without lowering her *armour*, then turn to 874.) If you are defeated, turn to 862.

843

Searching Daarko's remains, you find a leather pouch containing 100 gold crowns. You may also help yourself to one of the following special rewards:

Shadow-woven kris	Dark slayer vest	The craven's head
(main hand: dagger)	(chest)	(talisman)
+3 speed +5 brawn	+2 speed +4 brawn	+1 speed +1 brawn
Ability: deep wound	Ability: dominate	Ability: sidestep

When you have made your decision, turn to 811.

844

The air quickly becomes hot and stifling; the tingling from your arm intensifying as you descend into the musty tomb. At the foot of the stairs, you find yourself in a large stone chamber. Most of the ceiling is a crumbling ruin, the dark rock split by thick snaking roots and vines. Dust motes drift lazily through the twilit space, forming a hazy white veil as they swirl before Lansbury's pale light.

Nyms starts into the room, but Lansbury puts out her staff to stop him. 'Wait ...' Her attention is focused on the far side of the chamber, where something is moving.

You squint, trying to discern what it is. It appears to be a growth of some description, a mould or lichen, covering an entire side of the room. Parts of its rotted form are rising and falling, as if beating with some form of sentient life.

'Now, let's assume that isn't friendly,' says Nyms, grimacing with revulsion.

'It's a magic anomaly,' whispers Lansbury, glancing at her staff as its light begins to flicker. 'We should stay well away from it. Learn from those who were less fortunate ...' She nods to the paved floor of the chamber, where you notice several fleshy mounds smeared across the stone, punctuated by splintered shards of bone.

'We don't have to go near it,' says Caeleb firmly, pointing his sword in the direction of an archway in the west wall. 'I suggest we move on from here.'

Will you:

Investigate the magic anomaly?	818
Leave the room through the archway?	909

845

(Make a note of the word *companion* on your hero sheet.)

The creatures are strong – but they are slow. Sidestepping yet another sluggish attack, you turn and hurry back towards the shield, leaping and kicking off from its side to back-flip through the air. The creatures snarl and curse as you sail over their heads, slicing and blasting as you go. Twisting round mid-air, you drop onto the leader's back, throwing aside your weapons to rip one of its growths free. Black slime geysers from its ruptured body, as you take the pulsating parasite and wrap it around the decayer's throat. There is a sickening crunch as the rotted head snaps free of its body, rolling away into the dust.

The decayer shakes and convulses, then starts to topple backwards. You leap free at the last moment, ripping another parasite from its back. The unnatural growth is still spewing out spores from its gaping maw, surrounding you in a dense cloud of floating bombs. Your slow-witted foes stumble into them, igniting their own mouldy wrappings and engulfing themselves in flame.

Congratulations! The decayers have been defeated. You may now help yourself to one of the following rewards:

Parasitic plate	Decayer's wraps	Spore shoulders
(left hand: shield)	(chest)	(cloak)
+2 speed +4 armour	+2 speed +3 brawn	+2 speed +3 armour
Ability: leech	Ability: disease	Ability: spore cloud
(requirement: warrior)		(requirement: mage)

When you have made your decision, turn to **856**.

846

You find yourself back in the magic-lit passageway. Eager to return to your companions, you retrace your steps back through the tomb, to the room where you met Arthurian.

To your relief, the magic anomaly is still lurking in a corner of the rough-hewn chamber, its shimmering body reflected in the muddy water. The storm still vents its fury in the lightning-flecked skies above. Pulling your hood down low over your face, you step through the curtain of drumming rainwater and approach the anomaly.

You are uncertain what will happen. Somehow this anomaly was able to bring you back in time; will it return you to the present day, or will it take you to another time and place? You grit your teeth as you take a step closer ...

Sure enough, as soon as you move within range of the magical creature, its silken threads snap around you, pulling you at speed towards a brightening white light. Turn to 838.

847

Searching the ogre's filthy belongings, you find a leather pouch containing 50 gold crowns. You may also help yourself to one of the following special rewards:

Sacrum of carnage	Beast's backbone	Hulking shoulders
(main hand: fist weapon)	(chest)	(cloak)
+2 speed +5 brawn	+2 speed +4 armour	+2 speed +3 brawn
Ability: fatal blow	Ability: savagery	Ability: barbs

When you have made your decision, turn to 824.

848

You emerge in a high-ceilinged chamber. Torches flicker in sconces along the walls, illuminating a row of statues that stand solemn guard at either side of the room. These life-like sculptures appear to be Tor Knights, clad in full-body plate. Swords and shields rest at their side.

'Arthurian's tomb ...' Nyms spins on the spot, taking in his surroundings.

You follow your three companions down the sombre hall, towards a large stone door set in the far wall. It stands slightly ajar, leading through to a set of stairs.

'The necros did a good job of breaking and entering,' sighs Caeleb, eyeing up the stone door. Its entire surface is covered in spiralling runes and detailed, intricate script work. 'These doors were warded.'

'Yes, and they are over a thousand years old,' states Lansbury matter-of-factly. 'A child could have broken through these defences. It is nothing to be admired.' The medic hikes up her robes and starts down the stairs.

'Mages,' sighs Nyms. 'So competitive.'

He starts after Lansbury, with yourself and Caeleb bringing up the rear. Turn to 926.

849

Nyms is a skilled swordsman and more than capable of handling the necromancers. The bone angel, on the other hand ...

Your shadow mark ignites with a blazing fury as you throw yourself forwards, directly into the path of the beast. With a hellish screech, the bone angel's talons rake through the air, as sharp and deadly as any blade:

	Speed	Brawn	Armour	Health
Bone angel	13	11	11	90

Special abilities

♥ Terrible talons: For each · that you roll for your hero (either for attack speed or damage), they are caught by the bone angel's talons and must take 2 damage, ignoring *armour*. (If you have an ability that lets you re-roll dice, you may use this before determining the result.)

🛡 Holy aura: The medic's holy aura raises your *brawn* and *magic* by 2 in this combat.

🛡 Caeleb's shield: Your *armour* is raised by 2 for the duration of this combat.

If you defeat this infernal monster, turn to 906. If you are defeated, turn to 862.

850

As a mage you may also take the following item:

Bone fetish

(talisman)

+1 armour

Ability: necromancer career (see below)

You must have the bone fetish talisman equipped if you wish to learn the necromancer career. As soon as this item is unequipped or you learn a new career, you lose the abilities associated with this career.

The necromancer has the following abilities:

Shades (pa): At the start of combat, you automatically summon a group of shades to aid you. The shades add 2 to each dice of damage you roll, for the duration of the combat. Once the shades have been summoned, they remain in play until you sacrifice them (see below).

Sacrifice (co): You may use this ability after an opponent has rolled their damage dice/damage score, to instantly sacrifice your shades. The shades absorb all the damage instead and you are unharmed. This destroys your shades instantly.

Once you have made your decision, turn to 883.

You raise your weapons defensively. 'Who is it?' you call, flinching when you hear the sound of Lorcan's voice coming from your own lips.

Take the staff, fool.

And ringing inside your head.

'Shut up,' you growl between clenched teeth.

The figure steps forward out of the shadows. You had already guessed who it was – from the bulky armour and the lightning flickering across their warhammer. 'Mathis . . .'

The inquisitor has a mad look about his eyes, his movements sluggish from exhaustion. 'More Nevarin scum.' He gives his surroundings a wary once over, his gaze falling on the crumpled clothes that once belonged to Lorcan.

'Wait!' You lower your weapons, realising that the inquisitor is no longer seeing your own body, but that of the gaunt mage. 'It's me, Mathis. Remember? This is not my body!'

Mathis takes another step forward, bringing his warhammer up across his chest. He shakes his head, almost with regret. 'You are a demon. And you must be stopped.'

'But I saved your—'

The inquisitor charges, moving with a speed that belies his heavy armour. You barely have time to block the warrior's first blow, his second lifting you off your feet and carrying you across the room. You smash through a clay urn, showering the ground with broken pottery.

You stumble to your feet woozily, aware that your wounds are not healing. A quick glance at your shadow mark confirms that its magic is not responding – its usual radiance reduced to a dull glow.

I told you to take the staff.

'What are you doing?' you scowl angrily. 'Are you controlling the mark?'

We have to leave. Leave. Leave. Now!

The inquisitor charges again. You throw yourself aside at the last moment, his warhammer taking a huge gouge out the wall. He swings around, the head of the weapon slamming into your side. You are thrown backwards, tumbling across the broken rubble, your body wracked with pain. Something wet is running down your face. You put a shaking hand to it, surprised when it comes away coated in blood.

'Heal me,' you choke, spitting out a broken tooth. 'Do you want us both to die?'

I told you what to do.

You find your feet again, only to see Mathis closing once more. You tangle together, smashing through wood and glass. His head butts into your own, sending it snapping back. Then his hammer cracks across your ribs, eliciting a strangled cry of pain. By luck rather than design, you stumble back, avoiding his follow-up swing.

The shroud. The place between worlds. We must go! Go!

Lorcan's voice distracts you. The hammer smashes into your chest, hurling you back across the room. You crash down, spitting dust and blood, your hands grappling over broken rock and pottery. Then you feel something, cold to the touch.

Yes. Yes. Take the staff.

You struggle to raise your head. One eye is closed and it won't open – the other struggles to focus, the room reduced to shreds of colour, whirling and reeling in a sickening spin. Boots crunch through the debris as the inquisitor advances. You can hear his laboured breathing.

Take the staff. Just think of the possibilities, Nevarin. The shroud. The gateway to other worlds. Other dreams. Don't let it end like this.

'Heal me ...' you croak, wincing as you try and move your shattered body. 'Heal me.'

The boots crunch closer and then stop. Mathis stands over you, his warhammer raised. You look up, his blurred face swaying like a reflection in water. 'Finally demon, I will rid this world of your taint ...'

The warhammer comes down. You reach out and snatch the staff, gripping it to your chest. It flares into a brilliant golden light, the magic from your shadow mark pumping into it, filling it with new life. Your life...

Yes, yes! The shroud calls us ... the staff is working ...

The warhammer comes down. But it finds only rubble, crushing it to sand beneath its heavy weight. Mathis stumbles back, eyes wide with surprise. 'It can't be ...'

All that remains of you is a faint outline of smoke, curling into the dusty air.

You have simply vanished.

'Demons ...' he spins around, eyes scanning the shadows. 'Where are you, demon? Where did you go?' But the only answer he receives is the echo of his own voice. 'Impossible ...' He shifts round, looking back to where you had been lying. A tattered roll of parchment lies crumpled amongst the dust. He reaches down and picks it up, unravelling it to reveal a letter. A letter of recommendation for a young knight to apprentice with the great Avian Dale. His brow furrows as he spots your pack lying some metres away, its contents scattered throughout the rubble.

Mathis crumples the parchment in his fist. 'Wherever you go, Nevarin... I *will* find you. As the One God is my witness. This is not the end ...'

852

Just like the tinker's chest in the town of 'No Hope', the interior of this chest is larger on the inside, filled with a myriad of weapons, armour and trinkets. It is a far cry from the battered pots and pans in the trader's cart.

'Now do you believe me,' grins Waldo, leaning over your shoulder. 'I got a knack for finding treasure. And rare stuff, too.'

'I suspect these don't come cheap,' you say with a wry grin, as you lift out a gold-embroidered cloak.

'That depends. I got my rare items ... real beauties those, then I got my special deals.'

Will you:
Ask to see the special deals?	**914**
Ask to see the rare items?	**881**

853

'Look for yourself,' sneers Fetch, waving a hand towards the nearest wooden crate.

You give the assassin a long stare, still distrustful of his motives.

'No, you open the crate.' With a ring of steel, you draw your weapon and hold it to his throat.

'Very well,' he scowls, waving you away with the back of his hand. 'Does everything have to be so dramatic with you?'

'Sorry, did you miss the part where you were trying to kill me?'

Fetch looks back at you, his eyes bright beneath his hood. 'I call it self-preservation. Something that has kept me alive these many years. You're not so bad at it yourself.'

Grunting with discomfort, the assassin takes the lid off the crate and pushes it aside. 'Travelling leaves me weak, tired. I am not interested in playing games. See for yourself.'

You step closer and look into the crate. Resting amongst folds of linen are a number of jade figurines. You shrug your shoulders. 'Some nice ornaments. What is the big deal?'

Fetch throws open his arms, turning on the spot to take in the whole of the room. 'Here are treasures so rare and priceless that even the king of Valeron would crawl on his belly for a chance to possess them. These are Avian's. He is a collector.'

'And what does he plan to do with all this?' You scan the room, filled with hundreds and hundreds of similar boxes.

'It's not what he plans to do,' grins Fetch folding his arms. 'It is what he hopes to stop others from doing.'

You scowl. 'I hate riddles.'

Fetch walks back over to the door, his eyes lingering on your own. 'Riddles are all you deserve, shadow walker.'

Turn to 792 to ask another question.

854

You sprint to the end of the building, then kick off from its edge, soaring effortlessly over the glittering sea of bodies. You twist in mid-air, sending bolts of black fire into the ranks of shadow spawn, your dark magic ripping through their bodies and leaving charred craters in the earth.

As you fall out of your dive, you grab hold of the statue, swinging yourself around to land on the plinth, right next to the surprised inquisitor. 'You started without me,' you grin, drawing your weapons.

Mathis glares at you as he blocks yet another blast from the knight's bow.

'They weren't keen on waiting,' he scowls.

You put your back to the statue, your mind now focused on the nightmarish creations that are clambering to reach you. They look like ghouls, save their bodies have been fashioned from pure shadow, their red eyes burning with a ravenous evil.

'Ghasts,' snarls the inquisitor. He swings his warhammer in a deadly arc, sending four of the creatures spinning away in a sizzling explosion of holy light. 'Watch their claws.'

'Just watch those arrows!' you shout back, ducking as one goes zipping past, to smash into an advancing monster. 'I'll handle these!' With a snarl of fury, you hurl yourself against the devilish ghasts, hoping to buy time until aid can arrive. You must fight:

	Speed	Brawn	Armour	Health
Ghasts	16	9	7	140

Special abilities

🟣 A gathering of ghasts: The ghasts' sharp claws ignore your *armour*. (If you have *second skin* then you may use half of your *armour* score, rounding up, to absorb the damage).

🟣 Bolt from the blue: Roll a die at the end of each combat round. If you roll ⚁ or more, then Mathis has deflected the general's arrows with his shield. Otherwise, an arrow has got through and you must take 5 damage (ignoring *armour*) from the magical blast.

If you manage to survive to the start of the *seventh* combat round, then turn to 794. (Special achievement: If you defeat the ghasts before the end of the *sixth* round, then turn to 813). If you are defeated, then you may return to an earlier point. Restore your *health*, then turn to 885.

855

The general is a skilled fighter, matching you blow for blow – but a lucky opening allows you to step in past her guard, kicking her leg away and throwing her off balance. Too late, she tries to recover but your weapons knock her blades aside, your follow-up blow sending her helmet rattling away into the dirt. At last, you finally look upon your enemy's face. It would have been beautiful once, but now it is a ruin of pulpy, scarred flesh. Her flat stare holds no emotion – no remorse. 'Finish it,' she hisses.

You back away, shaking your head. 'It doesn't have to be like this.'

The woman laughs bitterly. 'It has always been like this. Do you even think we remember another way?'

You raise your shadow mark, its demonic glow surrounding your body. 'I wish I did...'

Before you can stop her, Sanrah snatches a dagger from the dust and lunges. Your reaction is pure instinct, blasting her away with your magic. The general's body snaps back, flipping over to crash down onto the dusty ground. There is a groan of pain then silence.

Slowly, from between the black plates of armour, her essence seeps out – the purple tendrils of magic snaking into the air. You contemplate letting them reform, allowing her to live again. But you have not the strength to deny your shadow mark. It greedily absorbs the general's essence, filling you with its power. If you are a mage turn to 871. If you are a warrior, turn to 882. If you are a rogue, turn to 887.

856

Suddenly, a bright flash of light draws your attention skywards. From out of the smog, you see white shapes swooping down over the ruined city, their vapour trails blazing bright like comets. Beneath them, a series of explosions swell out across the square, cutting a vicious swathe through the tightly-packed ranks of shadow spawn.

'The airborne regulars!' You punch the air as the mages hurtle past on their flying carpets.

Then, at the far side of the square, you hear the resonating blast of a horn. From your vantage point, it is difficult to see through the thronging masses, but it looks like a battalion of Ravenwing's militia have made it across the city. You catch the glimmer of polished armour and a fluttering standard, proudly displaying the black raven. Aid has finally arrived. Turn to 895.

The passageway is lined with torches, their crackling flames casting a ghoulish dance of shadows across the flagstones. You stagger onwards, teeth clenched against the throbbing pain that is coming from your shadow mark.

Lansbury walks at your side, watching you with a curious fascination. 'The inscriptions don't agree with you, do they?'

You look up, struggling to focus. 'I don't feel good, if that's what you mean.'

The medic nods. 'Yes, your mark is strong in demon magic. I wonder what it is truly capable of ... should your memory return.'

You wince as a hot pain shoots up your arm. You stagger into the wall, putting out a hand to regain your balance. 'Sometimes I am grateful that I do not remember.'

After several hundred metres, the passageway widens, ending in a tall pair of gilded doors. They already stand open, revealing a bright chamber beyond. With effort, you draw your weapons, preparing yourself for whatever danger might lurk in this new section of the tomb. Turn to 799.

858

Ravenwing's men pursue the routed shadow spawn, slashing and blasting at their fleeing enemy. The battle is won. But at what cost? You look around at the men that have remained behind – not only the wounded and the dead, but those who have simply hung back from exhaustion. Many have a haunted look about them, their bodies blackened by soot and grime. You can't imagine what devastation awaits beyond the walls of the city – where the doom orb's magic was turned against the camp. The men's expressions tell you enough.

Across the rubble-strewn square, you see Ravenwing supporting Lansbury, as he guides her to the shelter of a building. She looks exhausted from her efforts, her shoulders sagging, head hung low. You notice that Nyms is not with her.

'Nevarin!' Mathis is trudging through the rubble towards you. The inquisitor's armour is raked with black scars, his hair plastered to his head by blood and sweat. 'We have unfinished business, you and I.'

'Mathis? You frown, taking a step backwards. 'You are not yourself ...'

He raises his warhammer. 'Oh I am perfectly myself, demon!'

Suddenly, you catch movement out of the corner of your eye. A man is standing on the edge of a rooftop, his scarlet coat billowing in the wind. He raises his hand and suddenly you feel an invisible force closing in around you, pinning your arms and legs tightly together.

Then the man is moving, running through the air as quickly and deftly as if it was solid ground. And like a dog on leash, you find yourself being dragged after him, floating in a magical prison.

'More demons!' screams Mathis. 'Don't think you can escape!'

You are pulled across a broad plaza, its fountains and pathways now charred and cratered, towards an officious-looking building clinging to a rise of grey rock. You try and discern its purpose – but the invisible bonds shift, spinning you around. Then something hard strikes you across the head, plunging you into darkness. Turn to 928.

859

A winding staircase leads you down into a high-ceilinged chamber. Torches flicker in sconces along the walls, illuminating a row of statues that stand solemn guard along either side of the room. These life-like sculptures appear to be Tor Knights, clad in full-body plate. Swords and shields rest at their side.

Turning back to the entranceway, you see the barrier of magical light fade. Lansbury steps between the once-glowing pillars. 'Amateurs,' she mutters with disdain. 'Thinking they could keep me out!' Nyms and Caeleb follow her into the room.

'Took your time,' you grin, folding your arms and assuming a mocking pose.

Lansbury playfully slaps your arm as she continues past. 'We're not through this yet. I suggest you stay on your guard.'

As she marches away, Nyms offers you an apologetic smile. 'If it makes you feel any better, she never laughs at my jokes either.'

Pushing back your rain-soaked hood, you follow your three

companions down the hall, towards a large stone door set in the far wall. It stands slightly ajar, leading through to a set of stairs.

'The necros did a good job of breaking and entering,' sighs Caeleb, eyeing up the stone door. You note that its entire surface is covered in spiralling runes and detailed, intricate script work. 'These doors were warded.'

'Yes, and they are over a thousand years old,' states Lansbury matter-of-factly. 'A child could have broken through these defences. It is nothing to be admired.' The medic hikes up her robes and starts down the stairs.

'See what I mean?' grins Nyms. 'No fun at all.'

He starts after Lansbury, with yourself and Caeleb bringing up the rear. Turn to 926.

860

You join Lansbury, who is still studying the cart with a thoughtful expression.

'What do you think? Those runes ... did they tell you anything?'

The medic gives a deep sigh. 'I don't know. They are not of this world, if that is what you mean.' She traces a finger along a length of wood, forcing the sigils to glimmer briefly in the dull half-light. 'While not the same, I would say they share a common origin with ... this.' She reaches out and takes hold of your arm, tugging back the sleeve to reveal your branded skin.

You snatch your arm away defensively. 'A shadow mark?'

Lansbury shrugs. 'Some of the symbols on this cart follow a similar form, although I sense their purpose is different. I would say these runes have more to do with travel and safe passage, than ...' she glances down at your arm, '... murder.'

You tug back your sleeve, shamed and angered. 'I can't change the past.'

The medic holds up her hands, nodding. 'I know. I know. Forgive me, I'm sorry.'

You give her a hard look before shifting your attention back to the trader. 'And what of him? Is he a spy or not? If these are shadow runes, that makes him the enemy.'

'Oh, hardly.' Lansbury leans over the side of the cart and pulls out an old cooking pot. Holding it to her face, she peers at you through one of its many rusted holes. 'I don't think we need to be frightened of old pots just yet, do you?'

Will you:

Ask Nyms for his opinion on the trader?	898
Ask to see the trader's wares?	795

861

With a burst of magic, you propel yourself forward, aiming straight for the legion's general. As your shield sputters and dies, one of the arrows slams into your chest, sending you spinning back through the air. You land roughly, tumbling and sliding through the dust to finally lie in a smoking heap at the base of one of the craters.

The ground trembles as the general's mount advances. It is a huge, grey-scaled beast, its horned face sloping back to form a spiked crest. Along its flanks, black plates of steel are bolted into its flesh, oozing dark blood and rust.

Frantically, you scramble to your feet, tugging the arrow from your chest. You feel no pain, no discomfort, only an icy tingling as your shadow mark closes up the wound, flooding you with fresh energy.

'Nevarin!' The general reins in the armoured beast, its splayed feet skidding in the thick ash. 'You ... you fight against us?' The muffled voice is that of a young woman's – surprise evident in her tone.

You brush the dirt and dust from your clothes. 'What ever gave you that impression,' you sneer, drawing your weapons.

'Humph! So be it!' The general barks a word of command. The beast gives an answering roar as it lowers its head and starts to charge, looking to run you through with its horns:

	Speed	Brawn	Armour	Health
Styraxian steed	15	13	16/6	90

Special abilities

◗ Blindside: If you use a speed ability *and* win the combat round, you can strike at the steed's unprotected rear using the lower *armour* attribute (6). Otherwise, you are unable to outflank your foe and must strike against an *armour* of 16.

◗ Sharp shooter: The general is firing arrows in your direction. For each ⊡ result you roll for speed, you are hit by an arrow and must take 4 damage, ignoring *armour*. (If you have an ability that lets you change or reroll die results, you may use it to avoid this damage.)

If you manage to bring down the general's mount, then you must continue with the *health* that you have remaining. Turn to 809. If you are defeated, then you may return to an earlier point. Restore your *health*, then turn to 905.

862

Your eyes flutter open, the rain-drenched hills of the bone fields swaying before your blurred vision. Ahead of you, an indistinct shape moves quickly across the uneven terrain. As colours and detail swim into focus, you discern flowing robes and a bright staff of light.

You try and speak but the words clog at the back of your throat, producing little more than a guttural croak. The ground sways once again.

'They're awake,' mutters a voice close to your ear.

You are dropped to the earth, landing in the sodden ash. As you struggle for breath, you look up to see Caeleb standing over you, sweat and dirt staining his face. 'You aren't so light to carry, now get up.'

Nyms paces into view, looking around warily. 'We need to keep moving. Can you walk?' He glances your way, a grimace etched deep into his pale, narrow face.

'Get up!' snaps Caeleb, kicking ash in your direction. 'You have already slowed us down!'

In the distance you hear the shriek of some infernal creature.

'What happened?' you rasp, aware of a throbbing pain coming from your arm.

'Good question,' says Nyms, nervously tapping the pommels of his swords. 'We thought you were dead and then ...' He shrugs his shoulders.

'Demon magic!' Caeleb scowls, turning away.

'But the tomb ... our mission.' You push yourself back onto your feet, swaying slightly as you try and regain your balance.

'Zul's forces overwhelmed us,' states Lansbury, looking back to survey the dark skies. 'We were lucky to escape – but now they have scouts looking for us. We must hurry.'

Another deafening shriek dashes the uneasy silence. You take a tentative step forward, relieved to find that your strength is slowly starting to return. 'I'll be fine. Lead the way.'

Lansbury nods, before starting down into a narrow ravine. You follow, slipping on the loose stones and bones that carpet the ground. As you catch sight of a skull, grinning back at you from a mound of ash, you find yourself pondering your strange immortality. Return to the Act 3 map to continue your adventure.

863

Suddenly, a bright flash of light draws your attention skywards. From out of the smog, you see white shapes swooping down over the ruined city, their vapour trails blazing bright like comets. Beneath them, a series of explosions swell out across the square, cutting a vicious swathe through the tightly-packed ranks of shadow spawn.

'The airborne regulars!' You punch the air as the mages hurtle past on their flying carpets.

Then, at the far side of the square, you hear the resonating blast of a horn. From your vantage point, it is difficult to see through the thronging masses, but it looks like a battalion of Ravenwing's militia have made it across the city. You catch the glimmer of polished armour and a fluttering standard, proudly displaying the black raven. Aid has finally arrived. Turn to 884.

Quest: Waking the dead

'Remind me again why we're here?'

Nyms is huddled in his cloak, the cold rain dripping from the peaked brim of his hood. In the valley below, lies a vast necropolis – its crumbling buildings veiled by a ghostly mist.

Next to you, Caeleb gives a heavy sigh. 'I'm going on a hunch, nothing more. We've seen what Zul can do. His necros are raising the dead.'

'And you want us to do the same?' Nyms blows out his cheeks, rubbing his gloved hands together nervously. 'We've done some crazy things together, my friend, but this one ...'

Caeleb points to a large domed structure, looming tall and ominous amidst the swirling fog. 'That is Arthurian's tomb. He was a great warrior; the leader of the Tor Knights. It was his sacrifice that helped win the shadow war.'

'The last charge,' Nyms snorts. 'Always sounded like a suicide mission to me. A hundred knights against an army of thousands. No wonder they were cut to pieces.'

Caeleb brushes the wet hair from his eyes. 'They knew they would not survive, Nyms. But their sacrifice bought time – time for crucial reinforcements to arrive from Talanost. Without their sacrifice, the king's army would have been overrun.'

'Hmm, history does have a way of over-glorifying the past.'

Lansbury leans forward, scrutinising the tombs and ruins in the valley below. 'Let's concentrate on the facts. Zul is using necromancy to raise the Tor Knights – turning them against us. It is only a matter of time before his mages desecrate these tombs.' The elderly medic turns to Nyms. 'We cannot allow them to do this.'

'And the horn?' Nyms folds his arms stubbornly. 'I'm not risking my life for some fireside fable.'

Caeleb tugs his visor down. 'It's not a fable. Arthurian swore an oath with his last dying breath, that he would return to Valeron in its time of greatest need.'

'Oh really? And who was around to hear those grand words?' Nyms puts a hand to his ear, grinning. 'According to your famous legend, all the knights were wiped out – to the very last man.'

Caeleb shakes his head. 'You should read more, Nyms. It was Jorvic Moore, the Tor Knight's standard bearer. He was mortally wounded ... the medics couldn't save him, but he managed to return to the camp with Arthurian's horn – the one he used in battle a hundred times to sound his charge.'

Nyms rolls his eyes. 'And if we find this horn, he'll come along and help us battle Zul. That is what you're saying, right?'

Caeleb takes up his shield, its surface slick with rainwater. 'It comes down to faith, Nyms. I believe it's worth a try – at least.'

'And that's good enough for me,' you interject impatiently.

Beneath your clothing, you can feel the shadow mark burning ... eager for battle.

Nyms nods, glancing up at the broiling, storm-heavy sky. 'OK, you win. But really ... couldn't we have picked a better day for this?'

Caeleb draws his sword and starts down into the valley. Within seconds the plated warrior has vanished – swallowed up by the thick banks of white fog. Drawing your own weapons, you follow the knight's tracks through the sludgy black ash. Turn to 833.

865

Searching Daarko's remains, you find a leather pouch containing 100 gold crowns. You may also help yourself to one of the following special rewards:

Veil of dark synergies	Elemental greaves	Conduit of shadow
(cloak)	(feet)	(ring)
+2 speed +3 magic	+2 speed +2 armour	+3 magic
Ability: second wind	Ability: fire aura	Ability: overload

When you have made your decision, turn to 811.

You race from the mansion, struggling to keep your balance as the ground shifts and trembles beneath your feet. The booming sound has not abated, each thunderous bellow hinting at something impossibly large – and powerful – now loose in the city.

Stumbling through a series of rubble-filled halls, you finally make it out into the courtyard...

...to discover that day has turned to night.

Looking up, you see the cause of this dramatic change – a gargantuan orb-like creature hangs suspended above Talanost. You stagger, almost falling to your knees, as you struggle to take in its enormity. The orb is a moon-sized mass of bloated grey flesh, its underside swelling into a vast number of tubular protrusions. From each one, black smoke pumps out into the darkening skies, enveloping the city in a veil of smog.

'How did we miss that?' croaks Nyms, unable to tear his eyes away from the horror.

There is another thunderous boom from above, coming from the creature itself. Magic crackles over its body, coating it in a glimmering meshwork of light.

'Judah, protect us!' Mathis strides down the mansion stairs, his fists gripping his warhammer 'Avian, speak to me. What is that thing?'

The mage stands in the doorway, his eyes wide with astonishment. 'A doom orb. The most dangerous of the legion's creations.'

'Did that machine summon it here?' you ask confused.

Avian struggles to order his thoughts. 'I ... I think so ... I believe the machine was keeping it anchored ... in the shroud.' His gaze shifts to Mathis. 'Destroying the machine would have severed the link, pulling it back to our world. We should not have interfered!'

Before the inquisitor can reply, there is a deafening roar from above. The creature's tubes begin to swell, their sides flickering with spectral light – then, like a giant bellows, they deflate, expelling a huge blast of black fire from their gigantic apertures. The column of flame slams down in an area outside the city walls, sending up a vast cloud of ash and debris.

The resulting tremor forces you all to hug the ground.

'That must have been the camp,' chokes Lansbury. 'Ravenwing's forces …'

You catch her panicked expression. Then the world explodes in white light. You find yourself flying through the air, jagged rocks and broken masonry spiralling past you. Then you crash down on something hard, bones snapping and breaking beneath you. Before you can register the pain, your shadow mark flares into life, knitting your shattered body back together again.

As you stagger to your feet, you see a figure running towards you through the smoke. One of Ravenwing's guards. He looks frantic, as if he is being chased by something. A bright light flashes behind him, then he topples to the ground, his sword skittering away. You see that the back of his armour has been blown away, an arrow shaft protruding from his exposed back.

You hurry down the street, your magic slowly filling you with renewed strength. From somewhere up ahead, you can hear the clamour of battle – steel ringing on steel, and the wail of some bestial creature. The ground trembles as more explosions rip across the crumbling wasteland. You can't detect their source, but clearly they are not the work of the monstrous orb, whose attention seems focused on the camp beyond the city walls.

Your shadow mark flashes once again, feeding off your adrenaline and Daarko's absorbed magic. The world begins to blur as you race forward at impossible speed, your footfalls punching holes into the street. Ahead, you sight a ruined hall, one side reduced to a jagged slope of rubble. With a cry of exertion, you throw your body forwards, kicking off from a nearby wall to grab a splintered beam. You swing underneath it, somersaulting high into the air – the force of your momentum taking you spinning over the ravaged side of the hall, to alight on its roof.

Below you stretches Talanost's famous market square.

Once it might have been a joyous sight – a gaudy collision of colour and noise, of eager shoppers bustling down makeshift aisles, to the accompaniment of minstrels and the hawking cries of merchants. But today…

Today it is teeming with shadow spawn. Turn to **885**.

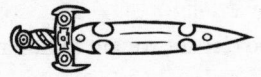

867

You take a hasty swipe at the stranger, who skitters back on his heels, dodging your blow with ease. It appears there may be more to this vagabond than meets the eye.

'I'm still sharp,' he cackles, watching you with dark, hungry eyes. 'This is another test. You try my faith!' (Turn to 816.)

868

(Make a note of the word *apprentice* on your hero sheet.)

These pitiful creatures are no match for your power. Overcome by a dark frenzy, you throw aside your weapons and launch yourself at the nearest scarron. Catching it around the tail, you spin around, dragging the creature with you, then proceed to use it as a club to pummel the rest of its nightmarish brood into a foul-smelling pulp. Once your grim work is done, you swing back your arms and then hurl your makeshift weapon into the advancing ranks of shadow spawn. 'And good riddance,' you scowl, flicking the goo from your hands.

Congratulations! With the scarrons defeated, you may now help yourself to one of the following special rewards:

The sting	**Scarron reapers**	**Fang of Vengos**
(main hand: spear)	(gloves)	(left hand: dagger)
+3 speed +5 brawn	+1 speed +4 magic	+2 speed +4 brawn
Ability: impale	Ability: piercing	Ability: venom
(requirement: warrior)	(requirement: mage)	(requirement: rogue)

When you have made your decision, turn to 927.

869

The icelock is defeated, her final scream accompanied by the ringing clink of ice on stone as Caeleb's magical prison is shattered.

You may now help yourself to one of the following rewards:

Witch's finger	Blood winter	Deep freeze
(left hand: wand)	(ring)	(main hand: staff)
+2 speed +3 magic	+1 brawn	+2 speed +3 magic
Ability: curse	Ability: leech	Ability: stun

When you have made your decision, turn to 808.

870

There was a time when you remember experiencing pain, exhaustion, even remorse – but now there is just the fire, filling every pore of your being, burning beneath the skin, blazing behind your berserk fury.

Lorcan is no match for you. With another swipe of your weapon, you knock his staff away, sending it skittering across the ground. The wounded mage sprawls backwards into the broken fragments of his stone guardians. He tries to roll over, to crawl away, but you plant a boot in his side, driving him back to the ground.

'He never told me ... never told me it would end this way,' pants the mage bitterly.

'This wasn't the ending I was expecting either,' you growl, standing over him. 'Any last requests?'

Lorcan smiles then, his scar twisting it back into a sneer. 'If I die ... I die on my terms, Nevarin.'

He throws himself forward, his body rushing out from the confines of his clothes in a torrent of dark energy. It slams into your shadow mark, pushing itself inside your skin, inside your body. You cry out in horror, clawing at the mark, trying to make it stop – but Lorcan is inside you now, his magic running through your veins ... whispering inside your head.

'You are me. I am you.'

Your shadow mark flashes, and suddenly you feel your body changing – the bones shifting and realigning, the skin and muscle flowing like liquid to mould itself anew. 'Stop this!' you cry, watching as your arms and hands transform before your very eyes, growing paler ... older; branched with dark veins.

You stagger towards the golden shield that the mage had discarded earlier. Holding it up, you turn its polished surface to look upon your reflection. The mage's face is staring back at you, his scar cutting down the left cheek, the mouth curled in a constant sneer. 'This is not me!' You hurl the shield away, clawing at your scarred head, where the hair grows in bristly grey tufts. 'This is not me!'

Lorcan has fused his essence with your own. You have gained the following special ability:

Windwalker (co): If you win a round, you can use all your attack speed dice for your damage score (adding your *brawn* or *magic* as normal). You can only use this ability once per combat. (Note: you cannot use modifier abilities to alter these dice results once they are used for your damage score.)

Behind you a door slams, followed by the rattle of metal as boots scrape across stone. You spin round, almost losing your footing as your new body shifts balance quicker than the old. A figure strides towards you, their armoured features obscured by shadow. 'Nevarin?'

If you have the word *rival* on your hero sheet, turn to 851. Otherwise, turn to 933.

871

Searching the general's armour, you find a leather pouch containing 150 gold crowns. You may also help yourself to one of the following special rewards:

Fortune's favour	Unstable element	Misery cord
(main hand: dagger)	(necklace)	(ring)
+2 speed +5 magic	+1 speed +2 armour	+2 magic +1 armour
Ability: radiance	Ability: disrupt	Ability: thorns

When you have made your decision, turn to 824.

You lurch to your feet, feeling dizzy and nauseous. As your hazy surroundings swim into focus, you see that you have been brought to a stone chamber. Light from a narrow window illuminates a jumbled assortment of boxes and crates, all dusted with a fine white sand.

You catch movement out of the corner of your eye. You spin round, expecting another attack. Instead you see Fetch limping away, towards the far side of the room. His breathing is ragged, the harsh gasps echoing in the shadowy chamber.

'Where are we?' you call after him angrily.

The robed assassin stops and turns. 'You are a long way from home, Nevarin,' he hisses.

Reaching to his belt, Fetch pulls out a short silver wand. With a pained grimace, he raises his arm and points the wand towards a corner of the room. Your eyes flick to the shadows, where a metal statue rests against the sandy wall.

'*Kymeet Malci*' snarls the assassin. There is a flash from the end of the wand. Bewildered, you glance back to the statue – and give a gasp of surprise. Lights are now flickering around its head, moving in a rapid arc as they build up speed. A second later and the lights are joined by a whirring sound coming from inside the plated chest.

'What is it?' you growl, backing away.

Fetch answers with a cold cackle of delight. 'Your doom, Nevarin!'

Suddenly, the armoured body jerks into life, its massive fists clenching and unclenching. You draw your weapons as the automaton staggers forward, knocking boxes and trunks aside with its steel arms. As it enters the band of light cast from the window, you see that it is fashioned from sheets of iron, bolted and riveted to form a crude human shape. Its head, however, is a whirring mass of cogs and wheels, spinning in a frenzied blur as magic crackles around the golem's glass eyes.

'Farewell, Nevarin.'

The strange assassin resumes his escape, leaving you to do battle with this outlandish guardian:

	Speed	Brawn	Armour	Health
Clockwerk	12	11	10	80

Special abilities

● Body of metal: The golem is immune to *piercing*, *impale*, *barbs*, *thorns*, *venom*, *disease* and *bleed*.

If you defeat the golem, turn to 891.

873

'Like the gate. Yes, yes. They made it. The elves.' He gestures to the alabaster statues, carved to resemble men and women, dressed in ornate headdresses and robes. 'We should not have ended such a great people.' He looks back at you, then at the staff. 'They were creators – made things. We could have learned so much from them. Instead, we take, take, take – put back the pieces again.'

'That still doesn't explain what it does,' you interject impatiently.

'The shroud, fool!' He snaps suddenly, veins cording in his neck. 'What else would it do? It takes me back there. Takes me back to the shroud.' He sucks in a deep breath. 'I still hear it. I still ... Yes, still hear the shroud. Still feel it calling. I hear him. He tells me what to do.'

'The shroud is a place of demons – of magic,' you insist. 'How is it possible to exist there? I thought it was dangerous.'

Lorcan looks at you intently. 'This is not real ... no, not real. The shroud is real. Where everything is possible. I have seen things... such wondrous things.' His words break into a cackle of maniacal laughter.

'You're insane,' you growl, your hands inching closer to your weapons. 'You speak of fever dreams. Nothing more.'

Lorcan's laughter dies. 'You don't think, Nevarin – don't think of the possibilities. I wish I could show you. Open your eyes. But you must die so that I can go home.'

Return to 928 to ask Lorcan another question, or turn to 939 to attack this deranged mage.

874

The icelock is defeated, her final scream accompanied by the ringing clink of ice on stone as Caeleb's magical prison is shattered.

You may now help yourself to one of the following special rewards:

Crown of ice	Hunger	Hoarfrost
(head)	(ring)	(main hand: staff)
+2 speed +3 magic	+2 brawn	+2 speed +3 magic
Ability: barbs	Ability: leech	Ability: chill touch

When you have made your decision, turn to 808.

875

Just like the tinker's chest in the town of 'No Hope', the interior of this chest is larger on the inside, filled with a myriad of weapons, armour and trinkets. It is a far cry from the battered pots and pans in the trader's cart.

'Now do you believe me,' grins Waldo, leaning over your shoulder. 'I got a knack for finding treasure. And rare stuff, too.'

'I suspect these don't come cheap,' you say with a wry grin, as you lift out a black coat, trimmed with silver and gold runes.

'That depends. I got my rare items . . .real beauties those, then I got my special deals.'

Will you:

Ask to see the special deals?	839
Ask to see the rare items?	903

876

Searching the ogre's filthy belongings, you find a leather pouch containing 50 gold crowns. You may also help yourself to one of the following special rewards:

Chains of the void	Seed of rage	Aged acromion
(necklace)	(talisman)	(main hand: wand)
+1 speed +1 magic	+2 magic	+2 speed +5 magic
Ability: shackled	Ability: dominate	Ability: rust

When you have made your decision, turn to 824.

877

After much effort, you finally manage to blast a hole in the membrane... but your success may be short-lived. The rupture is already closing back together again in an effort to heal itself.

Without hesitation, Avian throws the carpet forward, sending it careering towards the narrow gap. Your shoulders brush the gooey sides of the membrane as you sweep past, making it through the breach with scant seconds to spare.

'That was close!' you yell, ducking your head to avoid the ceiling of the tunnel. 'Tell me that's the last of those?'

'Hold on!' shouts Avian. 'We're almost there now. We have to destroy the brain!' Under his expert guidance, the carpet twists and turns through a tight forest of glowing stems, dodging the streaks of lightning that flicker between them.

Then, the forest is gone – the carpet shooting out into a huge, circular chamber dominated by a grey sphere of fatty tissue.

'That's it!' shouts Avian 'Prepare yourself! The brain will try and defend ...'

Suddenly, a wave of sizzling magic rumbles out across the chamber. It hits like a wall, slamming into the carpet and sending it spinning over through the air. You fall backwards, screaming out in agony as a thousand unseen needles lance into your body. With a whimpering cry, you crash down on the spongy floor of the cave, tears streaming from your eyes. 'Pain,' you gasp. 'I'd almost forgotten ...'

Frantically you look around for Avian. The mage is sprawled several metres away, the tattered remains of his carpet strewn across the ground. He is still breathing, but looks to be unconscious. You struggle to your feet, hurrying to his side as another wave of energy tears through the cave. You draw on your reserves of magic, summoning a temporary shield to absorb the blast.

As the energy dissipates, you lower your shield and hurry forward, using the momentary reprieve to press your own attack against the gargantuan brain of the doom orb:

	Speed	Magic	Armour	Health
Cerebral cortex	15	10	8	180

Special abilities

◗ Neural blast: At the end of each combat round, the cortex releases a neural blast. This automatically does 10 damage to your hero, ignoring *armour*.

◗ Magic shield: You can spend 2 *magic* to create a shield, to absorb the damage of the neural blast. Each time you use the shield, your *magic* score is lowered by 2 for the duration of the combat. If this reduces your *magic* to zero you fall unconscious and automatically lose the combat.

If you manage to destroy the cerebral cortex, restore any lowered attributes and then turn to 826.

878

As you hurtle into the room, you glimpse a stone tomb at its centre – and its carved lid, pushed to one side. A black-robed body goes flying through the air, to crack against the nearest wall. Your attention swings back to the centre of the room, where a broad-shouldered man dressed in a glowing white shroud is stalking towards another necromancer. They are cowering in fear, fumbling for the dagger at their waist.

'Squire! Squire!' bellows the man in the shroud. 'Where is my squire?' He looks around angrily, then starts back towards the mage.

Before the necromancer can free their weapon or cast a spell, the man has grabbed them around the throat. He lifts them up off the ground with ease.

'One God punish thee!' With a growl of anger, the man hurls the body across the room. You wince when your hear the mage's bones shatter on impact.

Nyms gives you a sideways glance. 'OK, this is new ...'

The man fixes his attention on your group, his brow furrowed.

'Squire! Bring me my broadsword.' He looks around distractedly. 'There are shadow spawn here and I must defend my home. Squire!'

'They have raised another Tor Knight,' hisses Caeleb. 'He still thinks he is in the past ...'

Around the room are a series of alcoves, surrounded by shimmering white runes. Within each alcove there is a weapon or a piece of armour. The man throws out his hand, his fingertips curling. There is a flash of magic from the nearest alcove and suddenly the sword, that was once resting within it, flies out and lands in his outstretched palm.

'If you need something doing,' he growls, 'do it yourself!' The knight raises his sword and charges towards you. 'For Valeron! For glory!'

You must now fight this crazed undead knight:

	Speed	Brawn	Armour	Health
Jorvic	12	13	10	100

Special abilities

To arms!: At the end of each combat round, Jorvic equips himself with another item from his armoury, boosting his attributes for the remainder of the combat. He equips these items in the following order:

* Breastplate – raises his *armour* by 2
* Cloak – raises his *speed* by 1
* Shield – raises his *armour* by 2
* Helm – raises his *armour* by 2
* Leg guards – raises his *armour* by 1

'Heal me!': Lansbury can heal you for 15 *health* any time during this combat. This ability can only be used once per combat.

Team effort: Nyms' sweeping strikes add 2 to your damage score. Caeleb uses his shield to defend you from harm. Your *armour* is raised by 2 for this battle.

If you manage to defeat the mighty warrior, turn to 916. If you are defeated, turn to 862.

879

'Oh, this one likes to party.'

Nyms frowns down at you as you stumble towards the rise.

The fury, the blood lust has abated – leaving you fatigued and exhausted. Your weapons are heavy in your hands; feet dragging through the thick black ash. Above you, columns of grey light break through the heavy storm cloud. The light is piercing – almost painful after the gloom of the crypt.

Most of all, you feel pain. From every inch of your body.

The dagger still protrudes from your thigh, where blood soaks through your clothing. Your shoulders throb and your lower back stings, but those pains are nothing to the burning coming from your arm. The shadow mark smoulders as if on fire, sending curling smoke drifting up into the chill air.

Nyms moves to help you, but the robed woman at his side stops him. It is Lansbury – Redguard's medic.

'One God protect us.'

She hurries to meet you, just as your knees buckle and you drop to the ground, emitting a grunt of agony.

'What possessed you to leave the camp?' asks Lansbury, looking you over with a concerned expression.

You don't have the strength to answer.

The elderly healer puts a hand to your thigh, fingers settling around the hilt of the dagger. 'Now, this is likely to hurt,' she says, with a hint of regret. 'But I'm afraid ... under the circumstances ...'

You scream with pain as hot fire races up your spine, forcing you to kick and jerk. Then there is a different heat ... soothing, comforting. You open your eyes to see Lansbury's healing energies closing up the wound. The heat washes across your body, numbing the other points of pain.

'Just the tonic,' grins Nyms, folding his arms.

You return the smile, flexing your shoulders. 'Good as new.'

Lansbury gives a weary sigh. 'You should not have been out here alone. It isn't safe.'

'You want to keep me on a leash, huh?' you add dryly.

Lansbury scowls. 'Don't answer back to your elders. Especially when they just saved your life.' She stands abruptly, brushing the dust from her skirts.

Nyms steps forward and offers out his hand. 'I don't think this one needed much saving, Lans. It's the enemy I feel sorry for.'

You grab his wrist, using the support to spring back onto your feet.

'So, what did you find?' asks Lansbury, looking back the way you came. 'Anything that will actually help our efforts here?' The medic's disdain is evident in her tone.

'I found a crypt. More a labyrinth than anything else, crawling with necros and ghouls. They're raising the dead.'

Nyms snorts. 'Tell us something we don't know.'

Lansbury rolls her eyes, as if in agreement.

'Look, I didn't find any rotten, old books, if that's what you're wondering,' you add tersely, glaring at the medic. 'I got ... distracted.'

'So we see!' Lansbury grabs hold of your arm and lifts it closer to her face. The purple sigils are still glowing with a purple light, although their fierce heat has now subsided.

'Do not give in to this,' she whispers, her eyes meeting your own. 'It is a dark thing. It is not what you are.'

'Then what am I?' you ask intently.

The medic looks about to answer, but then her resolve falters ... she shakes her head instead. 'Come, let us return to the camp before we are missed.' She slides her arm through your own and together you wander back towards the track, Nyms following at your side. Return to the map to continue your adventure.

880

You hammer against the creature's warded flesh, striking faster than its magic can heal. Finally, the beast crashes to the ground, its thick black blood pooling around your boots.

'Glad to see you're back on form,' grins Nyms, sheathing his blades.

You give him a sideways glance, aware that your shadow mark is still pulsing with its stolen energy. 'I had a little help from a friend.'

Lansbury lays her hands on Caeleb's chest, uttering words of holy magic. A soft white glow spreads out from her palms, pooling across his broken armour and knitting together the wounds beneath.

'Thank you,' he grunts, pushing himself back to his feet. He walks over to his shield and lifts it up. 'Not much use now,' he grimaces, turning the twisted metal around in his hands. 'What was that devilish thing anyway?'

You look down at the defeated shadow creature. If you wish, you may now help yourself to the following item:

Branded bracers
(gloves)
+2 brawn +2 armour
Ability: regrowth

You follow the others past the smashed flagstones at the centre of the room, making for the rune-bordered archway in the far wall.

Lansbury notices that you are prodding at your face, your expression dark.

'What troubles you, Nevarin?'

You glance her way. 'The Nevarin are shape-shifters – they can assume different bodies. What could ...' You pause, struggling to find the words. 'How do I know that this face, this body ... is even me?'

The medic stares at you, deep in thought. 'The truth is, you can't.'

A shiver runs up your spine. 'But how is it even possible – to assume the shape of another?'

Lansbury chews her bottom lip, pondering the question. 'Hmm, some magic you have forgotten, I think. Perhaps you share a common bond, a shared conscience, with the others of your kind ... through the mark.'

The thought sickens you, bringing bile to the back of your throat. 'I do not wish to share anything with their kind.'

Lansbury is silent, her attention shifting back to the decorative arch. You see that its keystone and several of the surrounding stones are smashed, disfiguring their runes.

'When in doubt, take the direct approach,' mutters Nyms, kicking at the loose rubble covering the floor. 'Is there anything they don't try and break?'

Caeleb has moved ahead and is now peering through the archway into the chamber beyond. He looks back over his shoulder, motioning your party to prepare for combat. Turn to 790.

881

'Craving more magic, eh?' The trader gives a low whistle. 'Well, I reckon these are just what you need.' He reaches inside the chest and produces three items, which he lays carefully before you. 'Now, magic like this,' he catches your eye, his mouth twisting into a smile, 'could win you a war. Tell me, how can anyone put a price on that?' He rubs his jaw thoughtfully. 'It pains me ... but, 900 gold crowns? Yes, that's a fair price. Risked my life for those little beauties.'

You may purchase any of the following items for 900 gold crowns each:

Slipstream gown	Talanost's reach	Boots of shielding
(chest)	(left-hand: wand)	(feet)
+2 speed +4 magic	+2 speed +4 magic	+2 speed +1 armour
Ability: overload	Ability: critical strike	Ability: deflect

After you have made your purchases, you can ask to see Waldo's special deals (turn to 914) or bid the trader farewell (turn to 789).

882

Searching the general's armour, you find a leather pouch containing 150 gold crowns. You may also help yourself to one of the following special rewards:

Retribution	Bone bow of grief	Bloodied chestguard
(main hand: sword)	(left hand: bow)	(chest)
+3 speed +6 brawn	+2 speed +5 brawn	+2 speed +4 armour
Ability: feral fury	Ability: puncture	Ability: bleed

When you have made your decision, turn to 824.

You pass around the back of the domed building, hoping to find an alternative entrance to Arthurian's tomb. However, as you gaze upon the wide expanse of mildewed stone, your hopes are dashed.

'Nice idea,' groans Nyms, pushing against a section of the wall. 'Were you hoping to find a secret door, Lans?'

You glance over your shoulder, waiting for the medic's retort. To your surprise to find that Lansbury isn't there.

'Over here!'

Your attention is drawn to a wedge-shaped mound of dirt, set away from the building. Lank yellow reeds and tangled thorns cover much of its surface. Lansbury is standing next to it, her staff pointed to a section of the mound.

'What have you found?' grumbles Nyms, walking over. 'A new herb for your collection?'

When you join the medic, you give a snort of surprise when you see the secret entrance that she has discovered. It is a slab of dark grey stone, set into the earth. Someone or something has pushed it inwards, revealing an ash-clogged set of stairs, leading down into darkness.

'A back entrance,' grins Lansbury. 'You just need to have faith.'

The medic utters a quick word of magic, summoning a brilliant white light to the tip of her staff. 'Care to join me?'

With a smug smile, the medic starts down the stairs. Nyms draws his swords and gives you an uneasy frown. 'I've a bad feeling about this.'

'That's not like you,' chuckles Caeleb, pushing him forwards into the earthen tunnel. 'Need me to hold your hand?'

Nyms gives Caeleb a playful shove as they head down the stairs.

You pause, your eyes shifting to your shadow mark, which has started to tingle beneath your skin. Not a good sign, you realise grimly.

Readying your own weapons, you follow the others into the secret passage, grateful – at least – to be finally out of the incessant rain. Turn to 844.

884

The inquisitor flings his shield away, then turns on you in a zealous rage. 'This changes nothing between us, shadow spawn,' he spits. You hear the creak of leather as his hands tighten around his mighty war-hammer. For a second, the rest of the battle is forgotten as you stare each other down, tensed ... ready to fight.

Then a voice cuts through the tension. It is Avian Dale. He circles past on a magic carpet, a trail of glittering light streaming behind him. 'We're heading for the doom orb,' he shouts. 'Are you with us?' Across the other side of the square, the airborne regulars have now gathered in tight formation, their glowing carpets streaking skywards, towards the gigantic sphere. Avian sweeps in closer, offering out his hand. 'If your magic is strong, I could use your aid, apprentice.'

If you have a *magic* score of 24 or above, you may accompany Avian Dale. (Turn to 921.) Otherwise, you decline, wishing to focus your efforts on the ground battle. (Turn to 905.)

885

For several moments, you struggle to comprehend what you are witnessing. You had been sure that the city had been cleared – that every last shadow spawn had been destroyed. But here, crammed into the market square, is a veritable horde of the vile creatures. And they look different – more powerful and demonic than any of the creatures you have encountered already.

Through the chaotic mass of black bodies, you see beacons of hope – your companions struggling against the endless tide. To your left, Lansbury is pinned against a wall, with Nyms lying at her feet. His hands are pressed to the side of his chest, his expression pained. The healer has summoned a shield of holy light to protect them – but it is being battered down by the creatures that surround her. They look like rotting undead, with parasitic growths sprouting from their decaying bandages. With her efforts focused solely on maintaining the shield, Lansbury is unable to heal Nyms' wounds.

To your right, Avian stands alone, encircled by a sizeable mound of blackened bodies. Overwhelmed by shadow spawn, he has now resorted to a similar magic shield, its green glow enfolding him in a protective dome. All around it, scorpion-like monsters are besieging the magic, spitting venom against its walls, and hammering at it with their barbed tails.

From the centre of the square, a white signal flare whizzes up into the dark skies, where it bursts into glittering shards of bright light. Following its trail, you see Mathis standing on the platform of a ruined statue. On all sides, shadowy ghouls are attempting to overwhelm his position, their sharp claws promising a painful end. The inquisitor is beating back their efforts with his warhammer, while using a filched shield to deflect incoming bolts of magic from the far side of the square. There, rising above the undulating tide of shadow spawn, is a black-armoured knight. They sit astride a giant four-legged beast, its black hide covered in thick plates of metal. In the knight's hands is a longbow fashioned from bone, which they are using to send a constant stream of magic towards the beleaguered inquisitor.

You must decide which of your companions you will aid.

Will you:

Help Lansbury and Nyms?	924
Help Avian Dale?	821
Help Inquisitor Mathis?	854

886

The room is a lot smaller than you had expected for such a grand entrance, however, what it contains more than makes up for any shortcomings. The entire space is filled with a dazzling array of treasures – goblets, caskets, statues, jewellery – its glittering radiance reflected a hundred-fold in the polished armour, arranged in racks along the walls.

You are left speechless, your eyes roving from one treasure to the next. Arthurian, on the other hand, appears less daunted by the impressive spectacle. He strides into the room, looking around intently.

'It must be here!' he snaps. He kicks over a statue in his haste to reach a velvet bag. Lifting it up, he spills the contents onto the floor.

You watch mesmerised as a stream of golden coins and fist-sized jewels rain across the floor. Snarling, he throws the empty bag aside, his eyes searching the room. Next, he marches over to a trunk, pulling out clothes and hurling them aside. He lifts up the empty box and turns it over, shaking it angrily.

'The mage said it would be here!' he growls, his head snapping round to focus on the next area of his search. He moves over to a silver casket and lifts it out of a sea of coins. Opening it up, he gives a maddened peel of laughter.

'Yes! Yes!' he casts the casket aside, raising his left fist to reveal an onyx necklace . Hanging on the end of it is a round pendant, its glassy centre swirling with black smoke. 'The witch's charm!'

'Wait!'

Before you can stop him, Arthurian throws back his arm and brings the pendant down hard against the nearest wall. It shatters, sending black smoke spiralling up into the air.

Arthurian gives a gasp, stumbling backwards. 'Yes. Yes ...'

His eyes grow wide, his mouth gagging open, gulping for breath. You move quickly to his side, catching him as he falls.

The body goes into spasm, gripped by a series of abrupt seizures. Then the warrior's eyes close and he is still, the body becoming limp in your arms.

'Arthurian?' Gently, you lay him down, aware that the warrior is no longer breathing. 'So, you finally got your wish,' you mutter sadly.

Your attention is caught by the silver crucifix resting against the grime-stained jerkin. You go to take it, when suddenly there is a flash of movement; Arthurian's hand snaps around your wrist, gripping it tightly.

As you wrestle to free yourself, you realise that the man's body is alive once again ... the chest is rising and falling with deep, ragged breaths; the lips part to give a low moan.

Then the eyes flick open.

Instead of Arthurian's steely gaze, you are met by dark pits of hatred.

'No!' You break the man's powerful grip, stumbling back into a clinking mound of gold and silver.

The stranger springs agilely to his feet, his right arm bursting into purple flames. 'What is this?' He stares at you intently, his brow creasing with a sudden confusion. 'Nevarin? Are you the one who brought me back here?' He draws the jewelled dagger from his belt. 'What foolishness is this?'

You realise that this must be the shadowstalker who tricked Arthurian; the one who stole his body and led his faithful knights to their deaths against the shadow legion.

'Yes,' you growl, your own shadow mark flaring with anger. 'Though I intend to send you back to the demon pit that spawned you!':

	Speed	Brawn	Armour	Health
Kelldred	13	10	8	90

Special abilities

🍷 Mark of fury: At the end of every combat round, your hero takes 3 health damage from the flames that surround the Nevarin. This ability ignores *armour*.

🍷 Heightened senses: You cannot use *evade*, *sidestep* or *vanish* in this combat.

If you defeat this sinister foe, turn to **892**. If you are defeated, turn to **796**.

887

Searching the general's armour, you find a leather pouch containing 150 gold crowns. You may also help yourself to one of the following special rewards:

Final solution	Heartache	Styrax sinew
(left hand: sword)	(necklace)	(ring)
+2 speed +5 brawn	+1 speed +1 brawn	+2 brawn +2 armour
Ability: acid	Ability: disrupt	Ability: webbed

When you have made your decision, turn to **824**.

888

As you land the killing blow, you step away from the robber, leaving him to fall to his knees on the muddy ground. His dagger drops from his hand, his pale fingers going to a cord around his throat.

'Judah protect me.' A flash of lightning picks out the silver crucifix he is now clutching between bloody fingers. When he looks up at you, he is smiling. 'Did I pass the test? Did I prove my faith?'

Then, with a cry of anguish, his body begins to unravel, spinning into black coils of shadow that rise up before you in a whirling column.

Your eyes widen in shock. 'It ... can't be!'

The robber was a Nevarin, just like yourself. There is a sharp tingling from your shadow mark. You tug back your sleeve to reveal the diamond-bodied serpents branded into your skin.

As you look back at the writhing mass of magic, you feel the familiar desire welling up inside of you – the overwhelming need to absorb the magic into your mark.

Will you:

Resist the urge?	806
Absorb the magic?	827

889

'Did they send you? Are you here to finish what you started?' The robber hisses like a cornered serpent, making a tentative lunge for you with the knife. You dodge away, watching him intently.

'Finish what?' you ask, frowning.

'Oh, games – yes, your kind like games.' The robber taps the side of his head with the hilt of his dagger. 'Get inside my head ... head, yes!'

'I'm not here to play games.' You raise your hands as a sign of submission. 'I am here to help you. Perhaps that is why I was brought here – to this place.' You speak slowly, emphasising each word in the hope that you can calm this crazed vagabond.

'Help?' he sneers. 'Why would you help me?'

You glance around at the dark chamber. 'I sense you are trapped here ... or perhaps you are looking for something that you can't find. Am I right?'

The robber steps back, looking momentarily disarmed. 'I just want what was mine.' You notice him tug his coat over his chest, trying to obscure a silver chain. Dangling on the end of it is a crucifix.

'And I'll help you, I promise.'

'Promises?' The robber snickers. 'It is already too late for me! I will not play these games!' He takes the dagger he is holding and, with a cry of defiant rage, he plunges the blade into his chest.

'No!' You rush forward, grabbing the robber by the lapels of his dirty coat. Blood flecks his lips as he looks up at you between his matted hair. 'I cannot die,' he rasps. 'I cannot die. What harm can you do to me?'

He laughs, crimson spit bubbling down his dirt-stained chin. 'You cannot harm me, demon!' Then, with a cry of anguish, his body begins to unravel, spinning into dark coils of shadow.

Your eyes widen in shock. 'No! It can't be!'

The robber is a Nevarin, just like yourself. There is a sharp tingling from your shadow mark. You tug back your sleeve to reveal the diamond-bodied serpents branded into your skin.

As you look back to the writhing mass of magic, you feel the familiar desire welling up inside of you – the overwhelming need to absorb the magic into your mark.

Will you:

Resist the urge?	806
Absorb the magic?	827

890

'I understand,' nods Avian. 'Then take this. I suspect you will have need of it.' He reaches into his robes and pulls out a metal globe. 'Something I made myself.' He tosses it to you.

'What is it?' you ask, snatching it out of the air. Turning it over in your hands, you discover that the globe's surface is perfectly smooth, without marking or decoration.

'It will project a shield around you, for a limited time,' explains the mage. 'Use it wisely.'

Portable shield (1 use)
(backpack)
Use any time in combat to raise a shield.
This shield will absorb 10 damage before
it is destroyed. Any further damage
is deducted from your own *health*

'Thank you.' You clasp Avian's hand.

The mage regards you gravely, as if troubled by something. 'You will travel to dark places, Nevarin. Of that I am sure.' He glances up at the doom orb, its magic glittering against the darkening sky. 'The time has come ...' He sighs, his gaze shifting back to you. 'I think you have fulfilled your apprenticeship, don't you?'

He raises his hands – and suddenly bright light flares around the edges of the carpet. A second later and the mage is speeding away, to join the rest of the airborne regulars gathering at the far side of the square.

You glance down at the globe, and at your own wearied expression reflected in its metallic surface. Indeed, you have come a long way since you first walked across the drawbridge at Avian's castle, presenting the mage with your letter of recommendation. 'Dark places ...' Pocketing Avian's gift, you turn your attention back to the square. Turn to 905.

891

You smash apart the golem's body, sending battered sheets of twisted metal careening across the room. Finally, you drive your magic into the beast's head, ripping apart the delicate array of cogs and wheels. With a wheezing low-pitched whirr, the automaton crashes to the ground in a pile of smoking body parts.

You may now help yourself to one of the following rewards:

Charged core	Meat grinder	Steel gear solid
(necklace)	(left hand: mace)	(left hand: shield)
+2 magic	+2 speed +3 brawn	+2 speed +3 armour
Ability: life spark	Ability: pound	Ability: retaliation
(requirement: mage)		(requirement: warrior)

When you have made your decision, turn to 805.

892

Your final blow hurls the Nevarin back against the wall, where he explodes into a swirling mass of shadow magic. Eagerly, you raise your mark and absorb his dark essence, revelling in the fiendish power that is now yours.

If you wish, you may change the ability of any one of your items to:

Usurper (mo): (only usable in hero vs. hero combat). Use any time during a combat to steal a speed or modifier ability that your opponent has already used. You may then play this same ability against them during the combat, based on the ability's description. *Usurper* can only be used once per combat.

Searching the treasure vault, you may also help yourself to one of the following items:

Justice	Cloak of ceremonies	Lion's tabard
(left hand: hammer)	(cloak)	(chest)
+2 speed +3 brawn	+2 speed +2 magic	+1 speed +2 brawn
Ability: knockdown	Ability: radiance	Ability: fearless
(requirement: warrior)		

You also fill your pockets with gold, before leaving the vault (you have gained 150 gold crowns). Turn to 846.

893

Searching Daarko's remains, you find a leather pouch containing 100 gold crowns. You may also help yourself to one of the following special rewards:

The dread mask	Boots of black fortune	Ring of rebirth
(head)	(feet)	(ring)
+1 speed +3 brawn	+2 speed +2 armour	+2 brawn
Ability: overpower	Ability: feint	Ability: kick start

When you have made your decision, turn to 811.

894

'A wise choice,' nods Lansbury. 'I'm glad to see someone listens to my counsel.'

Nyms starts past you, rolling his eyes as he does so. You grin back at him as you follow, with Lansbury and Caeleb bringing up the rear.

Moving quickly, you take a wide arc around the paved courtyard, keeping to the shadows of the smaller outbuildings. Most are grey and crumbling, their stonework clogged with weeds and thorny brambles.

As you pass around the side of the domed building, Nyms suddenly halts, dropping down for cover behind a fallen column. He waves for the rest of you to do the same.

'What is it?' you whisper, crouching beside him. 'I don't see ...'

Nyms puts a hand on your sleeve to silence you, and then nods towards a smaller tomb over to the left. As you scan its weed-choked stonework, you suddenly hear voices amidst the drumming rain. They appear to be coming from the other side of the tomb, obscured from view by a mouldering statue.

Will you:

Insist that the party investigates?	931
Ignore the distraction and continue onwards?	883

Lansbury lowers the shield, moving quickly to Nyms' side. The swordsman lies on his back, cursing as he kicks at the ground in pain.

'Stop struggling. Let me see,' insists the medic, bending close.

Nyms lifts his bloodied hands away, his breath rattling in his lungs. 'Got ... any miracles ... left?' he rasps.

For the briefest moment, you see surprise on the medic's face as she looks upon the full extent of the wound. Then she is lost in her art, pressing palms tight to his chest, weaving the skin and muscle back into place.

It takes only a few moments. Then Lansbury leans back with an exhausted sigh. 'It is done. Blessed be the light.'

With a groan, Nyms sits up on his elbows, looking down at the torn shreds of armour. Where there had once been an unsightly gash, there is now newly healed flesh. 'You know, Lans, I think I could become a believer.' He pushes himself back to his feet, retrieving his swords from the dust. 'That's almost as many lives as you now, Nevarin.'

'Well, don't grow too attached to your latest one,' you reply wryly, 'we're not out of this yet.' All around you, the shadow spawn are starting to regroup, their snarls and hollers rising once again.

'At least we won't be facing them alone,' states Lansbury, pointing. You follow her gaze to the battalion of magic carpets, sweeping over the battlefield. One of the riders looks familiar.

'Avian Dale!' You cry, waving a hand in the air. 'Over here!'

He breaks away from the others, gliding closer. 'We're heading for the doom orb,' he shouts. 'Are you with us?' Across the other side of the square, the rest of the airborne regulars are gathering in formation, preparing to take on the monstrous orb. Avian offers out his hand. 'If your magic is strong, I could use your aid, apprentice.'

If you have a *magic* score of 24 or above, you may accompany Avian Dale. (Turn to **921**.) Otherwise, you decline, wishing to focus your efforts on the ground battle. (Turn to **905**.)

896

It is Mathis. The inquisitor's armour is raked with black scars, his hair plastered to his face by blood and sweat. 'Nevarin,' he drawls, stumbling dizzily through the haze. 'I swore to the One God, the maker ... that I'd destroy all shadow spawn this day ...'

'Mathis?' You frown, taking a step backwards. 'You are not yourself ...'

He raises his warhammer. 'Oh I am perfectly myself, demon!'

Suddenly, you catch movement out of the corner of your eye. A man is standing on the edge of a rooftop, his scarlet coat billowing in the wind. He raises his hand and suddenly you feel the strange force closing in around you once again. You try and struggle, but the invisible bonds hold you fast.

Then the man is moving, running through the air as quickly and deftly as if it was solid ground. And like a dog on a leash, you find yourself being dragged after him, floating in a magical prison.

'I'll find you!' screams Mathis. 'I'll find you, demon!'

You are pulled across a broad plaza, its fountains and pathways now charred and cratered, towards an officious-looking building clinging to a rise of grey rock. You try and discern its purpose – but the invisible bonds shift, spinning you around. Then something hard strikes you across the head, plunging you into darkness. Turn to 928.

897

Determined not to allow the mysterious assassin to escape, you dive across the tomb in an effort to reach him. As black lightning streaks from his fingertips, you know you only have seconds to spare. Frantically, you grab hold of the man's robes, bunching the soft material in your fists.

'No!' You hear Lansbury cry out.

There is a flash of bright light and suddenly the room falls away into nothingness. Your stomach gives a lurch as you feel yourself rushing forwards at great speed ...

Another flash.

Freezing cold water splashes against your face, forcing you to recoil. As you stumble backwards, you see that your surroundings have changed. All around you, water pours over jagged black rocks, spilling out from a gorge high above you.

'What the ...?'

You look around frantically, having lost all sense of your bearings.

There is hard rock beneath your feet – a ledge, jutting out like a giant's tooth from a mossy cliff side. A few metres away a curtain of water breaks against its pitted edge, filling the air with a fine white spray. For a second, all you can hear is the roar of the waterfall. Then, you catch something else ... the scuffle of feet.

Spinning round, you see Fetch lunging for you with a knife. You react instantly, snatching his wrist and twisting it back, forcing him to drop the weapon.

'Fool!'

You feel the air around you charging with static ... the water roars loader in your ears, a deafening pain ... then there is another flash of white light. You find yourself falling forwards, hands flailing for something to hold onto. There is nothing to see – only a white light; piercing and cold.

Then a stone floor rushes up to meet you. Unable to stop yourself, you slam down hard with a cry of pain. Turn to 872.

898

Nyms studies the trader with a frown. 'I've heard of such things – charms that allow you to travel unseen or to confuse those that would seek to do you harm. I suspect this cart of his,' he taps one of the rickety-looking wheels with his foot, 'strange though it might sound, could have such a charm worked on it. Although, why anyone would want to give this junkyard that kind of attention ...'

He tilts his head, regarding the trader with a half-smile. 'In a camp full of the king's own, he would be even crazier than me to cause trouble. And as you know...that is a whole lot of crazy.'

The swordsman turns and pats you on the shoulder. 'Perhaps you should find out what he has to sell. I mean,' Nyms makes a show of looking you up and down, 'you could really do with the makeover.'

Will you:

Ask Lansbury about the strange runes?	860
Ask to see the trader's wares?	795

899

You expose your mark, dragging the spirit's shadowy remains towards the waiting jaws of your branded serpents. You have gained the following special ability:

Banshee's wail (co): Use this ability to stop your opponent rolling for damage when they have won a round. You can only use this ability once per combat.

Nyms shivers and looks away. 'I hate it when you do that.'

You laugh as the newly absorbed magic surges through your body, healing your wounds and swelling your corded muscles. You close your eyes, feeling yourself drifting away on the euphoric currents of magic, losing yourself to a void of darkness...

'Nevarin!'

You hear a voice but it is distant, distorted. It belonged to someone you once knew – but perhaps that was another life. You see others now, bodies shimmering like stars against the backdrop of night. Other Nevarin. Other faces. They slide past you, blurring into streaks of light. You try and focus but they are moving too quick, eluding you. All except one... standing alone, burning brighter than the rest. A man. His eyes widen with surprise as he turns to face you. You catch a scar running down his left cheek and a circlet of gold resting on his brow.

'Nevarin!'

You feel something tugging at you. Pulling you back.

With a gasp, you lurch forward, your eyes snapping open – to find Nyms' gaunt face inches from your own. 'Woah, you're back!' The rogue rocks back on his heels, surprised. 'What happened?' he asks, looking you over with concern. 'You just passed out cold.'

You try and remember, but the gossamer images are already fading from memory. 'The mark ...' You look down to see its swirling runes humming with energy, their bright glow shimmering across your body. 'It ... it was nothing,' you state hastily, clambering back to your feet.

As your gaze falls on the double doors leading deeper into the mansion, you can't help but feel that whatever lurks in this place, in this city, now knows you are coming.

'I've got a new plan,' says Nyms, his hands flexing around his weapons. 'You lead the way and I'll watch *your* back. How does that sound – better?'

You stride towards the double doors and fling them open, their runes of protection fizzing and hissing in protest. 'Do not worry, my friend. The time for skulking in shadows is over.' Turn to 936.

900

The blood-smeared passageway opens out onto a large, rectangular room. In each of its corners is a stone pedestal, above which an orb of green light hovers in mid-air, casting an eerie glow over the room's cluttered contents.

At the centre of the subterranean chamber is a tomb, bearing the effigy of Valentine D'Azzuro. The lid of the tomb is still intact. At the foot of it, two necromancers lie sprawled in the dust, their wounds coated with a bubbling green poison.

Around the edges of the room, smashed pottery and overturned chests litter the space. Several racks have been pulled down from the wall and their weapons lie strewn across the floor, joining the tattered scrolls and discarded books that have been tipped out of their cases and trunks.

There is the sound of angry cursing. A figure, previously hidden by the tomb, suddenly straightens into view – the ghostly-green light catches their features.

It is a hooded man, dressed in velvet-black robes. His long, pale fingers are curled around an object, which looks like a sceptre or rod. With a snarl, he tosses it aside ... then his head jerks around, as your party enter the room.

Your eyes meet and recognition dawns.

'Fetch!'

The hooded man mumbles another curse, then throws his arms up towards the ceiling. Black light flickers around his body.

'He's teleporting!' you cry, starting forward into the room.

'No!' shouts Lansbury. 'Do not go near it!'

Will you:

Grab Fetch before he can leave?	897
Heed the medic's warning?	802

901

It is Caeleb. The cavalier's armour is raked with black scars, his shield battered and dented. He staggers dizzily through the haze, his inscribed sword dragging through the dirt behind him. 'Nevarin,' he drawls, hobbling closer. 'I swore to Mathis ... to the One God ... that, I'd destroy all shadow spawn this day ...'

'Caeleb?' You shake your head in confusion. 'What madness is this? I'm not your enemy!'

Suddenly, you catch movement out of the corner of your eye. A man is standing on the edge of a rooftop, his scarlet coat billowing in the wind. He raises his hand and suddenly you feel the strange force closing in around you once again. You try and struggle, but the invisible bonds hold you fast.

Then the man is moving, running through the air as quickly and deftly as if it was solid ground. And like a dog on leash, you find yourself being dragged after him, floating in a magical prison.

'I'll find you!' screams Caeleb. 'I'll find you, demon!'

You are pulled across a broad plaza, its fountains and pathways now charred and cratered, towards an officious-looking building clinging to a rise of grey rock. You try and discern its purpose – but the invisible bonds shift, spinning you around. Then something hard strikes you across the head, plunging you into darkness. Turn to 928.

902

You find yourself back in the paved stone room – opposite you are the stairs that lead back up to the surface. Caeleb and Nyms have already passed beneath the archway in the west wall, their footfalls echoing back from the passageway beyond. Turn to 909.

903

'Really?' The trader gives a low whistle. 'Well, what I've got here will turn a few heads, even Lord Happy's over there.' He nods in Nyms' direction. 'Your friend does have a certain charm though, I'll give him that.' With a smirk, Waldo reaches inside the chest and produces three items, which he lays carefully before you. 'Now, tell me – how can anyone put a price on these?' He rubs his jaw thoughtfully. 'It pains me ... but, 900 gold crowns? Yes, that's a fair price. Risked my life for those little beauties.'

You may purchase any of the following items for 900 gold crowns each:

Confessor's coat	Talanost's edge	Reaper's fists
(chest)	(main-hand: sword)	(gloves)
+2 speed +4 brawn	+3 speed +5 brawn	+1 speed +3 brawn
Ability: fortitude	Ability: sear	Ability: critical strike

After you have made your purchases, you can ask to see Waldo's special deals (turn to 839) or bid the trader farewell (turn to 789).

904

The shadowstalker goes for a lunge, but stumbles losing her balance. You note that her breathing is laboured, her movements lacking the sharp focus you would normally associate with one of her kind.

'This place does not agree with us, does it?' you state dourly, feeling the heaviness dragging at your own limbs.

The shadowstalker rights herself, raising her magical blades once again. You see that both are dripping with a thick black poison. 'On the contrary, I find you considerably more intolerable, coward!' With a screeching cry, the stalker springs forward, her poisoned blades cutting deadly arcs of steel:

	Speed	Brawn	Armour	Health
Malaise	12	11	10	90

Special abilities

◗ Withering strikes: Each time you take health damage from Malaise's damage score, you must lower your *brawn* and *magic* by 1.

◗ Deadly venom: Once you have taken health damage from the shadowstalker, at the end of each combat round, you must automatically lose 3 *health*.

If you defeat Malaise, turn to 912. If you are defeated, turn to 862.

905

The shadow spawn surge forward, presenting a single, black wall of snarling death. You grip your weapons, waiting tensely for the inevitable. Above their horned helms and grisly standards, you see the last of the mages streaking towards the doom orb that hangs above Talanost. The dark moon of flesh and sinew is firing a torrent of black fire across the city. You can only assume that it is destroying the last of Ravenwing's camp and hampering any attempt at reinforcement.

Then the wave of shadow spawn crashes down upon you, drowning you in a mass of filthy bodies and snapping jaws. With a surge of magic, you break free – springing up into the air. Daarko's power is nearly spent, but there is just enough, pulsing within your shadow mark, to make a worthy last stand.

Great tentacles of shadow spiral out from the writhing serpents on your arm, smashing into the legion's ranks and sending bodies flying. A giant looms close, trying to bat you with its spiked club. You flip over, blasting it with bolts of magic. The giant gives a booming cry, as its smoking body crashes down, sending shadow spawn scampering in all directions.

You hang in the air, your magic surrounding you in a halo of purple light. From here, you are able to take in the battlefield. At the far side of the square, amidst the blackened craters inflicted by the airstrike, the dark general sits astride their armoured mount. The warrior has sighted you, levelling their bow to fire a stream of enchanted arrows in your direction. Your shield blocks the deadly projectiles, their magic fizzing and sparking harmlessly on impact. But you know that your barrier will not hold for long.

To your right, a knot of Ravenwing's forces are battling the shadow spawn. Even though they are outnumbered ten to one, they are managing to push back the enemy forces. Behind them, you see more warriors hurrying into the square – Ravenwing and Caeleb amongst them. Suddenly, a jagged boulder smashes down amongst their ranks, throwing up dust and sending them hurrying for cover. The missile came from the edge of the square, where an ogre-like monster is swinging a huge ball and chain in an angered frenzy, smashing up buildings and sending broken masonry toppling towards the knights.

Ravenwing and Caeleb emerge from the dust, attempting to close in on its position, but they are headed off by a group of shadow spawn. The ogre gives a deafening roar as it lumbers towards the fight, its heavy iron-shod boots crushing the stone beneath its feet.

Will you:

Attack the general?	861
Attack the ogre?	930

906

With the help of your allies, you are able to bring down the gigantic bone angel. While Lansbury administers healing to a wounded Caeleb, you search the rotted pile of flesh and bone. You may now help yourself to one of the following rewards:

Broken wings	Bone halo	Skull plate
(cloak)	(head)	(chest)
+2 speed +2 brawn	+2 speed +3 magic	+2 speed +3 armour
Ability: fearless	Ability: focus	Ability: dominate
		(requirement: warrior)

When you have made your decision, turn to **841**.

Ravenwing's men pursue the routed shadow spawn, slashing and blasting at their fleeing enemy. The battle is won. But at what cost? You look around at the men that have remained behind – not only the wounded and the dead, but those who have simply hung back from exhaustion. Many have a haunted look about them, their bodies blackened by soot and grime. You can't imagine what devastation awaits beyond the walls of the city – where the doom orb's magic was turned against the camp. The men's expressions tell you enough.

Across the rubble-strewn square, you see Mathis lying on his side. The inquisitor looks badly wounded. Possibly fatal. Caeleb kneels at his side, his ear pressed close to the warrior's fevered ramblings. Ravenwing stumbles past, helping to support an exhausted Lansbury. You notice that Nyms is not with her. The grizzled warrior glances your way, shaking his head sadly.

'Nevarin!' Caeleb trudges through the rubble towards you. The cavalier's armour is raked with black scars, his shield battered and dented. 'It's over for your kind,' he sneers, hobbling closer. 'I swore to Mathis ... to the One God ... that I'd destroy all shadow spawn this day ...'

'Caeleb?' You shake your head in confusion. 'What madness is this? I'm not your enemy.'

He raises his inscribed sword. 'Mathis told me everything ...'

Suddenly, you catch movement out of the corner of your eye. A man is standing on the edge of a rooftop, his scarlet coat billowing in the wind. He raises his hand and suddenly you feel an invisible force closing in around you, pinning your arms and legs tightly together.

Then the man is moving, running through the air as quickly and deftly as if it was solid ground. And like a dog on leash, you find yourself being dragged after him, floating in a magical prison.

'More demons!' screams Caeleb. 'Don't think you can escape!'

You are pulled across a broad plaza, its fountains and pathways now charred and cratered, towards an officious-looking building clinging to a rise of grey rock. You try and discern its purpose – but the invisible bonds shift, spinning you around. Then something hard strikes you across the head, plunging you into darkness. Turn to 928.

908

You are back in the tomb of Valentine D'Azzuro. While you recover from your ordeal, you recount your strange travels to Lansbury, Nyms and Caeleb. The latter is inspecting an antique sword as he listens to your story.

'What was this talisman he was so interested in?' he asks, turning the sword over to scrutinise the hilt.

You shrug your shoulders, before taking another gulp from Nym's water skin.

'It matters not,' states Lansbury stiffly. 'Whatever that creature is, it is no concern of ours.'

'He was a man,' you add, lowering the skin. 'Once.'

'He reeked of old magic. Old magic gone bad.'

You hand the skin back to Nyms before pushing yourself back to your feet. 'Avian trusted him, like he trusts me.'

Lansbury purses her lips, her back straightening.

'Now, now ...' Nyms steps around the medic, pointing to the archway with the tip of his sword. 'Can we save the drama for camp?'

You rub your shadow mark, which has started to burn again, beneath your skin. 'I have no mind to delay here.' Turn to 793.

909

You follow the corridor through into a wide circular chamber. It is nondescript save for a pattern of runes carved into the floor. Each one is surrounded by intricate lettering, the characters flowing in a spiralling array of designs. The effect would be almost hypnotic, if it wasn't for the dust and rubble that is strewn over most of the engraving. As you pass through, you see that someone or something has smashed many of the flagstones, disrupting the detailed scripture.

'The work of a fine inscriber,' comments Lansbury. 'Such a shame that its power has been broken.'

Caeleb has not halted, showing little interest in the runed tiles. Instead, he is intent on heading deeper into the tomb. As you follow him into a side passage, you hear a strangled cry from up ahead, accompanied by the ringing boom of a voice raised in anger.

'Looks like we've caught up with the necros,' mutters Nyms.

Caeleb doesn't slow, advancing down the corridor into the next chamber. Turn to 878.

910

The robber spits on the ground. 'What am I doing here?' he growls. 'Like you wouldn't know, demon!' He continues to circle you warily, the blade of his dagger glinting in the lantern-light. 'Did they send you? Are you here to finish what they started?' He hisses like a cornered serpent, making a tentative lunge for you with the knife. You dodge away, watching him intently.

'Finish what?' you ask, frowning.

'Oh games – yes, your kind like games.' The robber taps the side of his head with the hilt of his dagger. 'Get inside my head, yes!'

'I'm not here to play games.' You raise your hands as a sign of submission. 'I was brought here by some magic. Perhaps you were too.'

The robber shakes his head, sniggering. 'Witch magic. Took my soul ... stole my soul. If you cannot give it back, then you are no use to me!'

Before you can say anything, the robber comes running at you with his dagger. Turn to 816.

911

While Caeleb battles with the tutor, it is up to you to defeat the young mage and his ghoulish companion:

	Speed	Magic	Armour	Health
Apprentice	12	9	8	85

Special abilities

◆ Giblets: The zombie causes 3 health damage at the end of every combat round. This ability ignores *armour*. Once the acolyte is defeated, the zombie will no longer attack.

◗ Dark master: If you are a necromancer you can attempt to wrest control of the zombie. Roll a die at the start of each combat round. On a roll of a ⚅ you have won control. For the remainder of the combat, Giblets will inflict his damage on the apprentice instead.

If you defeat the apprentice, turn to 923. If you are defeated, turn to 862.

912

Your weapons clash together, scraping and sparking. It isn't long before both of you are sapped of strength – exhausted, the fight becomes more of an uncoordinated brawl. Amidst the flailing punches and desperate strikes, you knock the shadowstalker's mask away, revealing a porcelain white face framed by curls of dark hair. The woman's eyes are a brilliant blue – both beautiful and cold.

At last, pinning your enemy to one of the sword-clipped pillars, you drive home a fatal blow. In those final moments you look deep into the woman's crystal blue eyes, looking for some regret, some hint of humanity. But there is only a bitter hatred, festering like a poisoned wound ...

Then the face and body begin to change.

You jerk away in shock, watching with a mix of revulsion and fascination as the shadowstalker's physique broadens out, the skin reforming itself over shifting bones. Within seconds, you are looking upon your own face – staring back you with those same hard blue eyes.

The shadowstalker spits blood in your face.

'You are one of us,' your own voice growls with gusto. Then the eyes lose their fierce glimmer, the face becomes slack and the stalker's body slumps to the floor at your feet.

With shaking hands, you feel at your cheeks, tracing the familiar contours of your face. When you remove your hand, there is blood coating your fingers.

The air crackles with magic, as the stalker's body becomes a swirling mass of shadow. Feeling tired and numb, you can barely raise your arm – watching with a hollow detachment as the magic pours into your mark, healing your wounds and relieving you of the dull ache in your muscles.

All that remains of the stalker is their few paltry belongings. You find 30 gold crowns and can help yourself to one of the following rewards:

Scorn	Tainted wraps	Twisted treads
(main hand: sword)	(gloves)	(feet)
+2 speed +3 brawn	+1 speed +3 magic	+2 speed +2 brawn
Ability: immobilise	Ability: curse	Ability: trickster

When you have made your decision, turn to 919.

913

Your shadow mark flares bright as your grip on the assassin tightens. 'Tell me about the book. The Grimoire of Naraghost. Why was it so important?'

Fetch gives a wheezing cough. 'It does not concern you. Now release …'

'TELL ME!' you growl, shaking him angrily. 'I deserve to know. I risked my life to find it.'

'Very well,' hisses the assassin. 'It belonged to a navigator – one of the elves. My master had been searching for it for a very long time. Little did he know it had been right under his nose all along.'

'And your master? Who do you serve, Fetch?'

The man's pale lips curve into a smile. 'Avian Dale. I think you know him.'

You shake your head, scowling with contempt. 'Lies, that can't be true. Avian is a good man.'

'Know him so well do you? Let me tell you something about Avian. He has a special talent – a talent for finding people like us. Those who are broken and need fixing; those he can breathe new life into … give them fresh purpose.'

You release the assassin and back away, no longer certain if what he says is the truth or just more poison. 'And the book,' you ask, your voice little more than a whisper. 'Why did he need it? I thought it was evil.'

Fetch's glittering eyes fix on your own. 'It is evil, Nevarin. And that is why I lost it. To a demon.'

Your confused expression urges Fetch to say more.

'The book is a set of charts, to navigate through the shroud. It is how the elves used to travel between worlds, before they built the gates.'

'The shroud.' The word is familiar. You sift through your memories, trying to remember ... 'Lansbury. It has something to do with old magic.'

Fetch snorts. 'It is the birthplace of magic. It *is* magic. Anything that touches or passes through that place is changed ... and not always for the better.'

'And that's what happened to the book?' you ask intently. 'It was corrupted by this magic?'

Fetch gives a rasping laugh. 'You are learning fast, Nevarin. Yes, and before I could get the book to safety, something else – a demon changeling – took it from me.'

'And there was me thinking you had a gift for speedy getaways,' you add with a smirk. 'So, what happened?'

Fetch sneers, as if the explanation is beneath him. 'When I travel, I pass through the shroud, if only for an instant. The demon was waiting for me ... and on this occasion, I was not able to battle such a foe.'

You glance down at your shadow mark, burning hot beneath your skin. 'Is this ... part of that same magic?' you ask grimly, studying the glowing runes. 'Am I a demon, like that ... changeling?'

Fetch leans in close, his bright eyes narrowing. 'Yes, Nevarin. We are both demons.' Turn to 792.

914

'Yes, my special deals. Well let's take a look ...' He reaches inside the chest and produces three items, which he lays out on the ash-covered ground. 'For you, 450 gold crowns. I can't say fairer than that.'

You may purchase any of the following items for 450 gold crowns each:

Slipstream silk	**Wrath of ages**	**Chilblain's tears**
(cloak)	(ring)	(necklace)
+3 speed +2 magic	+2 magic	+1 magic +1 armour
Ability: surge	Ability: rust	Ability: piercing

After you have made your decision, you can ask to see Waldo's rare items (turn to 881) or bid the trader farewell (turn to 789).

915

'Ah, tired of my company already,' chuckles Fetch, with a mock expression of hurt. 'I forgot how impatient your kind can be.'

'I need to return to the tomb,' you state firmly. 'Zul's mages are raising the dead. We believe they're going for Arthurian next – the leader of the Tor Knights.'

Fetch rubs his chin thoughtfully. 'Yes, that would make sense.'

'Well?' you snap irritably. 'Can you travel back there or not?'

Fetch is silent for some time, studying you intently with his bright, piercing eyes. With a shrug of his shoulders, he finally appears to have reached a decision. 'My magic should now be strong enough to take us back. But I will not stay. I must return to Avian at Ravenwing's camp.'

'Fine.' You place a hand on the assassin's shoulder. 'I am ready.'

You wince as the air ignites around you, crackling with black lightning. It is followed by a blinding white flash . . .

A heartbeat later and you are lurching forwards into a cold dark room. Shapes whirl in a dizzying blur around you. Desperately you reach out, seeking to slow your momentum. Hands slide across slippery stone.

Then your knees buckle and you drop to the dusty floor, gasping for air.

'They're back!' shouts a voice.

You hear the scrape of metal and the rush of feet . . . somewhere amidst the spiralling haze you see figures moving. There is a loud crack and another flash of light.

'He got away,' snaps a female voice.

'Lansbury?' you croak hoarsely.

You feel yourself being lifted to your feet. Nyms' face appears inches from your own. 'You OK? Wake up.' A gloved hand takes hold of your chin, lifting your head up and forcing you to focus.

'Just a little ... travel sick,' you grimace.

The swordsman chuckles. 'Good, glad to have you back. Now, care to tell us what just happened?' Turn to 908.

916

Up close, it is apparent that this is no earthly knight. The man's face is pale – almost transparent – the eyes burning with a dull red light. As you deliver the final blow, you watch as the knight falls to his knees, his sword rattling to the ground. He looks up at you, eyes widening as if with a sudden recognition ...

Then the body diffuses into motes of light, which flicker and then are gone. The empty shroud and the knight's armour drop to the stone tiles.

You may now take one of the following rewards:

Stalwart shoulders	Ever-sharp	Funeral gown
(cloak)	(main hand: sword)	(chest)
+2 speed +2 armour	+3 speed +4 brawn	+1 speed +3 magic
Ability: might of stone	Ability: deep wound	Ability: charm
	(requirement: warrior)	

'This was Jorvic,' states Caeleb grimly, brushing the dust from the tomb's inscription. 'He was Arthurian's standard bearer.'

'Nut job if you ask me,' says Nyms, out of the corner of his mouth.

At the other end of the chamber is an arch, leading through into a dark passageway. Lansbury raises her glowing staff and leads the way. If you have the word *vault* written on your hero sheet, turn to 822. Otherwise, turn to 831.

917

'Stop dancin' around and let me hit ya!' snarls the ogre, attempting to crush you beneath its wrecking ball. As the huge weapon smashes into the ground, you leap onto it, racing up the rusted chain and hopping onto the beast's hairy shoulders. 'Wha ... what yer doing?'

The ogre tries to knock you away, but your weapons have already found a vital spot at the base of its neck. You flip away as the ogre drops to its knees, its eyes assuming a cross-eyed expression. Then it topples face down into the dust, its legs and arms splaying to either side. If you are a mage, turn to 876. If you are a warrior, turn to 801. If you are a rogue, turn to 847.

918

Ravenwing's men pursue the routed shadow spawn, slashing and blasting at their fleeing enemy. The battle is won. But at what cost? You look around at the men that have remained behind – not only the wounded and the dead, but those who have simply hung back from exhaustion. Many have a haunted look about them, their bodies blackened by soot and grime. You can't imagine what devastation awaits beyond the walls of the city – where the doom orb's magic was turned against the camp. The men's expressions tell you enough.

Across the rubble-strewn square, you see Mathis lying on his side. The inquisitor looks badly wounded. Possibly fatal. Caeleb kneels at his side, his ear pressed close to the warrior's fevered ramblings. Nyms stumbles past, helping to support an exhausted Lansbury. As he passes by, he nods a silent word of thanks. You return the gesture, glad that your companions are safe.

'Nevarin!' You look up, to see Caeleb trudging through the rubble towards you. The cavalier's armour is raked with black scars, his shield battered and dented. 'It's over for your kind,' he sneers, hobbling closer. 'I swore to Mathis ... to the One God ... that I'd destroy all shadow spawn this day...'

'Caeleb?' You shake your head in confusion. 'What madness is this? I'm not your enemy.'

He raises his inscribed sword. 'Mathis told me everything . . .'

Suddenly, you catch movement out of the corner of your eye. A man is standing on the edge of a rooftop, his scarlet coat billowing in the wind. He raises his hand and suddenly you feel an invisible force closing in around you, pinning your arms and legs tightly together.

Then the man is moving, running through the air as quickly and deftly as if it was solid ground. And like a dog on leash, you find yourself being dragged after him, floating in a magical prison.

'More demons!' screams Caeleb. 'Don't think you can escape!'

You are pulled across a broad plaza, its fountains and pathways now charred and cratered, towards an officious-looking building clinging to a rise of grey rock. You try and discern its purpose – but the invisible bonds shift, spinning you around. Then something hard strikes you across the head, plunging you into darkness. Turn to 928.

919

You step out from behind the pillars, your body glowing with your newly absorbed shadow magic. The hulking creature is pounding its massive fists against a shield of light that Lansbury has projected around herself and Caeleb. The warrior is lying on his back, injured. His shield rests several metres away, now a battered and twisted piece of metal.

Nyms is slashing at the monster's back with his swords, but as soon as each wound is delivered, they are healing. The swordsman already looks exhausted and desperate.

'What happened?' he calls over his shoulder.

You stride past him, towards the brute. 'Just grabbing a little pick-me-up.' With a savage cry, you charge into the fray, your shadow mark burning with demonic energy:

	Speed	Brawn	Armour	Health
Branded brute	13	14	8	110

Special abilities

🖤 Power of shadow: Your *brawn* and *magic* are raised by 5 for the duration of this combat.

♥ Dark runes: The creature's branded flesh helps it to heal. At the end of each combat round, the brute heals 3 *health*. This cannot take him above his starting *health* of 110.

If you defeat this mighty foe, turn to **880**. Otherwise turn to **862**.

920

'I am Arthurian, the king's son,' he says brokenly, gazing down at the glowing shadow mark. 'I was tricked by a Nevarin. He had some ... some kind of talisman.' He looks up, his eyes cold with anger. 'It was witch magic. It took my soul ... I became ... this.' He scowls, raising his branded arm. 'I became a shadow spawn!'

You frown, considering the man's words. 'You mean, you swapped bodies somehow?'

'These are matters for priests, not warriors. I am no scholar.' The man retrieves his jewelled dagger from the mud. 'I know what I saw. He became me ... Arthurian.' He gives a bitter laugh. 'And he led my men to their deaths.'

You blink, startled. 'You mean, when your men rode against the legion ... that wasn't you?'

'Why would I risk my men's lives?' he flares angrily. 'They were butchered! I tried to stop them but they only saw this ...' He hits the pommel of his dagger against the shadow mark. 'I was chased out of the camp like a common beggar. They thought me the enemy. I could convince no one ...'

You look around at the dark chamber, echoing with the storm.

'What date is this?' you ask nervously. You approach the entrance-way to the chamber, surprised to see that the mould-covered anomaly is still alive, its rotted body covering the exit.

'It has been seven months since the shadow war,' says Arthurian quietly. 'People have their freedom. They are rebuilding. But I ... I have nothing.'

You turn back, eyeing the chamber once again. As you suspected, in the corner of the room, you see the web-like anomaly that brought you here. Its silken strands ripple gently back and forth, glistening with droplets of light. 'I have travelled back in time,' you gasp, glancing up at the dark storm raging high above. 'Magic makes all things possible ...'

Your attention shifts back to Arthurian. 'And you were dead ... in my time. We thought you were a tomb robber. This is your tomb.'

The warrior pulls his coat back on, tugging the collars up around his chin. 'I am here to put right this wrong; to take what is mine.' He stoops down to retrieve his lantern. 'I have to believe that the One God sent you here.' He looks up, a sudden weariness apparent on his face. 'I will not have my faith tested again. Are you with me?'

Fascinated by the man's story, you agree to help him with his task. Turn to **840**.

921

You take Avian's hand, joining him on the magic carpet. 'I'll pilot – you're the cannon,' he says, crouching down at the front of the vehicle.

'Do you even know how to defeat that thing?' you ask, gazing up at the immense floating orb.

Avian glances over his shoulder. 'No. But that's never stopped me before. Here, you might need these.' He flips you a pair of goggles.

'Are you serious?'

Avian grins. 'Hold tight.'

The carpet gives a sudden lurch as it jolts forward, speeding across the battlefield. The wind roars in your ears as it begins to pick up speed, accelerating over the rooftops of the city. Then, everything is plunged into a thick, gritty blackness. You choke as you swallow a mouthful of the smog, the grime stinging your eyes. Taking the goggles, you quickly strap them over your face, rubbing the dirt from their visor as you try and focus.

'I don't see anything,' you shout, struggling to get your bearings.

Suddenly, you see flashes of magic ahead. Something hurtles past in a ball of flames, accompanied by a high-pitched scream. Then the smog begins to thin and you find yourself speeding over a landscape of grey, bulbous flesh. The doom orb.

With a sickening lurch, the carpet veers to the side, missing a tentacle-like appendage by scant inches. The sudden movement throws you off balance, forcing you to grip the edges of the carpet to steady yourself.

Around you, there are explosions of light, as the other mages sweep across the face of the orb, flinging spells at its immense body. But each time the spells hit its flesh, a meshwork of magic flashes into being, causing them to spark and fizzle uselessly. 'It has a shield!' you shout above the roar of the wind.

'I know,' cries Avian, taking the carpet down towards the surface. 'The shield is blocking magic... but we can get past it.'

A column of black fire bursts out from a crater-sized hole. Avian swerves aside, dodging the blast. Several of the other mages are less lucky however, their carpets slamming into the flames and exploding into balls of spinning light.

'There!' Avian points to something below. Squinting through your grime-stained goggles, you see a trench of fatty tissue stretching out across the face of the creature's body. The floor of the trench is dotted with hundreds of circular holes, some of which are opening and closing, occasionally expelling geysers of gas into the air. 'One of those should take us through into the brain.'

You do a double-take. 'Take us through to *what*?'

The carpet tilts into a sickening series of spins, finally levelling out as one of the open holes speeds towards you. A second later and you are zooming down a circular tunnel, its slime-covered walls streaking past in a pink-white blur.

'Do you know where you are going?' you yell hoarsely, aware that you are now inside a vast maze of tunnels, branching out through the innards of the beast.

Avian swerves, guiding the carpet into a smaller side passage, its floor and ceiling pulsing with blue light. 'We need to follow these neural pulses,' says Avian, deviating down another passageway where the light is rippling in dazzling halos.

'I've done some crazy things, mage – but this ...'

As you hurtle deeper into the doom orb, you become aware of an angry buzzing sound, getting louder and louder. Glancing back, you see a swarm of wasp-like creatures in close pursuit. 'We've got company!'

Avian looks back. 'Sentries. Hold on. We're almost—'

The mage's words are cut short as the carpet starts to brake suddenly, throwing you forwards. As you slam into Avian, you look over his shoulder to see what has caused the sudden interruption.

The tunnel ahead is covered by a large pink membrane, its bloated surface branched with veins. As the carpet slides to a halt next to it, you hear a loud hiss from above. Looking up, you see a cluster of tentacles dangling from the ceiling of the tunnel. Each one is secreting a glowing green resin, which starts to mist, forming dense clouds of vapour.

'Poison!' gasps Avian, summoning magic to his hands. 'We need to break through this membrane – quickly!'

'I think we have bigger problems ...' You spin round, as the buzzing sentries swarm closer, their abdomens tapering back into sword-sized stingers. In order to continue deeper into the orb, you will have to overcome its deadly defences:

	Speed	Magic	Armour	Health
Sentries	15	12	-	-
Membrane	-	-	19	80
Poison nodes	-	-	5	60

Special abilities

- Endless swarm: The sentries cannot be defeated – as soon as one falls, there is another to take its place. You will need to concentrate on breaking through the membrane.
- Poison nodes: At the end of every combat round, if the poison nodes are still alive, you must automatically lose 4 *health*.
- Avian's aid: You may add 2 to your damage score, for the duration of this combat.

If you win a combat round against the sentries, you can choose to apply your damage to the membrane or the poison nodes (or both, if you have an ability that lets you do so). Once the membrane is reduced to zero *health*, you have broken through and automatically win the combat.

If you manage to break through the membrane before the sentries and poison defeat you, turn to **877**.

The anomaly breaks apart into glittering strands of green magic, which streak towards your arm. As they hit the branded flesh, you feel a cold surge of power rush into your body. The magic is old and corrupted, but it is welcome all the same, feeding your muscles and enhancing your senses. When the last of the anomaly has been absorbed, you stumble back, half-gasping and half-laughing at your newfound power.

Lansbury is at your side, regarding you with a mixture of horror and fascination. Nyms on the other hand, is patting you on the back.

'Nice move,' he grins. 'And look – your way of finding secret doors is much more interesting.'

You look up, to see a square opening cut into the stone of the wall, previously covered by the magical growth. Caeleb helps you to your feet, watching you intently from between the slits of his helm.

'Are you OK?' he asks. 'Is that thing ... inside you now?'

You nod, lifting your arm to reveal the absorbed magic, flickering along the branded mark. Caeleb jerks his head away. 'It reeks of evil,' he growls.

'And it will be the death of you,' hisses Lansbury, knocking your arm away with her staff. Her face is flushed with both anger and upset. 'You have no idea of the magic you are playing with!'

Nyms shrugs his shoulders. 'No complaints here, I don't have to look at that disgusting snot-beast anymore. Now, what're we doing people? I say, secret room equals treasure.'

'And I say, we have more pressing concerns,' snaps Caeleb. 'We cannot let Zul's followers gain the upper hand.'

Will you:

Leave the chamber via the archway?	902
Investigate the secret room?	786

The apprentice is defeated, his ghoulish creation dropping to the ground in a jumble of blood-flecked bones. Meanwhile, Caeleb is still trading blows with the tutor, who has summoned a black blade into his hands. Deflecting the mage's desperate strikes with his shield, the cavalier thrusts his sword past the necromancer's guard, taking him down.

'Nice work,' grins Nyms, wandering over. He brushes the wet ash from his leathers. 'Anyone would think you no longer needed me.'

Caeleb kneels beside the necromancer, wiping his bloody sword against the mage's robes. 'And anyone would think a rogue couldn't dodge a fireball.' He looks up, his eyes glinting mischievously beneath his helm.

Nyms scowls, rubbing his right shoulder. 'Yeah, took me a bit by surprise, that's all.'

You cast a nervous glance over your shoulder, fearful that the battle might have drawn the attention of the bone sentry. But thankfully, there is no sign of the winged abomination. Sheathing your weapons, you search the body of the apprentice. You find 30 gold crowns and may help yourself to one of the following items:

Home brew (2 uses) (backpack)	Cracked spectacles (head)	Stink bomb (1 use) (backpack)
Use any time in combat to raise your *magic* by 3 for one combat round	+2 speed +2 magic Ability: focus	Use at the start of a combat round to reduce an opponent's *speed* by 2 for that round

If you are a mage, turn to 850. Otherwise, turn to 883.

You sprint to the end of the building, then kick off from its edge, soaring effortlessly over the glittering sea of bodies. You twist in mid-air, sending bolts of black fire into the ranks of shadow spawn, your dark magic ripping through their bodies and leaving charred craters in the earth.

As you level out into a dive, you draw your weapons, flipping over at the last moment to land in front of Lansbury's shield. Surrounding you are the decayers – giant-sized undead; their mummified bodies cloaked in a thick cloud of green noxious gas. From between the creatures' damp, rotted bandages, you see worm-like parasites twisting and snaking around their diseased bodies, spewing forth an endless swarm of deadly spores into the foul-smelling air.

'The spores!' shouts Lansbury desperately. 'They explode on contact. Keep them away from the shield!'

With a snarl of fury, you charge into the pestilent undead, hoping to buy time for your companions until help arrives. You must fight:

	Speed	Brawn	Armour	Health
Decayers	15	13	7	100
Spore cloud	-	-	4	40 (*)
Lansbury's shield	-	-	-	25

Special abilities

- A swarm of spores:* It takes three combat rounds for the spore cloud to reach the shield. At the end of the third combat round, the shield takes 1 damage for each *health* point the cloud has remaining. A new cloud is then released (with 40 *health*), taking 3 rounds to reach the shield (and so on).
- Disease: Once you have taken health damage from the decayers, at the end of every combat round you must automatically lose 2 *health*.
- Natural immunity: The spore cloud is immune to all passive effects, such as *bleed*, *burn* and *venom*.

In this combat, you roll against the decayers' speed. If you win, you can roll for damage against the decayers or the spore cloud (or both, if you have an ability that lets you do so). If you lose the round, then the decayers attack you.

If you manage to survive to the start of the *seventh* combat round, with Lansbury's shield still intact (i.e. it still has *health*), then turn to 832. (Special achievement: If you defeat the decayers before the end of the *sixth* round with the shield still intact, then turn to **845**). If you are defeated, then you may return to an earlier point. Restore your *health*, then turn to **885**.

925

The warrior's body collapses into a swirling vortex of purple light. Eagerly, you tug back your sleeve and expose your shadow mark to the magic. The runes writhe and twist beneath your skin as they greedily devour the ranger's essence, healing your wounds and gifting you with even greater power.

If you are a ranger, you may now learn the shadow ranger career (turn to **814**). Otherwise, turn to **834**.

926

At the foot of the stairs is a small square room. The floors, walls and ceiling are all fashioned from slabs of grey stone, inscribed with neat flowing script. You can feel the air around you pulsing with magic. The mark beneath your skin burns, as if on fire.

'What is this place?' you ask hoarsely, the air thick and suffocating.

'There is some residue of holy magic here,' says Lansbury, her eyes scanning the walls of engraved lettering. 'This inscriber knew their art.'

'Magic for what purpose?' enquires Nyms, nervously glancing from side to side. 'Hasn't done much to stop Zul and his mages.'

Lansbury furrows her brow, leaning closer to a section of the writing. 'Don't be so quick to judge, rogue. These were designed to absorb negative energy, to cleanse this place of taint.'

'Why?' asks Caeleb sceptically.

'This tomb was fashioned from magic, cut from the earth using geomancy.'

'But that is good, right?' Caeleb traces a line of script with a gloved finger.

'Not all magic comes from the One God, Caeleb,' replies the medic.

'Dwarf magic.' Nyms raises his twin swords and turns their blades to display their runes. 'Like these. Thought you holy people frowned on the old magic.'

'It has its uses, from time to time. These inscriptions are a cleansing rite ... to repel the demons that are drawn to such things.' She turns and stares at your arm, which is releasing a thick, dark smoke into the air. You look down at it in bewilderment, feeling suddenly dizzy and nauseous.

'Is this dwarf magic?' you croak. Your voice sounds distant ... detached.

Nyms moves to your side. 'You don't look so good.'

Lansbury takes your arm, studying your mark with a mixture of interest and unease. 'We should move on.'

There are two exits from the room, one to the north – leading onwards into a torch lit passageway – and a narrower side corridor to the east.

Will you:

Take the passage north?	857
Take the passage east?	836

927

Suddenly, a bright flash of light draws your attention skywards. From out of the smog, you see white shapes swooping down over the ruined city, their vapour trails blazing bright like comets. Beneath them, a series of explosions swell out across the square, cutting a vicious swathe through the tightly-packed ranks of shadow spawn.

'The airborne regulars!' You punch the air as the mages hurtle past on their flying carpets.

Then, at the far side of the square, you hear the resonating blast of a horn. From your vantage point, it is difficult to see through the thronging masses, but it looks like a battalion of Ravenwing's militia have made it across the city. You catch the glimmer of polished armour and a fluttering standard, proudly displaying the black raven. Aid has finally arrived. Turn to 828.

You awake to find yourself lying on your side. The room is dark and smoky – a vaulted hall lined with flickering oil lamps. A row of alabaster statues stand in silent vigil against one wall, their faces grim-set and mean. Next to them, the dim light catches on the bared ribcage of some ancient beast, its skeleton reconstructed and strung on wires. Its jaws hang open in a silent roar, the blade-sized teeth mirrored in the glass display cases that litter the rest of the dusty space.

'Oh yes. Be back soon. Oh yes ...'

You arch your neck, seeking the source of the voice. The man in the red coat is leaning over one of the cases. Shards of glass sparkle on the ground around his feet.

'Hush, hush. This is the one, yes? Just like he said – just like we thought.' He lifts out a rectangular shield, its lower end tapering to a point. He holds it awkwardly, turning it over in his hands. 'Are we sure? The sun, sun, sun.' He scratches the back of his head, where you see his grey hair balding around an ugly scar. 'Yes, like he said. Be back soon. So soon, pretty thing.'

He twists something set in the shield. There is a loud click, echoing in the empty chamber. Carefully, the man lifts a golden disc from out of the shield, fashioned to resemble a sun. He puts the shield aside and holds the disc aloft, gazing at its underside. 'Lily, lily, lotus ... lily, lily, lotus.' The man licks his lips, chuckling to himself as he turns it round, seemingly counting patterns carved into the gold. 'Lily, lily, lotus ... ah.' He touches something. There is a spark of magic and suddenly the disc begins to twist and fold in on itself, the sculptured rays of the sun forming the petals of a golden flower. Reaching into his coat, the man produces an ivory-and-gold rod which he slides into a hole beneath the head-piece, forming a wand-like staff. It flickers with golden light as soon as the two pieces connect.

'I was right,' the man sighs, shaking his head. His voice hints at disappointment. 'More magic. Need more ...'

You realise you still have your weapons. Gingerly, you shift your weight, preparing to spring at the man while he is still unawares. But even making this minuscule movement causes the man to flinch.

'I hear you. Scrape, scrape, scraping. Sound is so very loud. So very loud.' He spins round, his long coat snapping around his gaunt frame. 'Breathing much softer. Calm. Softer.' The man raises a finger and shakes it in a reprimanding fashion. 'You're not doing things you're supposed to.'

You realise that the man is clearly deranged. But there is something familiar about him. A thin scar cuts down his left cheek, disfiguring his mouth into a perpetual sneer. Resting against his forehead is a gold crown, shaped to resemble three entwined serpents.

'Who are you?' you rasp hoarsely. 'Why did you bring me here?'

'Many name, name, names,' he replies, his eyes glittering in the glow from the staff. 'In the shroud, the name doesn't matter, not so much. But ... Lorcan ... that's what they used to call me.' He points a trembling finger in your direction. 'And you. You're important because I have to kill you.'

Will you:

Ask why he has to kill you?	937
Ask if he is a Nevarin, like yourself?	934
Ask about the staff's purpose?	873
Ask about Daarko's strange machine?	819
Attack this deranged mage?	939

929

The dark warrior is a powerful opponent, bolstered by the healing of his necromantic minions. The deadly black axes slice through the dusty air, leaving streaks of crackling magic in their wake. But you are a Nevarin, fast and agile, your own powers heightened by the shadow mark that burns bright against your skin. While your allies are forced back by the warrior's unstoppable fury, you see an opening and spring forward, catching the flat of one of his sweeping blades and leaping again, to somersault behind him. Before the warrior has a chance to turn and defend himself, you strike with the full power of your strength and magic.

The warrior falls to his knees, his axes sparking and then winking out of existence. With a final pained gasp, the dark warrior vanishes, the armour clattering to the floor, empty.

Caeleb walks over and prods the runed armour with his foot, pushing the breastplate over to reveal an engraved insignia – a chalice, surrounded by a circle of seven stars.

'Arthurian's coat of arms ...' He shakes his head grimly. 'We were too late.'

Lansbury wrinkles her nose as she examines the armour. 'I don't think what we fought today was Arthurian. It was something else ... something that was using his body.'

Caeleb's expression hardens, his eyes coming to rest on the shattered remains of Arthurian's tomb. 'Zul will pay for this sacrilege.'

Lowering your weapons, you step over the rubble to search the bodies of Zul's followers. You find 50 gold crowns and may help yourself to one of the following rewards:

Twilight claw	Black widow	Stolen hope
(left hand: fist weapon)	(head)	(necklace)
+2 speed +3 brawn	+2 speed +2 brawn	+1 brawn +1 magic
Ability: rake	Ability: webbed	Ability: deceive

With little else of interest in the chamber, you leave Arthurian's tomb and head back into the bone fields. Return to the Act 3 quest map.

930

With a burst of magic, you propel yourself through the air, landing in a roll ahead of the charging ogre. The slow-witted beast shows no signs of slowing, its ball and chain spinning in a grey blur above its ugly head.

Your weapons fly into your hands as you prepare to take on this formidable opponent:

	Speed	Brawn	Armour	Health
The Wrecker	15	14	11	120

Special abilities

♥ Clobbering time: At the end of every combat round, the Wrecker spins his ball and chain. To avoid being hit, roll 4 dice. If the result is equal to or less than your *speed*, then you have avoided the wrecking ball. If the result is higher, you have been hit and must take 15 damage. You can use half your *armour* score (rounding up) to absorb this damage.

♥ Inquisitor's wrath: If you have the word *rival* on your hero sheet, then Mathis will wade into the combat at the start of round 3, adding 2 to your damage score for the remainder of the combat.

♥ Healer's gift: If you have the word *companion* on your hero sheet, then Lansbury will heal you once, any time during this combat, restoring 12 *health*.

If you manage to defeat the ogre, turn to **917**. If you are defeated, then you may return to an earlier point. Restore your *health*, then turn to **905**.

931

You draw your weapons and start towards to the tomb, intrigued as to the source of the voices. As you near, there is the crunch of booted feet – and suddenly two black-robed figures appear around the side of the tomb. One is shorter than the other, his rain-sodden hood pulled low over a youthful face. You note that his hands are raised and magic is flickering around the ends of his fingers. His companion appears to be a tutor of some sort, offering encouragement.

'Yes, that's it,' he states in an eager tone. 'You don't have to force the magic. Once the connection is made ...'

You freeze, aware that you are in full view of the mages, your sudden halt forcing Nyms to knock into you with a grunt.

The necromancers notice you, their eyes widening.

Like lightning, the tutor tugs a wand from his belt and aims it at you. There is a blinding flash of magic and then the sound of crackling flames. You are able to dodge aside, but Nyms takes the full force of the blast, reeling backwards into the sodden ash.

Caeleb races to your side, raising his shield as another bolt tears across the space, slamming harmlessly against the shield's runed steel.

Lansbury has hurried over to Nyms, who is groaning in pain. You see her hands flare with healing magic, as she passes a palm across his charred armour.

Then you hear a guttural snarl. Behind the young mage lurches a hunched, misshapen figure. It has the appearance of a ghoul: its body haphazardly formed from bones and rotted flesh. The creature shuffles forward, its scraggly arms ending in knife-like claws slick with rainwater. It is then that you realise that the young mage is controlling the beast. With a cruel grin, the youth raises his hand and extends a finger out in your direction. The ghoul's glowing eyes narrow to angry slits, then with a gibbering cackle of delight, it scampers towards you, its claws raised to strike. Turn to 911.

932

The doors are unlocked. Warily, you push them open, finding yourself in a vast, empty hall of white stone. You pause on the threshold, eyes scanning the high walls and vaulted ceiling.

At your bidding, your shadow mark pulses into life, flooding you with its power. You reach out, sensing for signs of shadow magic. The place reeks of it. But the tang of fear is more palpable. You look to Nyms, who is eyeing his surroundings nervously, his fingers drumming against the pommels of his blades.

'I have a bad feeling about this,' he mutters.

'Are you ... *afraid*?' you ask curiously. It is a sensation almost alien to you now.

Nyms bristles with affront. 'We don't all have your talent for coming back from the dead,' he replies sharply. 'Just watch my back.' His swords hiss out of their scabbards as he steps forward onto the marbled floor.

'No!' You put out a hand, but it is too late. The room swiftly darkens as shadows swirl from the corners of the room. They move with purpose, winding towards the centre of the chamber, where they coil together to form a spinning column of dark light.

'Allam's teeth, was it something I said?' growls Nyms.

'A trap,' you reply, edging cautiously forwards. 'Someone warded the door.'

As you approach, the column starts to shift and change, its centre moulding itself into the figure of a woman. She crosses her arms to her chest, allowing the shadows to wrap about her body, coating it in tattered folds of smoke and shadow.

Realising that you must destroy this dark spirit before it is at full strength, you raise your weapons and charge forward. As if in response, the woman throws back her head, her open mouth slowly distending into a yawning chasm of darkness.

'It's a banshee,' gasps Nyms. 'Don't let it scream, or we're done for!'

'Then let us silence it forever,' you reply, hurling your magic and steel against this sinister foe. You must fight:

	Speed	Brawn	Armour	Health
Banshee	14	13	8	76(*)

Special abilities

🛡 Gathering darkness:* The shadows are slowly merging together to form the banshee. At the end of each combat round, the banshee's *health* increases by 8. (Once the banshee is reduced to zero *health*, it can no longer heal.)

🛡 Wail of the banshee: Once the banshee's *health* reaches 100 or more, it will have gained sufficient strength to issue its call – alerting the mansion to your presence. This will immediately summon guards, who will quickly overwhelm you – losing you the combat.

If you are able to defeat the banshee before it can sound its alarm, turn to **899**.

933

You raise your weapons defensively. 'Who is it?' you call, flinching when you hear the sound of Lorcan's voice coming from your own lips.

Take the staff, fool.

And ringing inside your head.

'Shut up,' you growl between clenched teeth.

The figure steps forward out of the shadows. You had already guessed who it was – from the bulky armour and the dented shield. 'Caeleb ...'

The cavalier has a mad look about his eyes, his movements sluggish from exhaustion. 'More Nevarin scum.' He gives his surroundings a wary once over, his gaze falling on the crumpled clothes that once belonged to Lorcan.

'Wait!' You lower your weapons, realising that he is no longer seeing your own body, but that of the gaunt mage. 'It's me, Caeleb. Remember? We fought with Captain Redguard ... Nyms ... Lansbury. This is not my body!'

Caeleb takes another step forward, raising his scarred shield. In the other hand, a mighty broadsword hums with magic, its holy inscriptions glittering with a pale light. 'You are a demon. Mathis told me what you did.' He shakes his head, almost with regret. 'And you must be stopped.'

'Did what?' you insist.

'The machine. You brought the legion here. Just like you did before ... when you stole the Nexus.'

You shake your head in dismay. 'I did nothing to the machine. It was Mathis. He destroyed it – that's what brought the black guard to the city. He lied to you!'

'And what is *this*?' he scowls, waving the point of his sword across your new body. 'You are a trickster. Your magic is a dark thing ... evil.'

'Really?' You bristle with anger, hands clenching around your weapons. 'I don't remember you complaining when I was saving your life – saving everybody's life, all those times.'

Caeleb bares his teeth. 'While you live, there is still a shadow spawn in this city.'

'And what are planning to do about that?' you snipe. 'I do not wish to fight you, Caeleb. You are a friend. A companion. Do not make me ...'

The cavalier charges, moving with a startling speed. You barely have time to block the warrior's first blow, his sword scraping against your own. Then his shield cuts in, its metal rim catching you in the midriff and lifting you off your feet. You flail through the air, smashing through a clay urn and showering the ground with broken pottery.

'This has to end,' grunts the warrior, metal rattling as he advances. 'It ends today.'

You stumble to your feet woozily, aware that your wounds are not healing. A quick glance at your shadow mark confirms that its magic is not responding – its usual radiance reduced to a dull glow.

I told you to take the staff.

'What are you doing?' you scowl angrily. 'Are you controlling the mark?'

We have to leave. Leave. Leave. Now!

Caeleb charges again, leading with his shield. You sidestep, bringing your weapons across your body, hoping to knock him away. But they graze off metal, his shield blocking the blow. His sword quickly follows, swinging around in a cruel arc. You try and dodge the attack, taking a nick on the cheek. Another blow leaves a burning scratch across your leg.

'Stop this madness,' you cry, shaking with pain and anger. 'I am not what you think I am.'

His shield connects with your chest, sending you tumbling back into the broken rubble. As you struggle to rise, you become aware of something wet running down your face. You put a shaking hand to it, surprised when it comes away coated in blood.

'Heal me,' you choke, spitting out a broken tooth. 'Do you want us both to die?'

I told you what to do.

You find your feet again, only to see Caeleb closing once more. You tangle together, smashing through wood and glass. His head butts into your own, sending it snapping back. Then his shield cracks across your ribs, eliciting a strangled cry of pain. By luck rather than design, you stumble back, avoiding his follow-up swing.

The shroud. The place between worlds. We must go! Go!

Lorcan's voice distracts you. The rim of the shield smashes into your side, hurling you back across the room. You crash down, spitting dust and blood, your hands grappling over broken rock and pottery. Then you feel something, cold to the touch.

Yes. Yes. Take the staff.

You struggle to raise your head. One eye is closed and it won't open – the other struggles to focus, the room reduced to shreds of colour, whirling and reeling in a sickening spin. Boots crunch through the debris as the cavalier advances. You can hear his laboured breathing.

Take the staff. Just think of the possibilities, Nevarin. The shroud. The gateway to other worlds. Other dreams. Don't let it end like this.

'Heal me ...' you croak, wincing as you try and move your shattered body. 'Heal me.'

The boots crunch closer and then stop. Caeleb stands over you, his inscribed sword raised. You look up, his blurred face swaying like a reflection in water. 'Finally, demon, I will rid this world of your taint ...'

The sword hums as it slices down through the air.

'No!' You reach out and snatch the staff, gripping it to your chest. It flares into a brilliant golden light, the magic from your shadow mark pumping into it, filling it with new life. Your life ...

Yes, yes! The shroud calls us ... The staff is working ...

The sword slices through the rubble, lodging itself deep into the ground. Caeleb tugs it free, stumbling back in surprise. 'It can't be ...'

All that remains of you is a faint outline of smoke, curling into the dusty air.

You have simply vanished.

'Demons ...' he spins around, eyes scanning the shadows. 'Where are you, demon? Where did you go?' But the only answer he receives is the echo of his own voice. 'Impossible ...' He shifts round, looking back to where you had been lying. A tattered piece of parchment lies crumpled amongst the dust. He reaches down and picks it up, unravelling it to reveal a letter. A letter of recommendation for a young knight to apprentice with the great Avian Dale. His brow furrows as he spots your pack lying some metres away, its contents scattered throughout the rubble.

Caeleb crumples the parchment in his fist. 'Wherever you go, Nevarin ... I *will* find you. As the One God is my witness. This is not the end ...'

934

'They think us slaves. The Borellin-var.' The man glances down at his right hand, gripping the staff. You catch the glimmer of a shadow mark snaking around the wrist and palm. 'But in branding us, they made us gods.'

'Those creatures enslaved us,' you growl angrily, remembering your encounter with Sharroth. 'They destroyed our cities – our people. They tortured us. They made us no better than animals. There is nothing god-like about servitude to monsters!'

Lorcan waves his finger with a knowing smile. 'You've broken your bond with them. I feel it. Feel it like music under the skin. If you were to live …' He shakes his head, as if ridding it of some unwanted thought. 'No. The man tells me what to do. You … you must die so I can go home.'

Return to 928 to ask Lorcan another question, or turn to 939 to attack this deranged mage.

935

Your blows batter the warrior to his knees. From behind the mask, you hear a wheezing gasp as the magic that surrounds his body flickers and dies. 'I always knew … it would be you,' he pants. 'You were the … last ….the finest. You held out until … the end.'

You raise your weapons, ready to deliver the final blow.

'The legion took everything … and that is what broke you … made you the vessel for their power.' The warrior lifts a gloved hand to his mask. 'You cannot win this war, Nevarin. But I give to you … my strength.' He pulls the mask away – and suddenly a stream of black magic floods out from beneath the hood, slamming into your shadow mark. You stumble back, gasping for breath as the magic burns through your body, searing along each and every vein.

And then a scene, a memory, flashes before your eyes.

You stand before an empty shell of a building, blackened with soot. Flames still lick around its shattered walls, where bodies lie sprawled against the dark sand. You knew them. Family. And they have been taken from you. You look down, at the mark that shimmers along your arm, and the bloodied blade in your hand. It is then that you are reminded of what you have done – that this is your work. The laughter of your new master rings in your ears.

'You want to feel something, don't you?' spits Sharroth. The creature's immense shadow stretches across the sand. 'We will remake you, Nevarin. Together we will accomplish great things.'

Then the memory fades, joining the other indistinct fragments that torment you each and every day. If you are a mage turn to 865. If you are a warrior, turn to 893. If you are a rogue, turn to 843.

936

You pass through another hall into an opulent chamber, its walls lined with an extensive array of paintings and sculptures. Nearly all of them feature grisly scenes of battle or nightmarish monsters engaged in gruesome acts of cruelty and destruction.

'Quite the collector,' comments Nyms dryly. 'Dinner parties must be a scream.'

'This was Zul's home,' you reply, pointing to one of the larger paintings, which shows a portrait of the dark sorcerer, dressed in stately robes. 'Don't you sense it? His taint is everywhere ...'

A side door immediately draws your attention. Pushing it open, you find yourself at the top of a set of stairs, which wind down into a cold and fetid darkness.

'This way,' you nod, feeling the magic of your shadow mark quicken. 'They're below the mansion.'

'Oh good,' remarks Nyms, patting the head of one of the beastly sculptures. 'Can I make a suggestion?'

You glance over your shoulder, an eyebrow raised. 'Will I like it?'

A guilty grin twists his lips. 'I'm just saying – we could go back, wait for Mathis and the others. I mean, it might be nice to have some extra healing around. We don't know what's down there. If *these* things are anything to go by.' He turns on the spot, taking in the grisly display of art. 'Then some back up would be appreciated. What do you ... ' His words falter as he looks back across the room, realising that he no longer has an audience. You have already started down the stairs, the glow of your mark lighting the way. Turn to 807.

937

'For this,' grins the mage, tapping the side of the staff. 'Your power is strong – stronger than any I have seen.' He leans forward, the hollows in his face giving him a skull-like appearance. 'I absorb your essence then I am strong again. Yes? Make the staff work.' He nods his head quickly, his broken lips forming a mockery of a smile. 'There are no choices. No choices. He tells me to do it. He tells me ...'

'Who?' you ask sardonically, not too surprised that this crazed man is hearing 'voices' in his head.

'The man in the shroud,' grins the mage, pacing up and down. 'I don't hear him now, but I know he is there. He told me that this was here,' he shakes the staff. 'Tells me the truth of things.' The mage stops pacing, standing rigid, holding his breath. For a moment there is an uneasy silence.

You go to speak, but the man puts out a hand. 'Shush, listen. Sometimes ... I hear him, if I concentrate.' He frowns, then opens his eyes. 'I'll hear him again soon. I know I will. When I go home.'

Return to 928 to ask Lorcan another question, or turn to 939 to attack this deranged mage.

938

You expose your mark, dragging the Nevarin's shadowy remains towards the waiting jaws of your own branded serpents. You have gained the following special ability:

Snakes alive! (**sp**): You may entangle your opponent in coils of dark magic, lowering their *speed* by 2 for one combat round.

Across the hall, Nyms has dispatched the shadow spawn but is now fending off the magical attacks of the female mage. As you suspected, she is a Nevarin – and her mark has brought her back to life. You jump the distance, your body fuelled by your absorbed shadow magic – but as you land on the other side of the balcony, you discover your effort has been wasted. The swordsman has already landed a lucky blow, forcing the woman to stagger backwards. He follows up with a twin strike, driving both blades through her dark robes, exploding her body into flickering clouds of shadow.

You stride past him, lifting your shadow mark to drink in her essence, denying her a second chance to heal. Nyms shivers and looks away.

'I hate it when you do that.'

You close your eyes, feeling yourself drifting away on the euphoric currents of magic, losing yourself to a void of darkness ...

'Nevarin!'

You hear a voice but it is distant, distorted. It belonged to someone you once knew – but perhaps that was another life. You see others now, bodies shimmering like stars against the backdrop of night. Other Nevarin. Other faces. They slide past you, blurring into streaks of light. You try and focus but they are moving too quick, eluding you. All except one ... standing alone, burning brighter than the rest. A man. His eyes widen with surprise as he turns to face you. You catch a scar running down his left cheek and a circlet of gold resting on his brow.

'Nevarin!'

You feel something tugging at you. Pulling you back.

With a gasp, you lurch forward, your eyes snapping open – to find Nyms' gaunt face inches from your own. 'Woah, you're back!' The rogue rocks back on his heels, surprised. 'What happened?' he asks, looking you over with concern. 'You just passed out cold.'

You try and remember, but the gossamer images are already fading from memory. 'The mark ...' You look down to see its swirling runes humming with energy, their bright glow shimmering across your body. 'It... it was nothing,' you state hastily, clambering back to your feet. 'We need to move.'

Nyms snorts, nodding towards the corpses of the shadow spawn. 'Wouldn't be surprised if the whole mansion doesn't know we're here now.' He flashes you a crooked grin. 'So much for the stealthy approach, eh?'

'Agreed.' You spring over the balcony, dropping into the hall below. You land in a crouch, your mark blazing with fire. 'The time for skulking in shadows is over.' Turn to 936.

939

You clamber to your feet, keeping a wary eye on the mage. He regards you with interest, fingers drumming against the rod of his staff.

'There won't be a peaceful outcome to this, will there?' you sigh, drawing your weapons.

Lorcan shakes his head. 'I need your magic. To power the staff.'

'Then I can't give you what you want.'

There is a tense silence as you both eye each other – knowing that the next minute, the next few seconds, may decide both your fates.

You spring forward. The mage raises a hand, sending a concussive blast of air in your direction. It hits you in the stomach, blowing you back into one of the glass cases. You smash through it, tumbling over in an agile roll to land back on your feet.

'Agh! My magic is weak,' snarls Lorcan. 'I should have foreseen this … so ill-prepared. An oversight …' He continues muttering to himself as he aims the staff towards the nearest row of statues. Swirls of white mist drift from its flower-like head, settling around several of the alabaster figures. 'Defend your master!' cries the mage. He swings round to watch your next move, his shadow mark glowing with purple light.

You advance, crunching through the broken glass, aware that the stone figures are coming to life, staggering forward through a cloud of age-old dust. It is time to fight:

	Speed	*Magic*	*Armour*	*Health*
Lorcan	15	13	8	100
Statue	-	-	10	24
Statue	-	-	10	24
Statue	-	-	10	24

Special abilities

- Enduring spirit: At the end of each combat round, Lorcan heals 4 *health*. Once Lorcan's *health* has been reduced to zero, he cannot heal. (This ability cannot take him above his starting *health* of 100.)
- Stomping statues: At the end of each combat round, each surviving statue inflicts 4 damage to your hero, ignoring *armour*.
- Magic of the makers: When each statue is destroyed, their *magic* returns to the staff. For each statue destroyed, Lorcan's *speed*, *magic* and *armour* are increased by 1.
- Enchanted stone: The statues are immune to all passive effects, such as *bleed*, *burn* and *venom*.

If you win a combat round against Lorcan, you can choose to direct your damage towards the mage or one of the statues. If you defeat Lorcan, all remaining statues immediately crumble into dust.

If you manage to defeat this deranged opponent, turn to 870.

Glossary:
Special abilities

The following is a list of all the abilities associated with special items and hero careers.

The letters in brackets after each name refer to the type of ability – speed (sp), combat (co), modifier (mo), passive (pa).

Unless otherwise stated in the text, each ability can only be used *once* during a combat – even if you have multiple items with the same ability (i.e. if you have two items with the *piercing* ability, you can still only use *piercing* once per combat). The same rule applies to passive abilities (i.e. even if you have two items with the *venom* ability, you can only have one *venom* effect in play at a time).

Acid (mo): Add 1 to the result of each die you roll for your damage score, for the duration of the combat. (Note: if you have multiple items with *acid*, you can still only add 1 to the result.)

Adrenaline (sp): Use this ability to increase your *speed* by 2 for two combat rounds. This ability can only be used once per combat.

Ambidextrous (pa): You can equip main-hand swords in your left hand, and vice versa.

Avenging spirit (co): When you take health damage from your opponent's damage score / damage dice, you can inflict damage back to them equal to your *armour*. This ability ignores your opponent's *armour*. (Note: you cannot use modifier abilities to increase this damage.) You can only perform *Avenging spirit* once per combat.

Backfire (co): Instead of rolling for a damage score when you have won a round, you can use the *backfire* ability. This automatically inflicts 3 damage dice to your opponent, but it also does 2 damage dice to your hero, ignoring *armour*. You can only use this ability once per combat.

Barbs (pa): At the end of every combat round, you automatically inflict 1 damage to all of your opponents. This ability ignores *armour*.

Beep! Beep! (pa): Whenever you discover gold on your travels, you may automatically double the amount. Gold that is given to you by another character (for example, as a reward) cannot be doubled.

Black rain (co): (requires a bow in the left hand). Instead of rolling for a damage score after winning a round, you can use *black rain* to shower your enemies with dark magic. Roll 1 damage die and apply the result to each of your opponents, ignoring their *armour*. You can only use *black rain* once per combat.

Bleed (pa): If your damage dice / damage score causes health damage to your opponent, they continue to take a further point of damage at the end of each combat round. This damage ignores *armour*.

Blood rage (mo): If you win two consecutive combat rounds and cause health damage in both rounds, you automatically go into a *blood rage*. This increases your *brawn* by 2 for the remainder of the combat.

Bolt (co): Instead of rolling for damage, you can 'charge up' your wand. When you win your next round of combat you can then release the charge. This allows you to inflict 3 damage dice to one opponent, ignoring their *armour*. *Bolt* can only be used once per combat.

Brain drain (mo): You may spend *magic* to increase your damage score. For each *magic* point you spend, you may increase your damage score by 1. You can spend up to a maximum of 5 *magic* points (increasing your damage score by 5). Your *magic* is restored at the end of the combat. You can only use this ability once per combat.

Brutality (co): (see **Overpower**). You can only use *brutality* once per combat.

Bull's eye (mo): You may fire an arrow / bullet at your opponent before combat starts, automatically inflicting 1 damage die, ignoring a*rmour*. *Bull's eye* will also inflict any harmful passive abilities you have, such as *venom* and *bleed*. (Note: An assassin using *first strike* cannot use this ability.)

Burn (pa): All opponents who have suffered health damage from ignite automatically lose 1 *health* at the end of every combat round. This ability ignores *armour*.

Cat's speed (sp): This ability allows you to roll an extra die to determine your attack speed for one round of combat. You may only use this ability once per combat.

Cauterise (mo): This ability can be used any time in combat to remove all *venom*, *bleed* and *disease* effects that your hero is currently inflicted with. You can only use it once in combat – and once used, your hero is again susceptible to these effects.

Charge (sp): In the first round of combat, you may increase your *speed* by 2.

Charm (mo): You may re-roll one of your hero's die any time during a combat. You must accept the result of the second roll. If you have multiple items with the *charm* ability, each one gives you a re-roll.

Chill touch (sp): Use this ability to reduce your opponent's *speed* by 2 for one combat round. You can only use *chill touch* once per combat.

Cleansing light (pa): Automatically heals the hero for 2 *health* at the end of each combat round.

Cleave (co): Instead of rolling for a damage score after winning a round, you can use *cleave*. Roll 1 damage die and apply the result to each of your opponents, ignoring their *armour*. You can only use *cleave* once per combat.

Click your heels (sp): Raise your *speed* by 2 for one combat round. This ability can only be used once per combat.

Clymonistra's adornments: If your hero is wearing both pieces of Clymonistra's set (necklace and ring) then you may use the *vampirism* ability (see **Vampirism**).

Command (co): When an opponent wins a combat round, use the *command* power to instantly halt their attack, allowing you to roll for damage instead, as if you had won the combat round. You can only use *command* once per combat.

Corruption (co): If your damage score causes health damage to your opponent, you can inflict *corruption* on them, reducing either their *brawn* or *magic* by 2 points for the remainder of the combat. You can only use this ability once per combat.

Courage (sp): Use this ability to increase your *speed* by 4 for one combat round. You can only use this ability once per combat.

Cripple (co): If your damage score causes health damage to your opponent, you can also *cripple* them. This immediately lowers their *speed* score by 1 for the next three combat rounds. You can only use this ability once per combat.

Critical strike (mo): Change the result of all dice you have rolled for damage to a ⚁. You can only use this ability once per combat.

Curse (sp): (see **Webbed**). You can only use *curse* once per combat.

Dark pact (co): Sacrifice 4 *health* to charge your strike with shadow energy, increasing your damage score by 4. This ability can only be used once per combat.

Deadly poisons (mo): If you have the *venom* special ability, its damage is increased by 1 (causing 3 points of damage instead of only 2).

Deceive (mo): (see **Trickster**). You can only use *deceive* once per combat.

Deep wound (co): You can use the *deep wound* ability to roll an extra die when determining your damage score. You can only use this ability once per combat.

Deflect (co): (see **Overpower**). You can only use *deflect* once per combat.

Demolish (sp): This ability reduces the number of dice your opponent can roll for attack speed by 1, for one combat round only. It also lowers their *armour* by 1 for the remainder of the combat. You can only use *demolish* once per combat.

Disease (pa): If your damage dice / damage score causes health damage to your opponent, they continue to take 2 points of damage at the end of each combat round. This damage ignores *armour*.

Disrupt (co): If your damage score causes health damage to your opponent, you can also *disrupt* them. This immediately lowers their *magic* score by 3 for the remainder of the combat. You can only use this ability once per combat.

Dodge (co): Use this ability when you have lost a combat round, to avoid taking damage from your opponent. (Note: You will still take damage from passive abilities such as *bleed* or *venom*).

Dominate (mo): Change the result of *one* die you roll for damage to a ⚁. You can only use this ability once per combat.

Ebony and ivory: If your hero is equipped with both swords (ebony and ivory) then you may use the *cripple* ability (see **Cripple**).

Embers (pa): Your *burn* ability now does 2 damage to each opponent (instead of 1).

Ensnare (co): If your opponent has used a dodge ability (such as *evade*, *vanish* or *sidestep*) you can immediately ensnare them, allowing you to win back control of the round and roll for damage as normal (as if their ability had never been played). *Ensnare* can only be used once per combat.

Eureka (mo): Use any time in combat to raise your *speed*, *brawn* or *magic* score by 1 for one combat round. You can only use this ability once per combat.

Evade (co): (see **Dodge**). You can only use *evade* once per combat.

Execution (sp): (requires a sword in the main hand). Once an opponent's *health* is equal to or less than your *speed* score, you may automatically 'execute' them at the start of the combat round, reducing their *health* to zero. (Note: You can only execute a single opponent in each combat round.)

Expertise (mo): If, after winning a round, your opponent uses an ability that would strike back at you (such as *sideswipe*, *retaliation*, *riposte*, *overpower*, *deflect* and *brutality*) you can ignore the damage. You can only use *expertise* once per combat.

Fallen hero (mo): Use this ability to raise your *brawn* by 3 for one combat round and heal 10 *health*. This ability can only be used once per combat.

Fatal blow (co): Use *fatal blow* to ignore half of your opponent's *armour*, rounding up. This ability can only be used once per combat.

Fearless (sp): Use this ability to raise your *speed* by 2 for one combat round. This ability can only be used once per combat.

Feint (mo): You may re-roll some or all of your dice when rolling for attack speed. You may only use this ability once per combat.

Feral fury (co): You can use *feral fury* to roll an extra die when determining your damage score. You can only use this ability once per combat.

Finery of the fallen: If your hero is wearing both pieces of the fallen set (gauntlets and chest) then you may use the *fallen hero* ability (see **Fallen hero**).

Fire aura (pa): You are surrounded by magical flames. All opponents take 1 damage, ignoring *armour*, at the end of every combat round.

First cut (pa): This ability allows you to inflict 1 *health* damage to your opponent before combat begins. This ability ignores *armour*. (This ability cannot be used by assassins.)

First strike (pa): (requires a dagger in the main hand). Before combat begins you may automatically inflict 1 damage die to an opponent, ignoring *armour*. This will also inflict any harmful passive abilities you have, such as *venom* and *bleed*.

Focus (mo): Use any time in combat to raise your *magic* score by 3 for one combat round. You can only use this ability once per combat.

Fortitude (mo): Use any time in combat to raise your *brawn* or *armour* score by 3 for one combat round. You can only use *fortitude* once per combat.

Good taste (pa): Each time you use a backpack item to increase your *magic* in combat, roll 1 die and add the result to the item's benefit.

Gut ripper (mo): Change the result of all dice you have rolled for damage to a ⚅. You can only use *gut ripper* once per combat.

Hamstring (co): If your opponent has used a dodge ability (such as *evade*, *sidestep* or *vanish*), you can immediately use your *hamstring* ability to cancel their dodge, allowing you to roll for damage as normal (as if the dodge ability had never been played). *Hamstring* can only be used once per combat.

Haste (sp): (see **Cat's speed**). You can only use *haste* once per combat.

Haunt (co): Instead of rolling for a damage score, you can cast *haunt*. This summons a vengeful spirit to attack a single opponent. They will take 2 damage, ignoring *armour*, at the end of every combat round, until your hero rolls a double (for speed or damage). Then the spirit is dispelled. You can only cast *haunt* once per combat.

Head butt (co): Use this ability to prevent your opponent from rolling for damage. This automatically ends the combat round. You can only use *head butt* once per combat.

Heal (mo): You may instantly restore 4 *health* during a combat. This ability can only be used once per combat. If you have multiple items with the *heal* ability, each one can be used to restore 4 *health*.

Ice shards (co): If you win a combat round, instead of rolling for a damage score, you can shower a single opponent with *ice shards*. This automatically does damage equal to your *magic* score, ignoring your opponent's *armour*. *Ice shards* can only be used once per combat.

Ice shield (mo): Use this ability to add 1 die to your armour score for one combat round. This ability can only be used once per combat.

Ignite (co): If you win a combat round, instead of rolling for a damage score, you can cast *ignite*. Roll 2 damage dice and apply the result to each of your opponents, ignoring their *armour*. It also causes them to *burn*. *Ignite* can only be used once per combat. (Note: You cannot use modifier abilities to increase this damage.)

Immobilise (sp): (see **Webbed**). You can only use *immobilise* once per combat.

Impale (co): A penetrating blow that increases your damage score by 3. In the next combat round, your opponent's *speed* is lowered by 1. You can only use *impale* once per combat.

Iron will (mo): (see **Might of stone**). You can only use *iron will* once per combat.

Judgement (co): When you take health damage from your opponent's damage score/damage dice, you can inflict damage back to your opponent equal to half your *speed* score, rounding up. This ability ignores *armour*. You can only perform *judgement* once per combat.

Kick start (pa): When you lose your last point of *health*, a magical shock automatically brings you back to life, restoring you to 15 *health*. This also removes all passive effects on your hero. You can only use *kick start* once per combat.

Knockdown (sp): (see **Webbed**). You can only use *knockdown* once per combat.

Last laugh (mo): You may force your opponent to re-roll *all* of their dice (for either their attack speed or for their damage score). This ability can only be used once per combat and you must accept the re-rolled results.

Lay of the land (sp): You can now use the natural features of the land to your advantage. Add one extra die when rolling for your attack speed, for one combat round only.

Leech (pa): Every time your damage score/damage dice causes health damage to your opponent, you may restore 2 *health*. This cannot take you above your maximum *health*.

Life spark (pa): Every time you roll a double, you automatically heal 4 *health*. This cannot take you above your maximum *health*.

Lightning (pa): Every time you take health damage as a result of an opponent's damage score/damage dice, you automatically inflict 2 points of damage to them in return. This ability ignores *armour*. (Note: If you have multiple items with *lightning*, you still only inflict 2 damage.)

Loot master (pa): If you do not wish to choose a reward when you defeat an enemy, you may award yourself an extra 20 gold crowns instead.

Martyr (mo): Instead of taking the result of your opponent's damage, you can choose to lose 5 *health* instead. This ability can only be used once per combat.

Mend (mo): You can cast this spell any time in combat to automatically heal yourself or an ally for 15 *health*. This ability can only be used once per combat.

Merciless (pa): You may add 1 to each die you roll for your damage score if your opponent has been inflicted with *bleed*, *disease* or *venom*.

Midas touch (pa): Every time you destroy an item of equipment (by replacing it with a new item) you gain 30 gold crowns. This ability does not work on backpack items.

Might of stone (mo): You may instantly increase your *armour* score by 3 for one combat round. You can only use this ability once per combat.

Nature's revenge (co): Use this ability instead of rolling for a damage score, to automatically bind a single opponent in deadly thorns. This inflicts 2 damage dice to your opponent, ignoring *armour*. It also reduces their *speed* by 1 for the next combat round. This ability can only be used once per combat.

Nightwalker set: If your hero is wearing both pieces of nightwalker armour (chest and gloves) then you may use the *gut ripper* ability (see **Gut ripper**).

Overload (co): You can use the *overload* ability to roll an extra die when determining your damage score. You can only use this ability once per combat.

Overpower (co): This ability stops your opponent from rolling for damage, after they have won a round, and automatically inflicts 2 damage dice, ignoring *armour*, to your opponent. You can only perform *overpower* once per combat.

Parry (co): Use this ability to stop your opponent rolling for damage after they have won a round. This ability can only be used once per combat.

Patchwork pauper (pa): When replacing an item of equipment in your chest, gloves, cloak or feet locations on your hero sheet, you can keep the special ability from the old item but replace its name and attributes with those of the new item.

Piercing (co): Use *piercing* to ignore your opponent's *armour* and apply your full damage score to their *health*. This ability can only be used once per combat.

Poison mastery (pa): Health damage from the *venom* special ability is increased by 1 (causing 4 points of health damage instead of only 3).

Pound (co): A mighty blow that increases your damage score by 3. However, in the next combat round, you must lower your *speed* by 1. This ability can only be used once per combat.

Puncture (co): Instead of rolling for a damage score, you can puncture an opponent with a well-aimed arrow. This does 2 dice of damage, ignoring *armour*. It also reduces your opponent's *armour* by 1 for the remainder of the combat. You can only use *puncture* once per combat.

Quicksilver (sp): Increase your *speed* by 2 for one combat round. You can only use *quicksilver* once per combat.

Radiance (sp): Dazzle your foes, temporarily blinding them. This lowers your opponent's *speed* by 2 for one combat round. *Radiance* can only be used once per combat.

Raining blows (mo): Every time you get a ⚅ result when rolling for your damage score, you may automatically roll another die to add further damage. If you roll a ⚅ again, you may roll another die – and so on.

Rake (co): Instead of rolling for a damage score after winning a round, you can *rake* an opponent. This inflicts 3 damage dice, ignoring *armour*. (Note: You cannot use modifiers with this ability.) You can only use *rake* once per combat.

Reflect (co): If your opponent is a vampire then you can use the magic mirror to reflect any health damage that they would have inflicted back onto the vampire. This ability can only be used once per combat.

Regrowth (mo): You may instantly restore 6 *health* any time during combat. If you have multiple items with the *regrowth* ability, each one can be used to restore 6 *health*.

Retaliation (co): When your opponent's damage score/damage dice causes health damage, you can immediately retaliate by inflicting 1 damage dice back to them, ignoring *armour*. You can only use *retaliation* once per combat.

Riposte (co): (see **Retaliation**). You can only use *riposte* once per combat.

Royal regalia: If your hero is wearing both pieces of the majesty set (shoulders and greaves) then you may use the *cripple* ability (see **Cripple**).

Rust (co): If your damage score causes health damage to your opponent, you can also cast the spell *rust*. This lowers your opponent's *armour* by 2 for the remainder of the combat.

Sacrifice (co): You may use this ability after an opponent has rolled their damage dice/damage score, to instantly *sacrifice* your shades. The shades absorb all the damage instead and you are unharmed. This destroys your shades instantly.

Savagery (mo): You may raise your *brawn* or *magic* score by 2 for one combat round. You can only use *savagery* once per combat.

Sear (mo): Add 1 to the result of each die you roll for your damage score, for the duration of the combat. (Note: if you have multiple items with *sear*, you can still only add 1 to the result.)

Second sight (mo): Your reflexes are heightened. This lowers the result of each die your opponent rolls for damage by 2.

Second skin (pa): You are immune to the *piercing* ability. If an opponent uses *piercing*, you may use *armour* as normal to absorb the damage.

Second wind (mo): You may use *second wind* at any time to restore one speed ability that you or an ally has already played. This allows you/your ally to use that speed ability a second time in the same combat.

Seeing red (pa): If your *health* is reduced to 20 or less, you may add 2 to your *speed*. If you are healed and your *health* rises above 20, you lose your bonus.

Shackle (sp): (see **Webbed**). You can only use *shackle* once per combat.

Shades (pa): At the start of combat, you automatically summon a group of shades to aid you. The shades add 2 to each die of damage you roll, for the duration of the combat. Once the shades have been summoned, they remain in play until you sacrifice them.

Shadow fury (co): Use this ability to add the *speed* of both your weapons (main hand and left hand) to your damage score. This ability can only be used once per combat.

Shadow speed (mo): When rolling for your attack speed, all results of ⚀ can be changed to a ⚂.

Shield spin (pa): (requires a shield in the left hand). Each time your opponent gets a ⚀ when rolling for attack speed, they are hit by your shield, taking 1 damage die, ignoring *armour*. They cannot use a re-roll to avoid this.

Shield wall (co): (requires a shield in the left hand). Use this ability to double your armour score and inflict 1 damage die to your opponent, ignoring their *armour*. You can only use this ability once per combat.

Shock! (co): If your damage score causes health damage to your opponent, you can also electrocute them with the *shock!* ability. This inflicts 1 extra damage for every 2 points of *armour* your opponent is wearing, rounding up. (If your opponent had an *armour* of 15 they would take an extra 8 damage.) You can only use *shock!* once per combat.

Sidestep (co): (see **Dodge**). You can only use *sidestep* once per combat.

Sideswipe (co): (see **Retaliation**). You can only use *sideswipe* once per combat.

Slam (co): Use this ability to stop your opponent rolling for damage when they have won a round. In the next combat round, your opponent's *speed* is reduced by 1. You can only use this ability once per combat.

Spider sense (co): (see **Dodge**). You can only use *spider sense* once per combat.

Spindlesilk set: If your hero is wearing all three pieces of spindlesilk armour (chest, boots and cloak) then you may use the *spider sense* ability (see **Spider sense**).

Spore cloud (co): When your opponent's damage score / damage dice causes health damage, you can use *spore cloud* to inflict 2 damage dice back to them, ignoring *armour*. You can only use this ability once per combat.

Stake (sp): If your opponent is a vampire and their *health* is reduced to 10 or less, you may immediately stake them. This reduces their *health* to zero and you automatically win the combat.

Steadfast (pa): You are immune to *knockdown*. If an opponent has this ability, you can ignore it.

Steal (mo): Use this ability any time in combat to automatically raise one of your attributes (*speed*, *brawn*, *magic* or *armour*) to match your opponent's. The effect wears off at the end of the combat round. You can only use *steal* once per combat.

Stun (sp): (see **webbed**). You can only use *stun* once per combat.

Surge (co): A powerful attack that increases your *magic* score by 3. However, in the next combat round, you must lower your *speed* by 1. This ability can only be used once per combat.

Swamp legs (sp): Reduce your opponent's *speed* by 1 for one combat round. You can only use this ability once per combat.

Swift strikes (pa): (requires a sword in the main and left hand) For each ⚃ that you roll for your attack *speed*, you can inflict damage to any opponent equal to the *speed* of your fastest weapon (either main or left hand). This ability ignores *armour*.

Thorn armour (co): Use this ability to raise your *armour* by 3 for one combat round. It also inflicts 1 damage die, ignoring *armour*, to all your opponents (roll once and apply the same damage to each opponent). This ability can only be used once per combat.

Thorn fist (co): When your opponent's damage score/damage dice causes health damage, you can immediately retaliate using your *thorn fist*. This inflicts 2 damage dice back to them, ignoring *armour*. You can only use *thorn fist* once per combat.

Thorns (pa): At the end of every combat round, you automatically inflict 1 damage to all of your opponents. This ability ignores *armour*.

Time shift (sp): You may raise your *speed* to match your opponent's for three combat rounds. You cannot play another speed ability until *time shift* has faded. This ability can only be used once per combat.

Tourniquet (mo): This spell can be cast at any time to remove any *bleed, venom* and/or *disease* effects that you or an ally have been inflicted with. This ability can only be used once per combat.

Trickster (mo): You may swap one of your opponent's speed die for your own. You can only use *trickster* once per combat.

Usurper (mo): (only usable in hero vs. hero combat). Use any time during a combat to steal a speed or modifier ability that your opponent has already played. You may then play this ability against them during the combat, based on the ability's description. *Usurper* can only be used once per combat.

Vampirism (mo): When you inflict damage on your opponent, you can heal yourself for half the amount of *health* that your opponent has lost, rounding up. *Vampirism* can only be used once per combat.

Vanish (co): (see **Dodge**). Use *vanish* to turn invisible for several seconds, avoiding your opponent's damage. You can only use *vanish* once per combat.

Vanquish (mo): You may raise your *brawn* score by 2 for one combat round. You can only use *vanquish* once per combat.

Venom (pa): If your damage dice/damage score causes health damage to your opponent, they lose a further 2 *health* at the end of every combat round, for the remainder of the combat. This ability ignores *armour*.

Vitriol (pa): Use at the start of combat to coat your weapons in deadly bile. This does 1 damage to all combatants, including your hero, at the end of every combat round.

Webbed (sp): This ability reduces the number of dice your opponent can roll for attack speed by 1, for one combat round only. You can only use this ability once per combat.

Windblast (sp): (see **Webbed**). You can only use *windblast* once per combat.

Zapped! (sp): Use this ability to automatically shrink your opponent, making them weaker. Your opponent's *speed*, *brawn* and *magic* are lowered by 3 until the end of the combat round. Then the ability wears off and their stats are restored. You can only use this ability once per combat.